Pan Michael: An Historical Novel of Poland, the Ukraine, and Turkey; a Sequel to "With Fire and Sword" and "The Deluge".

Henryk Sienkiewicz

Popular Edition.

PAN MICHAEL.

BY

HENRYK SIENKIEWICZ.

Since Saint Michael leads the whole host of heaven, and has gained so many victories over the banners of hell, I prefer him as a patron.— THE DELUGE, Vol. I, p. 120.

PAN MICHAEL.

An Historical Novel

OF

POLAND, THE UKRAINE, AND TURKEY

A SEQUEL TO

"WITH FIRE AND SWORD" AND "THE DELUGE."

BY

HENRYK SIENKIEWICZ.

AUTHORIZED AND UNABRIDGED TRANSLATION FROM THE POLISH BY

JEREMIAH CURTIN.

BOSTON:
LITTLE, BROWN, AND COMPANY.
1898.

𝔘𝔫𝔦𝔳𝔢𝔯𝔰𝔦𝔱𝔶 𝔓𝔯𝔢𝔰𝔰:

John Wilson and Son, Cambridge, U.S.A.

TO

JOHN MURRAY BROWN, Esq.

My Dear Brown,—You read "With Fire and Sword" in manuscript; you appreciated its character, and your House published it. What you did for the first, you did later on for the other two parts of the trilogy. Remembering your deep interest in all the translations, I beg to inscribe to you the concluding volume, "Pan Michael."

JEREMIAH CURTIN.

Valentia Island, West Coast of Ireland,
    August 15, 1893.

From the author of "QUO VADIS."

Messrs Little, Brown and Company; Gentlemen

Having concluded with You an agreement concerning
my novels translated by M. Jeremiah Curtin, and published
by Your House, I have the honour to declare, that the
publication of these novels by other publishers would be
done against my will and interest. As far as I know,
I cannot put a legal stop to their publication by
others; but I think, that public opinion in your country
might in this case take the place of law. since the
feeling of commercial honor is so highly developed in
the United States.—

Your truly

Henryk Sienkiewicz

INTRODUCTION.

———◆———

THE great struggle begun by the Cossacks, and, after the victory at Korsun, continued by them and the Russian population of the Commonwealth, is described in "With Fire and Sword," from the ambush on the Omelnik[1] to the battle of Berestechko. In "The Deluge" the Swedish invasion is the argument, and a mere reference is made to the war in which Moscow and the Ukraine are on one side and the Commonwealth on the other. In "Pan Michael," the present volume and closing work of the trilogy, the invader is the Turk, whose forces, though victorious at Kamenyets, are defeated at Hotin.

"With Fire and Sword" covers the war of 1648–49, which was ended at Zborovo, where a treaty most hateful to the Poles was concluded between the Cossacks and the Commonwealth. In the second war there was only one great action, that of Berestechko (1651), an action followed by the treaty of Belaya Tserkoff, oppressive to the Cossacks and impossible of execution.

The main event in the interval between Berestechko and the war with Moscow was the siege and peace of Jvanyets, of which mention is made in the introduction to "With Fire and Sword."

After Jvanyets the Cossacks turned to Moscow and swore allegiance to the Tsar in 1654; in that year the war was begun to which reference is made in "The Deluge." In

[1] "With Fire and Sword," page 4.

addition to the Cossack cause Moscow had questions of her own, and invaded the Commonwealth with two separate armies; of these one moved on White Russia and Lithuania, the other joined the forces of Hmelnitski.

Moscow had rapid and brilliant success in the north. Smolensk, Orsha, and Vityebsk were taken in the opening campaign, as were Vilno, Kovno, and Grodno in the following summer. In 1655 White Russia and nearly all Lithuania came under the hand of the Tsar.

In view of Moscow's great victories, Karl Gustav made a sudden descent on the Commonwealth. The Swedish monarch became master of Great and Little Poland almost without a blow. Yan Kazimir fled to Silesia, and a majority of the nobles took the oath to Karl Gustav.

Moving from the Ukraine, Hmelnitski and Buturlin, the Tsar's voevoda, carried all before them till they encamped outside Lvoff; there the Cossack hetman gave audience to an envoy from Yan Kazimir, and was persuaded to withdraw with his army, thus leaving the king one city in the Commonwealth, a great boon, as was evident soon after.

When Swedish success was almost perfect, and the Commonwealth seemed lost, the Swedes laid siege to Chenstohova. The amazing defence of that sanctuary roused religious spirit in the Poles, who had tired of Swedish rigor; they resumed allegiance to Yan Kazimir, who returned and rallied his adherents at Lvoff, the city spared ·by Hmelnitski. In the attempt to strike his rival in that capital of Red Russia, Karl Gustav made the swift though calamitous march across Poland which Sienkiewicz has described in "The Deluge" so vividly.

Soon after his return from Silesia, the Polish king sent an embassy to the Tsar. Austria sent another to strengthen it and arrange a treaty or a truce on some basis.

Yan Kazimir was eager for peace with Moscow at any price, especially a price paid in promises. The Tsar desired peace on terms that would give the Russian part of the Commonwealth to Moscow, Poland proper to become a hereditary kingdom in which the Tsar himself or his heir would succeed Yan Kazimir, and thus give to both States the same sovereign, though different administrations.

An agreement was effected: the sovereign or heir of Moscow was to succeed Yan Kazimir, details of boundaries and succession to be settled by the Diet, both sides to refrain from hostilities till the Swedes were expelled, and neither to make peace with Sweden separately.

Austria forced the Swedish garrison out of Cracow, and then induced the Elector of Brandenburg to desert Sweden. She did this by bringing Poland to grant independence to Princely, that is, Eastern Prussia, where the elector was duke and a vassal of the Commonwealth. The elector, who at that time held the casting vote in the choice of Emperor, agreed in return for the weighty service which Austria had shown him to give his voice for Leopold, who had just come to the throne in Vienna.

Austria, having secured the imperial election at Poland's expense, took no further step on behalf of the Commonwealth, but disposed troops in Southern Poland and secured her own interests. The Elector, to make his place certain in the final treaty, took active part against Sweden. Peace was concluded in 1657 and ratified in 1660 at Oliva. With the expulsion of the Swedes the historical part of "The Deluge" is ended, no further reference being made to the main war between the Commonwealth and Moscow.

Since the Turkish invasion described in "Pan Michael" was caused by events in this main war, a short account of its subsequent course and its connection with Turkey is in order in this place.

Bogdan Hmelnitski dreaded the truce between Moscow and Poland. He feared lest the Poles, outwitting the Tsar, might recover control of the Cossacks; hence he joined the alliance which Karl Gustav had made with Rakotsy in 1657 to dismember the Commonwealth. Rakotsy was defeated, and the alliance failed; both Moscow and Austria were opposed to it.

In 1657 Hmelnitski died, and was succeeded as hetman by Vygovski, chancellor of the Cossack army, though Yuri, the old hetman's son, had been chosen during his father's last illness. Vygovski was a noble, with leanings toward Poland, though his career was firm proof that he loved himself better than any cause.

In the following year the new hetman made a treaty at Gadyach with the Commonwealth, and in conjunction with a Polish army defeated Prince Trubetskoi in a battle at Konotop. The Polish Diet annulled now the terms of the treaty concluded with Moscow two years before. Various reasons were alleged for this action; the true reason was that in 1655 the succession to the Polish crown had been offered to Austria, and, though refused in public audience, had been accepted in private by the Emperor for his son Leopold. In the following year Austria advised the Poles unofficially to offer this crown (already disposed of) to the Tsar, and thus induce him to give the Commonwealth a respite, and turn his arms against Sweden.

The Poles followed this advice; the Tsar accepted their offer. When the service required had been rendered the treaty was broken. In the same year, however, Vygovski was deposed by the Cossacks, the treaty of Gadyach rejected, and Yuri Hmelnitski made hetman. The Cossacks were again in agreement with Moscow; but the Poles spared no effort to bring Yuri to their side, and they succeeded through the deposed hetman, Vygovski, who adhered to the Commonwealth so far.

Both sides were preparing their heaviest blows at this juncture, and 1660 brought victory to the Poles. In the beginning of that year Moscow had some success in Lithuania, but was forced back at last toward Smolensk. The best Polish armies, trained in the Swedish struggle, and leaders like Charnyetski, Sapyeha, and Kmita, turned the scale in White Russia. In the Ukraine the Poles, under Lyubomirski and Pototski, were strengthened by Tartars and met the forces of Moscow under Sheremetyeff, with the Cossacks under Yuri Hmelnitski. At the critical moment, and during action, Yuri deserted to the Poles, and secured the defeat of Sheremetyeff, who surrendered at Chudnovo and was sent a Tartar captive to the Crimea.

In all the shifting scenes of the conflict begun by the resolute Bogdan, there was nothing more striking than the conduct and person of Yuri Hmelnitski, who renounced all the work of his father. Great, it is said, was the wonder of the Poles when they saw him enter their camp. Bogdan Hmelnitski, a man of iron will and striking presence, had filled the whole Commonwealth with terror; his son gave way at the very first test put upon him, and in person was, as the Poles said, a dark, puny stripling, more like a timid novice in a monastery than a Cossack. In the words of the captive voevoda, Sheremetyeff, he was better fitted to be a gooseherd than a hetman.

The Polish generals thought now that the conflict was over, and that the garrisons of Moscow would evacuate the Ukraine; but they did not. At this juncture the Polish troops, unpaid for a long time, refused service, revolted, formed what they called a "sacred league," and lived on the country. The Polish army vanished from the field, and after it the Tartars. Young Hmelnitski turned again to Moscow, and writing to the Tsar, declared that, forced by Cossack colonels, he had joined the Polish king, but wished to return to his former allegiance. Whatever his wishes may have been, he did not escape the Commonwealth; stronger men than he, and among them Vygovski, kept him well in hand. The Ukraine was split into two camps: that west of the river, or at least the Cossacks under Yuri Hmelnitski, obeyed the Commonwealth; the Eastern bank adhered to Moscow.

Two years later, Yuri, the helpless hetman, left his

office and took refuge in a cloister. He was succeeded by Teterya, a partisan of Poland, which now made every promise to the leading Cossacks, not as in the old time when the single argument was sabres.

East of the Dnieper another hetman ruled; but there the Poles could take no part in struggles for the office. The rivalry was limited to partisans of Moscow. Besides the two groups of Cossacks on the Dnieper, there remained the Zaporojians. Teterya strove to win these to the Commonwealth, and Yan Kazimir, the king, assembled all the forces he could rally and crossed the Dnieper toward the end of 1663. At first he had success in some degree, but in the following year led back a shattered, hungry army.

Teterya had received a promise from the Zaporojians that they would follow the example of the Eastern Ukraine. The king having failed in his expedition, Teterya declared that peace must be concluded between the Commonwealth and Moscow to save the Ukraine; that the country was reduced to ruin by all parties, neither one of which could subjugate the other; and that to save themselves the Cossacks would be forced to seek protection of the Sultan.

Doroshenko succeeded Teterya in the hetman's office, and began to carry out this Cossack project. In 1666 he sent a message to the Porte declaring that the Ukraine was at the will of the Sultan.

The Sultan commanded the Khan to march to the Ukraine. Toward the end of that year the Tartars brought aid to the Cossacks, and the joint army swept the field of Polish forces.

Meanwhile negotiations had been pending a long time between the Commonwealth and Moscow. An insurrection under Lyubomirski brought the Poles to terms touching boundaries in the north. In the south Moscow demanded, besides the line of the Dnieper, Kieff and a certain district around it on the west. This the Poles refused stubbornly till Doroshenko's union with Turkey induced them to yield Kieff to Moscow for two years. On this basis a peace of twenty years was concluded in 1667, at Andrussoff near Smolensk. This peace became permanent afterward, and Kieff remained with Moscow.

In 1668 Yan Kazimir abdicated, hoping to secure the succession to a king in alliance with France, and avoid a conflict with Turkey through French intervention. No foreign candidate, however, found sufficient support, and Olshovski,[1] the crafty and ambitious vice-chancellor, proposed at an opportune moment Prince Michael Vishnyevetski, son of the renowned Yeremi, and he was elected in 1669. The new king, of whom a short sketch is given in "The Deluge" (Vol. II. page 253), was, like Yuri Hmelnitski, the imbecile son of a terrible father. Elected by the lesser nobility in a moment of spite against magnates, he found no support among the latter. Without merit or influence at home, he sought support in Austria, and married a sister of the Emperor Leopold. Powerless in dealing with the Cossacks, to whom his name was detestable, without friends, except among the petty nobles, whose support in that juncture was more damaging than useful, he made a Turkish war certain. It came three years later, when the Sultan marched to support Doroshenko, and began the siege of Kamenyets, described in "Pan Michael."

After the fall of Kamenyets, the Turks pushed on to Lvoff, and dictated the peace of Buchach, which gave Podolia and the western bank of the Dnieper, except Kieff and its district, to the Sultan.

The battle of Hotin, described in the epilogue, made Sobieski king in 1674. This election was considered a triumph for France, an enemy of Austria at that time; and during the earlier years of his reign Sobieski was on the French side, and had sound reasons for this policy. In 1674 the Elector of Brandenburg attacked Swedish Pomerania; France supported Sweden, and roused Poland to

[1] The bishop who visited Zagloba at Ketling's house, see pages 121–126

oppose the Elector, who had fought against Yan Kazimir, his own suzerain. Sobieski, supported by subsidies from France, made levies of troops, went to Dantzig in 1677, concluded with Sweden a secret agreement to make common cause with her and attack the Elector. But in spite of subsidies, preparations, and treaties, the Polish king took no action. Sweden, without an ally, was defeated; Poland lost the last chance of recovering Prussia, and holding thereby an independent position in Europe.

The influence of Austria, the power of the church, and the intrigues of his own wife, bore away Sobieski. He deserted the alliance with France. To the end of his life he served Austria far better than Poland, though not wishing to do so, and died in 1696 complaining of this world, in which, as he said, "sin, malice, and treason are rampant."

JEREMIAH CURTIN.

CAHIRCIVEEN, COUNTY KERRY, IRELAND,
August 17, 1893.

NOTE. — The reign of Sobieski brought to an end that part of Polish history during which the Commonwealth was able to take the initiative in foreign politics. After Sobieski the Poles ceased to be a positive power in Europe.

I have not been able to verify the saying said to have been uttered by Sobieski at Vienna. In the text (page 401) he is made to say that Pani Wojnina (War's wife) may give birth to people, but Wojna (War) only destroys them. Who the Pani Wojnina was that Sobieski had in view I am unable to say at this moment, unless she was *Peace.*

PAN MICHAEL.

CHAPTER I.

AFTER the close of the Hungarian war, when the marriage of Pan Audrei Kmita and Panna Aleksandra Billevich was celebrated, a cavalier, equally meritorious and famous in the Commonwealth, Pan Michael Volodyovski, colonel of the Lauda squadron, was to enter the bonds of marriage with Panna Anna Borzobogati Krasienski.

But notable hindrances rose, which delayed and put back the affair. The lady was a foster-daughter of Princess Griselda Vishnyevetski, without whose permission Panna Anna would in no wise consent to the wedding. Pan Michael was forced therefore to leave his affianced in Vodokty, by reason of the troubled times, and go alone to Zamost for the consent and the blessing of the princess.

But a favoring star did not guide him: he did not find the princess in Zamost; she had gone to the imperial court in Vienna for the education of her son. The persistent knight followed her even to Vienna, though that took much time. When he had arranged the affair there successfully, he turned homeward in confident hope.

He found troubled times at home: the army was forming a confederacy; in the Ukraine uprisings continued; at the eastern boundary the conflagration had not ceased. New forces were assembled to defend the frontiers even in some fashion. Before Pan Michael had reached Warsaw, he received a commission issued by the voevoda of Rus. Thinking that the country should be preferred at all times to private affairs, he relinquished his plan of immediate marriage and moved to the Ukraine. He campaigned in those regions some years, living in battles, in unspeakable hardships and labor, having barely a chance on occasions to send letters to the expectant lady.

Next he was envoy to the Crimea; then came the unfortunate civil war with Pan Lyubomirski, in which Volodyovski fought on the side of the king against that traitor and infamous man; then he went to the Ukraine a second time under Sobieski.

From these achievements the glory of his name increased in such manner that he was considered on all sides as the first soldier of the Commonwealth, but the years were passing for him in anxiety, sighs, and yearning. At last 1668 came, when he was sent at command of the castellan to rest; at the beginning of the year he went for the cherished lady, and taking her from Vodokty, they set out for Cracow.

They were journeying to Cracow, because Princess Griselda, who had returned from the dominions of the emperor, invited Pan Michael to have the marriage at that place, and offered herself to be mother to the bride.

The Kmitas remained at home, not thinking to receive early news from Pan Michael, and altogether intent on a new guest that was coming to Vodokty. Providence had till that time withheld from them children; now a change was impending, happy and in accordance with their wishes.

That year was surpassingly fruitful. Grain had given such a bountiful yield that the barns could not hold it, and the whole land, in the length and the breadth of it, was covered with stacks. In neighborhoods ravaged by war the young pine groves had grown in one spring more than in two years at other times. There was abundance of game and of mushrooms in the forests, as if the unusual fruitfulness of the earth had been extended to all things that lived on it. Hence the friends of Pan Michael drew happy omens for his marriage also, but the fates ordained otherwise.

CHAPTER II.

On a certain beautiful day of autumn Pan Andrei Kmita was sitting under the shady roof of a summer-house and drinking his after-dinner mead; he gazed at his wife from time to time through the lattice, which was grown over with wild hops. Pani Kmita was walking on a neatly swept path in front of the summer-house. The lady was unusually stately; bright-haired, with a face serene, almost angelic. She walked slowly and carefully, for there was in her a fulness of dignity and blessing.

Pan Andrei gazed at her with intense love. When she moved, his look turned after her with such attachment as a dog shows his master with his eyes. At moments he smiled, for he was greatly rejoiced at sight of her, and he twirled his mustache upward. At such moments there appeared on his face a certain expression of glad frolicsomeness. It was clear that the soldier was fun-loving by nature, and in years of single life had played many a prank.

Silence in the garden was broken only by the sound of over-ripe fruit dropping to the earth and the buzzing of insects. The weather had settled marvellously. It was the beginning of September. The sun burned no longer with excessive violence, but cast yet abundant golden rays. In these rays ruddy apples were shining among the gray leaves and hung in such numbers that they hid the branches. The limbs of plum-trees were bending under plums with bluish wax on them.

The first movement of air was shown by the spider-threads fastened to the trees; these swayed with a breeze so slight that it did not stir even the leaves.

Perhaps it was that calm in the world which had so filled Pan Kmita with joyfulness, for his face grew more radiant each moment. At last he took a draught of mead and said to his wife, —

"Olenka, but come here! I will tell you something."

"It may be something that I should not like to hear."

"As God is dear to me, it is not. Give me your ear."

Saying this, he seized her by the waist, pressed his mustaches to her bright hair, and whispered, "If a boy, let him be Michael."

She turned away with face somewhat flushed, and whispered, "But you promised not to object to Heraclius."

"Do you not see that it is to honor Volodyovski ?"

"But should not the first remembrance be given to my grandfather ?"

"And my benefactor — H'm ! true — but the next will be Michael. It cannot be otherwise."

Here Olenka, standing up, tried to free herself from the arms of Pan Andrei; but he, gathering her in with still greater force, began to kiss her on the lips and the eyes, repeating at the same time, —

"O thou my hundreds, my thousands, my dearest love ! "

Further conversation was interrupted by a lad who appeared at the end of the walk and ran quickly toward the summer-house.

"What is wanted ? " asked Kmita, freeing his wife.

"Pan Kharlamp has come, and is waiting in the parlor," said the boy.

"And there he is himself !" exclaimed Kmita, at sight of a man approaching the summer-house. "For God's sake, how gray his mustache is ! Greetings to you, dear comrade ! greetings, old friend !"

With these words he rushed from the summer-house, and hurried with open arms toward Pan Kharlamp. But first Pan Kharlamp bowed low to Olenka, whom he had seen in old times at the court of Kyedani; then he pressed her hand to his enormous mustache, and casting himself into the embraces of Kmita, sobbed on his shoulder.

"For God's sake, what is the matter ? " cried the astonished host.

"God has given happiness to one and taken it from another," said Kharlamp. "But the reasons of my sorrow I can tell only to you."

Here he looked at Olenka; she, seeing that he was unwilling to speak in her presence, said to her husband, "I will send mead to you, gentlemen, and now I leave you."

Kmita took Pan Kharlamp to the summer-house, and seating him on a bench, asked, "What is the matter ? Are you in need of assistance ? Count on me as on Zavisha !" [1]

---

[1] A celebrated bishop of Cracow, famous for ambition and success.

"Nothing is the matter with me," said the old soldier, "and I need no assistance while I can move this hand and this sabre; but our friend, the most worthy cavalier in the Commonwealth, is in cruel suffering. I know not whether he is breathing yet."

"By Christ's wounds! Has anything happened to Volodyovski?"

"Yes," said Kharlamp, giving way to a new outburst of tears. "Know that Panna Anna Borzobogati has left this vale —"

"Is dead!" cried Kmita, seizing his head with both hands.

"As a bird pierced by a shaft."

A moment of silence followed, — no sound but that of apples dropping here and there to the ground heavily, and of Pan Kharlamp panting more loudly while restraining his weeping. But Kmita was wringing his hands, and repeated, nodding his head, —

"Dear God! dear God! dear God!"

"Your grace will not wonder at my tears," said Kharlamp, at last; "for if your heart is pressed by unendurable pain at the mere tidings of what happened, what must it be to me, who was witness of her death and her pain, of her suffering, which surpassed every natural measure?"

Here the servant appeared, bringing a tray with a decanter and a second glass on it; after him came Kmita's wife, who could not repress her curiosity. Looking at her husband's face and seeing in it deep suffering, she said straightway, —

"What tidings have you brought? Do not dismiss me. I will comfort you as far as possible, or I will weep with you, or will help you with counsel."

"Help for this will not be found in your head," said Pan Andrei; "and I fear that your health will suffer from sorrow."

"I can endure much. It is more grievous to live in uncertainty."

"Anusia is dead," said Kmita.

Olenka grew somewhat pale, and dropped on the bench heavily. Kmita thought that she would faint; but grief acted more quickly than the sudden announcement, and she began to weep. Both knights accompanied her immediately.

"Olenka," said Kmita, at last, wishing to turn his wife's

thoughts in another direction, "do you not think that she is in heaven ? "

"Not for her do I weep, but over the loss of her, and over the loneliness of Pan Michael. As to her eternal happiness, I should wish to have such hope for my own salvation as I have for hers. There was not a worthier maiden, or one of better heart, or more honest. O my Anulka![1] my Anulka, beloved! "

"I saw her death," said Kharlamp; "may God grant us all to die with such piety ! "

Here silence followed, as if some of their sorrow had gone with their tears; then Kmita said, "Tell us how it was, and take some mead to support you."

"Thank you," said Kharlamp; "I will drink from time to time if you will drink with me; for pain seizes not only the heart, but the throat, like a wolf, and when it seizes a man it might choke him unless he received some assistance. I was going from Chenstóhova to my native place to settle there quietly in my old age. I have had war enough; as a stripling I began to practise, and now my mustache is gray. If I cannot stay at home altogether, I will go out under some banner; but these military confederations to the loss of the country and the profit of the enemy, and these civil wars, have disgusted me thoroughly with arms. Dear God! the pelican nourishes its children with its blood, it is true ; but this country has no longer even blood in its breast. Sviderski[2] was a great soldier. May God judge him! "

"My dearest Anulka!" interrupted Pani Kmita, with weeping, "without thee what would have happened to me and to all of us ? Thou wert a refuge and a defence to me ! O my beloved Anulka!"

Hearing this, Kharlamp sobbed anew, but briefly, for Kmita interrupted him with a question, "But where did you meet Pan Michael ? "

"In Chenstohova, where he and she intended to rest, for they were visiting the shrine there after the journey. He told me at once how he was going from your place to Cracow, to Princess Griselda, without whose permission and blessing Anusia was unwilling to marry. The maiden was in good health at that time, and Pan Michael was as

---

[1] A diminutive of endearment for Anna. Anusia is another form.
[2] One of the chiefs of a confederacy formed against the king, Yan Kazimir, by soldiers who had not received their pay.

joyful as a bird. 'See,' said he, 'the Lord God has given me a reward for my labor!' He boasted also not a little, — God comfort him! — and joked with me because I, as you know, quarrelled with him on a time concerning the lady, and we were to fight a duel. Where is she now, poor woman?"

Here Kharlamp broke out again, but briefly, for Kmita stopped him a second time: "You say that she was well? How came the attack, then, so suddenly?"

"That it was sudden, is true. She was lodging with Pani Martsin Zamoyski, who, with her husband, was spending some time in Chenstohova. Pan Michael used to sit all the day with her; he complained of delay somewhat, and said they might be a whole year on the journey to Cracow, for every one on the way would detain him. And this is no wonder! Every man is glad to entertain such a soldier as Pan Michael, and whoever could catch him would keep him. He took me to the lady too, and threatened smilingly that he would cut me to pieces if I made love to her; but he was the whole world to her. At times, too, my heart sank, for my own sake, because a man in old age is like a nail in a wall. Never mind! But one night Pan Michael rushed in 'to me in dreadful distress: 'In God's name, can you find a doctor?' 'What has happened?' 'The sick woman knows no one!' 'When did she fall ill?' asked I. 'Pani Zamoyski has just given me word,' replied he. 'It is night now. Where can I look for a doctor, when there is nothing here but a cloister, and in the town more ruins than people?' I found a surgeon at last, and he was even unwilling to go; I had to drive him with weapons. But a priest was more needed then than a surgeon; we found at her bedside, in fact, a worthy Paulist, who, through prayer, had restored her to consciousness. She was able to receive the sacrament, and take an affecting farewell of Pan Michael. At noon of the following day it was all over with her. The surgeon said that some one must have given her something, though that is impossible, for witchcraft has no power in Chenstohova. But what happened to Pan Michael, what he said, — my hope is that the Lord Jesus will not account this to him, for a man does not reckon with words when pain is tearing him. You see," Pan Kharlamp lowered his voice, "he blasphemed in his forgetfulness."

"For God's sake, did he blaspheme?" inquired Kmita, in a whisper.

"He rushed out from her corpse to the ante-chamber, from the ante-chamber to the yard, and reeled about like a drunken man. He raised his hands then, and began to cry with a dreadful voice : 'Such is the reward for my wounds, for my toils, for my blood, for my love of country ! I had one lamb,' said he, 'and that one, O Lord, Thou didst take from me. To hurl down an armed man,' said he, 'who walks the earth in pride, is a deed for God's hand; but a cat, a hawk, or a kite can kill a harmless dove, and — '"

"By the wounds of God !" exclaimed Pani Kmita, "say no more, or you will draw misfortune on this house."

Kharlamp made the sign of the cross and continued, "The poor soldier thought that he had done service, and still this was his reward. Ah, God knows better what He does, though that is not to be understood by man's reason, nor measured by human justice. Straightway after this blasphemy he grew rigid and fell on the ground; and the priest read an exorcism over him, so that foul spirits should not enter him, as they might, enticed by his blasphemy."

"Did he come to himself quickly ?"

"He lay as if dead about an hour; then he recovered and went to his room; he would see no one. At the time of the burial I said to him, 'Pan Michael, have God in your heart.' He made me no answer. I stayed three days more in Chenstohova, for I was loath to leave him; but I knocked in vain at his door. He did not want me. I struggled with my thoughts: what was I to do, — try longer at the door, or go away ? How was I to leave a man without comfort ? But finding that I could do nothing, I resolved to go to Pan Yan Skshetuski. He is his best friend, and Pan Zagloba is his friend also; maybe they will touch his heart somehow, and especially Pan Zagloba, who is quick-witted, and knows how to talk over any man."

"Did you go to Pan Yan ?"

"I did, but God gave no luck, for he and Zagloba had gone to Kalish to Pan Stanislav. No one could tell when they would return. Then I thought to myself, 'As my road is toward Jmud, I will go to Pan Kmita and tell what has happened.'"

"I knew from of old that you were a worthy cavalier," said Kmita.

"It is not a question of me in this case, but of Pan Michael," said Kharlamp; "and I confess that I fear for him greatly lest his mind be disturbed."

"God preserve him from that!" said Pani Kmita.

"If God preserves him, he will certainly take the habit, for I tell you that such sorrow I have never seen in my life. And it is a pity to lose such a soldier as he, — it is a pity!"

"How a pity? The glory of God will increase thereby," said Pani Kmita.

Kharlamp's mustache began to quiver, and he rubbed his forehead.

"Well, gracious benefactress, either it will increase or it will not increase. Consider how many Pagans and heretics he has destroyed in his life, by which he, has surely delighted our Saviour and His Mother more than any one priest could with sermons. H'm! it is a thing worthy of thought! Let every one serve the glory of God as he knows best. Among the Jesuits legions of men may be found wiser than Pan Michael, but another such sabre as his there is not in the Commonwealth."

"True, as God is dear to me!" cried Kmita. "Do you know whether he stayed in Chenstohova?"

"He was there when I left; what he did later, I know not. I know only this: God preserve him from losing his mind, God preserve him from sickness, which frequently comes with despair, — he will be alone, without aid, without a relative, without a friend, without consolation."

"May the Most Holy Lady in that place of miracles save thee, faithful friend, who hast done so much for me that a brother could not have done more!"

Pani Kmita fell into deep thought, and silence continued long; at last she raised her bright head, and said, "Yendrek, do you remember how much we owe him?"

"If I forget, I will borrow eyes from a dog, for I shall not dare to look an honest man in the face with my own eyes."

"Yendrek, you cannot leave him in that state."

"How can I help him?"

"Go to him."

"There speaks a woman's honest heart; there is a noble woman," cried Kharlamp, seizing her hands and covering them with kisses.

But the advice was not to Kmita's taste; hence he began to twist his head, and said, "I would go to the ends of the earth for him, but — you yourself know — if you were well — I do not say — but you know. God preserve you from any accident! I should wither away from anxiety — A wife is above the best friend. I am sorry for Pan Michael but — you yourself know — "

"I will remain under the protection of the Lauda fathers. It is peaceful here now, and I shall not be afraid of any small thing. Without God's will a hair will not fall from my head; and Pan Michael needs rescue, perhaps."

"Oi, he needs it!" put in Kharlamp.

"Yendrek, I am in good health. Harm will come to me from no one; I know that you are unwilling to go — "

"I would rather go against cannon with an oven-stick!" interrupted Kmita.

"If you stay, do you think it will not be bitter for you here when you think, 'I have abandoned my friend'? and besides, the Lord God may easily take away His blessing in His just wrath."

"You beat a knot into my head. You say that He may take away His blessing? I fear that."

"It is a sacred duty to save such a friend as Pan Michael."

"I love Michael with my whole heart. The case is a hard one! If there is need, there is urgent need, for every hour in this matter is important. I will go at once to the stables. By the living God, is there no other way out of it? The Evil One inspired Pan Yan and Zagloba to go to Kalish. It is not a question with me of myself, but of you, dearest. I would rather lose all I have than be without you one day. Should any one say that I go from you not on public service, I would plant my sword-hilt in his mouth to the cross. Duty, you say? Let it be so. He is a fool who hesitates. If this were for any one else but Michael, I never should do it."

Here Pan Andrei turned to Kharlamp. "Gracious sir, I beg you to come to the stable; we will choose horses. And you, Olenka, see that my trunk is ready. Let some of the Lauda men look to the threshing. Pan Kharlamp, you must stay with us even a fortnight; you will take care of my wife for me. Some land may be found for you here in the neighborhood. Take Lyubich! Come to the stable. I will start in an hour. If 't is needful, 't is needful!"

CHAPTER III.

SOME time before sunset Pan Kmita set out, blessed by his tearful wife with a crucifix, in which splinters of the Holy Cross were set in gold; and since during long years the knight had been inured to sudden journeys, when he started, he rushed forth as if to seize Tartars escaping with plunder.

When he reached Vilno, he held on through Grodno to Byalystok, and thence to Syedlets. In passing through Lukov, he learned that Pan Yan had returned the day previous from Kalish with his wife and children, Pan Zagloba accompanying. He determined, therefore, to go to them; for with whom could he take more efficient counsel touching the rescue of Pan Michael?

They received him with surprise and delight, which were turned into weeping, however, when he told them the cause of his coming.

Pan Zagloba was unable all day to calm himself, and shed so many tears at the pond that, as he said himself afterward, the pond rose, and they had to lift the flood-gate. But when he had wept himself out, he thought deeply; and this is what he said at the council, —

"Yan, you cannot go, for you are chosen to the Chapter; there will be a multitude of cases, as after so many wars the country is full of unquiet spirits. From what you relate, Pan Kmita, it is clear that the storks[1] will remain in Vodokty all winter, since they are on the work-list and must attend to their duties. It is no wonder that with such housekeeping you are in no haste for the journey, especially since 't is unknown how long it may last. You have shown a great heart by coming; but if I am to give earnest advice, I will say : Go home; for in Michael's case a near confidant is called for, — one who will not be offended at a harsh answer, or because there is no wish to admit him. Patience is needful, and long experience; and your grace has only friendship for Michael, which in such a contingency is not enough.

---

[1] The story in Poland is that storks bring all the infants to the country.

But be not offended, for you must confess that Yan and I are older friends, and have passed through more adventures with him than you have. Dear God! how many are the times in which I saved him, and he me, from disaster!"

"I will resign my functions as a deputy," interrupted Pan Yan.

"Yan, that is public service!" retorted Zagloba, with sternness.

"God sees," said the afflicted Pan Yan, "that I love my cousin Stanislav with true brotherly affection; but Michael is nearer to me than a brother."

"He is nearer to me than any blood relative, especially since I never had one. It is not the time now to discuss our affection. Do you see, Yan, if this misfortune had struck Michael recently, perhaps I would say to you, 'Give the Chapter to the Devil, and go!' But let us calculate how much time has passed since Kharlamp reached Jmud from Chenstohova, and while Pan Andrei was coming from Jmud here to us. Now, it is needful not only to go to Michael, but to remain with him; not only to weep with him, but to persuade him; not only to show him the Crucified as an example, but to cheer his heart and mind with pleasant jokes. So you know who ought to go, — I! and I will go, so help me God! If I find him in Chenstohova, I will bring him to this place; if I do not find him, I will follow him even to Moldavia, and I will not cease to seek for him while I am able to raise with my own strength a pinch of snuff to my nostrils."

When they had heard this, the two knights fell to embracing Pan Zagloba; and he grew somewhat tender over the misfortune of Pan Michael and his own coming fatigues. Therefore he began to shed tears; and at last, when he had embraces enough, he said, —

"But do not thank me for Pan Michael; you are not nearer to him than I."

"Not for Pan Michael do we thank you," said Kmita; "but that man must have a heart of iron, or rather one not at all human, who would be unmoved at sight of your readiness, which in the service of a friend makes no account of fatigue and has no thought for age. Other men in your years think only of a warm corner; but you speak of a long journey as if you were of my years or those of Pan Yan."

Zagloba did not conceal his years, it is true; but, in general, he did not wish people to mention old age as an attendant of incapability. Hence, though his eyes were still red, he glanced quickly and with a certain dissatisfaction at Kmita, and answered, —

"My dear sir, when my seventy-seventh year was beginning, my heart felt a slight sinking, because two axes[1] were over my neck; but when the eighth ten of years passed me, such courage entered my body that a wife tripped into my brain. And had I married, we might see who would be first to have cause of boasting, you or I."

"I am not given to boasting," said Kmita; "but I do not spare praises on your grace."

"And I should have surely confused you as I did Revera Pototski, the hetman, in presence of the king, when he jested at my age. I challenged him to show who could make the greatest number of goat-springs one after the other. And what came of it? The hetman made three; the haiduks had to lift him, for he could not rise alone; and I went all around with nearly thirty-five springs. Ask Pan Yan, who saw it all with his own eyes."

Pan Yan, knowing that Zagloba had had for some time the habit of referring to him as an eye-witness of everything, did not wink, but spoke again of Pan Michael. Zagloba sank into silence, and began to think of some subject deeply; at last he dropped into better humor and said after supper, —

"I will tell you a thing that not every mind could hit upon. I trust in God that our Michael will come out of this trouble more easily than we thought at first."

"God grant! but whence did that come to your head?" inquired Kmita.

"H'm! Besides an acquaintance with Michael, it is necessary to have quick wit from nature and long experience, and the latter is not possible at your years. Each man has his own special qualities. When misfortune strikes some men, it is, speaking figuratively, as if you were to throw a stone into a river. On the surface the water flows, as it were, quietly; but the stone lies at the bottom and hinders the natural current, and stops it and tears it terribly, and it will lie there and tear it till all the water of that river flows into the Styx. Yan, you may be counted with such men; but there is more suffering in the world for them, since the pain, and the memory of what caused it, do not leave them. But

---

[1] This refers to the axelike form of the numeral 7.

others receive misfortune as if some one had struck them
with a fist on the shoulder. They lose their senses for the
moment, revive later on, and when the black-and-blue spot
is well, they forget it. Oi! such a nature is better in this
world, which is full of misfortune."

The knights listened with attention to the wise words of
Zagloba; he was glad to see that they listened with such
respect, and continued, —

"I know Michael through and through; and God is my
witness that I have no wish to find fault with him now, but
it seems to me that he grieves more for the loss of the
marriage than of the maiden. It is nothing that terrible
despair has come, though that too, especially for him, is a misfortune above misfortunes. You cannot even imagine what
a wish that man had to marry. There is not in him greed or
ambition of any kind, or selfishness: he has left what he had,
he has as good as lost his own fortune, he has not asked
for his salary; but in return for all his labors and services
he expected, from the Lord God and the Commonwealth,
only a wife. And he reckoned in his soul that such bread
as that belonged to him; and he was about to put it to
his mouth, when right there, as it were, some one sneered
at him, saying, 'You have it now! Eat it!' What wonder
that despair seized him? I do not say that he did not
grieve for the maiden; but as God is dear to me, he grieved
more for the marriage, though he would himself swear to
the opposite."

"That may be true," said Pan Yan.

"Wait! Only let those wounds of his soul close and
heal; we shall see if his old wish will not come again. The
danger is only in this, that now, under the weight of despair,
he may do something or make some decision which he
would regret later on. But what was to happen has happened, for in misfortune decision comes quickly. My
attendant is packing my clothes. I am not speaking to
dissuade you from going; I wished only to comfort you."

"Again, father, you will be a plaster to Michael," said
Pan Yan.

"As I was to you, you remember? If I can only find
him soon, for I fear that he may be hiding in some hermit-
age, or that he will disappear somewhere in the distant
steppes to which he is accustomed from childhood. Pan
Kmita, your grace criticises my age; but I tell you that if
ever a courier rushed on with despatches as I shall rush, then

command me when I return to unravel old silk, shell peas, or give me a distaff. Neither will hardships detain me, nor wonders of hospitality tempt me; eating, even drinking, will not stop me. You have not yet seen such a journey! I can now barely sit in my place, just as if some one were pricking me from under the bench with an awl. I have even ordered that my travelling-shirt be rubbed with goats' tallow, so as to resist the serpent."

CHAPTER IV.

PAN ZAGLOBA did not drive forward so swiftly, however, as he had promised himself and his comrades. The nearer he was to Warsaw, the more slowly he travelled. It was the time in which Yan Kazimir, king, statesman, and great leader, having extinguished foreign conflagration and brought the Commonwealth, as it were, from the depths of a deluge, had abdicated lordship. He had suffered everything, had endured everything, had exposed his breast to every blow which came from a foreign enemy; but when later on he aimed at internal reforms and instead of aid from the nation found only opposition and ingratitude, he removed from his anointed temples of his own will that crown which had become an unendurable burden to him.

The district and general diets had been held already; and Prajmovski, the primate, summoned the Convocation for November 5.

Great were the early efforts of various candidates, great the rivalry of various parties; and though it was the election alone which would decide, still, each one felt the uncommon importance of the Diet of Convocation. Therefore deputies were hastening to Warsaw, on wheels and on horseback, with attendants and servants; senators were moving to the capital, and with each one of them a magnificent escort.

The roads were crowded; the inns were filled, and discovery of lodgings for a night was connected with great delay. Places were yielded, however, to Zagloba out of regard for his age; but at the same time his immense reputation exposed him more than once to loss of time.

This was the way of it: He would come to some public house, and not another finger could be thrust into the place; the personage who with his escort had occupied the building would come out then, through curiosity to see who had arrived, and finding a man with mustaches and beard as white as milk, would say, in view of such dignity, —

"I beg your grace, my benefactor, to come with me for a chance bite."

Zagloba was no boor, and refused not, knowing that acquaintance with him would be pleasing to every man. When the host conducted him over the threshold and asked, "Whom have I the honor?" he merely put his hands on his hips, and sure of the effect, answered in two words, "Zagloba sum! (I am Zagloba)."

Indeed, it never happened that after those two words a great opening of arms did not follow, and exclamations, "I shall inscribe this among my most fortunate days!" And the cries of officers or nobles, "Look at him! that is the model, the *gloria et decus* (glory and honor) of all the cavaliers of the Commonwealth." They hurried together then to wonder at Zagloba; the younger men came to kiss the skirts of his travelling-coat. After that they drew out of the wagons kegs and vessels, and a *gaudium* (rejoicing) followed, continuing sometimes a number of days.

It was thought universally that he was going as a deputy to the Diet; and when he declared that he was not, the astonishment was general. But he explained that he had yielded his mandate to Pan Domashevski, so that younger men might devote themselves to public affairs. To some he related the real reason why he was on the road; but when others inquired, he put them off with these words, —

"Accustomed to war from youthful years, I wanted in old age to have a last drive at Doroshenko."

After these words they wondered still more at him, and to no one did he seem less important because he was not a deputy, for all knew that among the audience were men who had more power than the deputies themselves. Besides, every senator, even the most eminent, had in mind that, a couple of months later, the election would follow, and then every word of a man of such fame among the knighthood would have value beyond estimation.

They carried, therefore, Zagloba in their arms, and stood before him with bared heads, even the greatest lords. Pan Podlyaski drank three days with him; the Patses, whom he met in Kalushyn, bore him on their hands.

More than one man gave command to thrust into the old hero's hamper considerable gifts, from vodka and wine to richly ornamented caskets, sabres, and pistols.

Zagloba's servants too had good profit from this; and he, despite resolutions and promises, travelled so slowly that only on the third week did he reach Minsk.

2

But he did not halt for refreshments at Minsk. Driving to the square, he saw a retinue so conspicuous and splendid that he had not met such on the road hitherto : attendants in brilliant-colors ; half a regiment of infantry alone, for to the Diet of Convocation men did not go armed on horse-back, but these troops were in such order that the King of Sweden had not a better guard ; the place was filled with gilded carriages carrying tapestry and carpets to use in public houses on the way ; wagons with provision chests and supplies of food; with them were servants, nearly all foreign, so that in that throng few spoke an intelligible tongue.

Zagloba saw at last an attendant in Polish costume ; hence he gave order to halt, and sure of good entertainment, had put forth one foot already from the wagon, asking at the same time, " But whose retinue is this, so splendid that the king can have no better ? "

" Whose should it be," replied the attendant, " but that of our lord, the Prince Marshal of Lithuania ? "

" Whose ? " repeated Zagloba.

" Are you deaf ? Prince Boguslav Radzivill, who is going to the Convocation, but who, God grant, after the election will be elected."

Zagloba hid his foot quickly in the wagon. " Drive on ! " cried he. " There is nothing here for us ! "

And he went on, trembling from indignation.

" O Great God ! " said he, " inscrutable are Thy decrees ; and if Thou dost not shatter this traitor with Thy thunder-bolts, Thou hast in this some hidden designs which it is not permitted to reach by man's reason, though judging in human fashion, it would have been proper to give a good blow to such a bull-driver. But it is evident that evil is working in this most illustrious Commonwealth, if such traitors, without honor and conscience, not only receive no punishment, but ride in safety and power, — nay, exercise civil functions also. It must be that we shall perish, for in what other country, in what other State, could such a thing be brought to pass ? Yan Kazimir was a good king, but he forgave too often, and accustomed the wickedest to trust in impunity and safety. Still, that is not his fault alone. It is clear that in the nation civil conscience and the feeling of public virtue has perished utterly. Tfu ! tfu ! he a deputy ! In his infamous hands citizens place the integrity and safety of the country, — in those very hands with which he was rending it and fastening it in Swedish fetters. We shall be lost; it cannot be otherwise! Still more to make a king of him, the — But what! 't is evident that everything is possible among such people. He a deputy! For God's sake! But the law declares clearly that a man who fills offices in a foreign country cannot be a deputy; and he is a governor-general in princely Prussia under his mangy uncle. Ah, ha! wait, I have thee. And verifications at the Diet, what are they for? If I do not go to the hall and raise this question, though I am only a spectator, may I be turned this minute into a fat sheep, and my driver into a butcher! I will find among deputies men to support me. I know not, traitor, whether I can overcome such a potentate and exclude thee; but what I shall do will not help thy election, — that is sure. And Michael, poor fellow, must wait for me, since this is an action of public importance."

So thought Zagloba, promising himself to attend with care to that case of expulsion, and to bring over deputies in private; for this reason he hastened on more hurriedly to Warsaw from Minsk, fearing to be late for the opening of the Diet. But he came early enough. The concourse of deputies and other persons was so great that it was utterly impossible to find lodgings in Warsaw itself, or in Praga, or even outside the city; it was difficult too to find a place in a private house, for three or four persons were lodged in single rooms. Zagloba spent the first night in a shop, and it passed rather pleasantly; but in the morning, when he found himself in his wagon, he did not know well what to do.

"My God! my God!" said he, falling into evil humor, and looking around on the Cracow suburbs, which he had just passed; "here are the Bernardines, and there is the ruin of the Kazanovski Palace! Thankless city! I had to wrest it from the enemy with my blood and toil, and now it grudges me a corner for my gray head."

But the city did not by any means grudge Zagloba a corner for his gray head; it simply had n't one. Meanwhile a lucky star was watching over him, for barely had he reached the palace of the Konyetspolskis when a voice called from one side to his driver, "Stop!"

The man reined in the horses; then an unknown nobleman approached the wagon with gleaming face, and cried out, "Pan Zagloba! Does your grace not know me?"

Zagloba saw before him a man of somewhat over thirty years, wearing a leopard-skin cap with a feather, — an unerring mark of military service, — a poppy-colored under-coat, and a dark-red kontush, girded with a gold brocade belt. The face of the unknown was of unusual beauty: his complexion was pale, but burned somewhat by wind in the fields to a yellowish tinge; his blue eyes were full of a certain melancholy and pensiveness; his features were unusually symmetrical, almost too beautiful for a man. Notwithstanding his Polish dress, he wore long hair and a beard cut in foreign fashion. Halting at the wagon, he opened his arms widely; and Zagloba, though he could not remember him at once, bent over and embraced him. They pressed each other heartily, and at moments one pushed the other back so as to have a better look.

"Pardon me, your grace," said Zagloba, at last; "but I cannot call to mind yet."

"Hassling-Ketling!"

"For God's sake! The face seemed well known to me, but the dress has changed you entirely, for I saw you in old times in a Prussian uniform. Now you wear the Polish dress?"

"Yes; for I have taken as my mother this Commonwealth, which received me when a wanderer, almost in years of boyhood, and gave me abundant bread and another mother I do not wish. You do not know that I received citizenship after the war."

"But you bring me good news! So Fortune favored you in this?"

"Both in this and in something else; for in Courland, on the very boundary of Jmud, I found a man of my own name, who adopted me, gave me his escutcheon, and bestowed on me property. He lives in Svyenta in Courland; but on this side he has an estate called Shkudy, which he gave me."

"God favor you! Then you have given up war?"

"Only let the chance come, and I'll take my place without fail. In view of that, I have rented my land, and am waiting here for an opening."

"That is the courage that I like. Just as I was in youth, and I have strength yet in my bones. What are you doing now in Warsaw?"

"I am a deputy at the Diet of Convocation."

"God's wounds! But you are already a Pole to the bones!"

The young knight smiled. "To my soul, which is better."

"Are you married?"

Ketling sighed. "No."

"Only that is lacking. But I think — wait a minute! But has that old feeling for Panna Billevich gone out of your mind?"

"Since you know of that which I thought my secret, be assured that no new one has come."

"Oh, leave her in peace! She will soon give the world a young Kmita. Never mind! What sort of work is it to sigh when another is living with her in better confidence? To tell the truth, 't is ridiculous."

Ketling raised his pensive eyes. "I have said only that no new feeling has come."

"It will come, never fear! we'll have you married. I know from experience that in love too great constancy brings merely suffering. In my time I was as constant as Troilus, and lost a world of pleasure and a world of good opportunities; and how much I suffered!"

"God grant every one to retain such jovial humor as your grace!"

"Because I lived in moderation always, therefore I have no aches in my bones. Where are you stopping? Have you found lodgings?"

"I have a comfortable cottage, which I built after the war."

"You are fortunate; but I have been travelling through the whole city in vain since yesterday."

"For God's sake! my benefactor, you will not refuse, I hope, to stop with me. There is room enough; besides the house, there are wings and a commodious stable. You will find room for your servants and horses."

"You have fallen from heaven, as God is dear to me!"

Ketling took a seat in the wagon and they drove forward. On the way Zagloba told him of the misfortune that had met Pan Michael, and he wrung his hands, for hitherto he had not heard of it.

"The dart is all the keener for me," said he, at last; "and perhaps your grace does not know what a friendship sprang up between us in recent times. Together we went through all the later wars with Prussia, at the besieging of fortresses, where there were only Swedish garrisons. We went to the Ukraine and against Pan Lyubomirski, and after the death of the voevoda of Rus, to the Ukraine a second time under Sobieski, the marshal of the kingdom. The same saddle served us as a pillow, and we ate from the same dish; we were called Castor and Pollux. And only when he went for his affianced, did the moment of separation come. Who could think that his best hopes would vanish like an arrow in the air?"

"There is nothing fixed in this vale of tears," said Zagloba.

"Except steady friendship. We must take counsel and learn where he is at this moment. We may hear something from the marshal of the kingdom, who loves Michael as the apple of his eye. If he can tell nothing, there are deputies here from all sides. It cannot be that no man has heard of such a knight. In what I have power, in that I will aid you, more quickly than if the question affected myself."

Thus conversing, they came at last to Ketling's cottage, which turned out to be a mansion. Inside was every kind of order and no small number of costly utensils, either purchased, or obtained in campaigns. The collection of weapons especially was remarkable. Zagloba was delighted with what he saw, and said, —

"Oh, you could find lodgings here for twenty men. It was lucky for me that I met you. I might have occupied apartments with Pan Anton Hrapovitski, for he is an acquaintance and friend. The Patses also invited me, — they are seeking partisans against the Radzivills, — but I prefer to be with you."

"I have heard among the Lithuanian deputies," said Ketling, "that since the turn comes now to Lithuania, they wish absolutely to choose Pan Hrapovitski as marshal of the Diet."

"And justly. He is an honest man and a sensible one, but too good-natured. For him there is nothing more precious than harmony; he is only seeking to reconcile some man with some other, and that is useless. But tell me sincerely, what is Boguslav Radzivill to you?"

"From the time that Pan Kmita's Tartars took me captive at Warsaw, he has been nothing; for although he is a great lord, he is a perverse and malicious man. I saw enough of him when he plotted in Taurogi against that being superior to earth."

"How superior to earth? What are you talking of, man? She is of clay, and may be broken like any clay vessel. But that is no matter."

Here Zagloba grew purple from rage, till the eyes were starting from his head. "Imagine to yourself, that ruffian is a deputy!"

"Who?" asked in astonishment Ketling, whose mind was still on Olenka.

"Boguslav Radzivill! But the verification of powers, — what is that for? Listen: you are a deputy; you can raise the question. I will roar to you from the gallery in support; have no fear on that point. The right is with us; and if they try to degrade the right, a tumult may be raised in the audience that will not pass without blood."

"Do not do that, your grace, for God's sake! I will raise the question, for it is proper to do so; but God preserve us from stopping the Diet!"

"I will go to Hrapovitski, though he is lukewarm; but no matter, much depends on him as the future marshal. I will rouse the Patses. At least I will mention in public all Boguslav's intrigues. Moreover, I have heard on the road that that ruffian thinks of seeking the crown for himself."

"A nation would have come to its final decline and would not be worthy of life if such a man could become king," said Ketling. "But rest now, and on some later day we will go to the marshal of the kingdom and inquire about our friend."

CHAPTER V.

Some days later came the opening of the Diet, over which, as Ketling had foreseen, Pan Hrapovitski was chosen to preside; he was at that time chamberlain of Smolensk, and afterward voevoda of Vityebsk. Since the only question was to fix the time of election and appoint the supreme Chapter, and as intrigues of various parties could not find a field in such questions, the Diet was carried on calmly enough. The question of verification roused it merely a little in the very beginning. When the deputy Ketling challenged the election of the secretary of Belsk and his colleague, Prince Boguslav Radzivill, some powerful voice in the audience shouted "Traitor! foreign official!" After that voice followed others; some deputies joined them; and all at once the Diet was divided into two parties, — one striving to exclude the deputies of Belsk, the other to confirm their election. Finally a court was appointed to settle the question, and recognized the election. Still, the blow was a painful one to Prince Boguslav. This alone, that the Diet was considering whether the prince was qualified to sit in the chamber; this alone, that all his treasons and treacheries in time of the Swedish invasion were mentioned in public, — covered him with fresh disgrace in the eyes of the Commonwealth, and undermined fundamentally all his ambitious designs. For it was his calculation that when the partisans of Condé, Neuburgh, and Lorraine, not counting inferior candidates, had injured one another mutually, the choice might fall easily on a man of the country. Hence, pride and his sycophants told him that if that were to happen, the man of the country could be no other than a man endowed with the highest genius, and of the most powerful and famous family, — in other words, he himself.

Keeping matters in secret till the hour came, the prince spread his nets in advance over Lithuania, and just then he was spreading them in Warsaw, when suddenly he saw that in the very beginning they were torn, and such a broad rent made that all the fish might escape through it easily. He gritted his teeth during the whole time of the court; and since he could not wreak his vengeance on Ketling, as he was a deputy, he announced among his attendants a reward to him who would indicate that spectator who had cried out just after Ketling's proposal, "Traitor! foreign official!"

Zagloba's name was too famous to remain hidden long; moreover, he did not conceal himself in any way. The prince indeed raised a still greater uproar, but was disconcerted not a little when he heard that he was met by so popular a man and one whom it was dangerous to attack.

Zagloba too knew his own power; for when threats had begun to fly about, he said once at a great meeting of nobles, "I do not know if there would be danger to any one should a hair of my head fall. The election is not distant; and when a hundred thousand sabres of brothers are collected, there may easily be some making of mince-meat."

These words reached the prince, who only bit his lips and smiled sneeringly; but in his soul he thought that the old man was right. On the following day he changed his plans evidently with regard to the old knight, for when some one spoke of Zagloba at a feast given by the prince chamberlain, Boguslav said, —

"That noble is greatly opposed to me, as I hear; but I have such love for knightly people that even if he does not cease to injure me in future, I shall always love him."

And a week later the prince repeated the same directly to Pan Zagloba, when they met at the house of the Grand Hetman Sobieski. Though Zagloba preserved a calm face, full of courage, the heart fluttered a little in his breast at sight of the prince; for Boguslav had far-reaching hands, and was a man-eater of whom all were in dread. The prince called out, however, across the whole table, —

"Gracious Pan Zagloba, the report has come to me that you, though not a deputy, wished to drive me, innocent man, from the Diet; but I forgive you in Christian fashion, and should you ever need advancement, I shall not be slow to serve you."

"I merely stood by the Constitution," answered Zagloba, "as a noble is bound to do; as to assistance, at my age it is likely that the assistance of God is needed most, for I am near ninety."

"A beautiful age if its virtue is as great as its length, and this I have not the least wish to doubt."

"I served my country and my king without seeking strange gods."

The prince frowned a little. "You served against me too; I know that. But let there be harmony between us. All is forgotten, and this too, that you aided the private hatred of another against me. With that enemy I have still some accounts; but I extend my hand to your grace, and offer my friendship."

"I am only a poor man; the friendship is too high for me. I should have to stand on tiptoe, or spring to it; and that in old age is annoying. If your princely grace is speaking of accounts with Pan Kmita, my friend, then I should be glad from my heart to leave that arithmetic."

"But why so, I pray?" asked the prince.

"For there are four fundamental rules in arithmetic. Though Pan Kmita has a respectable fortune, it is a fly if compared with your princely wealth; therefore Pan Kmita will not consent to division. He is occupied with multiplication himself, and will let no man take aught from him; though he might give something to others, I do not think that your princely grace would be eager to take what he'd give you."

Though Boguslav was trained in word-fencing, still, whether it was Zagloba's argument or his insolence that astonished him so much, he forgot the tongue in his own mouth. The breasts of those present began to shake from laughter. Pan Sobieski laughed with his whole soul, and said,—

"He is an old warrior of Zbaraj. He knows how to wield a sabre, but is no common player with the tongue. Better let him alone."

In fact, Boguslav, seeing that he had hit upon an irreconcilable, did not try further to capture Zagloba; but beginning conversation with another man, he cast from time to time malign glances across the table at the old knight.

But Sobieski was delighted, and continued, "You are a master, lord brother,—a genuine master. Have you ever found your equal in this Commonwealth?"

"At the sabre," answered Zagloba, satisfied with the praise, "Volodyovski has come up to me; and Kmita too I have trained not badly."

Saying this, he looked at Boguslav; but the prince feigned not to hear him, and spoke diligently with his neighbor.

"Why!" said the hetman, "I have seen Pan Michael at work more than once, and would guarantee him even if the fate of all Christendom were at stake. It is a pity that a thunderbolt, as it were, has struck such a soldier."

"But what has happened to him?" asked Sarbyevski, the sword-bearer of Tsehanov.

"The maiden he loved died in Chenstohova," answered Zagloba; "and the worst is that I cannot learn from any source where he is."

"But I saw him," cried Pan Varshytski, the castellan of Cracow. "While coming to Warsaw, I saw him on the road coming hither also; and he told me that being disgusted with the world and its vanities, he was going to Mons Regius to end his suffering life in prayer and meditation."

Zagloba caught at the remnant of his hair. "He has become a monk of Camaldoli, as God is dear to me!" exclaimed he, in the greatest despair.

Indeed, the statement of the castellan had made no small impression on all. Pan Sobieski, who loved soldiers, and knew himself best how the country needed them, was pained deeply, and said after a pause, —

"It is not proper to oppose the free-will of men and the glory of God, but it is a pity to lose him; and it is hard for me to hide from you, gentlemen, that I am grieved. From the school of Prince Yeremi that was an excellent soldier against every enemy, but against the horde and ruffiandom incomparable. There are only a few such partisans in the steppes, such as Pan Pivo among the Cossacks, and Pan Rushchyts in the cavalry; but even these are not equal to Pan Michael."

"It is fortunate that the times are somewhat calmer," said the sword-bearer of Tsehanov, "and that Paganism observes faithfully the treaty of Podhaytse extorted by the invincible sword of my benefactor."

Here the sword-bearer inclined before Sobieski, who rejoiced in his heart at the public praise, and answered, "That was due, in the first instance, to the goodness of God, who permitted me to stand at the threshold of the Commonwealth, and cut the enemy somewhat; and in the second, to the courage of good soldiers who are ready for everything. That the Khan would be glad to keep the treaties, I know; but in the Crimea itself there are tumults against the Khan, and the Belgrod horde does not obey him at all. I have just received tidings that on the Moldavian boundary clouds are collecting, and that raids may come in; I have given orders to watch the roads carefully, but I have not soldiers sufficient. If I send some to one place, an opening is left in another. I need men trained specially and knowing the ways of the horde; this is why I am so sorry for Volodyovski."

In answer to this, Zagloba took from his temples the hands with which he was pressing his head, and cried, "But he will not remain a monk, even if I have to make an assault on Mons Regius and take him by force. For God's sake! I will go to him straightway to-morrow, and perhaps he will obey my persuasion; if not, I will go to the primate, to the prior. Even if I have to go to Rome, I will go. I have no wish to detract from the glory of God; but what sort of a monk would he be without a beard? He has as much hair on his face as I on my fist! As God is dear to me, he will never be able to sing Mass; or if he sings it, the rats will run out of the cloister, for they will think a tom-cat is wailing. Forgive me, gentlemen, for speaking what sorrow brings to my tongue. If I had a son, I could not love him as I do that man. God be with him! God be with him! Even if he were to become a Bernardine, but a monk of Camaldoli! As I sit here, a living man, nothing can come of this! I will go straightway to the primate to-morrow, for a letter to the prior."

"He cannot have made vows yet," put in the marshal, "but let not your grace be too urgent, lest he grow stubborn; and it is needful to reckon with this too, — has not the will of God appeared in his intention?"

"The will of God? The will of God does not come on a sudden; as the old proverb says, 'What is sudden is of the Devil.' If it were the will of God, I should have noted the wish long ago in him; and he was not a priest, but a dragoon. If he had made such a resolve while in full reason, in meditation and calmness, I should say nothing; but the will of God does not strike a despairing man as a falcon does a duck. I will not press him. Before I go I will meditate well with myself what to say, so that he may not play the fox to begin with; but in God is my hope. This little soldier has confided always more to my wit than his own, and will do the like this time, I trust, unless he has changed altogether."

CHAPTER VI.

NEXT day, Zagloba, armed with a letter from the primate, and having a complete plan made with Ketling, rang the bell at the gate of the monastery on Mons Regius. His heart was beating with violence at this thought, "How will Michael receive me?" and though he had prepared in advance what to say, he acknowledged himself that much depended on the reception. Thinking thus, he pulled the bell a second time; and when the key squeaked in the lock, and the door opened a little, he thrust himself into it straightway a trifle violently, and said to the confused young monk, —

"I know that to enter here a special permission is needed; but I have a letter from the archbishop, which you, *carissime frater*, will be pleased to give the reverend prior."

"It will be done according to the wish of your grace," said the doorkeeper, inclining at sight of the primate's seal.

Then he pulled a strap hanging at the tongue of a bell, and pulled twice to call some one, for he himself had no right to go from the door. Another monk appeared at that summons, and taking the letter, departed in silence. Zagloba placed on a bench a package which he had with him, then sat down and began to puff wonderfully. "Brother," said he, at last, "how long have you been in the cloister?"

"Five years," answered the porter.

"Is it possible? so young, and five years already! Then it is too late to leave, even if you wanted to do so. You must yearn sometimes for the world; the world smells of war for one man, of feasts for another, of fair heads for a third."

"Avaunt!" said the monk, making the sign of the cross with devotion.

"How is that? Has not the temptation to go out of the cloister come on you?" continued Zagloba.

The monk looked with distrust at the envoy of the archbishop, speaking in such marvellous fashion, and answered, "When the door here closes on any man, he never goes out."

"We'll see that yet! What is happening to Pan Volodyovski? Is he well?"

"There is no one here named in that way."

"Brother Michael?" said Zagloba, on trial. "Former
colonel of dragoons, who came here not long since."

"We call him Brother Yerzy; but he has not made his
vows yet, and cannot make them till the end of the term."

"And surely he will not make them; for you will not
believe, brother, what a woman's man he is! You could
not find another man so hostile to woman's virtue in all the
clois — I meant to say in all the cavalry."

"It is not proper for me to hear this," said the monk,
with increasing astonishment and confusion.

"Listen, brother; I do not know where you receive
visitors, but if it is in this place, I advise you to withdraw
a little when Brother Yerzy comes, — as far as that gate,
for instance, — for we shall talk here of very worldly
matters."

"I prefer to go away at once," said the monk.

Meanwhile Pan Michael, or rather Brother Yerzy,
appeared; but Zagloba did not recognize the approaching
man, for Pan Michael had changed greatly. To begin with,
he seemed taller in the long white habit than in the dragoon
jacket; secondly, his mustaches, pointing upward toward
his eyes formerly, were hanging down now, and he was
trying to let out his beard, which formed two little yellow
tresses not longer than half a finger; finally, he had grown
very thin and meagre, and his eyes had lost their former
glitter. He approached slowly, with his hands hidden on
his bosom under his habit, and with drooping head.

Zagloba, not recognizing him, thought that perhaps the
prior himself was coming; therefore he rose from the bench
and began, "Laudetur—" Suddenly he looked more closely,
opened his arms, and cried, "Pan Michael! Pan Michael!"

Brother Yerzy let himself be seized in the embrace;
something like a sob shook his breast, but his eyes remained
dry. Zagloba pressed him a long time; at last he began to
speak, —

"You have not been alone in weeping over your misfortune. I wept; Yan and his family wept; the Kmitas
wept. It is the will of God! be resigned to it, Michael.
May the Merciful Father comfort and reward you! You
have done well to shut yourself in for a time in these walls.
There is nothing better than prayer and pious meditation

in misfortune. Come, let me embrace you again! I can hardly see you through my tears."

And Zagloba wept with sincerity, moved at the sight of Pan Michael. "Pardon me for disturbing your meditation," said he, at last; "but I could not act otherwise, and you will do me justice when I give you my reasons. Ai, Michael! you and I have gone through a world of evil and of good. Have you found consolation behind these bars?"

"I have," replied Pan Michael, — "in those words which I hear in this place daily, and repeat, and which I desire to repeat till my death, *memento mori*. In death is consolation for me."

"H'm! death is more easily found on the battlefield than in the cloister, where life passes as if some one were unwinding thread from a ball, slowly."

"There is no life here, for there are no earthly questions; and before the soul leaves the body, it lives, as it were, in another world."

"If that is true, I will not tell you that the Belgrod horde are mustering in great force against the Commonwealth; for what interest can that have for you?"

Pan Michael's mustaches quivered on a sudden, and he stretched his right hand unwittingly to his left side; but not finding a sword there, he put both hands under his habit, dropped his head, and repeated, "Memento mori!"

"Justly, justly!" answered Zagloba, blinking his sound eye with a certain impatience. "No longer ago than yesterday Pan Sobieski, the hetman, said: 'Only let Volodyovski serve even through this one storm, and then let him go to whatever cloister he likes. God would not be angry for the deed; on the contrary, such a monk would have all the greater merit.' But there is no reason to wonder that you put your own peace above the happiness of the country, for *prima charitas ab ego* (the first love is of self)."

A long interval of silence followed; only Pan Michael's mustaches stood out somewhat and began to move quickly, though lightly.

"You have not taken your vows yet," asked Zagloba, at last, "and you can go out at any moment?"

"I am not a monk yet, for I have been waiting for the favor of God, and waiting till all painful thoughts of earth should leave my soul. His favor is upon me now; peace is returning to me. I can go out; but I have no wish to go, since the time is drawing near in which I can make

my vows with a clear conscience and free from earthly
desires."

"I have no wish to lead you away from this; on the
contrary, I applaud your resolution, though I remember
that when Yan in his time intended to become a monk, he
waited till the country was free from the storm of the
enemy. But do as you wish. In truth, it is not I who
will lead you away; for I myself in my own time felt a
vocation for monastic life. Fifty years ago I even began
my novitiate; I am a rogue if I did not. Well, God gave
me another direction. Only I tell you this, Michael, you
must go out with me now even for two days."

"Why must I go out? Leave me in peace!" said
Volodyovski.

Zagloba raised the skirt of his coat to his eyes and began
to sob. "I do not beg rescue for myself," said he, in a
broken voice, "though Prince Boguslav Radzivill is hunting me with vengeance; he puts his murderers in ambush
against me, and there is no one to defend and protect me,
old man. I was thinking that you — But never mind! I
will love you all my life, even if you are unwilling to
know me. Only pray for my soul, for I shall not escape
Boguslav's hands. Let that come upon me which has to
come; but another friend of yours, who shared every
morsel of bread with you, is now on his death-bed, and
wishes to see you without fail. He is unwilling to die
without you; for he has some confession to make on which
his soul's peace depends."

Pan Michael, who had heard of Zagloba's danger with
great emotion, sprang forward now, and seizing him by the
arms, inquired, "Is it Pan Yan?"

"No, not Yan, but Ketling!"

"For God's sake! what has happened to him?"

"He was shot by Prince Boguslav's ruffians while defending me; I know not whether he will be alive in twenty-four
hours. It is for you, Michael, that we have both fallen
into these straits, for we came to Warsaw only to think out
some consolation for you. Come for even two days, and
console a dying man. You will return later; you will
become a monk. I have brought the recommendation of
the primate to the prior to raise no impediment against
you. Only hasten, for every moment is precious."

"For God's sake!" cried Pan Michael; "what do I hear?
Impediments cannot keep me, for so far I am here only on

meditation. As God lives, the prayer of a dying man is sacred! I cannot refuse that."

"It would be a mortal sin!" cried Zagloba.

"That is true! It is always that traitor, Boguslav — But if I do not avenge Ketling, may I never come back! I will find those ruffians, and I will split their skulls! O Great God! sinful thoughts are already attacking me! *Memento mori!* Only wait here till I put on my old clothes, for it is not permitted to go out in the habit."

"Here are clothes!" cried Zagloba, springing to the bundle, which was lying there on the bench near them. "I foresaw everything, prepared everything! Here are boots, a rapier, a good overcoat."

"Come to the cell," said the little knight, with haste.

They went to the cell; and when they came out again, near Zagloba walked, not a white monk, but an officer with yellow boots to the knees, with a rapier at his side, and a white pendant across his shoulder. Zagloba blinked and smiled under his mustaches at sight of the brother at the door, who, evidently scandalized, opened the gate to the two.

Not far from the cloister and lower down, Zagloba's wagon was waiting, and with it two attendants. One was sitting on the seat, holding the reins of four well-attached horses; at these Pan Michael cast quickly the eye of an expert. The other stood near the wagon, with a mouldy, big-bellied bottle in one hand, and two goblets in the other.

"It is a good stretch of road to Mokotov," said Zagloba; "and harsh sorrow is waiting for us at the bedside of Ketling. Drink something, Michael, to gain strength to endure all this, for you are greatly reduced."

Saying this, Zagloba took the bottle from the hands of the man and filled both glasses with Hungarian so old that it was thick from age.

"This is a goodly drink," said Zagloba, placing the bottle on the ground and taking the goblets. "To the health of Ketling!"

"To his health!" repeated Pan Michael. "Let us hurry!"

They emptied the glasses at a draught.

"Let us hurry," repeated Zagloba. "Pour out, man!" said he, turning to the servant. "To the health of Pan Yan! Let us hurry!"

They emptied the goblets again at a draught, for there was real urgency.

"Let us take our seats!" cried Pan Michael.

"But will you not drink my health?" asked Zagloba, with a complaining voice.

"If quickly!"

And they drank quickly. Zagloba emptied the goblet at a breath, though there was half a quart in it, then without wiping his mustaches, he cried, "I should be thankless not to drink your health. Pour out, man!"

"With thanks!" answered Brother Yerzy.

The bottom appeared in the bottle, which Zagloba seized by the neck and broke into small pieces, for he never could endure the sight of empty vessels. Then he took his seat quickly, and they rode on.

The noble drink soon filled their veins with beneficent warmth, and their hearts with a certain consolation. The cheeks of Brother Yerzy were covered with a slight scarlet, and his glance regained its former vivacity. He stretched his hand unwittingly once, twice, to his mustaches, and turned them upward like awls, till at last they came near his eyes. He began meanwhile to gaze around with great curiosity, as if looking at the country for the first time. All at once Zagloba struck his palms on his knees and cried without evident reason, —

"Ho! ho! I hope that Ketling will return to health when he sees you! Ho! ho!"

And clasping Pan Michael around the neck, he began to embrace him with all his power. Pan Michael did not wish to remain in debt to Zagloba; he pressed him with the utmost sincerity. They went on for some time in silence, but in a happy one. Meanwhile the small houses of the suburbs began to appear on both sides of the road. Before the houses there was a great movement. On this side and that, townspeople were strolling, servants in various liveries, soldiers and nobles, frequently very well-dressed.

"Swarms of nobles have come to the Diet," said Zagloba; "for though not one of them is a deputy, they wish to be present, to hear and to see. The houses and inns are so filled everywhere that it is hard to find a room, and how many noble women are strolling along the streets! I tell you that you could not count them on the hairs of your beard. They are pretty too, the rogues, so that sometimes a man has the wish to slap his hands on his sides as a cock does his wings, and crow. But look! look at that brunette behind whom the haiduk is carrying the green shuba; is n't she splendid? Eh?"

Here Zagloba nudged Pan Michael in the side with his fist, and Pan Michael looked, moved his mustaches; his eyes glittered, but in that moment he grew shamefaced, dropped his head, and said after a brief silence, "Memento mori!"

But Zagloba clasped him again, and cried, "As you love me, *per amicitiam nostram* (by our friendship), as you respect me, get married. There are so many worthy maidens, get married!"

Brother Yerzy looked with astonishment on his friend. Zagloba could not be drunk, however, for many a time he had taken thrice as much wine without visible effect; therefore he spoke only from tenderness. But all thoughts of marriage were far away then from the head of Pan Michael, so that in the first instant astonishment overcame in him indignation; then he looked severely into the eyes of Zagloba and asked, —

"Are you tipsy?"

"From my whole heart I say to you, get married!"

Pan Michael looked still more severely. "Memento mori."

But Zagloba was not easily disconcerted. "Michael, if you love me, do this for me, and kiss a dog on the snout with your 'memento.' I repeat, you will do as you please, but I think in this way: Let each man serve God with that for which he was created; and God created you for the sword: in this His will is evident, since He has permitted you to attain such perfection in the use of it. In case He wished you to be a priest, He would have adorned you with a wit altogether different, and inclined your heart more to books and to Latin. Consider, too, that soldier saints enjoy no less respect in heaven than saints with vows, and they go campaigning against the legions of hell, and receive rewards from God's hands when they return with captured banners. All this is true; you will not deny it?"

"I do not deny it, and I know that it is hard to skirmish against your reasoning; but you also will not deny that for grief life is better in the cloister than in the world."

"If it is better, bah! then all the more should cloisters be shunned. Dull is the man who feeds mourning instead of keeping it hungry, so that the beast may die of famine as quickly as possible."

Pan Michael found no ready argument; therefore he was silent, and only after a while answered with a sad voice, "Do not mention marriage, for such mention only rouses fresh grief in me. My old desire will not revive, for it has passed away with tears; and my years are not suitable. My hair is beginning to whiten. Forty-two years, and twenty-five of them spent in military toil, are no jest, no jest!"

"O God, do not punish him for blasphemy! Forty-two years! Tfu! I have more than twice as many· on my shoulders, and still at times I must discipline myself to shake the heat out of my blood, as dust is shaken from clothing. Respect the memory of that dear dead one. You were good enough for her, I suppose? But for others are you too cheap, too old?"

"Give me peace! give me peace!" said Pan Michael, with a voice of pain; and the tears began to flow to his mustaches.

"I will not say another syllable," added Zagloba; "only give me the word of a cavalier that no matter what happens to Ketling you will stay a month with us. You must see Yan. If you wish afterward to return to the cloister, no one will raise an impediment."

"I give my word," said Pan Michael.

And they fell to talking of something else. Zagloba began to tell of the Diet, and how he had raised the question of excluding Prince Boguslav, and of the adventure with Ketling. Occasionally, however, he interrupted the narrative and buried himself in thoughts; they must have been cheerful, for from time to time he struck his knees with his palms, and repeated, —

"Ho! ho!"

But as he approached Mokotov, a certain disquiet appeared on his face. He turned suddenly to Pan Michael and said, "Your word is given, you remember, that no matter what happens to Ketling, you will stay a month with us."

"I gave it, and I will stay," said Pan Michael.

"Here is Ketling's house," cried Zagloba, — "a respectable place." Then he shouted to the driver, "Fire out of your whip! There will be a festival in this house to-day."

Loud cracks were heard from the whip. But the wagon had not entered the gate when a number of officers rushed from the ante-room, acquaintances of Pan Michael; among them also were old comrades from the days of Hmelnitski

and young officers of recent times. Of the latter were Pan
Vasilevski and Pan Novoveski, — youths yet, but fiery
cavaliers who in years of boyhood had broken away from
school and had been working at war for some years under
Pan Michael. These the little knight loved beyond
measure. Among the oldest was Pan Orlik of the shield
Novin, with a skull stopped with gold, for a Swedish
grenade had taken a piece of it on a time; and Pan
Rushchyts, a half-wild knight of the steppes, an incomparable partisan, second in fame to Pan Michael alone; and
a number of others. All, seeing the two men in the wagon,
began to shout, —

"He is there! he is there! Zagloba has conquered! He
is there!"

And rushing to the wagon, they seized the little knight
in their arms and bore him to the entrance, repeating,
"Welcome! dearest comrade, live for us! We have you;
we won't let you go! Vivat Volodyovski, the first cavalier, the ornament of the whole army! To the steppe with
us, brother! To the wild fields! There the wind will blow
your grief away."

They let him out of their arms only at the entrance. He
greeted them all, for he was greatly touched by that reception, and then he inquired at once, "How is Ketling? Is
he alive yet?"

"Alive! alive!" answered they, in a chorus, and the
mustaches of the old soldiers began to move with a strange
smile. "Go to him, for he cannot stay lying down; he is
waiting for you impatiently."

"I see that he is not so near death as Pan Zagloba said,"
answered the little knight.

Meanwhile they entered the ante-room and passed thence
to a large chamber, in the middle of which stood a table
with a feast on it; in one corner was a plank bed covered
with white horse-skin, on which Ketling was lying.

"Oh, my friend!" said Pan Michael, hastening toward
him.

"Michael!" cried Ketling, and springing to his feet as
if in the fulness of strength, he seized the little knight in
his embrace.

They pressed each other then so eagerly that Ketling
raised Volodyovski, and Volodyovski Ketling.

"They commanded me to simulate sickness," said the
Scot, "to feign death; but when I saw you, I could not

hold out. I am as well as a fish, and no misfortune has met me. But it was a question of getting you out of the cloister. Forgive, Michael. We invented this ambush out of love for you."

"To the wild fields with us!" cried the knights, again; and they struck with their firm palms on their sabres till a terrible clatter was raised in the room.

But Pan Michael was astounded. For a time he was silent, then he began to look at all, especially at Zagloba. "Oh, traitors!" exclaimed he, at last, "I thought that Ketling was wounded unto death."

"How is that, Michael?" cried Zagloba. "You are angry because Ketling is well? You grudge him his health, and wish death to him? Has your heart become stone in such fashion that you would gladly see all of us ghosts, and Ketling, and Pan Orlik, and Pan Rushchyts, and these youths, — nay, even Pan Yan, even me, who love you as a son?" Here Zagloba closed his eyes and cried still more piteously, "We have nothing to live for, gracious gentlemen; there is no thankfulness left in this world; there is nothing but callousness."

"For God's sake!" answered Pan Michael, "I do not wish you ill, but you have not respected my grief."

"Have pity on our lives!" repeated Zagloba.

"Give me peace!"

"He says that we show no respect to his grief; but what fountains we have poured out over him, gracious gentlemen! We have, Michael. I take God to witness that we should be glad to bear apart your grief on our sabres, for comrades should always act thus. But since you have given your word to stay with us a month, then love us at least for that month."

"I will love you till death," said Pan Michael.

Further conversation was interrupted by the coming of a new guest. The soldiers, occupied with Volodyovski, had not heard the arrival of that guest, and saw him only when he was standing in the door. He was a man enormous in stature, of majestic form and bearing. He had the face of a Roman emperor; in it was power, and at the same time the true kindness and courtesy of a monarch. He differed entirely from all those soldiers around him; he grew notably greater in face of them, as if the eagle, king of birds, had appeared among hawks, falcons, and merlins.

"The grand hetman!" cried Ketling, and sprang up, as the host, to greet him.

"Pan Sobieski!" cried others.

All heads were inclined in an obeisance of deep homage. All save Pan Michael knew that the hetman would come, for he had promised Ketling; still, his arrival had produced so profound an impression that for a time no one dared to speak first. That too was homage extraordinary. But Sobieski loved soldiers beyond all men, especially those with whom he had galloped over the necks of Tartar chambuls so often; he looked on them as his own family, and for this reason specially he had determined to greet Volodyovski, to comfort him, and finally, by showing such unusual favor and attention, to retain him in the ranks of the army. Therefore when he had greeted Ketling, he stretched out his hands at once to the little knight; and when the latter approached and seized him by the knees, Sobieski pressed the head of Pan Michael with his palms.

"Old soldier," said he, "the hand of God has bent thee to the earth, but it will raise thee, and give comfort. God aid thee! Thou wilt stay with us now."

Sobbing shook the breast of Pan Michael. "I will stay!" said he, with tears.

"That is well; give me of such men as many as possible. And now, old comrade, let us recall those times which we passed in the Russian steppes, when we sat down to feast under tents. I am happy among you. Now, our host, now!"

"Vivat Joannes dux!" shouted every voice.

The feast began and lasted long. Next day the hetman sent a cream-colored steed of great price to Pan Michael.

CHAPTER VII.

KETLING and Pan Michael promised each other to ride stirrup to stirrup again should occasion offer, to sit at one fire, and to sleep with their heads on one saddle. But meanwhile an event separated them. Not later than a week after their first greeting, a messenger came from Courland with notice that that Hassling who had adopted the youthful Scot and given him his property had fallen suddenly ill, and wished greatly to see his adopted son. The young knight did not hesitate; he mounted his horse and rode away. Before his departure he begged Zagloba and Pan Michael to consider his house as their own, and to live there until they were tired of it.

"Pan Yan may come," said he. "During the election he will come himself surely; even should he bring all his children, there will be room here for the whole family. I have no relatives; and even if I had brothers, they would not be nearer to me than you are."

Zagloba especially was gratified by these invitations, for he was very comfortable in Ketling's house; but they were pleasant for Pan Michael also. Pan Yan did not come, but Pan Michael's sister announced her arrival. She was married to Pan Makovetski, stolnik of Latychov. His messenger came to the residence of the hetman to inquire if any of his attendants knew of the little knight. Evidently Ketling's house was indicated to him at once.

Volodyovski was greatly delighted, for whole years had passed since he had seen his sister; and when he learned that, in absence of better lodgings, she had stopped at Rybaki in a poor little cottage, he flew off straightway to invite her to Ketling's house. It was dusk when he rushed into her presence; but he knew her at once, though two other women were with her in the room, for the lady was small of stature, like a ball of thread. She too recognized him; while the other women stood like two candles and looked at the greeting.

Pani Makovetski found speech first, and began to cry out in a thin and rather squeaking voice, "So many years, —

so many years! God give you aid, dearest brother! The moment the news of·your misfortune came, I sprang up at once to come hither; and my husband did not detain me, for a storm is threatening us from the side of Budjyak. People are talking also of the Belgrod Tartars; and surely the roads are growing black, for tremendous flocks of birds are appearing, and before every invasion it is that way. God console you, beloved, dear, golden brother! My husband must come to the election himself, so this is what he said: 'Take the young ladies, and go on before me. You will comfort Michael,' said he, 'in his grief; and you must hide your head somewhere from the Tartars, for the country here will be in a blaze, therefore one thing fits with another. Go,' said he, 'to Warsaw, hire good lodgings in time, so there may be some place to live in.' He, with men of those parts, is listening on the roads. There are few troops in the country; it is always that way with us. You, Michael, my loved one, come to the window, let me look in your face; your lips have grown thin, but in grief it cannot be otherwise. It was easy for my husband to say in Russia, 'Find lodgings!' but here there is nothing anywhere. We are in this hovel; you see it. I have hardly been able to get three bundles of straw to sleep on."

"Permit me, sister," said the little knight.

But the sister would not permit, and spoke on, as if a mill were rattling: "We stopped here; there was no other place. My host looks out of his eyes like a wolf; maybe they are bad people in the house. It is true that we have four attendants, — trusty fellows, — and we ourselves are not timid, for in our parts a woman must have a cavalier's heart, or she could not live there. I have a pistol which I carry always, and Basia[1] has two of them; but Krysia[2] does not like fire-arms. This is a strange place, though, and we prefer safer lodgings."

"Permit me, sister," repeated Volodyovski.

"But where do you live, Michael? You must help me to find lodgings, for you have experience in Warsaw."

"I have lodgings ready," interrupted Pan Michael, "and such good ones that a senator might occupy them with his retinue. I live with my friend, Captain Ketling, and will take you with me at once."

[1] Diminutive of Barbara.
[2] Diminutive of Krystina, or Christiana.

"But remember that there are three of us, and two servants and four attendants. But for God's sake! I have not made you acquainted with the company." Here she turned to her companions. "You know, young ladies, who he is, but he does not know you; make acquaintance even in the dark. The host has not heated the stove for us yet. This is Panna Krystina Drohoyovski, and that Panna Barbara Yezorkovski. My husband is their guardian, and takes care of their property; they live with us, for they are orphans. To live alone does not beseem such young ladies."

While his sister was speaking, Pan Michael bowed in soldier fashion; the young ladies, seizing their skirts with their fingers, courtesied, wherewith Panna Barbara nodded like a young colt.

"Let us take our seats in the carriage, and drive on!" said the little knight. "Pan Zagloba lives with me. I asked him to have supper prepared for us."

"That famous Pan Zagloba?" asked Panna Basia, all at once.

"Basia, be quiet!" said the lady. "I am afraid that there will be annoyance."

"Oh, if Pan Zagloba has his mind on supper," said the little knight, "there will be enough, even if twice as many were to come. And, young ladies, will you give command to carry out the trunks? I brought a wagon too for things, and Ketling's carriage is so wide that we four can sit in it easily. See what comes to my head; if your attendants are not drunken fellows, let them stay here till morning with the horses and larger effects. We'll take now only what things are required most."

"We need leave nothing," said the lady, "for our wagons are still unpacked; just attach the horses, and they can move at once. Basia, go and give orders!"

Basia sprang to the entrance; and a few "Our Fathers" later she returned with the announcement that all was ready.

"It is time to go," said Pan Michael.

After a while they took their seats in the carriage and moved on toward Mokotov. Pan Michael's sister and Panna Krysia occupied the rear seats; in front sat the little knight at the side of Basia. It was so dark already that they could not see one another's features.

"Young ladies, do you know Warsaw?" asked Pan Michael, bending toward Panna Krysia, and raising his voice above the rattle of the carriage.

"No," answered Krysia, in a low but resonant and agreeable voice. "We are real rustics, and up to this time have known neither famous cities nor famous men."

Saying this, she inclined her head somewhat, as if giving to understand that she counted Pan Michael among the latter; he received the answer thankfully. "A polite sort of maiden!" thought he, and straightway began to rack his head over some kind of compliment to be made in return.

"Even if the city were ten times greater than it is," said he at last, "still, ladies, you might be its most notable ornament."

"But how do you know that in the dark?" inquired Panna Basia, on a sudden.

"Ah, here is a kid for you!" thought Pan Michael.

But he said nothing, and they rode on in silence for some time; Basia turned again to the little knight and asked, "Do you know whether there will be room enough in the stable? We have ten horses and two wagons."

"Even if there were thirty, there would be room for them."

"Hwew! hwew!" exclaimed the young lady.

"Basia! Basia!" said Pani Makovetski, persuasively.

"Ah, it is easy to say, 'Basia, Basia!' but in whose care were the horses during the whole journey?"

Conversing thus, they arrived before Ketling's house. All the windows were brilliantly lighted to receive the lady. The servants ran out with Pan Zagloba at the head of them; he, springing to the wagon and seeing three women, inquired straightway, —

"In which lady have I the honor to greet my special benefactress, and at the same time the sister of my best friend, Michael?"

"I am she!" answered the lady.

Then Zagloba seized her hand, and fell to kissing it eagerly, exclaiming, "I beat with the forehead, — I beat with the forehead!"

Then he helped her to descend from the carriage, and conducted her with great attention and clattering of feet to the ante-room. "Let me be permitted to give greeting once more inside the threshold," said he, on the way.

Meanwhile Pan Michael was helping the young ladies to descend. Since the carriage was high, and it was difficult to find the steps in the darkness, he caught Panna Krysia by the waist, and bearing her through the air, placed her on the ground; and she, without resisting, inclined during the twinkle of an eye her breast on his, and said, " I thank you."

Pan Michael turned then to Basia; but she had already jumped down on the other side of the carriage, therefore he gave his arm to Panna Krysia. In the room acquaintance with Zagloba followed. He, at sight of the two young ladies, fell into perfect good-humor, and invited them straightway to supper. The platters were steaming already on the table; and as Pan Michael had foreseen, there was such an abundance that it would have sufficed for twice as many persons.

They sat down. Pan Michael's sister occupied the first place; next to her, on the right, sat Zagloba, and beyond him Panna Basia. Pan Michael sat on the left side near Panna Krysia. And now for the first time the little knight was able to have a good look at the ladies. Both were comely, but each in her own style. Krysia had hair as black as the wings of a raven, brows of the same color, deep-blue eyes; she was a pale brunette, but of complexion so delicate that the blue veins on her temples were visible. A barely discernible dark down covered her upper lip, showing a mouth sweet and attractive, as if put slightly forward for a kiss. She was in mourning, for she had lost her father not long before, and the color of her garments, with the delicacy of her complexion and her dark hair, lent her a certain appearance of pensiveness and severity. At the first glance she seemed older than her companion; but when he had looked at her more closely, Pan Michael saw that the blood of first youth was flowing under that transparent skin. The more he looked, the more he admired the distinction of her posture, the swanlike neck, and those proportions so full of maiden charms.

"She is a great lady," thought he, "who must have a great soul; but the other is a regular tomboy."

In fact, the comparison was just. Basia was much smaller than her companion, and generally minute, though not meagre; she was ruddy as a bunch of roses, and light-haired. Her hair had been cut, apparently after illness, and she wore it gathered in a golden net. But the hair would not sit quietly on her restless head; the ends of it were peeping out through every mesh of the net, and over her forehead formed an unordered yellow tuft which fell to her brows like the tuft of a Cossack, which, with her quick, restless eyes and challenging mien, made that rosy face like the face of a student who is only watching to embroil some one and go unpunished himself. Still, she was so shapely and fresh that it was difficult to take one's eyes from her; she had a slender nose, somewhat in the air, with nostrils dilating and active; she had dimples in her cheeks and a dimple in her chin, indicating a joyous disposition. But now she was sitting with dignity and eating heartily, only shooting glances every little while, now at Pan Zagloba, now at Volodyovski, and looking at them with almost childlike curiosity, as if at some special wonder.

Pan Michael was silent; for though he felt it his duty to entertain Panna Krysia, he did not know how to begin. In general, the little knight was not happy in conversation with ladies; but now he was the more gloomy, since these maidens brought vividly to his mind the dear dead one.

Pan Zagloba entertained Pani Makovetski, detailing to her the deeds of Pan Michael and himself. In the middle of the supper he fell to relating how once they had escaped with Princess Kurtsevich and Jendzian, four of them, through a whole chambul, and how, finally, to save the princess and stop the pursuit, they two had hurled themselves on the chambul.

Basia stopped eating, and resting her chin on her hand, listened carefully, shaking her forelock, at moments blinking, and snapping her fingers in the most interesting places, and repeating, "Ah, ah! Well, what next?" But when they came to the place where Kushel's dragoons rushed up with aid unexpectedly, sat on the necks of the Tartars, and rode on, slashing them, for three miles, she could contain herself no longer, but clapping her hands with all her might, cried, "Ah, I should like to be there, God knows I should!"

"Basia!" cried the plump little Pani Makovetski, with a strong Russian accent, "you have come among polite people; put away your 'God knows.' O Thou Great God! this alone is lacking, Basia, that you should cry, 'May the bullets strike me!'"

The maiden burst out into fresh laughter, resonant as silver, and cried, "Well, then, auntie, may the bullets strike me!"

"O my God, the ears are withering on me! Beg pardon of the whole company!" cried the lady.

Then Basia, wishing to begin with her aunt, sprang up from her place, but at the same time dropped the knife and the spoons under the table, and then dived down after them herself.

The plump little lady could restrain her laughter no longer; and she had a wonderful laugh, for first she began to shake and tremble, and then to squeak in a thin voice. All had grown joyous. Zagloba was in raptures. " You see what a time I have with this maiden," said Pani Makovetski.

" She is a pure delight, as God is dear to me !" exclaimed Zagloba.

Meanwhile Basia had crept out from under the table; she had found the spoons and the knife, but had lost her net, for her hair was falling into her eyes altogether. She straightened herself, and said, her nostrils quivering meanwhile, "Aha, lords and ladies, you are laughing at my confusion. Very well !"

"No one is laughing," said Zagloba, in a tone of conviction, " no one is laughing, — no one is laughing! We are only rejoicing that the Lord God has given us delight in the person of your ladyship."

After supper they passed into the drawing-room. There Panna Krysia, seeing a lute on the wall, took it down and began to run over the strings. Pan Michael begged her to sing.

" I am ready, if I can drive sadness from your soul."

" I thank you," answered the little knight, raising his eyes to her in gratitude.

After a while this song was heard : —

> "O knights, believe me,
> Useless is armor;
> Shields give no service;
> Cupid's keen arrows,
> Through steel and iron,
> Go to all hearts."

"I do not indeed know how to thank you," said Zagloba, sitting at a distance with Pan Michael's sister, and kissing her hands, "for coming yourself and bringing with you such elegant maidens that the Graces themselves might heat stoves for them. Especially does that little haiduk please my heart, for such a rogue drives away sorrow in such fashion that a weasel could not hunt mice better. In truth, what is grief unless mice gnawing the grains of joyousness placed in our hearts? You, my benefactress, should know that our late king, Yan Kazimir, was so fond of my comparisons that he could not live a day without them. I had to arrange for him proverbs and wise maxims. He used to have these repeated to him before bed-time, and by them it was that he directed his policy. But that is another matter. I hope too that our Michael, in company with these delightful girls, will forget altogether his un-happy misfortune. You do not know that it is only a week since I dragged him out of the cloister, where he wished to make vows; but I won the intervention of the nuncio him-self, who declared to the prior that he would make a dragoon of every monk in the cloister if he did not let Michael out straightway. There was no reason for him to be there. Praise be to God! Praise be to God! If not to-day, to-morrow some one of those two will strike such sparks out of him that his heart will be burning like punk."

Meanwhile Krysia sang on: —

> "If shields cannot save
> From darts a strong hero,
> How can a fair head
> Guard her own weakness?
> Where can she hide?"

"The fair heads have as much fear of those shafts as a dog has of meat," whispered Zagloba to Pan Michael's sister. "But confess, my benefactress, that you did not bring these titmice here without secret designs. They are maidens in a hundred! — especially that little haiduk. Would that I were as blooming as she! Ah, Michael has a cunning sister."

Pani Makovetski put on a very artful look, which did not, however, become her honest, simple face in the least, and said, "I thought of this and that, as is usual with us; shrewdness is not wanting to women. My husband had to come here to the election; and I brought the maidens beforehand, for with us there is no one to see unless Tartars. If anything lucky should happen to Michael from this, I would make a pilgrimage on foot to some wonder-working image."

"It will come; it will come!" said Zagloba.

"Both maidens are from great houses, and both have property; that, too, means something in these grievous times."

"There is no need to repeat that to me. The war has consumed Michael's fortune, though I know that he has some money laid up with great lords. We took famous booty more than once, gracious lady; and though that was placed at the hetman's discretion, still, a part went to be divided 'according to sabres,' as the saying is in our soldier speech. So much came to Michael's share more than once that if he had saved all his own, he would have to-day a nice fortune. But a soldier has no thought for to-morrow; he only frolics to-day. And Michael would have frolicked away all he had, were it not that I restrained him on every occasion. You say, then, gracious lady, that these maidens are of high blood?"

"Krysia is of senatorial blood. It is true that our castellans on the border are not castellans of Cracow, and there are some of whom few in the Commonwealth have heard; but still, whoso has sat once in a senator's chair bequeaths to posterity his splendor. As to relationship, Basia almost surpasses Krysia."

"Indeed, indeed! I myself am descended from a certain king of the Massagetes, therefore I like to hear genealogies."

"Basia does not come from such a lofty nest as that; but if you wish to listen, — for in our parts we can recount the relationship of every house on our fingers, — she is, in fact, related to the Pototskis and the Yazlovyetskis and the Lashches. You see, it was this way." Here Pan Michael's sister gathered in the folds of her dress and took a more convenient position, so that there might be no hindrance to any part of her favorite narrative; she spread out the fingers of one hand, and straightening the index finger of the other, made ready to enumerate the grandfathers and grandmothers. "The daughter of Pan Yakob Pototski, Elizabeth, from his second wife, a Yazlovyetski, married Pan Yan Smyotanko, banneret of Podolia."

"I have caulked that into my memory," said Zagloba.

"From that marriage was born Michael Smyotanko, also banneret of Podolia."

"H'm! a good office," said Zagloba.

"He was married the first time to a Dorohosto — no! to a Rojynski — no! to a Voronich! God guard me from forgetting!"

"Eternal rest to her, whatever her name was," said Zagloba, with gravity.

"And for his second wife he married Panna Lashch."

"I was waiting for that! What was the result of the marriage?"

"Their sons died."

"Every joy crumbles in this world."

"But of four daughters, the youngest, Anna, married Yezorkovski, of the shield Ravich, a commissioner for fixing the boundaries of Podolia; he was afterward, if I mistake not, sword-bearer of Podolia."

"He was, I remember!" said Zagloba, with complete certainty.

"From that marriage, you see, was born Basia."

"I see, and also that at this moment she is aiming Ketling's musket." In fact, Krysia and the little knight were occupied in conversation, and Basia was aiming the musket at the window for her own amusement.

Pani Makovetski began to shake and squeak at sight of that. "You cannot imagine what I pass through with that girl! She is a regular haydamak."

"If all the haydamaks were like her, I would join them at once."

"There is nothing in her head but arms, horses, and war. Once she broke out of the house to hunt ducks with a gun. She crept in somewhere among the rushes, was looking ahead of her; the reeds began to open — what did she see? The head of a Tartar stealing along through the reeds to the village. Another woman would have been terrified, and woe to her if she had not fired quickly; the Tartar dropped into the water. Just imagine, she laid him out on the spot; and with what? With duck-shot."

Here the lady began to shake again and laugh at the mishap of the Tartar; then she added, "And to tell the truth, she saved us all, for a whole chambul was advancing; but as she came and gave the alarm, we had time to escape to the woods with the servants. With us it is always so!"

Zagloba's face was covered with such delight that he half closed his eye for a moment; then he sprang up, hurried to the maiden, and before she saw him, he kissed her on the forehead. "This from an old soldier for that Tartar in the rushes," said he.

The maiden gave a sweeping shake to her yellow fore-lock. "Did n't I give him beans?" cried she, with her fresh, childish voice, which sounded so strangely in view of what she meant with her words.

"Oh, my darling little haydamak!" cried Zagloba, with emotion.

"But what is one Tartar? You gentlemen have cut them down by the thousand, and Swedes, and Germans, and Rakotsi's Hungarians. What am I before you, gentlemen, — before knights who have not their equals in the Commonwealth? I know that perfectly! Oho!"

"I will teach you to work with the sabre, since you have so much courage. I am rather heavy now, but Michael there, he too is a master."

The maiden sprang up in the air at such a proposal; then she kissed Zagloba on the shoulder and courtesied to the little knight, saying, "I give thanks for the promise. I know a little already."

But Pan Michael was wholly occupied talking with Krysia; therefore he answered inattentively, "Whatever you command."

Zagloba, with radiant face, sat down again near Pani Makovetski. "My gracious benefactress," said he, "I know well which Turkish sweetmeats are best, for I passed long years in Stambul; but I know this too, that there is just a world of people hungry for them. How has it happened that no man has coveted that maiden to this time?"

"As God lives, there was no lack of men who were courting them both. But Basia we call, in laughing, a widow of three husbands, for at one time three worthy cavaliers paid her addresses, — all nobles of our parts, and heirs, whose relationship I can explain in detail to you."

Saying this, Pani Makovetski spread out the fingers of her left hand and straightened her right index finger; but Zagloba inquired quickly, "And what happened to them?"

"All three died in war; therefore we call Basia a widow."

"H'm! but how did she endure the loss?"

"With us, you see, a case like that happens every day; and it is a rare thing for any man, after reaching ripe age, to pass away with his own death. Among us people even say that it is not befitting a nobleman to die otherwise than in the field. 'How did Basia endure it?' Oh, she whimpered a little, poor girl, but mostly in the stable; for when anything troubles her, she is off to the stable. I sent for her once and inquired, 'For whom are you crying?' 'For all three,' said she. I saw from the answer that no one of them pleased her specially. I think that as her head is stuffed with something else, she has not felt the will of God yet; Krysia has felt it somewhat, but Basia perhaps not at all."

"She will feel it!" said Zagloba. "Gracious benefactress, we understand that perfectly. She will feel it! she will feel it!"

"Such is our predestination," said Pani Makovetski.

"That is just it. You took the words out of my mouth."

Further conversation was interrupted by the approach of the younger society. The little knight had grown much emboldened with Krysia; and she, through evident goodness of heart, was occupied with him and his grief, like a physician with a patient. And perhaps for this very reason she showed him more kindness than their brief acquaintance permitted. But as Pan Michael was a brother of the stolnik's wife, and the young lady was related to the stolnik, no one was astonished. Basia remained, as it were, aside; and only Pan Zagloba turned to her unbroken attention. But however that might be, it was apparently all one to Basia whether some one was occupied with her or not. At first, she gazed with admiration on both knights; but with equal admiration did she examine Ketling's wonderful weapons distributed on the walls. Later she began to yawn somewhat; then her eyes grew heavier and heavier, and at last she said, —

"I am so sleepy that I may wake in the morning."

After these words the company separated at once; for the ladies were very weary from the journey, and were only waiting to have beds prepared. When Zagloba found himself at last alone with Pan Michael, he began first of all to wink significantly, then he covered the little knight with a shower of light fists. "Michael! what, Michael, hei? like turnips! Will you become a monk, what? That bilberry Krysia is a sweet one. And that rosy little haiduk, uh! What will you say of her, Michael?"

"What? Nothing!" answered the little knight.

"That little haiduk pleased me principally. I tell you that when I sat near her during supper I was as warm from her as from a stove."

"She is a kid yet; the other is ever so much more stately."

"Panna Krysia is a real Hungarian plum; but this one is a little nut! As God lives, if I had teeth! I wanted to say if I had such a daughter, I'd give her to no man but you. An almond, I say, an almond!"

Volodyovski grew sad on a sudden, for he remembered the nicknames which Zagloba used to give Anusia. She stood as if living before him there in his mind and memory, — her form, her small face, her dark tresses, her joyfulness, her chattering, and ways of looking. Both these were younger, but still she was a hundred times dearer than all who were younger.

The little knight covered his face with his palms, and sorrow carried him away the more because it was unexpected. Zagloba was astonished; for some time he was silent and looked unquietly, then he asked, "Michael, what is the matter? Speak, for God's sake!"

Volodyovski spoke, "So many are living, so many are walking through the world, but my lamb is no longer among them; never again shall I see her." Then pain stifled his voice; he rested his forehead on the arm of the sofa and began to whisper through his set lips, "O God! O God! O God!"

CHAPTER VIII.

BASIA insisted that Volodyovski should give her instruction in "fencing;" he did not refuse, though he delayed for
some days. He preferred Krysia; still, he liked Basia
greatly, so difficult was it, in fact, not to like her.

A certain morning the first lesson began, mainly because
of Basia's boasting and her assurances that she knew that
art by no means badly, and that no common person could
stand before her. "An old soldier taught me," said she;
"there is no lack of these among us; it is known too that
there are no swordsmen superior to ours. It is a question
if even you, gentlemen, would not find your equals."

"Of what are you talking?" asked Zagloba. "We have
no equals in the whole world."

"I should wish it to come out that even I am your equal.
I do not expect it, but I should like it."

"If it were firing from pistols, I too would make a trial,"
said Pani Makovetski, laughing.

"As God lives, it must be that the Amazons themselves
dwell in Latychov," said Zagloba. Here he turned to
Krysia: "And what weapon do you use best, your
ladyship?"

"None," answered Krysia.

"Ah, ha! none!" exclaimed Basia. And here, mimicking
Krysia's voice, she began to sing: —

> "'O knights, believe me,
> Useless is armor,
> Shields give no service;
> Cupid's keen arrows,
> Through steel and iron,
> Go to all hearts.'

"She wields arms of that kind; never fear," added Basia,
turning to Pan Michael and Zagloba. "In that she is a
warrior of no common skill."

"Take your place, young lady!" said Pan Michael, wishing to conceal a slight confusion.

"Oh, as God lives! if what I think should come true!"
cried Basia, blushing with delight.

And she stood at once in position with a light Polish
sabre in her right hand; the left she put behind her, and
with breast pushed forward, with raised head and dilated
nostrils, she was so pretty and so rosy that Zagloba
whispered to Pan Michael's sister, "No decanter, even
if filled with Hungarian a hundred years old, would delight
me so much with the sight of it."

"Remember," said the little knight to Basia, "that I will
only defend myself; I will not thrust once. You may
attack as quickly as you choose."

"Very well. If you wish me to stop, give the word."

"The fencing could be stopped without a word, if I
wished."

"And how could that be done?"

"I could take the sabre easily out of the hand of a
fencer like you."

"We shall see!"

"We shall not, for I will not do so, through politeness."

"There is no need of politeness in this case. Do it if
you can. I know that I have less skill than you, but still I
will not let that be done."

"Then you permit it?"

"I permit it."

"Oh, do not permit, sweetest haiduk," said Zagloba.
"He has disarmed the greatest masters."

"We shall see!" repeated Basia.

"Let us begin," said Pan Michael, made somewhat impatient by the boasting of the maiden.

They began. Basia thrust terribly, skipping around like
a pony in a field. Volodyovski stood in one place, making,
according to his wont, the slightest movements of the sabre,
paying but little respect to the attack.

"You brush me off like a troublesome fly!" cried the
irritated Basia.

"I am not making a trial of you; I am teaching you,"
answered the little knight. "That is good! For a fair
head, not bad at all! Steadier with the hand!"

"'For a fair head?' You call me a fair head! you do!
you do!"

But Pan Michael, though Basia used her most celebrated
thrusts, was untouched. Even he began to talk with Zagloba,
of purpose to show how little he cared for Basia's thrusts:
"Step away from the window, for you are in the lady's
light; and though a sabre is larger than a needle, she has
less experience with the sabre."

Basia's nostrils dilated still more, and her forelock fell to her flashing eyes. "Do you hold me in contempt?" inquired she, panting quickly.

"Not your person; God save me from that!"

"I cannot endure Pan Michael!"

"You learned fencing from a schoolmaster." Again he turned to Zagloba: "I think snow is beginning to fall."

"Here is snow! snow for you!" repeated Basia, giving thrust after thrust.

"Basia, that is enough! you are barely breathing," said Pani Makovetski. .

"Now hold to your sabre, for I will strike it from your hand."

"We shall see!"

"Here!" And the little sabre, hopping like a bird out of Basia's hands, fell with a rattle near the stove.

"I let it go myself without thinking! It was not you who did that!" cried the young lady, with tears in her voice; and seizing the sabre, in a twinkle she thrust again: "Try it now."

"There!" said Pan Michael. And again the sabre was at the stove. "That is enough for to-day," said the little knight.

Pani Makovetski began to bustle about and talk louder than usual; but Basia stood in the middle of the room, confused, stunned, breathing heavily, biting her lips and repressing the tears which were crowding into her eyes in spite of her. She knew that they would laugh all the more if she burst out crying, and she wished absolutely to restrain herself; but seeing that she could not, she rushed from the room on a sudden.

"For God's sake!" cried Pani Makovetski. "She has run to the stable, of course, and being so heated, will catch cold. Some one must go for her. Krysia, don't you go!"

So saying, she went out, and seizing a warm shuba in the ante-room, hurried to the stable; and after her ran Zagloba, troubled about his little haiduk. Krysia wished to go also, but the little knight held her by the hand. "You heard the prohibition. I will not let this hand go till they come back."

And, in fact, he did not let it go. But that hand was as soft as satin. It seemed to Pan Michael that a kind of warm current was flowing from those slender fingers into his bones, rousing in them an uncommon pleasantness; therefore he held them more firmly. A slight blush flew over Krysia's face. "I see that I am a prisoner taken captive."

"Whoever should take such a prisoner would not have reason to envy the Sultan, for the Sultan would gladly give half his kingdom for her."

"But you would not sell me to the Pagans ?"

"Just as I would not sell my soul to the Devil."

Here Pan Michael remarked that momentary enthusiasm had carried him too far, and he corrected himself: "As I would not sell my sister."

"That is the right word," said Krysia, seriously. "I am a sister in affection to your sister, and I will be the same to you."

"I thank you from my heart!" said Pan Michael, kissing her hand; "for I have great need of consolation."

"I know, I know," repeated the young lady; "I am an orphan myself." Here a small tear rolled down from her eyelid and stopped at the down on her lip.

Pan Michael looked on that tear, on the mouth slightly shaded, and said, "You are as kind as a real angel; I feel comforted already."

Krysia smiled sweetly: "May God reward you!"

"As God is dear to me."

The little knight felt meanwhile that if he should kiss her hand a second time, it would comfort him still more; but at that moment his sister appeared. "Basia took the shuba," said she, "but is in such confusion that she will not come in for anything. Pan Zagloba is chasing her through the whole stable."

In fact, Zagloba, sparing neither jests nor persuasion, not only followed Basia through the stable, but drove her at last to the yard, in hopes that he would persuade her to the warm house. She ran before him, repeating, "I will not go! Let the cold catch me! I will not go! I will not go!"

Seeing at last a pillar before the house with pegs, and on it a ladder, she sprang up the ladder like a squirrel, stopped, and leaned at last on the eave of the roof. Sitting there, she turned to Pan Zagloba and cried out half in laughter, "Well, I will go if you climb up here after me."

"What sort of a cat am I, little haiduk, to creep along roofs after you? Is that the way you pay me for loving you?"

"I love you too, but from the roof."

"Grandfather wants his way; grandmother will have hers. Come down to me this minute!"

"I will not go down!"

"It is laughable, as God is dear to me, to take defeat to heart as you do. Not you alone, angry weasel, but Kmita, who passed for a master of masters, did Pan Michael treat in this way, and not in sport, but in a duel. The most famous swordsmen — Italians, Germans, and Swedes — could not stand before him longer than during one 'Our Father,' and here such a gadfly takes the affair to heart. Fie! be ashamed of yourself! Come down, come down! Besides, you are only beginning to learn."

"But I cannot endure Pan Michael!"

"God be good to you! Is it because he is *exquisitissimus* in that which you yourself wish to know? You should love him all the more."

Zagloba was not mistaken. The admiration of Basia for the little knight increased in spite of her defeat; but she answered, "Let Krysia love him."

"Come down! come down!"

"I will not come down."

"Very well, stay there; but I will tell you one thing: it is not nice for a young lady to sit on a ladder, for she may give an amusing exhibition to the world."

"But that's not true," answered Basia, gathering in her skirts with her hand.

"I am an old fellow, — I won't look my eyes out; but I'll call everybody this minute, let others stare at you."

"I'll come down!" cried Basia.

With that, Zagloba turned toward the side of the house. "As God lives, somebody is coming!" said he.

In fact, from behind the corner appeared young Adam Novoveski, who, coming on horseback, had tied his beast at the side-gate and passed around the house himself, wishing to enter through the main door. Basia, seeing him, was on the ground in two springs, but too late. Unfortunately Pan Adam had seen her springing from the ladder, and stood confused, astonished, and covered with blushes like a young girl. Basia stood before him in the same way, till at last she cried out, —

"A second confusion!"

Zagloba, greatly amused, blinked some time with his sound eye; at length he said, "Pan Novoveski, a friend and subordinate of our Michael, and this is Panna Drabinovski (Ladder). Tfu! I wanted to say Yezorkovski."

Pan Adam recovered readily; and because he was a sol-

dier of quick wit, though young, he bowed, and raising his
eyes to the wonderful vision, said, "As God lives! roses
bloom on the snow in Ketling's garden."

But Basia, courtesying, muttered to herself, "For some
other nose than yours." Then she said very charmingly,
"I beg you to come in."

She went forward herself, and rushing into the room
where Pan Michael was sitting with the rest of the company, cried, making reference to the red kontush of Pan
Adam, "The red finch has come!" Then she sat at the
table, put one hand into the other, and pursed her mouth in
the style of a demure and strictly reared young lady.

Pan Michael presented his young friend to his sister and
Panna Krysia; and the friend, seeing another young lady
of equal beauty, but of a different order, was confused a
second time; he covered his confusion, however, with a bow,
and to add to his courage reached his hand to his mustache,
which had not grown much yet. Twisting his fingers above
his lip, he turned to Pan Michael and told him the object
of his coming. The grand hetman wished anxiously to see
the little knight. As far as Pan Adam could conjecture, it
was a question of some military function, for the hetman
had received letters recently from Pan Vilchkovski, from
Pan Silnitski, from Colonel Pivo, and other commandants
stationed in the Ukraine and Podolia, with reports of Crimean events which were not of favorable promise.

"The Khan himself and Sultan Galga, who made treaties
with us at Podhaytse," continued Pan Adam, "wish to observe the treaties; but Budjyak is as noisy as a bee-hive at
time of swarming. The Belgrod horde also are in an uproar;
they do not wish to obey either the Khan or Galga."

"Pan Sobieski has informed me already of that, and
asked for advice," said Zagloba. "What do they say now
about the coming spring?"

"They say that with the first grass there will be surely
a movement of those worms; that it will be necessary to
stamp them out a second time," replied Pan Adam, assuming the face of a terrible Mars, and twisting his mustache
till his upper lip reddened.

Basia, who was quick-eyed, saw this at once; therefore
she pushed back a little, so that Pan Adam might not see
her, and then twisted, as it were, her mustache, imitating
the youthful cavalier. Pan Michael's sister threatened with
her eyes, but at the same time she began to quiver, restrain-

ing her laughter with difficulty. Volodyovski bit his lips; and Krysia dropped her eyes till the long lashes threw a shadow on her cheeks.

"You are a young man," said Zagloba, "but a soldier of experience."

"I am twenty-two years old, and I have served the country seven years without ceasing; for I escaped to the field from the lowest bench in my fifteenth year," answered the young man.

"He knows the steppe, knows how to make his way through the grass, and to fall on the horde as a kite falls on grouse," said Pan Michael. "He is no common partisan! The Tartar will not hide from him in the steppe."

Pan Adam blushed with delight that praise from such famous lips met him in presence of ladies. He was withal not merely a falcon of the steppes, but a handsome fellow, dark, embrowned by the winds. On his face he bore a scar from his ear to his nose, which from this cut was thinner on one side than the other. He had quick eyes, accustomed to look into the distance, above them very dark brows, joined at the nose and forming, as it were, a Tartar bow. His head, shaven at the sides, was surmounted by a black, bushy forelock. He pleased Basia both in speech and in bearing; but still she did not cease to mimic him.

"As I live!" said Zagloba, "it is pleasant for old men like me to see that a new generation is rising up worthy of us."

"Not worthy yet," answered Pan Adam.

"I praise the modesty too. We shall see you soon receiving commands."

"That has happened already!" cried Pan Michael. "He has been commandant, and gained victories by himself."

Pan Adam began so to twist his mustache that he lacked little of pulling out his lip. And Basia, without taking her eyes from him, raised both hands also to her face, and mimicked him in everything. But the clever soldier saw quickly that the glances of the whole company were turning to one side, where, somewhat behind him, was sitting the young lady whom he had seen on the ladder, and he divined at once that something must be against him. He spoke on, as if paying no heed to the matter, and sought his mustache as before. At last he selected the moment, and wheeled around so quickly that Basia had no time either to turn her eyes from him, or to take her

hands from her face. She blushed terribly, and not knowing herself what to do, rose from the chair. All were confused, and a moment of silence followed.

Basia struck her sides suddenly with her hands: "A
third confusion!" cried she, with her silvery voice.

"My gracious lady," said Pan Adam, with animation, "I
saw at once that something hostile was happening behind
me. I confess that I am anxious for a mustache; but if I
do not get it, it will be because I shall fall for the country,
and in that event I hope I shall deserve tears rather than
laughter from your ladyship."

Basia stood with downcast eyes, and was the more put to
shame by the sincere words of the cavalier.

"You must forgive her," said Zagloba. "She is wild because she is young, but she has a golden heart."

And Basia, as if confirming Zagloba's words, said at once
in a low voice, "I beg your forgiveness most earnestly."

Pan Adam caught her hands that moment and fell to
kissing them. "For God's sake, do not take it to heart!
I am not some kind of barbarian. It is for me to beg pardon
for having dared to interrupt your amusement. We soldiers
ourselves are fond of jokes. *Mea culpa!* I will kiss those
hands again, and if I have to kiss them till you forgive me,
then, for God's sake, do not forgive me till evening!"

"Oh, he is a polite cavalier. You see, Basia!" said Pani
Makovetski.

"I see!" answered Basia.

"It is all over now," cried Pan Adam.

When he said this he straightened himself, and with
great resolution reached to his mustache from habit, but
suddenly remembered himself and burst out in hearty
laughter. Basia followed him; others followed Basia.
Joy seized all. Zagloba gave command straightway to
bring one and a second bottle from Ketling's cellar, and
all felt well. Pan Adam, striking one spur against the
other, passed his fingers through his forelock and looked
more and more ardently at Basia. She pleased him greatly.
He grew immensely eloquent; and since he had served with
the hetman, he had lived in the great world, therefore had
something to talk about. He told them of the Diet of Convocation, of its close, and how in the senate the stove had
tumbled down under the inquisitive spectators, to the great
amusement of all. He departed at last after dinner, with
his eyes and his soul full of Basia.

CHAPTER IX.

THAT same day Pan Michael announced himself at the quarters of the hetman, who gave command to admit the little knight, and said to him, "I must send Rushchyts to the Crimea to see what is passing there, and to stir up the Khan to observe his treaties. Do you wish to enter service again and take the command after Rushchyts? You, Vilchkovski, Silnitski, and Pivo will have an eye on Doroshenko, and on the Tartars, whom it is impossible to trust altogether at any time."

Pan Michael grew sad. He had served the flower of his life. For whole tens of years he had not known rest; he had lived in fire, in smoke, in toil, in sleeplessness, without a roof over his head, without a handful of straw to lie on. God knows what blood his sabre had not shed. He had not settled down; he had not married. Men who deserved a hundred times less were eating the bread of merit; had risen to honors, to offices, to starostaships. He was richer when he began to serve than he was then. But still it was intended to use him again, like an old broom. His soul was rent, because, when friendly and pleasant hands had been found to dress his wounds, the command was given to tear himself away and fly to the desert, to the distant boundaries of the Commonwealth, without a thought that he was so greatly wearied in soul. Had it not been for interruptions and service, he would have enjoyed at least a couple of years with Anusia. When he thought of all this, an immense bitterness rose in his soul; but since it did not seem to him worthy of a cavalier to mention his own services and dwell on them, he answered briefly, —

"I will go."

"You are not in service," said the hetman; "you can refuse. You know better yourself if this is too soon for you."

"It is not too soon for me to die," replied Pan Michael.

Sobieski walked a number of times through the chamber, then he stopped before the little knight and put his hand on his shoulder confidentially. "If your tears are not dried yet, the wind of the steppe will dry them for you. You have toiled, cherished soldier, all your life; toil on still further! And should it come ever to your head that you are forgotten, unrewarded, that rest is not granted you, that you have received not buttered toast, but a crust, not a starostaship, but wounds, not rest, but suffering only, set your teeth and say, 'For thee, O Country!' Other consolation I cannot give, for I have n't it; but though not a priest, I can give you the assurance that serving in this way, you will go farther on a worn-out saddle than others in a carriage and six, and that gates will be opened for you which will be closed before them."

"To thee, O Country!" said Pan Michael, in his soul, wondering at the same time that the hetman could penetrate his secret thoughts so quickly.

Pan Sobieski sat down in front of him and continued: "I do not wish to speak with you as with a subordinate, but as with a friend, — nay! as a father with a son. When we were in the fire at Podhaytse, and before that in the Ukraine; when we were barely able to prevent the preponderance of the enemy, — here, in the heart of the country, evil men in security, behind our shoulders, were attaining in turbulence their own selfish ends. Even in those days it came more than once to my head that this Commonwealth must perish. License lords it too much over order; the public good yields too often to private ends. This has never happened elsewhere in such a degree. These thoughts were gnawing me in the day in the field, and in the night in the tent, for I thought to myself: 'Well, we soldiers are in a woful condition; but this is our duty and our portion. If we could only know that with this blood which is flowing from our wounds, salvation was issuing also.' No! even that consolation there was not. Oh, I passed heavy days in Podhaytse, though I showed a glad face to you officers, lest you might think that I had lost hope of victory in the field. 'There are no men,' thought I, — 'there are no men who love this country really.' And it was to me as if some one had planted a knife in my breast, till a certain time — the last day at Podhaytse, when I sent you with two thousand to the attack against twenty-six thousand of the horde, and you all flew to apparent death, to certain slaughter, with such a shouting, with such willingness, as if you were going to a wedding — suddenly the thought came to me: 'Ah, these are my soldiers.' And

God in one moment took the stone from my heart, and in my eyes it grew clear. 'These,' said I, 'are perishing from pure love of the mother; they will not go to confederacies, nor to traitors. Of these I will form a sacred brotherhood; of these I will form a school, in which the young generation will learn. Their example will have influence; through them this ill-fated people will be reborn, will become free of selfishness, forget license, and be as a lion feeling wonderful strength in his limbs, and will astonish the world. Such a brotherhood will I form of my soldiers!'"

Here Sobieski flushed up, reared his head, which was like the head of a Roman Cæsar, and stretching forth his hands, exclaimed, "O Lord! inscribe not on our walls 'Mene, Tekel, Peres!' and permit me to regenerate my country!"

A moment of silence followed. Pan Michael sat with drooping head and felt that trembling had seized his whole body.

The hetman walked some time with quick steps through the room and then stopped before the little knight. "Examples are needed," said he, — "examples every day to strike the eye. Volodyovski, I have reckoned you in the first rank of the brotherhood. Do you wish to belong to it?"

The little knight rose and embraced the hetman's knees. "See," said he, with a voice of emotion, "when I heard that I had to march again, I thought that a wrong had been done, and that leisure for my suffering belonged to me; but now I see that I sinned, and I repent of my thought and am unable to speak, for I am ashamed."

The hetman pressed Pan Michael to his heart in silence. "There is a handful of us," said he; "but others will follow the example."

"When am I to go?" asked the little knight. "I could go even to the Crimea, for I have been there."

"No," answered the hetman; "to the Crimea I will send Pan Rushchyts. He has relations there, and even namesakes, likely cousins, who, seized in childhood by the horde, have become Mussulmans and obtained office among the Pagans. They will help him in everything. Besides, I need you in the field; there is no man your equal in dealing with Tartars."

"When have I to go?" repeated the little knight.

"In two weeks at furthest. I need to confer yet with the vice-chancellor of the kingdom and with the treasurer, to prepare letters for Rushchyts and give him instructions. But be ready, for I shall be urgent."

"I shall be ready from to-morrow."

"God reward you for the intention! but it is not needful to be ready so soon. Moreover, you will not go to stay long; for during the election, if only there is peace, I shall need you in Warsaw. You have heard of candidates. What is the talk among nobles?"

"I came from the cloister not long since, and there they do not think of worldly matters. I know only what Pan Zagloba has told me."

"True. I can obtain information from him; he is widely known among the nobles. But for whom do you think of voting?"

"I know not myself yet; but I think that a military king is necessary for us."

"Yes, yes! I have such a man too in mind, who by his name alone would terrify our neighbors. We need a military king, as was Stefan Batory. But farewell, cherished soldier! We need a military king. Do you repeat this to all. Farewell. God reward you for your readiness!"

Pan Michael took farewell and went out. On the road he meditated. The soldier, however, was glad that he had before him a week or two, for that friendship and consolation which Krysia gave was dear to him. He was pleased also with the thought that he would return to the election, and in general he went home without suffering. The steppes too had for him a certain charm; he was pining for them without knowing it. He was so used to those spaces without end, in which the horseman feels himself more a bird than a man.

"Well, I will go," said he, "to those measureless fields, to those stanitsas and mounds, to taste the old life again, make new campaigns with the soldiers, to guard those boundaries like a crane, to frolic in spring in the grass, — well, now, I will go, I will go!"

Meanwhile he urged on the horse and went at a gallop, for he was yearning for the speed and the whistle of the wind in his ears. The day was clear, dry, frosty. Frozen snow covered the ground and squeaked under the feet of the horse. Compressed lumps of it flew with force from his hoofs. Pan Michael sped forward so that his attendant, sitting on an inferior horse remained far behind. It was near sunset; a little later twilight was in the heavens, casting a violet reflection on the snowy expanse. On the ruddy sky the first twinkling stars came out; the moon hung in the form of a silver sickle. The road was empty; the knight passed an odd wagon and flew on without interruption. Only when he saw Ketling's house in the distance did he rein in his horse and let his attendant come up. All at once he saw a slender figure coming toward him. It was Krysia.

When he recognized her, Pan Michael sprang at once from his horse, which he gave to the attendant, and hurried up to the maiden, somewhat astonished, but still more delighted at sight of her. "Soldiers declare," said he, "that at twilight we may meet various supernatural beings, who are sometimes of evil, sometimes of good, omen; but for me there can be no better omen than to meet you."

"Pan Adam has come," answered Krysia; "he is passing the time with Basia and Pani Makovetski. I slipped out purposely to meet you, for I was anxious about what the hetman had to say."

The sincerity of these words touched the little knight to the heart. "Is it true that you are so concerned about me?" asked he, raising his eyes to her.

"It is," answered Krysia, with a low voice.

Pan Michael did not take his eyes from her; never before had she seemed to him so attractive. On her head was a satin hood; white swan's-down encircled her small, palish face, on which the moonlight was falling,—light which shone mildly on those noble brows, downcast eyes, long lids, and that dark, barely visible down above her mouth. There was a certain calm in that face and great goodness. Pan Michael felt at the moment that the face was a friendly and beloved one; therefore he said,—

"Were it not for the attendant who is riding behind, I should fall on the snow at your feet from thankfulness."

"Do not say such things," answered Krysia, "for I am not worthy; but to reward me say that you will remain with us, and that I shall be able to comfort you longer."

"I shall not remain," said Pan Michael.

Krysia stopped suddenly. "Impossible!"

"Usual soldier's service! I go to Russia and to the Wilderness."

"Usual service?" repeated Krysia. And she began to

5

hurry in silence toward the house. Pan Michael walked quickly at her side, a trifle confused. Somehow it was a little oppressive and dull in his mind. He wanted to say something; he wanted to begin conversation again; he did not succeed. But still it seemed to him that he had a thousand things to say to her, and that just then was the time, while they were alone and no one preventing.

"If I begin," thought he, "it will go on;" therefore he inquired all at once, "But is it long since Pan Adam came?"

"Not long," answered Krysia.

And again their conversation stopped.

"The road is not that way," thought Pan Michael. "While I begin in that fashion, I shall never say anything. But I see that sorrow has gnawed away what there was of my wit."

And for a time he hurried on in silence; his mustaches merely quivered more and more vigorously. At last he halted before the house and said, "Think, if I deferred my happiness so many years to serve the country, with what face could I refuse now to put off my own comfort?"

It seemed to the little knight that such a simple argument should convince Krysia at once; in fact, after a while she answered with sadness and mildness, "The more nearly one knows Pan Michael, the more one respects and honors him."

Then she entered the house. Basia's exclamations of "Allah! Allah!" reached her in the entrance. And when they came to the reception-room, they saw Pan Adam in the middle of it, blindfolded, bent forward, and with outstretched arms trying to catch Basia, who was hiding in corners and giving notice of her presence by cries of "Allah!" Pani Makovetski was occupied near the window in conversation with Zagloba.

The entrance of Krysia and the little knight interrupted the amusement. Pan Adam pulled off the handkerchief and ran to greet Volodyovski. Immediately after came Pani Makovetski, Zagloba, and the panting Basia.

"What is it? what is it? What did the hetman say?" asked one, interrupting another.

"Lady sister," answered Pan Michael, "if you wish to send a letter to your husband, you have a chance, for I am going to Russia."

"Is he sending you? In God's name, do not volunteer yet, and do not go," cried his sister, with a pitiful voice. "Will they not give you this bit of time?"

"Is your command fixed already?" asked Zagloba, gloomily. "Your sister says justly that they are threshing you as with flails."

"Rushchyts is going to the Crimea, and I take the squadron after him; for as Pan Adam has mentioned already, the roads will surely be black (with the enemy) in spring."

"Are we alone to guard this Commonwealth from thieves, as a dog guards a house?" cried Zagloba. "Other men do not know from which end of a musket to shoot, but for us there is no rest."

"Never mind! I have nothing to say," answered Pan Michael. "Service is service! I gave the hetman my word that I would go, and earlier or later it is all the same." Here Pan Michael put his finger on his forehead and repeated the argument which he had used once with Krysia, "You see that if I put off my happiness so many years to serve the Commonwealth, with what face can I refuse to give up the pleasure which I find in your company?"

No one made answer to this; only Basia came up, with lips pouting like those of a peevish child, and said, "I am sorry for Pan Michael."

Pan Michael laughed joyously. "God grant you happy fortune! But only yesterday you said that you could no more endure me than a wild Tartar."

"What Tartar? I did not say that at all. You will be working there against the Tartars, and we shall be lonely here without you."

"Oh, little haiduk, comfort yourself; forgive me for the name, but it fits you most wonderfully. The hetman informed me that my command would not last long. I shall set out in a week or two, and must be in Warsaw at the election. The hetman himself wishes me to come, and I shall be here even if Rushchyts does not return from the Crimea in May."

"Oh, that is splendid!"

"I will go with the colonel; I will go surely," said Pan Adam, looking quickly at Basia; and she said in answer, —

"There will be not a few like you. It is a delight for men to serve under such a commander. Go; go! It will be pleasanter for Pan Michael."

The young man only sighed and stroked his forelock with his broad palm; at last he said, stretching his hands, as if playing blind-man's-buff, "But first I will catch Panna Barbara! I will catch her most surely."

" Allah ! Allah !" exclaimed Basia, starting back.

Meanwhile Krysia approached Pan Michael, with face radiant and full of quiet joy. "But you are not kind, not kind to me, Pan Michael ; you are better to Basia than to me."

" I not kind ? I better to Basia ?" asked the knight, with astonishment.

" You told Basia that you were coming back to the election; if I had known that, I should not have taken your departure to heart."

" My golden — " cried Pan Michael. But that instant he checked himself and said, " My dear friend. I told you little, for I had lost my head."

CHAPTER X.

Pan Michael began to prepare slowly for his departure; he did not cease, however, to give lessons to Basia, whom he liked more and more, nor to walk alone with Krysia and seek consolation in her society. It seemed to him also that he found it; for his good-humor increased daily, and in the evening he even took part in the games of Basia and Pan Adam. That young cavalier became an agreeable guest at Ketling's house. He came in the morning or at midday, and remained till evening; as all liked him, they were glad to see him, and very soon they began to hold him as one of the family. He took the ladies to Warsaw, gave their orders at the silk shops, and in the evening played blindman's-buff and patience with them, repeating that he must absolutely catch the unattainable Basia before his departure.

But Basia laughed and escaped always, though Zagloba said to her, "If this one does not catch you at last, another man will."

It became clearer and clearer that just "this one" had resolved to catch her. This must have come even to the head of the haiduk herself, for she fell sometimes to thinking till the forelock dropped into her eyes altogether. Pan Zagloba had his reasons, according to which Pan Adam was not suitable. A certain evening, when all had retired, he knocked at Pan Michael's chamber.

"I am so sorry that we must part," said he, "that I have come to get a good look at you. God knows when we shall see each other again."

"I shall come in all certainty to the election," said the little knight, embracing his old friend, "and I will tell you why. The hetman wishes to have here the largest number possible of men beloved by the knighthood, so that they may capture nobles for his candidate; and because — thanks to God! — my name has some weight among our brethren, he wants me to come surely. He counts on you also."

"Indeed, he is trying to catch me with a large net; yet I see something, and though I am rather bulky, still I can creep out through any hole in that net. I will not vote for a Frenchman."

" Why ? "

" Because he would be for *absolutum dominium* (absolute rule)."

" Condé would have to swear to the *pacta conventa* like any other man; and he must be a great leader, — he is renowned for warlike achievement."

" With God's favor we have no need of seeking leaders in France. Pan Sobieski himself is surely no worse than Condé. Think of it, Michael; the French wear stockings like the Swedes; therefore, like them they of course keep no oaths. Carolus Gustavus was ready to take an oath every hour. For the Swedes to take an oath or crack a nut is all one. What does a pact mean when a man has no honesty ? "

" But the Commonwealth needs defence. Oh, if Prince Yeremi were alive ! We would elect him king with one voice."

" His son is alive, the same blood."

" But not the same courage. It is God's pity to look at him, for he is more like a serving-man than a prince of such worthy blood. If it were a different time ! But now the first virtue is regard for the good of the country. Pan Yan says the same thing. Whatever the hetman does, I will do, for I believe in his love of the Commonwealth as in the Gospel."

" It is time to think of that. It is too bad that you are going now."

" But what will you do ? "

" I will go to Pan Yan. The boys torment me at times; still, when I am away for a good while I feel lonely without them."

" If war comes after the election, Pan Yan too will go to it. Who knows ? You may take the field yourself; we may campaign yet together in Russia. How much good and evil have we gone through in those parts ! "

" True, as God is dear to me ! there our best years flowed by. At times the wish comes to see all those places which witnessed our glory."

" Then come with me now. We shall be cheerful together; in five months I will return to Ketling. He will be at home then, and Pan Yan will be here."

" No, Michael, it is not the time for me now; but I promise that if you marry some lady with land in Russia, I will go with you and see your installation."

Pan Michael was confused a little, but answered at once, "How should I have a wife in my head? The best proof that I have not is that I am going to the army."

"It is that which torments me; for I used to think, if not one, then another woman. Michael, have God in your heart; stop; where will you find a better chance than just at this moment? Remember that years will come later in which you will say to yourself: 'Each has his wife and his children, but I am alone, like Matsek's pear-tree, sticking up in the field.' And sorrow will seize you and terrible yearning. If you had married that dear one; if she had left children, — I should not trouble you; I should have some object for my affection and ready hope for consolation; but as things now are, the time may come when you will look around in vain for a near soul, and you will ask yourself, 'Am I living in a foreign country?'"

Pan Michael was silent; he meditated; therefore Zagloba began to speak again, looking quickly into the face of the little knight, "In my mind and my heart I chose first of all that rosy haiduk for you: to begin with, she is gold, not a maiden; and secondly, such venomous soldiers as you would give to the world have not been on earth yet."

"She is a storm; besides, Pan Adam wants to strike fire with her."

"That's it, — that's it! To-day she would prefer you to a certainty, for she is in love with your glory; but when you go, and he remains — I know he will remain, the rascal! for there is no war — who knows what will happen?"

"Basia is a storm! Let Novoveski take her. I wish him well, because he is a brave man."

"Michael!" said Zagloba, clasping his hands, "think what a posterity that would be!"

To this the little knight answered with the greatest simplicity, "I knew two brothers Bal whose mother was a Drohoyovski,[1] and they were excellent soldiers."

"Ah! I was waiting for that. You have turned in that direction?" cried Zagloba.

Pan Michael was confused beyond measure; at last he replied, "What do you say? I am turning to no side; but when I thought of Basia's bravery, which is really manlike,

---

[1] Drohoyovski is Panna Krysia's family name.

Krysia came to my mind at once; in her there is more of woman's nature. When one of them is mentioned, the other comes to mind, for they are both together."

"Well, well! God bless you with Krysia, though as God is dear to me, if I were young, I should fall in love with Basia to kill. You would not need to leave such a wife at home in time of war; you could take her to the field, and have her at your side. Such a woman would be good for you in the tent; and if it came to that, even in time of battle she would handle a musket. But she is honest and good. Oh, my haiduk, my little darling haiduk, they have not known you here, and have nourished you with thanklessness; but if I were something like sixty years younger, I should see what sort of a Pani Zagloba there would be in my house."

"I do not detract from Basia."

"It is not a question of detracting from her virtues, but of giving her a husband. But you prefer Krysia."

"Krysia is my friend."

"Your friend, not your friend*ess*?. That must be because she has a mustache. I am your friend; Pan Yan is; so is Ketling. You do not need a man for a friend, but a woman. Tell this to yourself clearly, and don't throw a cover over your eyes. Guard yourself, Michael, against a friend of the fair sex, even though that friend has a mustache; for either you will betray that friend, or you yourself will be betrayed. The Devil does not sleep, and he is glad to sit between such friends; as example of this, Adam and Eve began to be friends, till that friendship became a bone in Adam's throat."

"Do not offend Krysia, for I will not endure it in any way."

"God guard Krysia! There is no one above my little haiduk; but Krysia is a good maiden too. I do not attack her in any way, but I say this to you: When you sit near her, your cheeks are as flushed as if some one had pinched them, and your mustaches are quivering, your forelock rises, and you are panting and striking with your feet and stamping like a ring-dove; and all this is a sign of desires. Tell some one else about friendship; I am too old a sparrow for that talk."

"So old that you see that which is not."

"Would that I were mistaken! Would that my haiduk were in question! Michael, good-night to you. Take the haiduk; the haiduk is the comelier. Take the haiduk; take the haiduk!"

Zagloba rose and went out of the room.

Pan Michael tossed about the whole night; he could not sleep, for unquiet thoughts passed through his head all the time. He saw before him Krysia's face, her eyes with long lashes, and her lip with down. Dozing seized him at moments, but the vision did not vanish. On waking, he remembered the words of Zagloba, and called to mind how rarely the wit of that man was mistaken in anything. At times when half sleeping, half waking, the rosy face of Basia gleamed before him, and the sight calmed him; but again Krysia took her place quickly. The poor knight turns to the wall now, sees her eyes; turns to the darkness in the room, sees her eyes, and in them a certain languishing, a certain encouragement. At times those eyes are closing, as if to say, "Let thy will be done!" Pan Michael sat up in the bed and crossed himself. Toward morning the dream flew away altogether; then it became oppressive and bitter to him. Shame seized him, and he began to reproach himself harshly, because he did not see before him that beloved one who was dead; that he had his eyes, his heart, his soul, full not of her, but of the living. It seemed to him that he had sinned against the memory of Anusia, hence he shook himself once and a second time; then springing from the bed, though it was dark yet, he began to say his morning "Our Father."

When Pan Michael had finished, he put his finger on his forehead and said, "I must go as soon as possible, and restrain this friendship at once, for perhaps Zagloba is right." Then, more cheerful and calm, he went down to breakfast. After breakfast he fenced with Basia, and noticed, beyond doubt, for the first time, that she drew one's eyes, she was so attractive with her dilated nostrils and panting breast. He seemed to avoid Krysia, who, noting this, followed him with her eyes, staring from astonishment; but he avoided even her glance. It was cutting his heart; but he held out.

After dinner he went with Basia to the storehouse, where Ketling had another collection of arms. He showed her various weapons, and explained the use of them. Then they shot at a mark from Astrachan bows. The maiden was made happy with the amusement, and became giddier than ever, so that Pani Makovetski had to restrain her.

Thus passed the second day. On the third Pan Michael
went with Zagloba to Warsaw to the Danilovich Palace to
learn something concerning the time of his departure. In
the evening the little knight told the ladies that he would
go surely in a week. While saying this, he tried to speak
carelessly and joyfully. He did not even look at Krysia.
The young lady was alarmed, tried to ask him touching
various things; he answered politely, with friendliness,
but talked more with Basia.

Zagloba, thinking this to be the fruit of his counsel,
rubbed his hands with delight; but since nothing could
escape his eye, he saw Krysia's sadness. "She has changed,"
thought he; "she has changed noticeably. Well, that is
nothing,—the ordinary nature of fair heads. But Michael
has turned away sooner than I hoped. He is a man in a
hundred, but a whirlwind in love, and a whirlwind he will
remain."

Zagloba had, in truth, a good heart, and was sorry at once
for Panna Krysia. "I will say nothing to the maiden
directly," thought he, "but I must think out some consolation for her." Then, using the privilege of age and a
white head, he went to her after supper and began to stroke
her black, silky hair. She sat quietly, raising toward him
her mild eyes, somewhat astonished at his tenderness, but
grateful.

In the evening Zagloba nudged Pan Michael in the side
at the door of the little knight's room, "Well, what?" said
he. "No one can beat the haiduk?"

"A charming kid," answered Pan Michael. "She will
make as much uproar as four soldiers in the house,—a
regular drummer."

"A drummer? God grant her to go with your drum as
quickly as possible!"

"Good-night!"

"Good-night! Wonderful creatures, those fair heads!
Since you approached Basia a little, have you noted the
change in Krysia?"

"No, I have not," answered the little knight.

"As if some one had tripped her."

"Good-night," repeated Pan Michael, and went quickly to
his room.

Zagloba, in counting on the little knight's instability,
over-reckoned somewhat, and in general acted awkwardly
in mentioning the change in Krysia; for Pan Michael was

so affected that something seemed to seize him by the throat.

"And this is how I pay her for kindness, for comforting me in grief, like a sister," said he to himself. "Well, what evil have I done to her?" thought he, after a moment of meditation. "What have I done? I have slighted her for three days, which was rude, to say the least. I have slighted the cherished girl, the dear one. Because she wished to cure my wounds, I have nourished her with ingratitude. If I only knew," continued he, "how to preserve measure and restrain dangerous friendship, and not offend her; but evidently my wit is too dull for such management."

Pan Michael was angry at himself; but at the same time great pity rose in his breast. Involuntarily he began to think of Krysia as of a beloved and injured person. Anger against himself grew in him every moment.

"I am a barbarian, a barbarian!" repeated he. And Krysia overwhelmed Basia completely in his mind. "Let him who pleases take that kid, that wind-mill, that rattler," said he to himself, — "Pan Adam or the Devil, it is all one to me!"

Anger rose in him against Basia, who was indebted to God for her disposition; but it never came to his head once that he might wrong her more with this anger than Krysia with his pretended indifference. Krysia, with a woman's instinct, divined straightway that some change was taking place in Pan Michael. It was at once both bitter and sad for the maiden that the little knight seemed to avoid her; but she understood instantly that something must be decided between them, and that their friendship could not continue unmodified, but must become either far greater than it had been or cease altogether. Hence she was seized by alarm, which increased at the thought of Pan Michael's speedy departure. Love was not in Krysia's heart yet. The maiden had not come to self-consciousness on that point; but in her heart and in her blood there was a great readiness for love. Perhaps too she felt a light turning of the head. Pan Michael was surrounded with the glory of the first soldier in the Commonwealth. All knights were repeating his name with respect. His sister exalted his honor to the sky; the charm of misfortune covered him; and in addition, the young lady, living under the same roof with him, grew accustomed to his attraction.

Krysia had this in her nature, she was fond of being
loved; therefore when Pan Michael began in those recent
days to treat her with indifference, her self-esteem suffered
greatly; but having a good heart, she resolved not to show
an angry face or vexation, and to win him by kindness.
That came to her all the more easily, since on the following
day Pan Michael had a penitent mien, and not only did not
avoid Krysia's glance, but looked into her eyes, as if wishing to say, "Yesterday I offended you; to-day I implore
your forgiveness." He said so much to her with his eyes
that under their influence the blood flowed to the young
lady's face, and her disquiet was increased, as if with a
presentiment that very soon something important would
happen. In fact, it did happen. In the afternoon Pani
Makovetski went with Basia to Basia's relative, the wife of
the chamberlain of Lvoff, who was stopping in Warsaw;
Krysia feigned purposely a headache, for curiosity seized
her to know what she and Pan Michael would do if left to
themselves.

Zagloba did not go, it is true, to the chamberlain's wife,
but he had the habit of sleeping a couple of hours after
dinner, for he said that it saved him from fatness, and gave
him clear wit in the evening; therefore, after he had
chatted an hour or so, he began to prepare for his room.
Krysia's heart beat at once more unquietly. But what a
disillusion was awaiting her! Pan Michael sprang up, and
went out with Zagloba.

"He will come back soon," thought Krysia. And taking
a little drum, she began to embroider on it a gold top for
a cap to give Pan Michael at his departure. Her eyes rose,
however, every little while, and went to the Dantzig clock,
which stood in the corner of Ketling's room, and ticked
with importance.

But one hour and a second passed; Pan Michael was not
to be seen. Krysia placed the drum on her knees, and
crossing her hands on it, said in an undertone, "But before
he decides, they may come, and we shall not say anything,
or Pan Zagloba may wake."

It seemed to her in that moment that they had in truth
to speak of some important affair, which might be deferred
through the fault of Pan Michael. At last, however, his
steps were heard in the next room. "He is wandering
around," thought she, and began to embroider diligently
again.

Volodyovski was, in fact, wandering; he was walking through the room, and did not dare to come in. Meanwhile the sun was growing red and approaching its setting.

"Pan Michael!" called Krysia, suddenly.

He came in and found her sewing. "Did you call me?"

"I wished to know if some stranger was walking in the house; I have been here alone for two hours."

Pan Michael drew up a chair and sat on the edge of it. A long time elapsed; he was silent; his feet clattered somewhat as he pushed them under the table, and his mustache quivered. Krysia stopped sewing and raised her eyes to him; their glances met, and then both dropped their eyes suddenly.

When Pan Michael raised his eyes again, the last rays of the sun were falling on Krysia's face, and it was beautiful in the light; her hair gleamed in its folds like gold. "In a couple of days you are going?" asked she, so quietly that Pan Michael barely heard her.

"It cannot be otherwise."

Again a moment of silence, after which Krysia said, "I thought these last days that you were angry with me."

"As I live," cried Pan Michael, "I would not be worthy of your regard if I had been, but I was not."

"What was the matter?" asked Krysia, raising her eyes to him.

"I wish to speak sincerely, for I think that sincerity is always better than dissimulation; but I cannot tell how much solace you have poured into my heart, and how grateful I feel."

"God grant it to be always so!" said Krysia, crossing her hands on the drum.

To this Pan Michael answered with great sadness, "God grant! God grant— But Pan Zagloba told me—I speak before you as before a priest—Pan Zagloba told me that friendship with fair heads is not a safe thing, for a more ardent feeling may be hidden beneath it, as fire under ashes. I thought that perhaps Pan Zagloba was right. Forgive me, a simple soldier; another would have brought out the idea more cleverly, but my heart is bleeding because I have offended you these recent days, and life is not pleasant to me."

When he had said this, Pan Michael began to move his mustaches more quickly than any beetle. Krysia dropped her head, and after a while two tears rolled down her cheeks. "If it will be easier for you, I will conceal my sisterly affection." A second pair of tears, and then a third, appeared on her cheeks.

At sight of this, Pan Michael's heart was rent completely; he sprang toward Krysia, and seized her hands. The drum rolled from her knees to the middle of the room; the knight, however, did not care for that; he only pressed those warm, soft, velvety hands to his mouth, repeating, —

"Do not weep. For God's sake, do not weep!"

Pan Michael did not cease to kiss the hands even when Krysia put them on her head, as people do usually when embarrassed; but he kissed them the more ardently, till the warmth coming from her hair and forehead intoxicated him as wine does, and his ideas grew confused. Then not knowing himself how and when, his lips came to her forehead and kissed that still more eagerly; and then he pushed down to her tearful eyes, and the world went around with him altogether. Next he felt that most delicate down on her lip; and after that their mouths met and were pressed together with all their power. Silence fell on the room; only the clock ticked with importance.

Suddenly Basia's steps were heard in the ante-room, and her childlike voice repeating, "Frost! frost! frost!"

Pan Michael sprang away from Krysia like a frightened panther from his victim; and at that moment Basia rushed in with an uproar, repeating incessantly, "Frost! frost! frost!" Suddenly she stumbled against the drum lying in the middle of the room. Then she stopped, and looking with astonishment, now on the drum, now on Krysia, now on the little knight, said, "What is this? You struck each other, as with a dart?"

"But where is auntie?" asked Krysia, striving to bring out of her heaving breast a quiet, natural voice.

"Auntie is climbing out of the sleigh by degrees," answered Basia, with an equally changed voice. Her nostrils moved a number of times. She looked once more at Krysia and Pan Michael, who by that time had raised the drum, then she left the room suddenly.

Pani Makovetski rolled into the room; Pan Zagloba came downstairs, and a conversation set in about the wife of the chamberlain of Lvoff.

"I did not know that she was Pan Adam's godmother," said Pani Makovetski; "he must have made her his confidante, for she is persecuting Basia with him terribly."

"But what did Basia say?" asked Zagloba.

"'A halter for a dog!' She said to the chamberlain's lady: 'He has no mustache, and I have no sense; and it is not known which one will get what is lacking first.'"

"I knew that she would not lose her tongue; but who knows what her real thought is? Ah, woman's wiles!"

"With Basia, what is on her heart is on her lips. Besides, I have told you already that she does not feel the will of God yet; Krysia does, in a higher degree."

"Auntie!" said Krysia, suddenly.

Further conversation was interrupted by the servant, who announced that supper was on the table. All went then to the dining-room; but Basia was not there.

"Where is the young lady?" asked Pani Makovetski of the servant.

"The young lady is in the stable. I told the young lady that supper was ready; the young lady said, 'Well,' and went to the stable."

"Has something unpleasant happened to her? She was so gay," said Pani Makovetski, turning to Zagloba.

Then the little knight, who had an unquiet conscience, said, "I will go and bring her." And he hurried out. He found her just inside the stable-door, sitting on a bundle of hay. She was so sunk in thought that she did not see him as he entered.

"Panna Basia," said the little knight, bending over her.

Basia trembled as if roused from sleep, and raised her eyes, in which Pan Michael saw, to his utter astonishment, two tears as large as pearls. "For God's sake! What is the matter? You are weeping."

"I do not dream of it," cried Basia, springing up; "I do not dream of it! That is from frost." She laughed joyously, but the laughter was rather forced. Then, wishing to turn attention from herself, she pointed to the stall in which was the steed given Pan Michael by the hetman, and said with animation, "You say it is impossible to go to that horse? Now let us see!"

And before Pan Michael could restrain her, she had sprung into the stall. The fierce beast began to rear, to paw, and to put back his ears.

"For God's sake! he will kill you!" cried Pan Michael, springing after her.

But Basia had begun already to stroke with her palm the shoulder of the horse, repeating, "Let him kill! let him kill!"

But the horse turned to her his steaming nostrils and gave a low neigh, as if rejoiced at the fondling.

CHAPTER XI.

ALL the nights that Pan Michael had spent were nothing in comparison with the night after that adventure with Krysia. For, behold, he had betrayed the memory of his dead one, and he loved that memory. He had deceived the confidence of the living woman, had abused friendship, had contracted certain obligations, had acted like a man without conscience. Another soldier would have made nothing of such a kiss, or, what is more, would have twisted his mustache at thought of it; but Pan Michael was squeamish, especially since the death of Anusia, as is every man who has a soul in pain and a torn heart. What was left for him to do, then? How was he to act?

Only a few days remained until his departure; that departure would cut short everything. But was it proper to go without a word to Krysia, and leave her as he would leave any chamber-maid from whom he might steal a kiss? The brave heart of Pan Michael trembled at the thought. Even in the struggle in which he was then, the thought of Krysia filled him with pleasure, and the remembrance of that kiss passed through him with a quiver of delight. Rage against his own head seized him; still he could not refrain from a feeling of sweetness. And he took the whole blame on himself.

"I brought Krysia to that," repeated he, with bitterness and pain; "I brought her to it, therefore it is not just for me to go away without a word. What, then? Make a proposal, and go away Krysia's betrothed?"

Here the form of Anusia stood before the knight, dressed in white, and pale herself as wax, just as he had laid her in the coffin. "This much is due me," said the figure, "that you mourn and grieve for me. You wished at first to become a monk, to bewail me all your life; but now you are taking another before my poor soul could fly to the gates of heaven. Ah! wait, let me reach heaven first; let me cease looking at the earth."

And it seemed to the knight that he was a species of perjurer before that bright soul whose memory he should honor and hold as sacred. Sorrow and immeasurable shame seized him, and self-contempt. He desired death.

"Anulya,"[1] repeated he, on his knees, "I shall not cease to bewail thee till death; but what am I to do now?"

The white form gave no answer to that as it vanished like a light mist; and instead of it appeared in the imagination of the knight Krysia's eyes and her lip covered with down, and with it temptations from which the knight wished to free himself. So his heart was wavering in uncertainty, suffering, and torment. At moments it came to his head to go and confess all to Zagloba, and take counsel of that man whose reason could settle all difficulties. And he had foreseen everything; he had told beforehand what it was to enter into "friendship" with fair heads. But just that view restrained the little knight. He recollected how sharply he had called to Pan Zagloba, "Do not offend Panna Krysia, sir!" And now, who had offended Panna Krysia? Who was the man who had thought, "Is it not best to leave her like a chamber-maid and go away?"

"If it were not for that dear one up there, I would not hesitate a moment," thought the knight, "I should not be tormented at all; on the contrary, I should be glad in soul that I had tasted such delight." After a while he muttered, "I would take it willingly a hundred times." Seeing, however, that temptations were flocking around him, he shook them off again powerfully, and began to reason in this way: "It is all over. Since I have acted like one who is not desirous of friendship, but who is looking for satisfaction from Cupid, I must go by that road, and tell Krysia to-morrow that I wish to marry her."

Here he stopped awhile, then thought further thuswise: "Through which declaration the confidence of to-day will become quite proper, and to-morrow I can permit myself—" But at this moment he struck his mouth with his palm. "Tfu!" said he; "is a whole chambul of devils sitting behind my collar?"

But still he did not set aside his plan of making the declaration, thinking to himself simply: "If I offend the dear dead one, I can conciliate her with Masses and prayer; by this I shall show also that I remember her always, and will not cease in devotion. If people wonder and laugh at

[1] A diminutive of Anna, expressing endearment.

me because two weeks ago I wanted from sorrow to be a monk, and now have made a declaration of love to another, the shame will be on my side alone. If I make no declaration, the innocent Krysia will have to share my shame and my fault. I will propose to her to-morrow; it cannot be otherwise," said he, at last.

He calmed himself then considerably; and when he had repeated "Our Father," and prayed earnestly for Anusia, he fell asleep. In the morning, when he woke, he repeated, "I will propose to-day." But it was not so easy to propose, for Pan Michael did not wish to inform others, but to talk with Krysia first, and then act as was proper. Meanwhile Pan Adam arrived in the early morning, and filled the whole house with his presence.

Krysia went about as if poisoned; the whole day she was pale, worried, sometimes dropped her eyes, sometimes blushed so that the color went to her neck; at times her lips quivered as if she were going to cry; then again she was as if dreamy and languid. It was difficult for the knight to approach her, and especially to remain long alone with her. It is true he might have taken her to walk, for the weather was wonderful, and some time before he would have done so without any scruple; but now he dared not, for it seemed to him that all would divine on the spot what his object was, — all would think he was going to propose.

Pan Adam saved him. He took Pani Makovetski aside, conversed with her a good while touching something, then both returned to the room in which the little knight was sitting with the two young ladies and Pan Zagloba, and said, "You young people might have a ride in two sleighs, for the snow is sparkling."

At this Pan Michael inclined quickly to Krysia's ear and said, "I beg you to sit with me. I have a world of things to say."

"Very well," answered Krysia.

Then the two men hastened to the stables, followed by Basia; and in the space of a few "Our Fathers," the two sleighs were driven up before the house. Pan Michael and Krysia took their places in one, Pan Adam and the little haiduk in the other, and moved on without drivers.

When they had gone, Pani Makovetski turned to Zagloba and said, "Pan Adam has proposed for Basia."

"How is that?" asked Zagloba, alarmed.

"His godmother, the wife of the chamberlain of Lvoff,

is to come here to-morrow to talk with me ; Pan Adam himself has begged of me permission to talk with Basia, even
hintingly, for he understands himself that if Basia is not
his friend, the trouble and pains will be useless."

"It was for this that you, my benefactress, sent them
sleigh-riding ?"

"For this. My husband is very scrupulous. More than
once he has said to me, 'I will guard their property, but
let each choose a husband for herself ; if he is honorable,
I will not oppose, even in case of inequality of property.'
Moreover, they are of mature years and can give advice to
themselves."

"But what answer do you think of giving Pan Adam's
godmother ?"

"My husband will come in May. I will turn the affair
over to him ; but I think this way, — as Basia wishes, so
will it be."

"Pan Adam is a stripling !"

"But Michael himself says that he is a famous soldier,
noted already for deeds of valor. He has a respectable
property, and his godmother has recounted to me all his
relations. You see, it is this way : his great-grandfather
was born of Princess Senyut ; he was married the first
time to — "

"But what do I care for his relations ?" interrupted
Zagloba, not hiding his ill-humor; "he is neither brother
nor godfather to me, and I tell your ladyship that I have
predestined the little haiduk to Michael ; for if among
maidens who walk the world on two feet there is one
better or more honest than she, may I from this moment
begin to walk on all-four like a bear !"

"Michael is thinking of nothing yet ; and even if he were,
Krysia has struck his eye more. Ah! God, whose ways are
inscrutable, will decide this."

"But if that bare-lipped youngster goes away with
a water-melon,[1] I shall be drunk with delight," added
Zagloba.

Meanwhile in the two sleighs the fates of both knights
were in the balance. Pan Michael was unable to utter a
word for a long time ; at last he said to Krysia, "Do not
think that I am a frivolous man, or some kind of fop, for
not such are my years."

---

[1] To place a water-melon in the carriage of a suitor was one way of
refusing him.

Krysia made no answer.

"Forgive me for what I did yesterday, for it was from the good feeling which I have for you, which is so great that I was altogether unable to restrain it. My gracious lady, my beloved Krysia, consider who I am; I am a simple soldier, whose life has been passed in wars. Another would have prepared an oration beforehand, and then come to confidence; I have begun with confidence. Remember this also, that if a horse, though trained, takes the bit in his teeth and runs away with a man, why should not love, whose force is greater, run away with him? Love carried me away, simply because you are dear to me. My beloved Krysia, you are worthy of castellans and senators; but if you do not disdain a soldier, who, though in simple rank, has served the country not without some glory, I fall at your feet, I kiss your feet, and I ask, do you wish me? Can you think of me without repulsion?"

"Pan Michael!" answered Krysia. And her hand, drawn from her muff, hid itself in the hand of the knight.

"Do you consent?" asked Volodyovski.

"I do!" answered Krysia; "and I know that I could not find a more honorable man in all Poland."

"God reward you! God reward you, Krysia!" said the knight, covering the hand with kisses. "A greater happiness could not meet me. Only tell me that you are not angry at yesterday's confidence, so that I may find relief of conscience."

"I am not angry."

"Oh that I could kiss your feet!" cried Pan Michael.

They remained some time in silence; the runners were whistling on the snow, and snowballs were flying from under the horse's feet. Then Pan Michael said, "I marvel that you regard me."

"It is more wonderful," answered Krysia, "that you came to love me so quickly."

At this Pan Michael's face grew very serious, and he said, "It may seem ill to you that before I shook off sorrow for one, I fell in love with another. I own to you also, as if I were at confession, that in my time I have been giddy; but now it is different. I have not forgotten that dear one, and shall never forget her; I love her yet, and if you knew how much I weep for her, you would weep over me yourself."

Here voice failed the little knight, for he was greatly

moved, and perhaps for that reason he did not notice that
these words did not seem to make a very deep impression
on Krysia.

Silence followed again, interrupted this time by the lady:
" I will try to comfort you, as far as my strength permits."

" I loved you so soon," said Pan Michael, " because you
began from the first day to cure my wounds. What was I
to you? Nothing! But you began at once, because you had
pity in your heart for an unfortunate. Ah! I am thankful
to you, greatly thankful! Who does not know this will
perhaps reproach me, since I wished to be a monk in
November, and am preparing for marriage in December.
First, Pan Zagloba will be ready to jeer, for he is glad to
do that when occasion offers; but let the man jeer who is
able! I do not care about that, especially since the
reproach will not fall on you, but on me."

Krysia began to look at the sky thoughtfully, and said at
last, " Must we absolutely tell people of our engagement?"

" What is your meaning?"

" You are going away, it seems, in a couple of days?"

" Even against my will, I must go."

" I am wearing mourning for my father. Why should we
exhibit ourselves to the gaze of people? Let our engagement remain between ourselves, and people need not know
of it till you return from Russia. Are you satisfied?"

" Then I am to say nothing to my sister?"

" I will tell her myself, but after you have gone."

" And to Pan Zagloba?"

" Pan Zagloba would sharpen his wit on me. Ei, better
say nothing! Basia too would tease me; and she these
last days is so whimsical and has such changing humor as
never before. Better say nothing." Here Krysia raised
her dark-blue eyes to the heavens: " God is the witness
above us; let people remain uninformed."

" I see that your wit is equal to your beauty. I agree.
Then God is our witness. Amen! Now rest your shoulder
on me; for as soon as our contract is made, modesty is not
opposed to that. Have no fear! Even if I wished to
repeat yesterday's act, I cannot, for I must take care of
the horse."

Krysia gratified the knight, and he said, " As often as
we are alone, call me by name only."

" Somehow it does not fit," said she, with a smile. " I
never shall dare to do that."

"But I have dared."

"For Pan Michael is a knight, Pan Michael is daring, Pan Michael is a soldier."

"Krysia, you are my love!"

"Mich —" But Krysia had not courage to finish, and covered her face with her muff.

After a while Pan Michael returned to the house; they did not converse much on the road, but at the gate the little knight asked again, "But after yesterday's — you understand — were you very sad?"

"Oh, I was ashamed and sad, but had a wonderful feeling," added she, in a lower voice.

All at once they put on a look of indifference, so that no one might see what had passed between them. But that was a needless precaution, for no one paid heed to them. It is true that Zagloba and Pan Michael's sister ran out to meet the two couples, but their eyes were turned only on Basia and Pan Adam.

Basia was red, certainly, but it was unknown whether from cold or emotion; and Pan Adam was as if poisoned. Immediately after, too, he took farewell of the lady of the house. In vain did she try to detain him; in vain Pan Michael himself tried to persuade him to remain to supper: he excused himself with service and went away. That moment Pan Michael's sister, without saying a word, kissed Basia on the forehead; the young lady flew to her own chamber and did not return to supper.

Only on the next day did Zagloba make a direct attack on her and inquire, "Well, little haiduk, a thunderbolt, as it were, struck Pan Adam?"

"Aha!" answered she, nodding affirmatively and blinking.

"Tell me what you said to him."

"The question was quick, for he is daring; but so was the answer, for I too am daring. Is it not true?"

"You acted splendidly! Let me embrace you! What did he say? Did he let himself be beaten off easily?"

"He asked if with time he could not effect something. I was sorry for him, but no, no; nothing can come of that!"

Here Basia, distending her nostrils, began to shake her forelock somewhat sadly, as if in thought.

"Tell me your reasons," said Zagloba.

"He too wanted them, but it was of no use; I did not tell him, and I will tell no man."

"But perhaps," said Zagloba, looking quickly into her eyes, "you bear some hidden love in your heart. Hei?"

"A fig for love!" cried Basia. And springing from the place, she began to repeat quickly, as if wishing to cover her confusion, "I do not want Pan Adam! I do not want Pan Adam! I do not want any one! Why do you plague me? Why do you plague me, all of you?" And on a sudden she burst into tears.

Zagloba comforted her as best he could, but during the whole day she was gloomy and peevish. "Michael," said he at dinner, "you are going, and Ketling will come soon; he is a beauty above beauties. I know not how these young ladies will defend themselves, but I think this, when you come back, you will find them both dead in love."

"Profit for us!" said Volodyovski. "We'll give him Panna Basia at once."

Basia fixed on him the look of a wild-cat and said, "But why are you less concerned about Krysia?"

The little knight was confused beyond measure at these words, and said, "You do not know Ketling's power, but you will discover it."

"But why should not Krysia discover it? Besides, it is not I who sing, —

    'The fair head grows faint;
    Where will she hide herself?
    How will the poor thing defend herself?'"

Now Krysia was confused in her turn, and the little wasp continued, "In extremities I will ask Pan Adam to lend me his shield; but when you go away, I know not with what Krysia will defend herself, if peril comes on her."

Pan Michael had now recovered, and answered somewhat severely, "Perhaps she will find wherewith to defend herself better than you."

"How so?"

"For she is less giddy, and has more sedateness and dignity."

Pan Zagloba and the little knight's sister thought that the keen haiduk would come to battle at once; but to their great amazement, she dropped her head toward the plate, and after a while said, in a low voice, "If you are angry, I ask pardon of you and of Krysia."

CHAPTER XII.

As Pan Michael had permission to set out whenever he wished, he went to Anusia's grave at Chenstohova. After he had shed the last of his tears there, he journeyed on farther; and under the influence of fresh reminiscences it occurred to him that the secret engagement with Krysia was in some way too early. He felt that in sorrow and mourning there is something sacred and inviolable, which should not be touched, but permitted to rise heavenward like a cloud, and vanish in measureless space. Other men, it is true, after losing their wives, had married in a month or in two months; but they had not begun with the cloister, nor had misfortune met them at the threshold of happiness after whole years of waiting. But even if men of common mould do not respect the sacredness of sorrow, is it proper to follow their example?

Pan Michael journeyed forward then toward Russia, and reproaches went with him. But he was so just that he took all the blame on himself, and did not put any on Krysia; and to the many alarms which seized him was added this also, would not Krysia in the depth of her soul take that haste ill of him?

"Surely she would not act thus in my place," said Pan Michael to himself; "and having a lofty soul herself, beyond doubt, she seeks loftiness in others."

Fear seized the little knight lest he might seem to her petty; but that was vain fear. Krysia cared nothing for Pan Michael's mourning; and when he spoke to her too much concerning it, not only did it not excite sympathy in the lady, but it roused her self-love. Was not she, the living woman, equal to the dead one? Or, in general, was she of such small worth that the dead Anusia could be her rival? If Zagloba had been in the secret, he would have pacified Pan Michael certainly, by saying that women have not over-much mercy for one another.

After Volodyovski's departure, Panna Krysia was astonished not a little at what had happened, and at this, that the latch had fallen. In going from the Ukraine to Warsaw, where she had never been before, she had imagined that it would be different altogether. At the Diet of Convocation the escorts of bishops and dignitaries would meet; a brilliant knighthood would assemble from all sides of the Commonwealth. How many amusements and reviews would there be, how much bustle! and in all that whirl, in the concourse of knights, would appear some unknown "he," some knight such as maidens see only in dreams. This knight would flush up with love, appear under her windows with a lute; he would form cavalcades, love and sigh a long time, wear on his armor the knot of his loved one, suffer and overcome obstacles before he would fall at her feet and win mutual love.

But nothing of all that had come to pass. The haze, changing and colored, like a rainbow, vanished; a knight appeared, it is true, — a knight not at all common, heralded as the first soldier of the Commonwealth, a great cavalier, but not much, or indeed, not at all, like that "he." There were no cavalcades either, nor playing of lutes, nor tournaments, nor the knot on the armor, nor bustle, nor games, nor any of all that which rouses curiosity like a May dream, or a wonderful tale in the evening, which intoxicates like the odor of flowers, which allures as bait does a bird; from which the face flushes, the heart throbs, the body trembles. There was nothing but a small house outside the city; in the house Pan Michael; then intimacy grew up, and the rest of the vision disappeared as the moon disappears in the sky when clouds come and hide it. If that Pan Michael had appeared at the end of the story, he would be the desired one. More than once, when thinking of his fame, of his worth, of his valor, which made him the glory of the Commonwealth and the terror of its enemies, Krysia felt that, in spite of all, she loved him greatly; only it seemed to her that something had missed her, that a certain injustice had met her, a little through him, or rather through haste. That haste, therefore, had fallen into the hearts of both like a grain of sand; and since both were farther and farther from each other, that grain began to pain them somewhat. It happens frequently that something insignificant as a little thorn pricks the feelings of people, and in time either heals or festers more and more, and brings bitterness and pain, even to the greatest love. But in this case it was still far to pain and bitterness. For Pan Michael, the thought of Krysia was especially agreeable and soothing; and the thought of her followed him as his shadow follows a man. He thought too that the farther he went, the dearer she would become to him, and the more he would sigh and yearn for her. The time passed more heavily for her; for no one visited Ketling's house since the departure of the little knight; and day followed day in monotony and weariness.

Pani Makovetski counted the days before the election, waited for her husband, and talked only of him; Basia had put on a very long face. Zagloba reproached her, saying that she had rejected Pan Adam and was then wishing for him. In fact, she would have been glad if even he had come; but Novoveski said to himself, "There is nothing for me there," and soon he followed Pan Michael. Zagloba too was preparing to return to Pan Yan's, saying that he wished to see his boys. Still, being heavy, he put off his journey day after day; he explained to Basia that she was the cause of his delay, that he was in love with her and intended to seek her hand. Meanwhile he kept company with Krysia when Pan Michael's sister went with Basia to visit the wife of the chamberlain of Lvoff. Krysia never accompanied them in those visits; for the lady, notwithstanding her worthiness, could not endure Krysia. Frequently and often too Zagloba went to Warsaw, where he met pleasant company and returned more than once tipsy on the following day; and then Krysia was entirely alone, passing the dreary hours in thinking a little of Pan Michael, a little of what might happen if that latch had not fallen once and forever, and often, what did that unknown rival of Pan Michael look like, — the King's son in the fairy tale?

Once Krysia was sitting by the window and looking in thoughtfulness at the door of the room, on which a very bright gleam of the setting sun was falling, when suddenly a sleigh-bell was heard on the other side of the house. It ran through Krysia's head that Pani Makovetski and Basia must have returned; but that did not bring her out of meditation, and she did not even withdraw her eyes from the door. Meanwhile the door opened; and on the background of the dark depth beyond appeared to the eyes of the maiden some unknown man.

At the first moment it seemed to Krysia that she saw a picture, or that she had fallen asleep and was dreaming, such a wonderful vision stood before her. The unknown was young, dressed in black foreign costume, with a white

lace collar coming to his shoulders. Once in childhood
Krysia had seen Pan Artsishevski, general of the artillery
of the kingdom, dressed in such a costume; by reason of
the dress, as well as of his unusual beauty, the general had
remained long in her memory. Now, that young man before
her was dressed in like fashion; but in beauty he surpassed
Pan Artsishevski and all men walking the earth. His hair,
cut evenly over his forehead, fell in bright curls on both
sides of his face, just marvellously. He had dark brows,
definitely outlined on a forehead white as marble; eyes
mild and melancholy; a yellow mustache and a yellow,
pointed beard. It was an incomparable head, in which
nobility was united to manfulness, — the head at once of an
angel and a warrior. Krysia's breath was stopped in her
breast, for looking, she did not believe her own eyes, nor
could she decide whether she had before her an illusion or
a real man. He stood awhile motionless, astonished, or
through politeness feigning astonishment at Krysia; at last
he moved from the door, and waving his hat downward
began to sweep the floor with its plumes. Krysia rose, but
her feet trembled under her; and now blushing, now growing pale, she closed her eyes.

Meanwhile his voice sounded low and soft, "I am Ketling
of Elgin, — the friend and companion-at-arms of Pan Volodyovski. The servant has told me already that I have the
unspeakable happiness and honor to receive as guests under
my roof the sister and relatives of my Pallas; but pardon,
worthy lady, my confusion, for the servant told me nothing
of what my eyes see, and my eyes are overcome by the
brightness of your presence."

With such a compliment did the knightly Ketling greet
Krysia; but she did not repay him in like manner, for she
could not find a single word. She thought only that when
he had finished, he would incline surely a second time, for
in the silence she heard again the rustle of plumes on the
floor. She felt also that there was need, urgent need, to
make some answer and return compliment for compliment,
otherwise she might be held a simple woman; but meanwhile her breath fails her, the pulse is throbbing in her hands
and her temples, her breast rises and falls as if she were
suffering greatly. She opens her eyelids; he stands before
her with head inclined somewhat, with admiration and
respect in his wonderful face. With trembling hand Krysia
seizes her robe to make even a courtesy before the cavalier;

fortunately, at that moment cries of "Ketling! Ketling!" are heard behind the door, and into the room rushes, with open arms, the panting Zagloba.

The two men embraced each other then; and during that time the young lady tried to recover, and to look two or three times at the knight. He embraced Zagloba heartily, but with that unusual elegance in every movement which he had either inherited from his ancestors or acquired at the refined courts of kings and magnates.

"How are you?" cried Zagloba. "I am as glad to see you in your house as in my own. Let me look at you. Ah, you have grown thin! Is it not some love-affair? As God lives, you have grown thin. Do you know, Michael has gone to the squadron? Oh, you have done splendidly to come! Michael thinks no more of the cloister. His sister is living here with two young ladies, — maidens like turnips! Oh, for God's sake, Panna Krysia is here! I beg pardon for my words, but let that man's eyes crawl out who denies beauty to either of you; this cavalier has seen it already in your case."

Ketling inclined his head a third time, and said with a smile, "I left the house a barrack and find it Olympus; for I see a goddess at the entrance."

"Ketling! how are you?" cried a second time Zagloba, for whom one greeting was too little, and he seized him again in his arms. "Never mind," said he, "you have n't seen the haiduk yet. One is a beauty, but the other is honey! How are you, Ketling? God give you health! I will talk to you. It is you; very good. That is a delight to this old man. You are glad of your guests. Pani Makovetski has come here, for it was difficult to find lodgings in the time of the Diet; but now it is easier, and she will go out, of course, for it is not well for young ladies to lodge in a single man's house, lest people might look awry, and some gossip might come of the matter."

"For God's sake! I will never permit that! I am to Volodyovski not a friend, but a brother; and I may receive Pani Makovetski as a sister under my roof. To you, young lady, I shall turn for assistance, and if necessary will beg it here on my knees."

Saying this, Ketling knelt before Krysia, and seizing her hand, pressed it to his lips and looked into her eyes imploringly, joyously, and at the same time pensively; she began to blush, especially as Zagloba cried out straightway, "He

has barely come when he is on his knees before her. As
God lives! I'll tell Pani Makovetski that I found you in
that posture. Sharp, Ketling! See what court customs
are!"

"I am not skilled in court customs," whispered the lady,
in great confusion.

"Can I reckon on your aid?" asked Ketling.

"Rise, sir!"

"May I reckon on your aid? I am Pan Michael's
brother. An injury will be done him if this house is
abandoned."

"My wishes are nothing here," answered Krysia, with
more presence of mind, "though I must be grateful for
yours."

"I thank you!" answered Ketling, pressing her hand to
his mouth.

"Ah! frost out of doors, and Cupid is naked; but he •
would not freeze in this house," said Zagloba. "And I see
that from sighs alone there will be a thaw, — from nothing
but sighs."

"Spare us," said Krysia.

"I thank God that you have not lost your jovial humor,"
said Ketling, "for joyousness is a sign of health."

"And a clear conscience," added Zagloba. "'He grieves
who is troubled,' declares the Seer in Holy Writ. Nothing
troubles me, therefore I am joyous. Oh, a hundred Turks!
What do I behold? For I saw you in Polish costume with
a lynx-skin cap and a sabre, and now you have changed
again into some kind of Englishman, and are going around
on slim legs like a stork."

"For I have been in Courland, where the Polish dress is
not worn, and have just passed two days with the English
resident in Warsaw."

"Then you are returning from Courland?"

"I am. The relative who adopted me has died, and left
me another estate there."

"Eternal repose to him! He was a Catholic, of course?"

"He was."

"You have this consolation at least. But you will not
leave us for this property in Courland?"

"I will live and die here," answered Ketling, looking at
Krysia; and at once she dropped her long lashes on her
eyes.

Pani Makovetski arrived when it was quite dark; and

Ketling went outside the gate to meet her. He conducted the lady to his house with as much homage as if she had been a reigning princess. She wished on the following day to seek other quarters in the city itself; but her resolve was ineffective. The young knight implored, dwelt on his brotherhood with Pan Michael, and knelt until she agreed to stay with him longer. It was merely stipulated that Pan Zagloba should remain some time yet, to shield the ladies with his age and dignity from evil tongues. He agreed willingly, for he had become attached beyond measure to the haiduk; and besides, he had begun to arrange in his head certain plans which demanded his presence absolutely. The maidens were both glad, and Basia came out at once openly on Ketling's side.

"We will not move out to-day, anyhow," said she to Pan Michael's hesitating sister; "and if not, it is all the same whether we stay one day or twelve."

Ketling pleased her as well as Krysia, for he pleased all women; besides, Basia had never seen a foreign cavalier, except officers of foreign infantry, — men of small rank and rather common persons. Therefore she walked around him, shaking her forelock, dilating her nostrils, and looking at him with a childlike curiosity; so importunate was she that at last she heard the censure of Pani Makovetski. But in spite of the censure, she did not cease to investigate him with her eyes, as if wishing to fix his military value, and at last she turned to Pan Zagloba.

"Is he a great soldier?" asked she of the old man in a whisper.

"Yes; so that he cannot be more celebrated. You see he has immense experience, for, remaining in the true faith, he served against the English rebels from his fourteenth year. He is a noble also of high birth, which is easily seen from his manners."

"Have you seen him under fire?"

"A thousand times! He would halt for you in it without a frown, pat his horse on the shoulder, and be ready to talk of love."

"Is it the fashion to talk of love at such a time? Hei?"

"It is the fashion to do everything by which contempt for bullets is shown."

"But hand to hand, in a duel, is he equally great?"

"Yes, yes! a wasp; it is not to be denied."

"But could he stand before Pan Michael?"

"Before Michael he could not!"

"Ha!" exclaimed Basia, with joyous pride, "I knew that he could not. I thought at once that he could not." And she began to clap her hands.

"So, then, do you take Pan Michael's side?" asked Zagloba.

Basia shook her forelock and was silent; after a while a quiet sigh raised her breast. "Ei! what of that? I am glad, for he is ours."

"But think of this, and beat it into yourself, little haiduk," said Zagloba, "that if on the field of battle it is hard to find a better man than Ketling, he is most dangerous for maidens, who love him madly for his beauty. He is trained famously in love-making too."

"Tell that to Krysia, for love is not in my head," answered Basia, and turning to Krysia, she began to call, "Krysia! Krysia! Come here just for a word."

"I am here," said Krysia.

"Pan Zagloba says that no lady looks on Ketling without falling in love straightway. I have looked at him from every side, and somehow nothing has happened; but do you feel anything?"

"Basia, Basia!" said Krysia, in a tone of persuasion.

"Has he pleased you, eh?"

"Spare us! be sedate. My Basia, do not talk nonsense, for Ketling is coming."

In fact, Krysia had not taken her seat when Ketling approached and inquired, "Is it permitted to join the company?"

"We request you earnestly," answered Krysia.

"Then I am bold to ask, of what was your conversation?"

"Of love," cried Basia, without hesitation.

Ketling sat down near Krysia. They were silent for a time; for Krysia, usually self-possessed and with presence of mind, had in some wonderful way become timid in presence of the cavalier; hence he was first to ask, —

"Is it true that the conversation was of such a pleasant subject?"

"It was," answered Krysia, in an undertone.

"I shall be delighted to hear your opinion."

"Pardon me, for I lack courage and wit, so I think that I should rather hear something new from you."

"Krysia is right," said Zagloba. "Let us listen."

"Ask a question," said Ketling. And raising his eyes

somewhat, he meditated a little, then, although no one had questioned him, he began to speak, as if to himself: "Loving is a grievous misfortune; for by loving, a free man becomes a captive. Just as a bird, shot by an arrow, falls at the feet of the hunter, so the man struck by love has no power to escape from the feet of the loved one. To love is to be maimed; for a man, like one blind, does not see the world beyond his love. To love is to mourn; for when do more tears flow, when do more sighs swell the breast? When a man loves, there are neither dresses nor hunts in his head; he is ready to sit embracing his knees with his arms, sighing as plaintively as if he had lost some one near to him. Love is an illness; for in it, as in illness, the face becomes pale, the eyes sink, the hands tremble, the fingers grow thin, and the man thinks of death, or goes around in derangement, with dishevelled hair, talks with the moon, writes gladly the cherished name on the sand, and if the wind blows it away, he says, 'misfortune,' and is ready to sob."

Here Ketling was silent for a while; one would have said that he was sunk in musing. Krysia listened to his words with her whole soul, as if they were a song. Her lips were parted, and her eyes did not leave the pale face of the knight. Basia's forelock fell to her eyes, hence it could not be known what she was thinking of; but she sat in silence also.

Then Zagloba yawned loudly, drew a deep breath, stretched his legs, and said, "Give command to make boots for dogs of such love!"

"But yet," began the knight, anew, "if it is grievous to love, it is more grievous still not to love; for who without love is satisfied with pleasure, glory, riches, perfumes, or jewels? Who will not say to the loved one, 'I choose thee rather than a kingdom, than a sceptre, than health or long life'? And since each would give life for love willingly, love has more value than life." Ketling finished.

The young ladies sat nestling closely to each other, wondering at the tenderness of his speech and those conclusions of love foreign to Polish cavaliers, till Zagloba, who was napping at the end, woke and began to blink, looking now at one, now at another, now at the third; at last gaining presence of mind, he inquired in a loud voice, "What do you say?"

"We say good-night to you," said Basia.

7

"Ah! I know now we were talking of love. What was the conclusion?"

"The lining was better than the cloak."

"There is no use in denying that I was drowsy; but this loving, weeping, sighing — Ah, I have found another rhyme for it, — namely, sleeping, — and at this time the best, for the hour is advanced. Good-night to the whole company, and give us peace with your love. O my God, my God, while the cat is miauwing, she will not eat the cheese; but until she eats, her mouth is watering. In my day I resembled Ketling as one cup does another; and I was in love so madly that a ram might have pounded my back for an hour before I should have known it. But in old age I prefer to rest well, especially when a polite host not only conducts me to bed, but gives me a drink on the pillow."

"I am at the service of your grace," said Ketling.

"Let us go; let us go! See how high the moon is already. It will be fine to-morrow; it is glittering and clear as in the day. Ketling is ready to talk about love with you all night; but remember, kids, that he is road-weary."

"Not road-weary, for I have rested two days in the city. I am only afraid that the ladies are not used to night-watching."

"The night would pass quickly in listening to you," said Krysia.

Then they parted, for it was really late. The young ladies slept in the same room and usually talked long before sleeping; but this evening Basia could not understand Krysia, for as much as the first had a wish to speak, so much was the second silent and answered in half-words. A number of times too, when Basia, in speaking of Ketling, caught at an idea, laughing somewhat at him and mimicking him a little, Krysia embraced her with great tenderness, begging her to leave off that nonsense.

"He is host here, Basia," said she; "we are living under his roof; and I saw that he fell in love with you at once."

"Whence do you know that?" inquired Basia.

"Who does not love you? All love you, and I very much." Thus speaking, she put her beautiful face to Basia's face, nestled up to her, and kissed her eyes.

They went at last to their beds, but Krysia could not sleep for a long time. Disquiet had seized her. At times her heart beat with such force that she brought both hands to her satin bosom to restrain the throbbing. At times too, especially when she tried to close her eyes, it seemed to her that some head, beautiful as a dream, bent over her, and a low voice whispered into her ear, —

"I would rather have thee than a kingdom, than a sceptre, than health, than long life!"

CHAPTER XIII.

A FEW days later Zagloba wrote a letter to Pan Yan with the following conclusion, "If I do not go home before election, be not astonished. This will not happen through my lack of good wishes for you; but as the Devil does not sleep, I do not wish that instead of a bird something useless should remain in my hand. It will come out badly if when Michael returns, I shall not be able to say to him, 'That one is engaged, and the haiduk is free.' Everything is in the power of God; but this is my thought, that it will not be necessary then to urge Michael, nor to make long preparations, and that you will come when the engagement is made. Meanwhile, remembering Ulysses, I shall be forced to use stratagems and exaggerate more than once, which for me is not easy, since all my life I have preferred truth to every delight, and was glad to be nourished by it. Still, for Michael and the haiduk I will take this on my head, for they are pure gold. Now I embrace you both with the boys, and press you to my heart, commending you to the Most High God."

When he had finished writing, Zagloba sprinkled sand on the paper; then he struck it with his hand, read it once more, holding it at a distance from his eyes; then he folded it, took his seal ring from his finger, moistened it, and prepared to seal the letter, at which occupation Ketling found him.

"A good day to your grace!"

"Good-day, good-day!" said Zagloba. "The weather, thanks be to God, is excellent, and I am just sending a messenger to Pan Yan."

"Send an obeisance from me."

"I have done so already. I said at once to myself, 'It is necessary to send a greeting from Ketling. Both of them will be glad to receive good news.' It is evident that I have sent a greeting from you, since I have written a whole epistle touching you and the young ladies."

"How is that?" inquired Ketling.

Zagloba placed his palms on his knees, which he began to tap with his fingers; then he bent his head, and looking from under his brows at Ketling, said, "My Ketling, it is not necessary to be a prophet to know that where flint and steel are, sparks will flash sooner or later. You are a beauty above beauties, and even you would not find fault with the young ladies."

Ketling was really confused. "I should have to be wall-eyed or be a wild barbarian altogether," said he, "if I did not see their beauty, and do homage to it."

"But, you see," continued Zagloba, looking with a smile on the blushing face of Ketling, "if you are not a barbarian, it is not right for you to have both in view, for only Turks act like that."

"How can you suppose — "

"I do not suppose; I only say it to myself. Ha! traitor! you have so talked to them of love that pallor is on Krysia's lips this third day. It is no wonder; you are a beauty. When I was young myself, I used to stand in the frost under the window of a certain black brow; she was like Panna Krysia; and I remember how I used to sing, —

'You are sleeping there after the day;
And I am here thrumming my lute,
              Hòts! Hòts!'

If you wish, I will give you a song, or compose an entirely new one, for I have no lack of genius. Have you observed that Panna Krysia reminds one somewhat of Panna Bille-vich, except that Panna Billevich had hair like flax and had no down on her lip? But there are men who find superior beauty in that, and think it a charm. She looks with great pleasure on you. I have just written so to Pan Yan. Is it not true that she is like the former Panna Billevich?"

"I have not noticed the likeness, but it may be. In figure and stature she recalls her."

"Now listen to what I say. I am telling family secrets directly; but as you are a friend, you ought to know them. Be on your guard not to feed Volodyovski with ingratitude, for I and Pani Makovetski have predestined one of those maidens to him."

Here Zagloba looked quickly and persistently into Ket-ling's eyes, and he grew pale and inquired, "Which one?"

"Panna Krysia," answered Zagloba, slowly. And push-ing out his lower lip, he began to blink from under his frowning brow with his one seeing eye. Ketling was silent, and silent so long that at last Zagloba inquired, "What do you say to this?"

And Ketling answered with changed voice, but with emphasis, "You may be sure that I shall not indulge my heart to Michael's harm."

"Are you certain?"

"I have suffered much in life; my word of a knight that I will not indulge it."

Then Zagloba opened his arms to him: "Ketling, indulge your heart; indulge it, poor man, as much as you like, for I only wanted to try you. Not Panna Krysia, but the haiduk, have we predestined to Michael."

Ketling's face grew bright with a sincere and deep joy, and seizing Zagloba in his embrace, he held him long, then inquired, "Is it certain already that they are in love?"

"But who would not be in love with my haiduk, — who?" asked Zagloba.

"Then has the betrothal taken place?"

"There has been no betrothal, for Michael has barely freed himself from mourning; but there will be, — put that on my head. The maiden, though she evades like a weasel, is very much inclined to him, for with her the sabre is the main thing."

"I have noticed that, as God is dear to me!" interrupted Ketling, radiant.

"Ha! you noticed it? Michael is weeping yet for the other; but if any one pleases his spirit, it is certainly the haiduk, for she is most like the dead one, though she cuts less with her eyes, for she is younger. Everything is arranging itself well. I am the guarantee that these two weddings will be at election-time."

Ketling, saying nothing, embraced Zagloba again, and placed his beautiful face against his red cheeks, so that the old man panted and asked, "Has Panna Krysia sewed herself into your skin like that already?"

"I know not, — I know not," answered Ketling; "but I know this, that barely had the heavenly vision of her delighted my eyes when I said at once to myself that she was the one woman whom my suffering heart might love yet; and that same night I drove sleep away with sighs, and yielded myself to pleasant yearnings. Thenceforth she took possession of my being, as a queen does of an obedient and loyal country. Whether this is love or something else, I know not."

"But you know that it is neither a cap nor three yards of cloth for trousers, nor a saddle-girth, nor a crouper, nor sausage and eggs, nor a decanter of gorailka. If you are certain of this, then ask Krysia about the rest; or if you wish, I will ask her."

"Do not do that," said Ketling, smiling. "If I am to drown, let it seem to me, even a couple of days yet, that I am swimming."

"I see that the Scots are fine men in battle; but in love they are useless. Against women, as against the enemy, impetus is needful. 'I came, I saw, I conquered!' that was my maxim."

"In time, if my most ardent desires are to be accomplished, perhaps I shall ask you for friendly assistance; though I am naturalized, and of noble blood, still my name is unknown here, and I am not sure that Pani Makovetski —"

"Pani Makovetski?" interrupted Zagloba. "Have no fear about her. Pani Makovetski is a regular music-box. As I wind her, so will she play. I will go at her immediately; I must forewarn her, you know, so that she may not look awry at your approaches to the young lady. To such a degree is your Scottish method one, and ours another, I will not make a declaration straightway in your name, of course; I will say only that the maiden has taken your eye, and that it would be well if from that flour there should be bread. As God is dear to me, I will go at once; have no fear, for in every case I am at liberty to say what I like."

And though Ketling detained him, Zagloba rose and went out. On the way he met Basia, rushing along as usual, and said to her, "Do you know that Krysia has captured Ketling completely?"

"He is not the first man!" answered Basia.

"And you are not angry about it?"

"Ketling is a doll! — a pleasant cavalier, but a doll! I have struck my knee against the wagon-tongue; that is what troubles me."

Here Basia, bending forward, began to rub her knee, looking meanwhile at Zagloba, and he said, "For God's sake, be careful! Whither are you flying now?"

"To Krysia."

"But what is she doing?"

"She? For some time past she keeps kissing me, and rubs up to me like a cat."

"Do not tell her that she has captured Ketling."

"Ah! but can I hold out?"

Zagloba knew well that Basia would not hold out, and it was for that very reason that he forbade her. He went on, therefore, greatly delighted with his own cunning, and, Basia fell like a bomb into Krysia's chamber.

"I have smashed my knee; and Ketling is dead in love with you!" cried she, right on the threshold. "I did not see the pole sticking out at the carriage-house — and such a blow! There were flashes in my eyes, but that is nothing. Pan Zagloba begged me to say nothing to you about Ketling. I did not say that I would not; I have told you at once. And you were pretending to give him to me! Never fear; I know you — My knee pains me a little yet. I was not giving Pan Adam to you, but Ketling. Oho! He is walking through the whole house now, holding his head and talking to himself. Well done, Krysia; well done! Scot, Scot! kot, kot!"[1]

Here Basia began to push her finger toward the eye of her friend.

"Basia!" exclaimed Panna Krysia.

"Scot, Scot! kot, kot!"

"How unfortunate I am!" cried Krysia, on a sudden, and burst into tears.

After a while Basia began to console her; but it availed nothing, and the maiden sobbed as never before in her life. In fact, no one in all that house knew how unhappy she was. For some days she had been in a fever; her face had grown pale; her eyes had sunk; her breast was moving with short, broken breath. Something wonderful had taken place in her; she had dropped, as it were, into extreme weakness, and the change had come not gradually, slowly, but on a sudden. Like a whirlwind, like a storm, it had swept her away; like a flame, it had heated her blood; like lightning, it had flashed on her imagination. She could not, even for a moment, resist that power which was so mercilessly sudden. Calmness had left her. Her will was like a bird with broken wings.

Krysia herself knew not whether she loved Ketling or hated him; and a measureless fear seized her in view of that question. But she felt that her heart beat so quickly

[1] "Kot" means "cat," hence Basia's exclamations are, "Scot, Scot! cat. cat!"

only through him; that her head was thinking thus help-lessly only through him; that in her and above her it was full of him, — and no means of defence. Not to love him was easier than not to think of him; for her eyes were delighted with the sight of him, her ears were lost in listening to his voice, her whole soul was absorbed by him. Sleep did not free her from that importunate man, for barely had she closed her eyes when his head bent above her, whispering, "I would rather have thee than a king-dom, than a sceptre, than fame, than wealth." And that head was near, so near that even in the darkness blood-red blushes covered the face of the maiden. She was a Russian with hot blood; certain fires rose in her breast, — fires of which she had not known till that time that they could exist, and from the ardor of which she was seized with fear and shame, and a great weakness and a certain faintness at once painful and pleasant. Night brought her no rest. A weariness continually increasing gained control of her, as if after great toil.

"Krysia! Krysia! what is happening to thee?" cried she to herself. But she was as if in a daze and in unceas-ing distraction. Nothing had happened yet; nothing had taken place. So far she had not exchanged two words with Ketling alone; still, the thought of him had taken hold of her thoroughly; still, a certain instinct whispered unceasingly, "Guard thyself! Avoid him." And she avoided him.

Krysia had not thought yet of her agreement with Pan Michael, and that was her luck; she had not thought specially, because so far nothing had taken place, and because she thought of no one, — thought neither of her-self nor of others, but only of Ketling. She concealed this too in her deepest soul; and the thought that no one suspected what was taking place in her, that no one was occupied with her and Ketling at the same time, brought her no small consolation. All at once the words of Basia convinced her that it was otherwise, — that people were looking at them already, connecting them in thought, divining the position. Hence the disturbance, the shame and pain, taken together, overcame her will, and she wept like a little child.

But Basia's words were only the beginning of those various hints, significant glances, blinking of eyes, shaking of heads, finally, of those double meaning phrases which

Krysia must endure. This began during dinner. Pan
Michael's sister turned her gaze from Krysia to Ketling,
and from Ketling to Krysia, which she had not done
hitherto. Pan Zagloba coughed significantly. At times the
conversation was interrupted, — it was unknown wherefore;
silence followed, and once during such an interval Basia,
with dishevelled hair, cried out to the whole table, —

"I know something, but I won't tell!"

Krysia blushed instantly, and then grew pale at once, as
if some terrible danger had passed near her; Ketling too
bent his head. Both felt perfectly that that related to
them, and though they avoided conversation with each
other, so that people might not look at them, still it was
clear to both that something was rising between them;
that some undefined community of confusion was in process
of creation; that it would unite them and at the same time
keep them apart, for by it they lost freedom completely,
and could be no longer ordinary friends to each other.
Happily for them, no one gave attention to Basia's words.
Pan Zagloba was preparing to go to the city and return
with a numerous company of knights; all were intent on
that event.

In fact, Ketling's house was gleaming with light in the
evening; between ten and twenty officers came with music,
which the hospitable host provided for the amusement of
the ladies. Dancing of course there could not be, for it was
Lent, and Ketling's mourning was in the way; but they
listened to the music, and were entertained with conversation. The ladies were dressed splendidly. Pani Makovetski appeared in Oriental silk. The haiduk was arrayed in
various colors, and attracted the eyes of the military with
her rosy face and bright hair, which dropped at times over
her eyes; she roused laughter with the decision of her
speech, and astonished with her manners, in which Cossack
daring was combined with unaffectedness.

Krysia, whose mourning for her father was at an end,
wore a white robe trimmed with silver. The knights compared her, some to Juno, others to Diana; but none came
too near her; no man twirled his mustache, struck his heels,
or cast glances; no one looked at her with flashing eyes or
began a conversation about love. But soon she noticed that
those who looked at her with admiration and homage
looked afterward at Ketling; that some, on approaching
him, pressed his hand, as if congratulating him and giving

him good wishes; that he shrugged his shoulders and spread out his hands, as if in denial. Krysia, who by nature was watchful and keen, was nearly certain that they were talking to him of her, that they considered her as almost his affianced; and since she could not see that Pan Zagloba whispered in the ear of each man, she was at a loss to know whence these suppositions came. "Have I some-thing written on my forehead?" thought she, with alarm. She was ashamed and anxious. And then even words began to fly to her through the air, as if not to her, but still aloud. "Fortunate Ketling!" "He was born in a caul." "No wonder, for he is a beauty!" and similar words.

Other polite cavaliers, wishing to entertain her and say something pleasant, spoke of Ketling, praising him beyond measure, exalting his bravery, his kindness, his elegant manners, and ancient lineage. Krysia, whether willing or unwilling, had to listen, and involuntarily her eyes sought him of whom men were talking to her, and at times they met his eyes. Then the charm seized her with new force, and without knowing it, she was delighted at the sight of him; for how different was Ketling from all those rugged soldier-forms! "A king's son among his attendants," thought Krysia, looking at that noble, aristocratic head and at those ambitious eyes, full of a certain inborn melancholy, and on that forehead, shaded by rich golden hair. Her heart began to sink and languish, as if that head was the dearest on earth to her. Ketling saw this, and not wishing to increase her confusion, did not approach, as if another were sitting by her side. If she had been a queen, he could not have surrounded her with greater honor and higher attention. In speaking to her, he inclined his head and pushed back one foot, as if in sign that he was ready to kneel at any moment; he spoke with dignity, never jestingly, though with Basia, for example, he was glad to jest. In intercourse with Krysia, besides the greatest respect there was rather a certain shade of melancholy full of tenderness. Thanks to that respect, no other man permitted himself either a word too explicit, or a jest too bold, as if the conviction had been fixed upon every one that in dignity and birth she was higher than all others, — a lady with whom there was never politeness enough.

Krysia was heartily grateful to him for this. In general, the evening passed anxiously for her, but sweetly. When midnight approached, the musicians stopped playing, the ladies took farewell of the company, and among the knights goblets began to make the round frequently, and there followed a noisier entertainment, in which Zagloba assumed the dignity of hetman.

Basia went upstairs joyous as a bird, for she had amused herself greatly. Before she knelt down to pray she began to play tricks and imitate various guests; at last she said to Krysia, clapping her hands, —

"It is perfect that your Ketling has come! At least, there will be no lack of soldiers. Oho! only let Lent pass, and I will dance to kill. We'll have fun. And at your betrothal to Ketling, and at your wedding, well, if I don't turn the house over, let the Tartars take me captive! What if they should take us really! To begin with, there would be — Ha! Ketling is good! He will bring musicians for you; but with you I shall enjoy them. He will bring you new wonders, one after another, until he does this — "

Then Basia threw herself on her knees suddenly before Krysia, and encircling her waist with her arms, began to speak, imitating the low voice of Ketling: "Your ladyship! I so love you that I cannot breathe. I love you on foot and on horseback. I love you fasting and after breakfast. I love·you for the ages and as the Scots love. Will you be mine?"

"Basia, I shall be angry!" cried Krysia. But instead of growing angry, she caught Basia in her arms, and while trying, as it were, to lift her, she began to kiss her eyes.

CHAPTER XIV.

Pan Zagloba knew perfectly that the little knight was more inclined toward Krysia than Basia; but for that very reason he resolved to set Krysia aside. Knowing Pan Michael through and through, he was convinced that if he had no choice, he would turn infallibly to Basia, with whom the old noble himself was so blindly in love that he could not get it into his head how any man could prefer another to her. He understood also that he could not render Pan Michael a greater service than to get him his haiduk, and he was enchanted at thought of that match. He was angry at Pan Michael, at Krysia also; it was true he would prefer that Pan Michael should marry Krysia rather than no one, but he determined to do everything to make him marry the haiduk. And precisely because the little knight's inclination toward Krysia was known to him, he determined to make a Ketling of her as quickly as possible.

Still, the answer which Zagloba received a few days later from Pan Yan staggered him somewhat in his resolution. Pan Yan advised him to interfere in nothing, for he feared that in the opposite case great troubles might rise easily between the friends. Zagloba himself did not wish this, therefore certain reproaches made themselves heard in him; these he stilled in the following manner: —

"If Michael and Krysia were betrothed, and I had thrust Ketling between them like a wedge, then I say nothing. Solomon says, 'Do not poke your nose into another man's purse,' and he is right. But every one is free to wish. Besides, taking things exactly, what have I done? Let any one tell me what."

When he had said this, Zagloba put his hands on his hips, pouted his lips, and looked challengingly on the walls of his chamber, as if expecting reproaches from them; but since the walls made no answer, he spoke on: "I told Ketling that I had predestined the haiduk to Michael. But is this not permitted me? Maybe it is not true that I have predestined her! If I wish any other woman for Michael, may the gout bite me!"

The walls recognized the justice of Zagloba in perfect silence; and he continued further: "I told the haiduk that Ketling was brought down by Krysia; maybe that is not true? Has he not confessed; has he not sighed, sitting near the fire, so that the ashes were flying through the room! And what I saw, I have told others. Pan Yan has sound sense; but no one will throw my wit to the dogs. I know myself what may be told, and what would be better left in silence. H'm! he writes not to interfere in anything. That may be done also. Hereafter I will interfere in nothing. When I am a third party in presence of Krysia and Ketling, I will go out and leave them alone. Let them help themselves without me. In fact, I think they will be able. They need no help, for now they are so pushed toward each other that their eyes are growing white; and besides, the spring is coming, at which time not only the sun, but desires begin to grow warm. Well! I will leave them alone; but I shall see what the result will be."

And, in truth, the result was soon to appear. During Holy Week the entire company at Ketling's house went to Warsaw and took lodgings in the hotel on Dluga Street, to be near the churches and perform their devotions at pleasure, and at the same time to sate their eyes with the holiday bustle of the city. Ketling performed here the honors of host, for though a foreigner by origin, he knew the capital thoroughly and had many acquaintances in every quarter, through whom he was able to make everything easy. He surpassed himself in politeness, and almost divined the thoughts of the ladies he was escorting, especially Krysia. Besides, all had taken to loving him sincerely. Pan Michael's sister, forewarned by Zagloba, looked on him and Krysia with a more and more favorable eye; and if she had said nothing to the maiden so far, it was only because he was silent. But it seemed to the worthy "auntie" a natural thing and proper that the cavalier should win the lady, especially as he was a cavalier really distinguished, who was met at every step by marks of respect and friendship, not only from the lower but from the higher people; he was so capable of winning all to his side by his truly wonderful beauty, bearing, dignity, liberality, mildness in time of peace, and manfulness in war.

"What God will give, and my husband decide, will come to pass," said Pani Makovetski to herself; "but I will not cross these two."

Thanks to this decision, Ketling found himself oftener with Krysia and stayed with her longer than when in his own house. Besides, the whole company always went out together. Zagloba generally gave his arm to Pan Michael's sister, Ketling to Krysia, and Basia, as the youngest, went alone, sometimes hurrying on far ahead, then halting in front of shops to look at goods and various wonders from beyond the sea, such as she had never seen before. Krysia grew accustomed gradually to Ketling; and now when she was leaning on his arm, when she listened to his conversation or looked at his noble face, her heart did not beat in her breast with the former disquiet, presence of mind did not leave her, and she was seized not by confusion, but by an immense and intoxicating delight. They were continually by themselves; they knelt near each other in the churches; their voices were mingled in prayer and in pious hymns.

Ketling knew well the condition of his heart. Krysia, either from lack of decision or because she wished to tempt herself, did not say mentally, "I love him;" but they loved each other greatly. A friendship had sprung up between them; and besides love, they had immense regard for each other. Of love itself they had not spoken yet; time passed for them as a dream, and a serene sky was above them. Clouds of reproaches were soon to hide it from Krysia; but the present was a time of repose. Specially through intimacy with Ketling, through becoming accustomed to him, through that friendship which with love bloomed up between them, Krysia's alarms were ended, her impressions were not so violent, the conflicts of her blood and imagination ceased. They were near each other; it was pleasant for them in the company of each other; and Krysia, yielding herself with her whole soul to that agreeable present, was unwilling to think that it would ever end, and that to scatter those illusions it needed only one word [1] from Ketling, "I love." That word was soon uttered. Once, when Pan Michael's sister and Basia were at the house of a sick relative, Ketling persuaded Krysia and Pan Zagloba to visit the king's castle, which Krysia had not seen hitherto, and concerning whose curiosities wonders were related throughout the whole country. They went, then, three in company. Ketling's liberality

---

[1] In Polish, "I love" is one word, "Kocham."

had opened all doors, and Krysia was greeted by obeisances from the doorkeepers as profound as if she were
a queen entering her own residence. Ketling, knowing
the castle perfectly, conducted her through lordly halls
and chambers. They examined the theatre, the royal
baths; they halted before pictures representing the battles and victories gained by Sigismund and Vladislav over
the savagery of the East; they went out on the terraces,
from which the eye took in an immense stretch of country.
Krysia could not free herself from wonder; he explained
everything to her, but was silent from moment to moment,
and looking into her dark-blue eyes, he seemed to say with
his glance, "What are all these wonders in comparison
with thee, thou wonder? What are all these treasures in
comparison with thee, thou treasure?" The young lady
understood that silent speech. He conducted her to one
of the royal chambers, and stood before a door concealed
in the wall.

"One may go to the cathedral through this door. There
is a long corridor, which ends with a balcony not far from
the high altar. From this balcony the king and queen hear
Mass usually."

"I know that way well," put in Zagloba, "for I was a
confidant of Yan Kazimir. Marya Ludovika loved me
passionately; therefore both invited me often to Mass, so
that they might take pleasure in my company and edify
themselves with piety."

"Do you wish to enter?" asked Ketling, giving a sign to
the doorkeeper.

"Let us go in," said Krysia.

"Go alone," said Zagloba; "you are young and have
good feet; I have trotted around enough already. Go on,
go on; I will stay here with the doorkeeper. And even
if you should say a couple of 'Our Fathers,' I shall not be
angry at the delay, for during that time I can rest myself."

They entered. Ketling took Krysia's hand and led her
through a long corridor. He did not press her hand to his
heart; he walked calmly and collectedly. At intervals the
side windows threw light on their forms, then they sank
again in the darkness. Her heart beat somewhat, because
they were alone for the first time; but his calmness and
mildness made her calm also. They came out at last to the
balcony on the right side of the church, not far from the
high altar. They knelt and began to pray. The church

was silent and empty. Two candles were burning before the high altar, but all the deeper part of the nave was buried in impressive twilight. Only from the rainbow-colored panes of the windows various gleams entered and fell on the two wonderful faces, sunk in prayer, calm, like the faces of cherubim.

Ketling rose first and began to whisper, for he dared not raise his voice in the church. "Look," said he, "at this velvet-covered railing; on it are traces where the heads of the royal couple rested. The queen sat at that side, nearer the altar. Rest in her place."

"Is it true that she was unhappy all her life?" whispered Krysia, sitting down. "I heard her history when I was still a child, for it is related in all knightly castles. Perhaps she was unhappy because she could not marry him whom her heart loved."

Krysia rested her head on the place where the depression was made by the head of Marya Ludovika, and closed her eyes. A kind of painful feeling straitened her breast; a certain coldness was blown suddenly from the empty nave and chilled that calm which a moment before filled her whole being.

Ketling looked at Krysia in silence; and a stillness really churchlike set in. Then he sank slowly to her feet, and began to speak thus with a voice that was full of emotion, but calm: —

"It is not a sin to kneel before you in this holy place; for where does true love come for a blessing if not to the church? I love you more than life; I love you beyond every earthly good; I love you with my soul, with my heart; and here before this altar I confess that love to you."

Krysia's face grew pale as linen. Resting her head on the velvet back of the prayer-stool, the unhappy lady stirred not, but he spoke on: —

"I embrace your feet and implore your decision. Am I to go from this place in heavenly delight, or in grief which I am unable to bear, and which I can in no way survive?"

He waited awhile for an answer; but since it did not come, he bowed his head till he almost touched Krysia's feet, and evident emotion mastered him more and more, for his voice trembled, as if breath were failing his breast, —

"Into your hands I give my happiness and life. I expect mercy, for my burden is great."

"Let us pray for God's mercy!" exclaimed Krysia, suddenly, dropping on her knees.

Ketling did not understand her; but he did not dare to oppose that intention, therefore he knelt near her in hope and fear. They began to pray again. From moment to moment their voices were audible in the empty church, and the echo gave forth wonderful and complaining sounds.

"God be merciful!" said Krysia.

"God be merciful!" repeated Ketling.

"Have mercy on us!"

"Have mercy on us!"

She prayed then in silence; but Ketling saw that weeping shook her whole form. For a long time she could not calm herself; and then, growing quiet, she continued to kneel without motion. At last she rose and said, "Let us go."

They went out again into that long corridor. Ketling hoped that on the way he would receive some answer, and he looked into her eyes, but in vain. She walked hurriedly, as if wishing to find herself as soon as possible in that chamber in which Zagloba was waiting for them. But when the door was some tens of steps distant, the knight seized the edge of her robe.

"Panna Krysia!" exclaimed he, "by all that is holy — "

Then Krysia turned away, and grasping his hand so quickly that he had not time to show the least resistance, she pressed it in the twinkle of an eye to her lips. "I love you with my whole soul; but I shall never be yours!" and before the astonished Ketling could utter a word, she added, "Forget all that has happened."

A moment later they were both in the chamber. The doorkeeper was sleeping in one armchair, and Zagloba in the other. The entrance of the young people roused them. Zagloba, however, opened his eye and began to blink with it half consciously; but gradually memory of the place and the persons returned to him.

"Ah, that is you!" said he, drawing down his girdle. "I dreamed that the new king was elected, but that he was a Pole. Were you at the balcony?"

"We were."

"Did the spirit of Marya Ludovika appear to you, perchance?"

"It did!" answered Krysia, gloomily.

CHAPTER XV.

AFTER they had left the castle, Ketling needed to collect his thoughts and shake himself free from the astonishment into which Krysia's action had brought him. He took farewell of her and Zagloba in front of the gate, and they went to their lodgings. Basia and Pani Makovetski had returned already from the sick lady; and Pan Michael's sister greeted Zagloba with the following words, —

"I have a letter from my husband, who remains yet with Michael at the stanitsa. They are both well, and promise to be here soon. There is a letter to you from Michael, and to me only a postscript in my husband's letter. My husband writes also that the dispute with the Jubris about one of Basia's estates has ended happily. Now the time of provincial diets is approaching. They say that in those parts Pan Sobieski's name has immense weight, and that the local diet will vote as he wishes. Every man living is preparing for the election; but our people will all be with the hetman. It is warm there already, and rains are falling. With us in Verhutka the buildings were burned. A servant dropped fire; and because there was wind — "

"Where is Michael's letter to me?" inquired Zagloba, interrupting the torrent of news given out at one breath by the worthy lady.

"Here it is," said she, giving him a letter. "Because there was wind, and the people were at the fair — "

"How were the letters brought here?" asked Zagloba, again.

"They were taken to Ketling's house, and a servant brought them here. Because, as I say, there was wind — "

"Do you wish to listen, my benefactress?"

"Of course, I beg earnestly."

Zagloba broke the seal and began to read, first in an undertone, for himself, then aloud for all, —

"I send this first letter to you; but God grant that there will not be another, for posts are uncertain in this region, and I shall soon present myself personally among you. It is pleasant here in the field, but still my heart draws me tremendously toward you, and there is no end to thoughts and memories, wherefore solitude is dearer to me in this place than company. The promised work has passed, for the hordes sit quietly, only smaller bands are rioting in the fields; these also we fell upon twice with such fortune that not a witness of their defeat got away."

"Oh, they warmed them!" cried Basia, with delight. "There is nothing higher than the calling of a soldier!"

"Doroshenko's rabble" (continued Zagloba) "would like to have an uproar with us, but they cannot in any way without the horde. The prisoners confess that a larger chambul will not move from any quarter, which I believe, for if there was to be anything like this it would have taken place already, since the grass has been green for a week past, and there is something with which to feed horses. In ravines bits of snow are still hiding here and there; but the open steppes are green, and a warm wind is blowing, from which the horses begin to shed their hair, and this is the surest sign of spring. I have sent already for leave, which may come any day, and then I shall start at once. Pan Adam succeeds me in keeping guard, at which there is so little labor that Makovetski and I have been fox-hunting whole days, — for simple amusement, as the fur is useless when spring is near. There are many bustards, and my servant shot a pelican. I embrace you with my whole heart; I kiss the hands of my sister, and those of Panna Krysia, to whose good-will I commit myself most earnestly, imploring God specially to let me find her unchanged, and to receive the same consolation. Give an obeisance from me to Panna Basia. Pan Adam has vented the anger roused by his rejection at Mokotov on the backs of ruffians, but there is still some in his mind, it is evident. He is not wholly relieved. I commit you to God and His most holy love.

"P. S. I bought a lot of very elegant ermine from passing Armenians; I shall bring this as a gift to Panna Krysia, and for your haiduk there will be Turkish sweetmeats."

"Let Pan Michael eat them himself; I am not a child," said Basia, whose cheeks flushed as if from sudden pain.

"Then you will not be glad to see him? Are you angry at him?" asked Zagloba.

But Basia merely muttered something in low tones, and really settled down in anger, thinking some of how lightly Pan Michael was treating her, and a little about the bustard and that pelican, which roused her curiosity specially.

Krysia sat there during the reading with closed eyes, turned from the light; in truth, it was lucky that those present could not see her face, for they would have known at once that something uncommon was happening. That which took place in the church, and the letter of Pan

Volodyovski, were for her like two blows of a club. The wonderful dream had fled; and from that moment the maiden stood face to face with a reality as crushing as misfortune. She could not collect her thoughts to wait, and indefinite, hazy feelings were storming in her heart. Pan Michael, with his letter, with the promise of his coming, and with a bundle of ermine, seemed to her so flat that he was almost repulsive. On the other hand, Ketling had never been so dear. Dear to her was the very thought of him, dear his words, dear his face, dear his melancholy. And now she must go from love, from homage, from him toward whom her heart is struggling, her hands stretching forth, in endless sorrow and suffering, to give her soul and her body to another, who for this alone, that he is another, becomes wellnigh hateful to her.

"I cannot, I cannot!" cried Krysia, in her soul. And she felt that which a captive feels whose hands men are binding; but she herself had bound her own hands, for in her time she might have told Pan Michael that she would be his sister, nothing more.

Now the kiss came to her memory, — that kiss received and returned, — and shame, with contempt for her own self, seized her. Was she in love with Pan Michael that day? No! In her heart there was no love, and except sympathy there was nothing in her heart at that time but curiosity and giddiness, masked with the show of sisterly affection. Now she has discovered for the first time that between kissing from great love and kissing from impulse of blood, there is as much difference as between an angel and a devil. Anger as well as contempt was rising in Krysia; then pride began to storm in her and against Pan Michael. He too was at fault; why should all the penance, contrition, and disappointment fall upon her? Why should he too not taste the bitter bread? Has she not the right to say when he returns, "I was mistaken; I mistook pity for love. You also were mistaken; now leave me, as I have left you."

Suddenly fear seized her by the hair, — fear before the vengeance of the terrible man; fear not for herself, but for the head of the loved one, whom vengeance would strike without fail. In imagination she saw Ketling standing up to the struggle with that ominous swordsman beyond swordsmen, and then falling as a flower falls cut by a scythe; she sees his blood, his pale face, his eyes closed for the ages, and her suffering goes beyond every measure. She rose with all speed and went to her chamber to vanish from the eyes of people, so as not to hear conversation concerning Pan Michael and his approaching return. In her heart rose greater and greater animosity against the little knight. But Remorse and Regret pursued her, and did not leave her in time of prayer; they sat on her bed when, overcome with weakness, she lay in it, and began to speak to her.

"Where is he?" asked Regret. "He has not returned yet; he is walking through the night and wringing his hands. Thou wouldst incline the heavens for him, thou wouldst give him thy life's blood; but thou hast given him poison to drink, thou hast thrust a knife through his heart."

"Had it not been for thy giddiness, had it not been for thy wish to lure every man whom thou meetest," said Remorse, "all might be different; but now despair alone remains to thee. It is thy fault, — thy great fault! There is no help for thee; there is no rescue for thee now, — nothing but shame and pain and weeping."

"How he knelt at thy feet in the church!" said Regret, again. "It is a wonder that thy heart did not burst when he looked into thy eyes and begged of thee pity. It was just of thee to give pity to a stranger, but to the loved one, the dearest, what? God bless him! God solace him!"

"Were it not for thy giddiness, that dearest one might depart in joy," repeated Remorse; "thou mightest walk at his side, as his chosen one, his wife — "

"And be with him forever," added Regret.

"It is thy fault," said Remorse.

"Weep, O Krysia," cried Regret.

"Thou canst not wipe away that fault!" said Remorse, again.

"Do what thou pleasest, but console him," repeated Regret.

"Volodyovski will slay him!" answered Remorse, at once.

Cold sweat covered Krysia, and she sat on the bed. Bright moonlight fell into the room, which seemed somehow weird and terrible in those white rays.

"What is that?" thought Krysia. "There Basia is sleeping. I see her, for the moon is shining in her face; and I know not when she came, when she undressed and lay down. And I have not slept one moment; but my poor head is of no use, that is clear." Thus meditating, she lay down again; but Regret and Remorse sat on the edge of her bed, exactly like two goddesses, who were diving in at will through the rays of moonlight, or sweeping out again through its silvery abysses.

"I shall not sleep to-night," said Krysia to herself, and she began to think about Ketling, and to suffer more and more.

Suddenly the sorrowful voice of Basia was heard in the stillness of the night, "Krysia!"

"Are you not sleeping?"

"No, for I dreamed that some Turk pierced Pan Michael with an arrow. O Jesus! a deceiving dream. But a fever is just shaking me. Let us say the Litany together, that God may avert misfortune."

The thought flew through Krysia's head like lightning, "God grant some one to shoot him!" But she was astonished immediately at her own wickedness; therefore, though it was necessary for her to get superhuman power to pray at that particular moment for the return of Pan Michael, still she answered, —

"Very well, Basia."

Then both rose from their beds, and kneeling on their naked knees on the floor, began to say the Litany. Their voices responded to each other, now rising and now falling; you would have said that the chamber was changed into the cell of a cloister in which two white nuns were repeating their nightly prayers.

CHAPTER XVI.

NEXT morning Krysia was calmer; for among intricate and tangled paths she had chosen for herself an immensely difficult, but not a false one. Entering upon it, she saw at least whither she was going. But, first of all, she determined to have an interview with Ketling and speak with him for the last time, so as to guard him from every mishap. This did not come to her easily, for Ketling did not show himself for a number of consecutive days, and did not return at night.

Krysia began to rise before daylight and walk to the neighboring church of the Dominicans, with the hope that she would meet him some morning and speak to him without witnesses. In fact, she met him a few days later at the very door. When he saw her, he removed his cap and bent his head in silence. He stood motionless; his face was wearied by sleeplessness and suffering, his eyes sunk; on his temples there were yellowish spots; the delicate color of his face had become waxlike; he looked like a flower that is withering. Krysia's heart was rent at sight of him; and though every decisive step cost her very much, for she was not bold by nature, she was the first to extend the hand, and said, —

"May God comfort you and send you forgetfulness!"

Ketling took her hand, raised it to his forehead, then to his lips, to which he pressed it long and with all his force; then he said with a voice full of mortal sadness and of resignation, "There is for me neither solace nor forgetfulness."

There was a moment when Krysia needed all her self-control to restrain herself from throwing her arms around his neck and exclaiming, "I love thee above everything! take me." She felt that if weeping were to seize her she would do so; therefore she stood a long time before him in silence, struggling with her tears. At last she conquered herself and began to speak calmly, though very quickly, for breath failed her : —

"It may bring you some relief if I say that I shall belong to no one. I go behind the grating. Do not judge me harshly at any time, for as it is I am unhappy. Promise me, give me your word, that you will not mention your love for me to any one; that you will not acknowledge it; that you will not disclose to friend or relative what has happened. This is my last prayer. The time will come when you will know why I do this; then at least you will have the explanation. To-day I will tell you no more, for my sorrow is such that I cannot. Promise me this, — it will comfort me; if you do not, I may die."

"I promise, and give my word," answered Ketling.

"God reward you, and I thank you from my whole heart! Besides, show a calm face in presence of people, so that no one may have a suspicion. It is time for me to go. Your kindness is such that words fail to describe it. Henceforth we shall not see each other alone, only before people. Tell me further that you have no feeling of offence against me; for to suffer is one thing and to be offended another. You yield me to God, to no one else; keep this in mind."

Ketling wished to say something; but since he was suffering beyond measure, only indefinite sounds like groans came from his mouth; then he touched Krysia's temples with his fingers and held them for a while as a sign that he forgave her and blessed her. They parted then; she went to the church, and he to the street again, so as not to meet in the inn an acquaintance.

Krysia returned only in the afternoon; and when she came she found a notable guest, Bishop Olshovski, the vice-chancellor. He had come unexpectedly on a visit to Pan Zagloba, wishing, as he said himself, to become acquainted with such a great cavalier, "whose military pre-eminence was an example, and whose reason was a guide to the knights of that whole lordly Commonwealth." Zagloba was, in truth, much astonished, but not less gratified, that such a great honor had met him in presence of the ladies; he plumed himself greatly, was flushed, perspired, and at the same time endeavored to show Pani Makovetski that he was accustomed to such visits from the greatest dignitaries in the country, and that he made nothing of them. Krysia was presented to the prelate, and kissing his hands with humility, sat near Basia, glad that no one could see the traces of recent emotion on her face.

Meanwhile the vice-chancellor covered Zagloba so bountifully and so easily with praises that he seemed to be drawing new supplies of them continually from his violet sleeves embroidered with lace. "Think not, your grace," said he, "that I was drawn hither by curiosity alone to know the first man in the knighthood; for though admiration is a just homage to heroes, still men make pilgrimages for their own profit also to the place where experience and quick reason have taken their seats at the side of manfulness."

"Experience," said Zagloba, modestly, "especially in the military art, comes only with age; and for that cause perhaps the late Pan Konyetspolski, father of the banneret, asked me frequently for counsel, after him Pan Nikolai Pototski, Prince Yeremi Vishnyevetski, Pan Sapyeha, and Pan Charnyetski; but as to the title 'Ulysses,' I have always protested against that from considerations of modesty."

"Still, it is so connected with your grace that at times no one mentions your real name, but says, 'Our Ulysses,' and all divine at once whom the orator means. Therefore, in these difficult and eventful times, when more than one wavers in his thoughts and does not know whither to turn, whom to uphold, I said to myself, 'I will go and hear convictions, free myself from doubt, enlighten my mind with clear counsel.' You will divine, your grace, that I wish to speak of the coming election, in view of which every estimate of candidates may lead to some good; but what must one be which flows from the mouth of your grace? I have heard it repeated with the greatest applause among the knighthood that you are opposed to those foreigners who are pushing themselves on to our lordly throne. In the veins of the Vazas, as you explained, there flowed Yagellon blood, — hence they could not be considered as strangers; but those foreigners, as you said, neither know our ancient Polish customs nor will they respect our liberties, and hence absolute rule may arise easily. I acknowledge to your grace that these are deep words; but pardon me if I inquire whether you really uttered them, or is it public opinion that from custom ascribes all profound sentences to you in the first instance?"

"These ladies are witness," answered Zagloba; "and though this subject is not suited to their judgment, let them speak, since Providence in its inscrutable decrees has given them the gift of speech equally with us."

The vice-chancellor looked involuntarily on Pani Makovetski, and then on the two young ladies nestled up to each other. A moment of silence followed. Suddenly the silvery voice of Basia was heard, —

"I did not hear anything!"

Then she was confused terribly and blushed to her very
ears, especially when Zagloba said at once, "Pardon her,
your dignity. She is young, therefore giddy. But as to
candidates, I have said more than once that our Polish
liberty will weep by reason of these foreigners."

"I fear that myself," said the prelate; "but even if we
wished some Pole, blood of our blood and bone of our bone,
tell me, your grace, to what side should we turn our hearts?
Your grace's very thought of a Pole is great, and is spreading through the country like a flame; for I hear that everywhere in the diets which are not fettered by corruption one
voice is to be heard, 'A Pole, a Pole!'"

"Justly, justly!" interrupted Zagloba.

"Still," continued the vice-chancellor, "it is easier to
call for a Pole than to find a fit person; therefore let your
grace be not astonished if I ask whom you had in mind."

"Whom had I in mind?" repeated Zagloba, somewhat
puzzled; and pouting his lips, he wrinkled his brows. It
was difficult for him to give a sudden answer, for hitherto
not only had he no one in mind, but in general he had not
those ideas at all which the keen prelate had attributed to
him. Besides, he knew this himself, and understood that
the vice-chancellor was inclining him to some side; but he
let himself be inclined purposely, for it flattered him greatly.
"I have insisted only in principle that we need a Pole,"
said he at last; "but to tell the truth, I have not named
any man thus far."

"I have heard of the ambitious designs of Prince Boguslav
Radzivill," muttered the prelate, as if to himself.

"While there is breath in my nostrils, while the last drop
of blood is in my breast," cried Zagloba, with the force of
deep conviction, "nothing will come of that! I should not
wish to live in a nation so disgraced as to make a traitor
and a Judas its king."

"That is the voice not only of reason, but of civic virtue,"
muttered the vice-chancellor, again.

"Ha!" thought Zagloba, "if you wish to draw me, I will
draw you."

Then the vice-chancellor began anew: "When wilt thou
sail in, O battered ship of my country? What storms, what
rocks are in wait for thee? In truth, it will be evil if a
foreigner becomes thy steersman; but it must be so evidently, if among thy sons there is no one better." Here he

stretched out his white hands, ornamented with glittering rings, and inclining his head, said with resignation, "Then Condé, or he of Lorraine, or the Prince of Neuberg? There is no other outcome!"

"That is impossible! A Pole!" answered Zagloba.

"Who?" inquired the prelate.

Silence followed. Then the prelate began to speak again: "If there were even one on whom all could agree! Where is there a man who would touch the heart of the knighthood at once, so that no one would dare to murmur against his election? There was one such, the greatest, who had rendered most. service, — your worthy friend, O knight, who walked in glory as in sunlight. There was such a —"

"Prince Yeremi Vishnyevetski!" interrupted Zagloba.

"That is true. But he is in the grave."

"His son lives," replied Zagloba.

The vice-chancellor half closed his eyes, and sat some time in silence; all at once he raised his head, looked at Zagloba, and began to speak slowly: "I thank God for having inspired me with the idea of knowing your grace. That is it! the son of the great Yeremi is alive, — a prince young and full of hope, to whom the Commonwealth has a debt to pay. Of his gigantic fortune nothing remains but glory, — that is his only inheritance. Therefore in the present times of corruption, when every man turns his eyes only to where gold is attracting, who will mention his name, who will have the courage to make him a candidate? You? True! But will there be many like you? It is not wonderful that he whose life has been passed in heroic struggles on all fields will not fear to give homage to merit with his vote on the field of election; but will others follow his example?" Here the vice-chancellor fell to thinking, then raised his eyes and spoke on: "God is mightier than all. Who knows His decisions, who knows? When I think how all the knighthood believe and trust you, I see indeed with wonderment that a certain hope enters my heart. Tell me sincerely, has the impossible ever existed for you?"

"Never!" answered Zagloba, with conviction.

"Still, it is not proper to advance that candidacy too decidedly at first. Let the name strike people's ears, but let it not seem too formidable to opponents; let them rather laugh at it, and sneer, so that they may not raise too serious impediments. Perhaps, too, God will grant it to succeed quickly, when the intrigues of parties bring them to mutual destruction. Smooth the road for it gradually, your grace, and grow not weary in labor; for this is your candidate, worthy of your reason and experience. God bless you in these plans!"

"Am I to suppose," inquired Zagloba, "that your dignity has been thinking also of Prince Michael?"

The vice-chancellor took from his sleeve a small book on which the title "Censura Candidatorum" stood in large black letters, and said, "Read, your grace; let this letter answer for me."

Then the vice-chancellor began preparations for going; but Zagloba detained him and said, "Permit me, your dignity, to say something more. First of all, I thank God that the lesser seal is in hands which can bend men like wax."

"How is that?" asked the vice-chancellor, astonished.

"Secondly, I will tell your dignity in advance that the candidacy of Prince Michael is greatly to my heart, for I knew his father, and loved him and fought under him with my friends; they too will be delighted in soul at the thought that they can show the son that love which they had for the father. Therefore I seize at this candidacy with both hands, and this day I will speak with Pan Krytski, — a man of great family and my acquaintance, who is in high consideration among the nobles, for it is difficult not to love him. We will both do what is in our power; and God grant that we shall effect something!"

"May the angels attend you!" said the prelate; "if you do that, we have nothing more to say."

"With the permission of your dignity I have to speak of one thing more; namely, that your dignity should not think to yourself thuswise: 'I have put my own wishes into his mouth; I have talked into him this idea that he has found out of his own wit the candidacy of Prince Michael, — speaking briefly, I have twisted the fool in my hand as if he were wax.' Your dignity, I will advance the cause of Prince Michael, because it is to my heart, — that is what the case is; because, as I see, it is to the heart also of your dignity, — that is what the case is! I will advance it for the sake of his mother, for the sake of my friends; I will advance it because of the confidence which I have in the head" (here Zagloba inclined) "from which that Minerva sprang forth, but not because I let myself be persuaded, like a little boy, that the invention is mine; and in fine, not because I am a fool, but for the reason that when a wise man tells me a wise thing, old Zagloba says, 'Agreed!'"

Here the noble inclined once more. The vice-chancellor was confused considerably at first; but seeing the good-humor of the noble and that the affair was taking the turn so much desired, he laughed from his whole soul, then seizing his head with both hands, he began to repeat, —

"Ulysses! as God is dear to me, a genuine Ulysses! Lord brother, whoso wishes to do a good thing must deal with men variously; but with you I see it is requisite to strike the quick straightway. You have pleased my heart immensely."

"As Prince Michael has mine."

"May God give you health! Ha! I am beaten, but I am glad. You must have eaten many a starling in your youth. And this signet ring, — if it will serve to commemorate our *colloquium* —"

"Let that ring remain in its own place," said Zagloba.

"You will do this for me —"

"I cannot by any means. Perhaps another time — later on — after the election."

The vice-chancellor understood, and insisted no more; he went out, however, with a radiant face.

Zagloba conducted him to the gate, and returning, muttered, "Ha! I gave him a lesson! One rogue met another. But it is an honor. Dignitaries will outrun one another in coming to these gates. I am curious to know what the ladies think of this!"

The ladies were indeed full of admiration; and Zagloba grew to the ceiling, especially in the eyes of Pan Michael's sister, so that he had barely shown himself when she exclaimed with great enthusiasm, "You have surpassed Solomon in wisdom."

And Zagloba was very glad. "Whom have I surpassed, do you say? Wait, you will see hetmans, bishops, and senators here; I shall have to escape from them or hide behind the curtains."

Further conversation was interrupted by the entrance of Ketling.

"Ketling, do you want promotion?" cried Zagloba, still charmed with his own significance.

"No!" answered the knight, in sadness; "for I must leave you again, and for a long time."

Zagloba looked at him more attentively. " How is it that you are so cut down ? "

" Just for this, that I am going away."

" Whither ? "

" I have received letters from Scotland, from old friends of my father and myself. My affairs demand me there absolutely ; perhaps for a long time. I am grieved to part with all here — but I must."

Zagloba, going into the middle of the room, looked at Pan Michael's sister, then at the young ladies, and asked, " Have you heard ? In the name of the Father, Son, and Holy Ghost ! "

CHAPTER XVII.

THOUGH Zagloba received the news of Ketling's departure with astonishment, still no suspicion came into his
head; for it was easy to admit that Charles II. had remembered the services which the Ketlings had rendered the
throne in time of disturbance, and that he wished to show
his gratitude to the last descendant of the family. It
would seem even most wonderful were he to act otherwise. Besides, Ketling showed Zagloba certain letters from
beyond the sea, and convinced him decisively. In its way
that journey endangered all the old noble's plans, and he
was thinking with alarm of the future. Judging by his
letter, Volodyovski might return any day.

"The winds have blown away in the steppes the remnant
of his grief," thought Zagloba. "He will come back more
daring than when he departed; and because some devil is
drawing him more powerfully to Krysia, he is ready to
propose to her straightway. And then, — then Krysia will
say yes (for how could she say no to such a cavalier, and,
besides, the brother of Pani Makovetski?), and my poor,
dearest haiduk will be on the ice."

But Zagloba, with the persistence special to old people,
determined at all costs to marry Basia to the little knight.
Neither the arguments of Pan Yan, nor those which at
intervals he used on himself, had serious effect. At times
he promised mentally, it is true, not to interfere again in
anything; but he returned afterward involuntarily with
greater persistence to the thought of uniting this pair. He
meditated for whole days how to effect this; he formed
plans, he framed stratagems. And he went so far that
when it seemed to him that he had hit upon the means, he
cried out straightway, as if the affair were over, "May
God bless you!"

But now Zagloba saw before him almost the ruin of his
wishes. There remained nothing more to him but to
abandon all his efforts and leave the future to God's will;
for the shadow of hope that before his departure Ketling
would take some decisive step with reference to Krysia

could not remain long in Zagloba's head. It was only from sorrow and curiosity, therefore, that he determined to inquire of the young knight touching the time of his going, as well as what he intended to do before leaving the Commonwealth.

Having invited Ketling to a conversation, Zagloba said with a greatly grieved face, "A difficult case! Each man knows best what he ought to do, and I will not ask you to stay; but I should like to know at least something about your return."

"Can I tell what is waiting for me there, where I am going?" answered Ketling, — "what questions and what adventures? I will return sometime, if I can. I will stay there for good if I must."

"You will find that your heart will draw you back to us."

"God grant that my grave will be nowhere else but in the land which gave me all that it could give!"

"Ah, you see in other countries a foreigner is a step-child all his life; but our mother opens her arms to you at once, and cherishes you as her own son."

"Truth, a great truth. Ei! if only I could — For everything in the old country may come to me, but happiness will not come."

"Ah! I said to you, 'Settle down; get married.' You would not listen to me. If you were married, even if you went away, you would have to return, unless you wished to take your wife through the raging waves; and I do not suppose that. I gave you advice. Well, you would n't take it; you would n't take it."

Here Zagloba looked attentively at Ketling's face, wishing some definite explanation from him, but Ketling was silent; he merely hung his head and fixed his eyes on the floor.

"What is your answer to this?" asked Zagloba, after a while.

"I had no chance whatever of taking it," answered the young knight, slowly.

Zagloba began to walk through the room, then he stopped in front of Ketling, joined his hands behind his back, and said, "But I tell you that you had. If you had not, may I never from this day forward bind this body of mine with this belt here! Krysia is a friend of yours."

"God grant that she remain one, though seas be between us!"

9

"What does that mean ?"

"Nothing more ; nothing more."

"Have you asked her ?"

"Spare me.   As it is, I am so sad because I am going."

"Ketling, do you wish me to speak to her while there is time ?"

Ketling considered that if Krysia wished so earnestly that their feelings should remain secret, perhaps she might be glad if an opportunity were offered of denying them openly, therefore he answered, "I assure you that that is vain, and I am so far convinced that I have done everything to drive that feeling from my head ; but if you are looking for a miracle, ask."

"Ah, if you have driven her out of your head," said Zagloba, with a certain bitterness, "there is nothing indeed to be done.   Only permit me to remark that I looked on you as a man of more constancy."

Ketling rose, and stretching upward his two hands fever-ishly, said with violence unusual to him, "What will it help me to wish for one of those stars ?   I cannot fly up to it, neither can it come down to me.   Woe to people who sigh after the silver moon !"

Zagloba grew angry, and began to puff.   For a time he could not even speak, and only when he had mastered his anger did he answer with a broken voice, "My dear, do not hold me a fool ; if you have reasons to give, give them to me, as to a man who lives on bread and meat, not as to one who is mad, — for if I should now frame a fiction, and tell you that this cap of mine here is the moon, and that I cannot reach it with my hand, I should go around the city with a bare, bald head, and the frost would bite my ears like a dog. I will not wrestle with statements like that.   But I know this : the maiden lives three rooms distant from here ; she eats ; she drinks ; when she walks, she must put one foot before the other ; in the frost her nose grows red, and she feels hot in the heat ; when a mosquito bites her, she feels it ; and as to the moon, she may resemble it in this, that she has no beard.   But in the way that you talk, it may be said that a turnip is an astrologer.   As to Krysia, if you have not tried, if you have not asked her, it is your own fault ; but if you have ceased to love the girl, and now you are going away, saying to yourself 'moon,' then you may nourish any weed with your honesty as well as your wit, — that is the point of the question."

To this Ketling answered, "It is not sweet, but bitter in my mouth from the food which you are giving me. I go, for I must; I do not ask, because I have nothing to ask about. But you judge me unjustly, — God knows how unjustly!"

"Ketling! I know, of course, that you are a man of honor; but I cannot understand those ways of yours. In my time a man went to a maiden and spoke into her eyes with this rhyme, 'If you wish me, we will live together; if not, I will not buy you.'[1] Each one knew what he had to do; whoever was halting, and not bold in speech, sent a better man to talk than himself. I offered you my services, and offer them yet. I will go; I will talk; I will bring back an answer, and according to that, you will go or stay."

"I must go! it cannot be otherwise, and will not."

"You will return."

"No! Do me a kindness, and speak no more of this. If you wish to inquire for your own satisfaction, very well, but not in my name."

"For God's sake, have you asked her already?"

"Let us not speak of this. Do me the favor."

"Well, let us talk of the weather. May the thunderbolt strike you, and your ways! So you must go, and I must curse."

"I take farewell of you."

"Wait, wait! Anger will leave me this moment. My Ketling, wait, for I had something to say to you. When do you go?"

"As soon as I can settle my affairs. I should like to wait in Courland for the quarter's rent; and the house in which we have been living I would sell willingly if any one would buy it."

"Let Makovetski buy it, or Michael. In God's name! but you will not go away without seeing Michael?"

"I should be glad in my soul to see him."

"He may be here any moment. He may incline you to Krysia."

Here Zagloba stopped, for a certain alarm seized him suddenly. "I was serving Michael in good intent," thought he, "but terribly against his will; if discord is to rise between him and Ketling, better let Ketling go away." Here Zagloba rubbed his bald head with his hand; at last he

[1] In the original this forms a rhymed couplet.

added, "One thing and another was said out of pure good-
will. I have so fallen in love with you that I would be
glad to detain you by all means; therefore I put Krysia
before you, like a bit of bacon. But that was only through
good-will. What is it to me, old man? In truth, that was
only good-will, — nothing more. I am not match-making;
if I were, I would have made a match for myself. Ketling,
give me your face,[1] and be not angry."

Ketling embraced Zagloba, who became really tender, and
straightway gave command to bring the decanter, saying,
"We will drink one like this every day on the occasion of
your departure."

And they drank. Then Ketling bade him good-by and
went out. Immediately the wine roused fancy in Zagloba;
he began to meditate about Basia, Krysia, Pan Michael, and
Ketling, began to unite them in couples, to bless them; at
last he wished to see the young ladies, and said, "Well, I
will go and see those kids."

The young ladies were sitting in the room beyond the
entrance, and sewing. Zagloba, after he had greeted them,
walked through the room, dragging his feet a little; for
they did not serve him as formerly, especially after wine.
While walking, he looked at the maidens, who were sitting
closely, one near the other, so that the bright head of
Basia almost touched the dark one of Krysia. Basia
followed him with her eyes; but Krysia was sewing so
diligently that it was barely possible to catch the glitter of
her needle with the eye.

"H'm!" said Zagloba.

"H'm!" repeated Basia.

"Don't mock me, for I am angry."

"He'll be sure to cut my head off!" cried Basia, feigning terror.

"Strike! strike! I'll cut your tongue out, — that's
what I'll do!"

Saying this, Zagloba approached the young ladies, and
putting his hands on his hips, asked without any prelimi-
nary, "Do you want Ketling as husband?"

"Yes; five like him!" said Basia, quickly.

"Be quiet, fly! I am not talking to you. Krysia, the
speech is to you. Do you want Ketling as husband?"

Krysia had grown pale somewhat, though at first she

---

[1] That is, let me kiss you.

thought that Zagloba was asking Basia, not her; then she raised on the old noble her beautiful dark-blue eyes. "No," answered she, calmly.

"Well, 'pon my word! No! At least it is short. 'Pon my word!—'pon my word! And why do you not want him?"

"I want no one."

"Krysia, tell that to some one else," put in Basia.

"What brought the married state into such contempt with you?" continued Zagloba.

"Not contempt; I have a vocation for the convent," answered Krysia.

There was in her voice so much seriousness and such sadness that Basia and Zagloba did not admit even for a moment that she was jesting; but such great astonishment seized both that they began to look as if dazed, now on each other, now on Krysia.

"Well!" said Zagloba, breaking the silence first.

"I wish to enter a convent," repeated Krysia, with sweetness.

Basia looked at her once and a second time, suddenly threw her arms around her neck, pressed her rosy lips to her cheek, and began to say quickly, "Oh, Krysia, I shall sob! Say quickly that you are only talking to the wind; I shall sob, as God is in heaven, I shall!"

CHAPTER XVIII.

AFTER his interview with Zagloba, Ketling went to Pan
Michael's sister, whom he informed that because of urgent
affairs he must remain in the city, and perhaps too before
his final journey he would go for some weeks to Courland;
therefore he would not be able in person to entertain her
in his suburban house longer.   But he implored her to consider that house as her residence in the same way as hitherto,
and to occupy it with her husband and Pan Michael during
the coming election.   Pani Makovetski consented, for in
the opposite event the house would become empty, and
bring profit to no one.

After that conversation Ketling vanished, and showed himself no more either in the inn, or later in the neighborhood
of Mokotov, when Pan Michael's sister returned to the
suburbs with the young ladies.   Krysia alone felt that
absence; Zagloba was occupied wholly with the coming
election; while Basia and Pani Makovetski had taken the
sudden decision of Krysia to heart so much that they could
think of nothing else.

Still, Pani Makovetski did not even try to dissuade
Krysia; for in those times opposition to such undertak-
ings seemed to people an injury and an offence to God.
Zagloba alone, in spite of all his piety, would have had the
courage to protest, had it concerned him in any way; but
since it did not, he sat quietly, and he was content in spirit
that affairs had arranged themselves so that Krysia retired
from between Pan Michael and the haiduk.   Now Zagloba
was convinced of the successful accomplishment of his most
secret desires, and gave himself with all freedom to the
labors of the election; he visited the nobles who had come
to the capital, or he spent the time in conversations with the
vice-chancellor, with whom he fell in love at last, becoming
his trusted assistant.   After each such conversation he returned home a more zealous partisan of the "Pole," and a
more determined enemy of foreigners.   Accommodating himself to the instructions of the vice-chancellor, he remained
quietly in that condition so far, but not a day passed that

he did not win some one for the secret candidate, and that happened which usually happens in such cases, — he pushed himself forward so far that that candidacy became the second object in his life, at the side of the union of Basia and Pan Michael. Meanwhile they were nearer and nearer the election.

Spring had already freed the waters from ice; breezes warm and strong had begun to blow; under the breath of these breezes the trees were sprinkled with buds, and flocks of swallows were hovering around, to spring out at any moment, as simple people think, from the ocean of winter into the bright sunlight. Guests began to come to the election, with the swallows and other birds of passage. First of all came merchants, to whom a rich harvest of profit was indicated, in a place where more than half a million of people were to assemble, counting magnates with their forces, nobles, servants, and the army. Englishmen, Hollanders, Germans, Russians, Tartars, Turks, Armenians, and even Persians came, bringing stuffs, linen, damask, brocades, furs, jewels, perfumes, and sweetmeats. Booths were erected on the streets and outside the city, and in them was every kind of merchandise. Some "bazaars" were placed even in suburban villages; for it was known that the inns of the capital could not receive one tenth of the electors, and that an enormous majority of them would be encamped outside the walls, as was the case always during time of election. Finally, the nobles began to assemble so numerously, in such throngs, that if they had come in like numbers to the threatened boundaries of the Commonwealth, the foot of any enemy would never have crossed them.

Reports went around that the election would be a stormy one, for the whole country was divided between three chief candidates, — Condé, the Princes of Neuberg and of Lorraine. It was said that each party would endeavor to seat its own candidate, even by force. Alarm seized hearts; spirits were inflamed with partisan rancor. Some prophesied civil war; and these forebodings found faith, in view of the gigantic military legions with which the magnates had surrounded themselves. They arrived early, so as to have time for intrigues of all kinds. When the Commonwealth was in peril, when the enemy was putting the keen edge to its throat, neither king nor hetman could bring more than a wretched handful of troops against him; but now in spite of laws and enactments, the Radzivills alone came with an

army numbering between ten and twenty thousand men.
The Patses had behind them an almost equivalent force;
the powerful Pototskis were coming with no smaller
strength; other "kinglets" of Poland, Lithuania, and Russia were coming with forces but slightly inferior. "When
wilt thou sail in, O battered ship of my country?" repeated
the vice-chancellor, more and more frequently; but he himself had selfish objects in his heart. The magnates, with
few exceptions, corrupted to the marrow of their bones,
were thinking only of themselves and the greatness of their
houses, and were ready at any moment to rouse the tempest
of civil war.

The throng of nobles increased daily; and it was evident
that when, after the Diet, the election itself would begin,
they would surpass even the greatest force of the magnates.
But these throngs were incompetent to bring the ship of
the Commonwealth into calm waters successfully, for their
heads were sunk in darkness and ignorance, and their hearts
were for the greater part corrupted. The election therefore gave promise of being prodigious, and no one foresaw
that it would end only shabbily, for except Zagloba, even
those who worked for the "Pole" could not foresee to what
a degree the stupidity of the nobles and the intrigues of
the magnates would aid them; not many had hope to carry
through such a candidate as Prince Michael. But Zagloba
swam in that sea like a fish in water. From the beginning
of the Diet he dwelt in the city continually, and was at
Ketling's house only when he yearned for his haiduk; but
as Basia had lost much joyfulness by reason of Krysia's
resolve, Zagloba took her sometimes to the city to let her
amuse herself and rejoice her eyes with the sight of the
shops.

They went out usually in the morning; and Zagloba
brought her back not infrequently late in the evening. On
the road and in the city itself the heart of the maiden was
rejoiced at sight of the merchandise, the strange people,
the many-colored crowds, the splendid troops. Then her
eyes would gleam like two coals, her head turn as if on a
pivot; she could not gaze sufficiently, nor look around
enough, and overwhelmed the old man with questions by
the thousand. He answered gladly, for in this way he
showed his experience and learning. More than once a
gallant company of military surrounded the equipage in
which they were riding; the knighthood admired Basia's

beauty greatly, her quick wit and resolution, and Zagloba
always told them the story of the Tartar, slain with duck-
shot, so as to sink them completely in amazement and
delight.

A certain time Zagloba and Basia were coming home
very late; for the review of Pan Felix Pototski's troops
had detained them all day. The night was clear and warm;
white mists were hanging over the fields. Zagloba, though
always watchful, since in such a concourse of serving-men
and soldiers it was necessary to pay careful attention not
to strike upon outlaws, had fallen soundly asleep; the
driver was dozing also; Basia alone was not sleeping, for
through her head were moving thousands of thoughts and
pictures. Suddenly the tramp of a number of horses came
to her ears. Pulling Zagloba by the sleeve, she said, —

"Horsemen of some kind are pushing on after us."

"What? How? Who?" asked the drowsy Zagloba.

"Horsemen of some kind are coming."

"Oh! they will come up directly. The tramp of horses
is to be heard; perhaps some one is going in the same
direction —"

"They are robbers, I am sure!"

Basia was sure, for the reason that in her soul she was
eager for adventures, — robbers and opportunities for her
daring, — so that when Zagloba, puffing and muttering,
began to draw out from the seat pistols, which he took with
him always for "an occasion," she claimed one for herself.

"I shall not miss the first robber who approaches.
Auntie shoots wonderfully with a musket, but she cannot
see in the night. I could swear that those men are robbers!
Oh, if they would only attack us! Give me the pistol
quickly!"

"Well," answered Zagloba, "but you must promise not
to fire before I do, and till I say fire. If I give you a
weapon, you will be ready to shoot the noble that you
see first, without asking, 'Who goes there?' and then a
trial will follow."

"I will ask first, 'Who goes there?'"

"But if drinking-men are passing, and hearing a woman's
voice, say something impolite?"

"I will thunder at them out of the pistol! Isn't that
right?"

"Oh, man, to take such a water-burner to the city! I
tell you that you are not to fire without command."

"I will inquire, 'Who goes there?' but so roughly that they will not know me."

"Let it be so, then. Ha! I hear them approaching already. You may be sure that they are solid people, for scoundrels would attack us unawares from the ditch."

Since ruffians, however, really did infest the roads, and adventures were heard of not infrequently, Zagloba commanded the driver not to go among the trees which stood in darkness at the turn of the road, but to halt in a well-lighted place. Meanwhile the four horsemen had approached a number of yards. Then Basia, assuming a bass voice, which to her seemed worthy of a dragoon, inquired threateningly, —

"Who goes there?"

"Why have you stopped on the road?" asked one of the horsemen, who thought evidently that they must have broken some part of the carriage or the harness.

At this voice Basia dropped her pistol and said hurriedly to Zagloba, "Indeed, that is uncle. Oh, for God's sake!"

"What uncle?"

"Makovetski."

"Hei there!" cried Zagloba; "and are you not Pan Makovetski with Pan Volodyovski?"

"Pan Zagloba!" cried the little knight.

"Michael!"

Here Zagloba began to put his legs over the edge of the carriage with great haste; but before he could get one of them over, Volodyovski had sprung from his horse and was at the side of the equipage. Recognizing Basia by the light of the moon, he seized her by both hands and cried, —

"I greet you with all my heart! And where is Panna Krysia, and sister? Are all in good health?"

"In good health, thank God! So you have come at last!" said Basia, with a beating heart. "Is uncle here too? Oh, uncle!"

When she had said this, she seized by the neck Pan Makovetski, who had just come to the carriage; and Zagloba opened his arms meanwhile to Pan Michael. After long greetings came the presentation of Pan Makovetski to Zagloba; then the two travellers gave their horses to attendants and took their places in the carriage. Makovetski and Zagloba occupied the seat of honor; Basia and Pan Michael sat in front.

Brief questions and brief answers followed, as happens

usually when people meet after a long absence. Pan Makovetski inquired about his wife; Pan Michael once more
about the health of Panna Krysia; then he wondered at
Ketling's approaching departure, but he had not time to
dwell on that, for he was forced at once to tell of what he
had done in the border stanitsa, how he had attacked the
ravagers of the horde, how he was homesick, but how
wholesome it was to taste his old life.

"It seemed to me," said the little knight, "that the
Lubni times had not passed; that we were still together
with Pan Yan and Kushel and Vyershul; only when they
brought me a pail of water for washing, and gray-haired
temples were seen in it, could a man remember that he
was not the same as in old times, though, on the other hand,
it came to my mind that while the will was the same the
man was the same."

"You have struck the point!" replied Zagloba; "it is
clear that your wit has recovered on fresh grass, for
hitherto you were not so quick. Will is the main thing,
and there is no better drug for melancholy."

"That is true,—is true," added Pan Makovetski. "There
is a legion of well-sweeps in Michael's stanitsa, for there is
a lack of spring water in the neighborhood. I tell you,
sir, that when the soldiers begin to make those sweeps
squeak at daybreak, your grace would wake up with such a
will that you would thank God at once for this alone, that
you were living."

"Ah, if I could only be there for even one day!" cried
Basia.

"There is one way to go there," said Zagloba, — "marry
the captain of the guard."

"Pan Adam will be captain sooner or later," put in the
little knight.

"Indeed!" cried Basia, in anger; "I have not asked you
to bring me Pan Adam instead of a present."

"I have brought something else, nice sweetmeats. They
will be sweet for Panna Basia, and it is bitter there for
that poor fellow."

"Then you should have given him the sweets; let him
eat them while his mustaches are coming out."

"Imagine to yourself," said Zagloba to Pan Makovetski,
"these two are always in that way. Luckily the proverb
says, 'Those who wrangle, end in love.'"

Basia made no reply; but Pan Michael, as if waiting for

an answer, looked at her small face shone upon by the
bright light. It seemed to him so shapely that he thought
in spite of himself, "But that rogue is so pretty that she
might destroy one's eyes."

Evidently something else must have come to his mind at
once, for he turned to the driver and said, " Touch up the
horses there with a whip, and drive faster."

The carriage rolled on quickly after those words, so
quickly that the travellers sat in silence for some time; and
only when they came upon the sand did Pan Michael speak
again: "But the departure of Ketling surprises me. And
that it should happen to him, too, just before my coming and
before the election."

"The English think as much of our election as they do of
your coming," answered Zagloba. "Ketling himself is cut
from his feet because he must leave us."

Basia had just on her tongue, "Especially Krysia," but
something reminded her not to mention this matter nor the
recent resolution of Krysia. With the instinct of a woman
she divined that the one and the other might touch Pan
Michael at the outset; as to pain, something pained her,
therefore in spite of all her impulsiveness she held
silence.

"Of Krysia's intentions he will know anyhow," thought
she; "but evidently it is better not to speak of them now,
since Pan Zagloba has not mentioned them with a word."

Pan Michael turned again to the driver, "But drive
faster!"

"We left our horses and things at Praga," said Pan Makovetski to Zagloba, "and set out with two men, though it
was nightfall, for Michael and I were in a terrible hurry."

"I believe it," answered Zagloba. "Do you see what
throngs have come to the capital? Outside the gates are
camps and markets, so that it is difficult to pass. People
tell also wonderful things of the coming election, which I
will repeat at a proper time in the house to you."

Here they began to converse about politics. Zagloba was
trying to discover adroitly Makovetski's opinions; at last he
turned to Pan Michael and asked without ceremony, "And
for whom will you give your vote, Michael?"

But Pan Michael, instead of an answer, started as if
roused from sleep, and said, "I am curious to know if they
are sleeping, and if we shall see them to-day?"

"They are surely sleeping," answered Basia, with a sweet

and as it were drowsy voice. "But they will wake and come surely to greet you and uncle."

"Do you think so?" asked the little knight, with joy; and again he looked at Basia, and again thought involuntarily, "But that rogue is charming in this moonlight."

They were near Ketling's house now, and arrived in a short time. Pani Makovetski and Krysia were asleep; a few of the servants were up, waiting with supper for Basia and Pan Zagloba. All at once there was no small movement in the house; Zagloba gave command to wake more servants to prepare warm food for the guests.

Pan Makovetski wished to go straightway to his wife; but she had heard the unusual noise, and guessing who had come, ran down a moment later with her robe thrown around her, panting, with tears of joy in her eyes, and lips full of smiles; greetings began, embraces and conversation, interrupted by exclamations.

Pan Michael was looking continually at the door, through which Basia had vanished, and in which he hoped any moment to see Krysia, the beloved, radiant with quiet joy, bright, with gleaming eyes, and hair twisted up in a hurry; meanwhile, the Dantzig clock standing in the dining-room ticked and ticked, an hour passed, supper was brought, and the maiden beloved and dear to Pan Michael did not appear in the room.

At last Basia came in, but alone, serious somehow, and gloomy; she approached the table, and taking a light in her hand, turned to Pan Makovetski: "Krysia is somewhat unwell, and will not come; but she begs uncle to come, even near the door, so that she may greet him."

Pan Makovetski rose at once and went out, followed by Basia.

The little knight became terribly gloomy and said, "I did not think that I should fail to see Panna Krysia to-night. Is she really ill?"

"Ei! she is well," answered his sister; "but people are nothing to her now."

"Why is that?"

"Then has his grace, Pan Zagloba, not spoken of her intention?"

"Of what intention, by the wounds of God?"

"She is going to a convent."

Pan Michael began to blink like a man who has not heard all that is said to him; then he changed in the face, stood up, sat down again.　In one moment sweat covered his face with drops ; then he began to wipe it with his palms.　In the room there was deep silence.

" Michael ! " said his sister.

But he looked confusedly now on her, now on Zagloba, and said at last in a terrible voice, " Is there some curse hanging over me ? "

" Have God in your heart ! " cried Zagloba.

CHAPTER XIX.

ZAGLOBA and Pani Makovetski divined by that exclamation the secret of the little knight's heart; and when he sprang up suddenly and left the room, they looked at each other with amazement and disquiet, till at last the lady said, "For God's sake go after him! persuade him; comfort him; if not, I will go myself."

"Do not do that," said Zagloba. "There is no need of us there, but Krysia is needed; if he cannot see her, it is better to leave him alone, for untimely comforting leads people to still greater despair."

"I see now, as on my palm, that he was inclined to Krysia. See, I knew that he liked her greatly and sought her company; but that he was so lost in her never came to my head."

"It must be that he returned with a proposition ready, in which he saw his own happiness; meanwhile a thunderbolt, as it were, fell."

"Why did he speak of this to no one, neither to me, nor to you, nor to Krysia herself? Maybe the girl would not have made her vow."

"It is a wonderful thing," said Zagloba; "besides, he confides in me, and trusts my head more than his own; and not merely has he not acknowledged this affection to me, but even said once that it was friendship, nothing more."

"He was always secretive."

"Then though you are his sister, you don't know him. His heart is like the eyes of a sole, on top. I have never met a more outspoken man; but I admit that he has acted differently this time. Are you sure that he said nothing to Krysia?"

"God of power! Krysia is mistress of her own will, for my husband as guardian has said to her, 'If the man is worthy and of honorable blood, you may overlook his property.' If Michael had spoken to her before his departure, she would have answered yes or no, and he would have known what to look for."

"True, because this has struck him unexpectedly. Now give your woman's wit to this business."

"What is wit here? Help is needed."

"Let him take Basia."

"But if, as is evident, he prefers that one — Ha! if this had only come into my head."

"It is a pity that it did not."

"How could it when it did not enter the head of such a Solomon as you?"

"And how do you know that?"

"You advised Ketling."

"I? God is my witness, I advised no man. I said that he was inclined to her, and it was true; I said that he was a worthy cavalier, for that was and is true; but I leave match-making to women. My lady, as things are, half the Commonwealth is resting on my head. Have I even time to think of anything but public affairs? Often I have not a minute to put a spoonful of food in my mouth."

"Advise us this time, for God's mercy! All around I hear only this, that there is no head beyond yours."

"People are talking of this head of mine without ceasing; they might rest awhile. As to counsels, there are two: either let Michael take Basia, or let Krysia change her intention; an intention is not a vow."

Now Pan Makovetski came in; his wife told him everything straightway. The noble was greatly grieved, for he loved Pan Michael uncommonly and valued him; but for the time he could think out nothing.

"If Krysia will be obstinate," said he, rubbing his forehead, "how can you use even arguments in such an affair?"

"Krysia will be obstinate!" said Pani Makovetski. "Krysia has always been that way."

"What was in Michael's head that he did not make sure before departing?" asked Pan Makovetski. "As he left matters, something worse might have happened; another might have won the girl's heart in his absence."

"In that case, she would not have chosen the cloister at once," said Pani Makovetski. "However, she is free."

"True!" answered Makovetski.

But already it was dawning in Zagloba's head. If the secret of Krysia and Pan Michael had been known to him, all would have been clear to him at once; but without that knowledge it was really hard to understand anything. Still, the quick wit of the man began to break through the mist, and to divine the real reason and intention of Krysia and the despair of Pan Michael. After a while he felt sure that Ketling was involved in what had happened. His supposition lacked only certainty; he determined, therefore, to go to Michael and examine him more closely. On the road alarm seized him, for he thought thus to himself, —

"There is much of my work in this. I wanted to quaff mead at the wedding of Basia and Michael; but I am not sure that instead of mead, I have not provided sour beer, for now Michael will return to his former decision, and imitating Krysia, will put on the habit."

Here a chill came on Zagloba; so he hastened his steps, and in a moment was in Pan Michael's room. The little knight was pacing up and down like a wild beast in a cage. His forehead was terribly wrinkled, his eyes glassy; he was suffering dreadfully. Seeing Zagloba, he stopped on a sudden before him, and placing his hands on his breast, cried, —

"Tell me the meaning of all this!"

"Michael!" said Zagloba, "consider how many girls enter convents each year; it is a common thing. Some go in spite of their parents, trusting that the Lord Jesus will be on their side; but what wonder in this case, when the girl is free?"

"There is no longer any secret!" cried Pan Michael. "She is not free, for she promised me her love and hand before I left here."

"Ha!" said Zagloba; "I did not know that."

"It is true," repeated the little knight.

"Maybe she will listen to persuasion."

"She cares for me no longer; she would not see me," cried Pan Michael, with deep sorrow. "I hastened hither day and night, and she does not even want to see me. What have I done? What sins are weighing on me that the anger of God pursues me; that the wind drives me like a withered leaf? One is dead; another is going to the cloister. God Himself took both from me; it is clear that I am accursed. There is mercy for every man, there is love for every man, except me alone."

Zagloba trembled in his soul, lest the little knight, carried away by sorrow, might begin to blaspheme again, as once he blasphemed after the death of Anusia; therefore, to turn his mind in another direction, he called out, "Michael, do not doubt that there is mercy upon you also; and besides, you cannot know what is waiting for you to-morrow.

10

Perhaps that same Krysia, remembering your loneliness, will change her intention and keep her word to you. Secondly, listen to me, Michael. Is not this a consolation that God Himself, our Merciful Father, takes those doves from you, and not a man walking upon the earth? Tell me yourself if this is not better?"

In answer the little knight's mustaches began to tremble terribly; the noise of gritting came from his teeth, and he cried with a suppressed and broken voice, "If it were a living man! Ha! Should such a man be found, I would — Vengeance would remain."

"But as it is, prayer remains," said Zagloba. "Hear me, old friend; no man will give you better counsel. Maybe God Himself will change everything yet for the better. I myself — you know — wished another for you; but seeing your pain, I suffer together with you, and together with you will pray to God to comfort you, and incline the heart of that harsh lady to you again."

When he had said this, Zagloba began to wipe away tears; they were tears of sincere friendship and sorrow. Had it been in the power of the old man, he would have undone at that moment everything that he had done to set Krysia aside, and would have been the first to cast her into Pan Michael's arms.

"Listen," said he, after a while; "speak once more with Krysia; take your lament to her, your unendurable pain, and may God bless you! The heart in her must be of stone if she does not take pity on you; but I hope that she will. The habit is a praiseworthy thing, but not when made of injustice to others. Tell her that. You will see — Ei, Michael, to-day you are weeping, and to-morrow perhaps we shall be drinking at the betrothal. I am sure that will be the outcome. The young lady grew lonely, and therefore the habit came to her head. She will go to a cloister, but to one in which you will be ringing for the christening. Perhaps too she is affected a little with hypochondria, and mentioned the habit only to throw dust in our eyes. In every case, you have not heard of the cloister from her own lips, and if God grants, you will not. Ha, I have it! You agreed on a secret; she did not wish to betray it, and is throwing a blind in our eyes. As true as life, nothing else but woman's cunning."

Zagloba's words acted like balsam on the suffering heart of Pan Michael: hope entered him again; his eyes were filled with tears. For a long time he could not speak; but when he had restrained his tears he threw himself into the arms of his friend and said, "But will it be as you say?"

"I would bend the heavens for you. It will be as I say! Do you remember that I have ever been a false prophet? Do you not trust in my experience and wit?"

"You cannot even imagine how I love that lady. Not that I have forgotten the beloved dead one; I pray for her every day. But to this one my heart has grown fixed like fungus to a tree; she is my love. What have I thought of her away off there in the grasses, morning and evening and midday! At last I began to talk to myself, since I had no confidant. As God is dear to me, when I had to chase after the horde in the reeds, I was thinking of her when rushing at full speed."

"I believe it. From weeping for a certain maiden in my youth one of my eyes flowed out, and what of it did not flow out was covered with a cataract."

"Do not wonder; I came here, the breath barely in my body; the first word I hear,—the cloister. But still I have trust in persuasion and in her heart and her word. How did you state it? 'A habit is good'—but made of what?"

"But not when made of injustice to others."

"Splendidly said! How is it that I have never been able to make maxims? In the stanitsa it would have been a ready amusement. Alarm sits in me continually, but you have given me consolation. I agreed with her, it is true, that the affair should remain a secret; therefore it is likely that the maiden might speak of the habit only for appearance' sake. You brought forward another splendid argument, but I cannot remember it. You have given me great consolation."

"Then come to me, or give command to bring the decanter to this place. It is good after the journey."

They went, and sat drinking till late at night.

Next day Pan Michael arrayed his body in fine garments and his face in seriousness, armed himself with all the arguments which came to his own head, and with those which Zagloba had given him; thus equipped, he went to the dining-room, where all met usually at meal-time. Of the whole company only Krysia was absent, but she did not let people wait for her long; barely had the little knight swal-

lowed two spoonfuls of soup when through the open door
the rustle of a robe was heard, and the maiden came in.

She entered very quickly, rather rushed in. Her cheeks
were burning; her lids were dropped; in her face were
mingled fear and constraint. Approaching Pan Michael, she
gave him both hands, but did not raise her eyes at all, and
when he began to kiss those hands with eagerness, she grew
very pale; besides, she did not find one word for greeting.
But his heart filled with love, alarm, and rapture at sight of
her face, delicate and changeful as a wonder-working image,
at sight of that form shapely and beautiful, from which the
warmth of recent sleep was still beating; he was moved
even by that confusion and that fear depicted in her face.

"Dearest flower!" thought he, in his soul, "why do you
fear? I would give even my life and blood for you." But
he did not say this aloud, he only pressed his pointed mustaches so long to her hands that red traces were left on them.
Basia, looking at all this, gathered over her forehead her
yellow forelock of purpose, so that no one might notice
her emotion; but no one gave attention to her at that
time; all were looking at the pair, and a vexatious silence
followed.

Pan Michael interrupted it first. "The night passed for
me in grief and disquiet," said he; "for yesterday I saw
all except you, and such terrible tidings were told of you
that I was nearer to weeping than to sleep."

Krysia, hearing such outspoken words, grew still paler,
so that for a while Pan Michael thought that she would
faint, and said hurriedly, "We must talk of this matter;
but now I will ask no more, so that you may grow calm
and recover. I am no barbarian, nor am I a wolf, and God
sees that I have good-will toward you."

"Thank you!" whispered Krysia.

Zagloba, Pan Makovetski, and his wife began to exchange
glances, as if urging one another to begin the usual conversation; but for a long time no one was able to venture a
word; at last Zagloba began. "We must go to the city
to-day," said he, turning to the newly arrived. "It is
boiling there before the election, as in a pot, for every
man is urging his own candidate. On the road, I will tell
you to whom, in my opinion, we should give our votes."

No one answered, therefore Zagloba cast around an owl-
ish eye; at last he turned to Basia, "Well, Maybug, will
you go with us?"

"I will go even to Russia!" answered Basia, abruptly.

And silence followed again. The whole meal passed in similar attempts to begin a conversation that would not begin. At last the company rose. Then Pan Michael approached Krysia at once and said, —

"I must speak with you alone."

He gave her his arm and conducted her to the adjoining room, to that same apartment which was the witness of their first kiss. Seating Krysia on the sofa, he took his place near her, and began to stroke her hair as he would have stroked the hair of a child.

"Krysia!" said he, at last, with a mild voice. "Has your confusion passed? Can you answer me calmly and with presence of mind?"

Her confusion had passed, and besides, she was moved by his kindness; therefore she raised for a moment her eyes on him for the first time since his return. "I can," said she, in a low voice.

"Is it true that you have devoted yourself to the cloister?"

Krysia put her hands together and began to whisper imploringly, "Do not take this ill of me, do not curse me; but it is true."

"Krysia!" said the knight, "is it right to trample on the happiness of people, as you are trampling? Where is your word, where is our agreement? I cannot war with God, but I will tell you, to begin with, what Pan Zagloba told me yesterday, — that the habit should not be made of injustice to others. You will not increase the glory of God by injustice to me. God reigns over the whole world; His are all nations, His the lands and the sea and the rivers, the birds of the air and the beasts of the forests, the sun and the stars. He has all, whatsoever may come to the mind of man, and still more; but I have only you, beloved and dear; you are my happiness, my every possession. And can you suppose that the Lord God needs that possession? He, with such wealth, to tear away his only treasure from a poor soldier? Can you suppose that He will be rejoiced, and not offended? See what you are giving Him, — yourself. But you are mine, for you promised yourself to me; therefore you are giving Him that which belongs to another, that which is not your own: you are giving Him my weeping, my pain, my death. Have you a right to do so? Weigh this in your heart and in your mind; finally ask your own conscience. If I had offended you, if I had contemned you in love, if I had forgotten you, if I had committed crimes or offences — ah, I will not speak; I will not speak. But I went to the horde, to watch, to attack ravagers, to serve the country with my blood, with my health, with my time; and I loved you, I thought of you whole days and nights, and as a deer longs for waters, as a bird for the air, as a child for its mother, as a parent for its child, was I longing for you. And for all this what is the greeting, what the reward, that you have prepared for me? Krysia dearest, my friend, my chosen love, tell me whence is all this? Give me your reasons as sincerely, as openly, as I bring before you my reasons and my rights; keep faith with me; do not leave me alone with misfortune. You gave me this right yourself; do not make me an outlaw."

The unfortunate Pan Michael did not know that there is a right higher and older than all other human rights, in virtue of which the heart must and does follow love only; but the heart which ceases to love commits thereby the deepest perfidy, though often with as much innocence as the lamp quenches in which fire has burned out the oil. Not knowing this, Pan Michael embraced Krysia's knees, implored, and begged; but she answered him with floods of tears only because she could not answer with her heart.

"Krysia," said the knight, at last, while rising, "in your tears my happiness may drown; and I do not implore you for that, but for rescue."

"Do not ask me for a reason," answered Krysia, sobbing; "do not ask for a cause, since it must be this way, and cannot be otherwise. I am not worthy of such a man as you, and I have never been worthy. I know that I am doing you an injustice, and that pains me so terribly that, see! I cannot help myself. I know that this is an injustice. O God of greatness, my heart is breaking! Forgive me; do not leave me in anger! Pardon me; do not curse me!" When she had said this, Krysia threw herself on her knees before Pan Michael. "I know that I am doing you a wrong, but I implore of you condescension and pardon."

Here the dark head of Krysia bent to the floor. Pan Michael raised in one moment the poor weeping maiden, and placed her again on the sofa; but he began himself to pace up and down in the room, like one dazed. At times he stopped suddenly and pressed his fists to his temples; then again he walked; at last he stood before Krysia.

"Leave yourself time, and me some hope," said he. "Think that I too am not of stone. Why press red-hot iron against me without the least pity? Even though I knew not my own endurance, still when the skin hisses, pain pierces me. I cannot tell you how I suffer,—as God lives, I cannot. I am a simple man; my years have passed in war. Oh, for God's sake! O dear Jesus! In this same room our love began. Krysia, Krysia! I thought that you would be mine for life; and now there is nothing, nothing! What has taken place in you? Who has changed your heart? Krysia, I am just the same. And do you not know that for me this is a worse blow than for another, for I have already lost one love? O Jesus, what shall I tell her to move her heart? A man only torments himself, that is all. But leave me even hope! Do not take everything away at one time."

Krysia made no answer; but sobbing shook her more and more; the little knight stood before her, restraining at first his sorrow, and terrible anger. And only when he had broken that in himself, he said,—

"Leave me even hope! Do you hear me?"

"I cannot! I cannot!" answered Krysia.

Pan Michael went to the window and pressed his head against the cold glass. He stood a long time without motion; at last he turned, and advancing a couple of steps toward Krysia, he said in a very low voice,—

"Farewell! There is nothing for me here. Oh that it may be as pleasant for you as it is grievous for me! Know this, that I forgive you with my lips, and as God will grant, I will forgive you with my heart as well. But have more mercy on people's suffering, and a second time promise not. It cannot be said that I take happiness with me from these thresholds! Farewell!"

When Pan Michael had said this, his mustaches quivered; he bowed, and went out. In the next room were Makovetski and his wife and Zagloba; they sprang up at once as if to inquire, but he only waved his hand. "All to no use!" said he. "Leave me in peace!"

From that room a narrow corridor led to his own chamber; in that corridor, at the staircase leading to the young ladies' rooms, Basia stopped the way to the little knight. "May God console you and change Krysia's heart!" cried she, with a voice trembling from tears.

He went past without even looking at her, or saying a

word. Suddenly wild anger bore him away; bitterness
rose in his breast; he turned, therefore, and stood before
the innocent Basia with a face changed and full of derision. "Promise your hand to Ketling," said he, hoarsely,
"then cease to love him, trample on his heart, rend it, and
go to the cloister!"

"Pan Michael!" cried Basia, in amazement.

"Enjoy yourself, taste kisses, and then go to repent!
Would to God that you both were killed!"

That was too much for Basia. God alone knew how
much she had wrestled with herself for this wish which
she had given Pan Michael,—that God might change
Krysia's heart,—and in return an unjust condemnation
had met her, derision, insult, just at the moment in which
she would have given her blood to comfort the thankless
man. Therefore her soul stormed up in her as quickly as
a flame; her cheeks burned; her nostrils dilated; and
without an instant's thought, she cried, shaking her yellow
hair,—

"Know, sir, that *I* am not the one who is going to the
cloister for Ketling!"

When she had said this, she sprang on the stairs and
vanished from before the eyes of the knight. He stood
there like a stone pillar; after a while he began to rub his
eyes like a man who is waking from sleep.

Then he was thirsting for blood; he seized his sabre, and
cried with a terrible voice, "Woe to the traitor!"

A quarter of an hour later Pan Michael was rushing
toward Warsaw so swiftly that the wind was howling in
his ears, and lumps of earth were flying in a shower from
the hoofs of his horse.

CHAPTER XX.

PAN MAKOVETSKI, with his wife and Zagloba, saw Pan Michael riding away, and alarm seized all hearts; therefore they asked one another with their eyes, "What has happened; where is he going?"

"Great God!" cried Pani Makovetski; "he will go to the Wilderness, and we shall never see him again in life!"

"Or to the cloister, like that crazy woman," said Zagloba, in despair.

"Counsel is necessary here," said Makovetski.

With that the door opened and Basia burst into the room like a whirlwind, excited, pale, with fingers in both her eyes; stamping in the middle of the floor, like a little child, she began to scream, "Rescue! save! Pan Michael has gone to kill Ketling! Whoso believes in God, let him fly to stop him! Rescue! rescue!"

"What is the matter, girl?" cried Zagloba, seizing her hands.

"Rescue! Pan Michael will kill Ketling! Through me blood will be shed, and Krysia will die, all through me!"

"Speak!" cried Zagloba, shaking her. "How do you know? Why is it through you?"

"Because I told him in anger that they love each other; that Krysia is going behind the grating for Ketling's sake. Whoso believes in God, stop them! Go quickly; go all of you! Let us all go!"

Zagloba, not wont to lose time in such cases, rushed to the yard and gave command to bring the carriage out at once. Pani Makovetski wished to ask Basia about the astonishing news, for up to that moment she had not suspected the love between Krysia and Ketling; but Basia rushed after Zagloba to look to the harnessing of the horses. She helped to lead out the beasts and attach them to the carriage; at last, though bareheaded, she mounted the driver's seat before the entrance, where two men were waiting and already dressed for the road.

"Come down!" said Zagloba to her.

"I will not come down! Take your seats; you must take your seats; if not, I will go alone!" So saying, she took the reins, and they, seeing that the stubbornness of the girl might cause a considerable delay, ceased to ask her to come down.

Meanwhile the servant ran up with a whip; and Pani Makovetski succeeded in bringing out a shuba and cap to Basia, for the day was cold. Then they moved on. Basia remained on the driver's seat. Zagloba, wishing to speak with her, asked her to sit on the front seat; but she was unwilling, it may be through fear of being scolded. Zagloba therefore had to inquire from a distance, and she answered without turning her head.

"How do you know," asked he, "that which you told your uncle about those two?"

"I know all."

"Did Krysia tell you?"

"Krysia told me nothing."

"Then maybe the Scot did?"

"No, but I know; and that is why he is going to England. He fooled everybody but me."

"A wonderful thing!" said Zagloba.

"This is your work," said Basia; "you should not have pushed them against each other."

"Sit there in quiet, and do not thrust yourself into what does not belong to you," answered Zagloba, who was struck to the quick because this reproach was made in presence of Makovetski. Therefore he added after a while, "I push anybody! I advise! Look at that! I like such suppositions."

"Ah, ha! do you think you did not?" retorted the maiden.

They went forward in silence. Still, Zagloba could not free himself from the thought that Basia was right, and that he was in great part the cause of all that had happened. That thought grieved him not a little; and since the carriage jolted unmercifully, the old noble fell into the worst humor and did not spare himself reproaches.

"It would be the proper thing," thought he, "for Michael and Ketling to cut off my ears in company. To make a man marry against his will is the same as to command him to ride with his face to a horse's tail. That fly is right! If those men have a duel, Ketling's blood will be on me. What kind of business have I begun in my old age! Tfu, to the Devil! Besides, they almost fooled me, for I barely guessed why Ketling was going beyond the sea — and

that daw to the cloister; meanwhile the haiduk had long
before found out everything, as it seems." Here Zagloba
meditated a little, and after a while muttered, "A rogue,
not a maiden! Michael borrowed eyes from a crawfish to
put aside such as she for that doll!"

Meanwhile they had arrived at the city; but there their
troubles began really. None of them knew where Ketling
was lodging, or where Pan Michael might go; to look for
either was like looking for a particular poppy-seed in a
bushel of poppy-seeds. They went first to the grand hetman's. People told them there that Ketling was to start
that morning on a journey beyond the sea. Pan Michael
had come, inquired about the Scot, but whither the little
knight had gone, no one knew. It was supposed that he
might have gone to the squadron stationed in the field
behind the city.

Zagloba commanded to return to the camp; but there it
was impossible to find an informant. They went to every
inn on Dluga Street; they went to Praga; all was in vain.
Meanwhile night fell; and since an inn was not to be
thought of, they were forced to go home. They went back
in tribulation. Basia cried some; the pious Makovetski
repeated a prayer; Zagloba was really alarmed. He tried,
however, to cheer himself and the company.

"Ha!" said he, "we are distressed, and perhaps Michael
is already at home."

"Or killed!" said Basia. And she began to wail there
in the carriage, repeating, "Cut out my tongue! It was my
fault, my fault! Oh, I shall go mad!"

"Quiet there, girl! the fault is not yours," said Zagloba;
"and know this, — if any man is killed, it is not Michael."

"But I am sorry for the other. We have paid him
handsomely for his hospitality; there is nothing to be said
on that point. O God, O God!"

"That is the truth!" added Pan Makovetski.

"Let that rest, for God's sake! Ketling is surely nearer
to Prussia than to Warsaw by this time. You heard that
he is going away; I have hope in God too, that should he
meet Volodyovski they will remember old friendship, service rendered together. They rode stirrup to stirrup; they
slept on one saddle; they went together on scouting expeditions; they dipped their hands in one blood. In the whole
army their friendship was so famous that Ketling, by reason
of his beauty, was called Volodyovski's wife. It is impos-

sible that this should not come to their minds when they see each other."

"Still, it is this way sometimes," said the discreet Makovetski, "that just the warmest friendship turns to the fiercest animosity. So it was in our place when Pan Deyma killed Pan Ubysh, with whom he had lived twenty years in the greatest agreement. I can describe to you that unhappy event in detail."

"If my mind were more at ease, I would listen to you as gladly as I do to her grace, my benefactress, your grace's spouse, who has the habit also of giving details, not excepting genealogies; but what you say of friendship and animosity has stuck in my head. God forbid! God forbid that it should come true this time!"

"One was Pan Deyma, the other Pan Ubysh. Both worthy men and fellow-soldiers —"

"Oi, oi, oi!" said Zagloba, gloomily. "We trust in the mercy of God that it will not come true this time; but if it does, Ketling will be the corpse."

"Misfortune!" said Makovetski, after a moment of silence. "Yes, yes! Deyma and Ubysh. I remember it as if to-day. And it was a question also of a woman."

"Eternally those women! The first daw that comes will brew such beer for you that whoever drinks will not digest it," muttered Zagloba.

"Don't attack Krysia, sir!" cried Basia, suddenly.

"Oh, if Pan Michael had only fallen in love with you, none of this would have happened!"

Thus conversing, they reached the house. Their hearts beat on seeing lights in the windows, for they thought that Pan Michael had returned, perhaps. But Pani Makovetski alone received them; she was alarmed and greatly concerned. On learning that all their searching had resulted in nothing, she covered herself with bitter tears and began to complain that she should never see her brother again. Basia seconded her at once in these lamentations. Zagloba too was unable to master his grief.

"I will go again to-morrow before daylight, but alone," said he; "I may be able to learn something."

"We can search better in company," put in Makovetski.

"No; let your grace remain with the ladies. If Ketling is alive, I will let you know."

"For God's sake! We are living in the house of that man!" said Makovetski. "We must find an inn somehow to-morrow, or even pitch tents in the field, only not to live longer here."

"Wait for news from me, or we shall lose each other," said Zagloba. "If Ketling is killed —"

"Speak more quietly, by Christ's wounds!" said Pani Makovetski, "for the servants will hear and tell Krysia; she is barely alive as it is."

"I will go to her," said Basia.

And she sprang upstairs. Those below remained in anxiety and fear. No one slept in the whole house. The thought that maybe Ketling was already a corpse filled their hearts with terror. In addition, the night became close, dark; thunder began to roar and roll through the heavens; and later bright lightning rent the sky each moment. About midnight the first storm of the spring began to rage over the earth. Even the servants woke.

Krysia and Basia went from their chamber to the dining-room. There the whole company prayed and sat in silence, repeating in chorus, after each clap of thunder, "And the Word was made flesh!" In the whistling of the whirlwind was heard at times, as it were, a certain horse-tramp, and then fear and terror raised the hair on the heads of Basia, Pani Makovetski, and the two men; for it seemed to them that at any moment the door might open, and Pan Michael enter, stained with Ketling's blood. The usually mild Pan Michael, for the first time in his life, oppressed people's hearts like a stone, so that the very thought of him filled them with dread.

However, the night passed without news of the little knight. At daylight, when the storm had abated in a measure, Zagloba set out a second time for the city. That whole day was a day of still greater alarm. Basia sat till evening in the window in front of the gate, looking at the road along which Pan Zagloba might return.

Meanwhile the servants, at command of Pan Makovetski, were packing the trunks slowly for the road. Krysia was occupied in directing this work, for thus she was able to hold herself at a distance from the others. For though Pani Makovetski did not mention Pan Michael in the young lady's presence even by one word, still that very silence convinced Krysia that Pan Michael's love for her, their former secret engagement, and her recent refusal had been discovered; and in view of this, it was difficult to suppose that those people, the nearest to Pan Michael, were not offended and grieved. Poor Krysia felt that it must be so, that it was so, — that those hearts, hitherto loving, had withdrawn from her; therefore she wished to suffer by herself.

Toward evening the trunks were ready, so that it was possible to move that very day; but Pan Makovetski was waiting yet for news from Zagloba. Supper was brought; no one cared to eat it; and the evening began to drag along heavily, insupportably, and as silent as if all were listening to what the clock was whispering.

"Let us go to the drawing-room," said Pan Makovetski, at last. "It is impossible to stay here."

They went and sat down; but before any one had been able to speak the first word, the dogs were heard under the window.

"Some one is coming!" cried Basia.

"The dogs are barking as if at people of the house," said Pani Makovetski.

"Quiet!" said her husband. "There is a rattling of wheels!"

"Quiet!" repeated Basia. "Yes; it comes nearer every moment. That is Pan Zagloba."

Basia and Pan Makovetski sprang up and ran out. Pani Makovetski's heart began to throb; but she remained with Krysia, so as not to show by great haste that Pan Zagloba was bringing news of exceeding importance. Meanwhile the sound of wheels was heard right under the window, and then stopped on a sudden. Voices were heard at the entrance, and after a while Basia rushed into the room like a hurricane, and with a face as changed as if she had seen an apparition.

"Basia, who is that? Who is that?" asked Pani Makovetski, with astonishment.

But before Basia could regain her breath and give answer, the door opened; through it entered first Pan Makovetski, then Pan Michael, and last Ketling.

CHAPTER XXI.

KETLING was so changed that he was barely able to make a low obeisance to the ladies; then he stood motionless, with his hat at his breast, with his eyes closed, like a wonder-working image. Pan Michael embraced his sister on the way, and approached Krysia. The maiden's face was as white as linen, so that the light down on her lip seemed darker than usual; her breast rose and fell violently. But Pan Michael took her hand mildly and pressed it to his lips; then his mustaches quivered for a time, as if he were collecting his thoughts; at last he spoke with great sadness, but with great calmness, —

"My gracious lady, or better, my beloved Krysia! Hear me without alarm, for I am not some Scythian or Tartar, or a wild beast, but a friend, who, though not very happy himself, still desires your happiness. It has come out that you and Ketling love each other; Panna Basia in just anger threw it in my eyes. I do not deny that I rushed out of this house in a rage and flew to seek vengeance on Ketling. Whoso loses his all is more easily borne away by vengeance; and I, as God is dear to me, loved you terribly and not merely as a man never married loves a maiden. For if I had been married and the Lord God had given me an only son or a daughter, and had taken them afterward, I should not have mourned over them, I think, as I mourned over you."

Here Pan Michael's voice failed for a moment, but he recovered quickly; and after his mustache had quivered a number of times, he continued, "Sorrow is sorrow; but there is no help. That Ketling fell in love with you is not a wonder. Who would not fall in love with you? And that you fell in love with him, that is my fate; there is no reason either to wonder at that, for what comparison is there between Ketling and me? In the field he will say himself that I am not the worse man; but that is another matter. The Lord God gave beauty to one, withheld it from the other, but rewarded him with reflection. So when the wind on the road blew around me, and my first rage

had passed, conscience said straightway, Why punish
them? Why shed the blood of a friend? They fell in
love, that was God's will. The oldest people say that
against the heart the command of a hetman is nothing. It
was the will of God that they fell in love; but that they did
not betray, is their honesty. If Ketling even had known
of your promise to me, maybe I should have called to him,
'Quench!' but he did not know of it. What was his fault?
Nothing. And your fault? Nothing. He wished to depart; you wished to go to God. My fate is to blame, my
fate only; for the finger of God is to be seen now in this,
that I remain in loneliness. But I have conquered myself;
I have conquered!"

Pan Michael stopped again and began to breathe quickly,
like a man who, after long diving in water, has come out to
the air; then he took Krysia's hand. "So to love," said
he, "as to wish all for one's self, is not an exploit. 'The
hearts are breaking in all three of us,' thought I; 'better
let one suffer and give relief to the other two.' Krysia,
God give you happiness with Ketling! Amen. God give
you, Krysia, happiness with Ketling! It pains me a little,
but that is nothing — God give you — that is nothing — I
have conquered myself!"

The soldier said, "that is nothing," but his teeth gritted,
and his breath began to hiss through them. From the
other end of the room, the sobbing of Basia was heard.

"Ketling, come here, brother!" cried Volodyovski.

Ketling approached, knelt down, opened his arms, and
in silence, with the greatest respect and love, embraced
Krysia's knees.

But Pan Michael continued in a broken voice, "Press his
head. He has had his suffering too, poor fellow. God
bless you and him! You will not go to the cloister. I
prefer that you should bless me rather than have reason to
curse me. The Lord God is above me, though it is hard for
me now."

Basia, not able to endure longer, rushed out of the room,
seeing which, Pan Michael turned to Makovetski and his
sister. "Go to the other chamber," said he, "and leave
them; I too will go somewhere, for I will kneel down
and commend myself to the Lord Jesus." And he went
out.

Halfway down the corridor he met Basia, at the staircase,
on the very same place where, borne away by anger, she had

divulged the secret of Krysia and Ketling. But this time Basia stood leaning against the wall, choking from sobs.

At sight of this Pan Michael was touched at his own fate; he had restrained himself up to that moment as best he was able, but then the bonds of sorrow gave way, and tears burst from his eyes in a torrent. "Why do you weep?" cried he, pitifully.

Basia raised her head, thrusting, like a child, now one and now the other fist into her eyes, choking and gulping at the air with open mouth, and answered with sobbing, "I am so sorry! Oh, for God's sake! O Jesus! Pan Michael is so honest, so worthy! Oh, for God's sake!"

Pan Michael seized her hands and began kissing them from gratitude. "God reward you! God reward you for your heart!" said he. "Quiet; do not weep."

But Basia sobbed the more, almost to choking. Every vein in her was quivering from sorrow; she began to gulp for air more and more quickly; at last, stamping from excitement, she cried so loudly that it was heard through the whole corridor, "Krysia is a fool! I would rather have one Pan Michael than ten Ketlings! I love Pan Michael with all my strength, — better than auntie, better than uncle, better than Krysia!"

"For God's sake! Basia!" cried the knight. And wishing to restrain her emotion, he seized her in his embrace, and she nestled up to his breast with all her strength, so that he felt her heart throbbing like a wearied bird; then he embraced her still more firmly, and they remained so.

Silence followed.

"Basia, do you wish me?" asked the little knight.

"I do, I do, I do!" answered Basia.

At this answer transport seized him in turn; he pressed his lips to her rosy lips, and again they remained so.

Meanwhile a carriage rattled up to the house, and Zagloba rushed into the ante-room, then to the dining-room, in which Pan Makovetski was sitting with his wife. "There is no sign of Michael!" cried he, in one breath; "I looked everywhere. Pan Krytski said that he saw him with Ketling. Surely they have fought!"

"Michael is here," answered Pani Makovetski; "he brought Ketling and gave him Krysia."

The pillar of salt into which Lot's wife was turned had surely a less astonished face than Zagloba at that moment.

11

Silence continued for a while; then the old noble rubbed his eyes and asked, "What?"

"Krysia and Ketling are sitting in there together, and Michael has gone to pray," said Makovetski.

Zagloba entered the next room without a moment's hesitation; and though he knew of all, he was astonished a second time, seeing Ketling and Krysia sitting forehead to forehead. They sprang up, greatly confused, and had not a word to say, especially as the Makovetskis came in after Zagloba.

"A lifetime would not suffice to thank Michael," said Ketling, at last. "Our happiness is his work."

"God give you happiness!" said Makovetski. "We will not oppose Michael."

Krysia dropped into the embraces of Pani Makovetski, and the two began to cry. Zagloba was as if stunned. Ketling bowed to Makovetski's knees as to those of a father; and either from the onrush of thoughts, or from confusion, Makovetski said, "But Pan Deyma killed Pan Ubysh. Thank Michael, not me!" After a while he asked, "Wife, what was the name of that lady?"

But she had no time for an answer, for at that moment Basia rushed in, panting more than usual, more rosy than usual, with her forelock falling down over her eyes more than usual; she ran up to Ketling and Krysia, and thrusting her finger now into the eye of one, and now into the eye of the other, said, "Oh, sigh, love, marry! You think that Pan Michael will be alone in the world? Not a bit of it; I shall be with him, for I love him, and I have told him so. I was the first to tell him, and he asked if I wanted him, and I told him that I would rather have him than ten others; for I love him, and I'll be the best wife, and I will never leave him! I'll go to the war with him! I've loved him this long time, though I did not tell him, for he is the best and the worthiest, the beloved — And now marry for yourselves, and I will take Pan Michael, to-morrow, if need be — for —"

Here breath failed Basia.

All looked at her, not understanding whether she had gone mad or was telling the truth; then they looked at one another, and with that Pan Michael appeared in the door behind Basia.

"Michael," asked Makovetski, when presence of mind had restored his voice to him, "is what we hear true?"

"God has wrought a miracle," answered the little knight, with great seriousness, "and here is my comfort, my love, my greatest treasure."

After these words Basia sprang to him again like a deer.

Now the mask of astonishment fell from Zagloba's face, and his white beard began to quiver; he opened his arms widely and said, "God knows I shall sob! Haiduk and Michael, come hither!"

CHAPTER XXII.

HE loved her immensely; and she loved him in the same way. They were happy together, but had no children, though it was the fourth year of their marriage. Their lands were managed with great diligence. Pan Michael bought with his own and Basia's money a number of villages near Kamenyets; for these he paid a small price, since timid people in terror of Turkish invasion were glad to sell land in those regions. On his estates he introduced order and military discipline; he took the restless population in hand, rebuilt burned villages, established "fortalices," — that is, fortified houses, — in which he placed temporary garrisons; in one word, as formerly he had defended the country with success, so now he worked his lands with good profit, never letting the sword out of his hand.

The glory of his name was the best defence of his property. With some of the murzas he poured water on his sword and concluded brotherhood; others he subdued. Bands of disorderly Cossacks, scattered detachments of the horde, robbers from the steppes, highwaymen from the plains of Bessarabia, trembled at thought of the "Little Falcon;" therefore his herds of horses and flocks of sheep, his buffaloes and camels, lived without danger on the steppes. The enemy even respected his neighbors. His substance increased through the aid of his active wife. He was surrounded by the honor and affection of people. His native land had adorned him with office; the hetman loved him; the Pasha of Hotin clicked with his tongue in wonder at him; in the distant Crimea, in Bagchesarai, his name was repeated with honor. His land, war, and love were the three elements of his life.

The hot summer of 1671 found Pan Michael in Sokol, in Basia's paternal villages. That Sokol was the pearl of their estates. They entertained there ceremoniously and merrily Pan Zagloba, who, disregarding the toils of a journey unusual at his age, came to visit them, fulfilling his solemn promise given at their wedding. But the noisy feasts and the joy of the hosts at seeing a dear guest was soon interrupted by an order from the hetman directing Pan Michael to take command at Hreptyoff, to watch the Moldavian boundary, to listen to voices from the side of the desert, protect the place, intercept Tartar parties, and clear the region of robbers.

The little knight, as a soldier ever willing in the service of the Commonwealth, gave orders at once to his servants to drive the herds from the meadows, lade the camels, and be ready themselves in arms. Still, his heart was rent at thought of parting with his wife, for he loved her with the love of a husband and a father, and was hardly able to breathe without her; but he had no wish to take her to the wild and lonely deserts of Ushytsa and expose her to various perils. She, however, insisted on going with him.

"Think," said she, "whether it will be more dangerous for me to stay here than to live with you under the protection of troops. I do not wish another roof than your tent, since I married you to share fatigue, toil, and danger with you. Here alarm would gnaw me to death; but there, with such a soldier, I shall feel safer than the queen in Warsaw. Should it be needful to take the field with you, I shall take it. If you go alone, I shall not know sleep in this place; I shall not put food to my mouth; and finally, I shall not hold out, but fly as I am to Hreptyoff; and if you will not let me in, I will spend the night at the gate, and beg and cry till you take pity."

Pan Michael, seeing such affection, seized his wife by the arms and began to cover her rosy face with kisses, and she gave like for like. "I should not hesitate," said he, at last, "were it a question of standing on guard simply and attacking detachments of the horde. Really, there will be men enough, because one of the squadrons of the starosta of Podolia will go with me, and one of the chamberlain's squadrons; besides these, Motovidlo will come with Cossacks and the dragoons of Linkhauz. There will be about six hundred soldiers, and with camp-followers up to a thousand. But I fear this, which the braggarts at the Diet in Warsaw will not believe, but which we on the borders expect every hour, — namely, a great war with the whole power of Turkey. This Pan Myslishevski has confirmed, and the Pasha of Hotin repeats it every day; the hetman believes that the Sultan will not leave Doroshenko without succor, but will declare war against the Commonwealth; and then what should I do with you, my dearest flower, my reward from God's hand ? "

"What happens to you will happen to me. I wish no other fate than the fate which comes to you."

Here Zagloba broke his silence, and turning to Basia, said, "If the Turks capture you, whether you wish it or not, your fate will be different from Michael's. Ha! After the Cossacks, the Swedes, the Northerners, and the Brandenburg kennel — the Turk! I said to Olshovski, the vice-chancellor, 'Do not bring Doroshenko to despair, for only from necessity did he turn to the Turk.' Well, and what? They would not listen to me. They sent Hanenko against Doroshenko, and now Doroshenko, willing or unwilling, must crawl into the throat of the Turk, and, besides, lead him against us. You remember, Michael, that I forewarned Olshovski in your presence."

"You must have forewarned him some other time, for I do not remember that it was in my presence," said the little knight. "But what you say of Doroshenko is holy truth, for the hetman holds the same views; they say even that he has letters from Doroshenko written in that sense precisely. But as matters are, so they are; it is enough that it is too late now to negotiate. You have quick wit, however, and I should like to hear your opinion. Am I to take Basia to Hreptyoff, or is it better to leave her here? I must add too that the place is a terrible desert. It was always a wretched spot, but during twenty years so many Cossack parties and so many chambuls have passed through it, that I know not whether I shall find two beams fastened together. There is a world of ravines there, grown over with thickets, hiding-places, deep caves, and every kind of secret den in which robbers hide themselves by hundreds, not to mention those who come from Wallachia."

"Robbers, in view of such a force, are a trifle," said Zagloba. "Chambuls too are a trifle; for if strong ones march up, there will be a noise about them; and if they are small, you will rub them out."

"Well, now!" cried Basia; "is not the whole matter a trifle? Robbers are a trifle; chambuls are a trifle. With such a force Michael will defend me from all the power of the Crimea."

"Do not interrupt me in deliberation," said Zagloba; "if you do, I'll decide against you."

Basia put both palms on her mouth quickly, and dropped her head on her shoulder, feigning to fear Zagloba terribly, and though he knew that the dear woman was jesting, still her action pleased him; therefore he put his old hand on her bright head and said, "Have no fear; I will comfort you in this matter."

Basia kissed his hand straightway, for in truth much depended on his advice, which was so infallible that no one was ever led astray by it; he thrust both hands behind his belt, and glancing quickly with his seeing eye now on one, now on the other, said suddenly, "But there is no posterity here, none at all; how is that?" Here he thrust out his under-lip.

"The will of God, nothing more," said Pan Michael, dropping his eyes.

"The will of God, nothing more," said Basia, dropping her eyes.

"And do you wish for posterity?"

To this the little knight answered: "I will tell you sincerely, I do not know what I would give for children, but sometimes I think the wish vain. As it is, the Lord Jesus has sent happiness, giving me this kitten, — or as you call her, this haiduk, — and besides has blessed me with fame and with substance. I do not dare to trouble Him for greater blessings. You see it has come to my head more than once that if all people had their wishes accomplished, there would be no difference between this earthly Commonwealth and the heavenly one, which alone can give perfect happiness. So I think to myself that if I do not wait here for one or two sons, they will not miss me up there, and will serve and win glory in the old fashion under the heavenly hetman, the holy archangel Michael, in expeditions against the foulness of hell, and will attain to high office."

Here, moved at his own words and at that thought, the pious Christian-knight raised his eyes to heaven; but Zagloba listened to him with indifference, and did not cease to mutter sternly. At last he said, —

"See that you do not blaspheme. Your boast that you divine the intentions of Providence so well may be a sin for which you will hop around as peas do on a hot pan. The Lord God has a wider sleeve than the bishop of Cracow, but He does not like to have any one look in to see what He has prepared there for small people, and He does what

He likes; but do you see to that which concerns you, and
if you wish for posterity, keep your wife with you, instead
of leaving her."

When Basia heard this, she sprang with delight to the
middle of the room, and clapping her hands, began to repeat,
" Well, now ! we 'll keep together. I guessed at once that
your grace would come to my side; I guessed it at once.
We 'll go to Hreptyoff, Michael.   Even once you 'll take
me against the Tartars, — one little time, my dear, my
golden ! "

"There she is for you! Now she wants to go to an
attack!" cried the little knight.

"For with you I should not fear the whole horde."

" *Silentium !*" said Zagloba, turning his delighted eyes,
or rather his delighted eye, on Basia, whom he loved
immensely. " I hope too that Hreptyoff, which, by the way,
is not so far from here, is not the last stanitsa before the
Wilderness."

"No; there will be commands farther on, in Mohiloff
and Yampol; and the last is to be in Rashkoff," answered
Pan Michael.

"In Rashkoff? We know Rashkoff. It was from that
place that we brought Helena, Pan Yan's wife; and you remember that ravine in Valadynka, Michael. You remember
how I cut down that monster, or devil, Cheremis, who was
guarding her. But since the last garrison will be in Rashkoff, if the Crimea moves, or the whole Turkish power,
they will know quickly in Rashkoff, and will give timely
notice to Hreptyoff; there is no great danger then, for the
place cannot be surprised. I say this seriously; and you
know, besides, that I would rather lay down my old head
than expose her to any risk. Take her. It will be better
for you both. But Basia must promise that in case of a
great war she will let herself be taken even to Warsaw, for
there would be terrible campaigns and fierce battles,
besieging of camps, perhaps hunger, as at Zbaraj; in such
straits it is hard for a man to save his life, but what could
a woman do ? "

"I should be glad to fall at Michael's side," said Basia;
" but still I have reason, and know that when a thing is not
possible, it is not possible. Finally, it is Michael's will,
and not mine. This year he went on an expedition under
Pan Sobieski. Did I insist on going with him? No. Well,
if I am not prevented now from going to Hreptyoff with

Michael, in case a great war comes, send me wherever you like."

"His grace, Pan Zagloba, will take you to Podlyasye to Pan Yan's wife," said the little knight; "there indeed the Turk will not reach you."

"Pan Zagloba! Pan Zagloba!" answered the old noble, mocking him. "Am I a captain of home guards? Do not intrust your wives to Pan Zagloba, thinking that he is old, for he may turn out altogether different. Secondly, do you think that in case of war with the Turk, I shall go behind the stove in Podlyasye, and watch the roast meat lest it burn? I may be good for something else. I mount my horse from a bench, I confess; but when once in the saddle, I will gallop on the enemy as well as any young man. Neither sand nor sawdust is sprinkling out of me yet, glory be to God! I shall not go on a raid against Tartars, nor watch in the Wilderness, for I am not a scout; but in a general attack keep near me, if you can, and you will see splendid things."

"Do you wish to take the field again?"

"Do you not think that I wish to seal a famous life with a glorious death, after so many years of service? And what better could happen to me? Did you know Pan Dzevyantkevich? He, it is true, did not seem more than a hundred and forty years old, but he was a hundred and forty-two, and was still in service."

"He was not so old."

"He was. May I never move from this bench if he wasn't! I am going to a great war, and that's the end of it! But now I am going with you to Hreptyoff, for I love Basia."

Basia sprang up with radiant face and began to hug Zagloba, and he raised his head higher and higher, repeating, "Tighter, tighter!"

Pan Michael pondered over everything for a time yet and said at last: "It is impossible for us all to go together, since the place is a pure wilderness, and we should not find a bit of roof over our heads. I will go first, choose a place for a square, build a good enclosure with houses for the soldiers, and sheds for the officers' horses, which, being of finer stock, might suffer from change of climate; I will dig wells, open the roads, and clear the ravines from robber ruffians. That done, I'll send you a proper escort, and you will come. You will wait, perhaps, three weeks here."

Basia wished to protest; but Zagloba, seeing the justice of Pan Michael's words, said, "What is wise, is wise! Basia, we will stay here together and keep house, and our affair will not be a bad one. We must also make ready good supplies in some fashion, for, of course, you do not know that meads and wines never keep so well as in caves."

CHAPTER XXIII.

VOLODYOVSKI kept his word; in three weeks he finished the buildings and sent a notable escort, — one hundred Lithuanian Tartars from the squadron of Pan Lantskoronski and one hundred of Linkhauz's dragoons, who were led by Pan Snitko, of the escutcheon Hidden Moon. The Tartars were led by Capt. Azya Mellehovich, who was descended from Lithuanian Tartars, — a very young man, for he had barely reached twenty and some years. He brought a letter which the little knight had written, as follows, to his wife: —

"Baska, beloved of my heart! You may come now, for without you it is as if without bread; and if I do not wither away before you are here, I shall kiss your rosy face off. I am not stingy in sending men and experienced officers; but give priority in all to Pan Snitko, and admit him to our society, for he is *bene natus* (well-born), an inheritor of land, and an officer. As to Mellehovich, he is a good soldier, but God knows who he is. He could not become an officer in any squadron but the Tartar, for it would be easier elsewhere for any man to fling low birth at him. I embrace you with all my strength; I kiss your hands and feet. I have built a fortalice with one hundred circular openings. We have immense chimneys. For you and me there are several rooms in a house apart. There is an odor of rosin everywhere, and such legions of crickets that when they begin to chirp in the evening the dogs start up from sleep. If we had a little pea-straw, they might be got rid of quickly; perhaps you will have some placed in the wagons. There was no glass to be had, so we put membrane in the windows; but Pan Byaloglovski has a glazier in his command among the dragoons. You can get glass in Kamenyets from the Armenians; but, for God's sake! let it be handled with care to avoid breaking. I have had your room fitted with rugs, and it has a respectable look. I have had the robbers whom we caught in the ravines hanged, nineteen of them; and before you come, the number will reach half three-score. Pan Snitko will tell you how we live. I commend you to God and the Most Holy Lady, my dear soul."

Basia, after reading the letter, gave it to Zagloba, who, when he had glanced over it, began at once to show more consideration to Pan Snitko, — not so great, however, that

the other should not feel that he was speaking to a most
renowned warrior and a great personage, who admitted him
to confidence only through kindness. Moreover, Pan Snitko
was a good-natured soldier, joyous and most accurate in
service, for his life had passed in the ranks. He honored
Volodyovski greatly, and in view of Zagloba's fame he felt
small, and had no thought of exalting himself.

Mellehovich was not present at the reading of the letter,
for when he had delivered it, he went out at once, as if to
look after his men, but really from fear that they might
command him to go to the servants' quarters.

Zagloba, however, had time to examine him; and having
the words of Pan Michael fresh in his head, he said to
Snitko, "We are glad to see you. I pray you, Pan
Snitko, I know the escutcheon Hidden Moon, — a worthy
escutcheon. But this Tartar, what is his name?"

"Mellehovich."

"But this Mellehovich looks somehow like a wolf.
Michael writes that he is a man of uncertain origin, which
is a wonder, for all our Tartars are nobles, though Moham-
medans. In Lithuania I saw whole villages inhabited by
them. There people call them Lipki; but those here are
known as Cheremis. They have long served the Commonwealth faithfully in return for their bread; but during the
time of the peasant incursion many of them went over to
Hmelnitski, and now I hear that they are beginning to
communicate with the horde. That Mellehovich looks like
a wolf. Has Pan Volodyovski known him long?"

"Since the last expedition," said Pan Snitko, putting his
feet under the table, "when we were acting with Pan
Sobieski against Doroshenko and the horde; they went
through the Ukraine."

"Since the last expedition! I could not take part in that,
for Sobieski confided other functions to me, though later on
he was lonely without me. But your escutcheon is the
Hidden Moon! From what place is Mellehovich?"

"He says that he is a Lithuanian Tartar; but it is a
wonder to me that none of the Lithuanian Tartars knew
him before, though he serves in their squadron. From this
come stories of his uncertain origin, which his lofty
manners have not been able to prevent. But he is a good
soldier, though sullen. At Bratslav and Kalnik he rendered
great service, for which the hetman made him captain,
though he was the youngest man in the squadron. The

Tartars love him greatly, but he has no consideration among us, and why? Because he is very sullen, and, as you say, has the look of a wolf."

"If he is a great soldier and has shed blood," said Basia, "it is proper to admit him to our society, which my husband in his letter does not forbid." Here she turned to Pan Snitko: "Does your grace permit it?"

"I am the servant of my benefactress," said Snitko.

Basia vanished through the door; and Zagloba, drawing a deep breath, asked Pan Snitko, "Well, and how does the colonel's wife please you?"

The old soldier, instead of an answer, put his fists to his eyes, and bending in the chair, repeated, "Ai! ai! ai!" Then he stared, covered his mouth with his broad palm, and was silent, as if ashamed of his own enthusiasm.

"Sweet cakes, is n't she?" asked Zagloba.

Meanwhile "sweet cakes" appeared in the door, conducting Mellehovich, who was as frightened as a wild bird, and saying to him, "From my husband's letter and from Pan Snitko we have heard so much of your manful deeds that we are glad to know you more intimately. We ask you to our society, and the table will be laid presently."

"I pray you to come nearer," said Zagloba.

The sullen but handsome face of the young Tartar did not brighten altogether, but it was evident that he was thankful for the good reception, and because he was not commanded to remain in the servants' quarters. Basia endeavored of purpose to be kind to him, for with a woman's heart she guessed easily that he was suspicious and proud, that the chagrin which beyond doubt he had to bear often by reason of his uncertain descent pained him acutely. Not making, therefore, between him and Snitko any difference save that enjoined by Snitko's riper age, she inquired of the young captain touching those services owing to which he had received promotion at Kalnik. Zagloba, divining Basia's wish, spoke to him also frequently enough; and he, though at first rather distant in bearing, gave fitting answers, and his manners not only did not betray a vulgar man, but were even astonishing through a certain courtliness.

"That cannot be peasant blood, for not such would the spirit be," thought Zagloba to himself. Then he inquired aloud, "In what parts does your father live?"

"In Lithuania," replied Mellehovich, blushing.

"Lithuania is a large country. That is the same as if you had said in the Commonwealth."

"It is not in the Commonwealth now, for those regions have fallen away. My father has an estate near Smolensk."

"I had considerable possessions there too, which came to me from childless relatives; but I chose to leave them and side with the Commonwealth."

"I act in the same way," said Mellehovich.

"You act honorably," put in Basia.

But Snitko, listening to the conversation, shrugged his shoulders slightly, as if to say, "God knows who you are, and whence you came."

Zagloba, noticing this, turned again to Mellehovich, "Do you confess Christ, or do you live, — and I speak without offence, — live in vileness?"

"I have received the Christian faith, for which reason I had to leave my father."

"If you have left him for that reason, the Lord God will not leave you; and the first proof of His kindness is that you can drink wine, which you could not do if you had remained in error."

Snitko smiled; but questions touching his person and descent were clearly not to the taste of Mellehovich, for he grew reserved again. Zagloba, however, paid little attention to this, especially since the young Tartar did not please him much, for at times he reminded him, not by his face, it is true, but by his movements and glance, of Bogun, the famed Cossack leader.

Meanwhile dinner was served. The rest of the day was occupied in final preparations for the road. They started at daybreak, or rather when it was still night, so as to arrive at Hreptyoff in one day.

Nearly twenty wagons were collected, for Basia had determined to supply the larders of Hreptyoff bountifully; and behind the wagons followed camels and horses heavily laden, bending under the weight of meal and dried meat; behind the caravan moved a number of tens of oxen of the steppe and a flock of sheep. The march was opened by Mellehovich with his Tartars; the dragoons rode near a covered carriage in which sat Basia with Pan Zagloba. She wished greatly to ride a trained palfrey; but the old noble begged her not to do so, at least during the beginning and end of the journey.

"If you were to sit quietly," said he, "I should not

object; but you would begin right away to make your horse prance and show himself, and that is not proper to the dignity of the commander's wife."

Basia was happy and joyous as a bird. From the time of her marriage she had two great desires in life: one was to give Michael a son; the other to live with the little knight, even for one year, at some stanitsa near the Wilderness, and there, on the edge of the desert, to lead a soldier's life, to pass through war and adventures, to take part in expeditions, to see with her own eyes those steppes, to pass through those dangers of which she had heard so much from her youngest years. She dreamed of this when still a girl; and behold, those dreams were now to become reality, and moreover, at the side of a man whom she loved and who was the most famous partisan in the Commonwealth, of whom it was said that he could dig an enemy from under the earth.

Hence the young woman felt wings on her shoulders, and such a great joy in her breast that at moments the desire seized her to shout and jump; but the thought of decorum restrained her, for she had promised herself to be dignified and to win intense love from the soldiers. She confided these thoughts to Zagloba, who smiled approvingly and said, —

"You will be an eye in his head, and a great wonder, that is certain. A woman in a stanitsa is a marvel."

"And in need I will give them an example."

"Of what?"

"Of daring. I fear only one thing, — that beyond Hreptyoff there will be other commands in Mohiloff and Rashkoff, on to Yampol, and that we shall not see Tartars even for medicine."

"And I fear only this, — of course not for myself, but for you, — that we shall see them too often. Do you think that the chambuls are bound strictly to come through Rashkoff and Mohiloff? They can come directly from the East, from the steppes, or by the Moldavian side of the Dniester, and enter the boundaries of the Commonwealth wherever they wish, even in the hills beyond Hreptyoff, unless it is reported widely that I am living in Hreptyoff; then they will keep aside, for they know me of old."

"But don't they know Michael, or won't they avoid him?"

"They will avoid him unless they come with great

power, which may happen. But he will go to look for
them himself."

"I am sure of that. But is it a real desert in Hreptyoff?
The place is not so far away!"

"It could not be more real. That region was never
thickly settled, even in time of my youth. I went from
farm to farm, from village to village, from town to town.
I knew everything, was everywhere. I remember when
Ushytsa was what is called a fortified town. Pan Konyetspolski, the father, made me starosta there; but after that
came the invasion of the ruffians, and all went to ruin.
When we went there for Princess Helena, it was a desert;
and after that chambuls passed through it twenty times.
Pan Sobieski has snatched it again from the Cossacks and
the Tartars, as a morsel from the mouth of a dog. There
are only a few people there now, but robbers are living in
the ravines."

Here Zagloba began to look at the neighborhood and nod
his head, remembering old times. "My God!" said he,
"when we were going for Helena, it seemed to me that old
age was behind my girdle; and now I think that I was
young then, for nearly twenty-four years have passed.
Michael was a milksop at that time, and had not many
more hairs on his lip than I have on my fist. And this
region stands in my memory as if the time were yesterday.
Only these groves and pine woods have grown in places
deserted by tillers of the land."

In fact, just beyond Kitaigrod they entered dense pine
woods with which at that time the region was covered for
the greater part. Here and there, however, especially
around Studyenitsa, were open fields; and then they saw
the Dniester and a country stretching forward from that
side of the river to the heights, touching the horizon on the
Moldavian side. Deep ravines, the abodes of wild beasts
and wild men, intercepted their road; these ravines were at
times narrow and precipitous, at times wider, with sides
gently sloping and covered with thick brush. Mellehovich's
Tartars sank into them carefully; and when the rear of
the convoy was on the lofty brink, the van was already, as
it were, under the earth. It came frequently to Basia and
Zagloba to leave the carriage; for though Pan Michael had
cleared the road in some sort, these passages were dangerous. At the bottom of the ravine springs were flowing, or
swift rivulets were rushing, which in spring were swollen

with water from the snow of the steppes. Though the sun still warmed the pine woods and steppes powerfully, a harsh cold was hidden in those stone gorges, and seized travellers on a sudden. Pine-trees covered the rocky sides and towered on the banks, gloomy and dark, as if desiring to screen that sunken interior from the golden rays of the sun; but in places the edges were broken, trees thrown in wild disorder upon one another, branches twisted and broken into heaps, entirely dried or covered with red leaves and spines.

"What has happened to this forest?" asked Basia of Zagloba.

"In places there may be old fellings made by the former inhabitants against the horde, or by the ruffians against our troops; again in places the Moldavian whirlwinds rush through the woods; in these whirlwinds, as old people say, vampires, or real devils, fight battles."

"But has your grace ever seen devils fighting?"

"As to seeing, I have not seen them; but I have heard how devils cry to each other for amusement, 'U-ha! U-ha!' Ask Michael; he has heard them."

Basia, though daring, feared evil spirits somewhat, therefore she began to make the sign of the cross at once. "A terrible place!" said she.

And really in some ravines it was terrible; for it was not only dark, but forbidding. The wind was not blowing; the leaves and branches of trees made no rustle; there was heard only the tramp and snorting of horses, the squeak of wagons, and cries uttered by drivers in the most dangerous places. At times too, the Tartars or dragoons began to sing; but the desert itself was not enlivened with one sound of man or beast. If the ravines made a gloomy impression, the upper country, even where the pine woods extended, was unfolded joyously before the eyes of the caravan. The weather was autumnal, calm. The sun moved along the plain of heaven, unspotted by a cloud, pouring bountiful rays on the rocks, on the fields and the forest. In that gleam the pine-trees seemed ruddy and golden; and the spider-webs attached to the branches of trees, to the reeds and the grass, shone brightly, as if they were woven from sunbeams. October had come to the middle of its days; therefore, many birds, especially those sensitive to cold, had begun to pass from the Commonwealth to the Black Sea; in the heavens were to be seen rows

of storks flying with piercing cries, geese, and flocks of
teal.

Here and there floated high in the blue, on outspread
wings, eagles, terrible to inhabitants of the air; here and
there falcons, eager for prey, were describing circles slowly.
But there were not lacking, especially in the open fields,
those birds also which keep to the earth, and hide gladly in
tall grass.   Every little while flocks of rust-colored partridges flew noisily from under the steeds of the Tartars; a
number of times also Basia saw, though from a distance,
bustards standing on watch, at sight of which her cheeks
flushed, and her eyes began to glitter.

"I will go coursing with Michael!" cried she, clapping
her hands.

"If your husband were a sitter at home," said Zagloba,
"his beard would be gray soon from such a wife; but I
knew to whom I gave you.   Another woman would be
thankful at least, would n't she?"

Basia kissed Zagloba straightway on both cheeks, so that
he was moved and said, "Loving hearts are as dear to a
man in old age as a warm place behind the stove."   Then
he was thoughtful for a while and added, "It is a wonder
how I have loved the fair sex all my life; and if I had to
say why, I know not myself, for often they are bad and
deceitful and giddy.   But because they are as helpless as
children, if an injustice strikes one of them, a man's heart
pipes from pity.   Embrace me again, or not!"

Basia would have been glad to embrace the whole world;
therefore she satisfied Zagloba's wish at once, and they
drove on in excellent humor.   They went slowly, for the
oxen, going behind, could not travel faster, and it was dangerous to leave them in the midst of those forests with a
small number of men.   As they drew near Ushytsa, the
country became more uneven, the desert more lonely, and
the ravines deeper.   Every little while something was
injured in the wagons, and sometimes the horses were stubborn; considerable delays took place through this cause.
The old road, which led once to Mohiloff, was grown over
with forests during twenty years, so that traces of it could
barely be seen here and there; consequently they had to
keep to the trails beaten by earlier and later passages of
troops, hence frequently misleading, and also very difficult.
The journey did not pass either without accident.

On the slope of a ravine the horse stumbled under Melle-

hovich, riding at the head of the Tartars, and fell to the
stony bottom, not without injury to the rider, who cut the
crown of his head so severely that consciousness left him
for a time. Basia and Zagloba mounted led palfreys; and
Basia gave command to put the Tartar in the carriage and
drive carefully. Afterward she stopped the march at every
spring, and with her own hands bound his head with cloths
wet with cold spring-water. He lay for a time with closed
eyes, but opened them at last; and when Basia bent over him
and asked how he felt, instead of an answer he seized her
hand and pressed it to his white lips. Only after a pause,
as if collecting his thoughts and presence of mind, did he
say in Russian, —

"Oh, I am well, as I have not been for a long time."

The whole day passed in a march of this kind. The sun,
growing red at last and seeming immense, was descending
on the Moldavian side; the Dnieper was gleaming like a
fiery ribbon, and from the east, from the Wilderness, darkness was moving on slowly.

Hreptyoff was not far away, but it was necessary to give
rest to the horses, therefore they stopped for a considerable
halt. This and that dragoon began to chant prayers; the
Tartars dismounted, spread sheep-skins on the ground, and
fell to praying on their knees, with faces turned eastward.
At times "Allah! Allah!" sounded through all the ranks;
then again they were quiet; holding their palms turned
upward near their faces, they continued in attentive prayer,
repeating only from time to time drowsily and as if with a
sigh, "Lohichmen ah lohichmen!" The rays of the sun
fell on them redder and redder; a breeze came from the
west, and with it a great rustling in the trees, as if they
wished to honor before night Him who brings out on the
dark heavens thousands of glittering stars. Basia looked
with great curiosity at the praying of the Tartars; but at
the thought that so many good men, after lives full of toil,
would go straightway after death to hell's fire, her heart
was oppressed, especially since they, though they met
people daily who professed the true faith, remained of their
own will in hardness of heart.

Zagloba, more accustomed to those things, only shrugged
his shoulders at the pious considerations of Basia, and said,
"These sons of goats are not admitted to heaven, lest they
might take with them vile insects."

Then, with the assistance of his attendant, he put on a

coat lined with hanging threads, — an excellent defence
against evening cold, — and gave command to move on ; but
barely had the march begun when on the opposite heights
five horsemen appeared. The Tartars opened ranks at
once.

"Michael !" cried Basia, seeing the man riding in front.

It was indeed Volodyovski, who had come out with a few
horsemen to meet his wife. Springing forward, they
greeted each other with great joy, and then began to tell
what had happened to each.

Basia related how the journey had passed, and how Pan
Mellehovich had "sprained his reason[1] against a stone."
The little knight made a report of his activity in Hreptyoff,
in which, as he stated, everything was ready and waiting to
receive her, for five hundred axes had been working for
three weeks on buildings. During this conversation Pan
Michael bent from the saddle every little while, and seized
his young wife in his arms ; she, it was clear, was not very
angry at that, for she rode at his side there so closely that
the horses were nearly rubbing against each other.

The end of the journey was not distant ; meanwhile a
beautiful night came down, illuminated by a great golden
moon. But the moon grew paler as it rose from the steppes
to the sky, and at last its shining was darkened by a conflagration which blazed up brightly in front of the caravan.

"What is that ?" inquired Basia.

"You will see," said Volodyovski, "as soon as you have
passed that forest which divides us from Hreptyoff."

"Is that Hreptyoff already ?"

"You would see it as a thing on your palm, but the trees
hide it."

, They rode into a small forest; but they had not ridden
halfway through it when a swarm of lights appeared on the
other edge like a swarm of fireflies, or glittering stars.
Those stars began to approach with amazing rapidity ; and
suddenly the whole forest was quivering with shouts, —

"Vivat the lady ! Vivat her great mightiness ! vivat
our commandress ! vivat, vivat !"

These were soldiers who had hastened to greet Basia.
Hundreds of them mingled in one moment with the Tartars.
Each held on a long pole a burning taper, fixed in a split at
the end of the pole. Some had iron candlesticks on pikes,

[1] Injured his head.

from which burning rosin was falling in the form of long
fiery tears.

Basia was surrounded quickly with throngs of mustached
faces, threatening, somewhat wild, but radiant with joy.
The greater number of them had never seen Basia in their
lives; many expected to meet an imposing person; hence
their delight was all the greater at sight of that lady, almost
a child in appearance, who was riding on a white palfrey
and bent in thanks to every side her wonderful, rosy face,
small and joyous, but at the same time greatly excited by
the unlooked-for reception.

"I thank you, gentlemen," said she; "I know that this is
not for me." But her silvery voice was lost in the *vivats*,
and the forest was trembling from shouts.

The officers from the squadron of the starosta of Podolia
and the chamberlain of Premysl, Motovidlo's Cossacks and
the Tartars, mingled together. Each wished to see the lady
commandress, to approach her; some of the most urgent
kissed the edge of her skirt or her foot in the stirrup. For
these half-wild partisans, inured to raids and man-hunting,
to bloodshed and slaughter, that was a sight so unusual, so
new, that in presence of it their hard hearts were moved,
and some kind of feeling, new and unknown to them, was
roused in their breasts. They came to meet her out of love
for Pan Michael, wishing to give him pleasure, and perhaps
to flatter him; and behold! sudden tenderness seizes them.
That smiling, sweet, and innocent face, with gleaming eyes
and distended nostrils, became dear to them in one moment.
"That is our child!" cried old Cossacks, real wolves of the
steppe. "A cherub, Pan Commander." "She is a morning dawn! a dear flower!" shouted the officers. "We will
fall, one after another, for her!" And the Tartars, click-
ing with their tongues, put their palms to their broad breasts
and cried, "Allah! Allah!" Volodyovski was greatly
touched, but glad; he put his hands on his hips and was
proud of his Basia.

Shouts were heard continually. At last the caravan came
out of the forest, and before the eyes of the newly arrived
appeared firm wooden buildings, erected in a circle on high
ground. That was the stanitsa of Hreptyoff, as clearly
seen then as in daylight, for inside the stockade enormous piles were burning, on which whole logs had been
thrown. The square was full of fires, but smaller, so as not
to burn up the place. The soldiers quenched their torches;

then each drew from his shoulder, one a musket, another a gun, a third a pistol, and thundered in greeting to the lady. Musicians came too in front of the stockade : the starosta's band with crooked horns, the Cossacks with trumpets, drums, and various stringed instruments, and at last the Tartars, pre-eminent for squeaking pipes. The barking of the garrison dogs and the bellowing of terrified cattle added still to the uproar.

The convoy remained now in the rear, and in front rode Basia, having on one side her husband, and on the other Zagloba. Over the gate, beautifully ornamented with birch boughs, stood black, on membranes of bladder smeared with tallow and lighted from the inside, the inscription : —

> " May Cupid give you many happy moments !
> Dear guests, *crescite, multiplicamini !* "

" Vivant, floreant ! " cried the soldiers, when the little knight and Basia halted to read the inscription.

" For God's sake ! " said Zagloba, " I 'm a guest too; but if that wish for multiplication concerns me, may the crows pluck me if I know what to do with it."

But Pan Zagloba found a special transparency intended for himself, and with no small pleasure he read on it,—

> " Long live our great mighty Onufry Zagloba,
> The highest ornament of the whole knighthood ! "

Pan Michael was very joyful; the officers were invited to sup with him; and for the soldiers he gave command to roll out one and another keg of spirits. A number of bullocks fell also; these the men began at once to roast at the fires. They sufficed for all abundantly. Long into the night the stanitsa was thundering with shouts and musket-shots, so that fear seized the bands of robbers hidden in the ravines of Ushytsa.

CHAPTER XXIV.

PAN MICHAEL was not idle in his stanitsa, and his men lived in perpetual toil. One hundred, sometimes a smaller number, remained as a garrison in Hreptyoff; the rest were on expeditions continually. The more considerable detachments were sent to clear out the ravines of Ushytsa; and they lived, as it were, in endless warfare, for bands of robbers, frequently very numerous, offered powerful resistance, and more than once it was needful to fight with them regular battles. Such expeditions lasted days, and at times tens of days. Pan Michael sent smaller parties as far as Bratslav for news of the horde and Doroshenko. The task of these parties was to bring in informants, and therefore to capture them on the steppes. Some went down the Dniester to Mohiloff and Yampol, to maintain connection with commandants in those places; some watched on the Moldavian side; some built bridges and repaired the old road.

The country in which such a considerable activity reigned became pacified gradually; those of the inhabitants who were more peaceful, and less enamoured of robbery, returned by degrees to their deserted habitations, at first stealthily, then with more confidence. A few Jewish handicraftsmen came up to Hreptyoff itself; sometimes a more considerable Armenian merchant looked in; shopkeepers visited the place more frequently: Volodyovski had therefore a not barren hope that if God and the hetman would permit him to remain a longer time in command, that country which had grown wild would assume another aspect. That work was merely the beginning; there was a world of things yet to be done: the roads were still dangerous; the demoralized people entered into friendship more readily with robbers than with troops, and for any cause hid themselves again in the rocky gorges; the fords of the Dnieper were often passed stealthily by bands made up of Wallachians, Cossacks, Hungarians, Tartars, and God knows what people. These sent raids through the country, attacking in Tartar fashion villages and towns, gathering up everything which let itself be gathered; for a time yet it was impossible to drop a sabre from the hand in those regions, or to hang a musket on a nail; still a beginning was made, and the future promised to be favorable.

It was necessary to keep the most sensitive ear toward the eastern side. From Doroshenko's forces and his allied chambuls were detached at short intervals parties larger or smaller; and while attacking the Polish commands, they spread devastation and fire in the region about. But since these parties were independent, or at least seemed so, the little knight crushed them without fear of bringing a greater storm on the country; and without ceasing in his resistance, he sought them himself in the steppe so effectually that in time he made attack disgusting to the boldest.

Meanwhile Basia managed affairs in Hreptyoff. She was delighted immensely with that soldier-life which she had never seen before so closely, — the movement, marches, returns of expeditions, the prisoners. She told the little knight that she must take part in one expedition at least; but for the time she was forced to be satisfied with this, that she sat on her pony occasionally, and visited with her husband and Zagloba the environs of Hreptyoff. On such expeditions she hunted foxes and bustards; sometimes the fox stole out of the grass and shot along through the valleys. Then they chased him; but Basia kept in front to the best of her power, right after the dogs, so as to fall on the wearied beast first and thunder into his red eyes from her pistol. Pan Zagloba liked best to hunt with falcons, of which the officers had a number of pairs very well trained.

Basia accompanied him too; but after Basia Pan Michael sent secretly a number of tens of men to give aid in emergency, for though it was known always in Hreptyoff what men were doing in the desert for twenty miles around, Pan Michael preferred to be cautious. The soldiers loved Basia more every day, for she took pains with their food and drink; she nursed the sick and wounded. Even the sullen Mellehovich, whose head pained him continually, and who had a harder and a wilder heart than others, grew bright at the sight of her. Old soldiers were in raptures over her knightly daring and close knowledge of military affairs.

"If the Little Falcon were gone," said they, "she might take command, and it would not be grievous to fall under such a leader."

At times it happened too that when some disorder arose in the service during Pan Michael's absence, Basia reprimanded the soldiers, and obedience to her was great; old warriors were more grieved by reproval from her mouth than by punishment, which the veteran Pan Michael inflicted unsparingly for dereliction of duty. Great discipline reigned always in the command, for Volodyovski, reared in the school of Prince Yeremi, knew how to hold soldiers with an iron hand; and, moreover, the presence of Basia softened wild manners somewhat. Every man tried to please her; every man thought of her rest and comfort; hence they avoided whatever might annoy her.

In the light squadron of Pan Nikolai Pototski there were many officers, experienced and polite, who, though they had grown rough in continual wars and adventures, still formed a pleasant company. These, with the officers from other squadrons, often spent an evening with the colonel, telling of events and wars in which they had taken part personally. Among these Pan Zagloba held the first place. He was the oldest, had seen most and done much; but when, after one and the second goblet, he was dozing in a comfortable stuffed chair, which was brought for him purposely, others began. And they had something to tell, for there were some who had visited Sweden and Moscow; there were some who had passed their years of youth at the Saitch before the days of Hmelnitski; there were some who as captives had herded sheep in the Crimea; who in slavery had dug wells in Bagchesarai; who had visited Asia Minor; who had rowed through the Archipelago in Turkish galleys; who had beaten with their foreheads on the grave of Christ in Jerusalem; who had experienced every adventure and every mishap, and still had appeared again under the flag to defend to the end of their lives, to the last breath, those border regions steeped in blood.

When in November the evenings became longer and there was peace on the side of the broad steppe, for the grass had withered, they used to assemble in the colonel's house daily. Hither came Pan Motovidlo, the leader of the Cossacks, — a Russian by blood, a man lean as pincers and tall as a lance, no longer young; he had not left the field for twenty years and more. Pan Deyma came too, the brother of that one who had killed Pan Ubysh; and with them Pan Mushalski, a man formerly wealthy, but who, taken captive in early years, had rowed in a Turkish galley, and escaping from bondage, had left his property to others, and with sabre in hand was avenging his wrongs on the race of Mohammed. He was an incomparable bowman, who, when he chose, pierced with an arrow a heron in its lofty flight. There came also the two partisans, Pan Vilga and Pan Nyenashinyets, great soldiers, and Pan Hromyka and Pan Bavdynovich, and many others. When these began to tell tales and to throw forth words quickly, the whole Oriental world was seen in their narratives, — Bagchesarai and Stambul, the minarets and sanctuaries of the false prophet, the blue waters of the Bosphorus, the fountains, and the palace of the Sultan, the swarms of men in the stone city, the troops, the janissaries, the dervishes, and that whole terrible locust-swarm, brilliant as a rainbow, against which the Commonwealth with bleeding breast was defending the Russian cross, and after it all the crosses and churches in Europe.

The old soldiers sat in a circle in the broad room, like a flock of storks which, wearied with flying, had settled on some grave-mound of the steppe and were making themselves heard with great uproar. In the fireplace logs of pitch-pine were burning, casting out sharp gleams through the whole room. Moldavian wine was heated at the fire by the order of Basia; and attendants dipped it with tin dippers and gave it to the knights. From outside the walls came the calls of the sentries; the crickets, of which Pan Michael had complained, were chirping in the room and whistling sometimes in the chinks stuffed with moss; the November wind, blowing from the north, grew more and more chilly. During such cold it was most agreeable to sit in a comfortable, well-lighted room, and listen to the adventures of the knights.

On such an evening Pan Mushalski spoke as follows: —

"May the Most High have in His protection the whole sacred Commonwealth, us all, and among us especially her grace, the lady here present, the worthy wife of our commander, on whose beauty our eyes are scarcely worthy to gaze. I have no wish to rival Pan Zagloba, whose adventures would have roused the greatest wonder in Dido herself and her charming attendants; but if you, gentlemen, will give time to hear my adventures, I will not delay, lest I offend the honorable company.

"In youth I inherited in the Ukraine a considerable estate near Tarashcha. I had two villages from my mother in a peaceable region near Yaslo; but I chose to live in my father's place, since it was nearer the horde and more open to adventure. Knightly daring drew me toward the Saitch, but for us there was nothing there at that time; I went to the Wilderness in company with restless spirits, and experienced delight. It was pleasant for me on my lands; one thing alone pained me keenly, — I had a bad neighbor. He was a mere peasant, from Byalotserkov, who had been in his youth at the Saitch, where he rose to the office of kuren ataman, and was an envoy from the Cossacks to Warsaw, where he became a noble. His name was Didyuk. And you, gentlemen, must know that the Mushalskis derive their descent from a certain chief of the Samnites, called Musca, which in our tongue means *mucha* (fly). That Musca, after fruitless attacks on the Romans, came to the court of Zyemovit, the son of Piast, who renamed him, for greater convenience, Muscalski, which later on his posterity changed to Mushalski. Feeling that I was of such noble blood, I looked with great abomination on that Didyuk. If the scoundrel had known how to respect the honor which met him, and to recognize the supreme perfection of the rank of noble above all others, perhaps I might have said nothing. But he, while holding land like a noble, mocked at the dignity, and said frequently: 'Is my shadow taller now? I was a Cossack, and a Cossack I'll remain; but nobility and all you devils of Poles are that for me —' I cannot in this place relate to you, gentlemen, what foul gesture he made, for the presence of her grace, the lady, will not in any way permit me to do so. But a wild rage seized me, and I began to persecute him. He was not afraid; he was a resolute man, and paid me with interest. I would have attacked him with a sabre; but I did not like to do so, in view of his insignificant origin. I hated him as the plague, and he pursued me with venom. Once, on the square in Tarashcha, he fired at me, and came within one hair of killing me; in return, I opened his head with a hatchet. Twice I invaded his house with my servants, and twice he fell upon mine with his ruffians. He could not master me, neither could I overcome him. I wished to use law against him; bah! what kind of law is there in the Ukraine, when ruins of towns are still smoking? Whoever can summon ruffians in the Ukraine may jeer at the Commonwealth. So did he do, blaspheming besides this common mother of ours, not remembering for a moment that she, by raising him to the rank of noble, had pressed him to her bosom, given him privileges in virtue of which he owned land and that boundless liberty which he could not have had under any other rule. If we could have met in neighbor fashion, arguments would not have failed me; but we did not see each other except with a musket in one hand and a fire-brand in the other. Hatred increased in me daily, until I had grown yellow. I was thinking always of one thing, — how to seize him. I felt, however, that hatred was a sin; and I only wished, in return for his insults to nobility, to tear his skin with sticks, and then, forgiving him all his sins, as beseemed me, a true Christian, to give command to shoot him down simply. But the Lord God ordained otherwise.

"Beyond the village I had a nice bee farm, and went one day to look at it. The time was near evening. I was there barely the length of ten 'Our Fathers,' when some clamor struck my ears. I looked around. Smoke like a cloud was over the village. In a moment men were rushing toward me. The horde! the horde! And right there behind the men a legion, I tell you. Arrows were flying as thickly as drops in a rain shower; and wherever I looked, sheep-skin coats and the devilish snouts of the horde. I sprang to horse! But before I could touch the stirrup with my foot, five or six lariats were on me. I tore away, for I was strong then. *Nec Hercules!* Three months afterward I found myself with another captive in a Crimean village beyond Bagchesarai. Salma Bey was the name of my master. He was a rich Tartar, but a sullen man and cruel to captives. We had to work under clubs, to dig wells, and toil in the fields. I wished to ransom myself; I had the means to do so. Through a certain Armenian I wrote letters to Yaslo. I know not whether the letters were delivered, or the ransom intercepted; it is enough that nothing came. They took me to Tsargrad [1] and sold me to be a galley-slave.

"There is much to tell of that city, for I know not whether there is a greater and a more beautiful one in the world. People are there as numerous as grass on the steppe, or as stones in the Dniester; strong battlemented walls; tower after tower. Dogs wander through the city together with the people; the Turks do not harm them,

---

[1] The Tsar's city, — Constantinople.

because they feel their relationship, being dog brothers themselves. There are no other ranks with them but lords and slaves, and there is nothing more grievous than Pagan captivity. God knows whether it is true, but I heard in the galleys that the waters in Tsargrad, such as the Bosphorus, and the Golden Horn too, which enters the heart of the city, have come from tears shed by captives. Not a few of mine were shed there.

"Terrible is the Turkish power, and to no potentate are so many kings subject as to the Sultan. The Turks themselves say that were it not for Lehistan, — thus they name our mother, — they would have been lords of the earth long ago. 'Behind the shoulders of the Pole,' say they, 'the rest of the world live in injustice; for the Pole,' say they, 'lies like a dog in front of the cross, and bites our hands.' And they are right, for it is that way, and it will be that way. And we here in Hreptyoff and the commands farther on in Mohiloff, in Yampol, in Rashkoff, — what else are we doing? There is a world of wickedness in our Commonwealth; but still I think that God will account to us for this service sometime, and perhaps men too will account to us.

"But now I will return to what happened to me. The captives who live on land, in towns and villages, groan in less suffering than those who row in galleys. For the galley-slaves when once riveted on the bench near the oars are never unriveted, day or night, or festival; they must live there in chains till they die; and if the vessel goes down in a battle, they must go with it. They are all naked; the cold freezes them; the rain wets them; hunger pinches them; and for that there is no help but tears and terrible toil, for the oars are so heavy and large that two men are needed at one of them.

"They brought me in the night and riveted my chains, having put me in front of some comrade in misery whom in the darkness I could not distinguish. When I heard that beating of the hammer and the sound of the fetters, dear God! it seemed to me that they were driving the nails of my coffin; I would have preferred even that. I prayed, but hope in my heart was as if the wind had blown it away. A kavadji stifled my groans with blows; I sat there in silence all night, till day began to break. I looked then on him who was to work the same oar with me. O dear Jesus Christ! can you guess who was in front of me, gentlemen? Didyuk!

"I knew him at once, though he was naked, had grown thin, and the beard had come down to his waist, — for he had been sold long before to the galleys. I gazed on him, and he on me; he recognized me. We said not a word to each other. See what had come to us! Still, there was such rancor in both that not only did we not greet each other, but hatred burst up like a flame in us, and delight seized the heart of each that his enemy had to suffer the same things as he. That very day the galley moved on its voyage. It was strange to hold one oar with your bitterest enemy, to eat from one dish with him food which at home with us dogs would not eat, to endure the same tyranny, to breathe the same air, to suffer together, to weep face to face. We sailed through the Hellespont, and then the Archipelago. Island after island is there, and all in the power of the Turk. Both shores also, — a whole world! Oh, how we suffered! In the day, heat indescribable. The sun burned with such force that the waters seemed to flame from it; and when those flames began to quiver and dance on the waves, you would have said that a fiery rain was falling. Sweat poured from us, and our tongues cleaved to the roofs of our mouths. At night the cold bit us like a dog. Solace from no place; nothing but suffering, sorrow for lost happiness, torment and pain. Words cannot tell it. At one station in the Grecian land we saw from the galley famous ruins of a temple which the Greeks reared in old times. Column stands there by column; as if gold, that marble is yellow from age. All was seen clearly, for it was on a steep height, and the sky is like turquoise in Greece. Then we sailed on around the Morea. Day followed day, week followed week; Didyuk and I had not exchanged a word, for pride and rancor dwelt still in our hearts. But we began to break slowly under God's hand. From toil and change of air the sinful flesh was falling from our bones; wounds, given by the lash, were festering in the sun. In the night we prayed for death. When I dozed a little, I heard Didyuk say, 'O Christ, have mercy! Holy Most Pure, have mercy! Let me die.' He also heard and saw how I stretched forth my hands to the Mother of God and her Child. And here it was as if the sea had blown hatred from the heart. There was less of it, and then less. At last, when I had wept over myself, I wept over him. We looked on each other then differently. Nay! we began to help each other. When sweating and deathly weariness came on me, he rowed alone; when he

was in a similar state, I did the same for him. When they
brought a plate of food, each one considered that the other
ought to have it. But, gentlemen, see what the nature of
man is! Speaking plainly, we loved each other already,
but neither wished to say the word first. The rogue was in
him, the Ukraine spirit! We changed only when it had
become terribly hard for us and grievous, and we said
to-day, 'to-morrow we shall meet the Venetian fleet —'
Provisions too were scarce, and they spared everything on
us but the lash. Night came; we were groaning in quiet,
and he in his way, I in mine, were praying still more
earnestly. I looked by the light of the moon; tears were
flowing down his beard in a torrent. My heart rose, and I
said, 'Didyuk, we are from the same parts; let us forgive
each other our offences.' When he heard this, dear God!
didn't the man sob, and pull till his chains rattled! We
fell into each other's arms over the oar, kissing each other
and weeping. I cannot tell you how long we held each
other, for we forgot ourselves, but we were trembling
from sobs."

Here Pan Mushalski stopped, and began to remove something from around his eyes with his fingers. A moment of
silence followed; but the cold north wind whistled from
between the beams, and in the room the fire hissed and the
crickets chirped. Then Pan Mushalski panted, drew a
deep breath, and continued: —

"The Lord God, as will appear, blessed us and showed
us His favor; but at the time we paid bitterly for our
brotherly feeling. While we were embracing, we entangled
the chains so that we could not untangle them. The overseers came and extricated us, but the lash whistled above
us for more than an hour. They beat us without looking
where. Blood flowed from me, flowed also from Didyuk;
the two bloods mingled and went in one stream to the sea.
But that is nothing! it is an old story — to the glory of
God!

"From that time it did not come to my head that I was
descended from the Samnites, and Didyuk a peasant from
Byalotserkov, recently ennobled. I could not have loved my
own brother more than I loved him. Even if he had not
been ennobled, it would have been one to me, — though I
preferred that he should be a noble. And he, in old fashion,
as once he had returned hatred with interest, now returned
love. Such was his nature.

"There was a battle on the following day. The Venetians scattered to the four winds the Turkish fleet. Our galley, shattered terribly by a culverin, took refuge at some small desert island, simply a rock sticking out of the sea. It was necessary to repair it; and since the soldiers had perished, and hands were lacking, the officers were forced to unchain us and give us axes. The moment we landed I glanced at Didyuk; but the same thing was in his head that was in mine. 'Shall it be at once?' inquired he of me. 'At once!' said I; and without thinking further, I struck the chubachy on the head; and Didyuk struck the captain. After us others rose like a flame! In an hour we had finished the Turks; then we repaired the galley somehow, took our seats in it without chains, and the Merciful God commanded the winds to blow us to Venice.

"We reached the Commonwealth on begged bread. I divided my estate at Yaslo with Didyuk, and we both took the field again to pay for our tears and our blood. At the time of Podhaytse Didyuk went through the Saitch to join Sirka, and with him to the Crimea. What they did there and what a diversion they made, you, gentlemen, know.

"On his way home Didyuk, sated with vengeance, was killed by an arrow. I was left; and as often as I stretch a bow, I do it for him, and there are not wanting in this honorable company witnesses to testify that I have delighted his soul in that way more than once."

Here Pan Mushalski was silent, and again nothing was to be heard but the whistling of the north wind and the crackling of the fire. The old warrior fixed his glance on the flaming logs, and after a long silence concluded as follows: —

"Nalevaiko and Loboda have been; Hmelnitski has been; and now Doroshenko has come. The earth is not dried of blood; we are wrangling and fighting, and still God has sown in our hearts some seeds of love, and they lie in barren ground, as it were, till under the oppression and under the chain of the Pagan, till from Tartar captivity, they give fruit unexpectedly."

"Trash is trash!" said Zagloba, waking up suddenly.

CHAPTER XXV.

MELLEHOVICH was regaining health slowly; but because he had taken no part in expeditions and was sitting confined to his room, no one was thinking of the man. All at once an incident turned the attention of all to him.

Pan Motovidlo's Cossacks seized a Tartar lurking near the stanitsa in a certain strange manner, and brought him to Hreptyoff. After a strict examination it came out that he was a Lithuanian Tartar, but of those who, deserting their service and residence in the Commonwealth, had gone under the power of the Sultan. He came from beyond the Dniester, and had a letter from Krychinski to Mellehovich.

Pan Michael was greatly disturbed at this, and called the officers to council immediately. "Gracious gentlemen," said he, "you know well how many Tartars, even of those who have lived for years immemorial in Lithuania and here in Russia, have gone over recently to the horde, repaying the Commonwealth for its kindness with treason. Therefore we should not trust any one of them too much, and should follow their acts with watchful eye. We have here too a small Tartar squadron, numbering one hundred and fifty good horse, led by Mellehovich. I do not know this Mellehovich from of old; I know only this, that the hetman has made him captain for eminent services, and sent him here with his men. It was a wonder to me, too, that no one of you gentlemen knew him before his entrance into service, or heard of him. This fact, that our Tartars love him greatly and obey him blindly, I explained by his bravery and famous deeds; but even they do not know whence he is, nor who he is. Relying on the recommendation of the hetman, I have not suspected him of anything hitherto, nor have I examined him, though he shrouds himself in a certain secrecy. People have various fancies; and this is nothing to me, if each man performs his own duty. But, you see, Pan Motovidlo's men have captured a Tartar who was bringing a letter from Krychinski to Mellehovich; and I do not know whether you are aware, gentlemen, who Krychinski is?"

"Of course!" said Pan Nyenashinyets. "I know Krychinski personally, and all know him now from his evil fame."

"We were at school together —" began Pan Zagloba; but he stopped suddenly, remembering that in such an event Krychinski must be ninety years old, and at that age men were not usually fighting.

"Speaking briefly," continued the little knight, "Krychinski is a Polish Tartar. He was a colonel of one of our Tartar squadrons; then he betrayed his country and went over to the Dobrudja horde, where he has, as I hear, great significance, for there they hope evidently that he will bring over the rest of the Tartars to the Pagan side. With such a man Mellehovich has entered into relations, the best proof of which is this letter, the tenor of which is as follows." Here the little knight unfolded the letter, struck the top of it with his hand, and began to read : —

BROTHER GREATLY BELOVED OF MY SOUL, — Your messenger came to us and delivered —

"He writes Polish?" interrupted Zagloba.

"Krychinski, like all our Tartars, knows only Russian and Polish," said the little knight; "and Mellehovich also will surely not gnaw in Tartar. Listen, gentlemen, without interruption."

—and delivered your letter. May God bring about that all will be well, and that you will accomplish what you desire! We take counsel here often with Moravski, Aleksandrovich, Tarasovski, and Groholski, and write to other brothers, taking their advice too, touching the means through which that which you desire may come to pass most quickly. News came to us of how you suffered loss of health; therefore I send a man to see you with his eyes and bring us consolation. Maintain the secret carefully, for God forbid that it should be known prematurely! May God make your race as numerous as stars in the sky!

KRYCHINSKI.

Volodyovski finished, and began to cast his eyes around on those present; and since they kept unbroken silence, evidently weighing the gist of the letter with care, he said: "Tarasovski, Moravski, Groholski, and Aleksandrovich are all former Tartar captains, and traitors."

"So are Poturzynski, Tvorovski, and Adurovich," added Pan Snitko. "Gentlemen, what do you say of this letter?"

"Open treason! there is nothing here upon which to deliberate," said Pan Mushalski. "He is simply conspiring with Mellehovich to take our Tartars over to their side."

"For God's sake! what a danger to our command!" cried a number of voices. "Our Tartars too would give their souls for Mellehovich; and if he orders them, they will attack us in the night."

"The blackest treason under the sun!" cried Pan Deyma.

"And the hetman himself made that Mellehovich a captain!" said Pan Mushalski.

"Pan Snitko," said Zagloba, "what did I say when I looked at Mellehovich? Did I not tell you that a renegade and a traitor were looking with the eyes of that man? Ha! it was enough for me to glance at him. He might deceive all others, but not me. Repeat my words, Pan Snitko, but do not change them. Did I not say that he was a traitor?"

Pan Snitko thrust his feet back under the bench and bent his head forward, "In truth, the penetration of your grace is to be wondered at; but what is true, is true. I do not remember that your grace called him a traitor. Your grace said only that he looked out of his eyes like a wolf."

"Ha! then you maintain that a dog is a traitor, and a wolf is not a traitor; that a wolf does not bite the hand which fondles him and gives him to eat? Then a dog is a traitor? Perhaps you will defend Mellehovich yet, and make traitors of all the rest of us?"

Confused in this manner, Pan Snitko opened his eyes and mouth widely, and was so astonished that he could not utter a word for some time.

Meanwhile Pan Mushalski, who formed opinions quickly, said at once, "First of all, we should thank the Lord God for discovering such infamous intrigues, and then send six dragoons with Mellehovich to put a bullet in his head."

"And appoint another captain," added Nyenashinyets. "The reason is so evident that there can be no mistake."

To which Pan Michael added: "First, it is necessary to examine Mellehovich, and then to inform the hetman of these intrigues, for as Pan Bogush from Zyembitse told me, the Lithuanian Tartars are very dear to the marshal of the kingdom."

"But, your grace," said Pan Motovidlo, "a general inquiry will be a favor to Mellehovich, since he has never before been an officer."

"I know my authority," said Volodyovski, "and you need not remind me of it."

Then the others began to exclaim, "Let such a son stand before our eyes, that traitor, that betrayer!"

The loud calls roused Zagloba, who had been dozing somewhat; this happened to him now continually. He recalled quickly the subject of the conversation and said: "No, Pan Snitko; the moon is hidden in your escutcheon, but your wit is hidden still better, for no one could find it with a candle. To say that a dog, a faithful dog, is a traitor, and a wolf is not a traitor! Permit me, you have used up your wit altogether."

Pan Snitko raised his eyes to heaven to show how he was suffering innocently, but he did not wish to offend the old man by contradiction; besides, Volodyovski commanded him to go for Mellehovich; he went out, therefore, in haste, glad to escape in that way. He returned soon, conducting the young Tartar, who evidently knew nothing yet of the seizure of Krychinski's messenger. His dark and handsome face had become very pale, but he was in health and did not even bind his head with a kerchief; he merely covered it with a Crimean cap of red velvet. The eyes of all were as intent on him as on a rainbow; he inclined to the little knight rather profoundly, and then to the company rather haughtily.

"Mellehovich!" said Volodyovski, fixing on the Tartar his quick glance, "do you know Colonel Krychinski?"

A sudden and threatening shadow flew over the face of Mellehovich. "I know him!"

"Read," said the little knight, giving him the letter found on the messenger.

Mellehovich began to read; but before he had finished, calmness returned to his face. "I await your order," said he, returning the letter.

"How long have you been plotting treason, and what confederates have you?"

"Am I accused, then, of treason?"

"Answer; do not inquire," said the little knight, threateningly.

"Then I will give this answer: I have plotted no treason; I have no confederates; or if I have, gentlemen, they are men whom you will not judge."

Hearing this, the officers gritted their teeth, and straightway a number of threatening voices called, "More submissively, dog's son, more submissively! .You are standing before your betters!"

Thereupon. Mellehovich surveyed them with a glance in which cold hatred was glittering. "I am aware of what I owe to the commandant, as my chief," said he, bowing a second time to Volodyovski. "I know that I am held inferior by you, gentlemen, and I do not seek your society. Your grace" (here he turned to the little knight) "has asked me of confederates; I have two in my work: one is Pan Bogush, under-stolnik of Novgrod, and the other is the grand hetman of the kingdom."

When they heard these words, all were astonished greatly, and for a time there was silence; at last Pan Michael inquired, "In what way?"

"In this way," answered Mellehovich; "Krychinski, Moravski, Tvorovski, Aleksandrovich, and all the others went to the horde and have done much harm to the country; but they did not find fortune in their new service. Perhaps too their consciences are moved; it is enough that the title of traitor is bitter to them. The hetman is well aware of this, and has commissioned Pan Bogush, and also Pan Myslishevski, to bring them back to the banner of the Commonwealth. Pan Bogush has employed me in this mission, and commanded me to come to an agreement with Krychinski. I have at my quarters letters from Pan Bogush which your grace will believe more quickly than my words."

"Go with Pan Snitko for those letters and bring them at once."

Mellehovich went out.

"Gracious gentlemen," said the little knight, quickly, "we have offended this soldier greatly through over-hasty judgment; for if he has those letters, he tells the truth, and I begin to think that he has them. Then he is not only a cavalier famous through military exploits, but a man sensitive to the good of the country, and reward, not unjust judgments, should meet him for that. As God lives! this must be corrected at once."

The others were sunk in silence, not knowing what to say; but Zagloba closed his eyes, feigning sleep this time.

Meanwhile Mellehovich returned and gave the little knight Bogush's letter. Volodyovski read as follows:—

"I hear from all sides that there is no one more fitted than you for such a service, and this by reason of the wonderful love which those men bear to you. The hetman is ready to forgive them, and promises forgiveness from the Commonwealth. Communicate with Krychinski as frequently as possible through reliable people, and promise him a reward. Guard the secret carefully, for if not, as God lives, you would destroy them all. You may divulge the affair to Pan Volodyovski, for your chief can aid you greatly. Do not spare toil and effort, seeing that the end crowns the work, and be certain that our mother will reward your good-will with love equal to it."

"Behold my reward!" muttered the young Tartar, gloomily.

"By the dear God! why did you not mention a word of this to any one?" cried Pan Michael.

"I wished to tell all to your grace, but I had no opportunity, for I was ill after that accident. Before their graces" (here Mellehovich turned to the officers) "I had a secret which I was prohibited from telling; this prohibition your grace will certainly enjoin on them now, so as not to ruin those other men."

"The proofs of your virtue are so evident that a blind man could not deny them," said the little knight. "Continue the affair with Krychinski. You will have no hindrance in this, but aid, in proof of which I give you my hand as to an honorable cavalier. Come to sup with me this evening."

Mellehovich pressed the hand extended to him, and inclined for the third time. From the corners of the room other officers moved toward him, saying, "We did not know you; but whoso loves virtue will not withdraw his hand from you to-day."

But the young Tartar straightened himself suddenly, pushed his head back like a bird of prey ready to strike, and said, "I am standing before my betters." Then he went out of the room.

It was noisy after his exit. "It is not to be wondered at," said the officers among themselves; "his heart is indignant yet at the injustice, but that will pass. We must treat him differently. He has real knightly mettle in him. The hetman knew what he was doing. Miracles are happening; well, well!"

Pan Snitko was triumphing in silence; at last he could not restrain himself and said, "Permit me, your grace, but that wolf was not a traitor."

"Not a traitor?" retorted Zagloba. "He was a traitor, but a virtuous one, for he betrayed not us, but the horde. Do not lose hope, Pan Snitko; I will pray to-day for your wit, and perhaps the Holy Ghost will have mercy."

Basia was greatly comforted when Zagloba related the whole affair to her, for she had good-will and compassion for Mellehovich. "Michael and I must go," said she, "on the first dangerous expedition with him, for in this way we shall show our confidence most thoroughly."

But the little knight began to stroke Basia's rosy face and said, "O suffering fly, I know you! With you it is not a question of Mellehovich, but you would like to buzz off to the steppe and engage in a battle. Nothing will come of that!"

"Mulier insidiosa est (woman is insidious)!" said Zagloba, with gravity.

At this time Mellehovich was sitting in his own room with the Tartar messenger and speaking in a whisper. The two sat so near each other that they were almost forehead to forehead. A taper of mutton-tallow was burning on the table, casting yellow light on the face of Mellehovich, which, in spite of its beauty, was simply terrible; there were depicted on it hatred, cruelty, and a savage delight.

"Halim, listen!" whispered Mellehovich.

"Effendi," answered the messenger.

"Tell Krychinski that he is wise, for in the letter there was nothing that could harm me; tell him that he is wise. Let him never write more clearly. They will trust me now still more, all of them, the hetman himself, Bogush, Myslishevski, the command here, — all! Do you hear? May the plague stifle them!"

"I hear, Effendi."

"But I must be in Rashkoff first, and then I will return to this place."

"Effendi, young Novoveski will recognize you."

"He will not. He saw me at Kalnik, at Bratslav, and did not know me. He will look at me, wrinkle his brows, but will not recognize me. He was fifteen years old when I ran away from the house. Eight times has winter covered the steppes since that hour. I have changed. The old man would know me, but the young one will not know me. I will notify you from Rashkoff. Let Krychinski be ready, and hold himself in the neighborhood. You must have an understanding with the perkulabs. In Yampol, also, is our squadron. I will persuade Bogush to get an order from the hetman for me, that it will be easier for me to act on Krychinski from that place. But I must return hither, — I must! I do not know what will happen, how I shall manage. Fire burns me; in the night sleep flies from me. Had it not been for her, I should have died."

Mellehovich's lips began to quiver; and bending still again to the messenger, he whispered, as if in a fever, "Halim, blessed be her hands, blessed her head, blessed the earth on which she walks! Do you hear, Halim? Tell them there that through her I am well."

CHAPTER XXVI.

FATHER KAMINSKI had been a soldier in his youthful years and a cavalier of great courage; he was now stationed at Ushytsa and was reorganizing a parish. But as the church was in ruins, and parishioners were lacking, this pastor without a flock visited Hreptyoff, and remained there whole weeks, edifying the knights with pious instruction. He listened with attention to the narrative of Pan Mushalski, and spoke to the assembly a few evenings later as follows:—

"I have always loved to hear narratives in which sad adventures find a happy ending, for from them it is evident that whomever God's hand guides, it can free from the toils of the pursuer and lead even from the Crimea to a peaceful roof. Therefore let each one of you fix this in his mind: For the Lord there is nothing impossible, and let no one of you even in direst necessity lose trust in God's mercy. This is the truth!

"It was praiseworthy in Pan Mushalski to love a common man with brotherly affection. The Saviour Himself gave us an example when He, though of royal blood, loved common people and made many of them apostles and helped them to promotion, so that now they have seats in the heavenly senate.

"But personal love is one thing, and general love — that of one nation to another — is something different. The love which is general, our Lord, the Redeemer, observed no less earnestly than the other. And where do we find this love? When, O man, you look through the world, there is such hatred in hearts everywhere, as if people were obeying the commands of the Devil and not of the Lord."

"It will be hard, your grace," said Zagloba, "to persuade us to love Turks, Tartars, or other barbarians whom the Lord God Himself must despise thoroughly."

"I am not persuading you to that, but I maintain this: that children of the same mother should have love for one another; but what do we see? From the days of Hmelnitski, or for thirty years, no part of these regions is dried from blood."

"But whose fault is it?"

"Whoso will confess his fault first, him will God pardon."

"Your grace is wearing the robes of a priest to-day; but in youth you slew rebels, as we have heard, not at all worse than others."

"I slew them, for it was my duty as a soldier to do so; that was not my sin, but this, that I hated them as a pestilence. I had private reasons which I will not mention, for those are old times and the wounds are healed now. I repent that I acted beyond my duty. I had under my command one hundred men from the squadron of Pan Nyevodovski; and going often independently with my men, I burned, slaughtered, and hanged. You, gentlemen, know what times those were. The Tartars, called in by Hmelnitski, burned and slew; we burned and slew; the Cossacks left only land and water behind them in all places, committing atrocities worse than ours and the Tartars. There is nothing more terrible than civil war! What times those were no man will ever describe; enough that we and they fought more like mad dogs than men.

"Once news was sent to our command that ruffians had besieged Pan Rushitski in his fortalice. I was sent with my troops to the rescue. I came too late; the place was level with the ground. But I fell upon the drunken peasants and cut them down notably; only a part hid in the grain. I gave command to take these alive, to hang them for an example. But where? It was easier to plan than to execute; in the whole village there was not one tree remaining; even the pear-trees standing on the boundaries between fields were cut down. I had no time to make gibbets; a forest too, as that was a steppe-land, was nowhere in view. What could I do? I took my prisoners and marched on. 'I shall find a forked oak somewhere,' thought I. I went a mile, two miles, — steppe and steppe; you might roll a ball over it. At last we found traces of a village; that was toward evening. I gazed around; here and there a pile of coals, and besides gray ashes, nothing more. On a small hillside there was a cross, a firm oak one, evidently not long made, for the wood was not dark yet and glittered in the twilight as if it were afire. Christ was on it, cut out of tin plate and painted in such a way that only when you came from one side and saw the thinness of the plate could you know that not a real statue was hanging there; but in front the face was as if living, somewhat pale from pain; on the head a crown of thorns; the eyes were turned upward with wonderful sadness and pity. When I saw that cross, the thought flashed into my mind, 'There is a tree for you; there is no other,' but straightway I was afraid. In the name of the Father and the Son! I will not hang them on the cross. But I thought that I should comfort the eyes of Christ if I gave command in His presence to kill those who had spilled so much innocent blood, and I spoke thus: 'O dear Lord, let it seem to Thee that these men are those Jews who nailed Thee to the cross, for these are not better than those.' Then I commanded my men to drag the prisoners one by one to the mound under the cross. There were among them old men, gray-haired peasants, and youths. The first whom they brought said, 'By the Passion of the Lord, by that Christ, have mercy on me!' And I said in answer, 'Off with his head!' A dragoon slashed and cut off his head. They brought another; the same thing happened: 'By that Merciful Christ, have pity on me!' And I said again, 'Off with his head!' the same with the third, the fourth, the fifth; there were fourteen of them, and each implored me by Christ. Twilight was ended when we finished. I gave command to place them in a circle around the foot of the cross. Fool! I thought to delight the Only Son with this spectacle. They quivered awhile yet, — one with his hands, another with his feet, again one floundered like a fish pulled out of water, but that was short; strength soon left their bodies, and they lay quiet in a circle.

"Since complete darkness had come, I determined to stay in that spot for the night, though there was nothing to make a fire. God gave a warm night, and my men lay down on horse-blankets; but I went again under the cross to repeat the usual 'Our Father' at the feet of Christ and commit myself to His mercy. I thought that my prayer would be the more thankfully accepted, because the day had passed in toil and in deeds of a kind that I accounted to myself as a service.

"It happens frequently to a wearied soldier to fall asleep at his evening prayers. It happened so to me. The dragoons, seeing how I was kneeling with head resting on the cross, understood that I was sunk in pious meditation, and no one wished to interrupt me; my eyes closed at once, and a wonderful dream came down to me from that cross. I do not say that I had a vision, for I was not and am not worthy of that; but sleeping soundly, I saw as if I had been awake the whole Passion of the Lord. At sight of the suffering of the Innocent Lamb the heart was crushed in me, tears dropped from my eyes, and measureless pity took hold of me. 'O·Lord,' said I, 'I have a handful of good men. Dost Thou wish to see what our cavalry can do? Only beckon with Thy head, and I will bear apart on sabres in one twinkle those such sons, Thy executioners.' I had barely said this when all vanished from the eye; there remained only the cross, and on it Christ, weeping tears of blood. I embraced the foot of the holy tree then, and sobbed. How long this lasted, I know not; but afterward, when I had grown calm somewhat, I said again, 'O Lord, O Lord! why didst Thou announce Thy holy teaching among hardened Jews? Hadst Thou come from Palestine to our Commonwealth, surely we should not have nailed Thee to the cross, but would have received Thee splendidly, given Thee all manner of gifts, and made Thee a noble for the greater increase of Thy divine glory. Why didst Thou not do this, O Lord?'

"I raise my eyes, — this was all in a dream, you remember, gentlemen, — and what do I see? Behold, our Lord looks on me severely; He frowns, and suddenly speaks in a loud voice: 'Cheap is your nobility at this time; during war every low fellow may buy it, but no more of this! You are worthy of each other, both you and the ruffians; and each and the other of you are worse than the Jews, for you nail me here to the cross every day. Have I not enjoined love, even for enemies, and forgiveness of sins? But you tear each other's entrails like mad beasts. Wherefore I, seeing this, suffer unendurable torment. You yourself, who wish to rescue me, and invite me to the Commonwealth, what have you done? See, corpses are lying here around my cross, and you have bespattered the foot of it with blood; and still there were among them innocent persons, — young boys, or blinded men, who, having care from no one, followed others like foolish sheep. Had you mercy on them; did you judge them before death? No! You gave command to slay them all for my sake, and still thought that you were giving comfort to me. In truth, it is one thing to punish and reprove as a father punishes a son, or as an elder brother reproves a younger brother, and another to seek revenge without judgment, without measure, in punishing and without recognizing cruelty. It has gone so far in this land that wolves are more merciful than men; that the grass is sweating bloody dew; that the winds do not blow, but howl; that the rivers flow in tears, and people stretch forth their hands to death, saying, "Oh, our refuge!"'

"'O Lord,' cried I, 'are they better than we? Who has committed the greatest cruelty? Who brought in the Pagan?'

"'Love them while chastising,' said the Lord, 'and then the beam will fall from their eyes, hardness will leave their hearts, and my mercy will be upon you. Otherwise the on-rush of Tartars will come, and they will lay bonds upon you and upon them, and you will be forced to serve the enemy in suffering, in contempt, in tears, till the day in which you love one another. But if you exceed the measure in hatred, then there will not be mercy for one or the other, and the Pagan will possess this land for the ages of ages.'

"I grew terrified hearing such commands, and long I was unable to speak till, throwing myself on my face, I asked, 'O Lord, what have I to do to wash away my sins?' To this the Lord said, 'Go, repeat my words; proclaim love.' After that my dream ended.

"As night in summer is short, I woke up about dawn, all covered with dew. I looked; the heads were lying in a circle about the cross, but already they were blue. A won- derful thing, — yesterday that sight delighted me; to-day terror took hold of me, especially at sight of one youth, perhaps seventeen years of age, who was exceedingly beau- tiful. I ordered the soldiers to bury the bodies decently under that cross; from that day forth I was not the same man.

"At first I thought to myself, the dream is an illusion; but still it was thrust into my memory, and, as it were, took possession of my whole existence. I did not dare to suppose that the Lord Himself talked with me, for, as I have said, I did not feel myself worthy of that; but it might be that conscience, hidden in my soul in time of war, like a Tartar in the grass, spoke up suddenly, announcing God's will. I went to confession; the priest confirmed that supposition. 'It is,' said he, 'the evident will and forewarning of God; obey, or it will be ill with thee.'

"Thenceforth I began to proclaim love. But the officers laughed at me to my eyes. 'What!' said they, 'is this a priest to give us instruction? Is it little insult that these dog brothers have worked upon God? Are the churches that they have burned few in number; are the crosses that they have insulted not many ?   Are we to love them for this ? '   In one word, no one would listen to me.

"After Berestechko I put on these priestly robes so as to announce with greater weight the word and the will of God. For more than twenty years I have done this without rest. God is merciful; He will not punish me, because thus far my voice is a voice crying in the wilderness.

"Gracious gentlemen, love your enemies, punish them as a father, reprimand them as an elder brother, otherwise woe to them, but woe to you also, woe to the whole Commonwealth !

"Look around; what is the result of this war and the animosity of brother against brother ?   This land has become a desert; I have graves in Ushytsa instead of parishioners; churches, towns, and villages are in ruins; the Pagan power is rising and growing over us like a sea, which is ready to swallow even thee, O rock of Kamenyets."

Pan Nyenashinyets listened with great emotion to the speech of the priest, so that the sweat came out on his forehead; then he spoke thus, amid general silence : —

"That among Cossacks there are worthy cavaliers, a proof is here present in Pan Motovidlo, whom we all love and respect.   But when it comes to the general love, of which Father Kaminski has spoken so eloquently, I confess that I have lived in grievous sin hitherto, for that love was not in me, and I have not striven to gain it.   Now his grace has opened my eyes somewhat.   Without special favor from God I shall not find such love in my heart, because I bear there the memory of a cruel injustice, which I will relate to you briefly."

"Let us drink something warm," said Zagloba.

"Throw horn-beam on the fire," said Basia to the attendants.

And soon after the broad room was bright again with light, and before each of the knights an attendant placed a quart of heated beer.   All moistened their mustaches in it willingly; and when they had taken one and a second draught, Pan Nyenashinyets collected his voice again, and spoke as if a wagon were rumbling, —

"My mother when dying committed to my care a sister; Halshka was her name.   I had no wife nor children, therefore I loved that girl as the apple of my eye.   She was twenty years younger than I, and I had carried her in my arms. I looked on her simply as my own child. Later I went on a campaign, and the horde took her captive. When I came home I beat my head against the wall. My property had vanished in time of the invasion; but I sold what I had, put my last saddle on a horse, and went with Armenians to ransom my sister. I found her in Bagche-sarai. She was attached to the harem, not in the harem, for she was only twelve years of age then. I shall never forget the hour when I found thee, O Halshka. How thou didst embrace my neck! how thou didst kiss me in the eyes! But what! It turned out that the money I had brought was too little. The girl was beautiful. Yehu Aga, who carried her away, asked three times as much for her. I offered to give myself in addition, but that did not help. She was bought in the market before my eyes by Tugai Bey, that famous enemy of ours, who wished to keep her three years in his harem and then make her his wife. I returned, tearing my hair. On the road home I discovered that in a Tartar village by the sea one of Tugai Bey's wives was dwelling with his favorite son Azya. Tugai Bey had wives in all the towns and in many villages, so as to have everywhere a resting-place under his own roof. Hearing of this son, I thought that God would show me the last means of salvation for Halshka. At once I determined to bear away that son, and then exchange him for my sister; but I could not do this alone. It was necessary to assemble a band in the Ukraine, or the Wilderness, which was not easy, — first, because the name of Tugai Bey was terrible in all Russia, and secondly, he was helping the Cossacks against us. But not a few heroes were wandering through the steppes, — men looking to their own profit only and ready to go anywhere for plunder. I collected a notable party of those. What we passed through before our boats came out on the sea tongue cannot tell, for we had to hide before the Cossack commanders. But God blessed us. I stole Azya, and with him splendid booty. We returned to the Wilderness in safety. I wished to go thence to Kamenyets and commence negotiations with merchants of that place.

"I divided all the booty among my heroes, reserving for myself Tugai Bey's whelp alone; and since I had acted with such liberality, since I had suffered so many dangers with those men, had endured hunger with them, and risked my life for them, I thought that each one would spring into the fire for me, that I had won their hearts for the ages.

"I had reason to repent of that bitterly and soon. It had not come to my head that they tear their own ataman to pieces, to divide his plunder between themselves afterward; I forgot that among them there are no men of faith, virtue, gratitude, or conscience. Near Kamenyets the hope of a rich ransom for Azya tempted my followers. They fell on me in the night-time like wolves, throttled me with a rope, cut my body with knives, and at last, thinking me dead, threw me aside in the desert and fled with the boy.

"God sent me rescue and gave back my health; but my Halshka is gone forever. Maybe she is living there yet somewhere; maybe after the death of Tugai Bey another Pagan took her; maybe she has received the faith of Mohammed; maybe she has forgotten her brother; maybe her son will shed my blood sometime. That is my history."

Here Pan Nyenashinyets stopped speaking and looked on the ground gloomily.

"What streams of our blood and tears have flowed for these regions!" said Pan Mushalski.

"Thou shalt love thine enemies," put in Father Kaminski.

"And when you came to health did you not look for that whelp?" asked Zagloba.

"As I learned afterward," answered Pan Nyenashinyets, "another band fell on my robbers and cut them to pieces; they must have taken the child with the booty. I searched everywhere, but he vanished as a stone dropped into water."

"Maybe you met him afterward, but could not recognize him," said Basia.

"I do not know whether the child was as old as three years. I barely learned that his name was Azya. But I should have recognized him, for he had tattooed over each breast a fish in blue."

All at once Mellehovich, who had sat in silence hitherto, spoke with a strange voice from the corner of the room, "You would not have known him by the fish, for many Tartars bear the same sign, especially those who live near the water."

"Not true," answered the hoary Pan Hromyka; "after Berestechko we examined the carrion of Tugai Bey, — for it remained on the field; and I know that he had fish on his breast, and all the other slain Tartars had different marks."

"But I tell you that many wear fish."

"True; but they are of the devilish Tugai Bey stock."

Further conversation was stopped by the entrance of Pan Lelchyts, whom Pan Michael had sent on a reconnoissance that morning, and who had returned just then.

"Pan Commandant," said he in the door, "at Sirotski Brod, on the Moldavian side, there is some sort of band moving toward us."

"What kind of people are they?" asked Pan Michael.

"Robbers. There are a few Wallachians, a few Hungarians; most of them are men detached from the horde, altogether about two hundred in number."

"Those are the same of whom I have tidings that they are plundering on the Moldavian side," said Volodyovski. "The perkulab must have made it hot for them there, hence they are escaping toward us; but of the horde alone there will be about two hundred. They will cross in the night, and at daylight we shall intercept them. Pan Motovidlo and Mellehovich will be ready at midnight. Drive forward a small herd of bullocks to entice them, and now to your quarters."

The soldiers began to separate, but not all had left the room yet when Basia ran up to her husband, threw her arms around his neck, and began to whisper in his ear. He laughed, and shook his head repeatedly; evidently she was insisting, while pressing her arms around his neck with more vigor. Seeing this, Zagloba said, —

"Give her this pleasure once; if you do, I, old man, will clatter on with you."

CHAPTER XXVII.

INDEPENDENT detachments, occupied in robbery on both
banks of the Dniester, were made up of men of all nation-
alities inhabiting the neighboring countries. Runaway
Tartars from the Dobrudja and Belgrod hordes, wilder
still and braver than their Crimean brethren, always
preponderated in them; but there were not lacking
either Wallachians, Cossacks, Hungarians, Polish domestics
escaped from stanitsas on the banks of the Dniester. They
ravaged now on the Polish, now on the Moldavian side,
crossing and recrossing the boundary river, as they were
hunted by the perkulab's forces or by the commandants of
the Commonwealth. They had their almost inaccessible
hiding-places in ravines, forests, and caves. The main
object of their attacks was the herds of cattle and horses
belonging to the stanitsas; these herds did not leave the
steppes even in winter, seeking sustenance for themselves
under the snow. But, besides, the robbers attacked villages,
hamlets, settlements, smaller commands, Polish and even
Turkish merchants, intermediaries going with ransom to
the Crimea. These bands had their own order and their
leaders, but they joined forces rarely. It happened often
even that larger bands cut down smaller ones. They had
increased greatly everywhere in the Russian regions,
especially since the time of the Cossack wars, when
safety of every kind vanished in those parts. The bands
on the Dniester, reinforced by fugitives from the horde,
were peculiarly terrible. Some appeared numbering five
hundred. Their leaders took the title of "bey." They
ravaged the country in a manner thoroughly Tartar, and
more than once the commandants themselves did not know
whether they had to do with bandits or with advance
chambuls of the whole horde. Against mounted troops,
especially the cavalry of the Commonwealth, these bands
could not stand in the open field; but, caught in a trap,
they fought desperately, knowing well that if taken captive
the halter was waiting for them. Their arms were various.
Bows and guns were lacking them, which, however, were of
little use in night attacks. The greater part were armed

with daggers and Turkish yataghans, sling-shots, Tartar sabres, and with horse-skulls fastened to oak clubs with cords. This last weapon, in strong hands, did terrible service, for it smashed every sabre. Some had very long forks pointed with iron, some spears; these in sudden emergencies they used against cavalry.

The band which had halted at Sirotski Brod must have been numerous or must have been in extreme peril on the Moldavian side, since it had ventured to approach the command at Hreptyoff, in spite of the terror which the name alone of Pan Volodyovski roused in the robbers on both sides of the boundary. In fact, another party brought intelligence that it was composed of more than four hundred men, under the leadership of Azba Bey, a famous ravager, who for a number of years had filled the Polish and Moldavian banks with terror.

Pan Volodyovski was delighted when he knew with whom he had to do, and issued proper orders at once. Besides Mellehovich and Pan Motovidlo, the squadron of the starosta of Podolia went, and that of the under-stolnik of Premysl. They set out in the night, and, as it were, in different directions; for as fishermen who cast their nets widely, in order afterward to meet at one opening, so those squadrons, marching in a broad circle, were to meet at Sirotski Brod about dawn.

Basia assisted with beating heart at the departure of the troops, since this was to be her first expedition; and the heart rose in her at sight of those old wolves of the steppe. They went so quietly that in the fortalice itself it was possible not to hear them: the bridle-bits did not rattle; stirrup did not strike against stirrup, sabre against sabre; not a horse neighed. The night was calm and unusually bright. The full moon lighted clearly the heights of the stanitsa and the steppe, which was somewhat inclined toward every side; still, barely had a squadron left the stockade, barely had it glittered with silver sparks, which the moon marked on the sabres, when it had vanished from the eye like a flock of partridges into waves of grass. It seemed to Basia that they were sportsmen setting out on some hunt, which was to begin at daybreak, and were going therefore quietly and carefully, so as not to rouse the game too early. Hence great desire entered her heart to take part in that hunt.

Pan Michael did not oppose this, for Zagloba had inclined

him to consent. He knew besides that it was necessary to gratify Basia's wish sometime; he preferred therefore to do it at once, especially since the ravagers were not accustomed to bows and muskets. But they moved only three hours after the departure of the first squadrons, for Pan Michael had thus planned the whole affair. Pan Mushalski, with twenty of Linkhauz's dragoons and a sergeant, went with them, — all Mazovians, choice men, behind whose sabres the charming wife of the commandant was as safe as in her husband's room.

Basia herself, having to ride on a man's saddle, was dressed accordingly; she wore pearl-colored velvet trousers, very wide, looking like a petticoat, and thrust into yellow morocco boots; a gray overcoat lined with white Crimean sheep-skin and embroidered ornamentally at the seams; she carried a silver cartridge-box, of excellent work, a light Turkish sabre on a silk pendant, and pistols in her holsters. Her head was covered with a cap, having a crown of Venetian velvet, adorned with a heron-feather, and bound with a rim of lynx-skin; from under the cap looked forth a bright rosy face, almost childlike, and two eyes curious and gleaming like coals.

Thus equipped, and sitting on a chestnut pony, swift and gentle as a deer, she seemed a hetman's child, who, under guard of old warriors, was going to take the first lesson. They were astonished too at her figure. Pan Zagloba and Pan Mushalski nudged each other with their elbows, each kissing his hand from time to time, in sign of unusual homage for Basia; both of them, together with Pan Michael, allayed her fear as to their late departure.

"You do not know war," said the little knight, "and therefore reproach us with wishing to take you to the place when the battle is over. Some squadrons go directly; others must make a détour, so as to cut off the roads, and then they will join the others in silence, taking the enemy in a trap. We shall be there in time, and without us nothing will begin, for every hour is reckoned."

"But if the enemy takes alarm and escapes between the squadrons?"

"He is cunning and watchful, but such a war is no novelty to us."

"Trust in Michael," cried Zagloba; "for there is not a man of more practice than he. Their evil fate sent those bullock-drivers hither."

"In Lubni I was a youth," said Pan Michael; "and even then they committed such duties to me. Now, wishing to show you this spectacle, I have disposed everything with still greater care. The squadrons will appear before the enemy together, will shout together, and gallop against the robbers together, as if some one had cracked a whip."

"I! I!" piped Basia, with delight; and standing in the stirrups, she caught the little knight by the neck. "But may I gallop, too? What, Michael, what?" asked she, with sparkling eyes.

"Into the throng I will not let you go, for in the throng an accident is easy, not to mention this, — that your horse might stumble; but I have ordered to give rein to our horses immediately the band driven against us is scattered, and then you may cut down two or three men, and attack always on the left side, for in that way it will be awkward for the fugitive to strike across his horse at you, while you will have him under your hand."

"Ho! ho! never fear. You said yourself that I work with the sabre far better than Uncle Makovetski; let no one give me advice!"

"Remember to hold the bridle firmly," put in Zagloba. "They have their methods; and it may be that when you are chasing, the fugitive will turn his horse suddenly and stop, then before you can pass, he may strike you. A veteran never lets his horse out too much, but reins him in as he wishes."

"And never raise your sabre too high, lest you be exposed to a thrust," said Pan Mushalski.

"I shall be near her to guard against accident," said the little knight. "You see, in battle the whole difficulty is in this, that you must think of all things at once, — of your horse, of the enemy, of your bridle, the sabre, the blow, and the thrust, all at one time. For him who is trained this comes of itself; but at first even renowned fencers are frequently awkward, and any common fellow, if in practice, will unhorse a new man more skilled than himself. Therefore I will be at your side."

"But do not rescue me, and give command to the men that no one is to rescue me without need."

"Well, well! we shall see yet what your courage will be when it comes to a trial," answered the little knight, laughing.

"Or if you will not seize one of us by the skirts," finished Zagloba.

"We shall see!" said Basia, with indignation.

Thus conversing, they entered a place covered here and there with thicket. The hour was not far from daybreak, but it had become darker, for the moon had gone down. A light fog had begun to rise from the ground and conceal distant objects. In that light fog and gloom, the indistinct thickets at a distance took the forms of living creatures in the excited imagination of Basia. More than once it seemed to her that she saw men and horses clearly.

"Michael, what is that?" asked she, whispering, and pointing with her finger.

"Nothing; bushes."

"I thought it was horsemen. Shall we be there soon?"

"The affair will begin in something like an hour and a half."

"Ha!"

"Are you afraid?"

"No; but my heart beats with great desire. I, fear! Nothing and nothing! See, what hoar-frost lies there! It is visible in the dark."

In fact, they were riding along a strip of country on which the long dry stems of steppe-grass were covered with hoar-frost. Pan Michael looked and said, —

"Motovidlo has passed this way. He must be hidden not more than a couple of miles distant. It is dawning already!"

In fact, day was breaking. The gloom was decreasing. The sky and earth were becoming gray; the air was growing pale; the tops of the trees and the bushes were becoming covered, as it were, with silver. The farther clumps began to disclose themselves, as if some one were raising a curtain from before them one after another. Meanwhile from the next clump a horseman came out suddenly.

"From Pan Motovidlo?" asked Volodyovski, when the Cossack stopped right before them.

"Yes, your grace."

"What is to be heard?"

"They crossed Sirotski Brod, turned toward the bellowing of the bullocks, and went in the direction of Kalusik. They took the cattle, and are at Yurgove Polye."

"And where is Pan Motovidlo?"

"He has stopped near the hill, and Pan Mellehovich near Kalusik. Where the other squadrons are I know not."

"Well," said Volodyovski, "I know. Hurry to Pan

Motovidlo and carry the command to close in, and dispose
men singly as far as halfway from Pan Mellehovich.
Hurry!"

The Cossack bent in the saddle and shot forward, so
that the flanks of his horse quivered at once, and soon
he was out of sight. They rode on still more quietly,
still more cautiously. Meanwhile it had become clear
day. The haze which had risen from the earth about
dawn fell away altogether, and on the eastern side of the
sky appeared a long streak, bright and rosy, the rosiness
and light of which began to color the air on high land,
the edges of distant ravines, and the hill-tops. Then there
came to the ears of the horsemen a mingled croaking from
the direction of the Dniester; and high in the air before
them appeared, flying eastward, an immense flock of ravens.
Single birds separated every moment from the others, and
instead of flying forward directly began to describe circles,
as kites and falcons do when seeking for prey. Pan Zagloba
raised his sabre, pointing the tip of it to the ravens, and
said to Basia, —

"Admire the sense of these birds. Only let it come to a
battle in any place, straightway they will fly in from every
side, as if some one had shaken them from a bag. But let
the same army march alone, or go out to meet friends, the
birds will not come; thus are these creatures able to divine
the intentions of men, though no one assists them. The
wisdom of nostrils is not sufficient in this case, and so we
have reason to wonder."

Meanwhile the birds, croaking louder and louder, approached considerably; therefore Pan Mushalski turned to
the little knight and said, striking his palm on the bow,
"Pan Commandant, will it be forbidden to bring down one,
to please the lady? It will make no noise."

"Bring down even two," said Volodyovski, seeing how the
old soldier had the weakness of showing the certainty of
his arrows.

Thereupon the incomparable bowman, reaching behind his
shoulder, took out a feathered arrow, put it on the string,
and raising the bow and his head, waited.

The flock was drawing nearer and nearer. All reined in
their horses and looked with curiosity toward the sky. All
at once the plaintive wheeze of the string was heard, like
the twitter of a sparrow; and the arrow, rushing forth,
vanished near the flock. For a while it might be thought

that Mushalski had missed, but, behold, a bird reeled head downward, and was dropping straight toward the ground over their heads, then tumbling continually, approached nearer and nearer; at last it began to fall with outspread wings, like a leaf opposing the air. Soon it fell a few steps in front of Basia's pony. The arrow had gone through the raven, so that the point was gleaming above the bird's back.

"As a lucky omen," said Mushalski, bowing to Basia, "I will have an eye from a distance on the lady commandress and my great benefactress; and if there is a sudden emergency, God grant me again to send out a fortunate arrow. Though it may buzz near by, I assure you that it will not wound."

"I should not like to be the Tartar under your aim," answered Basia.

Further conversation was interrupted by Volodyovski, who said, pointing to a considerable eminence some furlongs away, "We will halt there."

After these words they moved forward at a trot. Halfway up, the little knight commanded them to lessen their pace, and at last, not far from the top, he held in his horse.

"We will not go to the very top," said he, "for on such a bright morning the eye might catch us from a distance; but dismounting, we will approach the summit, so that a few heads may look over."

When he had said this, he sprang from his horse, and after him Basia, Pan Mushalski, and a number of others. The dragoons remained below the summit, holding their horses; but the others pushed on to where the height descended in wall form, almost perpendicularly, to the valley. At the foot of this wall, which was a number of tens of yards in height, grew a somewhat dense, narrow strip of brushwood, and farther on extended a low level steppe; of this they were able to take in an enormous expanse with their eyes from the height. This plain, cut through by a small stream running in the direction of Kalusik, was covered with clumps of thicket in the same way that it was near the cliff. In the thickest clumps slender columns of smoke were rising to the sky.

"You see," said Pan Michael to Basia, "that the enemy is hidden there."

"I see smoke, but I see neither men nor horses," said Basia, with a beating heart.

" No ; for they are concealed by the thickets, though a
trained eye can see them. Look there : two, three, four, a
whole group of horses are to be seen, — one pied, another
all white, and from here one seems blue."

" Shall we go to them soon ? "

" They will be driven to us ; but we have time enough, for
to that thicket it is a mile and a quarter."

" Where are our men ? "

" Do you see the edge of the wood yonder ? The chamberlain's squadron must be touching that edge just now.
Mellehovich will come out of the other side in a moment.
The accompanying squadron will attack the robbers from
that cliff. Seeing people, they will move toward us, for
here it is possible to go to the river under the slope ; but on
the other side there is a ravine, terribly steep, through which
no one can go."

" Then they are in a trap ? "

" As you see."

" For God's sake ! I am barely able to stand still ! " cried
Basia ; but after a while she inquired, " Michael, if they
were wise, what would they do ? "

" They would rush, as if into smoke, at the men of the
chamberlain's squadron and go over their bellies. Then
they would be free. But they will not do that, for, first,
they do not like to rush into the eyes of regular cavalry ;
secondly, they will be afraid that more troops are waiting
in the forest ; therefore they will rush to us."

" Bah ! But we cannot resist them ; we have only twenty
men."

" But Motovidlo ? "

" True ! Ha ! but where is he ? "

Pan Michael, instead of an answer, cried suddenly, imitating a hawk. Straightway numerous calls answered him
from the foot of the cliff. These were Motovidlo's Cossacks, who were secreted so well in the thicket that Basia,
though standing right above their heads, had not seen them
at all. She looked for a while with astonishment, now
downward, now at the little knight ; suddenly her eyes
flashed with fire, and she seized her husband by the neck.

" Michael, you are the first leader on earth."

" I have a little training, that is all," answered Volodyovski, smiling. " But do not pat me here with delight, and
remember that a good soldier must be calm."

But the warning was useless ; Basia was as if in a fever.

She wished to sit straightway on her horse and ride down from the height to join Motovidlo's detachment; but Volodyovski delayed, for he wished her to see the beginning clearly. Meanwhile the morning sun had risen over the steppe and covered with a cold, pale yellow light the whole plain. The nearer clumps of trees were brightening cheerfully; the more distant and less distinct became more distinct; the hoar-frost, lying in the low places in spots, was disappearing every moment; the air had grown quite transparent, and the glance could extend to a distance almost without limit.

"The chamberlain's squadron is coming out of the grove," said Volodyovski; "I see men and horses."

In fact, horses began to emerge from the edge of the wood, and seemed black in a long line on the meadow, which was thickly covered with hoar-frost near the wood. The white space between them and the wood began to widen gradually. It was evident that they were not hurrying too much, wishing to give time to the other squadrons. Pan Michael turned then to the left side.

"Mellehovich is here too," said he. And after a while he said again, "And the men of the under-stolnik of Premysl are coming. No one is behind time two 'Our Fathers.' Not a foot should escape! Now to horse!"

They turned quickly to the dragoons, and springing into the saddles rode down along the flank of the height to the thicket below, where they found themselves among Motovidlo's Cossacks. Then they moved in a mass to the edge of the thicket, and halted, looking forward.

It was evident that the enemy had seen the squadron of the chamberlain, for at that moment crowds of horsemen rushed out of the grove growing in the middle of the plain, as deer rush when some one has roused them. Every moment more of them came out. Forming a line, they moved at first over the steppe by the edge of the grove; the horsemen bent to the backs of the horses, so that from a distance it might be supposed that that was merely a herd moving of itself along the grove. Clearly, they were not certain yet whether the squadron was moving against them, or even saw them, or whether it was a detachment examining the neighborhood. In the last event they might hope that the grove would hide them from the eyes of the on-coming party.

From the place where Pan Michael stood, at the head of

Motovidlo's men, the uncertain and hesitating movements of the chambul could be seen perfectly, and were just like the movements of wild beasts sniffing danger. When they had ridden half the width of the grove, they began to go at a light gallop. When the first ranks reached the open plain, they held in their beasts suddenly, and then the whole party did the same. They saw approaching from that side Mellehovich's detachment. Then they described a half-circle in the direction opposite the grove, and before their eyes appeared the whole Premysl squadron, moving at a trot.

Now it was clear to the robbers that all the squadrons knew of their presence and were marching against them. Wild cries were heard in the midst of the party, and disorder began. The squadrons, shouting also, advanced on a gallop, so that the plain was thundering from the tramp of their horses. Seeing this, the robber chambul extended in the form of a bench in the twinkle of an eye, and chased with what breath was in the breasts of their horses toward the elevation near which the little knight stood with Motovidlo and his men. The space between them began to decrease with astonishing rapidity.

Basia grew somewhat pale from emotion at first, and her heart thumped more powerfully in her breast; but knowing that people were looking at her, and not noticing the least alarm on any face, she controlled herself quickly. Then the crowd, approaching like a whirlwind, occupied all her attention. She tightened the rein, grasped her sabre more firmly, and the blood again flowed with great impulse from her heart to her face.

"Good!" said the little knight.

She looked only at him; her nostrils quivered, and she whispered, "Shall we move soon?"

"There is time yet," answered Pan Michael.

But the others are chasing on, like a gray wolf who feels dogs behind him. Now not more than half a furlong divides them from the thicket; the outstretched heads of the horses are to be seen, with ears lying down, and over them Tartar faces, as if grown to the mane. They are nearer and nearer. Basia hears the snorting of the horses; and they, with bared teeth and staring eyes, show that they are going at such speed that their breath is stopping. Volodyovski gives a sign, and the Cossack muskets, standing hedge-like, incline toward the onrushing robbers.

" Fire ! "

A roar, smoke : it was as if a whirlwind had struck a pile
of chaff.   In one twinkle of an eye the party flew apart in
every direction, howling and shouting.   With that the little
knight pushed out of the thicket, and at the same time
Mellehovich's squadron, and that of the chamberlain, closing
the circle, forced the scattered enemy to the centre again
in one group.   The horde seek in vain to escape singly ; in
vain they circle around ; they rush to the right, to the left,
to the front, to the rear ; the circle is closed up completely ;
the robbers come therefore more closely together in spite of
themselves.   Meanwhile the squadrons hurry up, and a
horrible smashing begins.

The ravagers understood that only he would escape with
his life who could batter his way through ; hence they fell
to defending themselves with rage and despair, though
without order and each for himself independently.   In the
very beginning they covered the field thickly, so great was
the fury of the shock.   The soldiers, pressing them and
urging their horses on in spite of the throng, hewed and
thrust with that merciless and terrible skill which only a
soldier by profession can have.   The noise of pounding was
heard above that circle of men, like the thumping of flails
wielded by a multitude quickly on a threshing-space.   The
horde were slashed and cut through their heads, shoulders,
necks, and through the hands with which they covered their
heads ; they were beaten on every side unceasingly, without quarter or pity.   They too struck, each with what he
had, with daggers, with sabres, with sling-shots, with horse-
skulls.   Their horses, pushed to the centre, rose on their
haunches, or fell on their backs.   Others, biting and whining,
kicked at the throng, causing confusion unspeakable.   After
a short struggle in silence, a howl was torn from the breasts
of the robbers ; superior numbers were bending them,
better weapons, greater skill.   They understood that there
was no rescue for them ; that no man would leave there,
not only with plunder, but with life.   The soldiers, warming up gradually, pounded them with growing force.   Some
of the robbers sprang from their saddles, wishing to slip
away between the legs of the horses.   These were trampled
with hoofs, and sometimes the soldiers turned from the
fight and pierced the fugitives from above ; some fell on
the ground, hoping that when the squadrons pushed toward
the centre, they, left beyond the circle, might escape by
flight.

In fact, the party decreased more and more, for every moment horses and men fell away. Seeing this, Azba Bey collected, as far as he was able, horses and men in a wedge, and threw himself with all his might on Motovidlo's Cossacks, wishing to break the ring at any cost. But they hurled him back, and then began a terrible slaughter. At that same time Mellehovich, raging like a flame, split the party, and leaving the halves to two other squadrons, sprang himself on the shoulders of those who were fighting with the Cossacks.

It is true that a part of the robbers escaped from the ring to the field through this movement and rushed apart over the plain, like a flock of leaves; but soldiers in the rear ranks who could not find access to the battle, through the narrowness of the combat, rushed after them straightway in twos and threes or singly. Those who were unable to break out went under the sword in spite of their passionate defence and fell near each other, like grain which harvesters are reaping from opposite sides.

Basia moved on with the Cossacks, piping with a thin voice to give herself courage, for at the first moment it grew a little dark in her eyes, both from the speed and the mighty excitement. When she rushed up to the enemy, she saw before her at first only a dark, moving, surging mass. An overpowering desire to close her eyes altogether was bearing her away. She resisted the desire, it is true; still she struck with her sabre somewhat at random. Soon her daring overcame her confusion; she had clear vision at once. In front she saw heads of horses, behind them inflamed and wild faces; one of these gleamed right there before her; Basia gave a sweeping cut, and the face vanished as quickly as if it had been a phantom. That moment the calm voice of her husband came to her ears.

"Good!"

That voice gave her uncommon pleasure; she piped again more thinly, and began to extend disaster, and now with perfect presence of mind. Behold, again some terrible head, with flat nose and projecting cheek-bones, is gnashing its teeth before her. Basia gives a blow at that one. Again a hand raises a sling-shot. Basia strikes at that. She sees some face in a sheepskin; she thrusts at that. Then she strikes to the right, to the left, straight ahead; and whenever she cuts, a man flies to the ground, tearing the bridle from his horse. Basia wonders that it is so easy; but it is

easy because on one side rides, stirrup to her stirrup, the
little knight, and on the other Pan Motovidlo. The first
looks carefully after her, and quenches a man as he would a
candle; then with his keen blade he cuts off an arm together
with its weapon; at times he thrusts his sword between
Basia and the enemy, and the hostile sabre flies upward as
suddenly as would a winged bird.

Pan Motovidlo, a phlegmatic soldier, guarded the other
side of the mettlesome lady; and as an industrious
gardener, going .among trees, trims or breaks off dry
branches, so he time after time brings down men to the
bloody earth, fighting as coolly and calmly as if his mind
were in another place. Both knew when to let Basia go
forward alone, and when to anticipate or intercept her.
There was watching over her from a distance still a third
man, — the incomparable archer, who, standing purposely at
a distance, put every little while the butt of an arrow on
the string, and sent an unerring messenger of death to the
densest throng.

But the pressure became so savage that Pan Michael
commanded Basia to withdraw from the whirl with some
men, especially as the half-wild horses of the horde began
to bite and kick. Basia obeyed quickly; for although eagerness was bearing her away, and her valiant heart urged her
to continue the struggle, her woman's nature was gaining
the upper hand of her ardor; and in presence of that
slaughter and blood, in the midst of howls, groans, and the
agonies of the dying, in an atmosphere filled with the odor
of flesh and sweat, she began to shudder. Withdrawing her
horse slowly, she soon found herself behind the circle of
combatants; hence Pan Michael and Pan Motovidlo, relieved
from guarding her, were able to give perfect freedom at last
to their soldierly wishes.

Pan Mushalski, standing hitherto at a distance, approached
Basia. "Your ladyship, my benefactress, fought really like
a cavalier," said he. "A man not knowing that you were
there might have thought that the Archangel Michael had
come down to help our Cossacks; and was smiting the dog
brothers. What an honor for them to perish under such a
hand, which on this occasion let it not be forbidden me to
kiss." So saying, Pan Mushalski seized Basia's hand and
pressed it to his mustache.

"Did you see? Did I do well, really?" inquired Basia,
catching the air in her distended nostrils and her mouth.

"A cat could not do better against rats. The heart rose in me at sight of you, as I love the Lord God. But you did well to withdraw from the fight, for toward the end there is more chance for an accident."

"My husband commanded me; and when leaving home, I promised to obey him at once."

"May my bow remain? No! it is of no use - now; besides, I will rush forward with the sabre. I see three men riding up; of course the colonel has sent them to guard your worthy person. Otherwise I would send; but I will go to the foot of the cliff, for the end will come soon, and I must hurry."

Three dragoons really came to guard Basia; seeing this, Pan Mushalski spurred his horse and galloped away. For a while Basia hesitated whether to remain in that place or ride around the steep cliff, and go to the eminence from which they had looked on the plain before the battle. But feeling great weariness, she resolved to remain.

The feminine nature rose in her more and more powerfully. About two hundred yards distant they were cutting down the remnant of the ravagers without mercy, and a black mass of strugglers was whirling with growing violence on the bloody place of conflict. Despairing cries rent the air; and Basia, so full of eagerness shortly before, had grown weak now in some way. Great fear seized her, so that she came near fainting, and only shame in presence of the dragoons kept her in the saddle; she turned her face from them to hide her pallor. The fresh air brought back her strength slowly and her courage, but not to that degree that she had the wish to spring in anew among the combatants. She would have done so to implore mercy for the rest of the horde. But knowing that that would be useless, she waited anxiously for the end of the struggle. And there they were cutting and cutting. The sound of the hacking and the cries did not cease for a moment. Half an hour perhaps had passed; the squadrons were closing in with greater force. All at once a party of ravagers, numbering about twenty, tore themselves free of the murderous circle, and rushed like a whirlwind toward the eminence.

Escaping along the cliff, they might in fact reach a place where the eminence was lost by degrees in the plain, and find on the high steppe their salvation; but in their way stood Basia with the dragoons. The sight of danger gave strength to Basia's heart at this moment, and self-control to

her mind. She understood that to stay where she was was
destruction; for the robbers with impetus alone could
overturn and trample her and her guards, not to mention
that they would bear them apart on sabres. The old
sergeant of dragoons was clearly of this view, for he seized
the bridle of Basia's pony, turned the beast, and cried with
voice almost desparing, —

" On, on ! serene lady ! "

Basia shot away like the wind; but the three faithful
soldiers stood like a wall on the spot, to hold back the
enemy even one moment, and give the beloved lady time to
put herself at a distance. Meanwhile soldiers galloped
after that band in immediate pursuit; but the circle hitherto
enclosing the ravagers hermetically was thereby broken;
they began to escape in twos, in threes, and then more
numerously. The enormous majority were lying on the
field, but some tens of them, together with Azba Bey, were
able to flee. All these rushed on in a body as fast as their
horses could gallop toward the eminence.

Three dragoons could not detain all the fugitives, — in fact,
after a short struggle they fell from their saddles; but the
cloud, running on behind Basia, turned to the slope of the
eminence and reached the high steppe. The Polish squadrons in the front ranks and the nearer Lithuanian Tartars
rushed with all speed some tens of steps behind them. On
the high steppe, which was cut across thickly by treacherous
clefts and ravines, was formed a gigantic serpent of those
on horseback, the head of which was Basia, the neck the
ravagers, and the continuation of the body Mellehovich
with the Lithuanian Tartars and dragoons, at the head of
which rushed Volodyovski, with his spurs in the side of his
horse, and terror in his soul.

At the moment when the handful of robbers had torn
themselves free of the ring, Volodyovski was engaged on
the opposite side of it; therefore Mellehovich preceded him
in the pursuit. The hair was standing on his head at the
thought that Basia might be seized by the fugitives; that
she might lose presence of mind, and rush straight toward
the Dniester; that any one of the robbers might reach her
with a sabre, a dagger, or a sling-shot, — and the heart was
sinking in him from fear for her life. Lying almost on the
neck of the horse, he was pale, with set teeth, a whirlwind
of ghastly thoughts in his head; he pricked his steed with
armed heels, struck him with the side of his sword, and
flew like a bustard before he rises to soar.

"God grant Mellehovich to come up! He is on a good horse. God grant him!" repeated he, in despair.

But his fears were ill founded, and the danger was not so great as it seemed to the loving knight. The question of their own skins was too near to the robbers; they felt the Lithuanian Tartars too close to their shoulders to pursue a single rider, even were that rider the most beautiful houri in the Mohammedan paradise, escaping in a robe set with jewels. Basia needed only to turn toward Hreptyoff to escape from pursuit; for surely the fugitives would not return to the jaws of the lion for her, while they had before them a river, with its reeds in which they could hide. The Lithuanian Tartars had better horses, and Basia was sitting on a pony incomparably swifter than the ordinary shaggy beasts of the horde, which were enduring in flight, but not so swift as horses of high blood. Besides, she not only did not lose presence of mind, but her daring nature asserted itself with all force, and knightly blood played again in her veins. The pony stretched out like a deer; the wind whistled in Basia's ears, and instead of fear, a certain feeling of delight seized her.

"They might hunt a whole year, and not catch me," thought she. "I'll rush on yet, and then turn, and either let them pass, or if they have not stopped pursuing, I will put them under the sabre."

It came to her mind that if the ravagers behind her were scattered greatly over the steppe, she might, on turning, meet one of them and have a hand-to-hand combat.

"Well, what is that?" said she to her valiant soul. "Michael has taught me so that I may venture boldly; if I do not, they will think that I am fleeing through fear, and will not take me on another expedition; and besides, Pan Zagloba will make sport of me."

Saying this to herself, she looked around at the robbers; but they were fleeing in a crowd. There was no possibility of single combat; but Basia wished to give proof before the eyes of the whole army that she was not fleeing at random and in frenzy. Remembering that she had in the holsters two excellent pistols carefully loaded by Michael himself before they set out, she began to rein in her pony, or rather to turn him toward Hreptyoff, while slacking his speed. But, oh, wonder! at sight of this the whole party of ravagers changed the direction of their flight somewhat, going more to the left, toward the edge of the eminence.

Basia, letting them come within a few tens of steps, fired twice at the nearest horses; then, turning, urged on at full gallop toward Hreptyoff.

But the pony had run barely some yards with the speed of a sparrow, when suddenly there darkened in front a cleft in the steppe. Basia pressed the pony with her spurs without hesitation, and the noble beast did not refuse, but sprang forward; only his fore feet caught somewhat the bank opposite. For a moment he strove violently to find support on the steep wall with his hind feet; but the earth, not sufficiently frozen yet, fell away, and the horse went down through the opening, with Basia. Fortunately the horse did not fall on her; she succeeded in freeing her feet from the stirrups, and, leaning to one side with all force, struck on a thick layer of moss, which covered the bottom of the chasm as if with a lining; but the shock was so violent that she fainted.

Pan Michael did not see the fall, for the horizon was concealed by the Lithuanian Tartars; but Mellehovich shouted with a terrible voice at his men to pursue the ravagers without stopping, and running himself to the cleft, disappeared in it. In a twinkle he was down from the saddle, and seized Basia in his arms. His falcon eyes saw her all in one moment, looking to see if there was blood anywhere; then they fell on the moss, and he understood that this had saved her and the pony from death. A stifled cry of joy was rent from the mouth of the young Tartar. But Basia was hanging in his arms; he pressed her with all his strength to his breast; then with pale lips he kissed her eyes time after time, as if wishing to drink them out of her head. The whole world whirled with him in a mad vortex; the passion concealed hitherto in the bottom of his breast, as a dragon lies concealed in a cave, carried him away like a storm.

But at that moment the tramp of many horses was heard in an echo from the lofty steppe, and approached more and more swiftly. Numerous voices were crying, "Here! in this cleft! Here!" Mellehovich placed Basia on the moss, and called to those riding up, —

"This way, this way!"

A moment later, Pan Michael was at the bottom of the cleft; after him Pan Zagloba, Mushalski, and a number of other officers.

"Nothing is the matter," cried the Tartar. "The moss saved her."

Pan Michael grasped his insensible wife by the hands; others ran for water, which was not near. Zagloba, seizing the temples of the unconscious woman, began to cry, —

"Basia, Basia, dearest! Basia!"

"Nothing is the matter with her," said Mellehovich, pale as a corpse.

Meanwhile Zagloba clapped his side, took a flask, poured gorailka on his palm, and began to rub her temples. Then he put the flask to her lips; this acted evidently, for before the men returned with water, she had opened her eyes and began to catch for air, coughing meanwhile, for the gorailka had burned the roof of her mouth and her throat. In a few moments she had recovered completely.

Pan Michael, not regarding the presence of officers and soldiers, pressed her to his bosom, and covered her hands with kisses, saying, "Oh, my love, the soul came near leaving me! Has nothing hurt? Does nothing pain you?"

"Nothing is the matter," said Basia. "Aha! I remember now that it grew dark in my eyes, for my horse slipped. But is the battle over?"

"It is. Azba Bey is killed. We will go home at once, for I am afraid that fatigue may overcome you."

"I feel no fatigue whatever." Then, looking quickly at those present, she distended her nostrils, and said, "But do not think, gentlemen, that I fled through fear. Oho! I did not even dream of it. As I love Michael, I galloped ahead of them only for sport, and then I fired my pistols."

"A horse was struck by those shots, and we took one robber alive," put in Mellehovich.

"And what?" asked Basia. "Such an accident may happen any one in galloping, is it not true? No experience will save one from that, for a horse will slip sometimes. Ha! it is well that you watched me, gentlemen, for I might have lain here a long time."

"Pan Mellehovich saw you first, and first saved you; for we were galloping behind him," said Volodyovski.

Basia, hearing this, turned to Mellehovich and reached her hand to him. "I thank you for good offices."

He made no answer, only pressed the hand to his mouth, and then embraced with submission her feet, like a peasant.

Meanwhile more of the squadron assembled at the edge of the cleft; Pan Michael simply gave orders to Mellehovich to form a circle around the few robbers who had hidden from pursuit, and then started for Hreptyoff. On the road Basia saw the field of battle once more from the height. The bodies of men and horses lay in places in piles, in places singly. Through the blue sky flocks of ravens were approaching more and more numerously, with great cawing, and coming down at a distance, waited till the soldiers, still going about on the plain, should depart.

"Here are the soldiers' gravediggers!" said Zagloba, pointing at the birds with his sabre; "let us only go away, and wolves will come too, with their orchestra, and will ring with their teeth over these dead men. This is a notable victory, though gained over such a vile enemy; for that Azba has ravaged here and there for a number of years. Commandants have hunted him like a wolf, always in vain, till at last he met Michael, and the black hour came on him."

"Is Azba Bey killed?"

"Mellehovich overtook him first; and I tell you if he did not cut him over the ear! The sabre went to his teeth."

"Mellehovich is a good soldier," said Basia. Here she turned to Zagloba, "And have you done much?"

"I did not chirp like a cricket, nor jump like a flea, for I leave such amusement to insects. But if I did not, men did not look for me among moss, like mushrooms; no one pulled my nose, and no one touched my face."

"I do not like you!" said Basia, pouting, and reaching involuntarily to her nose, which was red.

And he looked at her, smiled, and muttered, without ceasing to joke, "You fought valiantly, you fled valiantly, you went valiantly heels over head; and now, from pain in your bones, you will put away kasha so valiantly that we shall be forced to take care of you, lest the sparrows eat you up with your valor, for they are very fond of kasha."

"You are talking in that way so that Michael may not take me on another expedition. I know you perfectly!"

"But, but I will ask him to take you nutting always, for you are skilful, and do not break branches under you. My God, that is gratitude to me! And who persuaded Michael to let you go? I. I reproach myself now severely, especially since you pay me so for my devotion. Wait! you will cut stalks now on the square at Hreptyoff with a wooden sword! Here is an expedition for you! Another woman would hug the old man; but this scolding Satan frightens me first, and threatens me afterward."

Basia, without hesitating long, embraced Zagloba. He

was greatly delighted, and said, "Well, well! I must confess that you helped somewhat to the victory of to-day; for the soldiers, since each wished to exhibit himself, fought with terrible fury."

"As true as I live," cried Pan Mushalski, "a man is not sorry to die when such eyes are upon him."

"Vivat our lady!" cried Pan Nyenashinyets.

"Vivat!" cried a hundred voices.

"God give her health!"

Here Zagloba inclined toward her and muttered, "After faintness!"

And they rode forward joyously, shouting, certain of a feast in the evening. The weather became wonderful. The trumpeters played in the squadrons, the drummers beat their drums, and all entered Hreptyoff with an uproar.

CHAPTER XXVIII.

BEYOND every expectation, the Volodyovskis found guests
at the fortalice. Pan Bogush had come; he had determined
to fix his residence at Hreptyoff for some months, so as to
treat through Mellehovich with the Tartar captains Aleksandrovich, Moravski, Tvorovski, Krychinski, and others,
either of the Lithuanian or Ukraine Tartars, who had gone
to the service of the Sultan. Pan Bogush was accompanied
also by old Pan Novoveski and his daughter Eva, and by
Pani Boski, a sedate person, with her daughter, Panna
Zosia, who was young yet, and very beautiful. The sight of
ladies in the Wilderness and in wild Hreptyoff delighted,
but still more astonished, the soldiers. The guests, too, were
surprised at sight of the commandant and his wife; for
the first, judging from his extended and terrible fame, they
imagined to be some kind of giant, who by his very look
would terrify people, his wife as a giantess with brows
ever frowning and a rude voice. Meanwhile they saw
before them a little soldier, with a kindly and friendly face,
and also a tiny woman, rosy as a doll, who, in her broad
trousers and with her sabre, seemed more like a beautiful
boy than a grown person. None the less did the hosts
receive their visitors with open arms. Basia kissed heartily,
before presentation, the three women; when they told who
they were, and whence they had come, she said, —

"I should rejoice to bend the heavens for you, ladies, and
for you, gentlemen. I am awfully glad to see you! It is
well that no misfortune has met you on the road, for in our
desert, you see, such a thing is not difficult; but this very
day we have cut the ravagers to pieces."

Seeing then that Pani Boski was looking at her with increasing astonishment, she struck her sabre, and added with
great boastfulness, "Ah, but I was in the fight! Of course
I was. That's the way with us! For God's sake, permit
me, ladies, to go out and put on clothing proper to my sex,
and wash my hands from blood a little; for I am coming
from a terrible battle. Oh, if we had n't cut down Azba to-
day, perhaps you ladies would not have arrived without

accident at Hreptyoff. I will return in a moment, and Michael will be at your service meanwhile."

She vanished through the door; and then the little knight, who had greeted Pan Novoveski already, pushed up to Pani Boski. "God has given me such a wife," said he to her, "that she is not only a loving companion in the house, but can be a valiant comrade in the field. Now, at her command I offer my services to your ladyship."

"May God bless her in everything," answered Pani Boski, "as He has blessed her in beauty! I am Antonia Boski; I have not come to exact services from your grace, but to beg on my knees for aid and rescue in misfortune. Zosia, kneel down here too before the knight; for if he cannot help us, no man can."

Pani Boski fell on her knees then, and the comely Zosia followed her example; both, shedding ardent tears, began to cry, "Save us, knight! Have pity on orphans!"

A crowd of officers, made curious, drew near on seeing the kneeling women, and especially because the sight of the comely Zosia attracted them; the little knight, greatly confused, raised Pani Boski, and seated her on a bench. "In God's name," asked he, "what are you doing? I should kneel first before a worthy woman. Tell, your ladyship, in what I can render assistance, and as God is in heaven, I will not delay."

"He will do what he promises; I, on my part, offer myself! Zagloba *sum!* it is enough for you to know that!" said the old warrior, moved by the tears of the women.

Then Pani Boski beckoned to Zosia; she took quickly from her bosom a letter, which she gave to the little knight. He looked at the letter and said, "From the hetman!" Then he broke the seal and began to read: —

VERY DEAR AND BELOVED VOLODYOVSKI! — I send from the road to you, through Pan Bogush, my sincere love and instructions, which Pan Bogush will communicate to you personally. I have barely recovered from fatigues in Yavorov, when immediately another affair comes up. This affair is very near my heart, because of the affection which I bear soldiers, whom if I forgot, the Lord God would forget me. Pan Boski, a cavalier of great honor and a dear comrade, was taken by the horde some years since, near Kamenyets. I have given shelter to his wife and daughter in Yavorov; but their hearts are weeping, — one for a husband, the other for a father. I wrote through Pyotrovich to Pan Zlotnitski, our Resident in the

Crimea, to look for Pan Boski everywhere. They found him, it seems; but the Tartars hid him afterward, therefore he could not be given up with other prisoners, and doubtless is rowing in a galley to this time. The women, despairing and hopeless, have ceased to importune me; but I, on returning recently, and seeing their unappeased sorrow, could not refrain from attempting some rescue. You are near the place, and have concluded, as I know, brotherhood with many murzas. I send the ladies to you, therefore, and do you give them aid. Pyotrovich will go soon to the Crimea. Give him letters to those murzas with whom you are in brotherhood. I cannot write to the vizir or the Khan, for they are not friendly to me; and besides, I fear that if I should write, they would consider Boski a very eminent person, and increase the ransom beyond measure. Commend the affair urgently to Pyotrovich, and command him not to return without Boski. Stir up all your brothers; though Pagans, they observe plighted faith always, and must have great respect for you. Finally, do what you please; go to Rashkoff; promise three of the most considerable Tartars in exchange, if they return Boski alive. No one knows better than you all their methods, for, as I hear, you have ransomed relatives already. God bless you, and I will love you still more, for my heart will cease to bleed. I have heard of your management in Hreptyoff, that it is quiet there. I expected this. Only keep watch on Azba. Pan Bogush will tell you all about public affairs. For God's sake, listen carefully in the direction of Moldavia, for a great invasion will not miss us. Committing Pani Boski to your heart and efforts, I subscribe myself, etc.

Pani Boski wept without ceasing during the reading of the letter; and Zosia accompanied her, raising her blue eyes to heaven. Meanwhile, and before Pan Michael had finished, Basia ran in, dressed in woman's garments; and seeing tears in the eyes of the ladies, began to inquire with sympathy what the matter was. Therefore Pan Michael read the hetman's letter for her; and when she had listened to it carefully, she supported at once and with eagerness the prayers of the hetman and Pani Boski.

"The hetman has a golden heart," cried Basia, embracing her husband; "but we shall not show a worse one, Michael. Pani Boski will stay with us till her husband's return, and you will bring him in three months from the Crimea. In three or in two, is it not true?"

"Or to-morrow, or in an hour!" said Pan Michael, bantering. Here he turned to Pani Boski, "Decisions, as you see, are quick with my wife."

"May God bless her for that!" said Pani Boski. "Zosia, kiss the hand of the lady commandress."

But the lady commandress did not think of giving her

hands to be kissed; she embraced Zosia again, for in some way they pleased each other at once. "Help us, gracious gentlemen," cried she. "Help us, and quickly!"

"Quickly, for her head is burning!" muttered Zagloba.

But Basia, shaking her yellow forelock, said, "Not my head, but the hearts of those gentlemen are burning from sorrow."

"No one will oppose your honest intention," said Pan Michael; "but first we must hear Pani Boski's story in detail."

"Zosia, tell everything as it was, for I cannot, from tears," said the matron.

Zosia dropped her eyes toward the floor, covering them entirely with the lids; then she became as red as a cherry, not knowing how to begin, and was greatly abashed at having to speak in such a numerous assembly.

But Basia came to her aid. "Zosia, and when did they take Pan Boski captive?"

"Five years ago, in 1667," said Zosia, with a thin voice, without raising the long lashes from her eyes. And she began in one breath to tell the story: "There were no raids to be heard of at that time, and papa's squadron was near Panyovtsi. Papa, with Pan Bulayovski, was looking after men who were herding cattle in the meadows, and the Tartars came then on the Wallachian road, and took papa, with Pan Bulayovski; but Pan Bulayovski returned two years ago, and papa has not returned."

Here two tears began to flow down Zosia's cheeks, so that Zagloba was moved at sight of them, and said, "Poor girl! Do not fear, child; papa will return, and will dance yet at your wedding."

"But did the hetman write to Pan Zlotnitski through Pyotrovich?" inquired Volodyovski.

"The hetman wrote about papa to the sword-bearer of Poznan," recited Zosia; "and the sword-bearer and Pan Pyotrovich found papa with Aga Murza Bey."

"In God's name! I know that Murza Bey. I was in brotherhood with his brother," said Volodyovski. "Would he not give up Pan Boski?"

"There was a command of the Khan to give up papa; but Murza Bey is severe, cruel. He hid papa, and told Pan Pyotrovich that he had sold him long before into Asia. But other captives told Pan Pyotrovich that that was not true, and that the murza only said that purposely, so that he might abuse papa longer; for he is the cruellest of all the Tartars toward prisoners. Perhaps papa was not in the Crimea then; for the murza has his own galleys, and needs men for rowing. But papa was not sold; all the prisoners said that the murza would rather kill a prisoner than sell him."

"Holy truth!" said Pan Mushalski. "They know that Murza Bey in the whole Crimea. He is a very rich Tartar, but wonderfully venomous against our people, for four brothers of his fell in campaigns against us."

"But has he never formed brotherhood among our people?" asked Pan Michael.

"It is doubtful!" answered the officers from every side.

"Tell me once what that brotherhood is," said Basia.

"You see," said Zagloba, "when negotiations are begun at the end of war, men from both armies visit one another and enter into friendship. It happens then that an officer inclines to himself a murza, and a murza an officer; then they vow to each other life-friendship, which they call brotherhood. The more famous a man is, as Michael, for instance, or I, or Pan Rushchyts, who holds command in Rashkoff now, the more is his brotherhood sought. It is clear that such a man will not conclude brotherhood with some common fellow, but will seek it only among the most renowned murzas. The custom is this, — they pour water on their sabres and swear mutual friendship; do you understand?"

"And how if it comes to war afterward?"

"They can fight in a general war; but if they meet alone, if they are attacking as skirmishers, they will greet each other, and depart in friendship. Also if one of them falls into captivity, the other is bound to alleviate it, and in the worst case to ransom him; indeed, there have been some who shared their property with brothers. When it is a question of friends or acquaintances, or of finding some one, brothers go to brothers; and justice commands us to acknowledge that no people observe such oaths better than the Tartars. The word is the main thing with them, and such a friend you can trust certainly."

"But has Michael many such?"

"I have three powerful murzas," answered Volodyovski; "and one of them is from Lubni times. Once I begged him of Prince Yeremi. Aga Bey is his name; and even now, if he had to lay his head down for me, he would lay it down. The other two are equally reliable."

"Ah," said Basia, "I should like to conclude brother-hood with the Khan himself, and free all the prisoners."

"He would not be averse to that," said Zagloba; " but it is not known what reward he would ask of you."

"Permit me, gentlemen," said Pan Michael; "let us consider what we ought to do. Now listen; we have news from Kamenyets that in two weeks at the furthest Pyotro-vich will be here with a numerous escort. He will go to the Crimea with ransom for a number of Armenian merchants from Kamenyets, who at the change of the Khan were plundered and taken captive. That happened to Seferovich, the brother of Pretor. All those people are very wealthy; they will not spare money, and Pyotrovich will go well provided. No danger threatens him; for, first, winter is near, and it is not the time for chambuls, and, secondly, with him are going Naviragh, the delegate of the Patriarch of Echmiadzin, and the two Anardrats from Kaffa, who have a safe-conduct from the young Khan. I will give letters to Pyotrovich to the residents of the Com-monwealth and to my brothers. Besides, it is known to you, gentlemen, that Pan Rushchyts, the commandant at Rashkoff, has relatives in the horde, who, taken captive in childhood, have become thoroughly Tartar, and have risen to dignities. All these will move earth and heaven, will try negotiations; in case of stubbornness on the part of the murza, they will rouse the Khan himself against him, or perhaps they will twist the murza's head somewhere in secret. I hope, therefore, that if, which God grant, Pan Boski is alive, I shall get him in a couple of months with-out fail, as the hetman commands, and my immediate superior here present " (at this Pan Michael bowed to his wife).

His immediate superior sprang to embrace the little knight the second time. Pani and Panna Boski clasped their hands, thanking God, who had permitted them to meet such kindly people. Both became notably cheerful, therefore.

"If the old Khan were alive," said Pan Nyenashinyets, "all would go more smoothly; for he was greatly devoted to us, and of the young one they say the opposite. In fact, those Armenian merchants for whom Pan Pyotrovich is to go, were imprisoned in Bagchesarai itself during the time of the young Khan, and probably at his command."

"There will be a change in the young, as there was in

the old Khan, who, before he convinced himself of our honesty, was the most inveterate enemy of the Polish name," said Zagloba. "I know this best, for I was seven years under him in captivity. Let the sight of me give comfort to your ladyship," continued he, taking a seat near Pani Boski. "Seven years is no joke; and still I returned and crushed so many of those dog brothers that for each day of my captivity I sent at least two of them to hell; and for Sundays and holidays who knows if there will not be three or four? Ha!"

"Seven years!" repeated Pani Boski, with a sigh.

"May I die if I add a day! Seven years in the very palace of the Khan," confirmed Zagloba, blinking mysteriously. "And you must know that that young Khan is my —" Here he whispered something in the ear of Pani Boski, burst into a loud " Ha, ha, ha!" and began to stroke his knees with his palms; finally he slapped Pani Boski's knees, and said, "They were good times, were they not? In youth every man you met was an enemy, and every day a new prank, ha!"

The sedate matron became greatly confused, and pushed back somewhat from the jovial knight; the younger women dropped their eyes, divining easily that the pranks of which Pan Zagloba was talking must be something opposed to their native modesty, especially since the soldiers burst into loud laughter.

"It will be needful to send to Pan Rushchyts at once," said Basia, "so that Pan Pyotrovich may find the letters ready in Rashkoff."

"Hasten with the whole affair," added Pan Bogush, "while it is winter: for, first, no chambuls come out, and roads are safe; secondly, in the spring God knows what may happen."

"Has the hetman news from Tsargrad?" inquired Volodyovski.

"He has; and of this we must talk apart. It is necessary to finish quickly with those captains. When will Mellehovich come back? — for much depends on him."

"He has only to destroy the rest of the ravagers, and afterward bury the dead. He ought to return to-day or to-morrow morning. I commanded him to bury only our men, not Azba's; for winter is at hand, and there is no danger of infection. Besides, the wolves will clear them away."

"The hetman asks," said Pan Bogush, "that Mellehovich should have no hindrance in his work; as often as he wishes to go to Rashkoff, let him go. The hetman asks, too, to trust him in everything, for he is certain of his devotion. He is a great soldier, and may do us much good."

"Let him go to Rashkoff and whithersoever he pleases," said the little knight. "Since we have destroyed Azba, I have no urgent need of him. No large band will appear now till the first grass."

"Is Azba cut to pieces then?" inquired Novoveski.

"So cut up that I do not know if twenty-five men escaped; and even those will be caught one by one, if Mellehovich has not caught them already."

"I am terribly glad of this," said Novoveski, "for now it will be possible to go to Rashkoff in safety." Here he turned to Basia: "We can take to Pan Rushchyts the letters which her grace, our benefactress, has mentioned."

"Thank you," answered Basia; "there are occasions here continually, for men are sent expressly."

"All the commands must maintain communication," said Pan Michael. "But are you going to Rashkoff, indeed, with this young beauty?"

"Oh, this is an ordinary puss, not a beauty, gracious benefactor," said Novoveski; "and I am going to Rashkoff, for my son, the rascal, is serving there under the banner of Pan Rushchyts. It is nearly ten years since he ran away from home, and knocks at my fatherly clemency only with letters."

"I guessed at once that you were Pan Adam's father, and I was about to inquire; but we were so taken up with sorrow for Pani Boski. I guessed it at once, for there is a resemblance in features. Well, then, he is your son?"

"So his late mother declared; and as she was a virtuous woman, I have no reason for doubt."

"I am doubly glad to have such a guest as you. For God's sake, but do not call your son a rascal; for he is a famous soldier, and a worthy cavalier, who brings the highest honor to your grace. Do you not know that, after Pan Rushchyts, he is the best partisan in the squadron? Do you not know that he is an eye in the head of the hetman? Independent commands are intrusted to him, and he has fulfilled every function with incomparable credit."

Pan Novoveski flushed from delight. "Gracious Colonel," said he, "more than once a father blames his child only to let some one deny what he says; and I think that 't is impossible to please a parent's heart more than by such a denial. Reports have reached me already of Adam's good service; but I am really comforted now for the first time, when I hear these reports confirmed by such renowned lips. They say that he is not only a manful soldier, but steady, — which is even a wonder to me, for he was always a whirlwind. The rogue had a love for war from youth upward; and the best proof of this is that he ran away from home as a boy. If I could have caught him at that time, I would not have spared him. But now I must spare him; if not, he would hide for ten other years, and it is dreary for me, an old man, without him."

"And has he not been home during so many years?"

"He has not; I forbade him. But I have had enough of it, and now I go to him, since he, being in service, cannot come to me. I intended to ask of you and my benefactress a refuge for this maiden while I went to Rashkoff alone; but since you say that it is safe everywhere, I will take her. She is curious, the magpie, to see the world. Let her look at it."

"And let people look at her," put in Zagloba.

"Ah, they would have nothing to see," said the young lady, out of whose dark eyes and mouth, fixed as if for a kiss, something quite different was speaking.

"An ordinary puss, — nothing more than a puss!" said Pan Novoveski. "But if she sees a handsome officer, something may happen; therefore I chose to bring her with me rather than leave her, especially as it is dangerous for a girl at home alone. But if I go without her to Rashkoff, then let her grace give command to tie her with a cord, or she will play pranks."

"I was no better myself," said Basia.

"They gave her a distaff to spin," said Zagloba; "but she danced with it, since she had no one better to dance with. But you are a jovial man. Basia, I should like to have an encounter with Pan Novoveski, for I also am fond of amusement at times."

Meanwhile, before supper was served, the door opened, and Mellehovich entered. Pan Novoveski did not notice him at once, for he was talking with Zagloba; but Eva saw him, and a flame struck her face; then she grew pale suddenly.

"Pan Commandant," said Mellehovich to Pan Michael, "according to order, those men were caught."

"Well, where are they?"

"According to order, I had them hanged."

"Well done! And have your men returned?"

"A part remained to bury the bodies; the rest are with me."

At this moment Pan Novoveski raised his head, and great astonishment was reflected on his face. "In God's name, what do I see?" cried he. Then he rose, went straight to Mellehovich, and said, "Azya! And what art thou doing here, ruffian?"

He raised his hand to seize the Tartar by the collar; but in Mellehovich there was such an outburst in one moment as there is when a man throws a handful of powder into fire; he grew pale as a corpse, and seizing with iron grasp the hand of Novoveski, he said, "I do not know you! Who are you?" and pushed him so violently that Novoveski staggered to the middle of the room. For some time he could not utter a word from rage; but regaining breath, began to cry, —

"Gracious Commandant, this is my man, and besides that, a runaway. He was in my house from childhood. The ruffian denies! He is my man! Eva, who is he? Tell."

"Azya," said Eva, trembling in all her body.

Mellehovich did not even look at her. With eyes fixed on Novoveski, and with quivering nostril, he looked at the old noble with unspeakable hatred, pressing with his hand the handle of his knife. At the same time his mustaches began to quiver from the movement of his nostrils, and from under those mustaches white teeth were gleaming, like those of an angry wild beast.

The officers stood in a circle; Basia sprang in between Mellehovich and Novoveski. "What does this mean?" asked she, frowning.

"Pan Commandant," said Novoveski, "this is my man, Azya by name, and a runaway. Serving in youthful years in the Crimea, I found him half-alive on the steppe, and I took him. He is a Tartar. He remained twelve years in my house, and was taught together with my son. When my son ran away, this one helped me in management until he wished to make love to Eva; seeing this, I had him flogged: he ran away after that. What is his name here?"

"Mellehovich."

"He has assumed that name. He is called Azya, —

nothing more. He says that he does not know me; but I know him, and so does Eva."

"Your grace's son has seen him many times," said Basia. "Why did not he know him?"

"My son might not know him; for when he ran away from home, both were fifteen years old, and this one remained six years with me afterward, during which time he changed considerably, grew, and got mustaches. But Eva knew him at once. Gracious hosts, you will lend belief more quickly to a citizen than to this accident from the Crimea!"

"Pan Mellehovich is an officer of the hetman," said Basia; "we have nothing to do with him."

"Permit me; I will ask him. Let the other side be heard," said the little knight.

But Pan Novoveski was furious. "*Pan* Mellehovich! What sort of a *Pan* is he? — My serving-lad, who has hidden himself under a strange name. To-morrow I'll make my dog keeper of that *Pan*; the day after to-morrow I'll give command to beat that *Pan* with clubs. And the hetman himself cannot hinder me; for I am a noble, and I know my rights."

To this Pan Michael answered more sharply, and his mustaches quivered. "I am not only a noble, but a colonel, and I know my rights too. You can demand your man, by law, and have recourse to the jurisdiction of the hetman; but I command here, and no one else does."

Pan Novoveski moderated at once, remembering that he was talking, not only to a commandant, but to his own son's superior, and besides the most noted knight in the Commonwealth. "Pan Colonel," said he, in a milder tone, "I will not take him against the will of your grace; but I bring forward my rights, and I beg you to believe me."

"Mellehovich, what do you say to this?" asked Volodyovski.

The Tartar fixed his eyes on the floor, and was silent.

"That your name is Azya we all know," added Pan Michael.

"There are other proofs to seek," said Novoveski. "If he is my man, he has fish tattooed in blue on his breast."

Hearing this, Pan Nyenashinyets opened his eyes widely and his mouth; then he seized himself by the head, and cried, "Azya, Tugai Beyovich!"

All eyes were turned on him; he trembled throughout his

whole body, as if all his wounds were reopened, and he repeated, "That is my captive! That is Tugai Bey's son. As God lives, it is he."

But the young Tartar raised his head proudly, cast his wild-cat glance on the assembly, and pulling open suddenly the clothes on his bosom, said, "Here are the fish tattooed in blue. I am the son of Tugai Bey!"

16

CHAPTER XXIX.

ALL were silent, so great was the impression which the
name of the terrible warrior had made. Tugai Bey was
the man who, in company with the dreadful Hmelnitski,
had shaken the entire Commonwealth; he had shed a whole
sea of Polish blood; he had trampled the Ukraine, Volynia,
Podolia, and the lands of Galicia with the hoofs of horses;
had destroyed castles and towns, had visited villages with
fire, had taken tens of thousands of people captive. The
son of such a man was now there before the assembly in
the stanitsa of Hreptyoff, and said to the eyes of people:
"I have blue fish on my breast; I am Azya, bone of the
bone of Tugai Bey." But such was the honor among
people of that time for famous blood that in spite of the
terror which the name of the celebrated murza must have
called forth in the soul of each soldier, Mellehovich increased in their eyes as if he had taken on himself the
whole greatness of his father.

They looked on him with wonderment, especially the
women, for whom every mystery becomes the highest
charm; he too, as if he had increased in his own eyes
through his confession, grew haughty: he did not drop his
head a whit, but said in conclusion, —

"That noble" — here he pointed at Novoveski — "says
I am his man; but this is my reply to him: 'My father
mounted his steed from the backs of men better than you.'
He says truly also that I was with him, for I was, and
under his rods my back streamed with blood, which I shall
not forget, so help me God! I took the name of Mellehovich to escape his pursuit. But now, though I might
have gone to the Crimea, I am serving this fatherland
with my blood and health, and I am under no one but the
hetman. My father was a relative of the Khan, and in the
Crimea wealth and luxury were waiting for me; but I
remained here in contempt, for I love this fatherland,
I love the hetman, and I love those who have never
disdained me."

When he had said this, he bowed to Volodyovski, bowed
so low before Basia that his head almost touched her knees;

then, without looking on any one again, he took his sabre under his arm, and walked out.

For a time yet silence continued. Zagloba spoke first. "Ha! Where is Pan Snitko! But I said that a wolf was looking out of the eyes of that Azya; and he is the son of a wolf!"

"The son of a lion!" said Volodyovski; "and who knows if he has n't taken after his father?"

"As God lives, gentlemen, did you notice how his teeth glittered, just like those of old Tugai when he was in anger?" said Pan Mushalski. "By that alone I should have known him, for I saw old Tugai often."

"Not so often as I," said Zagloba.

"Now I understand," put in Bogush, "why he is so much esteemed among the Tartars of Lithuania and the South. And they remember Tugai's name as sacred. By the living God, if that man had the wish, he might take every Tartar to the Sultan's service, and cause us a world of trouble."

"He will not do that," answered Pan Michael, "for what he has said — that he loves the country and the hetman — is true; otherwise he would not be serving among us, being able to go to the Crimea and swim there in everything. He has not known luxury with us."

"He will not go to the Crimea," said Pan Bogush, "for if he had had the wish, he could have done so already; he met no hindrance."

"On the contrary," added Nyenashinyets, "I believe now that he will entice back all those traitorous captains to the Commonwealth again."

"Pan Novoveski," said Zagloba, suddenly, "if you had known that he was the son of Tugai Bey, perhaps then — perhaps so — what?"

"I should have commanded to give him, instead of three hundred, three thousand blows. May the thunderbolts shatter me if I would not have done so! Gracious gentlemen, it is a wonder to me that he, being Tugai Bey's whelp, did not run off to the Crimea. It must be that he discovered this only recently; for when with me he knew nothing about it. This is a wonder to me, I tell you it is; but for God's sake, do not trust him. I know him, gentlemen, longer than you do; and I will tell you only this much: the devil is not so slippery, a mad dog is not so irritable, a wolf is less malignant and cruel, than that man. He will pour tallow under the skins of you all yet."

"What are you talking about?" asked Mushalski. "We have seen him in action at Kalnik, at Uman, at Bratslav, and in a hundred other emergencies."

"He will not forget his own; he will have vengeance," said Novoveski.

"But to-day he slew Azba's ravagers. What are you telling us?".

Meanwhile Basia was all on fire, that history of Mellehovich occupied her so much; but she was anxious that the end should be worthy of the beginning; therefore, shaking Eva Novoveski, she whispered in her ear, "But you loved him, Eva? Own up; don't deny! You loved him. You love him yet, do you not? I am sure you do. Be outspoken with me. In whom can you confide, if not in me, a woman? There is almost royal blood in him. The hetman will get him, not one, but ten naturalizations. Pan Novoveski will not oppose. Undoubtedly Azya himself loves you yet. I know already; I know, I know. Never fear. He has confidence in me. I will put the question to him at once. He will tell me without torture. You loved him terribly; you love him yet, do you not?"

Eva was as if dazed. When Azya showed his inclination to her the first time, she was almost a child; after that she did not see him for a number of years, and had ceased to think of him. There remained with her the remembrance of him as a passionate stripling, who was half comrade to her brother, and half serving-lad. But now she saw him again; he stood before her a handsome hero and fierce as a falcon, a famous warrior, and, besides, the son of a foreign, it is true, but princely, stock. Therefore young Azya seemed to her altogether different; therefore the sight of him stunned her, and at the time dazzled and charmed her. Memories of him appeared before her as in a dream. Her heart could not love the young man in one moment, but in one moment she felt in it an agreeable readiness to love him.

Basia, unable to question her to the end, took her, with Zosia Boski, to an alcove, and began again to insist, "Eva, tell me quickly, awfully quickly, do you love him?"

A flame beat into the face of Eva. She was a dark-haired and dark-eyed maiden, with hot blood; and that blood flew to her cheeks at any mention of love.

"Eva," repeated Basia, for the tenth time, "do you love him?"

"I do not know," answered Eva, after a moment's hesitation.

"But you don't deny? Oho! I know. Do not hesitate. I told Michael first that I loved him, — no harm! and it was well. You must have loved each other terribly this long time. Ha! I understand now. It is from yearning for you that he has always been so gloomy; he went around like a wolf. The poor soldier withered away almost. What passed between you? Tell me."

"He told me in the storehouse that he loved me," whispered Eva.

"In the storehouse! What then?"

"Then he caught me and began to kiss me," continued she, in a still lower voice.

"Maybe I don't know him, that Mellehovich! And what did you do?"

"I was afraid to scream."

"Afraid to scream! Zosia, do you hear that? When was your loving found out?"

"Father came in, and struck him on the spot with a hatchet; then he whipped me, and gave orders to flog him so severely that he was a fortnight in bed."

Here Eva began to cry, partly from sorrow, and partly from confusion. At sight of this, the dark-blue eyes of the sensitive Zosia filled with tears, then Basia began to comfort Eva. "All will be well, my head on that! And I will harness Michael into the work, and Pan Zagloba. I will persuade them, never fear. Against the wit of Pan Zagloba nothing can stand; you do not know him. Don't cry, Eva dear, it is time for supper."

Mellehovich was not at supper. He was sitting in his own room, warming at the fire gorailka and mead, which he poured into a smaller cup afterward and drank, eating at the same time dry biscuits. Pan Bogush came to him late in the evening to talk over news.

The Tartar seated him at once on a chair lined with sheepskin, and placing before him a pitcher of hot drink, inquired, "But does Pan Novoveski still wish to make me his slave?"

"There is no longer any talk of that," answered the under-stolnik of Novgrod. "Pan Nyenashinyets might claim you first; but he cares nothing for you, since his sister is already either dead, or does not wish any change in her fate. Pan Novoveski did not know who you were

when he punished you for intimacy with his daughter.
Now he is going around like one stunned, for though your
father brought a world of evil on this country, he was a renowned warrior, and blood is always blood. As God lives,
no one will raise a finger here while you serve the country
faithfully, especially as you have friends on all sides."

"Why should I not serve faithfully?" answered Azya.
"My father fought against you; but he was a Pagan, while
I profess Christ."

"That's it, — that's it! You cannot return to the Crimea, unless with loss of faith, and that would be followed
by loss of salvation; therefore no earthly wealth, dignity,
or office could recompense you. In truth, you owe gratitude
both to Pan Nyenashinyets and Pan Novoveski, for the
first brought you from among Pagans, and the second reared
you in the true faith."

"I know," said Azya, "that I owe them gratitude, and I
will try to repay them. Your grace has remarked truly
that I have found here a multitude of benefactors."

"You speak as if it were bitter in your mouth when you
say that; but count yourself your well-wishers."

"His grace the hetman and you in the first rank, — that
I will repeat until death. What others there are, I know
not."

"But the commandant here? Do you think that he
would yield you into any one's hands, even though you were
not Tugai Bey's son? And Pani Volodyovski, I heard
what she said about you during supper. Even before,
when Novoveski recognized you, she took your part. Pan
Volodyovski would do everything for her, for he does not
see the world beyond her; a sister could not have more
affection for a brother than she has for you. During the
whole time of supper your name was on her lips."

The young Tartar bent his head suddenly, and began to
blow into the cup of hot drink; when he put out his somewhat blue lips to blow, his face became so Tartar-like that
Pan Bogush said, —

"As God is true, how entirely like Tugai Bey you were
this moment passes imagination. I knew him perfectly.
I saw him in the palace of the Khan and on the field; I
went to his encampment it is small to say twenty times."

"May God bless the just, and the plague choke evil-
doers!" said Azya. "To the health of the hetman!"

Pan Bogush drank, and said, "Health and long years! It

is true those of us who stand with him are a handful, but true soldiers. God grant that we shall not give up to those bread-skinners, who know only how to intrigue at petty diets, and accuse the hetman of treason to the king. The rascals! We stand night and day with our faces to the enemy, and they draw around kneading-troughs full of hashed meat and cabbage with millet, and are drumming on them with spoons, — that is their labor. The hetman sends envoy after envoy, implores reinforcements for Kamenyets. Cassandra-like, he predicts the destruction of Ilion and the people of Priam; but they have no thought in their heads, and are simply looking for an offender against the king."

"Of what is your grace speaking?"

"Nothing! I made a comparison of Kamenyets with Troy; but you, of course, have not heard of Troy. Wait a little; the hetman will obtain naturalization for you. The times are such that the occasion will not be wanting, if you wish really to cover yourself with glory."

"Either I shall cover myself with glory, or earth will cover me. You will hear of me, as God is in heaven!"

"But those men? What is Krychinski doing? Will they return, or not? What are they doing now?"

"They are in encampment, — some in Urzyisk, others farther on. It is hard to come to an agreement at present, for they are far from one another. They have an order to move in spring to Adrianople, and to take with them all the provisions they can carry."

"In God's name, that is important, for if there is to be a great gathering of forces in Adrianople, war with us is certain. It is necessary to inform the hetman of this at once. He thinks also that war will come, but this would be an infallible sign."

"Halim told me that it is said there among them that the Sultan himself is to be at Adrianople."

"Praised be the name of the Lord! And here with us hardly a handful of troops. Our whole hope in the rock of Kamenyets! Does Krychinski bring forward new conditions?"

"He presents complaints rather than conditions. A general amnesty, a return to the rights and privileges of nobles which they had formerly, commands for the captains, — is what they wish; but as the Sultan has offered them more, they are hesitating."

"What do you tell me? How could the Sultan give

them more than the Commonwealth? In Turkey there is
absolute rule, and all rights depend on the fancy of the
Sultan alone. Even if he who is living and reigning at
present were to keep all his promises, his successor might
break them or trample on them at will; while with us
privileges are sacred, and whoso becomes a noble, from him
even the king can take nothing."

"They say that they were nobles, and still they were
treated on a level with dragoons; that the starostas commanded them more than once to perform various duties,
from which not only a noble is free, but even an attendant."

"But if the hetman promises them."

"No one doubts the high mind of the hetman, and all
love him in their hearts secretly; but they think thus to
themselves: 'The crowd of nobles will shout down the hetman as a traitor; at the king's court they hate him; a
confederacy threatens him with impeachment. How can he
do anything?'"

Pan Bogush began to stroke his forelock. "Well,
what?"

"They know not themselves what to do."

"And will they remain with the Sultan?"

"No."

"But who will command them to return to the Commonwealth?"

"I."

"How is that?"

"I am the son of Tugai Bey."

"My Azya," said Pan Bogush, after a while, "I do not
deny that they may be in love with your blood and the
glory of Tugai Bey, though they are our Tartars, and Tugai
Bey was our enemy. I understand such things, for even
with us there are nobles who say with a certain pride that
Hmelnitski was a noble, and descended, not from the Cossacks, but from our people, — from the Mazovians. Well,
though such a rascal that in hell a worse is not to be found,
they are glad to recognize him, because he was a renowned
warrior. Such is the nature of man! But that your blood
of Tugai Bey should give you the right to command all
Tartars, for this I see no sufficient reason."

Azya was silent for a time; then he rested his palms on
his thighs, and said, "Then I will tell you; Krychinski and
other Tartars obey me. For besides this, that they are
simple Tartars and I a prince, there are resources and power

In me. But neither you know them, nor does the hetman himself know them."

"What resources, what power?"

"I do not know how to tell you," answered Azya, in Russian. "But why am I ready to do things that another would not dare? Why have I thought of that of which another would not have thought?"

"What do you say? Of what have you thought?"

"I have thought of this, — that if the hetman would give me the will and the right, I would bring back, not merely the captains, but would put half the horde in the service of the hetman. Is there little vacant land in the Ukraine and the Wilderness? Let the hetman only announce that if a Tartar comes to the Commonwealth he will be a noble, will not be oppressed in his faith, and will serve in a squadron of his own people, that all will have their own hetman, as the Cossacks have, and my head for it, the whole Ukraine will be swarming soon. The Lithuanian Tartars will come; they will come from the South; they will come from Dobrudja and Belgrod; they will come from the Crimea; they will drive their flocks, and bring their wives and children in wagons. Do not shake your head, your grace; they will come! — as those came long ago who served the Commonwealth faithfully for generations. In the Crimea and everywhere the Khan and the murzas oppress the people; but in the Ukraine they will have their sabres, and take the field under their own hetman. I swear to you that they will come, for they suffer from hunger there from time to time. Now, if it is announced among the villages that I, by the authority of the hetman, call them, — that Tugai Bey's son calls, — thousands will come here."

Pan Bogush seized his own head: "By the wounds of God, Azya, whence did such thoughts come to you? What would there be?"

"There would be in the Ukraine a Tartar nation, as there is a Cossack. You have granted privileges to the Cossacks, and a hetman. Why should you not grant them to us? You ask what there would be. There would not be what there is now, — a second Hmelnitski, — for we should have put foot at once on the throat of the Cossack; there would not be an uprising of peasants, slaughter and ruin; there would be no Doroshenko, for let him but rise, and I should be the first to bring him on a halter to the feet of the hetman. And should the Turkish power think to move against

us, we would beat the Sultan; were the Khan to threaten
raids, we would beat the Khan. Is it so long since the
Lithuanian Tartars, and those of Podolia, did the like,
though remaining in the Mohammedan faith? Why should
we do otherwise? We are of the Commonwealth, we are
noble. Now, calculate. The Ukraine in peace, the Cossacks
in check, protection against Turkey, a number of tens of
thousands of additional troops, — this is what I have been
thinking; this is what came to my head; this is why Krychinski, Adurovich, Moravski, Tarasovski, obey me; this is
why one half the Crimea will roll to those steppes when I
raise the call."

Pan Bogush was as much astonished and weighed down
by the words of Azya as if the walls of that room in which
they were sitting had opened on a sudden, and new, unknown regions had appeared to his eyes. For a long time
he could not utter a word, and merely gazed on the young
Tartar; but Azya began to walk with great strides up and
down in the room. At last he said, —

"Without me this cannot be done, for I am the son of
Tugai Bey; and from the Dnieper to the Danube there is
no greater name among the Tartars." After a while he
added: "What are Krychinski, Tarasovski, and others to
me? It is not a question of them alone, or of some thousands of Lithuanian or Podolian Tartars, but of the whole
Commonwealth. They say that in spring a great war will
rise with the power of the Sultan; but only give me permission, and I will cause such a seething among the Tartars
that the Sultan himself will scald his hands."

"In God's name, who are you, Azya?" cried Pan
Bogush.

The young man raised his head: "The coming hetman
of the Tartars!"

A gleam of the fire fell at that moment on Azya, lighting his
face, which was at once cruel and beautiful. And it seemed
to Pan Bogush that some new man was standing before
him, such was the greatness and pride beating from the
person of the young Tartar. Pan Bogush felt also that
Azya was speaking the truth. If such a proclamation of
the hetman were published, all the Lithuanian and Podolian
Tartars would return without fail, and very many of the
wild Tartars would follow them. The old noble knew passing well the Crimea, in which he had been twice as a captive,
and, ransomed by the hetman, had been afterward an

envoy; he knew the court of Bagchesarai; he knew the hordes living from the Don to the Dobrudja; he knew that in winter many villages were depopulated by hunger; he knew that the despotism and rapacity of the Khan's baskaks were disgusting to the murzas; that in the Crimea itself it came often to rebellion; he understood at once, then, that rich lands and privileges would entice without fail all those for whom it was evil, narrow, or dangerous in their old homesteads. They would be enticed most surely if the son of Tugai Bey raised the call. He alone could do this, — no other. He, through the renown of his father, might rouse villages, involve one half of the Crimea against the other half, bring in the wild horde of Belgrod, and shake the whole power of the Khan, — nay, even that of the Sultan. Should the hetman desire to take advantage of the occasion, he might consider Tugai Bey's son as a man sent by Providence itself.

Pan Bogush began then to look with another eye on Azya, and to wonder more and more how such thoughts could be hatched in his head. And the sweat was in drops like pearl on the forehead of the knight, so immense did those thoughts seem to him. Still, doubt remained yet in his soul; therefore he said, after a while, —

"And do you know that there would have to be war with Turkey over such a question?"

"There will be war as it is. Why did they command the horde to march to Adrianople? There will be war unless dissensions rise in the Sultan's dominions; and if it comes to taking the field, half the horde will be on our side."

"For every point the rogue has an argument," thought Pan Bogush. "It turns one's head," said he, after a while. "You see, Azya, in every case it is not an easy thing. What would the king say, what the chancellor, the estates, and all the nobles, for the greater part hostile to the hetman?"

"I need only the permission of the hetman on paper; and when we are once here, let them drive us out! Who will drive us out, and with what? You would be glad to squeeze the Zaporojians out of the Saitch, but you cannot in any way."

"The hetman will dread the responsibility."

"Behind the hetman will be fifty thousand sabres of the horde, besides the troops which he has in hand."

"But the Cossacks? Do you forget the Cossacks? They will begin opposition at once."

"We are needed here specially to keep a sword hanging over the Cossack neck. Through whom has Doroshenko support? Through the Tartars! Let me take the Tartars in hand, Doroshenko must beat with his forehead to the hetman."

Here Azya stretched out his palm and opened his fingers like the talons of an eagle; then he grasped after the hilt of his sabre. "This is the way we will show the Cossacks law! They will become serfs, and we will hold the Ukraine. Do you hear, Pan Bogush? You think that I am a small man; but I am not so small as it seems to Novoveski, the commandant of this place, and you, Pan Bogush. Behold, I have been thinking over this day and night, till I have grown thin, till my face is sunken. Look at it, your grace; it has grown black. But what I have thought out, I have thought out well; and therefore I tell you that in me there are resources and power. You see yourself that these are great things. Go to the hetman, but go quickly. Lay the question before him; let him give me a letter touching this matter, and I shall not care about the estates. The hetman has a great soul; the hetman will know that this is power and resource. Tell the hetman that I am Tugai Bey's son; that I alone can do this. Lay it before him, let him consent to it; but in God's name, let it be done in time, while there is snow on the steppe, before spring, for in spring there will be war! Go at once and return at once, so that I may know quickly what I am to do."

Pan Bogush did not observe even that Azya spoke in a tone of command, as if he were a hetman giving instructions to his officer. "To-morrow I will rest," said he; "and after to-morrow I will set out. God grant me to find the hetman in Yavorov! Decision is quick with him, and soon you will have an answer."

"What does your grace think, — will the hetman consent?"

"Perhaps he will command you to come to him; do not go to Rashkoff, then, at present, — you can go more quickly to Yavorov from this place. Whether he will agree, I know not; but he will take the matter under prompt consideration, for you present powerful reasons. By the living God, I did not expect this of you; but I see now that you are an uncommon man, and that the Lord God predestined you to greatness. Well, Azya, Azya! Lieutenant in a Tartar squadron, nothing more, and such things are in his head that fear seizes a man! Now I shall not wonder even if I see a heron-feather in your cap, and a bunchuk above you. I believe now what you tell me, — that these thoughts have been burning you in the night-time. I will go at once, the day after to-morrow; but I will rest a little. Now I will leave you, for it is late, and my head is as noisy as a saw-mill. Be with God, Azya! My temples are aching as if I had been drunk. Be with God, Azya, son of Tugai Bey!"

Here Pan Bogush pressed the thin hand of the Tartar, and turned toward the door; but on the threshold he stopped again, and said, "How is this? New troops for the Commonwealth; a sword ready above the neck of the Cossack; Doroshenko conquered; dissension in the Crimea; the Turkish power weakened; an end to the raids against Russia, — for God's sake!"

When he had said this, Pan Bogush went out. Azya looked after him a while, and whispered, "But for me a bunchuk, a baton, and, with consent or without, she. Otherwise woe to you!"

Then he finished the gorailka, and threw himself on to the bed, covered with skins. The fire had gone down in the chimney; but through the window came in the clear rays of the moon, which had risen high in the cold wintry sky. Azya lay for some time quietly, but evidently was unable to sleep. At last he rose, approached the window, and looked at the moon, sailing like a ship through the infinite solitudes of heaven. The young Tartar looked at it long; at last he placed his fists on his breast, pointed both thumbs upward, and from the mouth of him who barely an hour before had confessed Christ, came, in a half-chant, a half-drawl, in a melancholy key, —

"La Allah illa Allah! Mahomet Rossul Allah!"

CHAPTER XXX.

MEANWHILE Basia was holding counsel from early morning with her husband and Pan Zagloba how to unite two loving and straitened hearts. The two men laughed at her enthusiasm, and did not cease to banter her; still, yielding to her usually in everything, as to a spoiled child, they promised at last to assist her.

"The best thing," said Zagloba, "is to persuade old Novoveski not to take the girl with him to Rashkoff; tell him that the frosts have come, and that the road is not perfectly safe. Here the young people will see each other often, and fall in love with all their might."

"That is a splendid idea," cried Basia.

"Splendid or not," said Zagloba, "do not let them out of your sight. You are a woman, and I think this way, — you will solder them at last, for a woman carries her point always; but see to it that the Devil does not carry his point in the mean while. That would be a shame for you, since the affair is on your responsibility."

Basia began first of all to spit at Pan Zagloba, like a cat; then she said, "You boast that you were a Turk in your youth, and you think that every one is a Turk. Azya is not that kind."

"Not a Turk, only a Tartar. Pretty image! She would vouch for Tartar love."

"They are both thinking more of weeping, and that from harsh sorrow. Eva, besides, is a most honest maiden."

"Still, she has a face as if some one had written on her forehead, 'Here are lips for you!' Ho! she is a daw. Yesterday I fixed it in my mind that when she sits opposite a nice fellow, her sighs are such that they drive her plate forward time after time, and she must push it back again. A real daw, I tell you."

"Do you wish me to go to my own room?" asked Basia.

"You will not go when it is a question of match-making. I know you, — you 'll not go! But still 't is too early for you to make matches; for that is the business of women with gray hair. Pani Boski told me yesterday that when she saw you returning from the battle in trousers, she

thought that she was looking at Pani Volodyovski's son,
who had gone to the woods on an expedition. You do not love
dignity; but dignity, too, does not love you, which appears
at once from your slender form. You are a regular student,
as God is dear to me! There is another style of women in
the world now. In my time, when a woman sat down, the
chair squeaked in such fashion that you might think some
one had sat on the tail of a dog; but as to you, you might
ride bareback on a tom-cat without great harm to the beast.
They say, too, that women who begin to make matches will
have no posterity."

"Do they really say that?" asked the little knight,
alarmed.

But Zagloba began to laugh; and Basia, putting her rosy
face to the face of her husband, said, in an undertone, "Ah,
Michael, at a convenient time we will make a pilgrimage to
Chenstohova; then maybe the Most Holy Lady will change
matters."

"That is the best way indeed," said Zagloba.

Then they embraced at once, and Basia said, "But now
let us talk of Azya and poor Eva, of how we are to help
them. We are happy; let them be happy."

"When Novoveski goes away, it will be easier for
them," said the little knight; "for in his presence they
could not see each other, especially as Azya hates the old
man. But if the old man were to give him Eva, maybe,
forgetting former offences, they would begin to love each
other as son-in-law and father-in-law. According to my
head, it is not a question of bringing the young people
together, for they love each other already, but of bringing
over the old man."

"He is a misanthrope!" said Basia.

"Baska," said Zagloba, "imagine to yourself that you
had a daughter, and that you had to give her to some
Tartar —"

"Azya is a prince."

"I do not deny that Tugai Bey comes of high blood.
Ketling was a noble; still Krysia would not have married
him if he had not been naturalized."

"Then try to obtain naturalization for Azya."

"Is that an easy thing? Though some one were to
admit him to his escutcheon, the Diet would have to confirm
the choice; and for that, time and protection are necessary."

"I do not like this, — that time is needed, — for we could

find protection. Surely the hetman would not refuse it to
Azya, for he loves soldiers. Michael, write to the hetman.
Do you want ink, pen, paper? Write at once! I 'll bring
you everything, and a taper and the seal; and you will sit
down and write without delay."

"O Almighty God!" cried he, "I asked a sedate, sober
wife of Thee, and Thou didst give me a whirlwind!"

"Talk that way, talk; then I 'll die."

"Ah, your impatience!" cried the little knight, with
animation, — "your impatience, tfu! tfu! a charm for a
dog!" Here he turned to Zagloba: "Do you not know the
words of a charm?"

"I know them, and I 've told them," said Zagloba.

"Write!" cried Basia, "or I shall jump out of my
skin."

"I would write twelve letters, to please you, though I
know not what good that would be, for in this case the
hetman himself can do nothing; even with protection,
Azya can appear only at the right time. My Basia, Panna
Novoveski has revealed her secret to you, — very well!
But you have not spoken to Azya, and you do not know
to this moment whether he is burning with love for Eva
or not."

"He not burning! Why should n't he be burning, when he
kissed her in the storehouse? Aha!"

"Golden soul!" said Zagloba, smiling. "That is like
the talk of a newly born infant, except that you turn your
tongue better. My love, if Michael and I had to marry all
the women whom we happened to kiss, we should have to
join the Mohammedan faith at once, and I should be Sultan
of Turkey, and he Khan of the Crimea. How is that,
Michael, hei?"

"I suspected Michael before I was his," said Basia; and
thrusting her finger up to his eye, she began to tease him.
"Move your mustaches; move them! Do not deny! I
know, I know, and you know — at Ketling's."

The little knight really moved his mustaches to give himself courage, and at the same time to cover his confusion;
at last, wishing to change the conversation, he said, "And
so you do not know whether Azya is in love with Panna
Eva?"

"Wait; I will talk to him alone and ask him. But he is
in love, he must be in love! Otherwise I don't want to
know him."

"In God's name! she is ready to talk him into it," said Zagloba.

"And I will persuade him, even if I had to shut myself in with him daily."

"Inquire of him, to begin with," said the little knight. "Maybe at first he will not confess, for he is shy; that is nothing. You will gain his confidence gradually; you'll know him better; you'll understand him, and then only can you decide what to do." Here the little.knight turned to Zagloba: "She seems giddy, but she is quick."

"Kids are quick," said Zagloba, seriously.

Further conversation was interrupted by Pan Bogush, who rushed in like a bomb, and had barely kissed Basia's hands when he exclaimed, "May the bullets strike that Azya! I could not close my eyes the whole night. May the woods cover him!"

"What did Pan Azya bring against your grace?" asked Basia.

"Do you know what we were making yesterday?" And Pan Bogush, staring, began to look around on those present.

"What?"

"History! As God is dear to me, I do not lie."

"What history?"

"The history of the Commonwealth; that is, simply a great man. Pan Sobieski himself will be astonished when I lay Azya's ideas before him. A great man, I repeat to you; and I regret that I cannot tell you more, for I am sure that you would be as much astonished as I. I can only say that if what he has in view succeeds, God knows what he will be."

"For example," asked Zagloba, "will he be hetman?"

Pan Bogush put his hands on his hips: "That is it,—he will be hetman. I am sorry that I cannot tell you more. He will be hetman, and that's enough."

"Perhaps a dog hetman, or he will go with bullocks. Chabans have their hetmans also. Tfu! what is this that your grace is saying, Pan Under-Stolnik? That he is the son of Tugai Bey is true; but if he is to become hetman, what am I to become, or what will Pan Michael become, or your grace? Shall we become three kings at the birth of Christ, waiting for the abdication of Caspar, Melchior, and Baltazar? The nobles at least created me commander; I resigned the office, however, out of friendship

17

for Pavel,[1] but, as God lives, I don't understand your prediction."

"But I tell you that Azya is a great man."

"I said so," exclaimed Basia, turning toward the door, through which other guests at the stanitsa began to enter.

First came Pani Boski with the blue-eyed Zosia, and Pan Novoveski with Eva, who, after a night of bad sleep, looked more charming than usual. She had slept badly, for strange dreams had disturbed her; she dreamed of Azya, only he was more beautiful and insistent than of old. The blood rushed to her face at thought of this dream, for she imagined that every one would guess it in her eyes. But no one noticed her, since all had begun to say "good-day" to Pani Volody- ovski. Then Pan Bogush resumed his narrative touching Azya's greatness and destiny; and Basia was glad that Eva and Pan Novoveski must listen to it. In fact, the old noble had blown off his anger since his first meeting with the Tartar, and was notably calmer. He spoke of him no longer as his man. To tell the truth, the discovery that he was a Tartar prince and a son of Tugai Bey imposed upon him beyond measure. He heard with wonder of Azya's uncommon bravery, and how the hetman had in- trusted such an important function to him as that of bring- ing back to the service of the Commonwealth all the Lithuanian and Podolian Tartars. At times it seemed even to Pan Novoveski that they were talking of some one else besides Azya, to such a degree had the young Tartar become uncommon.

But Pan Bogush repeated every little while, with a very mysterious mien, "This is nothing in comparison with what is waiting for him; but I am not free to speak of it." And when the others shook their heads with doubt, he cried, "There are two great men in the Commonwealth, — Pan Sobieski and that Azya, son of Tugai Bey."

"By the dear God," said Pan Novoveski, made impatient at last, "prince or not prince, what can he be in this Com- monwealth, unless he is a noble? He is not naturalized yet."

"The hetman will get him ten naturalizations!" cried Basia.

Eva listened to these praises with closed eyes and a

---

[1] Zagloba refers here to Pavel Sapyeha, voevoda of Vilna, and grand hetman of Lithuania.

beating heart. It is difficult to say whether it would have beaten so feverishly for a poor and unknown Azya as for Azya the knight and man of great future. But that glitter captivated her; and the old remembrance of the kisses and the fresh dream went through her with a quiver of delight.

"So great and so celebrated," said Eva. "What wonder if he is as quick as fire!"

CHAPTER XXXI.

BASIA took the Tartar that very day to "an examination," following the advice of her husband; and fearing the shyness of Azya, she resolved not to insist too much at once. Still, he had barely appeared before her when she said, straight from the bridge, —

"Pan Bogush says that you are a great man; but I think that the greatest man cannot avoid love."

Azya closed his eyes, inclined his head, and said, "Your grace is right."

"I see that you are a man with a heart."

When she had said this, Basia began to shake her yellow forelock and blink, as if to say that she knew affairs of this kind well, and also hoped that she was not speaking to a man without knowledge. Azya raised his head and embraced with his glance her charming figure. She had never seemed so wonderful to him as on that day, when her eyes, gleaming from curiosity and animation, and the blushing child-like face, full of smiles, were raised toward his face. But the more innocent the face, the more charm did Azya see in it; the more did desire rise in his soul; the more powerfully did love seize and intoxicate him as with wine, and drive out all other desires, save this one alone, — to take her from her husband, bear her away, hold her forever at his breast, press her lips to his lips, feel her arms twined around his neck: to love, to love even to forget himself, even to perish alone, or perish with her. At thought of this the whole world whirled around with him; new desires crept up every moment from the den of his soul, like serpents from crevices in a cliff. But he was a man who possessed also great self-control; therefore he said in spirit, "It is impossible yet!" and he held his wild heart at check when he chose, as a furious horse is held on a lariat.

He stood before her apparently cold, though he had a flame in his mouth and eyes, and his deep pupils told all that his compressed lips refused to confess. But Basia, having a soul as pure as water in a spring, and besides a mind occupied entirely with something else, did not understand that speech; she was thinking in the moment what further to tell the Tartar; and at last, raising her finger, she said:

"More than one bears in his heart hidden love, and does not dare to speak of it to any one; but if he would confess his love sincerely, perhaps he might learn something good."

Azya's face grew dark for a moment; a wild hope flashed through his head like lightning; but he recollected himself, and inquired, "Of what does your grace wish to speak?"

"Another would be hasty with you," said Basia, "since women are impatient, and not deliberate; but I am not of that kind. As to helping, I would help you willingly, but I do not ask your confidence in a moment; I only say this to you: Do not hide; come to me even daily. I have spoken of this matter with my husband already; gradually you will come to know and see my good-will, and you will know that I do not ask through mere curiosity, but from sympathy, and because if I am to assist, I must be certain that you are in love. Besides, it is proper that you show it first; when you acknowledge it to me, perhaps I can tell you something."

Tugai Bey's son understood now in an instant how vain was that hope which had gleamed in his head a moment before; he divined at once that it was a question of Eva Novoveski, and all the curses on the whole family which time had collected in his vengeful soul came to his mouth. Hatred burst out in him like a flame; the greater, the more different were the feelings which had shaken him a moment earlier. But he recollected himself. He possessed not merely self-control, but the adroitness of Orientals. In one moment he understood that if he burst out against the Novoveskis venomously, he would lose the favor of Basia and the possibility of seeing her daily; but, on the other hand, he felt that he could not conquer himself — at least then — to such a degree as to lie to that desired one in the face of his own soul by saying that he loved another. Therefore, from a real internal conflict and undissembled suffering, he threw himself suddenly before Basia, and kissing her feet, began to speak thus: —

"I give my soul into the hands of your grace; I give my faith into the hands of your grace. I do not wish to do anything except what you command me; I do not wish to know any other will. Do with me what you like. I live in torment and suffering; I am unhappy. Have compassion on me; if not, I shall perish and be lost."

And he began to groan, for he felt immense pain, and unacknowledged desires burned him with a living flame. But Basia considered these words as an outburst of love for Eva, — love long and painfully hidden; therefore pity for the young man seized her, and two tears gleamed in her eyes.

"Rise, Azya!" said she to the kneeling Tartar. "I have always wished you well, and I wish sincerely to help you; you come of high blood, and they will surely not withhold naturalization in return for your services. Pan Novoveski will let himself be appeased, for now he looks with different eyes on you; and Eva —" Here Basia rose, raised her rosy, smiling face, and putting her hand at the side of her mouth, whispered in Azya's ear, — "Eva loves you."

His face wrinkled, as if from rage; he seized his hips with his hands, and without thinking of the astonishment which his exclamation might cause, he repeated a number of times in a hoarse voice, "Allah! Allah! Allah!" Then he rushed out of the room.

Basia looked after him for a moment. The cry did not astonish her greatly, for the Polish soldiers used it often; but seeing the violence of the young Tartar, she said to herself, "Real fire! He is wild after her." Then she shot out like a whirlwind to make a report to her husband, Pan Zagloba, and Eva.

She found Pan Michael in the chancery, occupied with the registry of the squadron stationed in Hreptyoff. He was sitting and writing, but she ran up to him and cried, "Do you know? I spoke to him. He fell at my feet; he is wild after her."

The little knight put down his pen and began to look at his wife. She was so animated and pretty that his eyes gleamed; and, smiling, he stretched his arms toward her. She, defending herself, repeated again, —

· "Azya is wild after Eva!"

"As I am after you," said the little knight, embracing her.

That same day Zagloba and Eva knew most minutely all her conversation with Azya. The young lady's heart yielded itself now completely to the sweet feeling, and was beating like a hammer at the thought of the first meeting, and still more at thought of what would happen when they should be alone. And she saw already the face of Azya at her knees, and felt his kisses on her hands, and her own faintness at the time when the head of a maiden bends toward the arms of the loved one, and her lips whisper, "I love." Meanwhile, from emotion and disquiet she kissed Basia's hands violently, and looked every moment at the door to see if she could behold in it the gloomy but shapely form of young Tugal Bey.

But Azya did not show himself, for Halim had come to him, — Halim, the old servant of his father, and at present a considerable murza in the Dobrudja. He had come quite openly, since it was known in Hreptyoff that he was the intermediary between Azya and those captains who had accepted service with the Sultan. They shut themselves up at once in Azya's quarters, where Halim, after he had given the requisite obeisances to Tugai Bey's son, crossed his hands on his breast, and with bowed head waited for questions.

"Have you any letters ?" asked Azya.

"I have none, Effendi. They commanded me to give everything in words."

"Well, speak."

"War is certain. In the spring we must all go to Adrianople. Commands are issued to the Bulgarians to take hay and barley there."

"And where will the Khan be ?"

"He will go straight by the Wilderness, through the Ukraine, to Doroshenko."

"What do you hear concerning the encampments ?"

"They are glad of the war, and are sighing for spring; there is suffering in the encampments, though the winter is only beginning."

"Is the suffering great ?"

"Many horses have died. In Belgrod men have sold themselves into slavery, only to live till spring. Many horses have died, Effendi; for in the fall there was little grass on the steppes. The sun burned it up."

"But have they heard of Tugai Bey's son ?"

"I have spoken as much as you permitted. The report went out from the Lithuanian and Podolian Tartars; but no one knows the truth clearly. They are talking too of this, — that the Commonwealth wishes to give them freedom and land, and call them to service under Tugai Bey's son. At the mere report all the villages that are poorer were roused. They are willing, Effendi, they are willing; but some explain to them that this is all untrue, that the Commonwealth will send troops against them, and that there is no son of Tugai Bey at all. There were merchants of ours in the Crimea; they said that some there were giving out, 'There is a son of Tugai Bey,' and the people were roused; others said, 'There is not,' and the people were restrained. But if it should go out that your grace calls them to freedom, land, and service, swarms would move. Only let it be free for me to speak."

Azya's face grew bright from satisfaction, and he began to walk with great strides up and down in the room; then he said, "Be in good health, Halim, under my roof. Sit down and eat."

"I am your servant and dog, Effendi," said the old Tartar.

Azya clapped his hands, whereupon a Tartar orderly came in, and, hearing the command, brought refreshments after a time, — gorailka, dried meat, bread, sweetmeats, and some handfuls of dried water-melon seeds, which, with sunflower seeds, are a tidbit greatly relished by Tartars.

"You are a friend, not a servant," said Azya, when the orderly retired. "Be well, for you bring good news; sit and eat."

Halim began to eat, and until he had finished, they said nothing; but he refreshed himself quickly, and began to glance at Azya, waiting till he should speak.

"They know here now who I am," said Azya, at length.

"And what, Effendi?"

"Nothing. They respect me still more. When it came to work, I had to tell them anyhow. But I delayed, for I was waiting for news from the horde, and I wished the hetman to know first; but Novoveski came, and he recognized me."

"The young one?" asked Halim, with fear.

"The old, not the young one. Allah has sent them all to me here, for the maiden is here. The Evil Spirit must have entered them. Only let me become hetman, I will play with them. They are giving me the maiden; very well, slaves are needed in the harem."

"Is the old man giving her?"

"No. *She* — she thinks that I love, not her, but the other."

"Effendi," said Halim, bowing, "I am the slave of your house, and I have not the right to speak before your face; but I recognized you among the Lithuanian Tartars; I told you at Bratslav who you are; and from that time I serve you faithfully. I tell others that they are to look on you as master; but though they love you, no one loves you as I do: is it free for me to speak?"

"Speak."

"Be on your guard against the little knight. He is famous in the Crimea and the Dobrudja."

"And, Halim, have you heard of Hmelnitski?"

"I have, and I served Tugai Bey, who warred with Hmelnitski against the Poles, ruined castles, and took property."

"And do you know that Hmelnitski took Chaplinski's wife from him, married her himself, and had children by her? What then? There was war; and all the troops of the hetmans and the king and the Commonwealth did not take her from Hmelnitski. He beat the hetmans and the king and the Commonwealth; and besides that, he was hetman of the Cossacks. And I, — what shall I be? Hetman of the Tartars. They must give me plenty of land, and some town as capital; around the town villages will rise on rich land, and in the villages good men with sabres, many bows and many sabres. And when I carry her away to my town, and have her for wife, the beauty, with whom will the power be? With me. Who will demand her? The little knight, — if he be alive. Even should he be alive, and howl like a wolf and beat with his forehead to the king with complaint, do you think that they would raise war with me for one bright tress? They have had such a war already, and half the Commonwealth was flaming with fire. Who will take her? Is it the hetman? Then I will join the Cossacks, will conclude brotherhood with Doroshenko, and give the country over to the Sultan. I am a second Hmelnitski; I am better than Hmelnitski: in me a lion is dwelling. Let them permit me to take her, I will serve them, beat the Cossacks, beat the Khan, and beat the Sultan; but if not, I will trample all Lehistan [1] with hoofs, take hetmans captive, scatter armies, burn towns, slay people. I am Tugai Bey's son; I am a lion."

Here Azya's eyes blazed with a red light; his white teeth glittered like those of old Tugai; he raised his hand and shook his threatening fist toward the north, and he was great and terrible and splendid, so that Halim bowed to him repeatedly, and said hurriedly, in a low voice, —

----

[1] Poland.

"Allah kerim!   Allah kerim!"[1]

Then silence continued for a long time. Azya grew calm
by degrees; at last he said, "Bogush came here. I revealed
to him my strength and resource; namely, to have in the
Ukraine, at the side of the Cossack nation, a Tartar nation,
and besides the Cossack hetman a Tartar hetman."

"Did he approve it?"

"He seized himself by the head, and almost beat with the
forehead; next day he galloped off to the hetman with the
happy news."

"Effendi," said Halim, timidly, "but if the Great Lion
should not approve it?"

"Sobieski?"

"Yes."

A ruddy light began to gleam again in Azya's eyes; but
it remained only during one twinkle. His face grew calm
immediately; then he sat on a bench, and resting his head
on his hands, fell into deep thought.

"I have weighed in my mind," said he, at last, "what
the grand hetman may answer when Bogush gives him the
happy news. The hetman is wise, and will consent. The
hetman knows that in spring there will be war with the
Sultan, for which there are neither men nor money in the
Commonwealth; and when Doroshenko and the Cossacks
are on the side of the Sultan, final destruction may come on
Lehistan, — and all the more that neither the king nor the
estates believe that there will be war, and are not hurrying
to prepare for it. I have an attentive ear here on everything; I know all, and Bogush makes no secret before me
of what they say at the hetman's headquarters. Pan Sobi·
eski is a great man; he will consent, for he knows that if
the Tartars come here for freedom and land, a civil war may
spring up in the Crimea and the steppes of the Dobrudja,
that the strength of the horde will decrease, and that the
Sultan himself must see to quieting those outbreaks.
Meanwhile, the hetman will have time to prepare himself
better; the Cossacks and Doroshenko will waver in loyalty
to the Sultan. This is the only salvation for the Commonwealth, which is so weak that even the return of a few
thousand Lithuanian Tartars means much for it. The hetman knows this; he is wise, he will consent."

"I bow before your reason," answered Halim; "but

---

[1] God is merciful! God is merciful!

what will happen if Allah takes from the Great Lion his light, or if Satan so blinds him with pride that he will reject your plans ? "

Azya pushed his wild face up to Halim's ear, and whispered, "You remain here now until the answer comes from the hetman; and till then I will not go to Rashkoff. If they reject my plans, I will send you to Krychinski and the others. You will give them the order to advance to this side of the river almost up to Hreptyoff, and to be in readiness; and I with my men here will fall on the command the first night I choose, and do this for them — " Here Azya drew his finger across his neck, and after a while added, " Fate, fate, fate ! "

Halim thrust his head down between his shoulders, and on his beast-like face an ominous smile appeared. " Allah ! And that to the Little Falcon ? "

" That to him first."

" And then to the Sultan's dominions ? "

" To the Sultan's dominions, — with her."

CHAPTER XXXII.

A FIERCE winter covered the forests with heavy snow-clusters and icicles, and filled ravines to their edges with drifts, so that the whole land seemed a single white plain. Great, sudden storms came, in which men and herds were lost under the pall of snow; roads grew misleading and perilous: still, Pan Bogush hastened with all his power to Yavorov to communicate Azya's great plans to the hetman as quickly as possible. A noble of the border, reared in continual danger of Cossacks and Tartars, penetrated with the thought of perils which threatened the country from insurrections, from raids, from the whole power of the Turks, he saw in those plans almost the salvation of the country; he believed sacredly that the hetman, held in homage by him, and by all men of the frontier, would not hesitate a moment when it was a question of the power of the Commonwealth: hence he rode forward with joy in his heart, in spite of snow-drifts, wrong roads, and tempests.

He dropped in at last on a Sunday, together with snow, at Yavorov, and having the good fortune to find Pan Sobieski at home, announced himself straightway, though attendants informed him that the hetman, busied night and day with expeditions and the writing of despatches, had barely time to take food. But beyond expectation, the hetman gave command to call him at once. Therefore, after he had waited only a short time, the old soldier bowed to the knees of his leader.

He found Pan Sobieski changed greatly, and with a face full of care; for those were well-nigh the most grievous years of his life. His name had not thundered yet through every corner of Christendom; but the fame of a great leader and a terrible crusher of the Mussulman encircled him already in the Commonwealth. Owing to that fame, the grand baton was confided to him in time, and the defence of the eastern boundary; but with the dignity of hetman they had given him neither money nor men. Still, victory had followed his steps hitherto as faithfully as his shadow follows a man. With a handful of troops he had won victory at Podhaytse; with a handful of troops he had passed

like a flame through the length and the breadth of the
Ukraine, rubbing into dust chambuls of many thousands,
capturing insurgent cities, spreading dread and terror of
the Polish name. But now there hung over the Commonwealth a war with the most terrible of the powers of that
period, for it was a war with the whole Mussulman world.
It was no longer a secret for Sobieski that since Doroshenko
had given up the Ukraine and the Cossacks to the Sultan,
the latter had promised to move Turkey, Asia Minor,
Arabia, and Egypt as far as the interior of Africa, to proclaim a sacred war, and go in his own person to demand the
new "pashalik" [1] from the Commonwealth. Destruction,
like a bird of prey, was floating over all Southern Russia,
and meanwhile there was disorder in the Commonwealth;
the nobles were uproarious in defence of their incompetent
king, and, assembled in armed camps, were ready for civil
war, if for any. The country, exhausted by recent conflicts
and military confederations, had become impoverished; envy
was storming in it; mutual distrust was rankling in men's
hearts.

No one wished to believe that war with the Mussulman
power was imminent; and they condemned the great leader
for spreading news about it purposely to turn men's minds
from home questions. He was condemned greatly for this
also, — that he was ready himself to call in the Turks, if only
to secure victory to his adherents. They made him simply
a traitor; and had it not been for the army, they would not
have hesitated to impeach him.

In view of the approaching war, to which thousands of
legions of wild people would march from the East, he was
without an army, — he had merely a handful, so small that
the Sultan's court counted more servants; he was without
money, without means of repairing the ruined fortresses,
without hope of victory, without possibility of defence,
without the conviction that his death, as formerly the
death of Jolkyevski, would rouse the torpid country and
give birth to an avenger. That was the reason that care
had settled on his forehead; and the lordly countenance, like
that of a Roman conqueror with a forehead in laurels,
bore traces of hidden pain and sleepless nights. But at
sight of Bogush a kindly smile brightened the face of the

---

[1] The territory governed by a pasha, in this case the lands of the
Cossacks.

hetman; he placed his hands on the shoulders of the man inclining before him, and said, —

"I greet you, soldier, I greet you! I had not hoped to see you so soon; but you are the dearer to me in Yavorov. Whence do you come, — from Kamenyets?"

"No, serene, great, mighty lord hetman, I have not even been at Kamenyets. I come straightway from Hreptyoff."

"What is my little soldier doing there? Is he well, and has he cleared the wilds of Ushytsa even somewhat?"

"The wilds are so peaceful that a child might pass through them in safety. The robbers are hanged, and in these last days Azba Bey with his whole party was cut to pieces, so that even a witness of the slaughter was not left. I arrived there on the very day of their destruction."

"I recognize Volodyovski: Rushchyts in Rashkoff is the only man who may compare with him. But what do they say in the steppes? Are there fresh tidings from the Danube?"

"There are, but of evil. There is to be a great muster of troops at Adrianople in the last days of winter."

"I know that already. There are no tidings now save of evil, — evil from the Commonwealth, evil from the Crimea and from Stambul."

"But not altogether, for I myself bring such good tidings that if I were a Turk or a Tartar I should surely mention a present."

"Well, then, you have fallen from heaven to me. Come, speak quickly, dispel my anxiety!"

"But if I am so frozen, your great mightiness, that the wit has stiffened in my head?"

The hetman clapped his hands, and commanded an attendant to bring mead. After a while they brought in a mouldy decanter, and candlesticks with burning tapers, for though the hour was still early, snowy clouds had made the air so gloomy that outside, as well as in the house, it was like nightfall.

The hetman poured out and drank to his guest; the latter, bowing low, emptied his glass, and said: "The first news is this, that Azya, who was to bring back to our service the captains of the Lithuanian Tartars and the Cheremis, is not called Mellehovich, he is a son of Tugai Bey."

"Of Tugai Bey?" asked Pan Sobieski, with amazement.

"Thus it is, your great mightiness. It has come out that Pan Nyenashinyets carried him away from the Crimea while a child, but lost him on the road home; and Azya, falling into possession of the Novoveskis, was reared at their house without knowing. that he was descended from such a father."

"It was a wonder to me that he, though so young, was held in such esteem among the Tartars. But now I understand; and the Cossacks too, even those who have remained faithful to the mother,[1] consider Hmelnitski as a kind of saint, and are proud of him."

"That is just it, just it; I told Azya the same thing," said Pan Bogush.

"Wonderful are the ways of God," said the hetman, after a while; "old Tugai shed rivers of blood in our country, and his son is serving it, — at least he serves it faithfully so far; but now I do not know whether he will not wish to taste Crimean greatness."

"Now? Now he is still more faithful; and here my second tidings begin, in which it may be that strength and resource and salvation for the suffering Commonwealth are contained. So help me God, I forgot fatigue and danger in view of these tidings, so as to let them out of my lips at the earliest moment, and console your troubled heart."

"I am listening eagerly," said Pan Sobieski.

Bogush began to explain Azya's plans, and presented them with such enthusiasm that he grew really eloquent. From time to time his hand, trembling from emotion, poured out a glass of mead, spilling the noble drink over the rim; and he spoke and spoke on. Before the astonished eyes of the grand hetman passed as it were clear pictures of the future; therefore thousands and tens of thousands of Tartars came for land and freedom, bringing their wives and children and their herds; therefore the astonished Cossacks, seeing the new power of the Commonwealth, bowed down to it obediently, bowed down to the king and the hetman; hence there was rebellion in the Ukraine no longer; hence raids, destructive as fire or flood, were advancing no longer on the old roads against Russia, — but at the side of the Polish and the Cossack armies moved over the measureless steppes, with the playing of trumpets and the rattle of drums, chambuls of Tartars, nobles of the Ukraine.

And for whole years carts after carts were advancing, and in them, in spite of the commands of Khan and Sultan,

---

[1] The Commonwealth.

were multitudes who preferred the black land of the
Ukraine and bread to their former hungry settlements.
And the power, hostile aforetime, was moving to the service of the Commonwealth. The Crimea became depopulated; their former power slipped out of the hands of the
Khan and the Sultan, and dread seized them; for from the
steppes, from the Ukraine, the new hetman of a new Tartar
nobility looked threateningly into their eyes, — a guardian
and faithful defender of the Commonwealth, the renowned
son of a terrible father, young Tugai Bey.

A flush came out on the countenance of Bogush; it
seemed that his own words bore him away, for at the end
he raised both hands and cried, —

"This is what I bring! This is what that dragon's whelp
has brooded out in the wild woods of Hreptyoff! All that
is needed now is to give him a letter and permission from
your great mightiness to spread a report in the Crimea and
on the Danube. Your great mightiness, if Tugai Bey's son
were to do nothing except to make an uproar in the Crimea
and on the Danube, to cause misunderstandings, to rouse
the hydra of civil war among the Tartars, to embroil some
camps against others, and that on the eve of conflict, I
repeat, he would render a great and undying service to the
Commonwealth."

But Pan Sobieski walked back and forth with long strides
through the room, without speaking. His lordly face was
gloomy, almost terrible; he strode, and it was to be seen
that he was conversing in his soul, — unknown whether
with himself or with God.

At last thou didst open some page in thy soul, grand
hetman, for thou gavest answer in these words to the
speaker : —

"Bogush, even if I had the right to give such a letter and
such permission, while I live I should not give them."

These words fell as heavily as if they had been of molten
lead or iron, and weighed so on Bogush that for a time he
was dumb, hung his head, and only after a long interval did
he groan out, —

"Why, your great mightiness, why?"

"First, I will tell you, as a statesman, that the name of
Tugai Bey's son might attract, it is true, a certain number
of Tartars, if land, liberty, and the rights of nobility were
offered them; but not so many would come as he and you
have imagined. And, besides, it would be an act of mad-

ness to call Tartars to the Ukraine, and settle new people there, when we cannot manage the Cossacks alone. You say that disputes and war will rise among them at once, that there will be a sword ready for the Cossack neck; but who will assure you that that sword would not be stained with Polish blood also? I have not known this Azya, hitherto; but now I perceive that the dragon of pride and ambition inhabits his breast, therefore I ask again, who will guarantee that there is not in him a second Hmelnitski? He will beat the Cossacks; but if the Commonwealth shall fail to satisfy him in something, and threaten him with justice and punishment for some act of violence, he will join the Cossacks, summon new hordes from the East, as Hmelnitski summoned Tugai Bey, give himself to the Sultan, as Doroshenko has done, and, instead of a new growth of power, new bloodshed and defeats will come on us."

"Your great mightiness, the Tartars, when they have become nobles, will hold faithfully to the Commonwealth."

"Were there few of the Lithuanian Tartars and Cheremis? They were nobles a long time, and went over to the Sultan."

"Their privileges were withheld from the Lithuanian Tartars."

"But what will happen if, to begin with, the Polish nobles, as is certain, oppose such an extension of their rights to others? With what face, with what conscience, will you give to wild and predatory hordes, who have been destroying our country continually, the power and the right to determine the fate of that country, to choose kings, and send deputies to the diets? Why give them such a reward? What madness has come to the head of this Tartar, and what evil spirit seized you, my old soldier, to let yourself bè so beguiled and seduced as to believe in such dishonor and such an impossibility?"

Bogush dropped his eyes, and said with an uncertain voice: —

"I knew beforehand that the estates would oppose; but Azya said that if the Tartars were to settle with permission of your great mightiness, they would not let themselves be driven out."

"Man! Why, he threatened, he shook his sword over the Commonwealth, and you did not see it!"

"Your great mightiness," said Bogush, in despair, "it might be arranged not to make all the Tartars nobles, only

the most considerable, and proclaim the rest free men.
Even in that situation they would answer the summons of
Tugai Bey's son."

"But why is it not better to proclaim all the Cossacks
free men? Cease, old soldier! I tell you that an evil spirit
has taken possession of you."

"Your great mightiness —"

"And I say further," here Pan Sobieski wrinkled his lion-
like forehead and his eyes gleamed, "even if everything
were to happen as you say, even if our power were to
increase through this action, even if war with Turkey were
to be averted, even if the nobles themselves were to call
for it, still, while this hand of mine wields a sabre and
can make the sign of the cross, never and never will I
permit such a thing! So help me God!"

"Why, your great mightiness?" repeated Bogush, wringing his hands.

"Because I am not only a Polish hetman, but a Christian
hetman, for I stand in defence of the Cross. And even if
those Cossacks were to tear the entrails of the Commonwealth more cruelly than ever, I will not cut the necks
of a blinded but still Christian people with the swords of
Pagans. For by doing so I should say 'raca' to our
fathers and grandfathers, to my own ancestors, to their
ashes, to the blood and tears of the whole past Commonwealth. As God is true! if destruction is waiting for us,
if our name is to be the name of a dead and not of a living
people, let our glory remain behind and a memory of that
service which God pointed out to us; let people who come in
after time say, when looking at those crosses and tombs:
'Here is Christianity; here they defended the Cross against
Mohammedan foulness, while there was breath in their
breasts, while the blood was in their veins; and they died
for other nations.' This is our service, Bogush. Behold,
we are the fortress on which Christ fixed His crucifix, and
you tell me, a soldier of God, nay, the commander of the
fortress, to be the first to open the gate and let in Pagans,
like wolves to a sheep-fold, and give the sheep, the flock of
Jesus, to slaughter. Better for us to suffer from chambuls;
better for us to endure rebellions; better for us to go to this
terrible war; better for me and you to fall, and for the
whole Commonwealth to perish, — than to put disgrace on
our name, to lose our fame, and betray that guardianship
and that service of God."

When he had said this, Pan Sobieski stood erect in all his grandeur; on his face there was a radiance such as must have been on that of Godfrey de Bouillon when he burst in over the walls of Jerusalem, shouting, "God wills it!" Pan Bogush seemed to himself dust before those words, and Azya seemed to him dust before Pan Sobieski, and the fiery plans of the young Tartar grew black and became suddenly in the eyes of Bogush something dishonest and altogether infamous. For what could he say after the statement of the hetman that it was better to fall than to betray the service of God? What argument could he bring? Therefore he did not know, poor knight, whether to fall at the knees of the hetman, or to beat his own breast, repeating, "*Mea culpa, mea maxima culpa.*"

But at that moment the sound of bells was given out from the neighboring Dominican monastery.

Hearing this, Pan Sobieski said, —

"They are sounding for vespers, Bogush; let us go and commit ourselves to God."

CHAPTER XXXIII.

As much as Pan Bogush hastened when going from Hreptyoff to the hetman, so much did he loiter on the way back.
He halted a week or two in each more considerable place;
he spent Christmas in Lvoff, and the New Year came on him
there. He carried, it is true, the hetman's instructions for
the son of Tugai Bey; but they contained merely injunc-
tions to finish the affair of the captains promptly, and a dry
and even threatening command to leave his great plans.
Pan Bogush had no reason to push on, for Azya could do
nothing among the Tartars without a document from the
hetman. He loitered, therefore, visiting churches along
the road, and doing penance because he had joined Azya's
plans.

Meanwhile guests had swarmed into Hreptyoff immediately after the New Year. From Kamenyets came Naviragh, a delegate from the patriarch of Echmiadzin, with
him the two Anardrats, skilful theologians from Kaffa,
and a numerous retinue. The soldiers wondered greatly at
the strange garments of these men, at the violet and red
Crimean caps, long shawls, velvet and silk, at their dark
faces, and the great gravity with which they strode, like
bustards or cranes, through the Hreptyoff stanitsa. Pan
Zaharyash Pyotrovich, famed for his continual journeys to
the Crimea, nay, to Tsargrad itself, and still more for the
eagerness with which he sought out and ransomed captives
in the markets of the East, accompanied, as interpreter,
Naviragh and the Anardrats. Pan Volodyovski counted
out to him at once the sum needful to ransom Pan Boski;
and since the wife had not money sufficient, he gave from
his own; Basia added her ear-rings with pearls, so as to
aid more efficiently the suffering lady and her charming
daughter. Pan Seferovich, pretor of Kamenyets, came
also, — a rich Armenian whose brother was groaning in
Tartar bonds, — and two women, still young and of beauty
far from inconsiderable, though somewhat dark, Pani
Neresevich and Pani Kyeremovich. Both were concerned
for their captive husbands.

The guests were for the greater part in trouble, but there were joyous ones also. Father Kaminski had sent, to remain for the carnival at Hreptyoff, under Basia's protection, his niece Panna Kaminski; and on a certain day Pan Novoveski the younger — that is, Pan Adam — burst in like a thunderbolt. When he had heard of the arrival of his father at Hreptyoff he obtained leave at once from Pan Rushchyts, and hastened to meet him.

Pan Adam had changed greatly during the last few years; first of all, his upper lip was shaded thickly by a short mustache, which did not cover his teeth, white as a wolf's teeth, but was handsome and twisted. Secondly, the young man, always stalwart, had now become almost a giant. It seemed that such a dense and bushy forelock could grow only on such an enormous head, and such an enormous head could find needful support only on fabulous shoulders. His face, always dark, was swarthy from the winds; his eyes were gleaming like coals; defiance was as if written on his features. When he seized a large apple he hid it so easily in his powerful palm that he could play "guess which one;" and when he put a handful of nuts on his knee and pressed them with his hand he made snuff of them. Everything in him went to strength; still he was lean, — his stomach was receding, but the chest above it was as roomy as a chapel. He broke horseshoes with ease, he tied iron rods around the necks of soldiers, he seemed even larger than he was in reality; when he walked, planks creaked under him; and when he stumbled against a bench, he knocked splinters from it.

In a word, he was a man in a hundred, in whom life, daring, and strength were boiling, as water in a caldron. Not being able to find room, in even such an enormous body, it seemed that he had a flame in his breast and his head, and involuntarily one looked to see if his forelock were not steaming. In fact, it steamed sometimes, for he was good at the goblet. To battle he went with a laugh which recalled the neighing of a charger; and he hewed in such fashion that when each engagement was over soldiers went to examine the bodies left by him, and wonder at his astonishing blows. Accustomed, moreover, from childhood to the steppe, to watchfulness and war, he was careful and foreseeing in spite of all his vehemence; he knew every Tartar stratagem, and, after Volodyovski and Rushchyts, was deemed the best partisan leader.

In spite of threats and promises, old Novoveski did not receive his son very harshly; for he feared lest he might go away again if offended, and not show himself for another eleven years. Besides, the selfish noble was satisfied at heart with that son who had taken no money from home, who had helped himself thoroughly in the world, won glory among his comrades, the favor of the hetman, and the rank of an officer, which no one else could have struggled to without protection. The father considered that this young man, grown wild in the steppes, might not bend before the importance of his father, and in such a case it was not best to expose it to the test. Therefore the son fell at his feet, as was proper; still he looked into his eyes, and at the first reproach he answered without ceremony, —

"Father, you have blame in your mouth, but at heart you are glad, and with reason. I have incurred no disgrace, — I ran away to the squadron; besides, I am a noble."

"But you may be a Mussulman," said the father, "since you did not show yourself at home for eleven years."

"I did not show myself through fear of punishment, which would be repugnant to my rank and dignity of officer. I waited for a letter of pardon; I saw nothing of the letter, you saw nothing of me."

"But are you not afraid at present?"

The young man showed his white teeth with a smile. "This place is governed by military power, to which even the power of a father must yield. Why should you not, my benefactor, embrace me, for you have a hearty desire to do so?"

Saying this, he opened his arms, and Pan Novoveski did not know himself what to do. Indeed, he could not quarrel with that son who went out of the house a lad, and returned now a mature man and an officer surrounded with military renown. And this and that flattered greatly the fatherly pride of Pan Novoveski; he hesitated only out of regard for his personal dignity.

But the son seized him; the bones of the old noble cracked in the bear-like embrace, and this touched him completely.

"What is to be done?" cried he, panting. "He feels, the rascal, that he is sitting on his own horse, and is not afraid. 'Pon my word! if I were at home, indeed I should not be so tender; but here, what can I do? Well, come on again."

And they embraced a second time, after which the young man began to inquire hurriedly for his sister.

"I gave command to keep her aside till I called her," said the father; "the girl will jump almost out of her skin."

"For God's sake, where is she?" cried the son, and opening the door he began to call so loudly that an echo answered, "Eva! Eva!" from the walls.

Eva, who was waiting in the next chamber, rushed in at once; but she was barely able to cry "Adam!" when strong arms seized her and raised her from the floor. The brother had loved her greatly always; in old times, while protecting her from the tyranny of their father, he took her faults on himself frequently, and received the floggings due her. In general the father was a despot at home, really cruel; therefore the maiden greeted now in that strong brother, not a brother merely, but her future refuge and protection. He kissed her on the head, on the eyes and hands; at times he held her at arms' length, looked into her face, and cried out with delight, —

"A splendid girl, as God is dear to me!" Then again, "See how she has grown! A stove,[1] not a maiden!"

Her eyes were laughing at him. They began to talk then very rapidly, of their long separation, of home and the wars. Old Pan Novoveski walked around them and muttered. The son made a great impression on him; but at times disquiet touching his own future authority seemed to seize him. Those were the days of great parental power, which grew to boundless preponderance afterward; but this son was that partisan, that soldier from the wild stanitsas, who, as Pan Novoveski understood at once, was riding on his own special horse. Pan Novoveski guarded his parental authority jealously. He was certain, however, that his son would always respect him, would give him his due; but would he yield always like wax, would he endure everything as he had endured when a stripling? "Bah!" thought the old man, "if I make up my mind to it, I'll treat him like a stripling. He is daring, a lieutenant; he imposes on me, as I love God." To finish all, Pan Novoveski felt that his fatherly affection was growing each minute, and that he would have a weakness for that giant of a son.

Meanwhile Eva was twittering like a bird, overwhelming

[1] That means as tall as a stove. The tile or porcelain stoves of eastern Europe are very high.

her brother with questions. " When would he come home;
and would n't he settle down, would n't he marry?" She
in truth does not know clearly, and is not certain; but as
she loves her father, she has heard that soldiers are given
to falling in love. But now she remembers that it was
Pani Volodyovski who said so. How beautiful and kind
she is, that Pani Volodyovski! A more beautiful and
better is not to be found in all Poland with a candle. Zosia
Boski alone might, perhaps, be compared with her.

" Who is Zosia Boski?" asked Pan Adam.

" She who with her mother is stopping here, whose father
was carried off by the Tartars. If you see her yourself you
will fall in love with her."

"Give us Zosia Boski!" cried the young officer.

The father and Eva laughed at such readiness.

" Love is like death," said Pan Adam: " it misses no one.
I was still smooth-faced, and Pani Volodyovski was a young
lady, when I fell terribly in love with her. Oi! dear God!
how I loved that Basia! But what of it! 'I will tell her
so,' thought I. I told her, and the answer was as if some
one had given me a slap in the face. Shu, cat away from
the milk! She was in love with Pan Volodyovski, it seems,
already; but what is the use in talking? — she was right."

" Why?" asked old Pan Novoveski.

" Why? This is why: because I, without boasting, could
meet every one else with the sabre; but he would not amuse
himself with me while you could say ' Our Father' twice.
And besides he is a partisan beyond compare, before whom
Rushchyts himself would take off his cap. What, Pan
Rushchyts? Even the Tartars love him. He is the greatest
soldier in the Commonwealth."

"And how he and his wife love each other! Ai, ai!
enough to make your eyes ache to look at them," put in
Eva.

" Ai, your mouth waters! Your mouth waters, for your
time has come too," exclaimed Pan Adam. And putting
his hands on his hips he began to nod his head, as a horse
does; but she answered modestly, —

" I have no thought of it."

" Well, there is no lack of officers and pleasant company
here."

" But," said Eva, "I do not know whether father has told
you that Azya is here."

" Azya Mellehovich, the Lithuanian Tartar? I know
him; he is a good soldier."

"But you do not know," said old Pan Novoveski, "that he is not Mellehovich, but that Azya who grew up with you."

"In God's name, what do I hear? Just think! Sometimes that came to my head too; but they told me that his name was Mellehovich, therefore I thought, 'Well, he is not the man.' Azya with the Tartars is a universal name. I had not seen him for so many years that I was not certain. Our Azya was rather ugly and short, and this one is a beauty."

"He is ours, ours!" said old Novoveski, "or rather not ours, for do you know what has come out, whose son he is?"

"How should I know?"

"He is the son of the great Tugai Bey."

The young man struck his powerful palms on his knees till the sound was heard through the house.

"I cannot believe my ears! Of the great Tugai Bey? If that is true, he is a prince and a relative of the Khan. There is no higher blood in the Crimea than Tugai Bey's."

"It is the blood of an enemy!"

"It was that in the father, but the son serves us; I have seen him myself twenty times in action. Ha! I understand now whence comes that devilish daring in him. Pan Sobieski distinguished him before the whole army, and made him a captain. I am glad from my soul to greet him, — a strong soldier; from my whole heart I will greet him."

"But be not too familiar with him."

"Why? Is he my servant, or ours? I am a soldier, he is a soldier; I am an officer, he is an officer. If he were some fellow of the infantry who commands his regiment with a reed, I should n't have a word to say; but if he is the son of Tugai Bey, then no common blood flows in him. He is a prince, and that is the end of it; the hetman himself will provide naturalization for him. How should I thrust my nose above him, when I am in brotherhood with Kulak Murza, with Bakchy Aga and Sukyman? None of these would be ashamed to herd sheep for Tugai Bey."

Eva felt a sudden wish to kiss her brother again; then she sat so near him that she began to stroke his bushy forelock with her shapely hand.

The entrance of Pan Michael interrupted this tenderness.

Pan Adam sprang up to greet the commanding officer, and began at once to explain that he had not paid his respects first of all to the commandant, because he had not come on service, but as a private person. Pan Michael embraced him cordially and said, —

"And who would blame you, dear comrade, if after so many years of absence you fell at your father's knees first of all? It would be something different were it a question of service; but have you no commission from Pan Rushchyts?"

"Only obeisances. Pan Rushchyts went down to Yagorlik, for they informed him that there were multitudes of horse-tracks on the snow. My commandant received your letter and sent it to the horde to his relatives and brothers, instructing them to search and make inquiries there; but he will not write himself. 'My hand is too heavy,' he says, 'and I have no experience in that art.'"

"He does not like writing, I know," said Pan Michael. "The sabre with him is always the basis." Here the mustaches of the little knight quivered, and he added, not without a certain boastfulness, "And still you were chasing Azba Bey two months for nothing."

"But your grace gulped him as a pike does a whiting," cried Pan Adam, with enthusiasm. "Well, God must have disturbed his mind, that when he had escaped from Pan Rushchyts, he came under your hand. He caught it!"

These words tickled the little knight agreeably, and wishing to return politeness for politeness, he turned to Pan Novoveski and said,—

"The Lord Jesus has not given me a son so far; but if ever He does, I should wish him to be like this cavalier."

"There is nothing in him!" answered the old noble,— "nothing, and that is the end of it."

But in spite of these words he began to puff from delight.

"Here is another great treat for me!"

Meanwhile the little knight stroked Eva's face, and said to her: "You see that I am no stripling; but my Basia is almost of your age; therefore I am thinking that at times she should have some pleasant amusement, proper for youthful years. It is true that all here love her beyond description, and you, I trust, see some reason for it."

"Beloved God!" said Eva, "there is not in the world another such woman! I have said that just now."

The little knight was rejoiced beyond measure, so that his face shone, and he asked, "Did you say that really ?"

"As I live she did !" cried father and son together.

"Well, then, array yourself in the best, for, without Basia's knowledge, I have brought an orchestra from Kamenyets. I ordered the men to hide the instruments in straw, and I told her that they were Gypsies who had come to shoe horses. This evening I'll have tremendous dancing. She loves it, she loves it, though she likes to play the dignified matron."

When he had said this, Pan Michael began to rub his hands, and was greatly pleased with himself.

CHAPTER XXXIV.

THE snow fell so thickly that it filled the stanitsa trench altogether, and settled on the stockade wall like a mound. Outside were night and a storm; but the chief room in Hreptyoff was blazing with light. There were two violins, a bass-viol, a flageolet, a French horn, and two bugles. The fiddlers worked away till they were turning in their seats. The cheeks of the flageolet player and the buglers were puffed out, and their eyes were bloodshot. The oldest officers sat on benches at the wall, one near another,—as gray doves sit before their cotes in a roof, — and while drinking mead and wine looked at the dancers.

Basia opened the ball with Pan Mushalski, who, despite advanced years, was as great a dancer as a bowman. Basia wore a robe of silver brocade edged with ermine, and resembled a newly blown rose in fresh snow. Young and old marvelled at her beauty, and the cry "Save us!" came involuntarily from the breasts of many; for though Panna Eva and Panna Zosia were somewhat younger, and beautiful beyond common measure, still Basia surpassed all. In her eyes delight and pleasure were flashing. As she swept past the little knight she thanked him for the entertainment with a smile; through her open rosy mouth gleamed white teeth, and she shone in her silver robe, glittering like a sun-ray or a star, and enchanted the eye and the heart with the beauty of a child, a woman, and a flower. The split sleeves of her robe fluttered after her like the wings of a great butterfly; and when, raising her skirt, she made an obeisance before her partner, you would think that she was floating on the earth like a vision, or one of those sprites which on bright nights in summer skip along the edges of ravines.

Outside, the soldiers pressed their stern mustached-faces against the lighted window-panes, and flattening their noses against the glass peered into the room. It pleased them greatly that their adored lady surpassed all others in beauty, for they held furiously to her side; they did not spare jests, therefore, and allusions to Panna Eva, or Panna

Zosia, and greeted with loud hurrahs every approach that Basia made to the window.

Pan Michael increased like bread-rising, and nodded his head, keeping time with Basia's movements; Pan Zagloba, standing near, held a tankard in his hand, tapped with his foot and dropped liquor on the floor; but at times he and the little knight turned and looked at each other with uncommon rapture and puffing.

But Basia glittered and glittered through the whole room, ever more joyous, ever more charming. Such for her was the Wilderness. Now a battle, now a hunt, now amusements, dancing and music, and a crowd of soldiers, — her husband the greatest among them, and he loving and beloved; Basia felt that all liked and admired her, gave her homage, — that the little knight was happy through that; and she herself felt as happy as birds feel when spring has come, and they rejoice and sing lustily and joyously in the air of May. The second couple were Azya and Eva Novoveski, who wore a crimson jacket. The young Tartar, completely intoxicated with the white vision glittering before him, spoke not one word to Eva; but she, thinking that emotion had stopped the voice in his breast, tried to give him courage by pressure of her hand, light at the beginning, and afterward stronger. Azya, on his part, pressed her hand so powerfully that hardly could she repress a cry of pain; but he did this involuntarily, for he thought only of Basia, he saw only Basia, and in his soul he repeated a terrible vow, that if he had to burn half Russia she should be his.

At times, when consciousness came to him somewhat, he felt a desire to seize Eva by the throat, stifle her, and gloat over her, because she pressed his hand, and because she stood between him and Basia. At times he pierced the poor girl with his cruel, falcon glance, and her heart began to beat with more power; she thought that it was through love that he looked at her so rapaciously.

Pan Adam and Zosia formed the third couple. She looked like a forget-me-not, and tripped along at his side with downcast eyes; he looked like a wild horse, and jumped like one. From under his shod heels splinters were flying; his forelock was soaring upward; his face was covered with ruddiness; he opened his nostrils wide like a Turkish charger, and sweeping Zosia around, as a whirlwind does a leaf, carried her through the air. The soul grew glad in him beyond measure, since he lived on the edge of the Wilderness whole months without seeing a woman. Zosia pleased him so much at first glance, that in a moment he was in love with her to kill. From time to time he looked at her downcast eyes, at her blooming cheeks, and just snorted at the pleasant sight; then all the more mightily did he strike fire with his heels; with greater strength did he hold her, at the turn of the dance, to his broad breast, and burst into a mighty laugh from excess of delight, and boiled and loved with more power every moment.

But Zosia had fear in her dear little heart; still, that fear was not disagreeable, for she was pleased with that whirlwind of a man who bore her along and carried her with him, — a real dragon! She had seen various cavaliers in Yavorov, but such a fiery one she had not met till that hour; and none danced like him, none swept her on so. In truth, a real dragon! What was to be done with him, since it was impossible to resist?

In the next couple, Panna Kaminski danced with a polite cavalier, and after her came the Armenians, — Pani Kyeremovich and Pani Neresevich, who, though wives of merchants, were still invited to the company, for both were persons of courtly manners, and very wealthy. The dignified Naviragh and the two Anardrats looked with growing wonder at the Polish dances; the old men at their mead cups made an increasing noise, like grasshoppers on stubble land. But the music drowned every voice, and in the middle of the room delight grew in all hearts.

Meanwhile Basia left her partner, ran panting to her husband, and clasped her hands before him.

"Michael," said she, "it is so cold outside the windows for the soldiers, give command to let them have a keg of gorailka."

He, being unusually jovial, fell to kissing her hands, and cried, —

"I would not spare blood to please you!"

Then he hurried out himself to tell the soldiers at whose instance they were to have the keg; for he wished them to thank Basia, and love her the more.

In answer, they raised such a shout that the snow began to fall from the roof; the little knight cried in addition, "Let the muskets roar there as a vivat to the Pani!" Upon his return to the room he found Basia dancing with

Azya. When the Tartar embraced that sweet figure with his arm, when he felt the warmth coming from her and her breath on his face, his pupils went up almost into his skull, and the whole world turned before his eyes; in his soul he gave up paradise, eternity, and for all the houris he wanted only this one.

Then Basia, when she noticed in passing the crimson jacket of Eva, curious to know if Azya had proposed yet, inquired, —

"Have you told her?"

"No."

"Why?"

"It is not time yet," said he, with a strange expression.

"But are you greatly in love?"

"To the death, to the death!" answered the Tartar, with a low but hoarse voice, like the croaking of a raven.

And they danced on, immediately after Pan Adam, who had pushed to the front. Others had changed partners, but Pan Adam did not let Zosia go; only at times he seated her on a bench to rest and recover breath, then he revelled again. At last he stopped before the orchestra, and holding Zosia with one arm, cried to the musicians, —

"Play the krakoviak! on with it!"

Obedient to command, they played at once. Pan Adam kept time with his foot, and sang with an immense voice, —

> "Lost are crystal torrents,
> In the Dniester River;
> Lost in thee, my heart is,
> Lost in thee, O maiden!
> U-há!"

And that "U-há" he roared out in such Cossack fashion that Zosia was drooping from fear. The dignified Naviragh, standing near, was frightened, the two learned Anardrats were frightened; but Pan Adam led the dance farther. Twice he made the circle of the room, and stopping before the musicians, sang of his heart again, —

> "Lost, but not to perish,
> Though the current snatch it;
> In the depth 't will seek out
> And bear back a gold ring.
> U-há!"

"Very pretty rhymes," cried Zagloba; "I am skilled in the matter, for I have made many such. Bark away, cavalier, bark away; and when you find the ring I will continue in this sense, —

> "Flint are all the maidens,
>   Steel are all the young men;
>   You 'll have sparks in plenty
>   If you strike with will.
>   U-há!"

"Vivat! vivat Pan Zagloba!" cried the officers, with a mighty voice, so that the dignified Naviragh was frightened, and the two learned Anardrats were frightened, and began to look at one another with exceeding amazement.

But Pan Adam went around twice more, and seated his partner at last on the bench, panting, and astonished at the boldness of her cavalier. He was very agreeable to her, so valiant and honest, a regular conflagration; but just because she had not met such a man hitherto, great confusion seized her, — therefore, dropping her eyes still lower, she sat in silence, like a little innocent.

"Why are you silent; are you grieving for something?" asked Pan Adam.

"I am; my father is in captivity," answered Zosia, with a thin voice.

"Never mind that," said the young man; "it is proper to dance! Look at this room; here are some tens of officers, and most likely no one of them will die his own death, but from arrows of Pagans or in bonds, — this one to-day, that to-morrow. Each man on these frontiers has lost some one, and we make merry lest God might think that we murmur at our service. That is it. It is proper to dance. Laugh, young lady! show your eyes, for I think that you hate me!"

Zosia did not raise her eyes, it is true; but she began to raise the corners of her mouth, and two dimples were formed in her rosy cheeks.

"Do you love me a little bit?" asked he.

And Zosia, in a still lower voice, said, "Yes; but —"

When he heard this, Pan Adam started up, and seizing Zosia's hands, began to cover them with kisses, and cry, —

"Lost! No use in talking; I love you to death! I don't want any one but you, my dearest beauty! Oh, save me, how I love you! In the morning I 'll fall at your mother's feet. What? — in the morning! I'll fall to-night, so as to be sure that you are mine!"

A tremendous roar of musketry outside the window drowned Zosia's answer. The delighted soldiers were firing, as a vivat for Basia; the window-panes rattled, the walls trembled. The dignified Naviragh was frightened a third time; the two learned Anardrats were frightened; but Zagloba, standing near, began to pacify them.

"With the Poles," said he to them, "there is never rejoicing without outcry and clamor."

In truth, it came out that all were just waiting for that firing from muskets to revel in the highest degree. The usual ceremony of nobles began now to give way to the wildness of the steppe. Music thundered again; dances burst out anew, like a storm; eyes were flashing and fiery; mist rose from the forelocks. Even the oldest went into the dance; loud shouts were heard every moment; and they drank and frolicked, — drank healths from Basia's slipper; fired from pistols at Eva's boot-heels. Hreptyoff shouted and roared and sang till daybreak, so that the beasts in the neighboring wilds hid from fear in the deepest thickets.

Since that was almost on the eve of a terrible war with the Turkish power, and over all these people terror and destruction were hanging, the dignified Naviragh wondered beyond measure at those Polish soldiers, and the two learned Anardrats wondered no less.

19

CHAPTER XXXV.

ALL slept late next morning, except the soldiers on guard
and the little knight, who never neglected service for pleasure. Pan Adam was on his feet early enough, for Panna
Zosia seemed still more charming to him after his rest.
Arraying himself handsomely, he went to the room in which
they had danced the previous evening to listen whether
there was not some movement or bustle in the adjoining
chambers where the ladies were.

In the chamber occupied by Pani Boski movement was
to be heard; but the impatient young man was so anxious
to see Zosia that he seized his dagger and fell to picking
out the moss and clay between the logs, so that, God willing, he might look through the chink with one eye at
Zosia.

Zagloba, who was just passing with his beads in his
hand, found him at this work, and knowing at once what
the matter was, came up on tiptoe and began to belabor
with the sandalwood beads the shoulders of the knight.

Pan Adam slipped aside and squirmed as if laughing;
but he was greatly confused, and the old man pursued him
and struck him continually.

"Oh, such a Turk! oh, Tartar! here it is for you; here
it is for you! I exorcise you! Where are your morals?
You want to see a woman? Here it is for you; here it is
for you!"

"My benefactor," cried Pan Adam, "it is not right to
make a whip out of holy beads. Let me go, for I had no
sinful intention."

"You say it is not right to strike with a rosary? Not
true! The palm on Palm Sunday is holy, and still people
strike with it. Ha! these were Pagan beads once and
belonged to Suban Kazi; but I took them from him at
Zbaraj, and afterward the apostolic nuncio blessed them.
See, they are genuine sandalwood!"

"If they are real sandalwood, they have an odor."

"Beads have an odor for me, and a girl for you. I must
dress your shoulders well yet, for there is nothing to drive
out the Devil like a chaplet."

"I had no sinful intention; upon my health I had not!"

"Was it only through piety that you were opening a chink?"

"Not through piety, but through love, which is so wonderful that I'm not sure that I shall not burst from it, as a bomb bursts. What is the use in pretending, when it is true? Flies do not trouble a horse in autumn as this affection troubles me."

"See that this is not sinful desire; for when I came in here you could not stand still, but were striking heel against heel as if you were standing on a firebrand."

"I saw nothing, as I love God sincerely, for I had only just begun to pick at the chink."

"Ah, youth! blood is not water! I, too, must at times even yet repress myself, for in me there is a lion seeking whom he may devour. If you have honorable intentions, you are thinking of marriage."

"Thinking of marriage? God of might! of what should I be thinking? Not only am I thinking, but 'tis as if some one were pricking me with an awl. Is it not known to your grace that I made a proposal to Panna Boski last evening, and I have the consent of my father?"

"The boy is of sulphur and powder! Hangman take thee! If that is the case, then the affair is quite different; but tell me, how was it?"

"Last evening Pani Boski went to her room to bring a handkerchief for Zosia, I after her. She turns around: 'Who is there?' And I, with a rush to her feet: 'Beat me, mother, but give me Zosia, — my happiness, my love!' But Pani Boski, when she recovered herself, said: 'All people praise you and think you a worthy cavalier; still, I will not give an answer to-day, nor to-morrow, but later; and you need the permission of your father.' She went out then, thinking that I was under the influence of wine. In truth, I had a little in my head."

"That is nothing; all had some in their heads. Did you not see the pointed caps sidewise on the heads of Naviragh and the Anardrats toward the end?"

"I did not notice them, for I was settling in my mind how to get my father's consent in the easiest way."

"Well, did it come hard?"

"Toward morning we both went to our room; and because it is well to hammer iron while it is hot, I thought to myself at once that it was necessary to feel, even from afar, how my father would look at the matter. 'Listen, father: I want Zosia terribly, and I want your consent; and if you don't give it, then, as God lives, I'll go to the Venetians to serve, and that's all you'll hear of me.' Then did not he fall on me with great rage: 'Oh, such a son!' said he; 'you can do without permission! Go to the Venetians, or take the girl, — only I tell you this, that I will not give you a copper, not only of my own, but of your mother's money, for it is all mine.' "

Zagloba thrust out his under-lip. "Oh, that is bad!"

"But wait. When I heard that, I said: 'But am I asking for money, or do I need it? I want your blessing, nothing more; for the property of Pagans that came to my sabre is enough to rent a good estate or purchase a village. What belongs to mother, let that be a dower for Eva; I will add one or two handfuls of turquoise and some silk and brocade, and if a bad year comes, I'll help my father with ready money.' My father became dreadfully curious then. 'Have you such wealth?' asked he. 'In God's name, where did you get it? Was it from plunder, for you went away as poor as a Turkish saint?'

" 'Fear God, father,' answered I. 'It is eleven years since I began to bring down this fist, and, as they say, it is not of the worst, and shouldn't it collect something? I was at the storming of rebel towns in which ruffiandom and the Tartars had piled up the finest plunder; I fought against murzas and robber bands: booty came and came. I took only what was recognized as mine without injustice to any; but it increased, and if a man didn't frolic, I should have had twice as much property as you got from your father.' "

"What did the old man say to that?" asked Zagloba, rejoicing.

"My father was amazed, for he had not expected this, and began straightway to complain of my wastefulness. 'There would be,' said he, 'an increase, but that this scatterer, this haughty fellow who loves only to plume himself and puts on the magnate, squanders all, saves nothing.' Then curiosity conquered him, and he began to ask particularly what I have; and seeing that I could travel quickly by smearing with that tar, I not only concealed nothing, but lied a little, though usually I will not over-color, for I think thus to myself: 'Truth is oats, and lying chopped straw.' My father bethought himself, and now for

plans : 'This or that [land] might have been bought,' said
he ; 'this or that lawsuit might have been kept up,' said he ;
'we might have lived at each side of the same boundary, and
when you were away I could have looked after everything.'
And my worthy father began to cry. 'Adam,' said he,
'that girl has pleased me terribly; she is under the protection of the hetman, — there may be some profit out of that,
too; but do you respect this my second daughter, and do not
squander what she has, for I should not forgive you at my
death-hour.' And I, my gracious benefactor, just roared at
the very suspicion of injustice to Zosia. My father and I
fell into each other's embraces, and wept till the first cock-
crow, precisely."

"The old rogue !" muttered Zagloba, then he added
aloud : "Ah, there may be a wedding soon, and new amusements in Hreptyoff, especially since it is carnival time."

"There would be one to-morrow if it depended on me,"
cried Pan Adam, abruptly; "but this is what : My leave will
end soon, and service is service, so I must return to Rashkoff. Well, Pan Rushchyts will give me another leave, I
know. But I am not certain that there will not be delays
on the part of the ladies. For when I push up to the old
one, she says, 'My husband is in captivity.' When I speak
to the daughter, she says, 'Papa is in captivity.' What of
that ? I do not keep that papa in bonds, do I ? I'm
terribly afraid of these obstacles; if it were not for that, I
would take Father Kaminski by the soutane and would n't
let him go till he had tied Zosia and me. But when women
get a thing into their heads you can't draw it out with
nippers. I'd give my last copper, I'd go in person for
'papa,' but I've no way of doing it. Besides, no one knows
where he is; maybe he is dead, and there is the work for
you ! If they ask me to wait for him, I might have to
wait till the Day of Judgment !"

"Pyotrovich, Naviragh, and the Anardrats will take the
road to-morrow; there will be tidings soon."

"Jesus save us ! Am I to wait for tidings ? There can
be nothing before spring; meanwhile I shall wither away,
as God is dear to me ! My benefactor, all have faith in
your wit and experience; knock this waiting out of the heads
of these women. My benefactor, in the spring there will
be war. God knows what will happen. Besides, I want
to marry Zosia, not 'papa;' why must I sigh to him ?"

"Persuade the women to go to Rashkoff and settle. There

it will be easier to get tidings, and if Pyotrovich finds Boski, he will be near you. I will do what I can, I repeat; but do you ask Pani Basia to take your part."

"I will not neglect that, I will not neglect, for devil —"

With that the door squeaked, and Pani Boski entered. But before Zagloba could look around, Pan Adam had already thundered down with his whole length at her feet, and occupying an enormous extent of the floor with his gigantic body, began to cry: —

"I have my father's consent. Give me Zosia, mother! Give me Zosia, give me Zosia, mother!"

"Give Zosia, mother," repeated Zagloba, in a bass voice.

The uproar drew people from the adjacent chambers; Basia came in, Pan Michael came from his office, and soon after came Zosia herself. It did not become the girl to seem to surmise what the matter was; but her face grew purple at once, and putting one hand in the other quickly she dropped them before her, pursed her mouth, and stood at the wall with downcast eyes. Pan Michael ran for old Novoveski. When he came he was deeply offended that his son had not committed the function to him, and had not left the affair to his eloquence, still he upheld the entreaty.

Pani Boski, who lacked, indeed, every near guardianship in the world, burst into tears at last, and agreed to Pan Adam's request to go to Rashkoff and wait there for her husband. Then, covered with tears, she turned to her daughter.

"Zosia," asked she, "are the plans of Pan Adam to your heart?"

All eyes were turned to Zosia. She was standing at the wall, her eyes fixed on the floor as usual, and only after some silence did she say, in a voice barely audible, —

"I will go to Rashkoff."

"My beauty!" roared Pan Adam, and springing to the maiden he caught her in his arms. Then he cried till the walls trembled, "Zosia is mine! She is mine, she is mine!"

CHAPTER XXXVI.

PAN ADAM started for Rashkoff immediately after his betrothal, to find and furnish quarters for Pani and Panna Boski; two weeks after his departure a whole caravan of Hreptyoff guests left the fortalice. It was compôsed of Naviragh, the two Anardrats, the Armenian women (Kyeremovich and Neresevich), Seferevich, Pani and Panna Boski, the two Pyotroviches, and old Pan Novoveski, without counting a number of Armenians from Kamenyets, and numerous servants, as well as armed attendants to guard wagons, draft horses, and pack animals. The Pyotroviches and the delegation of the patriarch of Echmiadzin were to rest simply at Rashkoff, receive news there concerning their journey, and move on toward the Crimea. The remainder of the company determined to settle in Rashkoff for a time, and wait, at least till the first thaws, for the return of the prisoners; namely, Boski, the younger Seferevich, and the two merchants whose wives were long waiting in sorrow.

That was a difficult road, for it lay through silent wastes and steep ravines. Fortunately abundant but dry snow formed excellent sleighing; the presence of commands in Mohiloff, Yampol, and Rashkoff insured safety. Azba Bey was cut to pieces, the robbers either hanged or dispersed; and the Tartars in winter, through lack of grass, did not go out on the usual roads.

Finally, Pan Adam had promised to meet them with a few tens of horses, if he should receive permission from Pan Rushchyts. They went, therefore, briskly and willingly; Zosia was ready to go to the end of the world for Pan Adam. Pani Boski and the two Armenian women were hoping for the speedy return of their husbands. Rashkoff lay, it is true, in terrible wilds on the border of Christendom; but still they were not going there for a lifetime, nor for a long stay. In spring war would come; war was mentioned on the borders everywhere. When their loved ones were found, they must return with the first warm breeze to save their heads from destruction.

Eva remained at Hreptyoff, detained by Pani Basia.
Pan Novoveski did not insist greatly on taking his daughter, especially as he was leaving her in the house of such
worthy people.

"I will send her most safely, or I will take her myself,"
said Basia, "rather I will take her myself, for I should like
to see once in my life that whole terrible boundary of which
I have heard so much from childhood. In spring, when the
roads will be black from chambuls, my husband would not
let me go; but now, if Eva stays here, I shall have a fair
pretext. In a couple of weeks I shall begin to insist, and in
three I shall have permission surely."

"Your husband, I hope, will not let you go in winter
unless with a good escort."

"If he can go, he will go with me ; if not, Azya will escort
us with a couple of hundred or more horses, for I hear that
he is to be sent to Rashkoff in every case."

The conversation ended with this, and Eva remained in
Hreptyoff. Basia, however, had other calculations besides
the reasons given to Pan Novoveski. She wished to lighten
for Azya an approach to Eva, for the young Tartar was
beginning to disquiet her. As often as he met Basia he
answered her queries, it is true, by saying that he loved
Eva, that his former feeling had not died; but when he was
with Eva he was silent. Meanwhile the girl had fallen in
love with him to desperation in that Hreptyoff desert. His
wild but splendid beauty, his childhood passed under the
strong hand of Novoveski, his princely descent, and that
prolonged mystery which had weighed upon him, finally his
military fame, had enchanted her thoroughly. She was
waiting merely for the moment to open to him her heart,
burning as a flame, and to say to him, "Azya, I have loved
thee from childhood," to fall into his arms and vow love to
him till death. Meanwhile he closed his teeth and was
silent.

Eva herself thought at first that the presence of her father
and brother restrained Azya from a confession. Later, disquiet seized her too, for if obstacles arose unavoidably on
the part of her father and brother, especially before Azya
had received naturalization, still he might open his heart to
her, and he was bound to do so the more speedily and sincerely the more obstacles were rising on their road.

But he was silent.

Doubt crept at last into the maiden's heart, and she began

to complain of her misfortune to Basia, who pacified her, saying : —

"I do not deny that he is a strange man, and wonderfully secretive; but I am certain that he loves you, for he has told me so frequently, and besides he looks on you not as on others."

To this Eva, shaking her head, answered gloomily : "Differently, that is certain; but I know not whether there is love or hatred in that gaze."

"Dear Eva, do not talk folly; why should he hate you ? "

"But why should he love me ? "

Here Basia began to pass her small hands over the maiden's face. "But why does Michael love me ? And why did your brother, when he had barely seen Zosia, fall in love with her ? "

"Adam has always been hasty."

"Azya is haughty, and dreads refusal, especially from your father; your brother, having been in love himself, would understand more quickly the torture of that feeling. This is how it is. Be not foolish, Eva; have no fear. I will stir up Azya well, and you 'll see how courageous he 'll be."

In fact, Basia had an interview with Azya that very day, after which she rushed in great haste to Eva.

"It is all over ! " cried she on the threshold.

"What ? " asked Eva, flushing.

"Said I to him, ' What are you thinking of, to feed me with ingratitude ? I have detained Eva purposely that you might take advantage of the occasion; but if you do not, know that in two, or at furthest three weeks, I will send her to Rashkoff. I may go myself with her, and you 'll be left in the lurch.' His face changed when he heard of the journey to Rashkoff, and he began to beat with his forehead to my feet. I asked him then what he had on his mind, and he answered : ' On the road I will confess what I have in my breast. On the road,' said he, 'will be the best occasion; on the road will happen what is to happen, what is pre-destined. I will confess all, I will disclose all, for I cannot live longer in this torment.' His lips began to quiver, so anxious was he before, for he has received some unfavor-able letters from Kamenyets. He told me that he must go to Rashkoff in every event, that there is an old command of the hetman to my husband touching that matter; but the period is not mentioned in the command, for it depends on negotiations which he is carrying on there with the captains.

'But now,' said he, 'the time is approaching, and I must go to them beyond Rashkoff, so that at the same time I can conduct your grace and Panna Eva.' I told him in answer that it was unknown whether I should go or not, for it would depend on Michael's permission. When he heard this he was frightened greatly. Ai, you are a fool, Eva! You say that he does n't love you, but he fell at my feet; and when he implored me to go, I tell you he just whined, so that I had a mind to shed tears over him. Do you know why he did that? He told me at once. 'I,' said he, 'will confess what I have in my heart; but without the prayers of your grace I shall do nothing with the Novoveskis, I shall only rouse anger and hatred in them against myself. My fate is in the hands of your grace, my suffering, my salvation; for if your grace will not go, then better that the earth swallowed me, or that living fire burned me.' That is how he loves you. Simply terrible to think of! And if you had seen how he looked at that moment you would have been frightened."

"No, I am not afraid of him," answered Eva, and she began to kiss Basia's hands. "Go with us; go with us!" repeated she, with emotion; "go with us! You alone can save us; you alone will not fear to tell my father; you alone can effect something. Go with us! I will fall at the feet of Pan Volodyovski to get leave for you. Without you, father and Azya will spring at each other with knives. Go with us; go with us!" And saying this, she dropped to Basia's knees and began to embrace them with tears.

"God grant that I go!" said Basia. "I will lay all before Michael, and will not cease to torment him. It is safe now to go even alone, and what will it be with such a numerous retinue! Maybe Michael himself will go; if not, he has a heart, and will give me permission. At first he will cry out against it; but just let me grow gloomy, he will begin to walk around me at once, look into my eyes, and give way. I should prefer to have him go too, for I shall be terribly lonely without him; but what is to be done? I will go anyhow to give you some solace. In this case it is not a question of my wishes, but of the fate of you and Azya. Michael loves you both, — he will consent."

After that interview with Basia, Azya flew to his own room, as full of delight and consolation as if he had gained health after a sore illness. A while before wild despair had been tearing his soul; that very morning he had received a dry and brief letter from Pan Bogush of the following contents : —

MY BELOVED AZYA, — I have halted in Kamenyets, and to Hreptyoff I will not go this time ; first, because fatigue has overcome me, and secondly, because I have no reason to go. I have been in Yavorov. The hetman not only refuses to grant you permission by letter to cover your mad designs with his dignity, but he commands you sternly, and under pain of losing his favor, to drop them at once. I, too, have decided that what you have told me is worthless. It would be a sin for a refined, Christian people to enter into such intrigues with Pagans ; and it would be a disgrace before the whole world to grant the privileges of nobility to malefactors, robbers, and shedders of innocent blood. Moderate yourself in this matter, and do not think of the office of hetman, since it is not for you, though you are Tugai Bey's son. But if you wish to re-establish promptly the favor of the hetman, be content with your office, and hasten especially that work with Krychinski, Adurovich, Tarasovski, and others, for thus you will render best service.

The hetman's statement of what you are to do, I send with this letter, and an official command to Pan Volodyovski, that there be no hindrance to you in going and coming with your men. You 'll have to go on a sudden to meet those captains, of course ; only hurry, and report to me carefully at Kamenyets, what you hear on the other bank. Commending you herewith to the favor of God, I remain, with unchanging good wishes,

MARTSIN BOGUSH OF ZYEMBLYTS,
UNDER-CARVER OF NOVGROD.

When the young Tartar received this letter, he fell into a terrible fury. First he crushed the letter in his hand into bits ; then he stabbed the table time after time with his dagger ; next he threatened his own life and that of the faithful Halim, who on his knees begged him to undertake nothing till he had recovered from rage and despair. That letter was a cruel blow to him. The edifices which his pride and ambition had reared, were as if blown up with powder ; his plans were destroyed. He might have become the third hetman in the Commonwealth, and held its fate in his hand ; and now he sees that he must remain an obscure officer, for whom the summit of ambition would be naturalization. In his fiery imagination he had seen crowds bowing down daily before him ; and now it will come to him to bow down before others. It is no good for him either that he is the son of Tugai Bey, that the blood of reigning warriors flows in his veins, that great thoughts are born in his soul — nothing — all nothing ! He will live unrecognized and die in some distant little fortalice forgotten. One word broke his wing; one "no" brought it about, that, henceforward, he will not be free to soar like an eagle to the firmament, but must crawl like a worm on the ground.

But all this is nothing yet, in comparison with the happiness which he has lost. She for the possession of whom he would have given blood and eternity; she for whom he was flaming like fire; she whom he loved with eyes, heart, soul, blood, — would never be his. That letter took from him her, as well as the baton of a hetman. Hmelnitski might carry off Chaplinski's wife; Azya, a hetman, might carry off another man's wife, and defend himself even against the whole Commonwealth, but how could that Azya take her, — Azya, a lieutenant of Lithuanian Tartars, serving under command of her husband?

When he thought of this, the world grew black before his eyes, — empty, gloomy; and the son of Tugai Bey was not sure but he would better die, than live without a reason to live, without happiness, without hope, without the woman he loved. This pressed him down the more terribly since he had not looked for such a blow; nay, considering the condition of the Commonwealth, he had become more convinced every day that the hetman would confirm those plans. Now his hopes were blown apart like mist before a whirlwind. What remained to him? To renounce glory, greatness, happiness; but he was not the man to do that. At the first moment the madness of anger and despair carried him away. Fire was passing through his bones and burning him fiercely; hence he howled and gnashed his teeth, and thoughts equally fiery and vengeful were flying through his head. He wanted revenge on the Commonwealth, on the hetman, on Pan Michael, even on Basia. He wanted to rouse his Tartars, cut down the garrison, all the officers, all Hreptyoff, kill Pan Michael, carry off Basia, go with her beyond the Moldavian boundary, and then down to the Dobrudja, and farther on, even to Tsargrad itself, even to the deserts of Asia.

But the faithful Halim watched over him, and he himself, when he had recovered from his first fury and despair, recognized all the impossibility of those plans. Azya in this too resembled Hmelnitski; as in Hmelnitski, so in him, a lion and a serpent dwelt in company. Should he attack Hreptyoff with his faithful Tartars, what would come of that? Would Pan Michael, who is as watchful as a stork, let himself be surprised; and even if he should, would that famous partisan let himself be slaughtered, especially as he had at hand more and better soldiers? Finally, suppose that Azya should finish Volodyovski, what would he do then? If he moves along the river toward Yagorlik, he must rub out the commands at Mohiloff, Yampol, and Rashkoff; if he crosses to the Moldavian bank, the perkulabs are there, friends of Volodyovski, and Habareskul of Hotin himself, his sworn friend. If he goes to Doroshenko, there are Polish commands at Bratslav; and the steppe, even in winter, is full of scouts. In view of all this, Tugai Bey's son felt his helplessness, and his malign soul belched forth flames first, and then buried itself in deep despair, as a wounded wild beast buries itself in a dark den of a cliff, and remained quiet. And as uncommon pain kills itself and ends in torpidity, so he became torpid at last.

Just then it was announced to him that the wife of the commandant wished to speak to him.

Halim did not recognize Azya when he returned from that conversation. Torpor had vanished from the Tartar's face, his eyes danced like those of a wild-cat, his face was gleaming, and his white teeth glittered from under his mustaches; in his wild beauty he was like the terrible Tugai Bey.

"My lord," inquired Halim, "in what way has God comforted thy soul?"

"Halim," said Azya, "God forms bright day after dark night, and commands the sun to rise out of the sea." Here he seized the old Tartar by the shoulders. "In a month she will be mine for the ages!"

And such a gleam issued from his dark face that he was beautiful, and Halim began to make obeisances.

"Oh, son of Tugai Bey, thou art great, mighty, and the malice of the unbeliever cannot overcome thee!"

"Listen!" said Azya.

"I am listening, son of Tugai Bey."

"I will go beyond the blue sea, where the snows lie only on the mountains, and if I return again to these regions it will be at the head of chambuls like the sands of the sea, as innumerable as the leaves in those wildernesses, and I will bring fire and sword. But thou, Halim, son of Kurdluk, wilt take the road to-day, wilt find Krychinski, and tell him to hasten with his men to the opposite bank over against Rashkoff. And let Adurovich, Moravski, Aleksandrovich,

Groholski, Tarasovski, with every man living of the Lithuanian Tartars and Cheremis, threaten the troops. Let
them notify the chambuls that are in winter quarters with
Doroshenko to cause great alarm from the side of Uman,
so that the Polish commands may go far into the steppe from
Mohiloff, Yampol, and Rashkoff. Let there be no troops
on that road over which I go, so that when I leave Rashkoff
there will remain behind me only ashes and burned ruins."

"God aid thee, my lord!" answered Halim.

And he began to make obeisances, and Tugai Bey's son
bent over him and repeated a number of times yet, —

"Hasten the messengers, hasten the messengers, for only
a month's time is left!"

He dismissed Halim then, and remaining alone began to
pray, for he had a breast filled with happiness and gratitude to God.

And while praying he looked involuntarily through the
window at his men, who were leading out their horses just
then to water them at the wells; the square was black
there was such a crowd. The Tartars, while singing their
monotonous songs in a low voice, began to draw the squeaking well-sweeps and to pour water into the trough. Steam
rose in two pillars from the nostrils of each horse and concealed his face. All at once Pan Michael, in a sheepskin
coat and cowhide boots, came out of the main building, and,
approaching the men, began to say something. They listened to him, straightening themselves and removing their
caps in contradiction to Eastern custom. At sight of him
Azya ceased praying, and muttered, —

"You are a falcon, but you will not fly whither I fly; you
will remain in Hreptyoff in grief and in sorrow."

After Pan Michael had spoken to the soldiers, he returned
to the building, and on the square was heard again the songs
of Tartars, the snorting of horses, and the plaintive and
shrill sound of well-sweeps.

CHAPTER XXXVII.

THE little knight, as Basia had foreseen, cried out against her plans at once when he learned them, said he never would agree to them, for he could not go himself and he would not let her go without him; but on all sides began then prayers and insistence which were soon to bend his decision.

Basia insisted less, indeed, than he expected, for she wished greatly to go with her husband, and without him the journey lost a part of its charm; but Eva knelt before the little knight, and kissing his hands implored him by his love for Basia to permit her to go.

"No other will dare approach my father," said she, "and mention such an affair, — neither I, nor Azya, nor even my brother. Basia alone can do it, for he refuses her nothing."

"Basia is no matchmaker," said Pan Michael, "and, besides, you must come back here; let her do this at your return."

"God knows what will happen before the return," answered Eva, with weeping, — "it is certain only that I shall die of suffering; but for such an orphan for whom no one has pity, death is best of all."

The little knight had a heart tender beyond measure, hence he began to walk up and down in the room. He wished above all not to part with his Basia, even for a day, and what must it be for two weeks! Still, it was clear that the prayers moved him deeply, for in a couple of days after those attacks he said one evening, —

"If I could only go with you! But that cannot be, for service detains me."

Basia sprang to him, and putting her rosy mouth to his cheek began to cry, —

"Go, Michael, go, go!"

"It is not possible by any means," answered Pan Michael, with decision.

And again two days passed. During this time the little knight asked advice of Zagloba as to what he ought to do; but Zagloba refused to give advice.

"If there are no other obstacles but your feelings," said he, "what have I to say? Decide yourself. The house will be empty here without the haiduk. Were it not for my age and the hard road, I would go myself, for there is no life without her."

"But you see there is really no hindrance: the weather is a little frosty, that is all; for the rest, it is quiet, there are commands along the road everywhere."

"In that case decide for yourself."

After that conversation Pan Michael began to hesitate again, and to weigh two things. He was sorry for Eva. He paused also over this, — is it proper to send the girl alone with Azya on such a long road? and still more over another point, — is it proper to withhold help from devoted people when the opportunity to give it is so easy? For what was the real difficulty? Basia's absence for two or three weeks. Even if it were only a question of pleasing Basia, by letting her see Mohiloff, Yampol, and Rashkoff, why not please her? Azya, in one event or another, must go with his squadron to Rashkoff; hence there would be a strong and even a superfluous guard in view of the destruction of the robbers, and the quiet during winter from the horde.

The little knight yielded more and more, seeing which the ladies renewed their insistence, — one representing the affair as a good deed and a duty, the other weeping and lamenting. Finally Azya bowed down before the commandant. He knew, he said, that he was unworthy of such a favor, but still he had shown so much devotion and attachment to the Volodyovskis that he made bold to beg for it. He owed much gratitude to both, since they did not permit men to insult him, even when he was not known as the son of Tugai Bey. He would never forget that the wife of the commandant had dressed his wounds, and had been to him not only a gracious lady, but as it were a mother. He had given proofs of his gratitude recently in the battle with Azba Bey, and with God's help in future he would lay down his head and shed the last drop of his blood for the life of the lady, if need be.

Then he began to tell of his old and unfortunate love for Eva. He could not live without that maiden; he had loved her through whole years of separation, though without hope, and he would never cease to love her. But between him and old Pan Novoveski there was an ancient hatred,

and the previous relation of servant and master separated
them, as it were, by a broad ravine. The lady alone could
reconcile them to each other; and if she could not do that,
she could at least shelter the dear girl from her father's
tyranny, from confinement and the lash.

Pan Michael would have preferred, perhaps, that Basia
had not interfered in the matter; but as he himself loved
to do good to people, he did not wonder at his wife's heart.
Still, he did not answer Azya affirmatively yet; he resisted
even additional tears from Eva; but he locked himself up
in the chancery and fell to thinking.

At last he came out to supper on a certain evening with
an agreeable expression of face, and after supper he asked
Azya suddenly, "Azya, when is it time for you to go?"

"In a week, your great mightiness," answered the Tartar,
unquietly. "Halim, it must be, will have concluded negotiations with Krychinski by that time."

"Give orders to repair the great sleigh, for you must
take two ladies to Rashkoff."

When she heard this, Basia began to clap her hands, and
rushed headlong to her husband. After her hurried Eva;
after Eva, Azya bowed down to the little knight's knees
with a wild outburst of delight, so that Pan Michael had to
free himself.

"Give me peace!" said he; "what is there wonderful?
When it's possible to help people, it is hard not to help
them, unless one is altogether heartless; and I am no tyrant.
But do you, Basia, return quickly, my love; and do you,
Azya, guard her faithfully; in this way you will thank me
best. Well, well, give me peace!"

Here his mustaches began to quiver, and then he said
more joyously, to give himself courage, —

"The worst are those tears of women; when I see tears
there is nothing left of me. But you, Azya, must thank not
only me and my wife, but this young lady, who has followed
me like a shadow, exhibiting her sorrow continually before
my eyes. You must pay her for such affection."

"I will pay her; I will pay her!" said Azya, with a
strange voice; and seizing Eva's hands, he kissed them so
violently that it might be thought he wished rather to bite
them.

"Michael!" cried Zagloba, suddenly, pointing to Basia,
"what shall we do here without her?"

"Indeed it will be grievous," said the little knight,

20

"God knows it will!" Then he added more quietly: "But the Lord God may bless my good action later. Do you understand?"

Meanwhile Basia pushed in between them her bright head full of curiosity.

"What are you saying?"

"Nothing," replied Zagloba; "we said that in spring the storks would come surely."

Basia began to rub her face to her husband's like a real cat. "Michael dear! I shall not stay long," said she, in a low voice.

After this conversation new councils were held during several days touching the journey. Pan Michael looked after everything himself, gave orders to arrange the sleigh in his presence, and line it with skins of foxes killed in autumn. Zagloba brought his own lap-robe, so that she might have wherewith to cover her feet on the road. Sleighs were to go with a bed and provisions; and Basia's pony was to go, so that she might leave her sleigh in dangerous places; for Pan Michael had a particular fear of the entrance to Mohiloff, which was really a breakneck descent. Though there was not the slightest likelihood of an attack, the little knight commanded Azya to take every precaution: to send men always a couple of furlongs in advance, and never pass the night on the road but in places where there were commands; to start at daylight, and not to loiter on the way. To such a degree did the little knight think of everything, that with his own hand he loaded the pistols for the holsters in Basia's saddle.

The moment of departure came at last. It was still dark when two hundred horse of the Lithuanian Tartars were standing ready on the square. In the chief room of the commandant's house movement reigned also. In the chimneys pitchy sticks were shooting up bright flames. The little knight, Pan Zagloba, Pan Mushalski, Pan Nyena-shinyets, Pan Hromyka, and Pan Motovidlo, and with them officers from the light squadrons, had come to say farewell. Basia and Eva, warm yet and ruddy from sleep, were drinking heated wine for the road. Pan Michael, sitting by his wife, had his arm around her waist; Zagloba poured out to her, repeating at each addition, "Take more, for the weather is frosty." Basia and Eva were dressed in male costume, for women travelled generally in that guise on the frontiers. Basia had a sabre; a wild-cat skin shuba bound with weasel-skin; an ermine cap with earlaps; very wide trousers looking like a skirt; and boots to her knees, soft and lined. To all this were to be added warm cloaks and shubas with hoods to cover the faces. Basia's face was uncovered yet, and astonished people as usual with its beauty. Some, however, looked appreciatively at Eva, who had a mouth formed as it were for kisses; and others did not know which to prefer, so charming seemed both to the soldiers, who whispered in one another's ears, —

"It is hard for a·man to live in such a desert! Happy commandant, happy Azya! Uh!"

The fire crackled joyfully in the chimneys; the crowing of cocks began; day approached gradually, rather frosty and clear; the roofs of the sheds and the quarters of the soldiers, covered with deep snow, took on a bright rose color.

From the square was heard the snorting of horses and the squeaking steps of soldiers and dragoons who had assembled from the sheds and lodgings to take farewell of Basia and the Tartars.

"It is time!" said Pan Michael at last.

Hearing this, Basia sprang from her place and fell into her husband's arms. He pressed his lips to hers, then held her with all his strength to his breast, kissed her eyes and forehead, and again her mouth. That moment was long, for they loved each other immensely.

After the little knight the turn came to Zagloba; then the other officers approached to kiss her hand, and she repeated with her childish voice, resonant as silver, —

"Be in good health, gentlemen; be in good health!"

She and Eva put on cloaks with openings instead of sleeves, and then shubas with hoods, and the two vanished altogether under these robes. The broad door was thrown open, a frosty steam rushed in, then the whole assembly found itself on the square.

Outside everything was becoming more and more visible from the snow and daylight.

Hoar-frost had settled on the hair of the horses and the sheepskin coats of the men; it seemed as though the whole squadron were dressed in white, and were sitting on white horses.

Basia and Eva took their seats in the fur-lined sleigh. The dragoons and the soldiers shouted for a happy journey to the departing.

At that sound a numerous flock of crows and ravens, which a severe winter had driven in near the dwellings of people, flew from the roofs, and with low croaking began to circle in the rosy air.

The little knight bent over the sleigh and hid his face in the hood covering the face of his wife. Long was that moment; at last he tore himself away from Basia, and, making the sign of the cross, exclaimed, —

"In the name of God!"

Now Azya rose in the stirrups; his wild face was gleaming from delight and the dawn. He waved his whirlbat, so that his burka rose like the wings of a bird of prey, and he cried with a piercing voice: —

"Move on!"

The hoofs squeaked on the snow; abundant steam came from the nostrils of the horses. The first rank moved slowly; after that the second, the third, and the fourth, then the sleigh, then the ranks of the whole detachment began to move across the sloping square to the gate.

The little knight blessed them with the Holy Cross; at last, when the sleigh had passed the gate, he put his hands around his mouth, and called, "Be well, Basia!"

But only the voices of muskets and the loud cawing of the dark birds gave him answer.

CHAPTER XXXVIII.

A DETACHMENT of Cheremis, some twenty in number, marched five miles in advance to examine the road and notify commandants of Pani Volodyovski's journey, so that quarters might be ready for her in each place. After this detachment came the main force of the Lithuanian Tartars, the sleigh with Basia and Eva, and another sleigh with servant-women; a small detachment closed the march. The road was heavy enough because of snowdrifts. Pine woods, which in winter do not lose their needle-like leaves, permit less snow to fall to the earth; but that forest along the bank of the Dniester, formed for the most part of oaks and other deciduous trees, stripped now of their natural covering, was packed halfway to the lower branches with snow. Snow had filled also the narrowest ravines; in places it had been lifted into waves whose curling summits seemed as if ready to tumble in an instant and be lost in the general white expanse. During the passage of difficult ravines and declivities the Tartars held the sleighs back with ropes; only on the lofty plains, where the wind had smoothed the snow surface, did they drive quickly in the track of the caravan, which with Naviragh and the two learned Anardrats had started earlier from Hreptyoff.

Travelling was difficult; not so difficult, however, as sometimes in those wild regions full of chasms, rivers, streams, and gullies. The ladies were rejoiced, therefore, that before deep night came they would be able to reach the precipitous ravine in the bottom of which stood Mohiloff; besides, there was promise of continued fair weather. After a ruddy dawn the sun rose, and all at once the plains, the ravines, and the forests were gleaming in its rays; the branches of the trees seemed coated with sparks; sparks glittered on the snow till the eyes ached from the brightness. From high points one could see out through open spaces, as through windows in that wilderness, the gaze reaching down to Moldavia was lost on a horizon white and blue, but flooded with sunlight.

The air was dry and sharp. In such an atmosphere men as well as beasts feel strength and health; in the ranks the horses snorted greatly, throwing rolls of steam from their nostrils; and the Tartars, though the frost so pinched their legs that they drew them under their skirts continually, sang joyful songs.

At last the sun rose to the very summit of the pavilion of the sky, and warmed the world somewhat. It was too hot for Basia and Eva under the fur in the sleigh. They loosened the covering on their heads, pushed back their hoods, showed their rosy faces to the light, and began to look around,—Basia on the country, and Eva searching for Azya. He was not near the sleigh; he was riding in advance with that detachment of Cheremis who were examining the road, and clearing away snow when necessary. Eva frowned because of this; but Basia, knowing military service through and through, said to console her:—

"They are all that way; when there is service, it is service. My Michael will not even look at me when military duty comes; and it would be ill were it otherwise, for if you are to love a soldier, let him be a good one."

"But will he be with us at the resting-place?" asked Eva.

"See lest you have too much of him. Did you not notice how joyful he was when we started? Light was beaming from him."

"I saw that he was very glad."

"But what will he be when he receives permission from your father?"

"Oi, what is in waiting for me? The will of God be done! though the heart dies in me when I think of father. If he shouts, if he becomes wilful and refuses permission, I shall have a fine life when I go home."

"Do you know, Eva, what I think?"

"What is it?"

"There is no trifling with Azya. Your brother might oppose with his force; but your father has no command. I think that if your father resists, Azya will take you anyhow."

"How is that?"

"Why, carry you off simply. There is no trifling with him, people say,—Tugai Bey's blood. You will be married by the first priest on the road. In another place it would be necessary to have banns, certificates, license; but here it is a wild country, all things are a little in Tartar fashion."

Eva's face brightened. "This is what I dread. Azya is ready for anything; this is what I dread," said she.

But Basia, turning her head, looked at her quickly, and burst out suddenly with her resonant, child-like laugh.

"You dread that just as a mouse dreads bacon. Oh, I know you!"

Eva, flushed already from the cold air, flushed still more, and said:—

"I should fear my father's curse, and I know that Azya is ready to disregard everything."

"Be of good courage," answered Basia, "besides me, you have your brother to help you. True love always comes to its own. Pan Zagloba told me that when Michael was n't even dreaming of me."

Conversation once begun, they vied with each other in talking,—one about Azya, the other about Michael. Thus a couple of hours passed, till the caravan halted for the first refreshment at Yaryshoff. Of a hamlet, wretched enough at all times, there remained, after the peasant incursion, only one public house, which was restored from the time that the frequent passage of soldiers began to promise certain profit. Basia and Eva found in it a passing Armenian merchant of Mohiloff origin, who was taking morocco to Kamenyets.

Azya wished to hurl him out of doors with the Wallachians and Tartars who were with him; but the women permitted him to remain, only his guard had to withdraw. When the merchant learned that the travelling lady was Pani Volodyovski, he began to bow down before her and praise her husband to the skies. Basia listened to the man with great delight. At last he went to his packs, and when he returned offered her a package of special sweetmeats and a little box full of odorous Turkish herbs good for various ailments.

"I bring this through gratitude," said he. "Till now we have not dared to thrust our heads out of Mohiloff, because Azba Bey ravaged so terribly, and so many robbers infested on this side all the ravines and on the Moldavian bank the meadows; but now the road is safe, and trading secure. Now we travel again. May God increase the days of the commandant of Hreptyoff, and make each day long enough for a journey from Mohiloff to Kamenyets, and let every hour be extended so as to seem a day! Our commandant, the field secretary, prefers to sit in Warsaw; but the commandant of Hreptyoff watched, and swept out the robbers, so that death is dearer to them now than the Dniester."

"Then is Pan Revuski not in Mohiloff?" asked Basia.

"He only brought the troops; I do not know if he remained three days. Permit, your great mightiness, here are raisins in this packet, and at this edge of it fruit such as is not found even in Turkey; it comes from distant Asia, and grows there on palms. The secretary is not in the town; but now there is no cavalry at all, for yesterday they went on a sudden toward Bratslav. But here are dates; may they be to the health of your great mightiness! Only Pan Gorzenski has remained with infantry."

"It is a wonder to me that all the cavalry have gone," said Basia, with an inquiring glance at Azya.

"They moved so the horses might not get out of training," answered Azya, calmly.

"In the town, people say that Doroshenko advanced unexpectedly," said the merchant.

Azya laughed. "But with what will he feed his horses, with snow?" said he to Basia.

"Pan Gorzenski will explain best to your great mightiness," added the merchant.

"I do not believe that it is anything," said Basia, after a moment's thought; "for if it were, my husband would be the first to know."

"Without doubt the news would be first in Hreptyoff," said Azya; "let your grace have no fear."

Basia raised her bright face to the Tartar, and her nostrils quivered.

"I have fear! That is excellent; what is in your head? Do you hear, Eva? — I have fear!"

Eva could not answer; for being by nature fond of dainties, and loving sweets beyond measure, she had her mouth full of dates, which did not prevent her, however, from looking eagerly at Azya; but when she had swallowed the fruit, she said, —

"Neither have I any fear with such an officer."

Then she looked tenderly and significantly into the eyes of young Tugai Bey; but from the time that she had begun to be an obstacle, he felt for her only secret repulsion and anger. He stood motionless, therefore, and said with downcast eyes, —

"In Rashkoff it will be seen if I deserve confidence."

And there was in his voice something almost terrible;

but as the two women knew so well that the young Tartar was thoroughly different in word and deed from other men, this did not rouse their attention. Besides, Azya insisted at once on continuing the journey, because the mountains before Mohiloff were abrupt, difficult of passage, and should be crossed during daylight.

They started without delay, and advanced very quickly till they reached those mountains. Basia wished then to sit on her horse; but at Azya's persuasion she stayed with Eva in the sleigh, which was steadied with lariats, and let down from the height with the greatest precaution. All this time Azya walked near the sleigh; but occupied altogether with their safety, and in general with the command, he spoke scarcely a word either to Basia or Eva. The sun went down, however, before they succeeded in passing the mountains; but the detachment of Cheremis, marching in advance, made fires of dry branches. They went down then among the ruddy fires and the wild figures standing near them. Beyond those figures were, in the gloom of the night and in the half-light of the flames, the threatening declivities in uncertain, terrible outlines. All this was new, curious; all had the appearance of some kind of dangerous and mysterious expedition, — wherefore Basia's soul was in the seventh heaven, and her heart rose in gratitude to her husband for letting her go on this journey to unknown regions, and to Azya because he had been able to manage the journey so well. Basia understood now, for the first time, the meaning of those military marches of which she had heard so much from soldiers, and what precipitous and winding roads were. A mad joyousness took possession of her. She would have mounted her pony assuredly, were it not that, sitting near Eva, she could talk with her and terrify her. Therefore when moving in a narrow, short turn the detachment in advance vanished from the eye and began to shout with wild voices, the stifled echo of which resounded among overhanging cliffs, Basia turned to Eva, and seizing her hands, cried, —

"Oh, ho! robbers from the meadows, or the horde!"

But Eva, when she remembered Azya, the son of Tugai Bey, was calm in a moment.

"The robbers in the horde respect and fear Azya," answered she. And later, bending to Basia's ear, she said, "Even to Belgrod, even to the Crimea, if with him!"

The moon had risen high in heaven when they were

issuing from the mountains. Then they beheld far down, and, as it were, at the bottom of a precipice, a collection of lights.

"Mohiloff is under our feet," said a voice behind Basia and Eva.

They looked around; it was Azya standing behind the sleigh.

"But does the town lie like that at the bottom of the ravine?" asked Basia.

"It does. The mountains shield it completely from winter winds," answered Azya, pushing his head between their heads. "Notice, your grace, that there is another climate here; it is warmer and calmer. Spring comes here ten days earlier than on the other side of the mountains, and the trees put forth their leaves sooner. That gray on the slopes is a vineyard; but the ground is under snow yet."

Snow was lying everywhere, but really the air was warmer and calmer. In proportion as they descended slowly toward the valley, lights showed themselves one after another, and increased in number every moment.

"A respectable place, and rather large," said Eva.

"It is because the Tartars did not burn it at the time of the peasant incursion. The Cossack troops wintered here, and Poles have scarcely ever visited the place."

"Who live here?"

"Tartars, who have their wooden mosque; for in the Commonwealth every man is free to profess his own faith. Wallachians live here, also Armenians and Greeks."

"I have seen Greeks once in Kamenyets," said Basia; "for though they live far away, they go everywhere for commerce."

"This town is composed differently from all others," said Azya; "many people of various nations come here to trade. That settlement which we see at a distance on one side is called Serby."

"We are entering already," said Basia.

They were, in fact, entering. A strange odor of skins and acid met their nostrils at once. That was the odor of morocco, at the manufacture of which all the inhabitants of Mohiloff worked somewhat, but especially the Armenians. As Azya had said, the place was different altogether from others. The houses were built in Asiatic fashion; they had windows covered with thick wooden lattice; in many houses there were no windows on the street, and only in the yards was seen the glitter of fires. The streets were not paved, though there was no lack of stone in the neighborhood. Here and there were buildings of strange form with latticed, transparent walls; those were drying-houses, in which fresh grapes were turned into raisins. The odor of morocco filled the whole place.

Pan Gorzenski, who commanded the infantry, had been informed by the Cheremis of the arrival of the wife of the commandant of Hreptyoff, and rode out on horseback to meet her. He was not young, and he stuttered; he lisped also, for his face had been pierced by a bullet from a long-barrelled janissary gun; therefore when he began to speak (stuttering every moment) of the star "which had risen in the heavens of Mohiloff," Basia came near bursting into laughter. But he received her in the most hospitable manner known to him. In the "fortalice" a supper was waiting for her, and a supremely comfortable bed on fresh and clean down, which he had taken by a forced loan from the wealthiest Armenians. Pan Gorzenski stuttered, it is true, but during the evening he related at the supper things so curious that it was worth while to listen.

According to him a certain disquieting breeze had begun to blow suddenly and unexpectedly from the steppes. Reports came that a strong chambul of the Crimean horde, stationed with Doroshenko, had moved all at once toward Haysyn and the country above that point; with the chambuls went some thousands of Cossacks. Besides, a number of other alarming reports had come from indefinite places. Pan Gorzenski did not attach great faith to these rumors, however. "For it is winter," said he; "and since the Lord God has created this earthly circle the Tartars move only in spring; then they form no camp, carry no baggage, take no food for their horses in any place. We all know that war with the Turkish power is held in the leash by frost alone, and that we shall have guests at the first grass; but that there is anything at present I shall never believe."

Basia waited patiently and long till Pan Gorzenski should finish. He stuttered, meanwhile, and moved his lips continually, as if eating.

"What do you think yourself of the movement of the horde toward Haysyn?" asked she at last.

"I think that their horses have pawed out all the grass from under the snow, and that they wish to make a camp in another place. Besides, it may be that the horde, living near Doroshenko's men, are quarrelling with them; it has always been so. Though they are allies and are fighting together, only let encampments stand side by side, and they fall to quarrelling at once in the pastures and at the bazaars."

"That is the case surely," said Azya.

"And there is another point," continued Pan Gorzenski; "the reports did not come directly through partisans, but peasants brought them; the Tartars here began to talk without evident reason. Three days ago Pan Yakubovich brought in from the steppes the first informants who confirmed the reports, and all the cavalry marched out immediately."

"Then you are here with infantry only?" inquired Azya.

"God pity us! — forty men! There is hardly any one to guard the fortalice; and if the Tartars living here in Mohiloff were to rise, I know not how I could defend myself."

"But why do they not rise against you?" inquired Basia.

"They do not, because they cannot in any way. Many of them live permanently in the Commonwealth with their wives and children, and they are on our side. As to strangers, they are here for commerce, not for war; they are good people."

"I will leave your grace fifty horse from my force," said Azya.

"God reward! You will oblige me greatly by this, for I shall have some one to send out to get intelligence. But can you leave them?"

"I can. We shall have in Rashkoff the parties of those captains who in their time went over to the Sultan, but now wish to resume obedience to the Commonwealth. Krychinski will bring three hundred horse certainly; and perhaps Adurovich, too, will come; others will arrive later. I am to take command over all by order of the hetman, and before spring a whole division will be assembled."

Pan Gorzenski inclined before Azya. He had known him for a long time, but had had small esteem for him, as being a man of doubtful origin. But knowing now that he was the son of Tugai Bey, for an account of this had been brought by the recent caravan in which Naviragh was travelling, Gorzenski honored in the young Tartar the blood of a great though hostile warrior; he honored in him, besides, an officer to whom the hetman had confided such significant functions.

Azya went out to give orders, and calling the sotnik David, said, —

"David, son of Skander, thou wilt remain in Mohiloff with fifty horse. Thou wilt see with thy eyes and hear with thy ears what is happening around thee. If the Little Falcon in Hreptyoff sends letters to me, thou wilt stop his messenger, take the letters from him, and send them with thy own man. Thou wilt remain here till I send an order to withdraw. If my messenger says, 'It is night,' thou wilt go out in peace; but if he says, 'Day is near,' thou wilt burn the place, cross to the Moldavian bank, and go whither I command thee."

"Thou hast spoken," answered David; "I will see with my eyes and hear with my ears; I will stop messengers from the Little Falcon, and when I have taken letters from them I will send those letters through our man to thee. I will remain till I receive an order; and if the messenger says to me, 'It is night,' I will go out quietly; if he says, 'Day is near,' I will burn the place, cross to the Moldavian bank, and go whither the command directs."

Next morning the caravan, less by fifty horse, continued the journey. Pan Gorzenski escorted Basia beyond the ravine of Mohiloff. There, after he had stuttered forth a farewell oration, he returned to Mohiloff, and they went on toward Yampol very hurriedly. Azya was unusually joyful, and urged his men to a degree that astonished Basia.

"Why are you in such haste?" inquired she.

"Every man hastens to happiness," answered Azya, "and mine will begin in Rashkoff."

Eva, taking these words to herself, smiled tenderly, and collecting courage, answered, "But my father?"

"Pan Novoveski will obstruct me in nothing," answered the Tartar, and gloomy lightning flashed through his face.

In Yampol they found almost no troops. There had never been any infantry there, and nearly all the cavalry had gone; barely a few men remained in the castle, or rather in the ruins of it. Lodgings were prepared, but Basia slept badly, for those rumors had begun to disturb her. She pondered over this especially, — how alarmed the little knight would be should it turn out that one of Doroshenko's chambuls had advanced really; but she strengthened herself with the

thought that it might be untrue. It occurred to her whether
it would not be better to return, taking for safety a part of
Azya's soldiers; but various obstacles presented themselves.
First, Azya, having to increase the garrison at Rashkoff,
could give only a small guard, hence, in case of real
danger, that guard might prove insufficient; secondly, two
thirds of the road was passed already; in Rashkoff there
was an officer known to her, and a strong garrison, which,
increased by Azya's detachment and by the companies of
those captains, might grow to a power quite important.
Taking all this into consideration, Basia determined to journey farther.

But she could not sleep. For the first time during that
journey alarm seized her, as if unknown danger were hanging over her head. Perhaps lodging in Yampol had its
share in those alarms, for that was a bloody and a terrible
place; Basia knew it from the narratives of her husband
and Pan Zagloba. Here had been stationed in Hmelnitski's
time the main forces of the Podolian cut-throats under Burlai; hither captives had been brought and sold for the
markets of the East, or killed by a cruel death; finally, in
the spring of 1651, during the time of a crowded fair, Pan
Stanislav Lantskoronski, the voevoda of Bratslav, had burst
in and made a dreadful slaughter, the memory of which was
fresh throughout the whole borderland of the Dniester.

Hence, there hung everywhere over the whole settlement
bloody memories; hence, here and there were blackened
ruins, and from the walls of the half-destroyed castle
seemed to gaze white faces of slaughtered Poles and Cossacks. Basia was daring, but she feared ghosts; it was
said that in Yampol itself, at the mouth of the Shumilovka,
and on the neighboring cataracts of the Dniester, great wailing was heard at midnight and groans, and that the water
became red in the moonlight as if colored with blood. The
thought of this filled Basia's heart with bitter alarm. She
listened, in spite of herself, to hear in the still night, in the
sounds of the cataract, weeping and groans. She heard only
the prolonged "watch call" of the sentries. Then she
remembered the quiet room in Hreptyoff, her husband, Pan
Zagloba, the friendly faces of Pan Nyenashinyets, Mushalski, Motovidlo, Snitko, and others, and for the first time
she felt that she was far from them, very far, in a strange
region; and such a homesickness for Hreptyoff seized her
that she wanted to weep. It was near morning when she

fell asleep, but she had wonderful dreams. Burlai, the cut-throats, the Tartars, bloody pictures of massacre, passed through her sleeping head; and in those pictures she saw continually the face of Azya, — not the same Azya, however, but as it were a Cossack, or a wild Tartar, or Tugai Bey himself.

She rose early, glad that night and the disagreeable visions had ended. She had determined to make the rest of the journey on horseback, — first, to enjoy the movement; second, to give an opportunity for free speech to Azya and Eva, who, in view of the nearness of Rashkoff, needed, of course, to settle the way of declaring everything to old Pan Novoveski, and to receive his consent. Azya held the stirrup with his own hand; he did not sit, however, in the sleigh with Eva, but went without delay to the head of the detachment, and remained near Basia.

She noticed at once that again the cavalry were fewer in number than when they came to Yampol; she turned therefore to the young Tartar and said, "I see that you have left some men in Yampol?"

"Fifty horse, the same as in Mohiloff," answered Azya.

"Why was that?"

He laughed peculiarly; his lips rose as those of a wicked dog do when he shows his teeth, and he answered only after a while.

"I wished to have those places in my power, and to secure the homeward road for your grace."

"If the troops return from the steppes, there will be forces there then."

"The troops will not come back so soon."

"Whence do you know that?"

"They cannot, because first they must learn clearly what Doroshenko is doing; that will occupy about three or four weeks."

"If that is the case you did well to leave those men."

They rode a while in silence. Azya looked from time to time at the rosy face of Basia, half concealed by the raised collar of her mantle and her cap, and after every glance he closed his eyes, as if wishing to fix that charming picture more firmly in his mind.

"You ought to talk with Eva," said Basia, renewing the conversation. "You talk altogether too little with her; she knows not what to think. You will stand before the face of Pan Novoveski soon; alarm even seizes me. You and

she should take counsel together, and settle how you are to
begin."

"I should like to speak first with your grace," said Azya,
with a strange voice.

"Then why not speak at once?"

"I am waiting for a messenger from Rashkoff; I thought
to find him in Yampol. I expect him every moment."

"But what," said Basia, "has the messenger to do with
our conversation?"

"I think that he is coming now," said the Tartar, avoiding an answer. And he galloped forward, but returned
after a while. "No; that is not he."·

In his whole posture, in his speech, in his look, in his
voice, there was something so excited and feverish that
unquietude was communicated to Basia; still the least
suspicion had not risen in her head yet. Azya's unrest
could be explained perfectly by the nearness of Rashkoff
and of Eva's terrible father; still, something oppressed
Basia, as if her own fate were in question. Approaching
the sleigh, she rode near Eva for a number of hours, speaking with her of Rashkoff, of old Pan Novoveski; of Pan
Adam, of Zosia Boski, finally of the region about them, which
was becoming a wilder and more terrible wilderness. It was,
in truth, a wilderness immediately beyond Hreptyoff; but
there at least a column of smoke rose from time to time on
the horizon, indicating some habitation. Here there were
no traces of man; and if Basia had not known that she was
going to Rashkoff, where people were living, and a Polish
garrison was stationed, she might have thought that they
were taking her somewhere into an unknown desert, into
strange lands at the end of the world.

Looking around at the country, she restrained her horse
involuntarily, and was soon left in the rear of the sleighs
and horsemen. Azya joined her after a while; and since he
knew the region well, he began to show her various places,
mentioning their names.

This did not last very long, however, for the earth began
to be smoky; evidently the winter had not such power in
that southern region as in woody Hreptyoff. Snow was
lying somewhat, it is true, in the valleys, on the cliffs, on
the edges of the rocks, and also on the hillsides turned
northward; but in general the earth was not covered, and
looked dark with groves, or gleamed with damp withered
grass. From that grass rose a light whitish fog, which,

extending near the earth, formed in the distance the counterfeit of great waters, filling the valleys and spreading widely over the plains; then that fog rose higher and higher, till at last it hid the sunshine, and turned a clear day into a foggy and gloomy one.

"There will be rain to-morrow," said Azya.

"If not to-day. How far is it to Rashkoff?"

Azya looked at the nearest place, barely visibly through the fog, and said, —

"From that point it is nearer to Rashkoff than to Yampol." And he breathed deeply, as if a great weight had fallen from his breast.

At that moment the tramp of a horse was heard from the direction of the cavalry, and some horseman was seen indistinctly in the fog.

"Halim! I know him," cried Azya.

Indeed, it was Halim, who, when he had rushed up to Azya and Basia, sprang from his horse and began to beat with his forehead toward the stirrup of the young Tartar.

"From Rashkoff?" inquired Azya.

"From Rashkoff, my lord," answered Halim.

"What is to be heard there?"

The old man raised toward Basia his ugly head, emaciated from unheard-of toils, as if wishing to inquire whether he might speak in her presence; but Tugai Bey's son said at once, —

"Speak boldly. Have the troops gone out?"

"They have. A handful remained."

"Who led them?"

"Pan Novoveski."

"Have the Pyotroviches gone to the Crimea?"

"Long ago. Only two women remained, and old Pan Novoveski with them."

"Where is Krychinski?"

"On the other bank of the river; he is waiting."

"Who is with him?"

"Adurovich with his company; both beat with the forehead to thy stirrup, O son of Tugai Bey, and give themselves under thy hand, — they, and all those who have not come yet."

"'T is well!" said Azya, with fire in his eyes. "Fly to Krychinski at once, and give the command to occupy Rashkoff."

"Thy will, lord."

Halim sprang on his horse in a moment, and vanished like a phantom in the fog. A terrible, ominous gleam issued from the face of Azya. The decisive moment had come, — the moment waited for, the moment of greatest happiness for him; but his heart was beating as if breath were failing him. He rode for a time in silence near Basia; and only when he felt that his voice would not deceive him did he turn toward her his eyes, inscrutable but bright, and say, —

"Now I will speak to your grace with sincerity."

"I listen," said Basia, scanning him carefully, as if she wished to read his changed countenance.

CHAPTER XXXIX.

Azya urged his horse up so closely to Basia's pony that his stirrup almost touched hers. He rode forward a few steps in silence; during this time he strove to calm himself finally, and wondered why calmness came to him with such effort, since he had Basia in his hands, and there was no human power which could take her from him. But he did not know that in his soul, despite every probability, despite every evidence, there glimmered a certain spark of hope that the woman whom he desired would answer with a feeling like his own. If that hope was weak, the desire for its object was so strong that it shook him as a fever. The woman would not open her arms, would not cast herself into his embrace, would not say those words over which he had dreamed whole nights: "Azya, I am thine;" she would not hang with her lips on his lips, — he knew this. But how would she receive his words? What would she say? Would she lose all feeling, like a dove in the claws of a bird of prey, and let him take her, just as the hapless dove yields itself to the hawk? Would she beg for mercy tearfully, or would she fill that wilderness with a cry of terror? Would there be something more, or something less, of all this? Such questions were storming in the head of the Tartar. But in every case the hour had come to cast aside feigning, pretences, and show her a truthful, a terrible face. Here was his fear, here his alarm. One moment more, and all would be accomplished.

Finally this mental alarm became in the Tartar that which alarm becomes most frequently in a wild beast, — rage; and he began to rouse himself with that rage. "Whatever happens," thought he, "she is mine, she is mine altogether; she will be mine to-morrow, and then will not return to her husband, but will follow me."

At this thought wild delight seized him by the hair, and he said all at once in a voice which seemed strange to himself, "Your grace has not known me till now."

"In this fog your voice has so changed," answered Basia, somewhat alarmed, "that it seems to me really as if another were speaking."

"In Mohiloff there are no troops, in Yampol none, in Rashkoff none. I alone am lord here, — Krychinski, Adurovich, and those others are my slaves; for I am a prince, I am the son of a ruler. I am their vizir, I am their highest murza; I am their leader, as Tugai Bey was; I am their khan; I alone have authority; all here is in my power."

"Why do you say this to me?"

"Your grace has not known me hitherto. Rashkoff is not far away. I wished to become hetman of the Tartars and serve the Commonwealth; but Sobieski would not permit it. I am not to be a Lithuanian Tartar any longer; I am not to serve under any man's command, but to lead great chambuls myself, against Doroshenko, or the Commonwealth, as your grace wishes, as your grace commands."

"How as I command? Azya, what is the matter with you?"

"This, that here all are my slaves, and I am yours. What is the hetman to me? I care not whether he has permitted or not. Say a word, your grace, and I will put Akkerman at your feet; and the Dobrudja, and those hordes which have villages there, and those which wander in the Wilderness, and those who are everywhere in winter quarters will be your slaves, as I am your slave. Command, and I will not obey the Khan of the Crimea, I will not obey the Sultan; I will make war on them with the sword, and aid the Commonwealth. I will form new hordes in these regions, and be khan over them, and you will be alone over me; to you alone will I bow down, beg for your favor and love."

When he had said this, he bent in the saddle, and, seizing the woman, half terrified, and, as it were, stunned by his words, he continued to speak in a hurried, hoarse voice: "Have you not seen that I love only you? Ah, but I have suffered my share! I will take you now! You are mine, and you will be mine! No one will tear you from my hands in this place — you are mine, mine, mine!"

"Jesus, Mary!" cried Basia.

But he pressed her in his arms as if wishing to smother her. Hurried breathing struggled from his lips, his eyes grew misty; at last he drew her out of the stirrups, off the saddle, put her in front of him, pressed her breast to his own, and his bluish lips, opening greedily, like the mouth of a fish, began to seek her mouth.

She uttered no cry, but began to resist with unexpected

strength; between them rose a struggle in which only the
panting of their breaths was to be heard. His violent movements and the nearness of his face restored her presence of
mind. An instant of such clear vision came to Basia as comes
to the drowning; she felt everything at once with the greatest vividness. Hence she felt first of all that the earth was
vanishing from under her feet, and a bottomless ravine opening, to which he was dragging her; she saw his desire, his
treason, her own dreadful fate, her weakness and helplessness; she felt alarm, and a ghastly pain and sorrow, and at
the same time there burst forth in her a flame of immense
indignation, rage, and revenge. Such was the courage and
spirit of that daughter of a knight, that chosen wife of the
most gallant soldier of the Commonwealth, that in that awful
moment she thought first of all, "I will have revenge," then
"I will save myself." All the faculties of her mind were
strained, as hair is straightened with terror on the head; and
that clearness of vision as in drowning became in her almost
miraculous. While struggling her hands began to seek for
weapons, and found at last the ivory butt of an Eastern pistol; but at the same time she had presence of mind to think
of this also, — that even if the pistol were loaded, even if
she should cock it, before she could bend her hand, before
she could point the barrel at his head, he would seize her
hand without fail, and take from her the last means of salvation. Hence she resolved to strike in another way.

All this lasted one twinkle of an eye. He indeed foresaw the attack, and put out his hand with the speed of a
lightning flash; but he did not succeed in calculating her
movement. The hands passed each other, and Basia, with
all the despairing strength of her young and vigorous arm,
struck him with the ivory butt of the pistol between the
eyes.

The blow was so terrible that Azya was not able even
to cry, and he fell backward, drawing her after him in
his fall.

Basia raised herself in a moment, and, springing on her
horse, shot off like a whirlwind in the direction opposite the
Dnieper, toward the broad steppes.

The curtain of fog closed behind her. The horse, dropping his ears, rushed on at random among the rocks, clefts,
ravines, and breaches. Any moment he might run into
some cleft, any moment he might crush himself and his
rider against a rocky corner; but Basia looked at nothing;

for her the most terrible danger was Azya and the Tartars. A wonderful thing it was, that now, when she had freed herself from the hands of the robber, and when he was lying apparently dead among the rocks, dread mastered all her feelings.   Lying with her face to the mane of the horse, shooting on in the fog, like a deer chased by wolves, she began to fear Azya more than when she was in his arms; and she felt terror and weakness and that which a helpless child feels, which, wandering where it wished, has gone astray, and is alone and deserted.   Certain weeping voices rose in her heart, and began, with groaning, with timidity, with complaint, and with pity, to call for protection: "Michael, save me!   Michael, save me!"

The horse rushed on and on; led by a wonderful instinct, he sprang over breaches, avoided with quick movement prominent cliff corners, until at last the stony ground ceased to sound under his feet; evidently he had come to one of those open "meadows" which stretched here and there among the ravines.

Sweat covered the horse, his nostrils were rattling loudly, but he ran and ran.

"Whither can I go?" thought Basia.   And that moment she answered herself: "To Hreptyoff."

But new alarm pressed her heart at thought of that long road lying through terrible wildernesses.   Quickly too she remembered that Azya had left detachments of his men in Mohiloff and Yampol.   Doubtless these were all in the conspiracy; all served Azya, and would seize her surely, and take her to Rashkoff; she ought, therefore, to ride far into the steppe, and only then turn northward, thus avoiding the settlements on the Dniester.

She ought to do this all the more for the reason that if men were sent to pursue her, beyond doubt they would go near the river; and meanwhile it might be possible to meet some of the Polish commands in the wide steppes, on their way to the fortresses.

The speed of the horse decreased gradually.   Basia, being an experienced rider, understood at once that it was necessary to give him time to recover breath, otherwise he would fall; she felt also that without a horse in those deserts she was lost.

She restrained, therefore, his speed, and went some time at a walk.   The fog was growing thin, but a cloud of hot steam rose from the poor beast.

Basia began to pray.

Suddenly she heard the neighing of a horse amid the fog a few hundred yards behind.

Then the hair rose on her head.

"Mine will fall dead, but so will that one!" said she, aloud; and again she shot on.

For some time her horse rushed forward with the speed of a dove pursued by a falcon, and he ran long, almost to the last of his strength; but the neighing was heard continually behind in the distance. There was in that neighing which came out of the fog something at once of immeasurable yearning and threatening; still, after the first alarm had passed, it came to Basia's mind that if some one were sitting on that horse he would not neigh, for the rider, not wishing to betray the pursuit, would stop the neighing.

"Can it be that that is only Azya's horse following mine?" thought Basia.

For the sake of precaution she drew both pistols out of the holsters; but the caution was needless. After a while something seemed black in the thinning mist, and Azya's horse ran up with flowing mane and distended nostrils. Seeing the pony, he began to approach him, giving out short and sudden neighs; and the pony answered immediately.

"Horse, horse!" cried Basia.

The animal, accustomed to the human hand, drew near and let itself be taken by the bridle. Basia raised her eyes to Heaven, and said: —

"The protection of God!"

In fact, the seizure of Azya's horse was a circumstance for her in every way favorable. To begin with, she had the two best horses in the whole detachment; secondly, she had a horse to change; and thirdly, the presence of the beast assured her that pursuit would not start soon. If the horse had run to the detachment, the Tartars, disturbed at sight of him, would have turned surely and at once to seek their leader; now it will not come to their heads that anything could befall him, and they will go back to look for Azya only when they are alarmed at his too prolonged absence.

"By that time I shall be far away," concluded Basia in her mind.

Here she remembered for the second time that Azya's detachments were stationed in Yampol and Mohiloff. "It is

necessary to go past through the broad steppe, and not ap-
proach the Dniester until in the neighborhood of Hreptyoff.
That terrible man has disposed his troops cunningly, but
God will save me."

Thus thinking, she collected her spirits and prepared to
continue her journey. At the pommel of Azya's saddle she
found a musket, a horn with powder, a box of bullets, a
box of hemp-seed which the Tartar had the habit of chewing continually. Basia, shortening the stirrups of Azya's
saddle to her own feet, thought to herself that during the
whole way she would live, like a bird, on those seeds, and
she kept them carefully near her.

She determined to avoid people and farms; for in those
wildernesses more evil than good was to be looked for from
every man. Fear oppressed her heart when she asked herself, "How shall I feed the horses?" They would dig grass
out from under the snow, and pluck moss from the crevices
of rocks, but might they not die from bad food and excessive travelling? Still, she could not spare them.

There was another fear: Would she not go astray in the
desert? It was easy to avoid that by travelling along the
Dniester, but she could not take that road. What would
happen were she to enter gloomy wildernesses, immense and
roadless? How would she know whether she was going
northward, or in some other direction, if foggy days were to
come, days without sunshine, and nights without stars?
The forests were swarming with wild beasts; she cared less
for that, having courage in her brave heart and having
weapons. Wolves, going in packs, might be dangerous, it
is true, but in general she feared men more than beasts, and
she feared to go astray most of all.

"Ah, God will show me the way, and will let me return to
Michael," said she, aloud. Then she made the sign of the
cross, wiped with her sleeve her face free from the moisture
which made her pale cheeks cold, looked with quick eyes
around the country, and urged her horse on to a gallop.

CHAPTER XL.

No one thought of searching for Tugai Bey's son; therefore he lay on the ground until he recovered consciousness. When he had come to his senses, he sat upright, and wishing to know what was happening to him, began to look around. But he saw the place as if in darkness; then he discovered that he was looking with only one eye, and badly with that one. The other was either knocked out, or filled with blood.

Azya raised his hands to his face. His fingers found icicles of blood stiff on his mustaches; his mouth too was full of blood which was suffocating him so that he had to cough and spit it out a number of times; a terrible pain pierced his face at this spitting; he put his fingers above his mustaches, but snatched them away with a groan of suffering.

Basia's blow had crushed the upper part of his nose, and injured his cheek-bone. He sat for a time without motion; then he began to look around with that eye in which some sight remained, and seeing a streak of snow in a cleft he crept up to it, seized a handful and applied it to his broken face.

This brought great relief straightway; and while the melting snow flowed down in red streaks over his mustaches, he collected another handful and applied it again. Besides, he began to eat snow eagerly, and that also brought relief to him. After a time the immense weight which he felt on his head became so much lighter that he called to mind all that had happened. But at the first moment he felt neither rage, anger, nor despair; bodily pain had deadened all other feelings, and left but one wish, — the wish to save himself quickly.

Azya, when he had eaten a number of handfuls more of snow, began to look for his horse; the horse was not there; then he understood that if he did not wish to wait till his men came to look for him, he must go on foot. Supporting himself on the ground with his hands, he tried to rise, but howled from pain and sat down again.

He sat perhaps an hour, and again began to make efforts. This time he succeeded in so far that he rose, and, resting his shoulders against the cliff, was able to remain on his feet; but when he remembered that he must leave the support and make one step, then, a second and a third in the empty expanse, a feeling of weakness and fear seized him so firmly that he almost sat down again.

Still he mastered himself, drew his sabre, leaned on it, and pushed forward; he succeeded. After some steps he felt that his body and feet were strong, that he had perfect command of them, only his head was, as it were, not his own, and like an enormous weight was swaying now to the right, now to the left, now to the front. He had a feeling also as if he were carrying that head, shaky and too heavy, with extraordinary care, and with extraordinary fear that he would drop it on the stones and break it.

At times, too, the head turned him around, as if it wished him to go in a circle. At times it became dark in his one eye; then he supported himself with both hands on the sabre. The dizziness of his head passed away gradually; but the pain increased always, and bored, as it were, into his forehead, into his eyes, into his whole head, till whining was forced from his breast. The echoes of the rocks repeated his groans, and he went forward in that desert, bloody, terrible, more like a vampire than a man.

It was growing dark when he heard the tramp of a horse in front.

It was the orderly coming for commands.

That evening Azya had strength to order pursuit; but immediately after he lay down on skins, and for three days could see no one except the Greek barber [1] who dressed his wounds, and Halim, who assisted the barber. Only on the fourth day did he regain his speech, and with it consciousness of what had happened.

Straightway his feverish thoughts followed Basia. He saw her fleeing among rocks and in wild places; she seemed to him a bird that was flying away forever; he saw her nearing Hreptyoff, saw her in the arms of her husband, and at that sight a pain carried him away which was more savage than his wound, and with the pain sorrow, and with the sorrow shame for the defeat which he had suffered.

---

[1] A barber in that age and in those regions took the place of a surgeon usually.

"She has fled, she has fled!" repeated he, continually; and rage stifled him so that at times presence of mind seemed to be leaving him again.

"Woe!" answered he, when Halim tried to pacify him, and give assurance that Basia could not escape pursuit; and he kicked the skins with which the old Tartar had covered him, and with his knife threatened him and the Greek. He howled like a wild beast, and tried to spring up, wishing to fly himself to overtake her, to seize her, and then from anger and wild love stifle her with his own hands.

At times he was wandering in delirium, and summoned Halim to bring the head of the little knight quickly, and to confine the commandant's wife, bound, there in that chamber. At times he talked to her, begged, threatened; then he stretched out his hands to draw her to him. At last he fell into a deep sleep, and slept for twenty-four hours; when he woke the fever had left him entirely, and he was able to see Krychinski and Adurovich.

They were anxious, for they knew not what to do. The troops which had gone out under young Novoveski were not to return, it is true, before two weeks; but some unexpected event might hasten their coming, and then it was necessary to know what position to take. It is true that Krychinski and Adurovich were simply feigning a return to the service of the Commonwealth; but Azya was managing the whole affair: he alone could give them directions what to do in emergency; he alone could explain on which side was the greatest profit, whether to return to the dominions of the Sultan or to pretend, or how long to pretend, that they were serving the Commonwealth. They both knew well that in the end of ends Azya intended to betray the Commonwealth; but they supposed that he might command them to wait for the war before disclosing their treason, so as to betray most effectively. His indications were to be a command for them; for he had put himself on them as a leader, as the head of the whole affair, the most crafty, the most influential, and, besides, renowned among all the hordes as the son of Tugai Bey.

They came hurriedly, therefore, to his bed, and bowed before him. With a bandaged face and only one eye, he was still weak, but his health was restored.

"I am sick," began he, at once. "The woman that I wished to take with me tore herself out of my hands, after wounding me with the butt of a pistol. She was the wife of

Volodyovski, the commandant; may pestilence fall on him
and all his race!"

"May it be as thou hast said!" answered the two captains.

"May God grant you, faithful men, happiness and
success!"

"And to thee also, oh, lord!" answered the captains.
Then they began to speak of what they ought to do.

"It is impossible to delay, or to defer the Sultan's service till war begins," said Azya; "after what has happened
with this woman they will not trust us, and will attack us
with sabres. But before they attack, we will fall upon this
place and burn it, for the glory of God. The handful of soldiers we will seize; the towns-people, who are subjects of the
Commonwealth, we will take captive, divide the goods of
the Wallachians, Armenians, and Greeks, and go beyond the
Dniester to the land of the Sultan."

Krychinski and Adurovich had lived as nomads among
the wildest hordes for a long time, had robbed with them,
and grown wild altogether; their eyes lighted up therefore.

"Thanks to you," said Krychinski, "we were admitted to
this place, which God now gives to us."

"Did Novoveski make no opposition?" asked Azya.

"Novoveski knew that we were passing over to the
Commonwealth, and knew that you were coming to meet us;
he looks on us as his men, because he looked on you as his
man."

"We remained on the Moldavian bank," put in Adurovich; "but Krychinski and I went as guests to him. He
received us as nobles, for he said: 'By your present acts
you extinguish former offence; and since the hetman for-
gives you on Azya's security, 't is not proper for me to look
askance at you.' He even wished us to enter the town; but
we said: 'We will not till Azya, Tugai Bey's son, brings
the hetman's permission.' But when he was going away
he gave us another feast, and begged us to watch over
the town."

"At that feast," added Krychinski, "we saw his father,
and the old woman who is searching for her captive husband, and that young lady whom Novoveski intends to
marry."

"Ah!" said Azya, "I did not think that they were all
here, and I brought Panna Novoveski."

He clapped his hands; Halim appeared at once, and Azya

said to him: "When my men see the flames in the place, let them fall on those soldiers in the fortalice, and cut their throats; let them bind the women and the old noble, and guard them till I give the order."

He turned to Krychinski and Adurovich, —

"I will not assist myself, for I am weak; still, I will mount my horse and look on. But, dear comrades, begin, begin!"

Krychinski and Adurovich rushed through the doorway at once. Azya went out after them, and gave command to lead a horse to him; then he rode to the stockade to look from the gate of the high fortalice on what would happen in the town.

Many of his men had begun to climb the wall to look through the stockade and sate their eyes with the sight of the slaughter. Those of Novoveski's soldiers who had not gone to the steppe, seeing the Lithuanian Tartars assembling, and thinking there was something to look at in the town, mixed with them without a shadow of fear or suspicion. Moreover, there were barely twenty of those soldiers; the rest were dispersed in the dram-shops.

Meanwhile the bands of Krychinski and Adurovich scattered through the place in the twinkle of an eye. The men in those bands were almost exclusively Lithuanian Tartars and Cheremis, therefore former inhabitants of the Commonwealth, for the greater part nobles; but since they had left its borders long before, during that time of wandering they had become much like wild Tartars. Their former clothing had gone to pieces, and they were dressed in sheepskin coats with the wool outside. These coats they wore next to their bodies, which were embrowned from the winds of the steppe and from the smoke of fires; but their weapons were better than those of wild Tartars, — all had sabres, all had bows seasoned in fire, and many had muskets. Their faces expressed the same cruelty and thirst for blood as those of their Dobrudja, Belgrod, or Crimean brethren.

Now scattering through the town, they began to run about in various directions, shouting shrilly, as if wishing by those shouts to encourage one another, and excite one another to slaughter and plunder. But though many of them had put knives in their mouths in Tartar fashion, the people of the place, composed as in Yampol of Wallachians, Armenians, Greeks, and partly of Tartar merchants, looked on them without any distrust. The shops were open; the merchants, sitting in front of their shops in Turkish fashion on benches, slipped their beads through their fingers. The cries of the Lithuanian Tartars merely caused men to look at them with curiosity, thinking that they were playing some game.

But all at once smoke rose from the corners of the market square, and from the mouth of all the Tartars came a howling so terrible that pale fear seized the Wallachians, Armenians, and Greeks, and all their wives and children.

Straightway a shower of arrows rained on the peaceful inhabitants. Their cries, the noise of doors and windows closed in a hurry, were mingled with the tramp of horses and the howling of the plunderers.

The market was covered with smoke. Cries of "Woe, woe!" were raised. At the same time the Tartars fell to breaking open shops and houses, dragging out terrified women by the hair; hurling into the street furniture, morocco, merchandise, beds from which feathers went up in a cloud; the groans of slaughtered men were heard, lamentation, the howling of dogs, the bellowing of cattle caught by fire in rear buildings; red tongues of flame, visible even in the daytime on the black rolls of smoke, were shooting higher and higher toward the sky.

In the fortalice Azya's cavalry-men hurled themselves at the very beginning on the infantry, who were defenceless for the greater part.

There was no struggle whatever; a number of knives were buried in each Polish breast without warning; then the heads of the unfortunates were cut off and borne to the hoofs of Azya's horse.

Tugai Bey's son permitted most of his men to join their brethren in the bloody work; but he himself stood and looked on.

Smoke hid the work of Krychinski and Adurovich; the odor of burnt flesh rose to the fortalice. The town was burning like a great pile, and smoke covered the view; only at times in the smoke was heard the report of a musket, like thunder in a cloud, or a fleeing man was seen, or a crowd of Tartars pursuing.

Azya stood still and looked on with delight in his heart; a stern smile parted his lips, under which the white teeth were gleaming: this smile was the more savage because it was mingled with pain from the drying wounds. Besides delight, pride, too, rose in the heart of Azya. He had cast from his breast that burden of feigning, and for the first time he gave rein to his hatred, concealed for long years; now he felt that he was himself, felt that he was the real Azya, the son of Tugai Bey. But at the same time there rose in him a savage regret that Basia was not looking at that fire, at that slaughter; that she could not see him in his new occupation. He loved her, but a wild desire for revenge on her was tearing him. "She ought to be standing right here by my horse," thought he, "and I would hold her by the hair; she would grasp at my feet, and then I would seize her and kiss her on the mouth, and she would be mine, mine! — my slave!"

Only the hope that perhaps that detachment sent in pursuit, or those which he left on the road, would bring her back, restrained him from despair. He clung to that hope as a drowning man to a plank, and that gave him strength; he could not think of losing her, for he was thinking too much of the moment in which he would find her and take her.

He remained at the gate till the slaughtered town had grown still. Stillness came soon, for the bands of Krychinski and Adurovich numbered almost as many heads as the town; therefore the burning outlasted the groans of men and roared on till evening. Azya dismounted and went with slow steps to a spacious room in the middle of which sheepskins were spread; on these he sat and awaited the coming of the two captains.

They came soon, and with them the sotniks. Delight was on the faces of all, for the booty had surpassed expectation; the town had grown much since the time of the peasant incursion, and was wealthy. They had taken about a hundred young women, and a crowd of children of ten years old and upward; these could be sold with profit in the markets of the East. Old women, and children too small and unfit for the road, were slaughtered. The hands of the Tartars were streaming with human blood, and their sheepskin coats had the odor of burning flesh. All took their seats around Azya.

"Only a pile of glowing embers behind us," said Krychinski. "Before the command returns we might go to Yampol; there is as much wealth of every kind there as in Rashkoff, — perhaps more."

"No," answered Azya, "men of mine are in Yampol who will burn the place; but it is time for us to go to the lands of the Khan and the Sultan."

"At thy command! We will return with glory and booty," said the captains and the sergeants.

"There are still women here in the fortalice, and that noble who reared me," said Azya. "A just reward belongs to them."

He clapped his hands and gave command to bring the prisoners.

They were brought without delay, — Pani Boski in tears; Zosia, pale as a kerchief; Eva and her father. Old Pan Novoveski's hands and feet were bound with ropes. All were terrified, but still more astonished at what had taken place. Eva was lost in conjectures as to what had become of Pani Volodyovski, and wondered why Azya had not shown himself. She, not knowing why there was slaughter in the town, nor why she and her friends were bound as captives, concluded that it was a question of carrying her away; that Azya, not wishing in his pride to beg her hand of her father, had fallen into a rage simply out of love for her, and had determined to take her by violence. This was all terrible in itself; but Eva, at least, was not trembling for her own life.

The prisoners did not recognize Azya, for his face was nearly concealed; but all the more did terror seize the knees of the women at the first moment, for they judged that wild Tartars had in some incomprehensible manner destroyed the Lithuanian Tartars and gained possession of Rashkoff. But the sight of Krychinski and Adurovich convinced them that they were still in the hands of Lithuanian Tartars.

They looked at one another some time in silence; at last old Pan Novoveski asked, with an uncertain but powerful voice, —

"In whose hands are we?"

Azya began to unwind the bandages from his head, and from beneath them his face soon appeared, beautiful on a time, though wild, deformed now forever, with a broken nose and a black and blue spot instead of an eye, — a face dreadful, collected in cold vengeance and with a smile like convulsive contortions. He was silent for a moment, then fixed his burning eye on the old man and said, —

"In mine, — in the hands of Tugai Bey's son."

But old Novoveski knew him before he spoke; and Eva also knew him, though the heart was straitened in her from terror and disgust at sight of that ghastly visage. The

maiden covered her eyes with her unbound hands; and the
noble, opening his mouth, began to blink with astonishment
and repeat, —

"Azya! Azya!"

"Whom your lordship reared, to whom you were a father,
and whose back streamed with blood under your parental
hand."

Blood rushed to the noble's head.

"Traitor," said he, "you shall answer for your deeds
before a judge. Serpent! I have a son yet."

"And you have a daughter," answered Azya, "for whose
sake you gave command to flog me to death; and this
daughter I will give now to the last of the horde, so that he
may have service and pleasure from her."

"Leader, give her to me!" cried Adurovich, on a sudden.

"Azya! Azya!" cried Eva, throwing herself at his feet,
"I have always —"

But he kicked her away with one foot, and Adurovich
seized her by the arms and began to drag her along the
floor. Pan Novoveski from purple became blue; the ropes
squeaked on his arms, as he twisted them, and from his
mouth came unintelligible words. Azya rose from the skins
and went toward him, at first slowly, then more quickly,
like a wild beast preparing to bound on its prey. At last
he came near, seized with the contorted fingers of one hand
the mustaches of old Novoveski, and with the other fell to
beating him without mercy on face and head.

A hoarse bellow was rent from his throat when the noble
fell to the floor; Azya knelt on Novoveski's breast, and
suddenly the bright gleam of a knife shone in the room.

"Mercy! rescue!" screamed Eva. But Adurovich struck
her on the head, and then put his broad hand on her mouth;
meanwhile Azya was cutting the throat of Pan Novoveski.

The spectacle was so ghastly that it chilled even the
breasts of the Tartars; for Azya, with calculated cruelty, drew
his knife slowly across the neck of the ill-fated noble, who
gasped and choked awfully. From his open veins the
blood spurted more and more violently on the hands of the
murderer and flowed in a stream along the floor. Then
the rattling and gurgling ceased by degrees; finally air was
wheezing in the severed throat, and the feet of the dying
man dug the floor in convulsive quivers.

Azya rose; his eyes fell now on the pale and sweet face
of Zosia Boski, who seemed dead, for she was hanging

22

senseless on the arm of a Tartar who was holding her, and he said, —

"I will keep this girl for myself, till I give her away or sell her."

Then he turned to the Tartars : "Now only let the pursuit return, and we will go to the lands of the Sultan."

The pursuit returned two days later, but with empty hands. Tugai Bey's son went, therefore, to the land of the Sultan with despair and rage in his heart, leaving behind him a gray and bluish pile of ruins.

CHAPTER XLI.

THE towns through which Basia passed in going from Hreptyoff to Rashkoff were separated from each other by ten or twelve Ukraine miles, [1] and that road by the Dniester was about thirty miles long. It is true that they started each morning in the dark, and did not stop till late in the evening; still, they made the whole journey, including time for refreshment, and in spite of difficult crossings and passages, in three days. People of that time and troops did not make such quick journeys usually; but whoso had the will, or was put to it, could make them. In view of this, Basia calculated that the journey back to Hreptyoff ought to take less time, especially as she was making it on horseback, and as it was a flight in which salvation depended on swiftness.

But she noted her error the first day, for unable to escape on the road by the Dniester, she went through the steppes and had to make broad circuits. Besides she might go astray, and it was probable that she would; she might meet with thawed rivers, impassable, dense forests, swamps not freezing even in winter; she might come to harm from people or beasts, — therefore, though she intended to push on continually, even at night, she was confirmed in the conviction in spite of herself that, even if all went well with her, God knew when she would be in Hreptyoff.

She had succeeded in tearing herself from the arms of Azya; but what would happen farther on? Doubtless anything was better than those infamous arms; still, at thought of what was awaiting her the blood became icy in her veins.

It occurred at once to her that if she spared the horses she might be overtaken by Azya's men, who knew those steppes thoroughly; and to hide from discovery, from pursuit, was almost impossible. They pursued Tartars whole days even in spring and summer when horses' hoofs left no trace on the snow or in soft earth; they read the steppe as an open book; they gazed over those plains like eagles; they

---

[1] Each nearly equal to five English miles.

knew how to sniff a trail in them like hunting dogs; their whole life was passed in pursuing. Vainly had Tartars gone time and again in the water of streams so as not to leave traces; Cossacks, Lithuanian Tartars, and Cheremis, as well as Polish raiders of the steppe, knew how to find them, to answer their "methods" with "methods," and to attack as suddenly as if they had sprung up through the earth. How was she to escape from such people unless to leave them so far in the rear that distance itself would make pursuit impossible? But in such an event her horses would fall.

"They will fall dead without fail, if they continue to go as they have gone so far," thought Basia, with terror, looking at their wet, steaming sides, and at the foam which was falling in flakes to the ground.

Therefore she slackened their speed from time to time and listened; but in every breath of wind, in the rustling of leaves on the edge of ravines, in the dry rubbing of the withered steppe reeds against one another, in the noise made by the wings of a passing bird, even in the silence of the wilderness, which was sounding in her ears, she heard voices of pursuit, and terrified urged on her horses again, and ran with wild impetus till their snorting declared that they could not continue at that speed.

The burden of loneliness and weakness pressed her down more and more. Ah! what an orphan she felt herself; what regret, as immense as unreasoning, rose in her heart for all people, the nearest and dearest, who had so forsaken her! Then she thought that surely it was God punishing her for her passion for adventures, for her hurrying to every hunt, to expeditions, frequently against the will of her husband; for her giddiness and lack of sedateness.

When she thought of this she wept, and raising her head began to repeat, sobbing, —

"Chastise, but do not desert me! Do not punish Michael! Michael is innocent."

Meanwhile night was approaching, and with it cold, darkness, uncertainty of the road, and alarm. Objects had begun to efface themselves, grow dim, lose definite forms, and also to become, as it were, mysteriously alive and expectant. Protuberances on lofty rocks looked like heads in pointed and round caps, — heads peering out from behind gigantic walls of some kind, and gazing in silence and malignity to see who was passing below. Tree

branches, stirred by the breeze, made motions like people:
some of these beckoned to Basia as if wishing to call her
and confide to her some terrible secret; others seemed to
speak and give warning: "Do not come near!" The trunks
of uprooted trees seemed like monstrous creatures crouching
for a spring. Basia was daring, very daring, but, like all
people of that period, she was superstitious. When darkness came down completely, the hair rose on her head, and
shivers passed through her body at thought of the unclean powers that might dwell in those regions. She feared
vampires especially; belief in them was spread particularly in the Dniester country by reason of nearness to
Moldavia, and just the places around Yampol and Rashkoff
were ill-famed in that regard. How many people there
left the world day by day through sudden death, without confession or absolution! Basia remembered all the
tales which the knights had told at Hreptyoff, on evenings at the fireside, — stories of deep valleys in which,
when the wind howled, sudden groans were heard of
"Jesus, Jesus!" of pale lights in which something was
snorting; of laughing cliffs; of pale children, suckling
infants with green eyes and monstrous heads,— infants
which implored to be taken on horseback, and when taken
began to suck blood; finally, of heads without bodies,
walking on spider legs; and most terrible of all those ghastli-
nesses, vampires of full size, or brukolaki, so called in
Wallachia, who hurled themselves on people directly.

Then she began to make the sign of the cross, and she
did not stop till her hand had grown weak; but even then
she repeated the litany, for no other weapons were effective
against unclean powers.

The horses gave her consolation, for they showed no
fear, snorting briskly. At times she patted her pony, as
if wishing in that way to convince herself that she was in a
real world.

The night, very dark at first, became clearer by degrees,
and at last the stars began to glimmer through the thin mist.
For Basia this was an uncommonly favorable circumstance, — first, because her fear decreased; and secondly,
because by observing the Great Bear, she could turn to the
north, or in the direction of Hreptyoff. Looking on the
region about, she calculated that she had gone a considerable distance from the Dniester; for there were fewer rocks,
more open country, more hills covered with oak groves, and

frequently broad plains. Time after time, however, she was forced to cross ravines, and she went down into them with fear in her heart, for in the depths of those places it was always dark, and a harsh, piercing cold was there. Some were so steep that she was forced to go around them; from this came great loss of time and an addition to the journey.

It was worse, however, with streams and rivers, and a whole system of these flowed from the East to the Dniester. All were thawed, and the horses snorted with fear when they went at night into strange water of unknown depth. Basia crossed only in places where the sloping bank allowed the supposition that the water, widely spread there, was shallow. In fact, it was so in most cases; at some crossings, however, the water reached halfway to the backs of her horses: Basia then knelt, in soldier fashion, on the saddle, and, holding to the pommel, tried not to wet her feet. But she did not succeed always in this, and soon a piercing cold seized her from feet to knees.

"God give me daylight, I will go more quickly," repeated she, from time to time.

At last she rode out onto a broad plain with a sparse forest, and seeing that the horses were barely dragging their legs, she halted for rest. Both stretched their necks to the ground at the same time, and putting forward one foot, began to pluck moss and withered grass eagerly. In the forest there was perfect silence, unbroken save by the sharp breathing of the horses and the crunching of the grass in their powerful jaws.

When they had satisfied, or rather deceived, their first hunger, both horses wished evidently to roll, but Basia might not indulge them in that. She dared not loosen the girths and come to the ground herself, for she wished to be ready at every moment for further flight.

She sat on Azya's horse, however, for her own had carried her from the last resting-place, and though strong, and with noble blood in his veins, he was more delicate than the other.

When she had changed horses, she felt a hunger after the thirst which she had quenched a number of times while crossing the rivers; she began therefore to eat the seeds which she had found in the bag at Azya's saddle-bow. They seemed to her very good, though a little bitter; she ate, thanking God for the unlooked-for refreshment.

But she ate sparingly, so that they might last to Hreptyoff. Soon sleep began to close her eyelids with irresistible power; and when the movement of the horse ceased to give warmth, a sharp cold pierced her. Her feet were perfectly stiff; she felt also an immeasurable weariness in her whole body, especially in her back and shoulders, strained with struggling against Azya. A great weakness seized her, and her eyes closed.

But after a while she opened them with effort. "No! In the daytime, in time of journeying, I will sleep," thought she; "but if I sleep now I shall freeze."

But her thoughts grew more confused, or came helter-skelter, presenting disordered images, — in which the forest, flight and pursuit, Azya, the little knight, Eva, and the last event were mingled together half in a dream, half in clear vision. All this was rushing on somewhere as waves rush driven by the wind; and she, Basia, runs with them, without fear, without joy, as if she were travelling by contract. Azya, as it were, was pursuing her, but at the same time was talking to her, and anxious about the horse; Pan Zagloba was angry because supper would get cold; Michael was showing the road; and Eva was coming behind in the sleigh, eating dates.

Then those persons became more and more effaced, as if a foggy curtain or darkness had begun to conceal them, and they vanished by degrees; there remained only a certain strange darkness, which, though the eye did not pierce it, seemed still to be empty, and to extend an immeasurable distance. This darkness penetrated every place, penetrated Basia's head, and quenched in it all visions, all thoughts, as a blast of wind quenches torches at night in the open air.

Basia fell asleep; but fortunately for her, before the cold could stiffen the blood in her veins, an unusual noise roused her. The horses started on a sudden; evidently somethir uncommon was happening in the forest.

Basia, regaining consciousness in one moment, grasped Azya's musket, and bending on the horse, with collected attention and distended nostrils, began to listen. Hers was a nature of such kind that every peril roused wariness at the first twinkle of an eye, daring and readiness for defence.

The noise which roused her was the grunting of wild pigs. Whether beasts were stealing up to the young pigs, or the old boars were going to fight, it is enough that the whole forest resounded immediately. That uproar took

place beyond doubt at a distance; but in the stillness of
night, and the general drowsiness, it seemed so near that
Basia heard not only grunting and squeals, but the loud
whistle of nostrils breathing heavily. Suddenly a breaking and tramp, the crash of broken twigs, and a whole herd,
though invisible to Basia, rushed past in the neighborhood,
and sank in the depth of the forest.

But in that incorrigible Basia, notwithstanding her terrible position, the feeling of a hunter was roused in a
twinkle, and she was sorry that she had not seen the herd
rushing by.

"One would like to see a little," said she, in her mind;
"but no matter! Riding in this way through forests, surely
I shall see something yet."

And only after that thought did she push on, remembering that it was better to see nothing and flee with all speed.

It was impossible to halt longer, because the cold seized
her more acutely, and the movement of the horse warmed
her a good deal, while wearying her comparatively little.
But the horses, having snatched merely some moss and
frozen grass, moved very reluctantly, and with drooping
heads. The hoar-frost in time of halting had covered their
sides, and it seemed that they barely dragged their legs
forward. They had gone, moreover, since the afternoon
rest almost without drawing breath.

When she had crossed the plain, with her eyes fixed on
the Great Bear in the heavens, Basia disappeared in the
forest, which was not very dense, but in a hilly region inter-
sected with narrow ravines. It became darker too; not only
because of the shade cast by spreading trees, but also because
a fog rose from the earth and hid the stars. She was forced
to go at random. The ravines alone gave some indication
that she was taking the right course, for she knew that they
all extended from the east toward the Dniester, and that by
crossing new ones, she was going continually toward the
north. But in spite of this indication, she thought, "I am
ever in danger of approaching the Dniester too nearly, or
of going too far from it. To do either is perilous: in the
first case, I should make an enormous journey; in the second,
I might come out at Yampol, and fall into the hands of my
enemies." Whether she was yet before Yampol, or just on
the heights above it, or had left that place behind, of this
she had not the faintest idea.

"There is more chance to know when I pass Mohiloff,"

said she; "for it lies in a great ravine, which extends far; perhaps I shall recognize it."

Then she looked at the sky and thought: "God grant me only to go beyond Mohiloff; for there Michael's dominion begins; there nothing will frighten me."

Now the night became darker. Fortunately snow was lying in the forest, and on the white ground she could distinguish the dark trunks of trees, see the lower limbs and avoid them. But Basia had to ride more slowly; therefore that terror of unclean powers fell on her soul again, — that terror which in the beginning of the night had chilled her blood as if with ice.

"But if I see gleaming eyes low down," said she to her frightened soul, "that's nothing! it will be a wolf; but if at the height of a man —" At that moment, she cried aloud, "In the name of the Father, Son —"

Was that, perhaps, a wild-cat sitting on a limb? It is sufficient that Basia saw clearly a pair of gleaming eyes, at the height of a man.

From fear, her eyes were covered with a mist; but when she looked again there was nothing to be seen, and nothing heard beyond a rustle among the branches, but her heart beat as loudly as if it would burst open her bosom.

And she rode farther; long, long, she rode, sighing for the light of day; but the night stretched out beyond measure. Soon after, a river barred her road again. Basia was already far enough beyond Yampol, on the bank of the Rosava; but without knowledge of where she was, she thought merely that if she continued to push forward to the north, she would soon meet a new river. She thought too that the night must be near its end; for the cold increased sensibly, the fog fell away, and stars appeared again, but dimmer, beaming with uncertain light.

At length darkness began to pale. Trunks of trees, branches, twigs, grew more visible. Perfect silence reigned in the forest, — the dawn had come.

After a certain time Basia could distinguish the color of the horses. At last in the east, among the branches of the trees, a bright streak appeared, — the day was there, a clear day.

Basia felt weariness immeasurable. Her mouth opened in continual yawning, and her eyes closed soon after; she slept soundly but a short time, for a branch, against which her head came, roused her. Happily the horses were going

very slowly, nipping moss by the way; hence the blow
was so slight that it caused her no harm. The sun had
risen, and was pale; its beautiful rays broke through
leafless branches. At sight of this, consolation entered
Basia's heart; she had left between her and pursuit so
many steppes, mountains, ravines, and a whole night.

"If those from Yampol, or Mohiloff, do not seize me,
others will not come up," said she to herself.

She reckoned on this too, — that in the beginning of her
flight she had gone by a rocky road, therefore hoofs could
leave no traces. But doubt began to seize her again. The
Lithuanian Tartars will find tracks even on stones, and will
pursue stubbornly, unless their horses fall dead; this last supposition was most likely. It was sufficient for Basia to look
at her own beasts; their sides had fallen in, their heads were
drooping, their eyes dim. While moving along, they dropped
their heads to the ground time after time, to seize moss, or nip
in passing red leaves withering here and there on the low oak
bushes. It must be too that fever was tormenting Basia,
for at all crossings she drank eagerly.

Nevertheless, when she came out on an open plain between two forests, she urged the wearied horses forward at
a gallop, and went at that pace to the next forest.

After she had passed that forest she came to a second
plain, still wider and more broken; behind hills at a distance of a mile or more smoke was rising, as straight as a
pine-tree, toward the sky. That was the first inhabited
place that Basia had met; for that country, excepting the
river-bank itself, was a desert, or rather had been turned
into a desert, not only in consequence of Tartar attacks, but
by reason of continuous Polish-Cossack wars. After the
last campaign of Pan Charnetski, to whom Busha fell a
victim, the small towns came to be wretched settlements,
the villages were overgrown with young forests; but after
Charnetski, there were so many expeditions, so many battles, so many slaughters, down to the most recent times, in
which the great Sobieski had wrested those regions from
the enemy. Life had begun to increase; but that one
tract through which Basia was fleeing was specially empty,
— only robbers had taken refuge there, but even they had
been well-nigh exterminated by the commands at Rashkoff,
Yampol, and Hreptyoff.

Basia's first thought at sight of this smoke was to ride
toward it, find a house or even a hut, or if nothing more,

a simple fire, warm herself and gain strength. But soon
it occurred to 'her that in those regions it was safer to
meet a pack of wolves than to meet men; men there were
more merciless and savage than wild beasts. Nay, it
behooved her to urge forward her horses, and pass that
forest haunt of men with all speed, for only death could
await her in that place.

At the very edge of the opposite forest Basia saw a small
stack of hay; so, paying no attention to anything, she
stopped at it to feed her horses. They ate greedily, thrusting their heads at once to their ears in the hay, and drawing
out great bunches of it. Unfortunately their bits hindered
them greatly; but Basia could not unbridle them, reasoning correctly in this way: —

"Where smoke is there must be a house; as there is a
stack here, they must have horses there on which they
could follow me, — therefore I must be ready."

She spent, however, about an hour at the stack, so that
the horses ate fairly well; and she herself ate some seeds.
She then moved on, and when she had travelled a number
of furlongs, all at once she saw before her two persons
carrying bundles of twigs on their backs.

One was a man not old, but not in his first youth, with a
face pitted with small-pox, and with crooked eyes, ugly,
repulsive, with a cruel, ferocious expression of face; the
other, a stripling, was idiotic. This was to be seen at the
first glance, by his stupid smile and wandering look.

Both threw down their bundles of twigs at sight of the
armed horseman, and seemed to be greatly alarmed. But
the meeting was so sudden, and they were so near, that they
could not flee.

"Glory be to God!" said Basia.

"For the ages of ages."

"What is the name of this farm?"

"What should its name be? There is the cabin."

"Is it far to Mohiloff?"

"We know not."

Here the man began to scrutinize Basia's face carefully.
Since she wore man's apparel he took her for a youth; insolence and cruelty came at once to his face instead of the
recent timidity.

"But why are you so young, Pan Knight?"

"What is that to you?"

"And are you travelling alone?" asked the peasant,
advancing a step.

"Troops are following me."

He halted, looked over the immense plain, and answered, —

"Not true. There is no one."

He advanced two steps; his crooked eyes gave out a sullen gleam, and arranging his mouth he began to imitate the call of a quail, evidently wishing to summon some one in that way.

All this seemed to Basia very hostile, and she aimed a pistol at his breast without hesitation, —

"Silence, or thou 'lt die!"

The man stopped, and, what is more, threw himself flat on the ground. The idiot did the same, but began to howl like a wolf from terror; perhaps he had lost his mind on a time from the same feeling, for now his howling recalled the most ghastly terror.

Basia urged forward her horses, and shot on like an arrow. Fortunately there was no undergrowth in the forest, and trees were far apart. Soon a new plain appeared, narrow, but very long. The horses had gained fresh strength from eating at the stack, and rushed like the wind.

"They will run home, mount their horses, and pursue me," thought Basia.

Her only solace was that the horses travelled well, and that the place where she met the men was rather far from the house.

"Before they can reach the house and bring out the horses, I, riding in this way, shall be five miles or more ahead."

That was the case; but when some hours had passed, and Basia, convinced that she was not followed, slackened speed, great fear, great depression, seized her heart, and tears came perforce to her eyes.

This meeting showed her what people in those regions were, and what might be looked for from them. It is true that this knowledge was not unexpected. From her own experience, and from the narratives at Hreptyoff, she knew that the former peaceful settlers had gone from those wilds, or that war had devoured them; those who remained were living in continual alarm, amid terrible civil disturbance and Tartar attacks, in conditions in which one man is a wolf toward another; they were living without churches or faith, without other principles than those of bloodshed and burning, without knowing any right but that of the strong hand; they had lost all human feelings, and grown wild, like the beasts of the forest. Basia knew this well; still, a human being, astray in the wilderness, harassed by cold and hunger, turns involuntarily for aid first of all to kindred beings. So did Basia when she saw that smoke indicating a habitation of people; following involuntarily the first impulse of her heart, she wished to rush to it, greet the inhabitants with God's name, and rest her wearied head under their roof. But cruel reality bared its teeth at her quickly, like a fierce dog. Hence her heart was filled with bitterness; tears of sorrow and disappointment came to her eyes.

"Help from no one but God," thought she; "may I meet no person again." Then she fell to thinking why that man had begun to imitate a quail. "There must be others there surely, and he wanted to call them." It came to her head that there were robbers in that tract, who, driven out of the ravines near the river, had betaken themselves to the wilds farther off in the country, where the nearness of broad steppes gave them more safety and easier escape in case of need.

"But what will happen," inquired Basia, "if I meet a number of men, or more than a dozen ? The musket, — that is one; two pistols, — two; a sabre, — let us suppose two more; but if the number is greater than this, I shall die a dreadful death."

And as in the previous night with its alarms she had wished day to come as quickly as possible, so now she looked with yearning for darkness to hide her more easily from evil eyes.

Twice more, during persistent riding, did it seem to her that she was passing near people. Once she saw on the edge of a high plain a number of cabins. Maybe robbers by vocation were not living in them, but she preferred to pass at a gallop, knowing that even villagers are not much better than robbers; another time she heard the sound of axes cutting wood.

The wished-for night covered the earth at last. Basia was so wearied that when she came to a naked steppe, free from forest, she said to herself, —

"Here I shall not be crushed against a tree; I will sleep right away, even if I freeze."

When she was closing her eyes it seemed to her that far off in the distance, in the white snow, she saw a number of black points which were moving in various directions. For a while longer she overcame her sleep. "Those are surely wolves," muttered she, quietly.

Before she had gone many yards, those points disappeared; then she fell asleep so soundly that she woke only when Azya's horse, on which she was sitting, neighed under her.

She looked around; she was on the edge of a forest, and woke in time, for if she had not waked she might have been crushed against a tree.

Suddenly she saw that the other horse was not near her.

"What has happened?" cried she, in great alarm.

But a very simple thing had happened. Basia had tied, it is true, the reins of her horse's bridle to the pommel of the saddle on which she was sitting; but her stiffened hands served her badly, and she was not able to knot the straps firmly; afterward the reins fell off, and the wearied horse stopped to seek food under the snow or lie down.

Fortunately Basia had her pistol at her girdle, and not in the holsters; the powder-horn and the bag with the rest of the seeds were also with her. Finally the misfortune was not too appalling; for Azya's horse, though he yielded to hers in speed, surpassed him undoubtedly in endurance of cold and labor. Still, Basia was grieved for her favorite horse, and at the first moment determined to search for him.

She was astonished, however, when she looked around the steppe and saw nothing of the beast, though the night was unusually clear.

"He has stopped behind," thought she, — "surely not gone ahead; but he must have lain down in some hollow, and that is why I cannot see him."

Azya's horse neighed a second time, shaking himself somewhat and putting back his ears; but from the steppe he was answered by silence.

"I will go and find him," said Basia.

And she turned, when a sudden alarm seized her, and a voice precisely as if human called, —

"Basia, do not go back!"

That moment the silence was broken by other and ill-omened voices near, and coming, as it were, from under the earth, howling, coughing, whining, groaning, and finally a ghastly squeal, short, interrupted. This was all the more terrible since there was nothing to be seen on the steppe. Cold sweat covered Basia from head to foot; and from her blue lips was wrested the cry, —

"What is that? What has happened?"

She divined at once, it is true, that wolves had killed her horse; but she could not understand why she did not see him, since, judging by the sounds, he was not more than five hundred yards behind.

There was no time to fly to the rescue, for the horse must be torn to pieces already; besides, she needed to think of her own life. Basia fired the pistol to frighten the wolves, and moved forward. While going she pondered over what had happened, and after a while it shot through her head that perhaps it was not wolves that had taken her horse, since those voices seemed to come from under the ground. At this thought a cold shiver went along her back; but dwelling on the matter more carefully, she remembered that in her sleep it had seemed to her that she was going down and then going up again.

"It must be so," said she; "I must have crossed in my sleep some ravine, not very steep. There my horse remained; and there the wolves found him."

The rest of the night passed without accident. Having eaten hay the morning before, the horse went with great endurance, so that Basia herself was amazed at his strength. That was a Tartar horse, — a "wolf hunter" of great stock, and of endurance almost without limit. During the short halts which Basia made, he ate everything without distinction, — moss, leaves; he gnawed even the bark of trees, and went on and on. Basia urged him to a gallop on the plains. Then he began to groan somewhat, and to breathe loudly when reined in; he panted, trembled, and dropped his head low from weariness, but did not fall. Her horse, even had he not perished under the teeth of the wolves, could not have endured such a journey. Next morning Basia, after her prayers, began to calculate the time.

"I broke away from Azya on Tuesday in the afternoon," said she to herself, "I galloped till night; then one night passed on the road; after that a whole day; then again a whole night, and now the third day has begun. A pursuit, even had there been one, must have returned already, and Hreptyoff ought to be near, for I have not spared the horses."

After a while she added, "It is time; it is time! God pity me!"

At moments a desire seized her to approach the Dniester, for at the bank it would be easier to learn where she was;

but when she remembered that fifty of Azya's men had remained with Pan Gorzenski in Mohiloff, she was afraid. It occurred to her that because she had made such a circuit she might not have passed Mohiloff yet. On the road, in so far as sleep had not closed her eyes, she tried, it is true, to note carefully whether she did not come on a very wide ravine, like that in which Mohiloff was situated; but she did not see such a place. However, the ravine in the interior might be narrow and altogether different from what it was at Mohiloff; might have come to an end or contracted at some furlongs beyond the town; in a word, Basia had not the least idea of where Mohiloff was.

Only she implored God without ceasing that it might be near, for she felt that she could not endure toil, hunger, sleeplessness, and cold much longer. During three days she had lived on seeds alone, and though she had spared them most carefully, still she had eaten the last kernel that morning, and there was nothing in the bag.

Now she could only nourish and warm herself with the hope that Hreptyoff was near. In addition to hope, fever was warming her. Basia felt perfectly that she had a fever; for though the air was growing colder, and it was even freezing, her hands and feet were as hot then as they had been cold at the beginning of the journey; thirst too tormented her greatly.

"If only I do not lose my presence of mind," said she to herself; "if I reach Hreptyoff, even with my last breath, see Michael, and then let the will of God be done."

Again she had to pass numerous streams or rivers, but these were either shallow or frozen; on some water was flowing, and there was ice underneath, firm and strong. But she dreaded these crossings most of all because the horse, though courageous, feared them evidently. Going into the water or onto the ice he snorted, put forward his ears, sometimes resisted, but when urged went warily, putting foot before foot slowly, and sniffing with distended nostrils. It was well on in the afternoon when Basia, riding through a thick pine-wood, halted before some river larger than others, and above all much wider. According to her supposition this might be the Ladava or the Kalusik. At sight of this her heart beat with gladness. In every case Hreptyoff must be near; had she passed it even, she might consider herself saved, for the country there was more inhabited and the people less to be feared. The river, as far as her eye could reach, had steep banks; only in one place was there a depression, and the water, dammed by ice, had gone over the bank as if poured into a flat and wide vessel. The banks were frozen thoroughly; in the middle a broad streak of water was flowing, but Basia hoped to find the usual ice under it.

The horse went in, resisting somewhat, as at every crossing, with head inclined, and smelling the snow before him. When she came to running water Basia knelt on the saddle, according to her custom, and held the saddle-bow with both hands. The water plashed under his hoofs. The ice was really firm; his hoof struck it as stone. But evidently the shoes had grown blunt on the long road, which was rocky in places, for the horse began to slip; his feet went apart, as if flying from under him. All at once he fell forward, and his nostrils sank in the water; then he rose, fell on his rump, rose again, but being terrified, began to struggle and strike desperately with his feet. Basia grasped the bridle, and with that a dull crack was heard; both hind legs of the horse sank through the ice as far as the haunches.

"Jesus, Jesus!" cried Basia.

The beast, with fore legs still on firm ice, made desperate efforts; but evidently the pieces on which he was resting began to move from under his feet, for he fell deeper, and began to groan hoarsely.

Basia had still time sufficient and presence of mind to seize the mane of the horse and reach the unbroken ice in front of him. She fell and was wet in the water; but rising and feeling firm ground under foot, she knew that she was saved. She wished to save the horse, and bending forward caught the bridle; and going toward the bank she pulled it with all her might.

But the horse sank deeper, could not free even his fore legs to grapple the ice, which was still unmoved. The reins were pulled harder every instant; but he sank more and more. He began to groan with a voice almost human, baring his teeth the while; his eyes looked at Basia with indescribable sadness, as if wishing to say to her: "There is no rescue for me; drop the reins ere I drag thee in!"

There was, in truth, no rescue for him, and Basia had to drop the reins.

When the horse disappeared beneath the ice she went to

23

the bank, sat down under a bush without leaves, and sobbed like a child.

Her energy was thoroughly broken for the moment. And besides that, the bitterness and pain which, after meeting with people, had filled her heart, overflowed it now with still greater force. Everything was against her,—uncertain roads, darkness, the elements, men, beasts; the hand of God alone had seemed to watch over her. In that kind, fatherly care she had put all her childlike trust; but now even that hand had failed her. This was a feeling to which Basia had not given such clear expression; but if she had not, she felt it all the more strongly in her heart.

What remained to her? Complaint and tears! And still she had shown all the valor, all the courage, all the endurance which such a poor, weak creature could show. Now, see, her horse is drowned,—the last hope of rescue, the last plank of salvation, the only thing living that was with her! Without that horse she felt powerless against the unknown expanse which separated her from Hreptyoff, against the pine-woods, ravines, and steppes; not only defenceless against the pursuit of men and beasts, but she felt far more lonely and deserted than before. She wept till tears failed her. Then came exhaustion, weariness, and a feeling of helplessness so great that it was almost equal to rest. Sighing deeply once and a second time, she said to herself,—

"Against the will of God I am powerless. I will die where I am."

And she closed her eyes, aforetime so bright and joyous, but now hollow and sunken.

In its own way, though her body was becoming more helpless every moment, thought was still throbbing in her head like a frightened bird, and her heart was throbbing also. If no one in the world loved her, she would have less regret to die; but all loved her so much.

And she pictured to herself what would happen when Azya's treason and his flight would become known: how they would search for her; how they would find her at last,—blue, frozen, sleeping the eternal sleep under a bush at the river. And all at once she called out,—

"Oh, but poor Michael will be in despair! Ei, ei!"

Then she implored him, saying that it was not her fault.

"Michael," said she, putting her arms around his neck, mentally, "I did all in my power; but, my dear, it was difficult. The Lord God did not will it."

And that moment such a heartfelt love for Michael possessed her, such a wish even to die near that dear head, that, summoning every force she had, she rose from the bank and walked on.

At first it was immensely difficult. Her feet had become unaccustomed to walking during the long ride; she felt as if she were going on stilts. Happily she was not cold; she was even warm enough, for the fever had not left her for a moment.

Sinking in the forest, she went forward persistently, remembering to keep the sun on her left hand. It had gone, in fact, to the Moldavian side; for it was the second half of the day, — perhaps four o'clock. Basia cared less now for approaching the Dniester, for it seemed to her always that she was beyond Mohiloff.

"If only I were sure of that; if I knew it!" repeated she, raising her blue, and at the same time inflamed, face to the sky. "If some beast or some tree would speak and say, 'It is a mile to Hreptyoff, two miles,'—I might go there perhaps."

But the trees were silent; nay more, they seemed to her unfriendly, and obstructed the road with their roots. Basia stumbled frequently against the knots and curls of those roots covered with snow. After a time she was burdened unendurably; she threw the warm mantle from her shoulders and remained in her single coat. Relieving herself in this way, she walked and walked still more hurriedly, — now stumbling, now falling at times in deeper snow. Her fur-lined morocco boots without soles, excellent for riding in a sleigh or on horseback, did not protect her feet well against clumps or stones; besides, soaked through repeatedly at crossings, and kept damp by the warmth of her feet now inflamed from fever, these boots were torn easily in the forest.

"I will go barefoot to Hreptyoff or to death!" thought Basia.

And a sad smile lighted her face, for she found comfort in this, that she went so enduringly; and that if she should be frozen on the road, Michael would have nothing to cast at her memory.

Therefore she talked now continually with her husband, and said once, —

"Ai, Michael dear! another would not have done so much; for example, Eva."

Of Eva she had thought more than once in that time of flight; more than once had she prayed for Eva. It was clear to her now, seeing that Azya did not love the girl, that her fate, and the fate of all the other prisoners left in Rashkoff, would be dreadful.

"It is worse for them than for me," repeated she, from moment to moment, and that thought gave fresh strength to her.

But when one, two, and three hours had passed, this strength decreased at every step. Gradually the sun sank behind the Dniester, and flooding the sky with a ruddy twilight, was quenched; the snow took on a violet reflection. Then that gold and purple abyss of twilight began to grow dark, and became narrower every moment; from a sea covering half the heavens it was changed to a lake, from a lake to a river, from a river to a stream, and finally gleaming as a thread of light stretched on the west, yielded to darkness.

Night came.

An hour passed. The pine-wood became black and mysterious; but, unmoved by any breath, it was as silent as if it had collected itself, and were meditating what to do with that poor, wandering creature. But there was nothing good in that torpor and silence; nay, there was insensibility and callousness.

Basia went on continually, catching the air more quickly with her parched lips; she fell, too, more frequently, because of darkness and her lack of strength.

She had her head turned upward; but not to look for the directing Great Bear, for she had lost altogether the sense of position. She went so as to go; she went because very clear and sweet visions before death had begun to fly over her.

For example, the four sides of the wood begin to run together quickly, to join and form a room, — the room at Hreptyoff. Basia is in it; she sees everything clearly. In the chimney a great fire is burning, and on the benches officers are sitting as usual: Pan Zagloba is chaffing Pan Snitko; Pan Motovidlo is sitting in silence looking into the flames, and when something hisses in the fire he says, in his drawling voice, "Oh, soul in purgatory, what needst thou?" Pan Mushalski and Pan Hromyka are playing dice with Michael. Basia comes up to them and says: "Michael, I will sit on the bench and nestle up to you a

little, for I am not myself." Michael puts his arm around
her. "What is the matter, kitten? But maybe —" And
he inclines to her ear and whispers something. But she
answers, "Ai, how I am not myself!" What a bright and
peaceful room that is, and how beloved is that Michael!
But somehow Basia is not herself, so that she is alarmed.

Basia is not herself to such a degree that the fever has
left her suddenly, for the weakness before death has overcome it. The visions disappear; presence of mind returns,
and with it memory.

"I am fleeing before Azya," said Basia to herself; "I
am in the forest at night. I cannot go to Hreptyoff. I am
dying."

After the fever, cold seizes her quickly, and goes through
her body to the bones. The legs bend under her, and she
kneels at last on the snow before a tree.

Not the least cloud darkens her mind now. She is terribly
sorry to lose life, but she knows perfectly that she is dying;
and wishing to commend her soul to God, she begins to say,
in a broken voice, —

"In the name of the Father and the Son —"

Suddenly certain strange, sharp, shrill, squeaking voices
interrupt further prayer; they are disagreeable and piercing
in the stillness of the night.

Basia opens her mouth. The question, "What is that?"
is dying on her lips. For a moment she places her trembling fingers to her face, as if not wishing to lend belief,
and from her mouth a sudden cry is wrested, —

"O Jesus, O Jesus! Those are the well-sweeps; that is
Hreptyoff! O Jesus!"

Then that being who was dying a little before springs
up, and panting, trembling, with eyes full of tears, and with
swelling bosom runs through the forest, falls, rises again,
repeating, —

"They are watering the horses! That is Hreptyoff!
Those are our well-sweeps! Even to the gate, even to the
gate! O Jesus! Hreptyoff — Hreptyoff!"

But here the forest grows thin, the snow-fields open, and
with them the slope, from which a number of glittering eyes
are looking on the running Basia.

But those were not wolves' eyes, — ah, those were Hreptyoff windows looking with sweet, bright, and saving light!
That is the "fortalice" there on the eminence, just that
eastern side turned to the forest!

·There was still a distance to go, but Basia did not know when she passed it. The soldiers standing at the gate on the village side did not know her in the darkness; but they admitted her, thinking her a boy sent on some message, and returning to the commandant. She rushed in with her last breath, ran across the square near the wells where the dragoons, returning just before from a reconnoissance, had watered their horses for the night, and stood at the door of the main building. The little knight and Zagloba were sitting just then astride a bench before the fire, and drinking krupnik.[1] They were talking of Basia, thinking that she was down there somewhere, managing in Rashkoff. Both were sad, for it was terribly dreary without her, and every day they were discussing about her return.

"God ward off sudden thaws and rains. Should they come, He alone knows when she would return," said Zagloba, gloomily.

"The winter will hold out yet," said the little knight; "and in eight or ten days I shall be looking toward Mohiloff for her every hour."

"I wish she had not gone. There is nothing for me here without her in Hreptyoff."

"But why did you advise the journey?"

"Don't invent, Michael! That took place with your head."

"If only she comes back in health."

Here the little knight sighed, and added, —

"In health, and as soon as possible."

With that the door squeaked, and a small, pitiful, torn creature, covered with snow, began to pipe plaintively at the threshold: —

"Michael, Michael!"

The little knight sprang up, but he was so astonished at the first moment that he stopped where he stood, as if turned to stone; he opened his arms, began to blink, and stood still.

"Michael! — Azya betrayed — he wanted to carry me away; but I fled, and — save — rescue!"

When she had said this, she tottered and fell as if dead, on the floor; Pan Michael sprang forward, raised her in his arms as if she had been a feather, and cried shrilly, —

---

[1] A hot drink made of gorailka, honey, and spices.

"Merciful Christ!"

But her poor head hung without life on his shoulder. Thinking that he held only a corpse in his arms, he began to cry with a ghastly voice, —

"Basia is dead! — dead! Rescue!"

CHAPTER XLII.

News of Basia's arrival flew like a thunderbolt through Hreptyoff; but no one except the little knight, Pan Zagloba, and the serving-women saw her that evening, or the following evenings. After that swoon on the threshold she recovered presence of mind sufficiently to tell in a few words at least what had happened, and how it had happened; but suddenly a new fit of fainting set in, and an hour later, though they used all means to revive her, though they warmed her, gave her wine, tried to give her food, she did not know even her husband, and there was no doubt that for her a long and grievous illness was beginning.

Meanwhile excitement rose in all Hreptyoff. The soldiers, learning that "the lady" had come home half alive, rushed out to the square like a swarm of bees; all the officers assembled, and whispering in low voices were waiting impatiently for news from the bedroom where Basia was lying. For a long time, however, it was impossible to learn anything. It is true that at times waiting-women hurried past, one to the kitchen for hot water, another to the dispensary for plasters, ointments, and herbs; but they let no one detain them. Uncertainty was weighing like lead on all hearts. Increasing crowds, even from the village, collected on the square; inquiries passed from mouth to mouth; men described Azya's treason, and said that "the lady" had saved herself by flight, had fled a whole week without food or sleep. At these tidings the breasts of all swelled with rage. At last a wonderful and terrible frenzy seized the assembly of soldiers; but they repressed it through fear of injuring the sick woman by an outburst.

At last, after long waiting, Pan Zagloba went out to the officers, his eyes red, and the remnant of the hair on his head standing up; they sprang to him in a crowd, and covered him at once with anxious questions in low tones.

"Is she alive; is she alive?"

"She is alive," said the old man; "but God knows whether she will live an hour."

Here the voice stuck in his throat; his lower lip quivered. Seizing his head with both hands, he dropped heavily on the bench, and suppressed sobbing heaved his breast.

At sight of this, Pan Mushalski caught in his embrace Pan Nyenashinyets, though he cared not much for him ordinarily, and began to moan quietly; Pan Nyenashinyets seconded him at once. Pan Motovidlo stared as if he were trying to swallow something, but could not; Pan Snitko fell to unbuttoning his coat with quivering fingers; Pan Hromyka raised his hands, and walked through the room. The soldiers, seeing through the windows these signs of despair, and judging that the lady had died already, began an outcry and lamentation. Hearing this, Zagloba fell into a sudden fury, and shot out like a stone from a sling to the square.

"Silence, you scoundrels! may the thunderbolts split you!" cried he, in a suppressed voice.

They were silent at once, understanding that the time for lamentation had not come yet; but they did not leave the square. Zagloba returned to the room, quieted somewhat, and sat again on the bench.

At that moment a waiting-woman appeared again at the door of the room.

Zagloba sprang toward her.

"How is it there?"

"She is sleeping."

"Is she sleeping? Praise be to God!"

"Maybe the Lord will grant —"

"What is the Pan Commandant doing?"

"The Pan Commandant is at her bedside."

"That is well. Go now for what you were sent."

Zagloba turned to the officers and said, repeating the words of the woman, —

"May the Most High God have mercy! She is sleeping! Some hope is entering me — Uf!"

And they sighed deeply in like manner. Then they gathered around Zagloba in a close circle and began to inquire, —

"For God's sake, how did it happen? What happened? How did she escape on foot?"

"At first she did not escape on foot," whispered Zagloba, "but with two horses, for she threw that dog from his saddle, — may the plague slay him!"

"I cannot believe my ears!"

"She struck him with the butt of a pistol between the eyes;

and as they were some distance behind no one saw them, and no one pursued. The wolves ate one horse, and the other was drowned under the ice. O Merciful Christ! She went, the poor thing, alone through forests, without eating, without drinking."

Here Pan Zagloba burst out crying again, and stopped his narrative for a time; the officers too sat down on benches, filled with wonder and horror and pity for the woman who was loved by all.

"When she came near Hreptyoff," continued Zagloba, after a while, "she did not know the place, and was preparing to die; just then she heard the squeak of the well-sweeps, knew that she was near us, and dragged herself home with her last breath."

"God guarded her in such straits," said Pan Motovidlo, wiping his moist mustaches. "He will guard her further."

"It will be so! You have touched the point," whispered a number of voices.

With that a louder noise came in from the square; Zagloba sprang up again in a rage, and rushed out through the doorway.

Head was thrust up to head on the square; but at sight of Zagloba and two other officers the soldiers pushed back into a half-circle.

"Be quiet, you dog souls!" began Zagloba, "or I'll command —"

But out of the half-circle stepped Zydor Lusnia, — a sergeant of dragoons, a real Mazovian, and one of Pan Michael's favorite soldiers. This man advanced a couple of steps, straightened himself out like a string, and said with a voice of decision, —

"Your grace, since such a son has injured our lady, as I live, we cannot but move on him and take vengeance; all beg to do this. And if the colonel cannot go, we will go under another command, even to the Crimea itself, to capture that man; and remembering our lady, we will not spare him."

A stubborn, cold, peasant threat sounded in the voice of the sergeant; other dragoons and attendants in the accompanying squadrons began to grit their teeth, shake their sabres, puff, and murmur. This deep grumbling, like the grumbling of a bear in the night, had in it something simply terrible.

The sergeant stood erect waiting for an answer; behind

him whole ranks were waiting, and in them was evident such obstinacy and rage that in presence of it even the ordinary obedience of soldiers disappeared.

Silence continued for a while; all at once some voice in a remoter line called out, —

"The blood of that one is the best medicine for 'the lady.'"

Zagloba's anger fell away, for that attachment of the soldiers to Basia touched him; and at that mention of medicine another plan flashed up in his head, — namely, to bring a doctor to Basia. At the first moment in that wild Hreptyoff no one had thought of a doctor; but nevertheless there were many of them in Kamenyets, — among others a certain Greek, a famous man, wealthy, the owner of a number of stone houses, and so learned that he passed everywhere as almost skilled in the black art. But there was a doubt whether he, being wealthy, would be willing to come at any price to such a desert, — he to whom even magnates spoke with respect.

Zagloba meditated for a short time, and then said, —

"A fitting vengeance will not miss that arch hound, I promise you that; and he would surely prefer to have his grace, the king, swear vengeance against him than to have Zagloba do it. But it is not known whether he is alive yet; for the lady, in tearing herself out of his hands, struck him with the butt of her pistol right in the brain. But this is not the time to think of him, for first we must save the lady."

"We should be glad to do it, even with our own lives," answered Lusnia.

And the crowd muttered again in support of the sergeant.

"Listen to me," said Zagloba. "In Kamenyets lives a doctor named Rodopul. You will go to him; you will tell him that the starosta of Podolia has sprained his leg at this place and is waiting for rescue. And if he is outside the wall, seize him, put him on a horse, or into a bag, and bring him to Hreptyoff without stopping. I will give command to have horses disposed at short distances apart, and you will go at a gallop. Only be careful to bring him alive, for we have no business with dead doctors."

A mutter of satisfaction was heard on every side; Lusnia moved his stern mustaches and said, —

"I will bring him surely, and I will not lose him till we come to Hreptyoff."

" Move on ! "

" I pray your grace — "

" What more ? "

" But if he should die of fright ? "

" He will not.　Take six men and move."

Lusnia shot away.　The others were glad to do something for the lady ; they ran to saddle the horses, and in a few " Our Fathers " six men were racing to Kamenyets.　After them others took additional horses, to be disposed along the road.

Zagloba, satisfied with himself, returned to the house.

After a while Pan Michael came out of the bedroom, changed, half conscious, indifferent to words of sympathy and consolation.　When he had informed Zagloba that Basia was sleeping continually, he dropped on the bench, and gazed with wandering look on the door beyond which she was lying.　It seemed to the officers that he was listening ; therefore all restrained their breathing, and a perfect stillness settled down in the room.

After a certain time Zagloba went on tiptoe to the little knight.

" Michael," said he, " I have sent to Kamenyets for a doctor ; but maybe it is well to send for some one else ? "

Volodyovski was collecting his thoughts, and apparently did not understand.

" For a priest," said Zagloba.　" Father Kaminski might come by morning."

The little knight closed his eyes, turned toward the fire, his face as pale as a kerchief, and said in a hurried voice, —

" Jesus, Jesus, Jesus ! "

Zagloba inquired no further, but went out and made arrangements.　When he returned, Pan Michael was no longer in the room.　The officers told Zagloba that the sick woman had called her husband, it was unknown whether in a fever or in her senses.

The old noble convinced himself soon, by inspection, that it was in a fever.

Basia's cheeks were bright red ; her eyes, though glittering, were dull, as if the pupils had mingled with the white ; her pale hands were searching for something before her, with a monotonous motion, on the coverlet.　Pan Michael was lying half alive at her feet.

From time to time the sick woman muttered something in a low voice, or uttered uncertain phrases more loudly ;

among them "Hreptyoff" was repeated most frequently: evidently it seemed to her at times that she was still on the road. That movement of her hands on the coverlet disturbed Zagloba especially, for in its unconscious monotony he saw signs of coming death. He was a man of experience, and many people had died in his presence; but never had his heart been cut with such sorrow as at sight of that flower withering so early.

Understanding that God alone could save that quenching life, he knelt at the bed and began to pray, and to pray earnestly.

Meanwhile Basia's breath grew heavier, and changed by degrees to a rattling. Volodyovski sprang up from her feet; Zagloba rose from his knees. Neither said a word to the other; they merely looked into each other's eyes, and in that look there was terror. It seemed to them that she was dying, but it seemed so only for some moments; soon her breathing was easier and even slower.

Thenceforth they were between fear and hope. The night dragged on slowly. Neither did the officers go to rest; they sat in the room, now looking at the door of the bedroom, now whispering among themselves, now dozing. At intervals a boy came in to throw wood on the fire; and at each movement of the latch they sprang from the bench, thinking that Volodyovski or Zagloba was coming, and they would hear the terrible words, "She is living no longer!"

At last the cocks crowed, and she was still struggling with the fever. Toward morning a fierce rain-storm burst forth; it roared among the beams, howled on the roof; at times the flames quivered in the chimney, casting into the room puffs of smoke and sparks. About daylight Pan Motovidlo stepped out quietly, for he had to go on a reconnoissance. At last day came pale and cloudy, and. lighted weary faces.

On the square the usual movement began. In the whistling of the storm were heard the tramp of horses on the planking of the stable, the squeak of the well-sweeps, and the voices of soldiers; but soon a bell sounded, — Father Kaminski had come.

When he entered, wearing his white surplice, the officers fell on their knees. It seemed to all that the solemn moment had come, after which death must follow undoubtedly. The sick woman had not regained consciousness; therefore the priest could not hear her confession. He only gave her extreme unction; then he began to console the little knight, and to persuade him to yield to the will of God. But there was no effect in that consolation, for no words could reach his pain.

For a whole day death hovered over Basia. Like a spider, which secreted in some gloomy corner of the ceiling crawls out at times to the light, and lets itself down on an unseen web, death seemed at times to come down right there over Basia's head; and more than once it seemed to those present that his shadow was falling on her forehead, that that bright soul was just opening its wings to fly away out of Hreptyoff, somewhere into endless space, to the other side of life. Then again death, like a spider, hid away under the ceiling, and hope filled their hearts.

But that was merely a partial and temporary hope, for no one dared to think that Basia would survive the attack. Pan Michael himself had no hope of her recovery; and this pain of his became so great that Zagloba, though suffering severely himself, began to be afraid, and to commend him to the care of the officers.

"For God's sake, look after him!" said the old man; "he may plunge a knife into his body."

This did not come, indeed, to Pan Michael's head; but in that rending sorrow and pain he asked himself continually, —

"How am I to stay behind when she goes? How can I let that dearest love go alone? What will she say when she looks around and does not find me near her?"

Thinking thus, he wished with all the powers of his soul to die with her; for as he could not imagine life for himself on earth without her, in like manner he did not understand that she could be happy in that life without him, and not yearn for him. In the afternoon the ill-omened spider hid again in the ceiling. The flush in Basia's cheeks was quenched, and the fever decreased to a degree that some consciousness came back to her.

She lay for a time with closed eyes, then, opening them, looked into the face of the little knight, and asked, —

"Michael, am I in Hreptyoff?"

"Yes, my love," answered Volodyovski, closing his teeth.

"And are you really near me?"

"Yes; how do you feel?"

"Ai, well."

It was clear that she herself was not certain that the

fever had not brought before her eyes deceptive visions; but from that moment she regained consciousness more and more.

In the evening Lusnia and his men came and shook out of a bag before the fort the doctor of Kamenyets, together with his medicines; he was barely alive. But when he learned that he was not in robber hands, as he thought, but was brought in that fashion to a patient, after a passing faintness he went to the rescue at once, especially as Zagloba held before him in one hand a purse filled with coin, in the other a loaded pistol, and said, —

"Here is the fee for life, and there is the fee for death."

That same night, about daybreak, the spider of ill-omen hid away somewhere for good; thereupon the decision of the doctor, "She will be sick a long time, but she will recover," sounded with joyful echo through Hreptyoff. When Pan Michael heard it first, he fell on the floor and broke into such violent sobbing that it seemed as though his bosom would burst. Zagloba grew weak altogether from joy, so that his face was covered with sweat, and he was barely able to exclaim, "A drink!" The officers embraced one another.

On the square the dragoons assembled again, with the escort and the Cossacks of Pan Motovidlo; it was hardly possible to restrain them from shouting. They wanted absolutely to show their delight in some fashion, and they began to beg for a number of robbers imprisoned in the cellars of Hreptyoff, so as to hang them for the benefit of the lady.

But the little knight refused.

CHAPTER XLIII.

BASIA suffered so violently for a week yet, that had it not
been for the assurance of the doctor both Pan Michael and
Zagloba would have admitted that the flame of her life
might expire at any moment. Only at the end of that time
did she become notably better; her consciousness returned
fully, and though the doctor foresaw that she would lie in
bed a month, or a month and a half, still it was certain that
she would return to perfect health, and gain her former
strength.

Pan Michael during her illness went hardly one step from
her pillow; he loved her after these perils still more, if
possible, and did not see the world beyond her. At times
when he sat near her, when he looked on that face, still thin
and emaciated but joyous, and those eyes, into which the
old fire was returning each day, he was beset by the wish
to laugh, to cry, and to shout from delight: —

"My only Basia is recovering; she is recovering!"

And he rushed at her hands, and sometimes he kissed
those poor little feet which had waded so valiantly through
the deep snows to Hreptyoff; in a word, he loved her
and honored her beyond estimation. He felt wonderfully
indebted to Providence, and on a certain time he said in
presence of Zagloba and the officers: —

"I am a poor man, but even were I to work off my arms
to the elbows, I will find money for a little church, even a
wooden one. And as often as they ring the bells in it, I will
remember the mercy of God, and the soul will be melting
within me from gratitude."

"God grant us first to pass through this Turkish war
with success," said Zagloba.

"The Lord knows best what pleases Him most," replied
the little knight: "if He wishes for a church He will preserve me; and if He prefers my blood, I shall not spare it,
as God is dear to me."

Basia with health regained her humor. Two weeks later
she gave command to open the door of her chamber a little
one evening; and when the officers had assembled in the
room, she called out with her silvery voice: —

"Good-evening, gentlemen! I shall not die this time, aha!"

"Thanks to the Most High God!" answered the officers, in chorus.

"Glory be to God, dear child!" exclaimed Pan Motovidlo, who loved Basia particularly with a fatherly affection, and who in moments of great emotion spoke always in Russian.[1]

"See, gentlemen," continued Basia, "what has happened! Who could have hoped for this? Lucky that it ended so."

"God watched over innocence," called the chorus again through the door.

"But Pan Zagloba laughed at me more than once, because I have more love for the sabre than the distaff. Well, a distaff or a needle would have helped me greatly! But did n't I act like a cavalier, did n't I?"

"An angel could not have done better!"

Zagloba interrupted the conversation by closing the door of the chamber, for he feared too much excitement for Basia. But she was angry as a cat at the old man, for she had a wish for further conversation, and especially to hear more praises of her bravery and valor. When danger had passed, and was merely a reminiscence, she was very proud of her action against Azya, and demanded praise absolutely. More than once she turned to the little knight, and pushing his breast with her finger said, with the mien of a spoiled child, —

"Praise for the bravery!"

And he, the obedient, praised her and fondled her, and kissed her on the eyes and on the hands, till Zagloba, though he was greatly affected himself in reality, pretended to be scandalized, and muttered, —

"Ah, everything will be as lax as grandfather's whip."

The general rejoicing in Hreptyoff over Basia's recovery was troubled only by the remembrance of the injury which Azya's treason had wrought in the Commonwealth, and the terrible fate of old Pan Novoveski, of Pani and Panna Boski, and of Eva. Basia was troubled no little by this, and with her every one; for the events at Rashkoff were known in detail, not only in Hreptyoff, but in Kamenyets and farther on. A few days before, Pan Myslishevski had

---

[1] Motovidlo's words are Russian in the original.

stopped in Hreptyoff; notwithstanding the treason of Azya,
Krychinski, and Adurovich, he did not lose hope of attracting to the Polish side the other captains. After Pan
Myslishevski came Pan Bogush, and later, news directly
from Mohiloff, Yampol, and Rashkoff itself.

In Mohiloff, Pan Gorzenski, evidently a better soldier than
orator, did not let himself be deceived. Intercepting Azya's
orders to the Tartars whom he left behind, Pan Gorzenski
fell upon them, with a handful of Mazovian infantry, and
cut them down or took them prisoners; besides, he sent a
warning to Yampol, through which that place was saved.
The troops returned soon after. So Rashkoff was the only
victim. Pan Michael received a letter from Pan Byaloglovski himself, giving a report of events there and other
affairs relating to the whole Commonwealth.

"It is well that I returned," wrote Pan Byaloglovski, among other
things, "for Novoveski, my second, is not in a state now to do duty.
He is more like a skeleton than a man, and we shall be sure to lose a
great cavalier, for suffering has crushed him beyond the measure of
his strength. His father is slain; his sister, in the last degree of
shame, given to Adurovich by Azya, who took Panna Boski for himself. Nothing can be done for them, even should there be success in
rescuing them from captivity. We know this from a Tartar who
sprained his shoulder in crossing the river; taken prisoner by our
men, he was put on the fire, and divulged everything. Azya, Krychinski, and Adurovich have gone to Adrianople. Novoveski is
struggling to follow without fail, saying that he must take Azya,
even from the centre of the Sultan's camp, and have vengeance. He
was always obstinate and daring, and there is no reason now to
wonder at him, since it is a question of Panna Boski, whose evil fate
we all bewail with tears, for she was a sweet maiden, and I do not
know the man whose heart she did not win. But I restrain Novoveski, and tell him that Azya himself will come to him; for war is
certain, and this also, that the hordes will move in the vanguard.
We have news from Moldavia from the perkulabs, and from Turkish
merchants as well, that troops are assembling already near Adrianople, — a great many of the horde. The Turkish cavalry, which
they call 'spahis,' are mustering too; and the Sultan himself is to
come with the janissaries. My benefactor, there will be untold
myriads of them; for the whole Orient is in movement, and we have
only a handful of troops. Our whole hope is in the rock of Kamenyets, which, God grant, is provisioned properly. In Adrianople
it is spring; and with us almost spring, for tremendous rains are
falling and grass is appearing. I am going to Yampol; for Rashkoff
is only a heap of ashes, and there is no place to incline one's head, or
anything to put into the mouth. Besides, I think that we shall be
withdrawn from all the forts."

The little knight had information of equal and even greater certainty, since it came from Hotin. He had sent it too a short time before to the hetman. Still, Byaloglovski's letter, coming from the remotest boundary, made a powerful impression on him, precisely because it confirmed that intelligence. But the little knight had no fears touching war, his fears were for Basia.

"The order of the hetman to withdraw the garrisons may come any day," said he to Zagloba; "and service is service. It will be necessary to move without delay; but Basia is in bed yet, and the weather is bad."

"If ten orders were to come," said Zagloba, "Basia is the main question; we will stay here until she recovers completely. Besides, the war will not begin before the end of the thaws, much less before the end of winter, especially as they will bring heavy artillery against Kamenyets."

"That old volunteer is always sitting within you," replied the little knight, with impatience; "you think an order may be delayed for private matters."

"Well, if an order is dearer to you than Basia, pack her into a wagon and march. I know, I know, you are ready at command to put her in with forks, if it appears that she is unable to sit in the wagon with her own strength. May the hangman take you with such discipline! In old times a man did what he could, and what he could n't he did n't do. You have kindness on your lips, but just let them cry, 'Haida on the Turk!' then you 'll spit out your kindness as you would a peachstone, and you will take that unfortunate woman on horseback with a lariat."

"I without pity for Basia! Fear the wounds of the Crucified!" cried the little knight.

Zagloba puffed angrily for a time, then looking at the suffering face of Pan Michael, he said, —

"Michael, you know that I say what I say out of love really parental for Basia. Otherwise would I be sitting here under the Turkish axe, instead of enjoying leisure in a safe place, which at my years no man could take ill of me? But who got Basia for you? If it shall be seen that it was not I, then command me to drink a vat of water without a thing to give taste to it."

"I could not repay you in a lifetime for Basia!" cried the little knight.

Then they took each other by the shoulders, and the best harmony began between them.

"I have planned," said the little knight, "that when war comes, you will take Basia to Pan Yan's place. Chambuls do not go that far."

"I will do so for you, though it would delight me to go against the Turk; for nothing disgusts me like that swinish nation which does not drink wine."

"I fear only one thing: Basia will try to be at Kamenyets, so as to be near me. My skin creeps at thought of this; but as God is God she will try."

"Do not let her try. Has little evil come already, because you indulge her in everything, and let her go on that expedition to Rashkoff, though I cried out against it immediately?"

"But that is not true! You said that you would not advise."

"When I say that I will not advise a thing, that is worse than if I had spoken against it."

"Basia ought to be wise now, but she will not. When she sees the sword over my head she will resist."

"Do not let her resist, I repeat. For God's sake, what sort of a straw husband are you?"

"I confess that when she puts her fists in her eyes and begins to cry, or just let her pretend to cry, the heart in me is like butter on a frying-pan. It must be that she has given me some herb. As to sending her, I will send her, for her safety is dearer to me than my own life; but when I think that I must torture her so the breath stops in me from pity."

"Michael, have God in your heart! Don't be led by the nose!"

"Bah! don't be led yourself. Who, if not you, said that I have no pity for her?"

"What's that?" asked Zagloba.

"You do not lack ingenuity, but now you are scratching behind your ear yourself."

"Because I'm thinking what better argument to use."

"But if she puts her fists in her eyes at once?"

"She will, as God is dear to me!" said Zagloba, with evident alarm.

And they were perplexed, for, to tell the truth, Basia had measured both perfectly. They had petted her to the last degree in her sickness, and loved her so much that the necessity of opposing her wish and desire filled them with fear. That Basia would not resist, and would yield with submission to the decree, both knew well; but not to mention Pan Michael, it would have been pleasanter for Zagloba to rush himself the third man on a whole regiment of janissaries, than to see her putting her little fists into her eyes.

CHAPTER XLIV.

On that same day there came to them aid infallible, as they thought, in the persons of guests unexpected and dear above all. The Ketlings came toward evening, without any previous intimation. The delight and astonishment at seeing them in Hreptyoff was indescribable; and they, learning on the first inquiry that Basia was returning to health, were comforted in an equal degree. Krysia rushed at once to the bedroom, and at the same moment exclamations and cries from there announced Basia's happiness to the little knight.

Ketling and Pan Michael embraced each other a long time; now they put each other out at arm's length, now they embraced again.

"For God's sake!" said the little knight. "I should be less pleased to receive the baton than to see you; but what are you doing in these parts?"

"The hetman has made me commander of the artillery at Kamenyets," said Ketling; "therefore I went with my wife to that place. Hearing there of the trials that had met you, I set out without delay for Hreptyoff. Praise be to God, Michael, that all has ended well! We travelled in great suffering and uncertainty, for we knew not whether we were coming here to rejoice or to mourn."

"To rejoice, to rejoice!" broke in Zagloba.

"How did it happen?" asked Ketling.

The little knight and Zagloba vied with each other in narrating; and Ketling listened, raising his eyes and his hands to heaven in wonderment at Basia's bravery.

When they had talked all they wished, the little knight fell to inquiring of Ketling what had happened to him, and he made a report in detail. After their marriage they had lived on the boundary of Courland; they were so happy with each other that it could not be better in heaven. Ketling in taking Krysia knew perfectly that he was taking "a being above earth," and he had not changed his opinion so far.

Zagloba and Pan Michael, remembering by this expression the former Ketling who expressed himself always in a courtly and elevated style, began to embrace him again; and when all three had satisfied their friendship, the old noble asked, —

"Has there come to that being above earth any earthly case which kicks with its feet and looks for teeth in its mouth with its finger?"

"God gave us a son," said Ketling; "and now again —"

"I have noticed," interrupted Zagloba. "But here everything is on the old footing."

Then he fixed his seeing eye on the little knight, whose mustaches quivered repeatedly.

Further conversation was interrupted by the coming of Krysia, who pointed to the door and said, —

"Basia invites you."

All went to the chamber together, and there new greetings began. Ketling kissed Basia's hand, and Pan Michael kissed Krysia's again; then all looked at one another with curiosity, as people do who have not met for a long time.

Ketling had changed in almost nothing, except that he had his hair cut closely, and that made him seem younger; but Krysia had changed greatly, at least considering the time. She was not so slender and willowy as before, and her face was paler, for which reason the down on her lip seemed darker; but she had the former beautiful eyes with unusually long lashes, and the former calmness of countenance. Her features, once so wonderful, had lost, however, their previous delicacy. The loss might be, it is true, only temporary; still, Pan Michael, looking at her and comparing her with his Basia, could not but think, —

"For God's sake, how could I fall in love with her when both were together? Where were my eyes?"

On the other hand, Basia seemed beautiful to Ketling; for she was really beautiful, with her golden, wayward forelock dropping toward her brows, with her complexion which, losing some of its ruddiness, had become after her illness like the leaf of a white rose. But now her face was enlivened somewhat by delight, and her delicate nostrils moved quickly. She seemed as youthful as if she had not yet reached maturity; and at the first glance it might be thought that she was some ten years younger than Ketling's wife. But her beauty acted on the sensitive Ketling only in this way, that he began to think with more tenderness of his wife, for he felt guilty with regard to her.

Both women related to each other all that could be told

in a short space of time; and the whole company, sitting
around Basia's bed, began to recall former days.   But that
conversation did not move somehow, for there were in those
former days delicate subjects, — the confidences of Pan
Michael with Krysia; and the indifference of the little
knight for Basia, loved later, and various promises and
various despairs.   Life in Ketling's house had a charm for
all, and left an agreeable memory behind; but to speak of it
was awkward.

Ketling changed the subject soon after: —

"I have not told you yet that on the road we stopped
with Pan Yan, who would not let us go for two weeks, and
entertained us so that in heaven it could not be better."

"By the dear God, how are they?" cried Zagloba.
"Then you found them at home?"

"We did; for Pan Yan had returned for a time from
the hetman's with his three elder sons, who serve in the
cavalry."

"I have not seen Pan Yan nor his family since the time
of your wedding," said the little knight.   "He was here in
the Wilderness, and his sons were with him; but I did not
happen to meet them."

"They are all very anxious to see you," said Ketling,
turning to Zagloba.

"And I to see them," replied the old man.   "But this is
how it is: if I am here, I am sad without them; if I go there,
I shall be sad without this weasel.   Such is human life; if
the wind does n't blow into one ear it will into the other.
But it is worse for the lone man, for if I had children I
should not be loving a stranger."

"You would not love your own children more than us,"
said Basia.

When he heard this Zagloba was greatly delighted, and
casting off sad thoughts, he fell at once into jovial humor;
when he had puffed somewhat he said, —

"Ha, I was a fool there at Ketling's; I got Krysia and
Basia for you two, and I did not think of myself.   There
was still time then."

Here he turned to the women, —

"Confess that you would have fallen in love with me,
both of you, and either one would have preferred me to
Michael or Ketling."

"Of course we should!" exclaimed Basia.

"Helena, Pan Yan's wife, too in her day would have

preferred me. Ha! it might have been. I should then have a sedate woman, none of your tramps, knocking teeth out of Tartars. But is she well ? "

"She is well, but a little anxious, for their two middle boys ran away to the army from school at Lukoff," said Ketling. "Pan Yan himself is glad that there is such mettle in the boys; but a mother is a mother almost always."

"Have they many children ? " inquired Basia, with a sigh.

"Twelve boys, and now the fair sex has begun," answered Ketling.

"Ha!" cried Zagloba, "the special blessing of God is on that house. I have reared them all at my own breast, like a pelican. I must pull the ears of those middle boys, for if they had to run away why did n't they come here to Michael? But wait, it must be Michael and Yasek who ran away. There was such a flock of them that their own father confounded their names; and you could n't see a crow for three miles around, for the rogues had killed every crow with their muskets. Bah, bah! you would have to look through the world for another such woman. 'Halska,' I used to say to her, 'the boys are getting too big for me, I must have new sport.' Then she would, as it were, frown at me; but the time came as if written down. Imagine to yourself, it went so far that if any woman in the country about could not get consolation, she borrowed a dress from Halska; and it helped her, as God is dear to me, it did."

All wondered greatly, and a moment of silence followed; then the voice of the little knight was heard on a sudden, —

"Basia, do you hear ? "

"Michael, will you be quiet ? " answered Basia.

But Michael would not be quiet, for various cunning thoughts were coming to his head. It seemed to him above all that with that affair another equally important might be accomplished; hence he began to talk, as it were to himself, carelessly, as about the commonest thing in the world, —

"As God lives, it would be well to visit Pan Yan and his wife; but he will not be at home now, for he is going to the hetman; but she has sense, and is not accustomed to tempt the Lord God, therefore she will stay at home."

Here he turned to Krysia. "The spring is coming, and the weather will be fine. Now it is too early for Basia, but a little later I might not be opposed, for it is a friendly obligation. Pan Zagloba would take you both there; in the fall, when all would be quiet, I would go after you."

"That is a splendid idea," exclaimed Zagloba; "I must go anyhow, for I have fed them with ingratitude. Indeed, I have forgotten that they are in the world, until I am ashamed."

"What do you say to this?" inquired Pan Michael, looking carefully into Krysia's eyes.

But she answered most unexpectedly, with her usual calmness, —

"I should be glad, but I cannot; for I will remain with my husband in Kamenyets, and will not leave him for any cause."

"In God's name, what do I hear?" cried Pan Michael. "You will remain in the fortress, which will be invested surely, and that by an enemy knowing no· moderation? I should not talk if the war were with some civilized enemy, but this is an affair with barbarians. But do you know what a captured city means, — what Turkish or Tartar captivity is? I do not believe my ears!"

"Still, it cannot be otherwise," replied Krysia.

"Ketling," cried the little knight, in despair, "is this the way you let yourself be mastered? O man, have God in your heart!"

"We deliberated long," answered Ketling, "and this was the end of it."

"And our son is in Kamenyets, under the care of a lady, a relative of mine. Is it certain that Kamenyets must be captured?" Here Krysia raised her calm eyes: "God is mightier than the Turk, — He will not betray our confidence; and because I have sworn to my husband not to leave him till death, my place is with him."

The little knight was terribly confused, for from Krysia he had expected something different altogether.

Basia, who from the very beginning of the conversation saw whither Michael was tending, laughed cunningly. She fixed her quick eyes on him, and said, —

"Michael, do you hear?"

"Basia, be quiet!" exclaimed the little knight, in the greatest embarrassment. Then he began to cast despairing glances at Zagloba, as if expecting salvation from him; but that traitor rose suddenly, and said, —

"We must think of refreshment, for it is not by word alone that man liveth." And he went out of the chamber.

Pan Michael followed quickly, and stopped him.

"Well, and what now?" asked Zagloba.

"Well, and what?"

"But may the bullets strike that Ketling woman! For God's sake, how is this Commonwealth not to perish when women are managing it?"

"Cannot you think out something?"

"Since you fear your wife, what can I think out for you? Get the blacksmith to shoe you, — that's what!"

CHAPTER XLV.

THE Ketlings stayed about three weeks.   At the expiration of that time Basia tried to leave her bed; but it appeared
that she could not stand on her feet yet. Health had returned
to her sooner than strength; and the doctor commanded her
to lie till all her vigor came back to her.   Meanwhile spring
came.   First a strong and warm wind, rising from the side of
the Wilderness and the Black Sea, rent and swept away that
veil of clouds as if it were a robe which had rotted from age,
and then began to gather and scatter those clouds through
the sky, as a shepherd dog gathers and scatters flocks of
sheep.   The clouds, fleeing before it, covered the earth frequently with abundant rain, which fell in drops as large as
berries.   The melting remnant of snow and ice formed
lakes on the flat steppe; from the cliffs ribbons of water
were falling; along the beds of ravines streams rose, —
and all those waters were flying with a noise and an outbreak and uproar to the Dniester, just as children fly with
delight to their mother.

Through the rifts between the clouds the sun shone every
few moments, — bright, refreshed, and as it were wet from
bathing in that endless abyss.

Then bright-green blades of grass began to rise through
the softened ground; the slender twigs of trees put forth
buds abundantly, and the sun gave heat with growing
power.   In the sky flocks of birds appeared, hence rows of
cranes, wild geese, and storks; then the wind began to bring
crowds of swallows; the frogs croaked in a great chorus in
the warmed water; the small birds were singing madly;
and through pine-woods and forests and steppes and ravines
went one great outcry, as if all Nature were shouting with
delight and enthusiasm, —

"Spring! U-há! Spring!"

But for those hapless regions spring brought mourning,
not rejoicing; death, not life. In a few days after the
departure of the Ketlings the little knight received the
following intelligence from Pan Myslishevski, —

"On the plain of Kuchunkaury the conflux of troops increases
daily. The Sultan has sent considerable sums to the Crimea. The

Khan is going with fifty thousand of the horde to assist Doroshenko. As soon as the floods dry, the multitude will advance by the Black Trail and the trail of Kuchman. God pity the Commonwealth!"

Volodyovski sent Pyentka, his attendant, to the hetman at once with these tidings. But he himself did not hasten from Hreptyoff. First, as a soldier, he could not leave that stanitsa without command of the hetman; second, he had spent too many years at "tricks" with the Tartars not to know that chambuls would not move so early. The waters had not fallen yet; grass had not grown sufficiently; and the Cossacks were still in winter quarters. The little knight expected the Turks in summer at the earliest; for though they were assembling already at Adrianople, such a gigantic tabor, such throngs of troops, of camp servants, such burdens, so many horses, camels, and buffaloes, advanced very slowly. The Tartar cavalry might be looked for earlier, — at the end of April or the beginning of May. It is true that before the main body, which counted tens of thousands of warriors, there fell always on the country detached chambuls and more or less numerous bands, as single drops of rain come before the great downpour; but the little knight did not fear these. Even picked Tartar horsemen could not withstand the cavalry of the Commonwealth in the open field; and what could bands do which at the mere report that troops were coming scattered like dust before a whirlwind?

In every event there was time enough; and even if there were not, Pan Michael would not have been greatly averse to rubbing against some chambuls in a way which for them would be equally painful and memorable.

He was a soldier, blood and bone, — a soldier by profession; hence the approach of a war roused in him thirst for the blood of his enemy, and brought to him calmness as well. Pan Zagloba was less calm, though inured beyond most men to great dangers in the course of his long life. In sudden emergencies he found courage; he had developed it besides by long though often involuntary practice, and had gained in his time famous victories; still, the first news of coming war always affected him deeply. But now when the little knight explained his own view, Zagloba gained more consolation, and even began to challenge the whole Orient, and to threaten it.

"When Christian nations war with one another," said he,

"the Lord Jesus Himself is sad, and all the saints scratch their heads, for when the Master is anxious the household is anxious; but whoso beats the Turk gives Heaven the greatest delight. I have it from a certain spiritual personage that the saints simply grow sick at sight of those dog brothers; and thus heavenly food and drink does not go to their profit, and even their eternal happiness is marred."

"That must be really so," answered the little knight. "But the Turkish power is immense, and our troops might be put on the palm of your hand."

"Still, they will not conquer the whole Commonwealth. Had Carolus Gustavus little power? In those times there were wars with the Northerners and the Cossacks and Rakotsi and the Elector; but where are they to-day? Besides, we took fire and sword to their hearths."

"That is true. Personally I should not fear this war, because, as I said, I must do something notable to pay the Lord Jesus and the Most Holy Lady for their mercy to Basia; only God grant me opportunity! But the question for me is this country, which with Kamenyets may fall into Pagan hands easily, even for a time. Imagine what a desecration of God's churches there would be, and what oppression of Christian people!"

"But don't talk to me of the Cossacks! The ruffians! They raised their hands against the mother; let that meet them which they wished for. The most important thing is that Kamenyets should hold out. What do you think, Michael, will it hold out?"

"I think that the starosta of Podolia has not supplied it sufficiently, and also that the inhabitants, secure in their position, have not done what behooved them. Ketling said that the regiments of Bishop Trebitski came in very scant numbers. But as God lives, we held out at Zbaraj behind a mere wretched trench, against great power; we ought to hold out this time as well, for that Kamenyets is an eagle's nest."

"An eagle's nest truly; but it is unknown if an eagle is in it, such as was Prince Yeremi, or merely a crow. Do you know the starosta of Podolia?"

"He is a rich man and a good soldier, but rather careless."

"I know him; I know him! More than once have I reproached him with that; the Pototskis wished at one time that I should go abroad with him for his education, so that he might learn fine manners from me. But I said : ' I will not go because of his carelessness, for never has he two straps to his boot; he was presented at court in my boots, and morocco is dear.' Later, in the time of Marya Ludovika, he wore the French costume; but his stockings were always down, and he showed his bare calves. He will never reach as high as Prince Yeremi's girdle."

"Another thing, the shopkeepers of Kamenyets fear a siege greatly; for trade is stopped in time of it. They would rather belong even to the Turks, if they could only keep their shops open."

"The scoundrels ! " said Zagloba.

And he and the little knight were sorely concerned over the coming fate of Kamenyets; it was a personal question concerning Basia, who in case of surrender would have to share the fate of all the inhabitants.

After a while Zagloba struck his forehead : " For God's sake ! " cried he, " why are we disturbed ? Why should we go to that mangy Kamenyets, and shut ourselves up there ? Is n't it better for you to stay with the hetman, and act in the field against the enemy ? And in such an event Basia would not go with you to the squadron, and would have to go somewhere besides Kamenyets, — somewhere far off, even to Pan Yan's house. Michael, God looks into my heart and sees what a desire I have to go against the Pagans; but I will do this for you and Basia, — I will take her away."

" I thank you," said the little knight. "The whole case is this : if I had not to be in Kamenyets, Basia would not insist; but what 's to be done when the hetman's command comes ? "

" What 's to be done when the command comes ? May the hangman tear all the commands ! What 's to be done ? Wait ! I am beginning to think quickly. Here it is : we must anticipate the command."

" How is that ? "

" Write on the spot to Pan Sobieski, as if reporting news to him, and at the end say that in the face of the coming war you wish, because of the love which you bear him, to be near his person and act in the field. By God's wounds, this is a splendid thought ! For, first of all, it is impossible that they will shut up such a partisan as you behind a wall, instead of using him in the field; and secondly, for such a letter the hetman will love you still more, and will wish to

have you near him. He too will need trusty soldiers.
Only listen: if Kamenyets holds out, the glory will fall to
the starosta of Podolia; but what you accomplish in the
field will go to the praise of the hetman. Never fear! the
hetman will not yield you to the starosta. He would rather
give some one else; but he will not give either you or me.
Write the letter; remind him of yourself. Ha! my wit is
still worth something, too good to let hens pick it up on
the dust-heap! Michael, let us drink something on the
occasion — or what! write the letter first."

Volodyovski rejoiced greatly indeed; he embraced Zagloba,
and thinking a while said, —

"And I shall not tempt hereby the Lord God, nor the
country, nor the hetman; for surely I shall accomplish much
in the field. I thank you from my heart! I think too that
the hetman will wish to have me at hand, especially after
the letter. But not to abandon Kamenyets, do you know
what I'll do? I'll fit up a handful of soldiers at my own
cost, and send them to Kamenyets. I'll write at once to
the hetman of this."

"Still better! But, Michael, where will you find the
men?"

"I have about forty robbers in the cellars, and I'll take
those. As often as I gave command to hang some one,
Basia tormented me to spare his life; more than once she
advised me to make soldiers of those robbers. I was
unwilling, for an example was needed; but now war is
on our shoulders, and everything is possible. Those are
terrible fellows, who have smelt powder. I will proclaim, too, that whoso from the ravines or the thickets
elects to join the regiment, will receive forgiveness for
past robberies. There will be about a hundred men; Basia
too will be glad. You have taken a great weight from
my heart."

That same day the little knight despatched a new messenger to the hetman, and proclaimed life and pardon to
the robbers if they would join the infantry. They joined
gladly, and promised to bring in others. Basia's delight
was unbounded. Tailors were brought from Ushytsa, from
Kamenyets, and from whence ever possible, to make uni-
forms. The former robbers were mustered on the square
of Hreptyoff. Pan Michael was rejoiced in heart at the
thought that he would act himself in the field against the
enemy, would not expose his wife to the danger of a siege,

and besides would render Kamenyets and the country noteworthy service.

This work had been going on a number of weeks when
one evening the messenger returned with a letter from Pan
Sobieski.

The hetman wrote as follows : —

BELOVED AND VERY DEAR VOLODYOVSKI, — Because you send
all news so diligently I cherish gratitude to you, and the country
owes you thanks. War is certain. I have news also from elsewhere
that there is a tremendous force in Kuchunkaury; counting the
horde, there will be three hundred thousand. The horde may march
any moment. The Sultan values nothing so much as Kamenyets.
The Tartar traitors will show the Turks every road, and inform
them about Kamenyets. I hope that God will give that serpent,
Tugai Bey's son, into your hands, or into Novoveski's, over whose
wrong I grieve sincerely. As to this, that you be near me, God
knows how glad I should be, but it is impossible. The starosta
of Podolia has shown me, it is true, various kindnesses since the election ; I wish, therefore, to send him the best soldiers, for the rock of
Kamenyets is to me as my own eyesight. There will be many there
who have seen war once or twice in their lives, and are like a man
who on a time has eaten some peculiar food which he remembers all
his life afterward ; a man, however, who has used it as his daily bread,
and might serve with experienced counsel, will be lacking, or if there
shall be such he will be without sufficient weight. Therefore I will
send you. Ketling, though a good soldier, is less known ; the inhabitants will have their eyes turned to you, and though the command
will remain with another, I think that men will obey you with readiness. That service in Kamenyets may be dangerous, but with us it
is a habit to be drenched in that rain from which others hide. There
is reward enough for us in glory, and a grateful remembrance ; but
the main thing is the country, to the salvation of which I need not
excite you.

This letter, read in the assembly of officers, made a great
impression ; for all wished to serve in the field rather than
in a fortress. Volodyovski bent his head.

"What do you think now, Michael?" asked Zagloba.

He raised his face, already collected, and answered with
a voice as calm as if he had met no disappointment in his
hopes, —

"I will go to Kamenyets. What have I to think?"

And it might have seemed that nothing else had ever been
in his head.

After a while his mustaches quivered, and he said, —

"Hei! dear comrades, we will go to Kamenyets, but we
will not yield it."

25

"Unless we fall there," said the officers. "One death to a man."

Zagloba was silent for some time; casting his eyes on those present, and seeing that all were waiting for what he would say, he puffed all at once, and said, —

"I will go with you. Devil take it!"

CHAPTER XLVI.

WHEN the earth had grown dry, and grass was flourishing, the Khan moved in person, with fifty thousand of the Crimean and Astrachan hordes, to help Doroshenko and the insurgents. The Khan himself, and his relatives, the petty sultans, and all the more important murzas and beys, wore kaftans as gifts from the Padishah, and went against the Commonwealth, not as they went usually, for booty and captives, but for a holy war with "fate," and the "destruction" of Lehistan (Poland) and Christianity.

Another and still greater storm was gathering at Adrianople, and against this deluge only the rock of Kamenyets was standing erect; for the rest of the Commonwealth lay like an open steppe, or like a sick man, powerless not only to defend himself, but even to rise to his feet. The previous Swedish, Prussian, Moscow, Cossack, and Hungarian wars, though victorious finally, had exhausted the Commonwealth. The army confederations and the insurrections of Lyubomirski of infamous memory had exhausted it, and now it was weakened to the last degree by court quarrels, the incapacity of the king, the feuds of magistrates, the blindness of a frivolous nobility, and the danger of civil war. In vain did the great Sobieski forewarn them of ruin, — no one would believe in war. They neglected means of defence; the treasury had no money, the hetman no troops. To a power against which alliances of all the Christian nations were hardly able to stand, the hetman could oppose barely a few thousand men.

Meanwhile in the Orient, where everything was done at the will of the Padishah, and nations were as a sword in the hand of one man, it was different altogether. From the moment that the great standard of the Prophet was unfurled, and the horse-tail standard planted on the gate of the seraglio and the tower of the seraskierat, and the ulema began to proclaim a holy war, half Asia and all Northern Africa had moved. The Padishah himself had taken his place in spring on the plain of Kuchunkaury, and was assembling forces greater than any seen for a long time on earth. A hundred thousand spahis and janissaries, the pick of the Turkish army, were stationed near his sacred person; and then troops began to gather from all the remotest countries and possessions. Those who inhabited Europe came earliest. The legions of the mounted beys of Bosnia came with colors like the dawn, and fury like lightning; the wild warriors of Albania came, fighting on foot with daggers; bands of Mohammedanized Serbs came; people came who lived on the banks of the Danube, and farther to the south beyond the Balkans, as far as the mountains of Greece. Each pasha led a whole army, which alone would have sufficed to overrun the defenceless Commonwealth. Moldavians and Wallachians came; the Dobrudja and Belgrod Tartars came in force; some thousands of Lithuanian Tartars and Cheremis came, led by the terrible Azya, son of Tugai Bey, and these last were to be guides through the unfortunate country, which was well known to them.

After these the general militia from Asia began to flow in. The pashas of Sivas, Brussa, Aleppo, Damascus, and Bagdad, besides regular troops, led armed throngs, beginning with men from the cedar-covered mountains of Asia Minor, and ending with the swarthy dwellers on the Euphrates and the Tigris. Arabians too rose at the summons of the Caliph; their burnooses covered as with snow the plains of Kuchunkaury; among them were also nomads from the sandy deserts, and inhabitants of cities from Medina to Mecca. The tributary power of Egypt did not remain at its domestic hearths. Those who dwelt in populous Cairo, those who in the evening gazed on the flaming twilight of the pyramids, who wandered through Theban ruins, who dwelt in those murky regions whence the sacred Nile issues forth, men whom the sun had burned to the color of soot, — all these planted their arms on the field of Adrianople, praying now to give victory to Islam, and destruction to that land which alone had shielded for ages the rest of the world against the adherents of the Prophet.

There were legions of armed men; hundreds of thousands of horses were neighing on the field; hundreds of thousands of buffaloes, of sheep and of camels, fed near the herds of horses. It might be thought that at God's command an angel had turned people out of Asia, as once he had turned Adam out of paradise, and commanded them to go to countries in which the sun was paler and the plains were covered in winter with snow. They went then with their herds, an innumerable swarm of white, dark, and black warriors. How many languages were heard there, how many different costumes glittered in the sun of spring! Nations wondered at nations; the customs of some were foreign to others, their arms unknown, their methods of warfare different, and faith alone joined those travelling generations; only when the muezzins called to prayer did those many-tongued hosts turn their faces to the East, calling on Allah with one voice.

There were more servants at the court of the Sultan than troops in the Commonwealth. After the army and the armed bands of volunteers marched throngs of shop-keepers, selling goods of all kinds; their wagons, together with those of the troops, flowed on like a river.

Two pashas of three tails, at the head of two armies, had no other work but to furnish food for those myriads; and there was abundance of everything. The sandjak of San-grytan watched over the whole supply of powder. With the army went two hundred cannon, and of these ten were "stormers," so large that no Christian king had the like. The Beglerbeys of Asia were on the right wing, the Euro-peans on the left. The tents occupied so wide an expanse that in presence of them Adrianople seemed no very great city. The Sultan's tents, gleaming in purple silk, satin, and gold embroidery, formed, as it were, a city apart. Around them swarmed armed guards, black eunuchs from Abyssinia, in yellow and blue kaftans; gigantic porters from the tribes of Kurdistan, intended for bearing bur-dens; young boys of the Uzbeks, with faces of uncommon beauty, shaded by silk fringes; and many other servants, varied in color as flowers of the steppe. Some of these were equerries, some served at the tables, some bore lamps, and some served the most important officials.

On the broad square around the Sultan's court, which in luxury and wealth reminded the faithful of paradise, stood courts less splendid, but equal to those of kings, — those of the vizir, the ulema, the pasha of Anatolia, and of Kara Mustafa, the young kaimakan, on whom the eyes of the Sultan and all were turned as upon the coming "sun of war."

Before the tents of the Padishah were to be seen the sacred guard of infantry, with turbans so lofty that the men wearing them seemed giants. They were armed with javelins fixed on long staffs, and short crooked swords. Their linen dwellings touched the dwellings of the Sultan.

Farther on were the camps of the formidable janissaries armed with muskets and lances, forming the kernel of the Turkish power. Neither the German emperor nor the French king could boast of infantry equal in number and military accuracy. In wars with the Commonwealth the nations of the Sultan, more enervated in general, could not measure strength with cavalry in equal numbers, and only through an immense numerical preponderance did they crush and conquer. But the janissaries dared to meet even regular squadrons of cavalry. They roused terror in the whole Christian world, and even in Tsargrad itself. Frequently the Sultan trembled before such pretorians, and the chief aga of those "lambs" was one of the most important dignitaries in the Divan.

After the janissaries came the spahis; after them the regular troops of the pashas, and farther on the common throng. All this camp had been for a number of months near Constantinople, waiting till its power should be completed by legions coming from the remotest parts of the Turkish dominions until the sun of spring should lighten the march to Lehistan by sucking out dampness from the earth.

The sun, as if subject to the will of the Sultan, had shone brightly. From the beginning of April until May barely a few warm rains had moistened the meadows of Kuchunkaury; for the rest, the blue tent of God hung without a cloud over the tent of the Sultan. The gleams of day played on the white linen, on the turbans, on the many-colored caps, on the points of the helmets and banners and javelins, on the camp and the tents and the people and the herds, drowning all in a sea of bright light. In the evening on a clear sky shone the moon, unhidden by fog, and guarded quietly those thousands who under its emblem were marching to win more and more new lands; then it rose higher in the heaven, and grew pale before the light of the fires. But when the fires were gleaming in the whole immeasurable expanse, when the Arab infantry from Damascus and Aleppo, called "massala djilari," lighted green, red, yellow, and blue lamps at the tents of the Sultan and the vizir, it might seem that a tract of heaven had fallen to the earth, and that those were stars glittering and twinkling on the plain.

Exemplary order and discipline reigned among those legions. The pashas bent to the will of the Sultan, like a reed in a storm; the army bent before them. Food was not wanting for men and herds. Everything was furnished in superabundance, everything in season. In exemplary order also were passed the hours of military exercise, of refreshment, of devotion. When the muezzins called to prayer from wooden towers, built in haste, the whole army turned to the East, each man stretched before himself a skin or a mat, and the entire army fell on its knees, like one man. At sight of that order and those restraints the hearts rose in the throngs, and their souls were filled with sure hope of victory.

The Sultan, coming to the camp at the end of April, did not move at once on the march. He waited more than a month, so that the waters might dry; during that time he trained the army to camp life, exercised it, arranged it, received envoys, and dispensed justice under a purple canopy. The kasseka, his chief wife, accompanied him on this expedition, and with her too went a court resembling a dream of paradise.

A gilded chariot bore the lady under a covering of purple silk; after it came other wagons and white Syrian camels, also covered with purple, bearing packs; houris and bayaderes sang songs to her on the road. When, wearied with the road, she was closing the silky lashes of her eyes, the sweet tones of soft instruments were heard at once, and they lulled her to sleep. During the heat of the day fans of peacock and ostrich feathers waved above her; priceless perfumes of the East burned before her tents in bowls from Hindostan. She was accompanied by all the treasures, wonders, and wealth that the Orient and the power of the Sultan could furnish, — houris, bayaderes, black eunuchs, pages beautiful as angels, Syrian camels, horses from the desert of Arabia; in a word, a whole retinue was glittering with brocade, cloth of silver and gold; it was gleaming like a rainbow from diamonds, rubies, emeralds, and sapphires. Nations fell prostrate before it, not daring to look at that face, which the Padishah alone had the right to see; and that retinue seemed to be either a supernatural vision or a reality, transferred by Allah himself from the world of visions and dream-illusions to the earth.

But the sun warmed the world more and more, and at last days of heat came. On a certain evening, therefore, the banner was raised on a lofty pole before the Sultan's tent, and a cannon-shot informed the army and the people of the

march to Lehistan. The great sacred drum sounded; all
the others sounded; the shrill voices of pipes were heard;
the pious, half-naked dervishes began to howl, and the river
of people moved on in the night, to avoid the heat of the sun
during daylight. But the army itself was to march only
in a number of hours after the earliest signal. First of all
went the tabor, then those pashas who provided food for
the troops, then whole legions of handicraftsmen, who had
to pitch tents, then herds of pack animals, then herds
destined for slaughter. The march was to last six hours
of that night and the following nights, and to be made in
such order that when soldiers came to a halt they should
always find food and a resting-place ready.

When the time came at last for the army to move, the
Sultan rode out on an eminence, so as to embrace with his
eyes his whole power, and rejoice at the sight. With him
were his vizir, the ulema, the young kaimakan, Kara Mustafa, the "rising sun of war," and a company of the infantry
guard. The night was calm and clear; the moon shone
brightly; and the Sultan might embrace with the eye all his
legions, were it not that no eye of man could take them all
in at once, — for on the march, though going closely together,
they occupied many miles.

Still he rejoiced in heart, and passing the beads of odorous sandal-wood through his fingers, raised his eyes to
Heaven in thanks to Allah, who had made him lord of so
many armies and so many nations. All at once, when the
front of the tabor had pushed almost out of sight, he interrupted his prayer, and turning to the young kaimakan,
Kara Mustafa, said, —

"I have forgotten who marches in the vanguard?"

"Light of paradise!" answered Kara Mustafa, "in the
vanguard are the Lithuanian Tartars and the Cheremis; and
thy dog Azya, son of Tugai Bey, is leading them."

CHAPTER XLVII.

Azya, the son of Tugai Bey, after a long halt on the plain of Kuchunkaury, was really marching with his men at the head of all the Turkish forces toward the boundary of the Commonwealth.

After the grievous blow which his plans and his person had received from the valiant hand of Basia, a fortunate star seemed to shine on him anew. First of all, he had recovered. His beauty, it is true, was destroyed forever: one eye had trickled out altogether, his nose was mashed, and his face, once like the face of a falcon, had become monstrous and terrible. But just that terror with which it filled people gave him still more consideration among the wild Tartars of the Dobrudja. His arrival made a great noise in the whole camp; his deeds grew in the narratives of men, and became gigantic. It was said that he had brought all the Lithuanian Tartars and Cheremis into the service of the Sultan; that he had outwitted the Poles, as no one had ever outwitted them; that he had burned whole towns along the Dniester, had cut off their garrisons, and had taken great booty. Those who were to march now for the first time to Lehistan; those who, coming from distant corners of the East, had not tried Polish arms hitherto; those whose hearts were alarmed at the thought that they would soon stand eye to eye with the terrible cavalry of the unbeliever, — saw in the young Azya a warrior who had conquered them, and made a fortunate beginning of war. The sight of the "hero" filled their hearts straightway with comfort; besides, as Azya was son of the terrible Tugai Bey, whose name had thundered through the Orient, all eyes were turned on him the more.

"The Poles reared him," said they; "but he is the son of a lion; he bit them and returned to the Padishah's service."

The vizir himself wished to see him; and the "rising sun of war," the young kaimakan, Kara Mustafa, enamoured of military glory and wild warriors, fell in love with him.- Both inquired diligently of him concerning the Commonwealth, the hetman, the armies, and Kamenyets; they rejoiced at his answers, seeing from them that war would be easy; that to the Sultan it must bring victory, to the Poles defeat, and to them the title of Ghazi (conqueror). Hence Azya had frequent opportunities later to fall on his face to the vizir, to sit at the threshold of the kaimakan's tent, and received from both numerous gifts in camels, horses, and weapons.

The grand vizir gave him a kaftan of silver brocade, the possession of which raised him in the eyes of all Lithuanian Tartars and Cheremis. Krychinski, Adurovich, Moravski, Groholski, Tarasovski, Aleksandrovich, — in a word, all those captains who had once dwelt in the Commonwealth and served it, but now returned to the Sultan, — placed themselves without a question under the command of Tugai Bey's son, honoring in him both the prince by descent and the warrior who had received a kaftan. He became, therefore, a notable murza; and more than two thousand warriors, incomparably better than the usual Tartars, obeyed his nod. The approaching war, in which it was easier for the young murza to distinguish himself than for any one else, might carry him high; he might find in it dignities, renown, power.

But still Azya bore poison in his soul. To begin with, it pricked his pride that the Tartars, in comparison with the Turks themselves, especially the janissaries and spahis, had little more significance than dogs compared with hunters. He had significance himself, but the Tartars in general were considered worthless cavalry. The Turk used them, at times he feared them, but in the camp he despised them. Azya, noticing this, kept his men apart from the general Tartar mass, as if they formed a separate, a better kind of army; but with this he brought on himself straightway the indignation of the Dobrudja and Belgrod murzas, and was not able to convince various Turkish officers that the Lithuanian Tartars were really better in any way than chambuls of the horde. On the other hand, reared in a Christian country, among nobles and knights, he could not inure himself to the manners of the East. In the Commonwealth he was only an ordinary officer and of the last arm of the service; but still, when meeting superiors or even the hetman, he was not obliged to humble himself as here, where he was a murza and the leader of all the companies of

Lithuanian Tartars. Here he had to fall on his face before the vizir; he had to touch the ground with his forehead in the friendly tent of the kaimakan; he had to prostrate himself before the pashas, before the ulema, before the chief aga of the janissaries. Azya was not accustomed to this. He remembered that he was the son of a hero; he had a wild soul full of pride, aiming high, as eagles aim; hence he suffered sorely.

But the recollection of Basia burned him with fire most of all. He cared not that one weak hand had hurled from his horse him who at Bratslav, at Kalnik, and a hundred other places had challenged to combat and stretched in death the most terrible skirmishers of the Zaporojia; he cared not for the shame, the disgrace! But he loved that woman beyond measure and thought; he wanted her in his tent, to look at her, to beat her, to kiss her. If it were in his choice to be Padishah and rule half the world, or to take her in his arms, feel with his heart the warmth of her blood, the breath of her face, her lips with his lips, he would prefer her to Tsargrad, to the Bosphorus, to the title of Khalif. He wanted her because he loved her; he wanted her because he hated her. The more she was foreign to him, the more he wanted her; the more she was pure, faithful, untainted, the more he wanted her. More than once when he remembered in his tent that he had kissed those eyes one time in his life, in the ravine after the battle with Azba Bey, and that at Rashkoff he had felt her breast on his, the madness of desire carried him away. He knew not what had become of her, whether she had perished on the road or not. At times he found solace in the thought that she had died. At times he thought, "It had been better not to carry her away, not to burn Rashkoff, not to come to the service of the Sultan, but to stay in Hreptyoff, and even look at her."

But the unfortunate Zosia Boski was in his tent. Her life passed in low service, in shame and continual terror, for in Azya's heart there was not a drop of pity for her. He simply tormented her because she was not Basia. She had, however, the sweetness and charm of a field flower; she had youth and beauty: therefore he sated himself with that beauty; but he kicked her for any cause, or flogged her white body with rods. In a worse hell she could not be, for she lived without hope. Her life had begun to bloom in Rashkoff, to bloom like spring with the flower of love for

Pan Adam. She loved him with her whole soul; she loved that knightly, noble, and honest nature with all her faculties; and now she was the plaything and the captive of that one-eyed monster. She had to crawl at his feet and tremble like a beaten dog, look into his face, look at his hands to see if they were not about to seize a club or a whip; she had to hold back her breath and her tears.

She knew well that there was not and could not be mercy for her; for though a miracle were to wrest her from those terrible hands, she was no longer that former Zosia, white as the first snows, and able to repay love with a clean heart. All that had passed beyond recovery. But since the dreadful disgrace in which she was living was not due to the least fault of hers, — on the contrary, she had been hitherto a maiden stainless as a lamb, innocent as a dove, trusting as a child, simple, loving, — she did not understand why this fearful injustice was wrought on her, an injustice which could not be recompensed; why such inexorable anger of God was weighing upon her; and this mental discord increased her pain, her despair. And so days, weeks, and months passed. Azya came to the plain of Kuchunkaury in winter, and the march to the boundary of the Commonwealth began only in June. All this time passed for Zosia in shame, in torment, in toil. For Azya, in spite of her beauty and sweetness, and though he kept her in his tent, not only did not love her, but rather he hated her because she was not Basia. He looked on her as a common captive; therefore she had to work like a captive. She watered his horses and camels from the river; she carried water for his ablutions, wood for the fire; she spread the skins for his bed; she cooked his food. In other divisions of the Turkish armies women did not go out of the tents through fear of the janissaries, or through custom; but the camp of the Lithuanian Tartars stood apart, and the custom of hiding women was not common among them, for having lived formerly in the Commonwealth, they had grown used to something different. The captives of common soldiers, in so far as soldiers had captives, did not even cover their faces with veils. It is true that women were not free to go beyond the boundaries of the square, for beyond those boundaries they would have been carried off surely; but on the square itself they could go everywhere safely, and occupy themselves with camp housekeeping.

Notwithstanding the heavy toil, there was for Zosia even
a certain solace in going for wood, or to the river to water
the horses and camels; for she feared to cry in the tent, and
on the road she could give vent to her tears with impunity.
Once, while going with arms full of wood, she met her
mother, whom Azya had given to Halim. They fell into
each other's arms, and it was necessary to pull them apart;
and though Azya flogged Zosia afterward, not sparing even
blows of rods on her head, still the meeting was dear to her.
Another time, while washing handkerchiefs and foot-cloths
for Azya at the ford, Zosia saw Eva at a distance going with
pails of water. Eva was groaning under the weight of the
pails; her form had changed greatly and grown heavier,
but her features, though shaded with a veil, reminded Zosia
of Adam, and such pain seized her heart that consciousness left her for the moment. Still, they did not speak to
each other from fear.

That fear stifled and mastered gradually all Zosia's
feelings, till at last it stood alone in place of her desires,
hopes, and memory. Not to be beaten had become for her
an object. Basia in her place would have killed Azya with
his own knife on the first day, without thinking of what
might come afterwards; but the timid Zosia, half a child
yet, had not Basia's daring. And it came at last to this,
that she considered it fondness if the terrible Azya, under
the influence of momentary desire, put his deformed face
near her lips. Sitting in the tent, she did not take her
eyes from him, wishing to learn whether he was angry
or not, following his movements, striving to divine his
wishes.

When she foresaw evil, and when from under his
mustaches, as in the case of Tugai Bey, the teeth began to
glitter, she crept to his feet almost senseless from terror,
pressed her pale lips to them, embracing convulsively his
knees and crying like an afflicted child, —

"Do not beat me, Azya! forgive me; do not beat!"

He forgave her almost never; he gloated over her, not only
because she was not Basia, but because she had been the
betrothed of Novoveski. Azya had a fearless soul; yet so
awful were the accounts between him and Pan Adam that
at thought of that giant, with vengeance hardened in his
heart, a certain disquiet seized the young Tartar. There
was to be war; they might meet, and it was likely that they
would meet. Azya was not able to avoid thinking of this;

and because these thoughts came to him at sight of Zosia,
he took vengeance on her, as if he wished to drive away his
own alarm with blows of rods.

At last the time came when the Sultan gave command to
march. Azya's men were to move in the vanguard, and
after them the whole legion of Dobrudja and Belgrod
Tartars. That was arranged between the Sultan, the vizir,
and the kaimakan. But in the beginning all went to the
Balkans together. The march was comfortable, for by
reason of the heat which was setting in, they marched only
in the night, six hours from one resting-place to the other.
Tar-barrels were burning along their road, and the massala
djirali lighted the way for the Sultan with colored lights.
The swarms of people flowed on like a river, through
boundless plains; filled the depressions of valleys like
locusts, covered the mountains. After the armed men went
the tabors, in them the harems; after the tabors herds
without number.

But in the swamps at the foot of the Balkans the gilded
and purple chariot of the kasseka was mired so that twelve
buffaloes were unable to draw it from the mud. "That is
an evil omen, lord, for thee and for the whole army," said
the chief mufti to the Sultan. "An evil omen," repeated
the half-mad dervishes in the camp. The Sultan was
alarmed, and decided to send all women out of the camp
with the marvellous kasseka.

The command was announced to the armies. Those of
the soldiers who had no place to which they might send
captives, and from love did not wish to sell them to
strangers, preferred to kill them. Merchants of the caravan-
serai bought others by the thousand, to sell them afterward
in the markets of Stambul and all the places of nearer Asia.
A great fair, as it were, lasted for three days. Azya offered
Zosia for sale without hesitation; an old Stambul merchant,
a rich person, bought her for his son.

He was a kindly man, for at Zosia's entreaties and tears
he bought her mother from Halim; it is true that he got
her for a trifle. The next day both wandered on toward
Stambul, in a line with other women. In Stambul Zosia's
lot was improved, without ceasing to be shameful. Her
new owner loved her, and after a few months he raised
her to the dignity of wife. Her mother did not part
from her.

Many people, among them many women, even after a long

time of captivity, returned to their country. There was also some person, who by all means, through Armenians, Greek merchants, and servants of envoys from the Commonwealth, sought Zosia too, but without result. Then these searches were interrupted on a sudden; and Zosia never saw her native land, nor the faces of those who were dear to her. She lived till her death in a harem.

CHAPTER XLVIII.

EVEN before the Turks marched from Adrianople, a great movement had begun in all the stanitsas on the Dniester. To Hreptyoff, the stanitsa nearest to Kamenyets, couriers of the hetman were hastening continually, bringing various orders; these the little knight executed himself, or if they did not relate to him, he forwarded them through trusty people. In consequence of these orders the garrison of Hreptyoff was reduced notably. Pan Motovidlo went with his Cossacks to Uman to aid Hanenko, who, with a handful of Cossacks faithful to the Commonwealth, struggled as best he could with Doroshenko and the Crimean horde which had joined him. Pan Mushalski, the incomparable bowman, Pan Snitko of the escutcheon Hidden Moon, Pan Nyenashinyets, and Pan Hromyka, led a squadron and Linkhauz's dragoons to Batog of unhappy memory, where was stationed Pan Lujetski, who, aided by Hanenko, was to watch Doroshenko's movements; Pan Bogush received an order to remain in Mohiloff till he could see chambuls with the naked eye. The instructions of the hetman were seeking eagerly the famous Pan Rushchyts, whom Volodyovski alone surpassed as a partisan; but Pan Rushchyts had gone to the steppes at the head of a few tens of men, and vanished as if in water. They heard of him only later, when wonderful tidings were spread, that around Doroshenko's tabor and the companies of the horde an evil spirit, as it were, was hovering, which carried away daily single warriors and smaller companies. It was suspected that this must be Pan Rushchyts, for no other except the little knight could attack in that manner. In fact, it was Pan Rushchyts.

As decided before, Pan Michael had to go to Kamenyets; the hetman needed him there, for he knew him to be a soldier whose coming would comfort the hearts, while it roused the courage, of the inhabitants and the garrison. The hetman was convinced that Kamenyets would not hold out; with him the question was simply that it should hold out as long as possible, — that is, till the

Commonwealth could assemble some forces for defence. In this conviction he sent to evident death, as it were, his favorite soldier, the most renowned cavalier of the Commonwealth.

He sent the most renowned warrior to death, and he did not grieve for him. The hetman thought always, what he said later on at Vienna, that Pani Wojnina [1] might give birth to people, but that Wojna (war) only killed them. He was ready himself to die; he thought that to die was the most direct duty of a soldier, and that when a soldier could render famous service by dying, death was to him a great reward and favor. The hetman knew also that the little knight was of one conviction with himself.

Besides, he had no time to think of sparing single soldiers when destruction was advancing on churches, towns, the country, the whole Commonwealth; when, with forces unheard of, the Orient was rising against Europe to conquer all Christendom, which, shielded by the breast of the Commonwealth, had no thought of helping that Commonwealth. The only question possible for the hetman was that Kamenyets should cover the Commonwealth, and then the Commonwealth the remainder of Christendom.

This might have happened had the Commonwealth been strong, had disorder not exhausted it. But the hetman had not troops enough even for reconnoissances, not to mention war. If he hurried some tens of soldiers to one place, there was an opening made in another, through which an invading wave might pour in without obstacle. The detachments of sentries posted by the Sultan at night in his camp outnumbered the squadrons of the hetman. The invasion moved from two directions,—from the Dnieper and the Danube. Because Doroshenko, with the whole horde of the Crimea, was nearer, and had inundated the country already, burning and slaying, the chief squadrons had gone against him; on the other hand, people were lacking for simple reconnoissances. While in such dire straits the hetman wrote the following few words to Pan Michael,—

"I did think to send you to Rashkoff near the enemy, but grew afraid, because the horde, crossing by seven fords from the Moldavian bank, will occupy the country, and you could not reach Kamenyets, where there is absolute need of you. Only yesterday I remembered Novoveski, who is a trained soldier and daring, and because a man

---

[1] See note after introduction.

in despair is ready for everything, I think that he will serve me
effectively. Send him whatever light cavalry you can spare; let him
go as far as possible, show himself everywhere, and give out reports
of our great forces, when before the eyes of the enemy; let him
appear here and there suddenly, and not let himself be captured. It
is known how they will come; but if he sees anything new, he is to
inform you at once, and you will hurry off without delay an informant
to me, and to Kamenyets. Let Novoveski move quickly, and be you
ready to go to Kamenyets, but wait where you are till news comes
from Novoveski in Moldavia."

Since Pan Adam was living at Mohiloff for the time, and,
as report ran, was to come to Hreptyoff in any case, the
little knight merely sent word to him to hasten, because a
commission from the hetman was waiting for him.

Pan Adam came three days later. His acquaintances
hardly knew him, and thought that Pan Byaloglovski had
good reason to call him a skeleton. He was no longer that
splendid fellow, high-spirited, joyous, who on a time used
to rush at the enemy with outbursts of laughter, like the
neighing of a horse, and gave blows with just such a sweep
as is given by the arm of a windmill. He had grown lean,
sallow, dark, but in that leanness he seemed a still greater
giant. While looking at people, he blinked as if not
recognizing his nearest acquaintances; it was needful also
to repeat the same thing two or three times to him, for he
seemed not to understand at first. Apparently grief was
flowing in his veins instead of blood; evidently he strove
not to think of certain things, preferring to forget them, so
as not to run mad.

It is true that in those regions there was not a man, not a
family, not an officer of the army, who had not suffered evil
from Pagan hands, who was not bewailing some acquaintance, friend, near and dear one; but on Pan Adam there had
burst simply a whole cloud of misfortunes. In one day he
had lost father and sister, and besides, his betrothed, whom
he loved with all the power of his exuberant spirit. He
would rather that his sister and that dearly beloved girl
had both died; he would rather they had perished from the
knife or in flames. But their fate was such that in comparison with the thought of them the greatest torment was
nothing for Pan Adam. He strove not to think of their
fate, for he felt that thinking of it bordered on insanity; he
strove, but he failed.

In truth, his calmness was only apparent. There was no

resignation whatever in his soul, and at the first glance it was evident to any man that under the torpor there was something ominous and terrible, and, should it break forth, that giant would do something awful, just as a wild element would. That was as if written on his forehead explicitly, so that even his friends approached him with a certain timidity; in talking with him, they avoided reference to the past.

The sight of Basia in Hreptyoff opened closed wounds in him, for while kissing her hands in greeting, he began to groan like an aurochs that is mortally wounded, his eyes became bloodshot, and the veins in his neck swelled to the size of cords. When Basia, in tears and affectionate as a mother, pressed his head with her hands, he fell at her feet, and could not rise for a long time. But when he heard what kind of office the hetman had given him, he became greatly enlivened; a gleam of ominous joy flashed up in his face, and he said, —

"I will do that, I will do more!"

"And if you meet that mad dog, give him a skinning!" put in Zagloba.

Pan Adam did not answer at once; he only looked at Zagloba; sudden bewilderment shone in his eyes; he rose and began to go toward the old noble, as if he wished to rush at him.

"Do you believe," said he, "that I have never done evil to that man, and that I have always been kind to him?"

"I believe, I believe!" said Zagloba, pushing behind the little knight hurriedly. "I would go myself with you, but the gout bites my feet."

"Novoveski," asked the little knight, "when do you wish to start?"

"To-night."

"I will give you a hundred dragoons. I will remain here myself with another hundred and the infantry. Go to the square!"

They went out to give orders. Zydor Lusnia was waiting at the threshold, straightened out like a string. News of the expedition had spread already through the square; the sergeant therefore, in his own name and the name of his company, began to beg the little colonel to let him go with Pan Adam.

"How is this? Do you want to leave me?" asked the astonished Volodyovski.

"Pan Commandant, we made a vow against that son of a such a one; and perhaps he may come into our hands."

"True! Pan Zagloba has told me of that," answered the little knight.

Lusnia turned to Novoveski, —

"Pan Commandant!"

"What is your wish?"

"If we get him, may I take care of him?"

Such a fierce, beastly venom was depicted on the face of the Mazovian that Novoveski inclined at once to Volodyov· ski, and said entreatingly, —

"Your grace, let me have this man!"

Pan Michael did not think of refusing; and that same evening, about dusk, a hundred horsemen, with Novoveski at their head, set out on the journey.

They marched by the usual road through Mohiloff and Yampol. In Yampol they met the former garrison of Rashkoff, from which two hundred men joined Novoveski by order of the hetman; the rest, under command of Pan Byalo-glovski, were to go to Mohiloff, where Pan Bogush was stationed. Pan Adam marched to Rashkoff.

The environs of Rashkoff were a thorough waste; the town itself had been turned into a pile of ashes, which the winds had blown to the four sides of the world; its scant number of inhabitants had fled before the expected storm. It was already the beginning of May, and the Dobrudja horde might show itself at any time; therefore it was unsafe to remain in those regions. In fact, the hordes were with the Turks, on the plain of Kuchunkaury; but men around Rashkoff had no knowledge of that, therefore every one of the former inhabitants, who had escaped the last slaughter, carried off his head in good season whithersoever seemed best to him.

Along the road Lusnia was framing plans and stratagems, which in his opinion Pan Adam should adopt if he wished to outwit the enemy in fact and successfully. He detailed these ideas to the soldiers with graciousness.

"You know nothing of this matter, horse-skulls," said he; "but I am old, I know. We will go to Rashkoff; we will hide there and wait. The horde will come to the crossing; small parties will cross first, as is their custom, because the chambul stops and waits till they tell if 't is safe; then we will slip out and drive them before us to Kamenyets."

"But in this way we may not get that dog brother," remarked one of the men in the ranks.

"Shut your mouth!" said Lusnia. "Who will go in the vanguard if not the Lithuanian Tartars?"

In fact, the previsions of the sergeant seemed to be coming true. When he reached Rashkoff Pan Adam gave the soldiers rest. All felt certain that they would go next to the caves, of which there were many in the neighborhood, and hide there till the first parties of the enemy appeared. But the second day of their stay the commandant brought the squadron to its feet, and led it beyond Rashkoff.

"Are we going to Yagorlik, or what?" asked the sergeant in his mind.

Meanwhile they approached the river just beyond Rashkoff, and a few "Our Fathers" later they halted at the so-called "Bloody Ford." Pan Adam, without saying a word, urged his horse into the water and began to cross to the opposite bank. The soldiers looked at one another with astonishment.

"How is this,—are we going to the Turks?" asked one of another. But these were not "gracious gentlemen" of the general militia, ready to summon a meeting and protest, they were simple soldiers inured to the iron discipline of stanitsas; hence the men of the first rank urged their horses into the water after the commandant, and then those in the second and third did the same. There was not the least hesitation. They were astonished that, with three hundred horse, they were marching against the Turkish power, which the whole world could not conquer; but they went. Soon the water was plashing around the horses' sides; the men ceased to wonder then, and were thinking simply of this, that the sacks of food for themselves and the horses should not get wet. Only on the other bank did they begin to look at one another again.

"For God's sake, we are in Moldavia already!" said they, in quiet whispers.

And one or another looked behind, beyond the Dniester, which glittered in the setting sun like a red and golden ribbon. The river cliffs, full of caves, were bathed also in the bright gleams. They rose like a wall, which at that moment divided that handful of men from their country. For many of them it was indeed the last parting.

The thought went through Lusnia's head that maybe the commandant had gone mad; but it was the commandant's affair to command, his to obey.

Meanwhile the horses, issuing from the water, began to

snort terribly in the ranks. " Good health ! good health !"
was heard from the soldiers. They considered the snorting
of good omen, and a certain consolation entered their hearts.

"Move on !" commanded Pan Adam.

The ranks moved, and they went toward the setting sun
and toward those thousands, to that swarm of people, to
those nations gathered at Kuchunkaury. .

CHAPTER XLIX.

PAN ADAM'S passage of the Dniester, and his march with three hundred sabres against the power of the Sultan, which numbered hundreds of thousands of warriors, were deeds which a man unacquainted with war might consider pure madness; but they were only bold, daring deeds of war, having chances of success.

To begin with, raiders of those days went frequently against chambuls a hundred times superior in numbers; they stood before the eyes of the enemy, and then vanished, cutting down pursuers savagely. Just as a wolf entices dogs after him at times, to turn at the right moment and kill the dog pushing forward most daringly, so did they. In the twinkle of an eye the beast became the hunter, started, hid, waited, but though pursued, hunted too, attacked unexpectedly, and bit to death. That was the so-called " method with Tartars," in which each side vied with the other in stratagems, tricks, and ambushes. The most famous man in this method was Pan Michael, next to him Pan Rushchyts, then Pan Pivo, then Pan Motovidlo; but Novoveski, practising from boyhood in the steppes, belonged to those who were mentioned among the most famous, hence it was very likely that when he stood before the horde he would not let himself be taken.

The expedition had chances of success too, for the reason that beyond the Dniester there were wild regions in which it was easy to hide. Only here and there, along the rivers, did settlements show themselves, and in general the country was little inhabited; nearer the Dniester it was rocky and hilly; farther on there were steppes, or the land was covered with forests, in which numerous herds of beasts wandered, from buffaloes, run wild, to deer and wild boars. Since the Sultan wished before the expedition " to feel his power and calculate his forces," the hordes dwelling on the lower Dniester, those of Belgrod, and still farther those of Dobrudja, marched at command of the Padishah to the south of the Balkans, and after them followed the Karalash of Moldavia, so that the country had become still more

deserted, and it was possible to travel whole weeks without
being seen by any person.

Pan Adam knew Tartar customs too well not to know
that when the chambuls had once passed the boundary of
the Commonwealth they would move more warily, keeping diligent watch on all sides; but there in their own
country they would go in broad columns without any precaution. And they did so, in fact; there seemed to the
Tartars a greater chance to meet death than to meet in the
heart of Bessarabia, on the very Tartar boundary, the troops
of that Commonwealth which had not men enough to
defend its own borders.

Pan Adam was confident that his expedition would astonish the enemy first of all, and hence do more good than the
hetman had hoped; secondly, that it might be destructive
to Azya and his men. It was easy for the young lieutenant
to divine that they, since they knew the Commonwealth
thoroughly, would march in the vanguard, and he placed his
main hope in that certainty. To fall unexpectedly on Azya
and seize him, to rescue perhaps his sister and Zosia, to
snatch them from captivity, accomplish his vengeance, and
then perish in war, was all that the distracted soul of
Novoveski wished for.

Under the influence of these thoughts and hopes, Pan
Adam freed himself from torpor, and revived. His march
along unknown ways, arduous labor, the sweeping wind
of the steppes, and the dangers of the bold undertaking
increased his health, and brought back his former strength.
The warrior began to overcome in him the man of misfortune. Before that, there had been no place in him for anything except memories and suffering; now he had to think
whole days of how he was to deceive and attack.

After they had passed the Dniester the Poles went on a
diagonal, and down toward the Pruth. In the day they hid
frequently in forests and reeds; in the night they made
secret and hurried marches. So far the country was not
much inhabited, and, occupied mainly by nomads, was empty
for the greater part. Very rarely did they come upon fields
of maize, and near them houses.

Marching secretly, they strove to avoid larger settlements,
but often they stopped at smaller ones composed of one,
two, three, or even a number of cottages; these they entered
boldly, knowing that none of the inhabitants would think of
fleeing before them to Budjyak, and forewarning the Tartars.

Lusnia, however, took care that this should not happen; but soon he omitted the precaution, for he convinced himself that those few settlements, though subject, as it were, to the Sultan, were looking for his troops with dread; and secondly, that they had no idea what kind of people had come to them, and took the whole detachment for Kara-lash parties, who were marching after others at command of the Sultan.

The inhabitants furnished without opposition corn, bread, and dried buffalo-meat. Every cottager had his flock of sheep, his buffaloes and horses, secreted near the rivers. From time to time appeared also very large herds of buffa-loes, half wild, and followed by a number of herdsmen. These herdsmen lived in tents on the steppe, and remained in one place only while they found grass in abundance. Frequently they were old Tartars. Pan Adam surrounded them with as much care as if they were a chambul; he did not spare them, lest they might send down toward Budjyak a report of his march. Tartars, especially after he had inquired of them concerning the roads, or rather the road-less country, he slew without mercy, so that not a foot escaped. He took then from the herds as many cattle as he needed, and moved on.

The detachment went southward; they met now more frequently herds guarded by Tartars almost exclusively, and in rather large parties. During a march of two weeks Pan Adam surrounded and cut down three bands of shep-herds, numbering some tens of men. The dragoons always took the sheepskin coats of these men, and cleaning them over fires, put them on, so as to resemble wild herdsmen and shepherds. In another week they were all dressed like Tartars, and looked exactly like a chambul. There remained to them only the uniform weapons of regular cavalry; but they kept their jackets in the saddle-straps, so as to put them on when returning. They might be recognized near at hand by their yellow Mazovian mus-taches and blue eyes; but from a distance a man of the greatest experience might be deceived at sight of them, all the more since they drove before them the cattle which they needed as food.

Approaching the Pruth, they marched along its left bank. Since the trail of Kuchman was in a region too much stripped, it was easy to foresee that the legions of the Sultan and the horde in the vanguard would march

through Falezi, Hush, Kotimore, and only then by the Wallachian trail, and either turn toward the Dniester, or go
straight as the cast of a sickle through all Bessarabia, to
come out on the boundary of the Commonwealth near
Ushytsa. Pan Adam was so certain of this that, caring
nothing for time, he went more and more slowly, and with
increasing care, so as not to come too suddenly on chambuls.
Arriving at last at the river forks formed by the Sarata
and the Tekich, he stopped there for a long time, first, to
give rest to his horses and men, and second, to wait in a
well-sheltered place for the vanguard of the horde.

The place was well sheltered and carefully chosen, for all
the inner and outer banks of the two rivers were covered
partly with the common cornel-bush, and partly with dogwood. This thicket extended as far as the eye could reach,
covering the ground in places with dense brushwood, in
places forming groups of bushes, between which were empty
spaces, commodious for camping. At that season the trees
and bushes had cast their blossoms, but in the early spring
there must have been a sea of white and yellow flowers.
The place was uninhabited, but swarming with beasts,
such as deer and rabbits, and with birds. Here and there,
at the edge of a spring, they found also bear tracks. One
man at the arrival of the detachment killed a couple of
sheep. In view of this, Lusnia promised himself a sheep
hunt; but Pan Adam, wishing to lie concealed, did not
permit the use of muskets, — the soldiers went out to
plunder with spears and axes.

Later on they found near the water traces of fires, but
old ones, probably of the past year. It was evident that
nomads looked in there from time to time with their herds,
or perhaps Tartars came to cut cornel-wood for slung
staffs. But the most careful search did not discover a
living soul. Pan Adam decided not to go farther, but to
remain there till the coming of the Turkish troops.

They laid out a square, built huts, and waited. At the
edges of the wood sentries were posted; some of these
looked day and night toward Budjyak, others toward the
Pruth in the direction of Falezi. Pan Adam knew that he
would divine the approach of the Sultan's armies by certain
signs; besides, he sent out small detachments, led by himself most frequently. The weather favored excellently the
halt in that dry region. The days were warm, but it was
easy to avoid heat in the shade of the thicket; the nights

were clear, calm, moonlight, and then the groves were
quivering from the singing of nightingales. During such
nights Pan Adam suffered most, for he could not sleep; he
was thinking of his former happiness, and pondering on the
present days of disaster. He lived only in the thought
that when his heart was sated with vengeance he would
be happier and calmer. Meanwhile the time was approaching in which he was to accomplish that vengeance
or perish.

Week followed week spent in finding food in wild places,
and in watching. During that time they studied all the
trails, ravines, meadows, rivers, and streams, gathered in
again a number of herds, cut down some small bands of
nomads, and watched continually in that thicket, like a wild
beast waiting for prey. At last the expected moment came.

A certain morning they saw flocks of birds covering the
earth and the sky. Bustards, ptarmigans, blue-legged quails,
hurried through the grass to the thicket; through the sky
flew ravens, crows, and even water-birds, evidently frightened on the banks of the Danube or the swamps of the
Dobrudja. At sight of this the dragoons looked at one
another; and the phrase, "They are coming! they are coming!" flew from mouth to mouth. Faces grew animated at
once, mustaches began to quiver, eyes to gleam, but in that
animation there was not the slightest alarm. Those were all
men for whom life had passed in "methods;" they only
felt what a hunting dog feels when he sniffs game.
Fires were quenched in a moment, so that smoke might not
betray the presence of people in the thicket; the horses
were saddled; and the whole detachment stood ready for
action.

It was necessary so to measure time as to fall on the
enemy during a halt. Pan Adam understood well that
the Sultan's troops would not march in dense masses,
especially in their own country, where danger was altogether unlikely. He knew, too, that it was the custom of
vanguards to march five or ten miles before the main
army. He hoped, with good reason, that the Lithuanian
Tartars would be first in the vanguard.

For a certain time he hesitated whether to advance to
meet them by secret roads, well known to him, or to wait
in the woods for their coming. He chose the latter,
because it was easier to attack from the woods unexpectedly.
Another day passed, then a night, during which not only

birds came in swarms, but beasts came in droves to the woods. Next morning the enemy was in sight.

South of the wood stretched a broad though hilly meadow, which was lost in the distant horizon. On that meadow appeared the enemy, and approached the wood rather quickly. The dragoons looked from the trees at that dark mass, which vanished at times, when hidden by hills, and then appeared again in all its extent.

Lusnia, who had uncommonly sharp eyesight, looked some time with effort at those crowds approaching; then he went to Novoveski, and said, —

"Pan Commandant, there are not many men; they are only driving herds out to pasture."

Pan Adam convinced himself soon that Lusnia was right, and his face shone with gladness.

"That means that their halting-place is five or six miles from this grove," said he.

"It does," answered Lusnia. "They march in the night, evidently to gain shelter from heat, and rest in the day; they are sending the horses now to pasture till evening."

"Is there a large guard with the horses?"

Lusnia pushed out again to the edge of the wood, and did not return for a longer time. At last he came back and said, —

"There are about fifteen hundred horses and twenty-five men with them. They are in their own country; they fear nothing, and do not put out strong watches."

"Could you recognize the men?"

"They are far away yet, but they are Lithuanian Tartars. They are in our hands already."

"They are," said Pan Adam.

In fact, he was convinced that not a living foot of those men would escape. For such a leader as he, and such soldiers as he led, that was a very light task.

Meanwhile the herdsmen had driven the beasts nearer and nearer to the forest. Lusnia thrust himself out once again to the border, and returned a second time. His face was shining with cruelty and gladness.

"Lithuanian Tartars," whispered he.

Hearing this, Pan Adam made a noise like a falcon, and straightway a division of dragoons pushed into the depth of the wood. There they separated into two parties, one of which disappeared in a defile, so as to come out behind the herd and the Tartars; the other formed a half-circle, and waited.

All this was done so quietly that the most trained ear could not have caught a sound; neither sabre nor spur rattled; no horse neighed; the thick grass on the ground dulled the tramp of hoofs; besides, even the horses seemed to understand that the success of the attack depended on silence, for they were performing such service not for the first time. Nothing was heard from the defile and the brushwood but the call of the falcon, lower every little while and less frequent.

The herd of Tartar horses stopped before the wood, and scattered in greater or smaller groups on the meadow. Pan Adam himself was then near the edge, and followed all the movements of the herdsmen. The day was clear, and the time before noon, but the sun was already high, and cast heat on the earth. The horses rolled; later on, they approached the wood. The herdsmen rode to the edge of the grove, slipped down from their horses, and let them out on lariats; then seeking the shade and cool places, they entered the thicket, and lay down under the largest bushes to rest.

Soon a fire burst up in a flame; when the dry sticks had turned into coals and were coated with ashes, the herdsmen put half a colt on the coals, and sat at a distance themselves to avoid the heat. Some stretched on the grass; others talked, sitting in groups, Turkish fashion; one began to play on a horn. In the wood perfect silence reigned; the falcon called only at times.

The odor of singed flesh announced at last that the roast was ready. Two men drew it out of the ashes, and dragged it to a shady tree; there they sat in a circle cutting the meat with their knives, and eating with beastly greed. From the half-raw strips came blood, which settled on their fingers, and flowed down their beards.

When they had finished eating, and had drunk sour mare's milk out of skins, they felt satisfied. They talked awhile yet; then their heads and limbs became heavy.

Afternoon came. The heat flew down from heaven more and more. The forest was varied with quivering streaks of light made by the rays of the sun penetrating dense places. Everything was silent; even the falcons ceased to call.

A number of Tartars stood up and went to look at the horses; others stretched themselves like corpses on a battlefield, and soon sleep overpowered them. But their sleep after meat and drink was rather heavy and uneasy, for at times one groaned deeply, another opened his lids for a moment, and repeated, "Allah, Bismillah!"

All at once on the edge of the wood was heard some low but terrible sound, like the short rattle of a stifled man who had no time to cry. Whether the ears of the herdsmen were so keen, or some animal instinct had warned them of danger, or finally, whether Death had blown with cold breath on them, it is enough that they sprang up from sleep in one moment.

"What is that? Where are the men at the horses?" they began to inquire of one another. Then from a thicket some voice said in Polish, —

"They will not return."

That moment a hundred and fifty men rushed in a circle at the herdsmen, who were frightened so terribly that the cry died in their breasts. An odd one barely succeeded in grasping his dagger. The circle of attackers covered and hid them completely. The bush-quivered from the pressure of human bodies, which struggled in a disorderly group. The whistle of blades, panting, and at times groaning or wheezing were heard, but that lasted one twinkle of an eye; and all was silent.

"How many are alive?" asked a voice among the attackers.

"Five, Pan Commandant."

"Examine the bodies; lest any escape, give each man a knife in the throat, and bring the prisoners to the fire."

The command was obeyed in one moment. The corpses were pinned to the turf with their own knives; the prisoners, after their feet had been bound to sticks, were brought around the fire, which Lusnia had raked so that coals, hidden under ashes, would be on the top.

The prisoners looked at this preparation and at Lusnia with wild eyes. Among them were three Tartars of Hreptyoff who knew the sergeant perfectly. He knew them too, and said, —

"Well, comrades, you must sing now; if not, you will go to the other world on roasted soles. For old acquaintance' sake I will not spare fire on you."

When he had said this he threw dry limbs on the fire, which burst out at once in a tall blaze.

Pan Adam came now, and began the examination. From confessions of the prisoners it appeared that what the young lieutenant had divined earlier was true. The Lithuanian

Tartars and Cheremis were marching in the vanguard
before the horde, and before all the troops of the Sultan.
They were led by Azya, son of Tugai Bey, to whom was
given command over all the parties. They, as well as the
whole army, marched at night because of the heat; in the
day they sent their herds out to pasture. They threw out
no pickets, for no one supposed that troops could attack
them even near the Dniester, much less at the Pruth, right
at the dwellings of the horde; they marched comfortably,
therefore, with their herds and with camels, which carried
the tents of the officers. The tent of Murza Azya was easily
known, for it had a bunchuk fixed on its summit, and the
banners of the companies were fastened near it in time of
halt. The camp was four or five miles distant; there were
about two thousand men in it, but some of them had
remained with the Belgrod horde, which was marching
about five miles behind.

Pan Adam inquired further touching the road which would
lead to the camp best, then how the tents were arranged, and
last, of that which concerned him most deeply.

"Are there women in the tent?"

The Tartars trembled for their lives. Those of them who
had served in Hreptyoff knew perfectly that Pan Adam was
the brother of one of those women, and was betrothed to
the other; they understood, therefore, what rage would
seize him when he knew the whole truth.

That rage might fall first on them; they hesitated, therefore, but Lusnia said at once, —

"Pan Commandant, we'll warm their soles for the dog
brothers; then they will speak."

"Thrust their feet in the fire!" said Pan Adam.

"Have mercy!" cried Eliashevich, an old Tartar from
Hreptyoff. "I will tell all that my eyes have seen."

Lusnia looked at the commandant to learn if he was to
carry out the threat notwithstanding this answer; but Pan
Adam shook his head, and said to Eliashevich, —

"Tell what thou hast seen."

"We are innocent, lord," answered Eliashevich; "we went
at command. The murza gave your gracious sister to Pan
Adurovich, who had her in his tent. I saw her in Kuchunkaury when she was going for water with pails; and I helped
her to carry them, for she was heavy —"

"Woe!" muttered Pan Adam.

"But the other lady our murza himself had in his tent.

We did not see her so often; but we heard more than once how she screamed, for the murza, though he kept her for his pleasure, beat her with rods, and kicked her."

Pan Adam's lips began to quiver.

Eliashevich barely heard the question.

"Where are they now?"

"Sold in Stambul."

"To whom?"

"The murza himself does not know certainly. A command came from the Padishah to keep no women in camp. All sold their women in the bazaar; the murza sold his."

The explanation was finished, and at the fire silence set in; but for some time a sultry afternoon wind shook the limbs of the trees, which sounded more and more deeply. The air became stifling; on the edge of the horizon, black clouds appeared, dark in the centre, and shining with a copper-color on the edges.

Pan Adam walked away from the fire, and moved like one demented, without giving an account to himself of where he was going. At last he dropped with his face to the ground, and began to tear the earth with his nails, then to gnaw his own hands, and then to gasp as if dying. A convulsion twisted his gigantic body, and he lay thus for hours. The dragoons looked at him from a distance; but even Lusnia dared not approach him.

Concluding that the commandant would not be angry at him for not sparing the Tartars, the terrible sergeant, impelled by pure inborn cruelty, stuffed their mouths with grass, so as to avoid noise, and slaughtered them like bullocks. He spared Eliashevich alone, supposing that he would be needed to guide them. When he had finished this work, he dragged away from the fire the bodies, still quivering, and put them in a row; he went then to look at the commandant.

"Even if he has gone mad," muttered Lusnia, "we must get that one."

Midday had passed, the afternoon hours as well, and the day was inclining toward evening. But those clouds, small at first, occupied now almost the whole heavens, and were growing ever thicker and darker without losing that copper-colored gleam along the edges. Their gigantic rolls turned heavily, like millstones on their own axes; then they fell on one another, crowded one another, and pushing one another from the height, rolled in a dense mass lower and

lower toward the earth. The wind struck at times, like a
bird of prey with its wings, bent the cornel-trees and the
dogwood to the earth, tore away a cloud of leaves, and bore
it apart with rage; at times it stopped as if it had fallen
into the ground. During such intervals of silence there was
heard in the gathering clouds a certain ominous rattling,
wheezing, rumbling; you would have said that legions of
thunders were gathering within them and ranging for
battle, grumbling in deep voices while rousing rage and
fury in themselves, before they would burst out and strike
madly on the terrified earth.

"A storm, a storm is coming!" whispered the dragoons
to one another.

The storm was coming. The air grew darker each
instant.

Then on the east, from the side of the Dniester, thunder
rose and rolled with an awful outbreak along the heavens,
till it went far away, beyond the Pruth; there it was silent
for a moment, but springing up afresh, rushed toward the
steppes of Budjyak, and rolled along the whole horizon.

First, great drops of rain fell on the parched grass. At
that moment Pan Adam stood before the dragoons.

"To horse!" cried he, with a mighty voice.

And at the expiration of as much time as is needed to
say a hurried "Our Father," he was moving at the head of a
hundred and fifty horsemen. When he had ridden out of
the woods, he joined, near the herd of horses, the other
half of his men, who had been standing guard at the field-
side, to prevent any herdsmen from escaping by stealth to
the camp. The dragoons rushed around the herd in the
twinkle of an eye, and giving out wild shouts, peculiar to
Tartars, moved on, urging before them the panic-stricken
horses.

The sergeant held Eliashevich on a lariat, and shouted in
his ear, trying to outsound the roar of the thunder, —

"Lead us on dog blood, and straight, or a knife in thy
throat!"

Now the clouds rolled so low that they almost touched
the earth. On a sudden they burst, like an explosion in a
furnace, and a raging hurricane was let loose; soon a blind-
ing light rent the darkness, a thunder-clap came, and after
it a second, a third; the smell of sulphur spread in the air,
and again there was darkness. Terror seized the herd of
horses. The beasts, driven from behind by the wild shouts

of the dragoons, ran with distended nostrils and flowing mane, scarcely touching the earth in their onrush; the thunder did not cease for a moment; the wind roared, and the horses raced on madly in that wind, in that darkness, amid explosions in which the earth seemed to be breaking. Driven by the tempest and by vengeance, they were like a terrible company of vampires or evil spirits in that wild steppe.

Space fled before them. No guide was needed, for the herd ran straight to the camp of the Tartars, which was nearer and nearer. But before they had reached it, the storm was unchained, as if the sky and the earth had gone mad. The whole horizon blazed with living fire, by the gleam of which were seen the tents standing on the steppe; the world was quivering from the roar of thunders; it seemed that the clouds might burst any moment and tumble to the earth. In fact, their sluices were opened, and floods of rain began to deluge the steppe. The downfall was so dense that a few paces distant nothing could be seen, and from the earth, inflamed by the heat of the sun, a thick mist was soon rising.

Yet a little while, and herd and dragoons will be in the camp.

But right before the tents the herd split, and ran to both sides in wild panic; three hundred breasts gave out a fearful shriek; three hundred sabres glittered in the flame of the lightning, and the dragoons fell on the tents.

Before the outburst of the torrent, the Tartars saw in the lightning-flashes the on-coming herd; but none of them knew what terrible herdsmen were driving. Astonishment and alarm seized them; they wondered why the herd should rush straight at the tents; then they began to shout to frighten them away. Azya himself pushed aside the canvas door, and in spite of the rain, went out with anger on his threatening face. But that instant the herd split in two, and, amid torrents of rain and in the fog, certain fierce forms looked black and many times greater in number than the horseherds; then the terrible cry, "Slay, kill!" was heard.

There was no time for anything, not even to guess what had happened, not even to be frightened. The hurricane of men, more dreadful and furious by far than the tempest, whirled on to the camp. Before Tugai Bey's son could retreat one step toward his tent, some power more than human, as you would have said, raised him from the earth.

Suddenly he felt that a dreadful embrace was squeezing him, that from its pressure his bones were bending and his ribs breaking; soon he saw, as if in mist, a face rather than which he would have seen Satan's, and fainted.

By that time the battle had begun, or rather the ghastly slaughter. The storm, the darkness, the unknown number of the assailants, the suddenness of the attack, and the scattering of the horses were the cause that the Tartars scarcely defended themselves. The madness of terror simply took possession of them. No one knew whither to escape, where to hide himself. Many had no weapons at hand; the attack found many asleep. Therefore, stunned, bewildered, and terrified, they gathered into dense groups, crowding, overturning, and trampling one another. The breasts of horses pushed them down, threw them to the ground; sabres cut them, hoofs crushed them. A storm does not so break, destroy, and lay waste a young forest, wolves do not eat into a flock of bewildered sheep, as the dragoons trampled and cut down those Tartars. On the one hand, bewilderment, on the other, rage and vengeance, completed the measure of their misfortune. Torrents of blood were mingled with the rain. It seemed to the Tartars that the sky was falling on them, that the earth was opening under their feet. The flash of lightning, the roar of thunder, the noise of rain, the darkness, the terror of the storm, answered to the dreadful outcries of the slaughtered. The horses of the dragoons, seized also with fear, rushed, as if maddened, into the throng, breaking it and stretching the men on the ground. At length the smaller groups began to flee, but they had lost knowledge of the place to such a degree that they fled around on the scene of struggle, instead of fleeing straight forward; and frequently they knocked against one another, like two opposing waves, struck one another, overturned one another, and went under the sword. At last the dragoons scattered the remnant of them completely, and slew them in the flight, taking no prisoners, and pursuing without mercy till the trumpets called them back from pursuit.

Never had an attack been more unexpected, and never a defeat more terrible. Three hundred men had scattered to the four winds of the world nearly two thousand cavalry, surpassing incomparably in training the ordinary chambuls. The greater part of them were lying flat in red pools of blood and rain. The rest dispersed, hid their heads, thanks to the darkness, and escaped on foot, at random, not certain that they would not run under the knife a second time. The storm and the darkness assisted the victors, as if the anger of God were fighting on their side against traitors.

Night had fallen completely when Pan Adam moved out at the head of his dragoons, to return to the boundaries of the Commonwealth. Between the young lieutenant and Lusnia, the sergeant, went a horse from the herd. On the back of this horse lay, bound with cords, the leader of all the Lithuanian Tartars, — Azya, the son of Tugai Bey, with broken ribs. He was alive, but in a swoon. Both looked at him from time to time as carefully and anxiously as if they were carrying a treasure, and were fearful of losing it.

The storm began to pass. On the heavens, legions of clouds were still moving, but in intervals between them, stars were beginning to shine, and to be reflected in lakes of water, formed on the steppe by the dense rain. In the distance, in the direction of the Commonwealth, thunder was still roaring from time to time.

CHAPTER L.

THE fugitive Tartars carried news to the Belgrod horde of the disaster. Couriers from them took the news to the Ordu i Humayun, — that is, to the Sultan's camp, — where it made an uncommon impression.

Pan Adam had no need, it is true, to flee too hurriedly with his booty to the Commonwealth, for not only did no one pursue him at the first moment, but not even for the two succeeding days. The Sultan was so astonished that he knew not what to think. He sent Belgrod and Dobrudja chambuls at once to discover what troops were in the vicinity. They went unwillingly, for with them it was a question of their òwn skins. Meanwhile the tidings, given from mouth to mouth, grew to be the account of a considerable overthrow. Men inhabiting the depth of Asia or Africa, who had not gone hitherto with war to Lehistan, and who heard from narratives of the terrible cavalry of the unbelievers, were seized with fright at the thought that they were already in presence of that enemy who did not wait for them within his own boundaries, but sought them in the very dominions of the Padishah; the grand vizir himself, and the "future sun of war," the kaimakan, Kara Mustafa, did not know either what to think of the attack. How that Commonwealth, of whose weakness they had the minutest accounts, could assume all at once the offensive, no Turkish head could explain. It is enough that henceforth the march seemed less secure, and less like a triumph. At the council of war the Sultan received the vizir and the kaimakan with a terrible countenance.

"You have deceived me," said he. "The Poles cannot be so weak, since they seek us even here. You told me that Sobieski would not defend Kamenyets, and now he is surely in front of us, with his whole army."

The vizir and kaimakan tried to explain to their lord that this might be some detached band of robbers; but in view of the muskets and of straps, in which there were dragoon jackets, they did not believe that themselves. The recent expedition of Sobieski to the Ukraine, daring beyond every measure, but for all that victorious, permitted the supposition that the terrible leader intended to anticipate the enemy this time as well as the other.

"He has no troops," said the grand vizir to the kaimakan, while coming out from the council; "but there is a lion in him which knows nothing of fear. If he has collected even a few thousand, and is here, we shall march in blood to Hotin."

"I should like to measure strength with him," said young Kara Mustafa.

"May God avert from you misfortune!" answered the grand vizir.

By degrees, however, the Belgrod and Dobrudja chambuls convinced themselves that there were not only no large bodies of troops, but no troops at all in the neighborhood. They discovered the trail of a detachment numbering about three hundred horse, which moved hurriedly toward the Dniester. The Tartars, remembering the fate of Azya's men, made no pursuit, out of fear of an ambush. The attack remained as something astonishing and unexplained; but quiet came back by degrees to the Ordu i Humayun, and the armies of the Padishah began again to advance like an inundation.

Meanwhile, Pan Adam was returning safely with his living booty to Rashkoff. He went hurriedly, but as experienced scouts learned on the second day that there was no pursuit, he advanced, notwithstanding his haste, at a gait not to weary the horses over-much. Azya, fastened with cords to the back of the horse, was always between Pan Adam and Lusnia. He had two ribs broken, and had become wonderfully weak, for even the wound given him by Basia in the face opened from his struggle with Pan Adam and from riding with head hanging down. The terrible sergeant was careful that he should not die before reaching Rashkoff, and thus baffle revenge. The young Tartar wanted to die. Knowing what awaited him, he determined first of all to kill himself with hunger, and would not take food; but Lusnia opened his set teeth with a knife, and forced into his mouth gorailka and Moldavian wine, in which biscuits, rubbed to dust, had been mixed. At the places of halting, they threw water on his face, lest the wounds of his eye and his nose, on which flies and gnats had settled thickly during the journey, should mortify, and bring premature death to the ill-fated man.

Pan Adam did not speak to him on the road. Once only, at the beginning of the journey, when Azya, at the price of his freedom and life, offered to return Zosia and Eva, did the lieutenant say to him, —

"Thou liest, dog! Both were sold by thee to a merchant of Stambul, who will sell them again in the bazaar."

And straightway they brought Eliashevich, who said in presence of all, —

"It is so, Effendi. You sold her without knowing to whom; and Adurovich sold the bagadyr's [1] sister, though she was with child by him."

After these words, it seemed for a while to Azya that Novoveski would crush him at once in his terrible grasp. Afterwards, when he had lost all hope, he resolved to bring the young giant to kill him in a transport of rage, and in that way spare himself future torment; since Novoveski, unwilling to let his captive out of sight, rode always near him, Azya began to boast beyond measure and shamelessly of all that he had done. He told how he had killed old Novoveski, how he had kept Zosia Boski in the tent, how he gloated over her innocence, how he had torn her body with rods, and kicked her. The sweat rolled off the pale face of Pan Adam in thick drops. He listened; he had not the power, he had not the wish to go away. He listened eagerly, his hands quivered, his body shook convulsively; still he mastered himself, and did not kill.

But Azya, while tormenting his enemy, tormented himself, for his narratives brought to his mind his present misfortune. Not long before, he was commanding men, living in luxury, a murza, a favorite of the young kaimakan; now, lashed to the back of a horse, and eaten alive by flies, he was travelling on to a terrible death. Relief came to him when, from the pain of his wounds, and from suffering, he fainted. This happened with growing frequency, so that Lusnia began to fear that he might not bring him alive. But they travelled night and day, giving only as much rest to the horses as was absolutely needful, and Rashkoff was ever nearer and nearer. Still the horned soul of the Tartar would not leave the afflicted body. But during the last days he was in a continual fever, and at times he fell into an oppressive sleep. More than once in that fever or sleep he dreamed that he was still in Hreptyoff, that he had

[1] Hero.

to go with Volodyovski to a great war; again that he was
conducting Basia to Rashkoff; again that he had borne her
away, and hidden her in his tent; at times in the fever he saw
battles and slaughter, in which, as hetman of the Polish
Tartars, he was giving orders from under his bunchuk.
But awakening came, and with it consciousness. Opening
his eyes, he saw the face of Novoveski, the face of Lusnia,
the helmets of the dragoons, who had thrown aside the
sheepskin caps of the horseherds; and all that reality
was so dreadful that it seemed to him a genuine nightmare.
Every movement of the horse tortured him; his wounds
burned him increasingly; and again he fainted. Pierced
with pain, he recovered consciousness, to fall into a fever,
and with it into a dream, to wake up again.

There were moments in which it seemed to him impossible that he, such a wretched man, could be Azya, the son
of Tugai Bey; that his life, which was full of uncommon
events, and which seemed to promise a great destiny, was to
end with such suddenness, and so terribly.

At times too it came to his head that after torments
and death he would go straightway to paradise; but
because once he had professed Christianity, and had lived
long among Christians, fear seized him at the thought of
Christ.   Christ would have no pity on him; if the Prophet
had been mightier than Christ, he would not have given
him into the hands of Pan Adam. Perhaps, however, the
Prophet would show pity yet, and take the soul out of
him before Pan Adam would kill him with torture.

Meanwhile, Rashkoff was at hand. They entered a
country of cliffs, which indicated. the vicinity of the
Dniester. Azya in the evening fell into a condition half
feverish, half conscious, in which illusions were mingled
with reality. It seemed to him that they had arrived, that
they had stopped, that he heard around him the words
"Rashkoff! Rashkoff!" Next it seemed to him that he
heard the noise of axes cutting wood.

Then he felt that men were dashing cold water on his
head, and then for a long time they were pouring gorailka
into his mouth. After that he recovered entirely. Above
him was a starry night, and around him many torches were
gleaming. To his ears came the words, —

"Is he conscious?"

"Conscious. He seems in his mind."

And that moment he saw above him the face of Lusnia.

"Well, brother," said the sergeant, in a calm voice, "the hour is on thee!"

Azya was lying on his back and breathing freely, for his arms were stretched upward at both sides of his head, by reason of which his expanded breast moved more freely and received more air than when he was lying lashed to the back of the horse. But he could not move his hands, for they were tied above his head to an oak staff which was placed at right angles to his shoulders, and were bound with straw steeped in tar. Azya divined in a moment why this was done; but at that moment he saw other preparations also, which announced that his torture would be long and ghastly. He was undressed from his waist to his feet; and raising his head somewhat, he saw between his naked knees a freshly trimmed, pointed stake, the larger end of which was placed against the butt of a tree. From each of his feet there went a rope ending with a whiffletree, to which a horse was attached. By the light of the torches Azya could see only the rumps of the horses and two men, standing somewhat farther on, who evidently were holding the horses by the head.

The hapless man took in these preparations at a glance; then, looking at the heavens, it is unknown why, he saw stars and the gleaming crescent of the moon.

"They will draw me on," thought he.

And at once he closed his teeth so firmly that a spasm seized his jaws. Sweat came out on his forehead, and at the same time his face became cold, for the blood rushed away from it. Then it seemed to him that the earth was fleeing from under his shoulders, that his body was flying and flying into some fathomless abyss. For a while he lost consciousness of time, of place, and of what they were doing to him. The sergeant opened Azya's mouth with a knife, and poured in more gorailka.

He coughed and spat out the burning liquor, but was forced to swallow some of it. Then he fell into a wonderful condition: he was not drunk; on the contrary, his mind had never been clearer, nor his thought quicker. He saw what they were doing, he understood everything; but an uncommon excitement seized him, as it were,—impatience that all was lasting so long, and that nothing was beginning yet.

Next heavy steps were heard near by, and before him stood Pan Adam. At sight of him all the veins in the

Tartar quivered. Lusnia he did not fear; he despised him
too much. But Pan Adam he did not despise; indeed, he had
no reason to despise him; on the contrary, every look of his
face filled Azya's soul with a certain superstitious dread
and repulsion. He thought to himself at that moment, "I
am in his power; I fear him!" and that was such a terrible
feeling that under its influence the hair stiffened on the
head of Tugai Bey's son.

"For what thou hast done, thou wilt perish in torment,"
said Pan Adam.

The Tartar gave no answer, but began to pant audibly.

Novoveski withdrew, and then followed a silence which
was broken by Lusnia.

"Thou didst raise thy hand on the lady," said he, with
a hoarse voice; "but now the lady is at home with her
husband, and thou art in our hands. Thy hour has come!"

With those words the act of torture began for Azya.
That terrible man learned at the hour of his death that
his treason and cruelty had profited nothing. If even
Basia had died on the road, he would have had the consolation
that though not in his, she would not be in any man's
possession; and that solace was taken from him just then,
when the point of the stake was at an ell's length from his
body. All had been in vain. So many treasons, so much
blood, so much impending punishment for nothing, — for
nothing whatever!

Lusnia did not know how grievous those words had made
death to Azya; had he known, he would have repeated them
during the whole journey.

But there was no time for regrets then; everything
must give way before the execution. Lusnia stooped down,
and taking Azya's hips in both his hands to give them
direction, called to the men holding the horses, —

"Move! but slowly and together!"

The horses moved; the straightened ropes pulled Azya's
legs. In a twinkle his body was drawn along the earth
and met the point of the stake. Then the point commenced
to sink in him, and something dreadful began, — something
repugnant to nature and the feelings of man. The bones of
the unfortunate moved apart from one another; his body gave
way in two directions; pain indescribable, so awful that it
almost bounds on some monstrous delight, penetrated
his being. The stake sank more and more deeply. Azya
fixed his jaws, but he could not endure; his teeth were

bared in a ghastly grin, and out of his throat came the cry, "A! a! a!" like the croaking of a raven.

"Slowly!" commanded the sergeant.

Azya repeated his terrible cry more and more quickly.

"Art croaking?" inquired the sergeant.

Then he called to the men, —

"Stop! together! There, it is done," said he, turning to Azya, who had grown silent at once, and in whose throat only a deep rattling was heard.

The horses were taken out quickly; then men raised the stake, planted the large end of it in a hole prepared purposely, and packed earth around it. The son of Tugai Bey looked from above on that work. He was conscious. That hideous species of punishment is in this the more dreadful, that victims drawn on to the stake live sometimes three days. Azya's head was hanging on his breast; his lips were moving, smacking, as if he were chewing something and tasting it. He felt then a great faintness, and saw before him, as it were, a boundless, whitish mist, which, it is unknown wherefore, seemed to him terrible; but in that mist he recognized the faces of the sergeant and the dragoons, he saw that he was on the stake, that the weight of his body was sinking him deeper and deeper. Then he began to grow numb from the feet, and began to be less and less sensitive to pain.

At times darkness hid from him that whitish mist; then he blinked with his one seeing eye, wishing to see and behold everything till death. His gaze passed with particular persistence from torch to torch, for it seemed to him that around each flame there was a rainbow circle.

But his torture was not ended; after a while the sergeant approached the stake with an auger in his hand, and cried to those standing near, —

"Lift me up."

Two strong men raised him aloft. Azya began to look at him closely, blinking, as if he wished to know what kind of man was climbing up to his height. Then the sergeant said, —

"The lady knocked out one eye, and I promised myself to bore out the other."

When he had said this, he put the point into the pupil, twisted once and a second time, and when the lid and delicate skin surrounding the eye were wound around the spiral of the auger, he jerked.

Then from the two eye-sockets of Azya two streams of
blood flowed, and they flowed like two streams of tears
down his face. His face itself grew pale and still paler.
The dragoons extinguished the torches in silence, as if in
shame that light had shone on a deed of such ghastliness;
and from the crescent of the moon alone fell silvery though
not very bright rays on the body of Azya. His head fell
entirely on his breast; but his hands, bound to the oak staff,
and enveloped in straw steeped in tar, were pointing toward
the sky, as if that son of the Orient were calling the
vengeance of the Turkish crescent on his executioners.

"To horse!" was heard from Pan Adam.

Before mounting the sergeant ignited, with the last torch,
those uplifted hands of the Tartar; and the detachment
moved toward Yampol. Amid the ruins of Rashkoff, in
the night and the desert, Azya, the son of Tugai Bey,
remained on the lofty stake, and he gleamed there a long
time.

CHAPTER LI.

THREE weeks later, at midday, Pan Adam was in Hreptyoff. He had made the journey from Rashkoff so slowly because he had crossed to the other side of the Dnieper many times, while attacking chambuls and the perkulab's people along the river, at various stanitsas. These informed the Sultan's troops afterward that they had seen Polish detachments everywhere, and had heard of great armies, which surely would not wait for the coming of the Turks at Kamenyets, but would intercept their march, and meet them in a general battle.

The Sultan, who had been assured of the helplessness of the Commonwealth, was greatly astonished; and sending Tartars, Wallachians, and the hordes of the Danube in advance, he pushed forward slowly, for in spite of his measureless strength, he had great fear of a battle with the armies of the Commonwealth.

Pan Adam did not find Volodyovski in Hreptyoff, for the little knight had followed Motovidlo to assist the starosta of Podlyasye against the Crimean horde and Doroshenko. There he gained great victories, adding new glory to his former renown. He defeated the stern Korpan, and left his body as food to beasts on the open plain; he crushed the terrible Drozd, and the manful Malyshka, and the two brothers Siny, celebrated Cossack raiders, also a number of inferior bands and chambuls.

But when Pan Adam arrived, Pani Volodyovski was just preparing to go with the rest of the people and the tabor to Kamenyets, for it was necessary to leave Hreptyoff, in view of the invasion. Basia was grieved to leave that wooden fortalice, in which she had experienced many evils, it is true, but in which the happiest part of her life had been passed, with her husband, among loving hearts, famous soldiers. She was going now, at her own request, to Kamenyets, to unknown fortunes and dangers involved in the siege. But since she had a brave heart, she did not yield to sorrow, but watched the preparations carefully, guarding the soldiers and the tabor. In this she was aided

by Zagloba, who in every necessity surpassed all in understanding, together with Pan Mushalski, the incomparable
bowman, who was besides a soldier of valiant hand and
uncommon experience.

All were delighted at the arrival of Pan Adam, though
they knew at once, from the face of the knight, that he had
not freed Eva or the sweet Zosia from Pagan captivity.
Basia bewailed the fate of the two ladies with bitter tears,
for they were to be looked·on as lost. Sold, it was
unknown to whom, they might be taken from the markets
of Stambul to Asia Minor, to islands under Turkish rule,
or to Egypt, and be confined there in harems ; hence it was
not only impossible to ransom them, but even to learn
where they were.

Basia wept; the wise Pan Zagloba wept; so did Pan
Mushalski, the incomparable bowman. Pan Adam alone had
dry eyes, for tears had failed him already. But when he
told how he had gone down to Tykich near the Danube,
had cut to pieces the Lithuanian Tartars almost at the
side of the horde and the Sultan, and had seized Azya,
the evil enemy, the two old men rattled their sabres, and
said, —

"Give him hither ! Here, in Hreptyoff, should he die."

"Not in Hreptyoff," said Pan Adam. "Rashkoff is the
place of his punishment, that is the place where he should
die ; and the sergeant here found a torment for him which
was not easy."

He described then the death which Azya had died, and
they listened with terror, but without pity.

"That the Lord God pursues crime is known," said
Zagloba at last ; "but it is a wonder that the Devil protects
his servants so poorly."

Basia sighed piously, raised her eyes, and after a short
meditation answered, —

"He does, for he lacks strength to stand against the
might of God."

"Oh, you have said it," remarked Pan Mushalski, "for
if, which God forfend, the Devil were mightier than the
Lord, all justice, and with it the Commonwealth, would
vanish."

"I am not afraid of the Turks, — first, because they are
such sons, and secondly, they are children of Belial,"
answered Zagloba.

All were silent for a while. Pan Adam sat on the bench

with his palms on his knees, looking at the floor with glassy eyes.

"It must have been some consolation," said Pan Mushalski, turning to him; "it is a great solace to accomplish a proper vengeance."

"Tell us, has it consoled you really? Do you feel better now?" asked Basia, with a voice full of pity.

The giant was silent for a time, as if struggling with his own thoughts; at last he said, as if in great wonderment, and so quietly that he was almost whispering, —

"Imagine to yourself, as God is dear to me, I thought that I should feel better if I were to destroy him. I saw him on the stake, I saw him when his eye was bored out, I said to myself that I felt better; but it is not true, not true."

Here Pan Adam embraced his hapless head with his hands, and said through his set teeth, —

"It was better for him on the stake, better with the auger in his eye, better with fire on his hands, than for me with that which is sitting within me, which is thinking and remembering within me. Death is my one consolation; death, death, that is the truth."

Hearing this, Basia's valiant and soldier heart rose quickly, and putting her hands on the head of the unfortunate man, she said, —

"God grant it to you at Kamenyets; for you say truly, it is the one consolation."

He closed his eyes then, and began to repeat, —

"Oh, that is true, that is true; God repay you!"

That same afternoon they all started for Kamenyets.

Basia, after she had passed the gate, looked around long and long at that fortalice, gleaming in the light of the evening; at last, signing herself with the holy cross, she said, —

"God grant that it come to us to return to thee, dear Hreptyoff, with Michael! God grant that nothing worse be waiting for us!"

And two tears rolled down her rosy face. A peculiar strange grief pressed all hearts; and they moved forward in silence. Meanwhile darkness came.

They went slowly toward Kamenyets, for the tabor advanced slowly. In it went wagons, herds of horses, bullocks, buffaloes, camels; army servants watched over the herds. Some of the servants and soldiers had married

in Hreptyoff, hence there was not a lack of women in the
tabor. There were as many troops as under Pan Adam,
and besides, two hundred Hungarian infantry, which body
the little knight had equipped at his own cost, and had
trained. Basia was their patron; and Kalushevski, a good
officer, led them. There were no real Hungarians in that
infantry, which was called Hungarian only because it had
a Hungarian uniform. The non-commissioned officers were
"veterans," soldiers of the dragoons; but the ranks were
composed of robber bands which had been sentenced to
the rope. Life was granted the men on condition that they
would serve in the infantry, and with loyalty and bravery
efface their past sins. There were not wanting among
them also volunteers who had left their ravines, meadows,
and similar robber haunts, preferring to join the service of
the "Little Falcon" of Hreptyoff rather than feel his sword
hanging over their heads. These men were not over-tract-
able, and not sufficiently trained yet; but they were brave,
accustomed to hardships, dangers, and bloodshed. Basia
had an uncommon love for this infantry, as for Michael's
child; and in the wild hearts of those warriors was soon
born an attachment for the wonderful and kind lady. Now
they marched around her carriage with muskets on their
shoulders and sabres at their sides, proud to guard the
lady, ready to defend her madly in case any chambul
should bar their way.

But the road was still free, for Pan Michael had more
foresight than others, and, besides, he had too much love for
his wife to expose her to danger through delay. The journey
was made, therefore, quietly. Leaving Hreptyoff in the
afternoon, they journeyed till evening, then all night; the
next day in the afternoon they saw the high cliffs of
Kamenyets.

At sight of them, and at sight of the bastions of the
fort adorning the summits of the cliffs, great consolation
entered their hearts at once; for it seemed to them impossible that any hand but God's own could break that eagle's
nest on the summit of projecting cliffs surrounded by the
loop of the river. It was a summer day and wonderful.
The towers of the churches looking out from behind the
cliffs were gleaming like gigantic lights; peace, calm, and
gladness were on that serene region.

"Basia," said Zagloba, "more than once the Pagans have
gnawed those walls, and they have always broken their

teeth on them. Ha! how many times have I myself seen how they fled, holding themselves by the snout, for they were in pain. God grant it to be the same this time!"

"Surely it will," said the radiant Basia.

"One of their sultans, Osman, was here. It was — I remember the case as if to-day — in the year 1621. He came, the pig's blood, just over there from that side of the Smotrych, from Hotin, stared, opened his mouth, looked and looked; at last he asked, 'But who fortified that place so?' 'The Lord God,' answered the vizir. 'Then let the Lord God take it, for I am not a fool!' And he turned back on the spot."

"Indeed, they turned back quickly!" put in Pan Mushalski.

"They turned back quickly," said Zagloba; "for we touched them up in the flanks with spears, and afterward the knighthood bore me on their hands to Pan Lubomirski."

"Then were you at Hotin?" asked the incomparable bowman. "Belief fails me, when I think where have you not been, and what have you not done."

Zagloba was offended somewhat and said: "Not only was I there, but I received a wound, which I can show to your eyes, if you are so curious; I can show it directly, but at one side, for it does not become me to boast of it in the presence of Pani Volodyovski."

The famous bowman knew at once that Zagloba was making sport of him; and as he did not feel himself competent to overcome the old noble by wit, he inquired no further, and turned the conversation.

"What you say is true," said he: "when a man is far away, and hears people saying, 'Kamenyets is not supplied, Kamenyets will fall,' terror seizes him; but when he sees Kamenyets, consolation comes to him."

"And besides, Michael will be in Kamenyets," cried Basia.

"And maybe Pan Sobieski will send succor."

"Praise be to God! it is not so ill with us, not so ill. It has been worse, and we did not yield."

"Though it were worse, the point is in this, not to lose courage. They have not devoured us, and they will not while our courage holds out," said Zagloba.

Under the influence of these cheering thoughts they grew silent. But Pan Adam rode up suddenly to Basia;

his countenance, usually threatening and gloomy, was now smiling and calm. He had fixed his gazing eyes with devotion on Kamenyets bathed in sunbeams, and smiled without ceasing.

The two knights and Basia looked at him with wonder, for they could not understand how the sight of that fortress had taken every weight from his soul with such suddenness; but he said,—

"Praise be to the name of the Lord! there was a world of suffering, but now gladness is near me!" Here he turned to Basia. "They are both with the mayor, Tomashevich; and it is well that they have hidden there, for in such a fortress that robber can do nothing to them."

"Of whom are you speaking?" asked Basia, in terror.

"Of Zosia and Eva."

"God give you aid!" cried Zagloba; "do not give way to the Devil."

But Pan Adam continued, "And what they say of my father, that Azya killed him, is not true either."

"His mind is disturbed," whispered Pan Mushalski.

"Permit me," said Pan Adam again; "I will hurry on in advance. I am so long without seeing them that I yearn for them."

When he had said this he began to nod his gigantic head toward both sides; then he pressed his horse with his heels, and moved on. Pan Mushalski, beckoning to a number of dragoons, followed him, so as to keep an eye on the madman. Basia hid her rosy face in her hands, and soon hot tears began to flow through her fingers.

"He was as good as gold, but such misfortunes surpass human power. Besides, the soul is not revived by mere vengeance."

Kamenyets was seething with preparations for defence. On the walls, in the old castle and at the gates, especially at the Roman gates, "nations" inhabiting the town were laboring under their mayors, among whom the Pole Tomashevich took the first place, and that because of his great daring and his rare skill in handling cannon. At the same time Poles, Russians, Armenians, Jews, and Gypsies, working with spades and pickaxes, vied with one another. Officers of various regiments were overseers of the work; sergeants and soldiers assisted the citizens; even nobles went to work, forgetting that God had created their hands for the sabre alone, giving all other work to people of

insignificant estate. Pan Humyetski, the banneret of
Podolia, gave an example himself which roused tears, for
he brought stones with his own hands in a wheelbarrow.
The work was seething in the town and in the castle.
Among the crowds the Dominicans, the Jesuits, the brethren of Saint Francis, and the Carmelites circled about among
the crowds, blessing the efforts of people. Women brought
food and drink to those laboring; beautiful Armenian
women, the wives and daughters of rich merchants, and
Jewesses from Karvaseri, Jvanyets, Zinkovtsi, Dunaigrod,
attracted the eyes of the soldiers.

But the entrance of Basia arrested the attention of the
throngs more than all. There were surely many women of
more distinction in Kamenyets, but none whose husband
was covered with more military glory. They had heard
also in Kamenyets of Pani Volodyovski herself, as of a
valiant lady who feared not to dwell on a watch-tower in
the Wilderness among wild people, who went on expeditions
with her husband, and who, when carried away by a Tartar,
had been able to overcome him and escape safely from his
robber hands. Her fame, therefore, was immense. But those
who did not know her, and had not seen her hitherto,
imagined that she must be some giantess, breaking horseshoes and crushing armor. What was their astonishment
when they saw a small, rosy, half childlike face!

"Is that Pani Volodyovski herself, or only her little
daughter?" asked people in the crowds. "Herself,"
answered those who knew her. Then admiration seized
citizens, women, priests, the army. They looked with no
-less wonder on the invincible garrison of Hreptyoff, on the
dragoons, among whom Pan Adam rode calmly, smiling
with wandering eyes, and on the terrible faces of the bandits turned into Hungarian infantry. But there marched
with Basia a few hundred men who were worthy of praise,
soldiers by trade; courage came therefore to the towns-
people. "That is no common power; they will look boldly
into the eyes of the Turks," cried the people in the crowd.
Some of the citizens, and even of the soldiers, especially in
the regiment of Bishop Trebitski, which regiment had come
recently to Kamenyets, thought that Pan Michael himself
was in the retinue, therefore they raised cries, —

"Long live Pan Volodyovski!"

"Long live our defender! The most famous cavalier!"

"Vivat Volodyovski! vivat!"

Basia listened, and her heart rose; for nothing can be dearer to a woman than the fame of her husband, especially when it is sounding in the mouths of people in a great city. "There are so many knights here," thought Basia, "and still they do not shout to any but my Michael." And she wanted to shout herself in the chorus, "Vivat Volodyovski!" but Zagloba told her that she should bear herself like a person of distinction, and bow on both sides, as queens do when they are entering a capital. And he, too, saluted, now with his cap, now with his hand; and when acquaintances began to cry "vivat" in his honor, he answered to the crowds, —

"Gracious gentlemen, he who endured Zbaraj will hold out in Kamenyets!"

According to Pan Michael's instructions, the retinue went to the newly built cloister of the Dominican nuns. The little knight had his own house in Kamenyets; but since the cloister was in a retired place which cannon-balls could hardly reach, he preferred to place his dear Basia there, all the more since he expected a good reception as a benefactor of the cloister. In fact, the abbess, Mother Victoria, the daughter of Stefan Pototski, voevoda of Bratslav, received Basia with open arms. From the embraces of the abbess she went at once to others, and greatly beloved ones, — to those of her aunt, Pani Makovetski, whom she had not seen for some years. Both women wept; and Pan Makovetski, whose favorite Basia had always been, wept too. Barely had they dried these tears of tenderness when in rushed Krysia Ketling, and new greetings began; then Basia was surrounded by the nuns and noble women, known and unknown, — Pani Bogush, Pani Stanislavski, Pani Kalinovski, Pani Hotsimirski, Pani Humyetski, the wife of the banneret of Podolia, a great cavalier. Some, like Pani Bogush, inquired about their husbands; others asked what Basia thought of the Turkish invasion, and whether, in her opinion, Kamenyets would hold out. Basia saw with great delight that they looked on her as having some military authority, and expected consolation from her lips. Therefore she was not niggardly in giving.

"No one says," replied she, "that we cannot hold out against the Turks. Michael will be here to-day or to-morrow, at furthest in a couple of days; and when he occupies himself with the defences, you ladies may sleep quietly. Besides, the fortress is tremendously strong; in this matter, thank God, I have some knowledge."

The confidence of Basia poured consolation into the hearts of the women; they were reassured specially by the promise of Pan Michael's arrival. Indeed, his name was so respected that, though it was evening, officers of the place began to come at once with greetings to Basia. After the first salutations, each inquired when the little knight would come, and if really he intended to shut himself up in Kamenyets. Basia received only Major Kvasibrotski, who led the infantry of the Bishop of Cracow; the secretary, Revuski, who succeeded Pan Lanchynski, or rather, occupied his place, was at the head of the regiment, and Ketling. The doors were not open to others that day, for the lady was road-weary, and, besides, she had to occupy herself with Pan Adam. That unfortunate young man had fallen from his horse before the very cloister, and was carried to a cell in unconsciousness. They sent at once for the doctor, the same who had cured Basia at Hreptyoff. The doctor declared that there was a serious disease of the brain, and gave little hope of Pan Adam's recovery.

Basia, Pan Mushalski, and Zagloba talked till late in the evening about that event, and pondered over the unhappy lot of the knight.

"The doctor told me," said Zagloba, "that if he recovers and is bled copiously, his mind will not be disturbed, and he will bear misfortune with a lighter heart."

"There is no consolation for him now," said Basia.

"Often it would be better for a man not to have memory," remarked Pan Mushalski; "but even animals are not free from it."

Here the old man called the famous bowman to account for that remark.

"If you had no memory you could n't go to confession," said he; "and you would be the same as a Lutheran, deserving hell-fire. Father Kaminski has warned you already against blasphemy; but say the Lord's prayer to a wolf, and the wolf would rather be eating a sheep."

"What sort of wolf am I?" asked the famous bowman. "There was Azya; he was a wolf."

"Did n't I say that?" asked Zagloba. "Who was the first to say, that's a wolf?"

"Pan Adam told me," said Basia, "that day and night he hears Eva and Zosia calling to him 'save;' and how can he save? It had to end in sickness, for no man can endure such pain. He could survive their death; he cannot survive their shame."

"He is lying now like a block of wood; he knows nothing of God's world," said Pan Mushalski; "and it is a pity, for in battle he was splendid."

Further conversation was interrupted by a servant, who announced that there was a great noise in the town, for the people were assembling to look at the starosta of Podolia, who was just making his entrance with a considerable escort and some tens of infantry.

"The command belongs to him," said Zagloba. "It is valiant on the part of Pan Pototski to prefer this to another place, but as of old I would that he were not here. He is opposed to the hetman; he did not believe in the war; and now who knows whether it will not come to him to lay down his head."

"Perhaps other Pototskis will march in after him," said Pan Mushalski.

"It is evident that the Turks are not distant," answered Zagloba. "In the name of the Father, Son, and Holy Ghost, God grant the starosta of Podolia to be a second Yeremi, and Kamenyets a second Zbaraj!"

"It must be; if not, we shall die first," said a voice at the threshold.

Basia sprang up at the sound of that voice, and crying "Michael!" threw herself into the little knight's arms.

Pan Michael brought from the field much important news, which he related to his wife in the quiet cell before he communicated it to the military council. He had destroyed utterly a number of smaller chambuls, and had whirled around the Crimean camp and that of Doroshenko with great glory to himself. He had brought also some tens of prisoners, from whom they might select informants as to the power of the Khan and Doroshenko.

But other men had less success. The starosta of Podlyasye, at the head of considerable forces, was destroyed in a murderous battle; Motovidlo was beaten by Krychinski, who pursued him to the Wallachian trail, with the aid of the Belgrod horde and those Tartars who survived Pan Adam's victory at Tykich. Before coming to Kamenyets, Pan Michael turned aside to Hreptyoff, wishing, as he said, to look again on that scene of his happiness.

"I was there," said he, "right after your departure; the place had not grown cold yet, and I might have come up with you easily, but I crossed over to the Moldavian bank at Ushytsa, to put my ear toward the steppe. Some chambuls have crossed already, but are afraid that if they come out at Pokuta, they will strike on people unexpectedly. Others are moving in front of the Turkish army, and will be here soon. There will be a siege, my dove, — there is no help for it; but we will not surrender, for here every one is defending not only the country, but his own private property."

When he had said this, he took his wife by the shoulders, and kissed her on the cheeks; that day they talked no more with each other.

Next morning Pan Michael repeated his news at Bishop Lantskoronski's before the council of war, which, besides the bishop, was formed of Pan Mikolai Pototski, starosta of Podolia, Pan Lantskoronski, chamberlain of Podolia, Pan Revuski, secretary of Podolia, Pan Humyetski, Ketling, Makovetski, Major Kvasibrotski, and a number of other officers. To begin with, Volodyovski was not pleased with the declaration of Pan Pototski, that he would not take the command on himself, but confide it to a council.

"In sudden emergencies, there must be one head and one will," said the little knight. "At Zbaraj there were three men to whom command belonged by office, still they gave it to Prince Yeremi, judging rightly that in danger it is better to obey one."

These words were without effect. In vain did the learned Ketling cite, as an example, the Romans, who, being the greatest warriors in the world, invented dictatorship. Bishop Lantskoronski, who did not like Ketling, — for he had fixed in his mind, it is unknown why, that, being a Scot by origin, Ketling must be a heretic at the bottom of his soul, — retorted that the Poles did not need to learn history from immigrants; they had their own mind too, and did not need to imitate the Romans, to whom they were not inferior in bravery and eloquence, or if they were, it was very little. "As there is more blaze," said the bishop, "from an armful of wood than from one stick, so there is more watchfulness in many heads than in one." Herewith he praised the "modesty" of Pan Pototski, though others understood it to be rather fear of responsibility, and from himself he advised negotiations.

When this word was uttered, the soldiers sprang from their seats as if scalded. Pan Michael, Ketling, Makovetski, Kvasibrotski, set their teeth and touched their sabres. "But I believe," said voices, "that we did not

come here for negotiations!" "His robe protects the nego-
tiator!" cried Kvasibrotski; "the church is your place,
not this council!" and there was an uproar.

Thereupon the bishop rose and said in a loud voice: "I
should be the first to give my life for the church and
my flock; but if I have mentioned negotiations and wish to
temporize, God be my judge, it is not because I wish
to surrender the fortress, but to win time for the hetman
to collect reinforcements. The name of Pan Sobieski is
terrible to the Pagans; and though he has not forces sufficient, still let the report go abroad that he is advancing,
and the Mussulman will leave Kamenyets soon enough."
And since he spoke so powerfully, all were silent; some
were even rejoiced, seeing that the bishop had not surrender in his mind.

Pan Michael spoke next: "The enemy, before he besieges
Kamenyets, must crush Jvanyets, for he cannot leave a
defensive castle behind his shoulders. Therefore, with
permission of the starosta, I will undertake to enclose
myself in Jvanyets, and hold it during the time which
the bishop wishes to gain through negotiations. I will
take trusty men with me; and Jvanyets will last while
my life lasts."

Whereupon all cried out: "Impossible! You are needed
here! Without you the citizens will lose courage, and
the soldiers will not fight with such willingness. In no
way is it possible! Who has more experience? Who
passed through Zbaraj? And when it comes to sorties,
who will lead the men? You would be destroyed in
Jvanyets, and we should be destroyed here without you."

"The command has disposal of me," answered Pan
Michael.

"Send to Jvanyets some daring young man, who would
be my assistant," said the chamberlain of Podolia.

"Let Novoveski go!" said a number of voices.

"Novoveski cannot go, for his head is burning," answered Pan Michael; "he is lying on his bed, and knows
nothing of God's world."

"Meanwhile, let us decide," said the bishop, "where
each is to have his place, and what gate he is to defend."

All eyes were turned to the starosta, who said: "Before I
issue the commands, I am glad to hear the opinions of
experienced soldiers; since Pan Volodyovski here is superior
in military experience, I call on him first."

Pan Michael advised, first of all, to put good garrisons in the castles before the town, for he thought that the main force of the enemy would be turned specially on them. Others followed his opinion. There were sixteen hundred men of infantry, and these were disposed in such manner that Pan Myslishevski occupied the right side of the castle; the left, Pan Humyetski, famous for his exploits at Hotin. Pan Michael took the most dangerous position on the side toward Hotin; lower down was placed Serdyuk's division. Major Kvasibrotski covered the side toward Zinkovtsi; the south was held by Pan Vansovich; and the side next the court by Captain Bukar, with Pan Krasinski's men. These were not volunteers indifferent in quality, but soldiers by profession, excellent, and in battle so firm that artillery fire was no more to them than the sun's heat to other men. Serving in the armies of the Commonwealth, which were always small in number, they were accustomed from youthful years to resist an enemy of ten times their force, and considered this as something natural. The general management of the artillery of the castle was under Ketling, who surpassed all in the art of aiming cannon. Chief command in the castle was to be with the little knight, with whom the starosta left the freedom of making sorties as often as there should be need and possibility.

These men, knowing now where each would stand, were rejoiced heartily, and raised a considerable shout, shaking their sabres at the same time. Thus they showed their willingness. Hearing this, the starosta said to his own soul, —

"I did not believe that we could defend ourselves, and I came here without faith, listening only to my conscience; who knows, however, but we may repulse the enemy with such soldiers? The glory will fall on me, and they will herald me as a second Yeremi; in such an event it may be that a fortunate star has brought me to this place."

And as before he had doubted of the defence, so now he doubted of the capture of Kamenyets; hence his courage increased, and he began to advise more readily the strengthening of the town.

It was decided to station Pan Makovetski at the Russian gate, in the town itself, with a handful of nobles, Polish towns-people, more enduring in battle than others, and with them a few tens of Armenians and Jews. The Lutsk

gate was confided to Pan Grodetski, with whom Pan Juk
and Pan Matchynski took command of artillery. The
guard of the square before the town-house was commanded
by Lukash Dzevanovski; Pan Hotsimirski had command of
the noisy Gypsies at the Russian gate. From the bridge
to the house of Pan Sinitski, the guards were commanded
by Pan Kazimir Humyetski. And farther on were to have
their quarters Pan Stanishevski, and at the Polish gate
Pan Martsin Bogush, and at the Spij bastion Pan Skar-
zinski, and Pan Yatskovski there at the side of the
Byaloblotski embrasures; Pan Dubravski and Pan Pye-
trashevski occupied the butcher's bastion. The grand
intrenchment of the town was given to Tomashevich, the
Polish mayor, the smaller to Pan Yatskovski; there was
an order to dig a third one, from which later a certain
Jew, a skilful gunner, annoyed the Turks greatly.

These arrangements made, all the council went to sup
with the starosta, who at that entertainment honored Pan
Michael particularly with place, wine, food, and conversation, foreseeing that for his action in the siege posterity
would add to the title of "Little Knight" that of "Hector
of Kamenyets." Volodyovski declared that he wished to
serve earnestly, and in view of that intended to make a
certain vow in the cathedral; hence he prayed the bishop
to let him make it on the morrow.

The bishop, seeing that public profit might come from
the vow, promised willingly.

Next morning there was a solemn service in the cathedral. Knights, nobles, soldiers, and common people heard
it with devotion and elevation of spirit. Pan Michael
and Ketling lay each in the form of a cross before the
altar; Krysia and Basia were kneeling near by beyond
the railing, weeping, for they knew that that vow might
bring danger to the lives of their husbands.

At the end of Mass, the bishop turned to the people with
the monstrance; then the little knight rose, and kneeling
on the steps of the altar, said with a moved but calm
voice, —

"Feeling deep gratitude for the special benefactions and
particular protection which I have received from the Lord
God the Most High, and from His only Son, I vow and
take oath that as He and His Son have aided me, so will I
to my last breath defend the Holy Cross. And since
command of the old castle is confided to me, while I am

alive and can move hands and feet, I will not admit to the castle the Pagan enemy, who live in vileness, nor will I leave the wall, nor will I raise a white rag, even should it come to me to be buried there under ruins. So help me God and the Holy Cross! Amen!"

A solemn silence reigned in the church; then the voice of Ketling was heard.

"I promise," said he, "for the particular benefactions which I have experienced in this fatherland, to defend the castle to the last drop of my blood, and to bury myself under its ruins, rather than let a foot of the enemy enter its walls. And as I take this oath with a clean heart and out of pure gratitude, so help me God and the Holy Cross! Amen!"

Here the bishop held down the monstrance, and gave it to Volodyovski to kiss, then to Ketling. At sight of this the numerous knights in the church raised a buzz. Voices were heard: "We will all swear!" "We will lie one upon another!" "This fortress will not fall!" "We will swear!" "Amen, amen, amen!" Sabres and rapiers came out with a gritting from the scabbard, and the church became bright from the steel. That gleam shone on threatening faces and glittering eyes; a great, indescribable enthusiasm seized the nobles, soldiers, and people. Then all the bells were sounded; the organ roared; the bishop intoned, "Sub Tuum præsidium;" a hundred voices thundered in answer; and thus they prayed for that fortress which was the watchtower of Christendom and the key of the Commonwealth.

At the conclusion of the service Ketling and Pan Michael went out of the church hand in hand. Blessings and praise were given them on the way, for no one doubted that they would die rather than surrender the castle. Not death, however, but victory and glory seemed to float over them; and it is likely that among all those people they alone knew how terrible the oath was with which they had bound themselves. Perhaps also two loving hearts had a presentiment of the destruction which was hanging over their heads, for neither Basia nor Krysia could gain self-composure; and when at last Pan Michael found himself in the cloister with his wife, she, choking from tears, and sobbing like a little child, nestled up to his breast, and said in a broken voice, —

"Remember — Michael — God keep misfortune from you — I — I — know not what — will become of me!"

And she began to tremble from emotion; the little knight was moved greatly too. After a time he said,—

"But, Basia, it was necessary."

"I would rather die!" said Basia.

Hearing this, the little knight's mustaches quivered more and more quickly, and he repeated a number of times,—

"Quiet, Basia, quiet." Then at last he said, to calm the woman loved above all,—

"And do you remember that when the Lord God brought you back to me, I said thus, 'Whatever return is proper, O Lord God, I promise Thee. After the war, if I am alive, I will build a chapel; but during the war I must do something noteworthy, so as not to feed Thee with ingratitude'? What is a castle? It is little for such a benefaction. The time has come. Is it proper that the Saviour should say to Himself, 'His promise is a plaything'? May the stones of the castle crush me before I break my word of a cavalier, given to God. It is necessary, Basia; and that is the whole thing. Let us trust in God, Basia."

CHAPTER LII.

THAT day Pan Michael went out with squadrons to assist Pan Vasilkovski, who had hastened on toward Hrynchuk, for news came that the Tartars had made an attack there, binding people, taking cattle, but not burning villages, so as not to rouse attention. Pan Vasilkovski soon scattered them, rescued the captives, and took prisoners. Pan Michael led these prisoners to Jvanyets, commissioning Pan Makovetski to torture them, and write down in order their confessions, so as to forward them to the hetman and the king. The Tartars confessed that, at command of the perkulab, they had crossed the boundary with Captain Styngan and Wallachians; but though burnt, they could not tell how far away the Sultan was at that time with all his forces, for, advancing in irregular bands, they did not maintain connection with the main army.

All, however, were at one in the statement that the Sultan had moved in force, that he was marching to the Commonwealth, and would be at Kamenyets soon. For the future defenders of Kamenyets there was nothing new in these confessions; but since in the king's palace they did not believe that there would be war, the chamberlain determined to send these prisoners, together with their statements, to Warsaw.

The scouting parties returned in good spirits from their first expedition. In the evening came the secretary of Habareskul, Pan Michael's Tartar brother, and the senior perkulab of Hotin. He brought no letters, for the perkulab was afraid to write; but he gave command to tell his brother Volodyovski, "the sight of his eye and the love of his heart," to be on his guard, and if Kamenyets had not troops enough for defence, to leave the town under some pretext, for the Sultan had been expected for two days with his whole force in Hotin.

Pan Michael sent his thanks to the perkulab, and rewarding the secretary, sent him home; he informed the commandants immediately of the approaching danger. Activity on works in the town was redoubled; Pan Hieronim

Lantskoronski moved without a moment's delay to his
Jvanyets, to have an eye on Hotin.

Some time passed in waiting; at last, on the second day
of August, the Sultan halted at Hotin. His regiments
spread out like a sea without shores; and at sight of the
last town lying within the Padishah's dominions, Allah!
Allah! was wrested from hundreds of thousands of throats.
On the other side of the Dniester lay the defenceless
Commonwealth, which those countless armies were to cover
like a deluge, or devour like a flame. Throngs of warriors,
unable to find places in the town, disposed themselves on
the fields, — on those same fields, where some tens of years
earlier, Polish sabres had scattered an equally numerous
army of the Prophet. It seemed now that the hour of
revenge had come; and no one in those wild legions, from
the Sultan to the camp servant, had a feeling that for the
Crescent those fields would be ill-omened a second time.
Hope, nay, even certainty of victory rejoiced every heart.
Janissaries and spahis, crowds of general militia from the
Balkans, from the mountains of Rhodope, from Rumelia,
from Pelion and Ossa, from Carmel and Lebanon, from the
deserts of Arabia, from the banks of the Tigris, from the
plains of the Nile, and the burning sands of Africa, giving
out wild shouts, prayed to be led at once to the " infidel
bank." But muezzins began to call from the minarets of
Hotin to prayer; therefore all were silent. A sea of heads
in turbans, caps, fezes, burnooses, kefis, and steel helmets
inclined toward the earth ; and through the fields went the
deep murmur of prayer, like the sound of countless swarms
of bees, and borne by the wind, it flew forward over the
Dniester toward the Commonwealth.

Then drums, trumpets, and pipes were heard, giving
notice of rest. Though the armies had marched slowly and
comfortably, the Padishah wished to give them, after the
long journey from Adrianople, a rest at the river. He performed ablutions himself in a clear spring flowing not far
from the town, and rode thence to the konak of Hotin;
but on the fields they began to pitch tents which soon
covered, as with snow, the immeasurable extent of the
country about.

The day was beautiful, and ended serenely. After the
last evening prayers, the camp went to rest. Thousands
and hundreds of thousands of fires were gleaming. From
the small castle opposite, in Jvanyets, men looked on the

light of these fires with alarm, for they were so wide-spread that the soldiers who went to reconnoitre said in their account, "It seemed to us that all Moldavia was under the fires." But as the bright moon rose higher in the starry sky, all died out save the watch-fires, the camp became quiet, and amid the silence of the night were heard only the neighing of horses and the bellowing of buffaloes, feeding on the meadows of Taraban.

But next morning, at daybreak, the Sultan commanded the janissaries and Tartars to cross the Dniester, and occupy Jvanyets, the town as well as the castle. The manful Pan Hieronim Lantskoronski did not wait behind the walls for them, but having at his side forty Tartars, eighty men of Kieff, and one squadron of his own, struck on the janissaries at the crossing; and in spite of a rattling fire from their muskets, he broke that splendid infantry, and they began to withdraw toward the river in disorder. But meanwhile, the chambul, reinforced by Lithuanian Tartars, who had crossed at the flank, broke into the town. Smoke and cries warned the brave chamberlain that the place was in the hands of the enemy. He gave command, therefore, to withdraw from the crossing, and succor the hapless inhabitants. The janissaries, being infantry, could not pursue, and he went at full speed to the rescue. He was just coming up, when, on a sudden, his own Tartars threw down their flag, and went over to the enemy. A moment of great peril followed. The chambul, aided by the traitors, and thinking that treason would bring confusion, struck hand to hand, with great force, on the chamberlain. Fortunately, the men of Kieff, roused by the example of their leader, gave violent resistance. The squadron broke the enemy, who were not in condition to meet regular Polish cavalry. The ground before the bridge was soon covered with corpses, especially of Lithuanian Tartars, who, more enduring than ordinary men of the horde, kept the field. Many of them were cut down in the streets later on. Lantskoronski, seeing that the janissaries were approaching from the water, sent to Kamenyets for succor, and withdrew behind the walls.

The Sultan had not thought of taking the castle of Jvanyets that day, thinking justly that he could crush it in the twinkle of an eye, at the general crossing of the armies. He wished only to occupy that point; and supposing the detachments which he sent to be amply sufficient, he sent no more, either of the janissaries or the horde. Those who

were on the other bank of the river occupied the place a
second time after the squadron had withdrawn behind the
walls.   They did not burn the town, so that it might serve
in future as a refuge for their own, or for other detachments, and began to work in it with sabres and daggers.
The janissaries seized young women in soldier fashion; the
husbands and children they cut down with axes; the
Tartars were occupied in taking plunder.

At that time the Poles saw from the bastion of the castle
that cavalry was approaching from the direction of Kamenyets.   Hearing this, Lantskoronski went out on the bastion
himself, with a field-glass, and looked long and carefully.
At last he said, —

"That is light cavalry from the Hreptyoff garrison; the
same cavalry with which Vasilkovski went to Hrynchuk.
Clearly they have sent him out this time.   I see volunteers.
It must be Humyetski!

"Praise be to God!" cried he, after a while.   "Volodyovski himself is there, for I see dragoons.   Gracious
gentlemen, let us rush out again from behind the walls, and
with God's help, we will drive the enemy, not only from
the town, but from this side of the river."

Then he ran down with what breath he had, to draw up
his men of Kieff and the squadron.   Meanwhile the Tartars
first in the town saw the approaching squadron, and shouting shrilly, "Allah!" began to gather in a chambul.   Drums
and whistles were heard in all the streets.   The janissaries
stood in order with that quickness in which few infantry on
earth could compare with them.

The chambul flew out of the place as if blown by a whirlwind, and struck the light squadron.   The chambul itself,
not counting the Lithuanian Tartars, whom Lantskoronski
had injured considerably, was three times more numerous
than the garrison of Jvanyets and the approaching squadrons
of reinforcement, hence it did not hesitate to spring on Pan
Vasilkovski; but Pan Vasilkovski, a young, irrepressible
man, who hurled himself against every danger with as much
eagerness as blindness, commanded his soldiers to go at
the highest speed, and flew on like a column of wind, not
even observing the number of the enemy.   Such daring
troubled the Tartars, who had no liking whatever for hand-
to-hand combat.   Notwithstanding the shouting of murzas
riding in the rear, the shrill whistle of pipes, and the
roaring sound of drums calling to "kesim," — that is, to

hewing heads from unbelievers, — they began to rein in, and hold back their horses. Evidently the hearts grew faint in them every moment, as did also their eagerness. Finally, at the distance of a bow-shot from the squadron, they opened on two sides, and sent a shower of arrows at the on-rushing cavalry.

Pan Vasilkovski, knowing nothing of the janissaries, who had formed beyond the houses toward the river, rushed with undiminished speed behind the Tartars, or rather behind one half the chambul. He came up, closed, and fell to slashing down those who, having inferior horses, could not flee quickly. The second half of the chambul turned then, wishing to surround him; but at that moment the volunteers rushed up, and the chamberlain came with his men of Kieff. The Tartars, pressed on so many sides, scattered like sand, and then began a rushing about, — that is, the pursuit of a group by a group, of a man by a man, — in which many of the horde fell, especially by the hand of Pan Vasilkovski, who struck blindly at whole crowds, just as a lark-falcon strikes sparrows or bunting.

But Pan Michael, a cool and keen soldier, did not let the dragoons out of his hand. Like a hunter who holds trained, eager dogs in strong leashes, not letting them go at a common beast, but only when he sees the flashing eyes and white teeth of a savage old boar, so the little knight, despising the fickle horde, was watching to see if spahis, janissaries, or some other chosen cavalry were not behind them. -

Pan Lantskoronski rushed to him with his men of Kieff.

"My benefactor," cried he, "the janissaries are moving toward the river; let us press them!"

Pan Michael drew his rapier and commanded, "Forward!"

Each dragoon drew in his reins, so as to have his horse in hand; then the rank bent a little, and moved forward as regularly as if on parade. They went first at a trot, then at a gallop, but did not let their horses go yet at highest speed. Only when they had passed the houses built toward the water, east of the castle, did they see the white felt caps of the janissaries, and know that they had to do not with volunteer, but with regular janissaries.

"Strike!" cried Volodyovski.

The horses stretched themselves, almost rubbing the

29

ground with their bellies, and hurled back lumps of hard earth with their hoofs.

The janissaries, not knowing what power was approaching to the succor of Jvanyets, were really withdrawing toward the river. One detachment, numbering two hundred and some tens of men, was already at the bank, and its first ranks were stepping onto scows; another detachment of equal force was going quickly, but in perfect order. When they saw the approaching cavalry they halted, and in one instant turned their faces to the enemy. Their muskets were lowered in a line, and a salvo thundered as at a review. What is more, these hardened warriors, considering that their comrades at the shore would support them with musketry, not only did not retreat after the volley, but shouted, and following their own smoke, struck in fury with their sabres on the cavalry. That was daring of which the janissaries alone were capable, but for which they paid dearly, because the riders, unable to restrain the horses, even had they the wish, struck them as a hammer strikes, and breaking them in a moment, scattered destruction and terror. The first rank fell under the force of the blow, as grain under a whirlwind. It is true that many fell only from the impetus, and these, springing up, ran in disorder to the river, from which the second detachment gave fire repeatedly, aiming high, so as to strike the dragoons over the heads of their comrades.

After a while there was evident hesitation among the janissaries at the scows, and also uncertainty whether to embark or follow the example of the other detachment, and engage hand to hand with the cavalry. But they were restrained from the last step by the sight of fleeing groups, which the cavalry pushed with the breasts of horses, and slashed so terribly that its fury could only be compared with its skill. At times such a group, when too much pressed, turned in desperation and began to bite, as a beast at bay bites when it sees that there is no escape for it. But just then those who were standing at the bank could see as on their palms that it was impossible to meet that cavalry with cold weapons, so far superior were they in the use of them The defenders were cut with such regularity and swiftness that the eye could not follow the motion of the sabres. As when men of a good household, shelling peas well dried, strike industriously and quickly on the threshing-floor, so that the whole barn is thundering with the noise of the blows and the kernels are jumping toward every side, so did the whole river-bank thunder with sabre-blows, and the groups of janissaries, slashed without mercy, sprang hither and thither in every direction.

Pan Vasilkovski hurled himself forward at the head of this cavalry, caring nothing for his own life. But as a trained reaper surpasses a young fellow much stronger than he, but less skilled at the sickle,— for when the young man is toiling, and streams of sweat cover him, the other goes forward constantly, cutting down the grain evenly before him,— so did Pan Michael surpass the wild youth Vasilkovski. Before striking the janissaries he let the dragoons go ahead, and remained himself in the rear somewhat, to watch the whole battle. Standing thus at a distance, he looked carefully, but every little while he rushed into the conflict, struck, directed, then again let the battle push away from him; again he looked, again he struck. As usual in a battle with infantry, so it happened then, that the cavalry in rushing on passed the fugitives. A number of these, not having before them a road to the river, returned in flight to the town, so as to hide in the sunflowers growing in front of the houses; but Pan Michael saw them. He came up with the first two, and distributed two light blows between them; they fell at once, and digging the earth with their heels, sent forth their souls with their blood through the open wounds. Seeing this, a third fired at the little knight from a janissary musket, and missed; but the little knight struck him with his sword-edge between nose and mouth, and this deprived him of precious life. Then, without loitering, Pan Michael sprang after the others; and not so quickly does a village youth gather mushrooms growing in a bunch, as he gathered those men before they ran to the sunflowers. Only the last two did soldiers of Jvanyets seize; the little knight gave command to keep these two alive.

When he had warmed himself a little, and saw that the janissaries were hotly pressed at the river, he sprang into the thick of the battle, and coming up with the dragoons, began real labor. Now he struck in front, now he turned to the right or the left, gave a thrust with his blade and looked no farther; each time a white cap fell to the ground. The janissaries began to crowd from before him with an outcry; he redoubled the swiftness of his blows; and though he remained calm himself, no eye could follow the movements of his sabre, and know when he would strike or when he would thrust, for his sabre described one bright circle around him.

Pan Lantskoronski, who had long heard of him as a master above masters, but had not seen him hitherto in action, stopped fighting and looked on with amazement; unable to believe his own eyes, he could not think that one man, though a master, and famous, could accomplish so much. He seized his head, therefore, and his comrades around only heard him repeating continually, "As God lives, they have told little of him yet!" And others cried, "Look at him, for you will not see that again in this world!" But Pan Michael worked on.

The janissaries, pushed to the river, began now to crowd in disorder to the scows. Since there were scows enough, and fewer men were returning than had come, they took their places quickly and easily. Then the heavy oars moved, and between the janissaries and the bank was formed an interval of water which widened every instant. But from the scows guns began to thunder, whereupon the dragoons thundered in answer from their muskets; smoke rose over the water in cloudlets, then stretched out in long strips. The scows, and with them the janissaries, receded every moment. The dragoons, who held the field, raised a fierce shout, and threatening with their fists, called, —

"Ah, thou dog, off with thee! off with thee!"

Pan Lantskoronski, though the balls were plashing still, seized Pan Michael by the shoulders right at the bank.

"I did not believe my eyes," said he, "those, my benefactor, are wonders which deserve a golden pen!"

"Native ability and training," answered Pan Michael, "that's the whole matter! How many wars have I passed through?"

Then returning Lantskoronski's pressure, he freed himself, and looking at the bank, cried, —

"Look, your grace; you will see another power."

The chamberlain turned, and saw an officer drawing a bow on the bank. It was Pan Mushalski.

Hitherto the famous bowman had been struggling with others in hand-to-hand conflicts with the enemy; but now, when the janissaries had withdrawn to such a distance that bullets and pistol-balls could not reach them, he drew his bow, and standing on the bank at its highest point he tried the string first with his finger, when it twanged sharply; he placed on it the feathered arrow — and aimed.

At that moment Pan Michael and Lantskoronski looked at him. It was a beautiful picture. The bowman was sitting on his horse; he held his left hand out straight before him, in it the bow, as if in a vice. The right hand he drew with increasing force to the nipple of his breast, till the veins were swelling on his forehead, and he aimed carefully. In the distance were visible, under a cloud of smoke, a number of scows moving on the river, which was very high, from snow melting on the mountains, and was so transparent that the scows and the janissaries sitting on them were reflected in the water. Pistols on the bank were silent; eyes were turned on Pan Mushalski, or looked in the direction in which his murderous arrow was to go.

Now the string sounded loudly, and the feathered arrow left the bow. No eye could catch its flight; but all saw perfectly how a sturdy janissary, standing at an oar, threw out his arms on a sudden, and turning on the spot, dropped into the river. The transparent surface spurted up from his weight; and Pan Mushalski said, —

"For thee, Didyuk." Then he sought another arrow. "In honor of the hetman," said he to his comrades. They held their breath; after a while the air whistled again, and a second janissary fell on the scow.

On all the scows the oars began to move more quickly; they struck the clear river vigorously; but the famous bowman turned with a smile to the little knight, —

"In honor of the worthy wife of your grace!"

A third time the bow was stretched; a third time he sent out a bitter arrow; and a third time it sank half its shaft's length in the body of a man. A shout of triumph thundered on the bank, a shout of rage from the scows. Then Pan Mushalski withdrew; and after him followed other victors of the day, and went to the town.

While returning, they looked with pleasure on the harvest of that day. Few of the horde had perished, for they had not fought well even once; and put to flight, they recrossed the river quickly. But the janissaries lay to the number of some tens of men, like bundles of firmly bound grain. A few were struggling yet, but all had been stripped by the servants of the chamberlain. Looking at them, Pan Michael said, —

"Brave infantry! the men move to the conflict like wild

boars; but they do not know beyond half what the Swedes do."

"They fired as a man would crack nuts," said the chamberlain.

"That came of itself, not through training, for they have no general training. They were of the Sultan's guard, and they are disciplined in some fashion; besides these there are irregular janissaries, considerably inferior."

"We have given them a keepsake! God is gracious, that we begin the war with such a noteworthy victory."

But the experienced Pan Michael had another opinion.

"This is a small victory, insignificant," said he. "It is good to raise courage in men without training and in towns-people, but will have no result."

"But do you think courage will not break in the Pagans?"

"In the Pagans courage will not break," said Pan Michael.

Thus conversing, they reached Jvanyets, where the people gave them the two captured janissaries who had tried to hide from Pan Michael in the sunflowers.

One was wounded somewhat, the other perfectly well and full of wild courage. When he reached the castle, the little knight, who understood Turkish well, though he did not speak it fluently, asked Pan Makovetski to question the man. Pan Makovetski asked if the Sultan was in Hotin himself, and if he would come soon to Kamenyets.

The Turk answered clearly, but insolently, —

"The Padishah is present himself. They said in the camp that to-morrow Halil Pasha and Murad Pasha would cross, taking engineers with them. To-morrow, or after to-morrow, the hour of destruction will come on you."

Here the prisoner put his hands on his hips, and, confident in the terror of the Sultan's name, continued, —

"Mad Poles! how did you dare at the side of the Sultan to fall on his people and strike them? Do you think that hard punishment will miss you? Can that little castle protect you? What will you be in a few days but captives? What are you this day but dogs springing in the face of your master?"

Pan Makovetski wrote down everything carefully; but Pan Michael, wishing to temper the insolence of the prisoner, struck him on the face at the last words. The Turk was confused, and gained respect for the little knight straight-way, and in general began to express himself more decently.

When the examination was over, and they brought him to the hall, Pan Michael said, —

"It is necessary to send these prisoners and their confession on a gallop to Warsaw, for at the king's court they do not believe yet that there will be war."

"And what do you think, gentlemen, did that prisoner tell the truth, or did he lie altogether?"

"If it please you, gentlemen," said Volodyovski, "it is possible to scorch his heels. I have a sergeant who executed Azya, the son of Tugai Bey, and who in these matters is *exquisitissimus*; but, to my thinking, the janissary has told the truth in everything. The crossing will begin soon; we cannot stop it, — no! even if there were a hundred times as many of us. Therefore nothing is left but to assemble, and go to Kamenyets with the news."

"I have done so well at Jvanyets that I would shut myself up in the castle with pleasure," said the chamberlain, "were I sure that you would come from time to time with succor from Kamenyets. After that, let happen what would!"

"They have two hundred cannon," said Pan Michael; "and if they bring over two heavy guns, this castle will not hold out one day. I too wished to shut myself up in it, but now I know that to be useless."

Others agreed with the little knight. Pan Lantskoronski, as if to show courage, insisted for a time yet on staying in Jvanyets; but he was too experienced a soldier not to see that Volodyovski was right. At last he was interrupted by Pan Vasilkovski, who, coming from the field, rushed in quickly.

"Gracious gentlemen," said he, "the river is not to be seen; the whole Dneister is covered with rafts."

"Are they crossing?" inquired all at once.

"They are, as true as life! The Turks are on the rafts, and the chambuls in the ford, the men holding the horses' tails."

Pan Lantskoronski hesitated no longer; he gave orders at once to sink the old howitzer, and either to hide the other things, or take them to Kamenyets. Pan Michael sprang to his horse, and went with his men to a distant height to look at the crossing.

Halil Pasha and Murad Pasha were crossing indeed. As far as the eye reached, it saw scows and rafts, pushed forward by oars, with measured movement, in the clear water.

Janissaries and spahis were moving together in great numbers; vessels for crossing had been prepared at Hotin a long time. Besides, great masses of troops were standing on the shore at a distance. Pan Michael supposed that they would build a bridge; but the Sultan had not moved his main force yet. Meanwhile Pan Lantskoronski came up with his men, and they marched toward Kamenyets with the little knight. Pan Pototski was waiting in the town for them. His quarters were filled, with higher officers; and before his quarters both sexes were assembled, unquiet, careworn, curious.

"The enemy is crossing, and Jvanyets is occupied!" said the little knight.

"The works are finished, and we are waiting," answered Pan Pototski.

The news went to the crowd, who began to roar like a river.

"To the gates! to the gates!" was heard through the town. "The enemy is in Jvanyets!" Men and women ran to the bastions, expecting to see the enemy; but the soldiers would not let them go to the places appointed for service.

"Go to your houses!" cried they to the crowds; "you will hinder the defence. Soon will your wives see the Turks near at hand."

Moreover, there was no alarm in the town, for already news had gone around of the victory of that day, and news naturally exaggerated. The soldiers told wonders of the meeting.

"Pan Volodyovski defeated the janissaries, the Sultan's own guard," repeated all mouths. "It is not for Pagans to measure strength with Pan Volodyovski. He cut down the pasha himself. The Devil is not so terrible as he is painted! And they did not withstand our troops. Good for you, dog-brothers! Destruction to you and your Sultan!"

The women showed themselves again at the intrenchments and bastions, but laden with flasks of gorailka, wine, and mead. This time they were received willingly; and gladness began among the soldiers. Pan Pototski did not oppose this; wishing to sustain courage in the men and cheerfulness, because there was an inexhaustible abundance of ammunition in the town and the castle, he permitted them to fire salvos, hoping that these sounds of joy would confuse the enemy not a little, should they hear them.

Pan Michael remained at the quarters of the starosta till nightfall, when he mounted his horse and was escaping in secret with his servant to the cloister, wishing to be with his wife as soon as possible. But his attempts came to nothing, for he was recognized, and dense crowds surrounded his horse. Shouts and vivats began. Mothers raised their children to him. "There he is! look at him, remember him!" repeated many voices. They admired him immensely; but people unacquainted with war were astonished at his diminutive stature. It could not find place in the heads of the towns-people that a man so small, and with such a pleasant face, could be the most terrible soldier of the Commonwealth, — a soldier whom none could resist. But he rode among the crowds, and smiled from time to time, for he was pleased. When he came to the cloister, he fell into the open arms of Basia.

She knew already of his deeds done that day and all his masterly blows; the chamberlain of Podolia had just left the cloister, and, as an eye-witness, had given her a detailed report. Basia, at the beginning of the narrative, called the women present in the cloister hence, — the abbess and the wives of Makovetski, Humyetski, Ketling, Hotsimirski; and as the chamberlain went on, she began to plume herself immensely before them. Pan Michael came just after the women had gone.

When greetings were finished, the wearied knight sat down to supper. Basia sat at his side, placed food on his plate, and poured mead into his goblet. He ate and drank willingly, for he had put almost nothing in his mouth the whole day. In the intervals he related something too; and Basia, listening with gleaming eyes, shook her head, according to custom, asking, —

"Ah, ha! Well? and what?"

"There are strong men among them, and very fierce; but it is hard to find a Turk who's a swordsman," said the little knight.

"Then I could meet any of them?"

"You might, only you will not, for I will not take you."

"Even once in my life! You know, Michael, when you go outside the walls, I am not even alarmed; I know that no one can reach you."

"But can't they shoot me?"

"Be quiet! Isn't there a Lord God? You will not let them cut you down, — that is the main thing."

"I will not let one or two slay me."

" Nor three, Michael, nor four."

" Nor four thousand," said Zagloba, mimicking her. " If
you knew, Michael, what she did when the chamberlain
was telling his story. I thought I should burst from
laughter. As God is dear to me! she snorted just like a
goat, and looked into the face of each woman in turn to
see if she was delighted in a fitting manner. In the end
I was afraid that the goat would go to butting, — no very
polite spectacle."

The little knight stretched himself after eating, for he
was considerably tired; then suddenly he drew Basia to him
and said, —

" My quarters in the castle are ready, but I do not wish
to return. I might stay here to-night, I suppose."

" As you like, Michael," said she, dropping her eyes.

" Ha!" said Zagloba, " they look on me here as a mush-
room, not a man, for the abbess invites me to live in the
nunnery. But I 'll pay her, my head on that point! Have
you seen how Pani Hotsimirski is ogling me? She is a
widow — very well — I won't tell you any more."

" I think I shall stay," said the little knight.

" If you will only rest well," said Basia.

" Why should n't he rest?" asked Zagloba.

" Because we shall talk, and talk, and talk."

Zagloba wishing to go to his own room, turned to look
for his cap; at last, when he had found it, he put it on his
head and said, " You will not talk, and talk, and talk."
Then he went out.

CHAPTER LIII.

NEXT morning, at daybreak, the little knight went to Kuyahin and captured Buluk Pasha, — a notable warrior among the Turks. The whole day passed for him in labor on the field, a part of the night in counsel with Pan Pototski, and only at first cock-crow did he lay down his wearied head to sleep a little. But he was barely slumbering sweetly and deeply when the thunder of cannon roused him. The man Pyentka, from Jmud, a faithful servant of Pan Michael, almost a friend, came into the room.

"Your grace," said he, "the enemy is before the town."

"What guns are those?" asked the little knight.

"Our guns, frightening the Pagans. There is a considerable party driving off cattle from the field."

"Janissaries or cavalry?"

"Cavalry. Very black. Our side is frightening them with the Holy Cross; for who knows but they are devils?"

"Devils or no devils, we must be at them," said the little knight. "Go to the lady, and tell her that I am in the field. If she wishes to come to the castle to look out, she may, if she comes with Pan Zagloba, for I count most on his discretion."

Half an hour later Pan Michael rushed into the field at the head of dragoons and volunteer nobles, who calculated that it would be possible to exhibit themselves in skirmishing. From the old castle the cavalry were to be seen perfectly, in number about two thousand, composed in part of spahis, but mainly of the Egyptian guard of the Sultan. In this last served wealthy and generous mamelukes from the Nile. Their mail in gleaming scales, their bright kefis, woven with gold, on their heads, their white burnooses and their weapons set with diamonds, made them the most brilliant cavalry in the world. They were armed with darts, set on jointed staffs, and with swords and knives greatly curved. Sitting on horses as swift as the wind, they swept over the field like a rainbow-colored cloud, shouting, whirling, and winding between their fingers the deadly darts. The Poles in the castle could not look at them long enough.

Pan Michael pushed toward them with his cavalry. It was difficult, however, for both sides to meet with cold weapons, since the cannon of the castle restrained the Turks, and they were too numerous for the little knight to go to them, and have a trial beyond the reach of Polish cannon. For a time, however, both sides circled around at a distance, shaking their weapons and shouting loudly. But at last this empty threatening became clearly disagreeable to the fiery sons of the desert, for all at once single horse-men began to separate from the mass and advance, calling loudly on their opponents. Soon they scattered over the field, and glittered on it like flowers which the wind drives in various directions. Pan Michael looked at his own men.

"Gracious gentlemen," said he, "they are inviting us. Who will go to the skirmish?"

The fiery cavalier, Pan Vasilkovski, sprang out first; after him Pan Mushalski, the infallible bowman, but also in hand-to-hand conflict an excellent skirmisher; after these went Pan Myazga of the escutcheon Prus, who dur-ing the full speed of his horse could carry off a finger-ring on his lance; after Pan Myazga galloped Pan Teodor Paderevski, Pan Ozevich, Pan Shmlud-Plotski, Prince Ovsyani, and Pan Murkos-Sheluta, with a number of good cavaliers; and of the dragoons there went also a group, for the hope of rich plunder incited them, but more than all the peerless horses of the Arabs. At the head of the dragoons went the stern Lusnia; and gnawing his yellow mustache, he was choosing at a distance the wealthiest enemy.

The day was beautiful. They were perfectly visible; the cannon on the walls became silent one after another, till at last all firing had ceased, for the gunners were fear-ful of injuring some of their own men; they preferred also to look at the battle rather than fire at scattered skir-mishers. The two sides rode toward each other at a walk, without hastening, then at a trot, not in a line, but irregu-larly, as suited each man. At length, when they had ridden near to each other, they reined in their horses, and fell to abusing each other, so as to rouse anger and daring.

"You'll not grow fat with us, Pagan dogs!" cried the Poles. "Your vile Prophet will not protect you!"

The others cried in Turkish and Arabic. Many Poles knew both languages, for, like the celebrated bowman, many had gone through grievous captivity; therefore when Pagans blasphemed the Most Holy Lady with special insolence, anger raised the hair on the servants of Mary, and they urged on their horses, wishing to take revenge for the insult to her name.

Who struck the first blow and deprived a man of dear life?

Pan Mushalski pierced first with an arrow a young bey, with a purple kefi on his head, and dressed in a silver scaled armor, clear as moonlight. The painful shaft went under his left eye, and entered his head half the length of its shaft; he, throwing back his beautiful face and spreading his arms, flew from the saddle. The archer, putting his bow under his thigh, sprang forward and cut him yet with the sabre; then taking the bey's excellent weapons, and driving his horse with the flat of his sword toward the castle, he called loudly in Arabic, —

"I would that he were the Sultan's own son. He would rot here before you would play the last kindya."

When the Turks and Egyptians heard this they were terribly grieved, and two beys sprang at once toward Mushalski; but from one side Lusnia, who was wolf-like in fierceness, intercepted their way, and in the twinkle of an eye bit to death one of them. First he cut him in the hand; and when the bey stooped for his sabre, which had fallen, Lusnia almost severed his head with a terrible blow on the neck. Seeing which, the other turned his horse swift as wind to escape, but that moment Pan Mushalski took the bow again from under his thigh, and sent after the fugitive an arrow; it reached him in his flight, and sank almost to the feathers between his shoulders.

Pan Shmlud-Plotski was the third to finish his enemy, striking him with a sharp hammer on the helmet. He drove in with the blow the silver and velvet lining of the steel; and the bent point of the hammer stuck so tightly in the skull that Pan Plotski could not draw it forth for a time. Others fought with varied fortune; still, victory was mainly with the nobles, who were more skilled in fencing. But two dragoons fell from the powerful hand of Hamdi Bey, who slashed then Prince Ovsyani with a curved sword through the face, and stretched him on the field. Ovsyani moistened his native earth with his princely blood. Hamdi turned then to Pan Sheluta, whose horse had thrust his foot into the burrow of a hamster. Sheluta, seeing death inevitable, chose to meet the terrible horseman on foot, and sprang to the ground. But Hamdi, with the breast of his horse, over-turned the Pole, and reached the arm of the falling man with the very end of his blade. The arm dropped; that instant Hamdi rushed farther through the field in search of opponents.

But in many there was not courage to measure with him, so greatly and evidently did he surpass all in strength. The wind raised his white burnoose on his shoulders, and bore it apart like the wings of a bird of prey; his gilt worked armor threw an ominous gleam on his almost black face, with its wild and flashing eyes; a curved sabre glittered above his head, like the sickle of the moon on a clear night.

The famed archer let out two arrows at him; but both merely sounded on his armor with a groaning, and fell without effect on the grass. Pan Mushalski began to hesitate whether to send forth a third shaft against the neck of the steed, or rush on the bey with his sabre. But while he was thinking of this on the way, the bey saw him and urged on his black stallion.

Both met in the middle of the field. Pan Mushalski, wish-ing to show his great strength and take Hamdi alive, struck up his sword with a powerful blow and closed with him; he seized the bey's throat with one hand, with the other his pointed helmet, and drew him from his horse. But the girth of his own saddle broke; the incomparable bowman turned with it, and dropped to the ground. Hamdi struck the falling man with the hilt of his sword on the head and stunned him. The spahis and mamelukes, who had feared for Hamdi, shouted with joy; the Poles were grieved greatly. Then the opposing sides sprang toward one another in dense groups, — one side to seize the bowman, the other to defend even his body.

So far the little knight had taken no part in the skirmish, for his dignity of colonel did not permit that; but seeing the fall of Mushalski and the preponderance of Hamdi, he resolved to avenge the archer and give courage to his own men. Inspired with this thought, he put spurs to his horse, and swept across the field as swiftly as a sparrow-hawk goes to a flock of plover, circling over stubble. Basia, look-ing through a glass, saw him from the battlements, and cried at once to Zagloba, who was near her, —

"Michael is flying! Michael is flying!"

"You see him," cried the old warrior. "Look carefully; see where he strikes the first blow. Have no fear!"

The glass shook in Basia's hand. Though, as there was no discharge in the field yet from bows or janissary guns, she was not alarmed over-much for the life of her husband, still, enthusiasm, curiosity, and disquiet seized her. Her soul and heart had gone out of her body that moment, and were flying after him. Her breast was heaving quickly; a bright flush covered her face. At one moment she had bent over the battlement so far that Zagloba seized her by the waist, lest she might fall to the fosse.

"Two are flying at Michael!" cried she.

"There will be two less!" said Zagloba.

Indeed, two spahis came out against the little knight. Judging from his uniform, they knew that he was a man of note, and seeing the small stature of the horseman they thought to win glory cheaply. The fools! they flew to sure death; for when they had drawn near he did not even rein in his horse, but gave them two blows, apparently as light as when a mother in passing gives a push apiece to two children. Both fell on the ground, and clawing it with their fingers, quivered like two lynxes which death-dealing arrows have struck simultaneously.

The little knight flew farther toward horsemen racing through the field, and began to spread dreadful disaster. As when after Mass a boy comes in with a pewter extinguisher fixed to a staff, and quenches one after another the candles on the altar, and the altar is buried in shadow, so Pan Michael quenched right and left brilliant horsemen, Egyptian and Turkish, and they sank in the darkness of death. The Pagans recognized a master above masters, and their hearts sank within them. One and another withdrew his horse, so as not to meet with the terrible leader; the little knight rushed after the fugitives like a venomous wasp, and pierced one after another with his sting.

The men at the castle artillery began to shout joyously at sight of this. Some ran up to Basia, and borne away with enthusiasm, kissed the hem of her robe; others abused the Turks.

"Basia, restrain yourself!" cried Zagloba, every little while, holding her continually by the waist; but Basia wanted to laugh and cry, and clap her hands, and shout and look, and fly to her husband in the field.

He continued to carry off spahis and Egyptian beys till at last cries of "Hamdi! Hamdi!" were heard throughout the whole field. The adherents of the Prophet called loudly for their greatest warrior to measure himself with that terrible little horseman, who seemed to be death incarnate.

Hamdi had seen the little knight for some time; but noting his deeds, he was simply afraid of him. It was a terror to risk at once his great fame and young life against such an ominous enemy; therefore he feigned not to see him, and began to circle around at the other end of the field. He had just finished Pan Yalbryk and Pan Kos when despairing cries of "Hamdi! Hamdi!" smote his ear. He saw then that he could hide himself no longer, that he must win immeasurable glory or lay down his life; at that moment he gave forth a shout so shrill that all the rocks answered with an echo, and he urged on toward the little knight a horse as swift as a whirlwind.

Pan Michael saw him from a distance, and pressed also with his heels his Wallachian bay. Others ceased the armed argument. At the castle Basia, who had seen just before all the deeds of the terrible Hamdi, grew somewhat pale, in spite of her blind faith in the little knight, the unconquerable swordsman; but Zagloba was thoroughly at rest.

"I would rather be the heir of that Pagan than that Pagan himself," said he to Basia, sententiously.

Pyentka, the slow Lithuanian, was so certain of his lord that not the least anxiety darkened his face; but seeing Hamdi rushing on, he began to hum a popular song, —

"O thou foolish, foolish house-dog,
That's a gray wolf from the forest.
Why dost thou rush forward to him
If thou canst not overcome him?"

The men closed in the middle of the field between two ranks, looking on from a distance. The hearts of all died in them for a moment. Then serpentine lightning flashed in the bright sun above the heads of the combatants; but the curved blade flew from the hand of Hamdi like an arrow urged by a bowstring; he bent toward the saddle, as if pierced with a blade-point, and closed his eyes. Pan Michael seized him by the neck with his left hand, and placing the point of his sabre at the armpit of the Egyptian, turned toward his own men. Hamdi gave no resistance; he even urged his horse forward with his heel, for he felt

the point between his armpit and the armor. He went as
if stunned, his hands hanging powerless, and from his
eyes tears began to fall. Pan Michael gave him to the
cruel Lusnia, and returned himself to the field.

But in the Turkish companies trumpets and pipes were
sounded, — a signal of retreat to the skirmishers. They
began to withdraw toward their own forces, taking with
them shame, vexation, and the memory of the terrible
horseman.

"That was Satan!" said the spahis and mamelukes to
one another. "Whoso meets that man, to him death is
predestined! Satan, no other!"

The Polish skirmishers remained awhile to show that
they held the field; then, giving forth three shouts of victory, they withdrew under cover of their guns, from which
Pan Pototski gave command to renew fire. But the Turks
began to retreat altogether. For a time yet their burnooses gleamed in the sun, and their colored kefis and
glittering head-pieces; then the blue sky hid them.

On the field of battle there remained only the Turks
and Poles slain with swords. Servants came out from
the castle to collect and bury the Poles. Then ravens
came to labor at the burial of the Pagans, but their stay
was not long, for that evening new legions of the Prophet
frightened them away.

30

CHAPTER LIV.

ON the following day, the vizir himself arrived before Kamenyets at the head of a numerous army of spahis, janissaries, and the general militia from Asia. It was supposed at once, from the great number of his forces, that he would storm the place; but he wished merely to examine the walls. Engineers came with him to inspect the fortress and earthworks. Pan Myslishevski went out this time against the vizir with infantry and a division of mounted volunteers. They began to skirmish again; the action was favorable for the besieged, though not so brilliant as on the first day. Finally, the vizir commanded the janissaries to move to the walls for a trial. The thunder of cannon shook at once the town and the castle. When the janissaries were near the quarters of Pan Podchaski, all fired at once with a great outburst; but as Pan Podchaski answered from above with very well-directed shots, and there was danger that cavalry might flank the janissaries, they retreated on the Jvanyets road, and returned to the main camp.

In the evening, a certain Cheh (Bohemian) stole into the town; he had been a groom with the aga of the janissaries, and being bastinadoed, had deserted. From him the Poles learned that the Turks had fortified themselves in Jvanyets, and occupied broad fields on this side of Dlujek. They asked the fugitive carefully what the general opinion among the Turks was, — did they think to capture Kamenyets or not? He answered that there was good courage in the army, and the omens were favorable. A couple of days before, there had risen on a sudden from the earth in front of the Sultan's pavilion, as it were a pillar of smoke, slender below, and widening above in the form of a mighty bush. The muftis explained that that portent signified that the glory of the Padishah would reach the heavens, and that he would be the ruler to crush Kamenyets, — an obstacle hitherto invincible. That strengthened hearts greatly in the army. "The Turks," continued the fugitive, "fear Pan Sobieski, and succor; from time past they bear in mind the peril of meeting the troops of the Commonwealth in the open field, though they are willing to meet Venetians, Hungarians, or any other people. But since they have information that there are no troops in the Commonwealth, they think generally that they will take Kamenyets, though not without trouble. Kara Mustafa, the kaïmakan, has advised to storm the walls straightway; but the more prudent vizir prefers to invest the town with regular works, and cover it with cannon-balls. The Sultan, after the first skirmishes, has inclined to the opinion of the vizir; therefore it is proper to look for a regular siege."

Thus spoke the deserter. Hearing this news, Pan Pototski and the bishop, the chamberlain, Pan Volodyovski, and all the other chief officers were greatly concerned. They had counted on storms, and hoped with the defensiveness of the place to repulse them with great loss to the enemy. They knew from experience that during storms assailants suffer great losses; that every attack which is repulsed shakes their courage, and adds boldness to the besieged. As the knights at Zbaraj grew enamoured at last of resistance, of battles and sorties, so the inhabitants of Kamenyets might acquire love for battle, especially if every attack ended in defeat for the Turks and victory for the town. But a regular siege, in which the digging of approaches and mines, the planting of guns in position, mean everything, might only weary the besieged, weaken their courage, and make them inclined to negotiation. It was difficult also to count on sorties, for it was not proper to strip the walls of soldiers, and the servants or townspeople, led beyond the walls, could hardly stand before janissaries.

Weighing this, all the superior officers were greatly concerned, and to them a happy result of the defence seemed less likely. In fact, it had small chance of success, not only in view of the Turkish power, but in view of themselves. Pan Volodyovski was an incomparable soldier and very famous, but he had not the majesty of greatness. Whoso bears the sun in himself is able to warm all everywhere; but whoso is a flame, even the most ardent, warms only those who are nearest. So it was with the little knight. He did not know how to pour his spirit into others, and could not, just as he could not give his own skill with the sword. Pan Pototski, the supreme chief, was not a warrior, besides, he lacked faith in himself, in others, in the Commonwealth. The bishop counted on negotiations mainly; his brother had a heavy hand, but also a mind not much lighter. Relief was impossible, for the hetman, Pan Sobieski, though great, was then without power. Without power was the king, without power the whole Commonwealth.

On the 16th of August came the Khan with the horde, and Doroshenko with his Cossacks, and occupied an enormous area on the fields, beginning with Orynin. Sufan Kazi Aga invited Pan Myslishevski that day to an interview, and advised him to surrender the place, for if he did he would receive such favorable conditions as had never been heard of in the history of sieges. The bishop was curious to know what those favors were; but he was shouted down in the council, and a refusal was sent back in answer. On August 18, the Turks began to advance, and with them the Sultan.

They came on like a measureless sea, — infantry, janissaries, spahis. Each pasha led the troops of his own pashalik, therefore inhabitants of Europe, Asia, and Africa. Behind them came an enormous camp with loaded wagons drawn by mules and buffaloes. That hundred-colored swarm, in various dresses and arms, moved without end. From dawn till night those leaders marched without stopping, moved from one place to another, stationed troops, circled about in the fields, pitched tents, which occupied such a space that from the towers and highest points of Kamenyets it was possible in no wise to see fields free from canvas. It seemed to people that snow had fallen and filled the whole region about them. The camp was laid out during salvos of musketry, for the janissaries shielding that work did not cease to fire at the walls of the fortress; from the walls an unbroken cannonade answered. Echoes were thundering from the cliffs; smoke rose and covered the blue of the sky. Toward evening Kamenyets was enclosed in such fashion that nothing save pigeons could leave it. Firing ceased only when the first stars began to twinkle.

For a number of succeeding days firing from the walls and at the walls continued without interruption. The result was great damage to the besiegers; the moment a considerable group of janissaries collected within range, white smoke bloomed out on the walls, balls fell among the janissaries, and they scattered as a flock of sparrows when some one sends fine shot at them from a musket. Meanwhile the Turks, not knowing evidently that in both castles and in the town there were guns of long range, pitched their tents too near. This was permitted, by the advice of Pan Michael; and only when time of rest came, and troops, escaping from heat, had crowded into those tents, did the walls roar with continuous thunder. Then rose a panic; balls tore tents, broke poles, struck soldiers, hurled around sharp fragments of rocks. The janissaries withdrew in dismay and disorder, crying with loud voices; in their retreat they overturned other tents, and carried alarm with them everywhere. On the men disordered in this way Pan Michael fell with cavalry, and cut them till strong bodies of horsemen came to their aid. Ketling directed this fire mainly; besides him, the Polish mayor made the greatest havoc among the Pagans. He bent over every gun, applied the match himself, and covering his eyes with his hand, looked at the result of the shot, and rejoiced in his heart that he was working so effectively.

The Turks were digging approaches, however, making intrenchments and fixing heavy guns in them. But before they began to fire from these guns, an envoy of the Turks came under the walls, and fastening to a dart a letter from the Sultan, showed it to the besieged. Dragoons were sent out; these brought the envoy at once to the castle. The Sultan, summoning the town to surrender, exalted his own might and clemency to the skies.

"My army" (wrote he) "may be compared to the leaves of the forest and the sands of the sea. Look at the heavens; and when you see the countless stars, rouse fear in your hearts, and say one to another, 'Behold, such is the power of the believers!' But because I am a sovereign, gracious above other sovereigns, and a grandson of the God of Justice, I receive my right from above. Know that I hate stubborn men; do not oppose, then, my will; surrender your town. If you resist, you will all perish under the sword, and no voice of man will rise against me."

They considered long what response to give to that letter, and rejected the impolitic counsel of Zagloba to cut off a dog's tail and send it in answer. They despatched a clever man skilled in Turkish; Yuritsa was his name. He bore a letter which read as follows: —

"We do not wish to anger the Sultan, but we do not hold it our duty to obey him, for we have not taken oath to him, but to our own lord. Kamenyets we will not surrender, for an oath binds us to defend the fortresses and churches while our lives last."

After this answer the officers went to their places on the walls. Bishop Lantskoronski and the starosta took advantage of this, and sent a new letter to the Sultan, asking of him an armistice for four weeks. When news of this went along the gates, an uproar and clatter of sabres began. "But I believe," repeated this man and that, "that we are here burning at the guns, and behind our shoulders they are sending letters without our knowledge, though we are members of the council." At the evening kindya the officers went in a body to the starosta, with the little knight and Pan Makovetski at their head, both greatly afflicted at what had happened.

"How is this?" asked Makovetski. "Are you thinking already of surrender, that you have sent a new envoy? Why has this happened without our knowledge?"

"In truth," added the little knight, "since we are called to a council, it is not right to send letters without our knowledge. Neither will we permit any one to mention surrender; if any one wishes to mention it, let him withdraw from authority."

While speaking he was terribly roused; being a soldier of rare obedience, it caused him the utmost pain to speak thus against his superiors. But since he had sworn to defend the castle till his death he thought, "It behooves me to speak thus."

The starosta was confused and answered, "I thought this was done with general consent."

"There is no consent. We will die here!" cried a number of voices.

"I am glad to hear that," said the starosta; "for in me faith is dearer than life, and cowardice has never come near me, and will not. Remain, gracious gentlemen, to supper; we will come to agreement more easily."

But they would not remain.

"Our place is at the gates, not at the table," said the little knight.

At this time the bishop arrived, and learning what the question was, turned at once to Pan Makovetski and Volodyovski.

"Worthy men!" said he, "each has the same thing at heart as you, and no one has mentioned surrender. I sent to ask for an armistice of four weeks; I wrote as follows: 'During that time we will send to our king for succor, and await his instructions, and further that will be which God gives.'"

When the little knight heard this he was excited anew, but this time because rage carried him away, and scorn at such a conception of military matters. He, a soldier since childhood, could not believe his ears, could not believe that any man would propose a truce to an enemy, so as to have time himself to send for succor.

The little knight looked at Makovetski and then at other officers; they looked at him. "Is this a jest?" asked a number of voices. Then all were silent.

"I fought through the Tartar, Cossack, Moscow, and Swedish wars," said Pan Michael, at last, "and I have never heard of such reasons. The Sultan has not come hither to please us, but himself. How will he consent to an armistice, when we write to him that at the end of that time we expect aid?"

"If he does not agree, there will be nothing different from what there is now," said the bishop.

"Whoso begs for an armistice exhibits fear and weakness, and whoso looks for succor mistrusts his own power. The Pagan dog believes this of us from that letter, and thereby irreparable harm has been done."

"I might be somewhere else," said the bishop; "and because I did not desert my flock in time of need, I endure reprimand."

The little knight was sorry at once for the worthy prelate; therefore he took him by the knees, kissed his hands, and said, —

"God keep me from giving any reprimand here; but since there is a council, I utter what experience dictates to me."

"What is to be done, then? Let the fault be mine; but what is to be done? How repair the evil?" asked the bishop.

"How repair the evil?" repeated Volodyovski.

And thinking a moment, he raised his head joyously, —

"Well, it is possible. Gracious gentlemen, I pray you to follow me."

He went out, and after him the officers. A quarter of an

hour later all Kamenyets was trembling from the thunder
of cannon. Volodyovski rushed out with volunteers; and
falling upon sleeping janissaries in the approaches, he
slashed them till he scattered and drove the whole force
to the tabor.

Then he returned to the starosta, with whom he found the
bishop. "Here," said he, joyously, — "here is help for
you."

CHAPTER LV.

AFTER that sortie the night was passed in desultory firing; at daylight it was announced that a number of Turks were standing near the castle, waiting till men were sent out to negotiate. Happen what might, it was needful to know what they wanted; therefore Pan Makovetski and Pan Myslishevski were appointed at the council to go out to the Pagans.

A little later Pan Kazimir Humyetski joined them, and they went forth. There were three Turks, — Muhtar Bey, Salomi, the pasha of Rushchuk, and the third Kozra, an interpreter. The meeting took place under the open sky outside the gate of the castle. The Turks, at sight of the envoys, began to bow, putting their finger-tips to their hearts, mouths, and foreheads; the Poles greeted them politely, asking why they had come. To this Salomi answered, —

" Dear men ! a great wrong has been done to our lord, over which all who love justice must weep; and for which He who was before the ages will punish you, if you do not correct it straightway. Behold, you sent out of your own will Yuritsa, who beat with the forehead to our vizir and begged him for a cessation of arms. When we, trusting in your virtue, went out of the trenches, you began to fire at us from cannon, and rushing out from behind walls, covered the road with corpses as far as the tents of the Padishah; which proceeding cannot remain without punishment, unless you surrender at once the castles and the town, and show great regret and repentance."

To this Makovetski gave answer, —

" Yuritsa is a dog, who exceeded his instructions, for he ordered his attendant to hang out a white flag, for which he will be judged. The bishop on his own behalf inquired privately if an armistice might be arranged; but you did not cease to fire in time of sending those letters. I myself am a witness of that, for broken stones wounded me in the mouth; wherefore you have not the right to ask us to cease firing. If you come now with an armistice ready, it is well; if not, tell your lord, dear men, that we will defend the walls and the town as before, until we perish, or what is more certain, till you perish, in these rocks. We have nothing further to give you, except wishes that God may increase your days, and permit you to live to old age."

After this conversation the envoys separated straightway. The Turks returned to the vizir; Makovetski, Humyetski, and Myslishevski to the castle. They were covered with questions as to how they had sent off the envoys. They related the Turkish declaration.

"Do not receive it, dear brothers," said Kazimir Humyetski. "In brief, these dogs wish that we should give up the keys of the town before evening."

To this many voices gave answer, repeating the favorite expression, —

"That Pagan dog will not grow fat with us. We will not surrender; we will drive him away in confusion. We do not want him."

After such a decision, all separated; and firing began at once. The Turks had succeeded already in putting many heavy guns in position; and their balls, passing the "breastworks," began to fall into the town. Cannoneers in the town and the castles worked in the sweat of their foreheads the rest of the day and all night. When any one fell, there was no man to take his place; there was a lack also of men to carry balls and powder. Only before daybreak did the uproar cease somewhat. But barely was the day growing gray in the east, and the rosy gold-edged belt of dawn appearing, when in both castles the alarm was sounded. Whoso was sleeping sprang to his feet; drowsy throngs came out on the streets, listening carefully. "They are preparing for an assault," said some to others, pointing to the side of the castle." "But is Pan Volodyovski there?" asked alarmed voices. "He is, he is!" answered others.

In the castles they rang the chapel bells, and rattling of drums was heard on all sides. In the half-light, half-darkness of morning, when the town was comparatively quiet, those voices seemed mysterious and solemn. At that moment the Turks played the "kindya;" one band gave the sounds to another, and they ran in that way, like an echo, through the whole immense tabor. The Pagan swarms began to move around the tents. At the rising day the towering intrenchments, ditches, and approaches came out of the darkness, stretching in a long line at the side of the castle. The heavy Turkish guns roared at once along

Its whole length; the cliffs of the Smotrych roared back in thundering echo; and the noise was as awful and terrible as if all the thunders in the storehouse of heaven had flashed and shot down together, bringing with them the dome of clouds to the·earth.

That was a battle of artillery. The town and the castles gave mighty answers. Soon smoke veiled the sun and the light; the Turkish works were invisible. Kamenyets was hidden; only one gray enormous cloud was to be seen, filled in the interior with lightning, with thunder and roaring. But the Turkish guns carried farther than those of the town. Soon death began to cut people down in Kamenyets. A number of cannon were dismounted. In service at the arquebuses, two or three men fell at a time. A Franciscan Father, who was blessing the guns, had his nose and part of his lip carried off by a wedge from under a cannon; two very brave Jews who assisted in working that cannon were killed.

But the Turkish guns struck mainly at the intrenchment of the town. Pan Kazimir Humyetski sat there like a salamander, in the greatest fire and smoke: one half of his company had fallen; nearly all of those who remained were wounded. He himself lost speech and hearing; but with the aid of the Polish mayor he forced the enemy's battery to silence, at least until new guns were brought to replace the old ones.

A day passed, a second, a·third; and that dreadful "colloquium" of cannon did not cease for an instant. The Turks changed gunners four times a day; but in the town the very same men had to work all the time without sleep, almost without food, stifled from smoke; many were wounded from broken stones and fragments of cannon carriages. The soldiers endured; but the hearts began to weaken in the inhabitants. It was necessary at last to drive them with clubs to the cannon, where they fell thickly. Happily, in the evening of the third day and through the night following, from Thursday till Friday, the main cannonading was turned on the castles.

They were both covered, but especially the old one, with bombs from great mortars, which, however, "harmed little, since in darkness each bomb was discernible, and a man could avoid it." But toward evening, when such weariness seized men that they fell off their feet from drowsiness, they perished often enough.

The little knight, Ketling, Myslishevski, and Kvasibrotski answered the Turkish fire from the castles. The
starosta looked in at them repeatedly, and advanced amid a
hail of bullets, anxious, but regardless of danger.

Toward evening, however, when the fire had increased
still more, Pan Pototski approached Pan Michael.

"Gracious Colonel," said he, "we shall not hold out."

"While they confine themselves to firing we shall hold
out," answered the little knight; "but they will blow us
out of here with mines, for they are making them."

"Are they really mining?" asked the starosta, in
alarm.

"Seventy cannon are playing, and their thunder is almost
unceasing; still, there are moments of quiet. When such
a moment comes, put down your ear carefully and listen."

At that time it was not needful to wait long, especially
as an accident came to their aid. One of the Turkish siege-
guns burst; that caused a certain disorder. They sent from
other intrenchments to inquire what had happened, and
there was a lull in cannonading.

Pan Michael and the starosta approached the very end of
one of the projections of the castle, and began to listen.
After a certain time their ears caught clearly enough the
resonant sound of hammers in the cliff.

"They are pounding," said the starosta.

"They are pounding," said the little knight.

Then they were silent. Great alarm appeared on the
face of the starosta; he raised his hands and pressed his
temples. Seeing this, Pan Michael said, —

"This is a usual thing in all sieges. At Zbaraj they
were digging under us night and day."

The starosta raised his hand: "What did Prince
Yeremi do?"

"He withdrew from intrenchments of wide circuit
into narrower ones."

"But what should we do?"

"We should take the guns, and with them all that is
movable, and transfer them to the old castle; for the old
one is founded on rocks that the Turks cannot blow up with
mines. I have thought always that the new castle would
serve merely for the first resistance; after that we must
blow it up with powder, and the real defence will begin
in the old one."

A moment of silence followed; and the starosta bent his
anxious head again.

"But if we have to withdraw from the old castle, where shall we go?" asked he, with a broken voice.

At that, the little knight straightened himself, and pointed with his finger to the earth: "I shall go there."

At that moment the guns roared again, and a whole flock of bombs began to fly to the castle; but as darkness was in the world, they could be seen perfectly. Pan Michael took leave of the general, and went along the walls. Going from one battery to another, he encouraged men everywhere, gave advice; at last, meeting with Ketling, he said, —

"Well, how is it?"

Ketling smiled pleasantly.

"It is clear as day from the bombs," said he, pressing the little knight's hand. "They do not spare fire on us."

"A good gun of theirs burst. Did you burst it?"

"I did."

"I am terribly sleepy."

"And I too, but there is no time."

"Ai," said Pan Michael; "and the little wives must be frightened; at thought of that, sleep goes away."

"They are praying for us," said Ketling, raising his eyes toward the flying bombs.

"God give them health!" said Pan Michael.

"Among earthly women," began Ketling, "there are none —"

But he did not finish, for the little knight, turning at that moment toward the interior of the castle, cried suddenly, in a loud voice, —

"For God's sake! Save us! What do I see?"

And he sprang forward.

Ketling looked around with astonishment. At a few paces distant, in the court of the castle, he saw Basia, with Zagloba and the Lithuanian, Pyentka.

"To the wall! to the wall!" cried the little knight, dragging them as quickly as possible to the cover of the. battlements. "For God's sake!"

"Ha!" said Zagloba, with a broken voice, and panting; "help yourself here with such a woman, if you please. I remonstrate with her, saying, 'You will destroy yourself and me.' I kneel down, — no use. Was I to let her go alone? Uh! No help, no help! 'I will go; I will go,' said I. Here she is for you!"

Basia had fear in her face, and her brow was quivering as if before weeping. But it was not bombs that she feared, nor the whizzing of balls, nor fragments of stones, but the anger of her husband. Therefore she clasped her hands like a child fearing punishment, and exclaimed, with sobbing voice, —

"I could not, Michael dear; as I love you, I could not. Be not angry, Michael. I cannot stay there when you are perishing here. I cannot; I cannot!"

He had begun to be angry indeed, and had cried, "Basia, you have no fear of God!" but sudden tenderness seized him, his voice stuck in his throat; and only when that dearest bright head was resting on his breast, did he say, —

"You are my faithful friend until death;" and he embraced her.

But Zagloba, pressing up to the wall, said to Ketling: "And yours wished to come, but we deceived her, saying that we were not coming. How could she come in such a condition? A general of artillery will be born to you. I'm a rogue if it will not be a general. Well, on the bridge from the town to the castle, the bombs are falling like peas. I thought I should burst, — from anger, not from fear. I slipped on sharp pieces of shell, and cut my skin. I shall not be able to sit down without pain for a week. The nuns will have to rub me, without minding modesty. Uf! But those rascals are shooting. May the thunderbolts shoot them away! Pan Pototski wants to yield the command to me. Give the soldiers a drink, or they will not hold out. See that bomb! It will fall somewhere near us. Hide yourself, Basia! As God lives, it will fall near!"

But the bomb fell far away, not near, for it fell on the roof of the Lutheran church in the old castle. Since the dome was very strong, ammunition had been carried in there; but this missile broke the dome, and set fire to the powder. A mighty explosion, louder than the thunder of cannon, shook the foundations of both castles. From the battlement, voices of terror were heard. Polish and Turkish cannon were silent.

Ketling left Zagloba, and Volodyovski left Basia. Both sprang to the walls with all the strength in their limbs. For a time it was heard how both gave commands with panting breasts; but the rattle of drums in the Turkish trenches drowned their commands.

"They will make an assault!" whispered Zagloba.

In fact, the Turks, hearing the explosion, imagined apparently that both castles were destroyed, the defenders partly buried in the ruins, and partly seized with fear. With that thought, they prepared for the storm. Fools! they knew not that only the Lutheran church had gone into the air. The explosion had produced no other effect than the shock; not even a gun had fallen from its carriage in the new castle. But in the intrenchments the rattle of drums grew more and more hurried. Crowds of janissaries pushed out of the intrenchments, and ran with quick steps toward the castle. Fires in the castle and in the Turkish trenches were quenched, it is true; but the night was clear, and in the light of the moon a dense mass of white caps were visible, sinking and rising in the rush, like waves stirred by wind. A number of thousands of janissaries and several hundred volunteers were running forward with rage and the hope of certain victory in their hearts; but many of them were never again to see the minarets of Stambul, the bright waters of the Bosphorus, and the dark cypresses of the cemeteries.

Pan Michael ran, like a spirit, along the walls. "Don't fire! Wait for the word!" cried he, at every gun.

The dragoons were lying flat at the battlements, panting with rage. Silence followed; there was no sound but that of the quick tread of the janissaries, like low thunder. The nearer they came, the more certain they felt of taking both castles at a blow. Many thought that the remnant of the defenders had withdrawn to the town, and that the battlements were empty. When they had run to the fosse, they began to fill it with fascines and bundles of straw, and filled it in a twinkle. On the walls, the stillness was unbroken.

But when the first ranks stood on the stuff with which the fosse had been filled, in one of the battlement openings a pistol-shot was heard; then a shrill voice shouted, —

"Fire!"

At the same time both bulwarks, and the prolongation joining them, gleamed with a long flash of flame. The thunder of cannon, the rattle of musketry, and the shouts of the assailants were mingled. When a dart, hurled by the hand of a strong beater, sinks half its length in the belly of a bear, he rolls himself into a bundle, roars, struggles, flounders, straightens, and again rolls himself; thus precisely did the throng of janissaries and volunteers. Not one shot of the defenders was wasted. Cannon loaded with grape laid men flat as a pavement, just as a fierce wind

levels standing grain with one breath.   Those who attacked
the extension, joining the bulwarks, found themselves under
three fires, and seized with terror, became a disordered mass
in the centre, falling so thickly that they formed a quivering mound.   Ketling poured grape-shot from two cannon
into that group; at last, when they began to flee, he closed,
with a rain of lead and iron, the narrow exit between the
bulwarks.

The attack was repulsed on the whole line, when the
janissaries, deserting the fosse, ran, like madmen, with a
howl of terror.   They began in the Turkish intrenchments
to hurl flaming tar buckets and torches, and burn artificial
fires, making day of night, so as to illuminate the road for
the fugitives, and to make pursuit difficult for a sortie.

Meanwhile Pan Michael, seeing that crowd enclosed
between the bulwarks, shouted for his dragoons, and went
out against them.   The unfortunate Turks tried once more
to escape through the exit; but Ketling covered them so
terribly that he soon blocked the place with a pile of bodies
as high as a wall.   It remained to the living to perish; for
the besieged would not take prisoners, hence they began to
defend themselves desperately.   Strong men collected in
little groups (two, three, five), and supporting one another
with their shoulders, armed with darts, battle-axes, daggers,
and sabres, cut madly.   Fear, terror, certainty of death,·
despair, was changed in them into one feeling of rage.
The fever of battle seized them.   Some rushed in fury
single-handed on the dragoons.   These were borne apart
on sabres in a twinkle.   That was a struggle of two furies;
for the dragoons, from toil, sleeplessness, and hunger, were
possessed by the anger of beasts against an enemy that
they surpassed in skill in using cold weapons; hence
they spread terrible disaster.

Ketling, wishing on his part to make the scene of struggle
more visible, gave command to ignite tar buckets, and in
the light of them could be seen irrestrainable Mazovians
fighting against janissaries with sabres, dragging them by
the heads and beards.   The savage Lusnia raged specially,
like a wild bull.   At the other wing. Pan Michael himself
was fighting; seeing that Basia was looking at him from
the walls, he surpassed himself.   As when a venomous
weasel breaks into grain where a swarm of mice are living,
and makes terrible slaughter among them, so did the little
knight rush like a spirit of destruction among the janis-

saries. His name was known to the besiegers already, both from previous encounters and from the narratives of Turks in Hotin. There was a general opinion that no man who met him could save himself from death; hence many a janissary of those enclosed between the bulwarks, seeing Pan Michael suddenly in front, did not even defend himself, but closing his eyes, died under the thrust of the little knight's rapier, with the word "kismet" on his lips. Finally resistance grew weak; the remnant of the Turks rushed to that wall of bodies which barred the exit, and there they were finished.

The dragoons returned now through the filled fosse with singing, shouting, and panting, with the odor of blood on them; a number of cannon-shots were fired from the Turkish intrenchments and the castle; then silence followed. Thus ended that artillery battle which lasted some days, and was crowned by the storm of the janissaries.

"Praise be to God," said the little knight, "there will be rest till the morning kindya at least, and in justice it belongs to us."

But that was an apparent rest only, for when night was still deeper they heard in the silence the sound of hammers beating the cliff.

"That is worse than artillery," said Ketling, listening.

"Now would be the time to make a sortie," said the little knight; "but 't is impossible; the men are too weary. They have not slept and they have not eaten, though they had food, for there was no time to take it. Besides, there are always some thousands on guard with the miners, so that there may be no opposition from our side. There is no help but to blow up the new castle ourselves, and withdraw to the old one."

"That is not for to-day," answered Ketling. "See, the men have fallen like sheaves of grain, and are sleeping a stone sleep. The dragoons have not even wiped their swords."

"Basia, it is time to go home and sleep," said the little knight.

"I will, Michael," answered Basia, obediently; "I will go as you command. But the cloister is closed now; I should prefer to remain and watch over your sleep."

"It is a wonder to me," said the little knight, "that after such toil sleep has left me, and I have no wish whatever to rest my head."

31

"Because you have roused your blood among the janissaries," said Zagloba. "It was always so with me; after a
battle I could never sleep in any way. But as to Basia,
why should she drag herself to a closed gate? Let her
remain here till morning."

Basia pressed Zagloba with delight; and the little knight,
seeing how much she wished to stay, said, —

"Let us go to the chambers."

They went in; but the place was full of lime-dust, which
the cannon-balls had raised by shaking the walls. It was
impossible to stay there, so they went out again, and took
their places in a niche made when the old gate had been
walled in. Pan Michael sat there, leaning against the
masonry. Basia nestled up to him, like a child to its
mother. The night was in August, warm and fragrant.
The moon illuminated the niche with a silver light; the
faces of the little knight and Basia were bathed in its rays.
Lower down, in the court of the castle, were groups of
sleeping soldiers and the bodies of those slain during the
cannonade, for there had been no time yet for their burial.
The calm light of the moon crept over those bodies, as if
that hermit of the sky wished to know who was sleeping
from weariness merely, and who had fallen into the eternal
slumber. Farther on was outlined the wall of the main
castle, from which fell a black shadow on one half of the
courtyard. Outside the walls, from between the bulwarks,
where the janissaries lay cut down with sabres, came the
voices of men. They were camp followers and those of the
dragoons to whom booty was dearer than slumber; they
were stripping the bodies of the slain. Their lanterns were
gleaming on the place of combat like fireflies. Some of
them called to one another; and one was singing in an
undertone a sweet song not beseeming the work to which
he was given at the moment: —

> "Nothing is silver, nothing is gold to me now,
>   Nothing is fortune.
>   Let me die at the fence, then, of hunger,
>   If only near thee."

But after a certain time that movement began to decrease,
and at last stopped completely. A silence set in which was
broken only by the distant sound of the hammers breaking
the cliffs, and the calls of the sentries on the walls. That
silence, the moonlight, and the night full of beauty delighted

Pan Michael and Basia. A yearning came upon them, it is
unknown why, and a certain sadness, though pleasant. Basia
raised her eyes to her husband; and seeing that his eyes
were open, she said, —

"Michael, you are not sleeping."

"It is a wonder, but I cannot sleep."

"It is pleasant for you here?"

"Pleasant. But for you?"

Basia nodded her bright head. "Oh, Michael, so pleasant! ai, ai! Did you not hear what that man was
singing?"

Here she repeated the last words of the little song, —

> "Let me die at the fence, then, of hunger,
>   If only near thee."

A moment of silence followed, which the little knight
interrupted, —

"But listen, Basia."

"What, Michael?"

"To tell the truth, we are wonderfully happy with each
other; and I think if one of us were to fall, the other would
grieve beyond measure."

Basia understood perfectly that when the little knight
said "if one of us were to fall," instead of *die*, he had
himself only in mind. It came to her head that maybe
he did not expect to come out of that siege alive, that he
wished to accustom her to that termination; therefore a
dreadful presentiment pressed her heart, and clasping her
hands, she said, —

"Michael, have pity on yourself and on me!"

The voice of the little knight was moved somewhat,
though calm.

"But see, Basia, you are not right," said he; "for if you
only reason the matter out, what is this temporal existence? Why break one's neck over it? Who would be
satisfied with tasting happiness and love here when all
breaks like a dry twig, — who?"

But Basia began to tremble from weeping, and to repeat, —

"I will not hear this! I will not! I will not!"

"As God is dear to me, you are not right," repeated the
little knight. "Look, think of it: there above, beyond
that quiet moon, is a country of bliss without end. Of such
a one speak to me. Whoever reaches that meadow will draw
breath for the first time, as if after a long journey, and will

feed in peace. When my time comes, — and that is a soldier's affair, — it is your simple duty to say to yourself: 'That is nothing! Michael is gone. True, he is gone far, farther than from here to Lithuania; but that is nothing, for I shall follow him.' Basia, be quiet; do not weep. The one who goes first will prepare quarters for the other; that is the whole matter."

Here there came on him, as it were, a vision of coming events; for he raised his eyes to the moonlight, and continued, —

"What is this mortal life? Grant that I am there first, waiting till some one knocks at the heavenly gate. Saint Peter opens it. I look; who is that? My Basia! Save us! Oh, I shall jump then! Oh, I shall cry then! Dear God, words fail me. And there will be no tears, only endless rejoicing; and there will be no Pagans, nor cannon, nor mines under walls, only peace and happiness. Ai, Basia, remember, this life is nothing!"

"Michael, Michael!" repeated Basia.

And again came silence, broken only by the distant, monotonous sound of the hammers.

"Basia, let us pray together," said Pan Michael, at last.

And those two souls began to pray. As they prayed, peace came on both; and then sleep overcame them, and they slumbered till the first dawn.

Pan Michael conducted Basia away before the morning kindya to the bridge joining the old castle with the town. In parting, he said, —

"This life is nothing! remember that, Basia."

CHAPTER LVI.

THE thunder of cannon shook the castles and the town immediately after the kindya. The Turks had dug a fosse at the side of the castle, five hundred yards long; in one place, at the very wall, they were digging deeply. From that fosse there went against the walls an unceasing fire from janissary muskets. The besieged made screens of leather bags filled with wool; but as long balls and bombs were hurled continually from the intrenchments, bodies fell thickly around the cannon. At one gun a bomb killed six men of Volodyovski's infantry at once; at other guns men were falling continually. Before evening the leaders saw that they could hold out no longer, especially as the mines might be exploded any moment. In the night, therefore, the captains led out their companies, and before morning they had transferred, amid unbroken firing, all the guns, powder, and supplies of provisions to the old castle. That, being built on a rock, could hold out louger, and there was special difficulty in digging under it. Pan Michael, when consulted on this matter at the council, declared that if no one would negotiate, he was ready to defend it a year. His words went to the town, and poured great consolation into hearts, for people knew that the little knight would keep his word even at the cost of his life.

At the evacuation of the new castle, strong mines were put under both bulwarks and the front. These exploded with great noise about noon, but caused no serious loss to the Turks; for, remembering the lesson of the day before, they had not dared yet to occupy the abandoned place. But both bulwarks, the front and the main body of the new castle, formed one gigantic pile of ruins. These ruins rendered difficult, it is true, approach to the old castle; but they gave perfect protection to sharpshooters, and, what is worse, to the miners, who, unterrified at sight of the mighty cliff, began to bore a new mine. Skilful Italian and Hungarian engineers, in the service of the Sultan, were overseers of this work, which advanced rapidly. The besieged could not strike the enemy either from cannon or musket, for

they could not see them. Pan Michael was thinking of a
sortie, but he could not undertake it immediately; the
soldiers were too tired. Blue lumps as large as biscuits had
formed on the right shoulders of the dragoons, from bringing gunstocks against them continually. Some could hardly
move their arms. It became evident that if boring were
continued some time without interruption, the chief gate of
the castle would be blown into the air beyond doubt. Foreseeing this, Pan Michael gave command to make a high wall
behind the gate, and said, without losing courage, —

"But what do I care? If the gate is blown up, we will
defend ourselves behind the wall; if the wall is blown up,
we'll have a second one made previously, and so on, as long
as we feel an ell of ground under our feet."

"But when the ell is gone, what then?" asked the
starosta.

"Then we shall be gone too," said the little knight.

Meanwhile he gave command to hurl hand-grenades at
the enemy; these caused much damage. Most effective
in this work was Lieutenant Dembinski, who killed Turks
without number, until a grenade ignited too soon, burst in
his hand, and tore it off. In this manner perished Captain
Schmit. Many fell from the Turkish artillery, many from
musket-shots fired by janissaries hidden in the ruins of the
new castle. During that time they fired rarely from the
guns of the castle; this troubled the council not a little.
"They are not firing; hence it is evident that Volodyovski
himself has doubts of the defence." Such was the general
opinion. Of the officers no man dared to say first that it
remained only to seek the best conditions, but the bishop,
free of military ambition, said this openly; but previously
Pan Vasilkovski was sent to the starosta for news from the
castle. He answered, "In my opinion the castle cannot
hold out till evening, but here they think otherwise."

After reading this answer, even the officers began to say,
"We have done what we could. No one has spared himself,
but what is impossible cannot be done; it is necessary to
think of conditions."

These words reached the town, and brought together a
great crowd of people. This multitude stood before the
town-hall, alarmed, silent, rather hostile than inclined to
negotiations. Some rich Armenian merchants were glad in
their hearts that the siege would be ended and trading
begin; but other Armenians, long settled in the Common-

wealth and greatly inclined to it, as well as Poles and Russians, wished to defend themselves. "Had we wished to surrender, we should have surrendered at first," was whispered here and there; "we could have received much, but now conditions will not be favorable, and it is better to bury ourselves under ruins."

The murmur of discontent became ever louder, till all at once it turned into shouts of enthusiasm and vivats.

What had happened ? On the square Pan Michael appeared in company with Pan Humyetski, for the starosta had sent them of purpose to make a report of what had happened in the castle. Enthusiasm seized the crowd. Some shouted as if the Turks had already broken into the town; tears came to the eyes of others at sight of the idolized knight, on whom uncommon exertions were evident. His face was black from powder-smoke, and emaciated, his eyes were red and sunken; but he had a joyous look. When he and Humyetski had made their way at last through the crowd, and entered the council, they were greeted joyously. The bishop spoke at once.

"Beloved brothers," said he, "*Nec Hercules contra plures!* The starosta has written us already that you must surrender."

To this Humyetski, who was very quick to action and of great family, not caring for people, said sharply: "The starosta has lost his head; but he has this virtue, that he exposes it to danger. As to the defence, let Pan Volodyovski describe it; he is better able to do so."

All eyes were turned to the little knight, who was greatly moved, and said, —

"For God's sake, who speaks of surrender ? Have we not sworn to the living God to fall one upon another ? "

"We have sworn to do what is in our power, and we have done it," answered the bishop.

"Let each man answer for what he has promised! Ketling and I have sworn not to surrender the castle till death, and we will not surrender; for if I am bound to keep the word of a cavalier to every man, what must I do to God, who surpasses all in majesty ? "

"But how is it with the castle ? We have heard that there is a mine under the gate. Will you hold out long ? " asked numerous voices.

"There is a mine under the gate, or there will be; but there is a good wall behind the gate, and I have given com-

mand to put falconets on it. Dear brothers, fear God's
wounds; remember that in surrendering you will be forced
to surrender churches into the hands of Pagans, who will
turn them into mosques, to celebrate foulness in them.
How can you speak of surrender with such a light heart?
With what conscience do you think of opening before the
enemy a gate to the heart of the country? I am in the
castle and fear no mines; and you here in the town, far
away, are afraid! By the dear God! we will not surrender
while we are alive. Let the memory of this defence
remain among those who come after us, like the memory
of Zbaraj."

"The Turks will turn the castle into a pile of ruins,"
said some voice.

"Let them turn it. We can defend ourselves from a
pile of ruins."

Here patience failed the little knight somewhat.

"And I will defend myself from a pile of ruins, so help
me God! Finally, I tell you that I will not surrender the
castle. Do you hear?"

"But will you destroy the town?" asked the bishop.

"If to go against the Turks is to destroy it, I prefer to
destroy it. I have taken my oath; I will not waste more
words; I will go back among cannon, for they defend the
Commonwealth instead of betraying it."

Then he went out, and after him Humyetski, who
slammed the door. Both hastened greatly, for they felt
really better among ruins, corpses, and balls than among
men of little faith. Pan Makovetski came up with them
on the way.

"Michael," said he, "tell the truth, did you speak of
resistance only to increase courage, or will you be able
really to hold out in the castle?"

The little knight shrugged his shoulders. "As God is
dear to me! Let the town not surrender, and I will defend
the castle a year."

"Why do you not fire? People are alarmed on that
account, and talk of surrender."

"We do not fire, because we are busy with hand-grenades,
which have caused considerable harm in the mines."

"Listen, Michael, have you in the castle such defence
that you could strike at the Russian gate in the rear? — for
if, which God prevent, the Turks break through, they will
come to the gate. I am watching with all my force;

but with towns-people only, without soldiers, I cannot succeed."

To which the little knight answered: "Fear not, dear brother; I have fifteen cannon turned to that side. Be at rest too concerning the castle. Not only shall we defend ourselves, but when necessary we will give you reinforcement at the gates."

When he heard this, Makovetski was delighted greatly, and wished to go away, when the little knight detained him, and asked further, —

"Tell me, you are oftener at these councils, do they only wish to try us, or do they intend really to give Kamenyets into the hands of the Sultan?"

Makovetski dropped his head. "Michael," said he, "answer truly now, must it not end in that? We shall resist awhile yet, a week, two weeks, a month, two months, but the end will be the same."

Volodyovski looked at him gloomily, then raising his hands cried, —

"And thou too, Brutus, against me? Well, in that case swallow your shame alone; I am not used to such diet."

And they parted with bitterness in their hearts.

The mine under the main gate of the old castle exploded soon after Pan Michael's return. Bricks and stones flew; dust and smoke rose. Terror dominated the hearts of the gunners. For a while the Turks rushed into the breach, as rush sheep through the open gate of a sheepfold, when the shepherd and his assistants urge them in with whips. But Ketling breathed on that crowd with cartridges from six cannon, prepared previously on the wall; he breathed once, a second, a third time, and swept them out of the court. Pan Michael, Humyetski, and Myslishevski hurried up with infantry and dragoons, who covered the walls as quickly as flies on a hot day cover the carcass of a horse or an ox. A struggle began then between muskets and janissary guns. Balls fell on the wall as thickly as falls rain, or kernels of wheat which a strong peasant hurls from his shovel. The Turks were swarming in the ruins of the new castle; in every depression, behind every fragment, behind every stone, in every opening of the ruin, they sat in twos, threes, fives, and tens, and fired without a moment's intermission. From the direction of Hotin came new reinforcements continually. Regiment followed regiment, and crouching down among the ruins began fire immediately. The new castle was as if paved with turbans. At times those masses of turbans sprang up suddenly with a terrible outcry, and ran to the breach; but then Ketling raised his voice, the bass of the cannon drowned the rattle of musketry, and a storm of grapeshot with whistling and terrible rattling confused the crowd, laid them on the ground, and closed up the breach with a quivering mass of human flesh. Four times the janissaries rushed forward; four times Ketling hurled them back and scattered them, as a storm scatters a cloud of leaves. Alone amid fire, smoke, showers of earth-clods, and bursting grenades, he was like an angel of war. His eyes were fixed on the breach, and on his serene forehead not the slightest anxiety was evident. At times he seized the match from the gunner and touched the priming; at times he covered his eyes with his hand and observed the effect of the shot; at times he turned with a smile to the Polish officers and said, —

"They will not enter."

Never was rage of attack repulsed with such fury of defence. Officers and soldiers vied with one another. It seemed that the attention of those men was turned to everything save death; and death cut down thickly. Pan Humyetski fell, and Pan Mokoshytski, commander of the men of Kieff. At last the white-haired Pan Kalushovski seized his own breast with a groan; he was an old friend of Pan Michael, as mild as a lamb, but a soldier as terrible as a lion. Pan Michael caught the falling man, who said, "Give your hand, give your hand quickly!" then he added, "Praise be to God!" and his face grew as white as his beard. That was before the fourth attack. A party of janissaries had come inside the breach, or rather they could not go out by reason of the too thickly flying missiles. Pan Michael sprang on them at the head of his infantry, and they were beaten down in a moment with the butts of muskets.

Hour followed hour; the fire did not weaken. But meanwhile news of the heroic defence was borne through the town, exciting enthusiasm and warlike desire. The Polish inhabitants, especially the young men, began to call on one another, to look at one another, and give mutual encouragement. "Let us go to the castle with assistance! Let us go; let us go! We will not let our brothers perish! Come, boys!" Such voices were heard on the square and at the gates; soon a few hundred men, armed in any fashion, but with daring in their hearts, moved toward the bridge. The Turks turned on the young men a terrible fire, which stretched many dead; but a part passed, and they began to work on the wall against the Turks with great zeal.

This fourth attack was repulsed with fearful loss to the Turks, and it seemed that a moment of rest must come. Vain hope! The rattle of janissary musketry did not cease till evening. Only when the evening kindya was played, did the cannon grow silent, and the Turks leave the ruins of the new castle. The remaining officers went then from the wall to the other side. The little knight, without losing a moment, gave command to close up the breach with whatever materials they could find, — hence with blocks of timber, with fascines, with rubbish, with earth. Infantry, cavalry, dragoons, common soldiers, and officers vied with one another, regardless of rank. It was thought that Turkish guns might renew fire at any moment; but that was a day of great victory for the besieged over the besiegers. The faces of all the besieged were bright; their souls were flaming with hope and desire of further victories.

Ketling and Pan Michael, taking each other by the hands after their labor, went around the square and the walls, bent out through the battlements, to look at the courtyard of the new castle and rejoice at the bountiful harvest.

" Body lies there near body," said the little knight, pointing to the ruins; "and at the breach there are such piles that you would need a ladder to cross them. That is the work of your cannon, Ketling."

"The best thing," answered Ketling, "is that we have repaired that breach; the approach is closed to the Turks, and they must make a new mine. Their power is boundless as the sea, but such a siege for a month or two must become bitter to them."

"By that time the hetman will help us. But come what may, you and I are bound by oath," said the little knight.

At that moment they looked into each other's eyes, and Pan Michael asked in a lower voice, "And have you done what I told you?"

"All is ready," whispered Ketling, in answer; "but I think it will not come to that, for we may hold out very long here, and have many such days as the present."

"God grant us such a morrow!"

"Amen!" answered Ketling, raising his eyes to heaven. The thunder of cannon interrupted further conversation.

Bombs began to fly against the castle again. Many of them burst in the air, however, and went out like summer lightning.

Ketling looked with the eye of a judge. "At that trench over there from which they are firing," said he, "the matches have too much sulphur."

"It is beginning to smoke on other trenches," said Volodyovski.

And, in fact, it was. As, when one dog barks in the middle of a still night, others begin to accompany, and at last the whole village is filled with barking, so one cannon in the Turkish trenches roused all the neighboring guns, and a crown of bombs encircled the besieged place. This time, however, the enemy fired at the town, not the castle; but from three sides was heard the piercing of mines. Though the mighty rock had almost baffled the efforts of miners, it was clear that the Turks had determined at all cost to blow that rocky nest into the air.

At the command of Ketling and Pan Michael, the defenders began to hurl hand-grenades again, guided by the noise of the hammers. But at night it was impossible to know whether that means of defence caused any damage. Besides, all turned their eyes and attention to the town, against which were flying whole flocks of flaming birds. Some missiles burst in the air; but others, describing a fiery circle in the sky, fell on the roofs of houses. At once a reddish conflagration broke the darkness in a number of places. The Church of St. Catherine was burning, also the Church of St. George in the Russian quarter, and soon the Armenian Cathedral was burning; this, however, had been set on fire during the day; it was merely ignited again by the bombs. The fire increased every moment and lighted up all the neighborhood. The outcry from the town reached the old castle. One might suppose that the whole town was burning.

"That is bad," said Ketling, "for courage will fail in the inhabitants."

"Let everything burn," said the little knight; "if only the rock is not crushed from which we may defend ourselves."

Now the outcry increased. From the cathedral the fire spread to the Armenian storehouses of costly merchandise. These were built on the square belonging to that nationality; great wealth was burning there in gold, silver, divans, furs, and rich stuffs. After a while, tongues of fire appeared here and there over the houses.

Pan Michael was disturbed greatly. "Ketling," said he, "look to the hurling of grenades, and injure work in the mines as much as possible. I will hurry to the town, for my heart is suffering for the Dominican nuns. Praise be to God that the Turks leave the castle in quiet, and that I can be absent!"

In the castle there was not, in truth, at that moment much to do; hence the little knight sat on his horse and rode away. He returned only after two hours in company with Pan Mushalski, who after that injury sustained at the hands of Hamdi Bey, recovered, and came now to the fortress, thinking that during storms he might cause notable loss to the Pagans, and gain glory immeasurable.

"Be welcome!" said Ketling. "I was alarmed. How is it with the nuns?"

"All is well," answered the little knight. "Not one bomb has burst there. The place is very quiet and safe."

"Thank God for that! But Krysia is not alarmed?"

"She is as quiet as if at home. She and Basia are in one cell, and Pan Zagloba is with them. Pan Adam, to whom consciousness has returned, is here too. He begged to come with me to the castle; but he is not able to stand long on his feet yet. Ketling, go there now, and I will take your place here."

Ketling embraced Pan Michael, for his heart drew him greatly to Krysia, and gave command to bring his horse at once. But before they brought the horse, he inquired of the little knight what was to be heard in the town.

"The inhabitants are quenching the fire very bravely," answered the little knight; "but when the wealthier Armenian merchants saw their goods burning, they sent deputations to the bishop and insisted on surrender. Hearing of this, I went to the council, though I had promised myself not to go there again. I struck in the face the man who insisted most on surrender: for this the bishop rose in anger against me. The situation is bad, brother; cowardice is seizing people more and more, and our readiness for defence is for them cheaper and cheaper. They give blame and not praise, for they say that we are exposing the place in vain. I heard too that they attacked Makovetski because he opposed negotiations. The bishop himself said to him,

'We are not deserting faith or king; but what can further resistance effect? See,' said he, 'what will be after it, — desecrated shrines, honorable ladies insulted, and innocent children dragged captive. With a treaty,' said he, 'we can assure their fate and obtain free escape.' So spoke the bishop. The starosta nodded and said, 'I would rather perish, but this is true.'"

"The will of God be done!" said Ketling.

But Pan Michael wrung his hands. "And if that were even true," cried he, "but God is witness that we can defend ourselves yet."

Now they brought Ketling's horse. He mounted quickly.

"Carefully through the bridge," said Pan Michael at parting, "for the bombs fall there thickly."

"I will return in an hour," said Ketling; and he rode away.

Pan Michael started to go around the walls with Mushalski. In three places hammering was heard; hence the besieged were throwing hand-grenades from three places. On the left side of the castle Lusnia was directing that work.

"Well, how is it going with you?" inquired Volodyovski.

"Badly, Pan Commandant," said the sergeant: "the pig-bloods are sitting in the cliff, and only sometimes at the entrance does a piece of shell hurt a man. We have n't done much."

In other places the case was still worse, especially as the sky had grown gloomy and rain was falling, from which the wicks in the grenades were growing damp. Darkness too hindered the work.

Pan Michael drew Mushalski aside somewhat, and halting, said on a sudden, "But listen! If we should try to smother those moles in their burrows?"

"That seems to me certain death, for whole regiments of janissaries are guarding them. But let us try!"

"Regiments are guarding them, it is true; but the night is very dark, and confusion seizes them quickly. Just think, they are talking of surrender in the town. Why? Because, they say to us, 'There are mines under you; you are not defending yourselves.' We should close their lips if to-night we could send the news, 'There is no longer a mine!' For such a cause is it worth while to lay down one's head or not?"

Pan Mushalski thought a moment, and cried, "It is worth while! As God lives, it is!"

"In one place they began to hammer not long ago," said Pan Michael; "we will leave those undisturbed, but here and on that side they have dug in very deeply. Take fifty dragoons; I will take the same number; and we will try to smother them. Have you the wish?"

" I have, and it is increasing. I will take spikes in my belt to spike cannon; perhaps on the road I may find some."

"As to finding, I doubt that, though there are some falconets standing near; but take the spikes. We will only wait for Ketling; he knows better than others how to succor in a sudden emergency."

Ketling came as he had promised; he was not behind time one moment. Half an hour later two detachments of dragoons, of fifty men each, went to the breach, slipped out quickly, and vanished in the darkness. Ketling gave command to throw grenades for a short time yet; then he ceased work and waited. His heart was beating unquietly, for he understood well how desperate the undertaking was. A quarter of an hour passed, half an hour, an hour: it seemed that they ought to be there already and to begin; meanwhile, putting his ear to the ground, he heard the quiet hammering perfectly.

Suddenly at the foot of the castle, on the left side, there was a pistol-shot, which in the damp air, in view of the firing from the trenches, did not make a loud report, and might have passed without rousing the attention of the garrison had not a terrible uproar succeeded it. "They are there," thought Ketling; "but will they return?" And then sounded the shouts of men, the roar of drums, the whistle of pipes, — finally the rattle of musketry, hurried and very irregular. The Turks fired from all sides and in throngs; evidently whole divisions had run up to succor the miners. As Pan Michael had foreseen, confusion seized the janissaries, who, fearing to strike one another, shouted loudly, fired at random, and often in the air. The uproar and firing increased every moment. When martens, eager for blood, break into a sleeping hen-house at night, a mighty uproar and cackling rise in the quiet building: confusion like that set in all at once round the castle. The Turks began to hurl bombs at the walls, so as to clear up the darkness. Ketling pointed guns in the direction of the Turkish troops on guard, and answered with grape-shot. The Turkish approaches blazed; the walls blazed. In the town the alarm was beaten, for the people believed

universally that the Turks had burst into the fortress. In the
trenches the Turks thought that a powerful sortie was
attacking all their works simultaneously; and a general
alarm spread among them. Night favored the desperate
enterprise of Pan Michael and Mushalski, for it had grown
very dark. Discharges of cannon and grenades rent only
for instants the darkness, which was afterward blacker.
Finally, the sluices of heaven opened suddenly, and down
rushed torrents of rain. Thunder outsounded the firing,
rolled, grumbled, howled, and roused terrible echoes in
the cliffs. Ketling sprang from the wall, ran at the
head of fifteen or twenty men to the breach, and waited.
But he did not wait long. Soon dark figures swarmed
in between the timbers with which the opening was barred.

"Who goes there?" cried Ketling.

"Volodyovski," was the answer. And the two knights
fell into each other's embrace.

"What! How is it there?" asked the officers, rushing
out to the breach.

"Praise be to God! the miners are cut down to the last
man; their tools are broken and scattered. Their work is
for nothing."

"Praise be to God! Praise be to God!"

"But is Mushalski with his men?"

"He is not here yet."

"We might go to help him. Gracious gentlemen, who
is willing?"

But that moment the breach was filled again. Mushalski's men were returning in haste, and decreased in
number considerably, for many of them had fallen from
bullets. But they returned joyously, for with an equally
favorable result. Some of the soldiers had brought back
hammers, drills, and pickaxes as a proof that they had been
in the mine itself.

"But where is Mushalski?" asked Pan Michael.

"True; where is Pan Mushalski?" repeated a number of
voices.

The men under command of the celebrated bowman
stared at one another; then a dragoon, who was wounded
severely, said, with a weak voice, —

"Pan Mushalski has fallen. I saw him when he fell.
I fell at his side; but I rose, and he remained."

The knights were grieved greatly on hearing of the bowman's death, for he was one of the first cavaliers in the

armies of the Commonwealth. They asked the dragoon
again how it had happened; but he was unable to answer,
for blood was flowing from him in a stream, and he fell
to the ground like a grain-sheaf.

The knights began to lament for Pan Mushalski.

"His memory will remain in the army," said Pan Kvasibrotski, "and whoever survives the siege will celebrate his
name."

"There will not be born another such bowman," said a
voice.

"He was stronger in the arm than any man in Hreptyoff,"
said the little knight. "He could push a thaler with his
fingers into a new board. Pan Podbipienta, a Lithuanian,
alone surpassed him in strength; but Podbipienta was killed
in Zbaraj, and of living men none was so strong in the
hands, unless perhaps Pan Adam."

"A great, great loss," said others. "Only in old times
were such cavaliers born."

Thus honoring the memory of the bowman, they mounted
the wall. Pan Michael sent a courier at once with news to
the starosta and the bishop that the mines were destroyed,
and the miners cut down by a sortie. This news was
received with great astonishment in the town, but — who
could expect it? — with secret dislike. The starosta and
the bishop were of opinion that those passing triumphs
would not save Kamenyets, but only rouse the savage lion
still more. They could be useful only in case surrender
were agreed on in spite of them; therefore the two leaders
determined to continue further negotiations.

But neither Pan Michael nor Ketling admitted even for
a moment that the happy news could have such an effect.
Nay, they felt certain now that courage would enter the
weakest hearts, and that all would be inflamed with desire
for a passionate resistance. It was impossible to take the
town without taking the castle first; therefore if the castle
not merely resisted, but conquered, the besieged had not
the least need to negotiate. There was plenty of provisions, also of powder; in view of this it was only needful
to watch the gates and quench fires in the town.

During the whole siege this was the night of most joy
for Pan Michael and Ketling. Never had they had such
great hope that they would come out alive from those
Turkish toils, and also bring out those dearest heads in
safety.

"A couple of storms more," said the little knight, "and as God is in heaven the Turks will be sick of them, and will prefer to force us with famine. And we have supplies enough here. September is at hand; in two months rains and cold will begin. Those troops are not over-enduring; let them get well chilled once, and they will withdraw."

"Many of them are from Ethiopian countries," said Ketling, "or from various places where pepper grows; and any frost will nip them. We can hold out two months in the worst case, even with storms. It is impossible too to suppose that no succor will come to us. The Commonwealth will return to its senses at last; and even if the hetman should not collect a great force, he will annoy the Turk with attacks."

"Ketling! as it seems to me, our hour has not struck yet."

"It is in the power of God, but it seems to me also that it will not come to that."

"Even if some one has fallen, such as Pan Mushalski. Well, there is no help for it! I am terribly sorry for Mushalski, though he died a hero's death."

"May God grant us no worse one, if only not soon! for I confess to you, Michael, I should be sorry for — Krysia."

"Yes, and I too for Basia; we will work earnestly, and maybe there is mercy above us. I am very glad in soul for some reason. We must do a notable deed to-morrow as well."

"The Turks have made protections of plank. I have thought of a method used in burning ships; the rags are now steeping in tar, so that to-morrow before noon we will burn all those works."

"Ah!" said the little knight, "then I will lead a sortie. During the fire there will be confusion in every case, and it will not enter their heads that there can be a sortie in daylight. To-morrow may be better than to-day, Ketling."

Thus did they converse with swelling hearts, and then went to rest, for they were greatly wearied. But the little knight had not slept three hours when Lusnia roused him.

"Pan Commandant," said the sergeant, "we have news."

"What is it?" cried the watchful soldier, springing up in one moment.

"Pan Mushalski is here."

"For God's sake! what do you tell me?"

"He is here. I was standing at the breach, and heard

some one calling from the other side in Polish, 'Do not fire; it is I.' I looked; there was Pan Mushalski coming back dressed as a janissary."

"Praise be to God!" said the little knight; and he sprang up to greet the bowman.

It was dawning already. Pan Mushalski was standing outside the wall in a white cap and armor, so much like a real janissary that one's eyes were slow in belief. Seeing the little knight, he hurried to him, and began to greet him joyously.

"We have mourned over you already!" cried Volodyovski.

With that a number of other officers ran up, among them Ketling. All were amazed beyond description, and interrupted one another asking how he came to be in Turkish disguise.

"I stumbled," said he, "over the body of a janissary when I was returning, and struck my head against a cannon-ball; though I had a cap bound with wire, I lost consciousness at once. My head was tender after that blow which I got from Hamdi Bey. When I came to myself I was lying on a dead janissary, as on a bed. I felt my head; it was a trifle sore, but there was not even a lump on it. I took off my cap; the rain cooled my head, and I thought: 'This is well for us. It would be a good plan to take that janissary's uniform, and stroll among the Turks. I speak their tongue as well as Polish, and no one could discover me by my speech; my face is not different from that of a janissary. I will go and listen to their talk.' Fear seized me at times, for I remembered my former captivity; but I went. The night was dark; there was barely a light here and there. I tell you, gentlemen, I went among them as if they had been my own people. Many of them were lying in trenches under cover; I went to them. This and that one asked, 'Why are you strolling about?' 'Because I cannot sleep,' answered I. Others were talking in crowds about the siege. There is great consternation. I heard with my own ears how they complained of our Hreptyoff commandant here present," at this Pan Mushalski bowed to Volodyovski. "I repeat their *ipsissima verba*" (very words), "because an enemy's blame is the highest praise. 'While that little dog,' said they, thus did the dog brothers call your grace, — 'while that little dog defends the castle, we shall not capture it.' Others said, 'Bullets and iron do not harm him; but death blows from him as from a pestilence.'

Then all in the crowd began to complain: 'We alone fight,' said they, 'and other troops are doing nothing; the volunteers are lying with their bellies to the sky. The Tartars are plundering; the spahis are strolling about the bazaars. The Padishah says to us, "My dear lambs;" but it is clear that we are not over-dear to him, since he sends us here to the shambles. We will hold out,' said they, 'but not long; then we will go back to Hotin, and if they do not let us go, some lofty heads may fall.' "

"Do you hear, gracious gentlemen?" cried Volodyovski. "When the janissaries mutiny, the Sultan will be frightened, and raise the siege."

"As God is dear to me, I tell the pure truth," said Mushalski. "Rebellion is easy among the janissaries, and they are very much dissatisfied. I think that they will try one or two storms more, and then will gnash their teeth at their aga, the kaimakan, or even the Sultan himself."

"So it will be," cried the officers.

"Let them try twelve storms; we are ready," said others.

They rattled their sabres and looked with bloodshot eyes at the trenches, while drawing deep breaths; hearing this, the little knight whispered with enthusiasm to Ketling, "A new Zbaraj! a new Zbaraj!"

But Pan Mushalski began again: "I have told you what I heard. I was sorry to leave them, for I might have heard more; but I was afraid that daylight might catch me. I went then to those trenches from which they were not firing; I did this so as to slip by in the dark. I look; I see no regular sentries, only groups of janissaries strolling, as everywhere. I go to a frowning gun; no one says anything. You know that I took spikes for the cannon. I push a spike into the priming quickly; it won't go in, — it needs a blow from a hammer. But since the Lord God gave some strength to my hand (you have seen my experiments more than once), I pressed the spike; it squeaked a little, but went in to the head. I was terribly glad."

"As God lives! did you do that? Did you spike the great cannon?" asked men on every side.

"I spiked that and another, for the work went so easily that I was sorry to leave it; and I went to another gun. My hand is a little sore, but the spike went in."

"Gracious gentlemen," cried Pan Michael, "no one here has done greater things; no one has covered himself with such glory. Vivat Pan Mushalski!"

"Vivat! vivat!" repeated the officers.

After the officers the soldiers began to shout. The Turks in their trenches heard those shouts, and were alarmed; their courage fell the more. But the bowman, full of joy, bowed to the officers, and showed his mighty palm, which was like a shovel; on it were two blue spots. "True, as God lives! you have the witness here," said he.

"We believe!" cried all. "Praise be to God that you came back in safety!"

"I passed through the planking," continued the bowman. "I wanted to burn that work; but I had nothing to do it with."

"Do you know, Michael," cried Ketling, "my rags are ready. I am beginning to think of that planking. Let them know that we attack first."

"Begin! begin!" cried Pan Michael.

He rushed himself to the arsenal, and sent fresh news to the town: "Pan Mushalski was not killed in the sortie, for he has returned, after spiking two heavy guns. He was among the janissaries, who think of rebelling. In an hour we shall burn their woodworks; and if it be possible to make at the same time a sortie, I will make it."

The messenger had not crossed the bridge when the walls were trembling from the roar of cannon. This time the castle began the thundering dialogue. In the pale light of the morning the flaming rags flew like blazing banners, and fell on the woodwork. The moisture with which the night rain had covered the wood helped nothing. Soon the timbers caught fire, and were burning. After the rags Ketling hurled bombs. The wearied crowds of janissaries left the trenches in the first moments. They did not play the kindya. The vizir himself appeared at the head of new legions; but evidently doubt had crept even into his heart, for the pashas heard how he muttered, —

"Battle is sweeter to those men than sleep. What kind of people live in that castle?"

In the army were heard on all sides alarmed voices repeating, "The little dog is beginning to bite! The little dog is beginning to bite!"

CHAPTER LVII.

THAT happy night, full of omens of victory, was followed by August 26, — the day most important in the history of that war. In the castle they expected some great effort on the part of the Turks. In fact, about sunrise there was heard such a loud and mighty hammering along the left side of the castle as never before. Evidently the Turks were hurrying with a new mine, the largest of all. Strong detachments of troops were guarding that work from a distance. Swarms began to move in the trenches. From the multitude of colored banners with which the field on the side of Dlujek had bloomed as with flowers, it was known that the vizir was coming to direct the storm in person. New cannon were brought to the intrenchments by janissaries, countless throngs of whom covered the new castle, taking refuge in its fosses and ruins, so as to be in readiness for a hand-to-hand struggle.

As has been said, the castle was the first to begin the converse with cannon, and so effectually that a momentary panic rose in the trenches. But the bimbashes rallied the janissaries in the twinkle of an eye; at the same time all the Turkish cannon raised their voices. Bombs, balls, and grapeshot were flying; at the heads of the besieged flew rubbish, bricks, plaster; smoke was mingled with dust, the heat of fire with the heat of the sun. Breath was failing in men's breasts; sight left their eyes. The roar of guns, the bursting of bombs, the biting of cannon-balls on the rocks, the uproar of the Turks, the cries of the defenders, formed one terrible concert which was accompanied by the echoes of the cliffs. The castle was covered with missiles; the town, the gates, all the bastions, were covered. But the castle defended itself with rage; it answered thunders with thunders, shook, flashed, smoked, roared, vomited fire, death, and destruction, as if Jove's anger had borne it away, — as if it had forgotten itself amid flames; as if it wished to drown the Turkish thunders and sink in the earth, or else triumph.

In the castle, among flying balls, fire, dust, and smoke, the little knight rushed from cannon to cannon, from one wall to another, from corner to corner; he was like a destroying flame. He seemed to double and treble himself: he was everywhere. He encouraged; he shouted. When a gunner fell he took his place, and rousing confidence in men, ran again to some other spot. His fire was communicated to the soldiers. They believed that this was the last storm, after which would come peace and glory; faith in victory filled their breasts. Their hearts grew firm and resolute; the madness of battle seized their minds. Shouts and challenges issued every moment from their throats. Such rage seized some that they went over the wall to close outside with the janissaries hand to hand.

The janissaries, under cover of smoke, went twice to the breach in dense masses; and twice they fell back in disorder after they had covered the ground with their bodies. About midday the volunteer and irregular janissaries were sent to aid them; but the less trained crowds, though pushed from behind with darts, only howled with dreadful voices, and did not wish to go against the castle. The kaimakan came; that did no good. Every moment threatened disorder, bordering on panic. At last the men were withdrawn; and the guns alone worked unceasingly as before, hurling thunder after thunder, lightning after lightning.

Whole hours were spent in this manner. The sun had passed the zenith, and rayless, red, and smoky, as if veiled by haze, looked at that struggle.

About three o'clock in the afternoon the roar of guns gained such force that in the castle the loudest words shouted in the ear were not audible. The air in the castle became as hot as in a stove. The water which they poured on the cannon turned into steam, mixing with the smoke and hiding the light; but the guns thundered on.

Just after three o'clock, the largest Turkish culverines were broken. Some "Our Fathers" later, the mortar standing near them burst, struck by a long shot. Gunners perished like flies. Every moment it became more evident that that irrepressible castle was gaining in the struggle, that it would roar down the Turkish thunder, and utter the last word of victory.

The Turkish fire began to weaken gradually.

"The end will come!" shouted Volodyovski, with all his might, in Ketling's ear. He wished his friend to hear those words amid the roar.

"So I think," answered Ketling. "To last till to-morrow, or longer?"

"Perhaps longer. Victory is with us to-day."

"And through us. We must think of that new mine."

The Turkish fire was weakening still more.

"Keep up the cannonade!" cried Volodyovski. And he sprang among the gunners. "Fire, men!" cried he, "till the last Turkish gun is silent! To the glory of God and the Most Holy Lady! To the glory of the Commonwealth!"

The soldiers, seeing that the storm was nearing its end, gave forth a loud shout, and with the greater enthusiasm fired at the Turkish trenches.

"We'll play an evening kindya for you, dog brothers," cried many voices.

Suddenly something wonderful took place. All the Turkish guns ceased at once, as if some one had cut them off with a knife. At the same time, the musketry fire of the janissaries ceased in the new castle. The old castle thundered for a time yet; but at last the officers began to look at one another, and inquire, —

"What is this? What has happened?"

Ketling, alarmed somewhat, ceased firing also.

"Maybe there is a mine under us which will be exploded right away," said one of the officers.

Volodyovski pierced the man with a threatening glance, and said, "The mine is not ready; and even if it were, only the left side of the castle could be blown up by it, and we will defend ourselves in the ruins while there is breath in our nostrils. Do you understand?"

Silence followed, unbroken by a shot from the trenches or the town. After thunders from which the walls and the earth had been quivering, there was something solemn in that silence, but something ominous also. The eyes of each were intent on the trenches; but through the clouds of smoke nothing was visible. Suddenly the measured blows of hammers were heard on the left side.

"I told you that they are only making the mine," said Pan Michael. "Sergeant, take twenty men and examine for me the new castle," commanded he, turning to Lusnia.

Lusnia obeyed quickly, took twenty men, and vanished in a moment beyond the breach. Silence followed again, broken only by groans here and there, or the gasp of the dying, and the pounding of hammers. They waited rather long. At last the sergeant returned.

"Pan Commandant," said he, "there is not a living soul in the new castle."

Volodyovski looked with astonishment at Ketling. "Have they raised the siege already, or what? Nothing can be seen through the smoke."

But the smoke, blown by the wind, became thin, and at last its veil was broken above the town. At the same moment a voice, shrill and terrible, began to shout from the bastion, —

"Over the gates are white flags! We are surrendering!"

Hearing this, the soldiers and officers turned toward the town. Terrible amazement was reflected on their faces; the words died on the lips of all; and through the strips of smoke they were gazing toward the town. But in the town, on the Russian and Polish gates, white flags were really waving. Farther on, they saw one on the bastion of Batory.

The face of the little knight became as white as those flags waving in the wind.

"Ketling, do you see?" whispered he, turning to his friend.

Ketling's face was pale also. "I see," replied he.

And they looked into each other's eyes for some time, uttering with them everything which two soldiers like them, without fear or reproach, had to say, — soldiers who never in life had broken their word, and who had sworn before the altar to die rather than surrender the castle. And now, after such a defence, after a struggle which recalled the days of Zbaraj, after a storm which had been repulsed, and after a victory, they were commanded to break their oath, to surrender the castle, and live.

As, not long before, hostile balls were flying over the castle, so now hostile thoughts were flying in a throng through their heads. And sorrow simply measureless pressed their hearts, — sorrow for two loved ones, sorrow for life and happiness; hence they looked at each other as if demented, as if dead, and at times they turned glances full of despair toward the town, as if wishing to be sure that their eyes were not deceiving them, — to be sure that the last hour had struck.

At that time horses' hoofs sounded from the direction of the town; and after a while Horaim, the attendant of the starosta, rushed up to them.

"An order to the commandant!" cried he, reining in his horse.

Volodyovski took the order, read it in silence, and after a time, amid silence as of the grave, said to the officers, —

"Gracious gentlemen, commissioners have crossed the river in a boat, and have gone to Dlujek to sign conditions. After a time they will come here. Before evening we must withdraw the troops from the castle, and raise a white flag without delay."

No one answered a word. Nothing was heard but quick breathing.

At last Kvasibrotski said, "We must raise the white flag. I will muster the men."

Here and there the words of command were heard. The soldiers began to take their places in ranks, and shoulder arms. The clatter of muskets and the measured tread roused echoes in the silent castle.

Ketling pushed up to Pan Michael. "Is it time?" inquired he.

"Wait for the commissioners; let us hear the conditions! Besides, I will go down myself."

"No, I will go! I know the places better; I know the position of everything."

"The commissioners are returning! The commissioners are returning!"

The three unhappy envoys appeared in the castle after a certain time. They were Grushetski, judge of Podolia, the chamberlain Revuski, and Pan Myslishevski, banneret of Chernigoff. They came gloomily, with drooping heads; on their shoulders were gleaming kaftans of gold brocade, which they had received as gifts from the vizir.

Volodyovski was waiting for them, resting against a gun turned toward Dlujek. The gun was hot yet, and steaming. All three greeted him in silence.

"What are the conditions?" asked he.

"The town will not be plundered; life and property are assured to the inhabitants. Whoever does not choose to remain has the right to withdraw and betake himself to whatever place may please him."

"And Kamenyets?"

The commissioners dropped their heads: "Goes to the Sultan forever."

The commissioners took their way, not toward the bridge, for throngs of people had blocked the road, but toward the southern gate at the side. When they had descended, they sat in the boat which was to go to the Polish gate. In the low place lying along the river between the cliffs, the janissaries began to appear. Greater and greater streams of people flowed from the town, and occupied the place opposite the old bridge. Many wished to run to the castle; but the outgoing regiments restrained them, at command of the little knight.

When Volodyovski had mustered the troops, he called Pan Mushalski and said to him, —

"Old friend, do me one more service. Go this moment to my wife, and tell her from me — " Here the voice stuck in the throat of the little knight for a while. "And say to her from me — " He halted again, and then added quickly, "This life is nothing!"

The bowman departed. After him the troops went out gradually. Pan Michael mounted his horse and watched over the march. The castle was evacuated slowly, because of the rubbish and fragments which blocked the way.

Ketling approached the little knight. "I will go down," said he, fixing his teeth.

"Go! but delay till the troops have marched out. Go!"

Here they seized each other in an embrace which lasted some time. The eyes of both were gleaming with an uncommon radiance. Ketling rushed away at last toward the vaults.

Pan Michael took the helmet from his head. He looked awhile yet on the ruin, on that field of his glory, on the rubbish, the corpses, the fragments of walls, on the breastwork, on the guns; then raising his eyes, he began to pray. His last words were, "Grant her, O Lord, to endure this patiently; give her peace!"

Ah! Ketling hastened, not waiting even till the troops had marched out; for at that moment the bastions quivered, an awful roar rent the air; bastions, towers, walls, horses, guns, living men, corpses, masses of earth, all torn upward with a flame, and mixed, pounded together, as it were, into one dreadful cartridge, flew toward the sky.

Thus died Volodyovski, the Hector of Kamenyets, the first soldier of the Commonwealth.

In the monastery of St. Stanislav stood a lofty catafalque in the centre of the church; it was surrounded with gleaming tapers, and on it lay Pan Volodyovski in two coffins, one of lead and one of wood. The lids had been fastened, and the funeral service was just ending.

It was the heartfelt wish of the widow that the body should rest in Hreptyoff; but since all Podolia was in the hands of the enemy, it was decided to bury it temporarily in Stanislav, for to that place the "exiles" of Kamenyets had been sent under a Turkish convoy, and there delivered to the troops of the hetman.

All the bells in the monastery were ringing. The church was filled with a throng of nobles and soldiers, who wished to look for the last time at the coffin of the Hector of Kamenyets, and the first cavalier of the Commonwealth. It was whispered that the hetman himself was to come to the funeral; but as he had not appeared so far, and as at any moment the Tartars might come in a chambul, it was determined not to defer the ceremony.

Old soldiers, friends or subordinates of the deceased, stood in a circle around the catafalque. Among others were present Pan Mushalski, the bowman, Pan Motovidlo, Pan Snitko, Pan Hromyka, Pan Nyenashinyets, Pan Novoveski, and many others, former officers of the stanitsa. By a marvellous fortune, no man was lacking of those who had sat on the evening benches around the hearth at Hreptyoff; all had brought their heads safely out of that war, except the man who was their leader and model. That good and just knight, terrible to the enemy, loving to his own; that swordsman above swordsmen, with the heart of a dove, — lay there high among the tapers, in glory immeasurable, but in the silence of death. Hearts hardened through war were crushed with sorrow at that sight; yellow gleams from the tapers shone on the stern, suffering faces of warriors, and were reflected in glittering points in the tears dropping down from their eyelids.

Within the circle of soldiers lay Basia, in the form of a cross, on the floor, and near her Zagloba, old, broken, decrepit, and trembling. She had followed on foot from Kamenyets the hearse bearing that most precious coffin, and now the moment had come when it was necessary to give that coffin to the earth. Walking the whole way, insensible, as if not belonging to this world, and now at the catafalque, she repeated with unconscious lips, "This life is nothing!" She repeated it because that beloved one had commanded her, for that was the last message which he had sent her; but in that repetition and in those expressions were mere sounds, without substance, without truth, without meaning and solace. No; "This life is nothing" meant merely regret, darkness, despair, torpor, merely misfortune incurable, life beaten and broken, — an erroneous announcement that there was nothing above her, neither mercy nor hope; that there was merely a desert, and it will be a desert which God alone can fill when He sends death.

They rang the bells; at the great altar Mass was at its end. At last thundered the deep voice of the priest, as if calling from the abyss: "*Requiescat in pace!*" A feverish quiver shook Basia, and in her unconscious head rose one thought alone, "Now, now, they will take him from me!" But that was not yet the end of the ceremony. The knights had prepared many speeches to be spoken at the lowering of the coffin; meanwhile Father Kaminski ascended the pulpit, — the same who had been in Hreptyoff frequently, and who in time of Basia's illness had prepared her for death.

People in the church began to spit and cough, as is usual before preaching; then they were quiet, and all eyes were turned to the pulpit. The rattling of a drum was heard on the pulpit.

The hearers were astonished. Father Kaminski beat the drum as if for alarm; he stopped suddenly, and a deathlike silence followed. Then the drum was heard a second and a third time; suddenly the priest threw the drumsticks to the floor of the church, and called, —

"Pan Colonel Volodyovski!"

A spasmodic scream from Basia answered him. It became simply terrible in the church. Pan Zagloba rose, and aided by Mushalski bore out the fainting woman.

Meanwhile the priest continued: "In God's name, Pan Volodyovski, they are beating the alarm! there is war, the enemy is in the land! — and do you not spring up, seize your sabre, mount your horse? Have you forgotten your former virtue? Do you leave us alone with sorrow, with alarm?"

The breasts of the knights rose; and a universal weeping broke out in the church, and broke out several times again, when the priest lauded the virtue, the love of country, and the bravery of the dead man. His own words carried the preacher away. His face became pale; his forehead was covered with sweat; his voice trembled. Sorrow for the little knight carried him away, sorrow for Kamenyets, sorrow for the Commonwealth, ruined by the hands of the followers of the Crescent; and finally he finished his eulogy with this prayer : —

"O Lord, they will turn churches into mosques, and chant the Koran in places where till this time the Gospel has been chanted. Thou hast cast us down, O Lord; Thou hast turned Thy face from us, and given us into the power of the foul Turk. Inscrutable are Thy decrees; but who, O Lord, will resist the Turk now? What armies will war with him on the boundaries? Thou, from whom nothing in the world is concealed, — Thou knowest best that there is nothing superior to our cavalry! What cavalry can move for Thee, O Lord, as ours can? Wilt Thou set aside defenders behind whose shoulders all Christendom might glorify Thy name? O kind Father, do not desert us! show us Thy mercy! Send us a defender! Send a crusher of the foul Mohammedan! Let him come hither; let him stand among us; let him raise our fallen hearts! Send him, O Lord!"

At that moment the people gave way at the door; and into the church walked the hetman, Pan Sobieski. The eyes of all were turned to him; a quiver shook the people; and he went with clatter of spurs to the catafalque, lordly, mighty, with the face of a Caesar. An escort of iron cavalry followed him.

"Salvator!" cried the priest, in prophetic ecstasy.

Sobieski knelt at the catafalque, and prayed for the soul of Volodyovski.

EPILOGUE.

MORE than a year after the fall of Kamenyets, when the dissensions of parties had ceased in some fashion, the Commonwealth came forth at last in defence of its eastern boundaries; and it came forth offensively. The grand hetman, Sobieski, marched with thirty-one thousand cavalry and infantry to Hotin, in the Sultan's territory, to strike on the incomparably more powerful legions of Hussein Pasha, stationed at that fortress.

The name of Sobieski had become terrible to the enemy. During the year succeeding the capture of Kamenyets the hetman accomplished so much, injured the countless army of the Padishah to such a degree, crushed out so many chambuls, rescued such throngs of captives, that old Hussein, though stronger in the number of his men, though standing at the head of chosen cavalry, though aided by Kaplan Pasha, did not dare to meet the hetman in the open field, and decided to defend himself in a fortified camp.

The hetman surrounded that camp with his army; and it was known universally that he intended to take it in an offensive battle. Some thought surely that it was an undertaking unheard of in the history of war to attack a superior with an inferior army when the enemy was protected by walls and trenches. Hussein had a hundred and twenty guns, while in the whole Polish camp there were only fifty. The Turkish infantry was threefold greater in number than the power of the hetman; of janissaries alone, so terrible in hand-to-hand conflict, there were eighty thousand. But the hetman believed in his star, in the magic of his name, — and finally in the men whom he led. Under him marched regiments trained and tempered in fire, — men who had grown up from years of childhood in the bustle of war, who had passed through an uncounted number of expeditions, campaigns, sieges, battles. Many of them remembered the terrible days of Hmelnitski, of Zbaraj and Berestechko; many had gone through all the wars, Swedish, Prussian, Moscovite, civil, Danish, and Hungarian. With him were the escorts of magnates, formed of veterans only; there were soldiers from the

stanitsas, for whom war had become what peace is for other
men, — the ordinary condition and course of life. Under
the voevoda of Rus were fifteen squadrons of hussars, —
cavalry considered, even by foreigners, as invincible; there
were light squadrons, the very same at the head of which
the hetman had inflicted such disasters on detached Tartar
chambuls after the fall of Kamenyets; there were finally
the land infantry, who rushed on janissaries with the butts
of their muskets, without firing a shot.

War had reared those veterans, for it had reared whole
generations in the Commonwealth; but hitherto they had
been scattered, or in the service of opposing parties. Now,
when internal agreement had summoned them to one camp
and one command, the hetman hoped to crush with such
soldiers the stronger Hussein and the equally strong Kaplan.
These old soldiers were led by trained men whose names
were written more than once in the history of recent wars,
in the changing wheel of defeats and victories.

The hetman himself stood at the head of them all like
a sun, and directed thousands with his will; but who were
the other leaders who at this camp in Hotin were to
cover themselves with immortal glory? There were the
two Lithuanian hetmans, — the grand hetman, Pats, and the
field hetman, Michael Kazimir Radzivill. These two joined
the armies of the kingdom a few days before the battle,
and now, at command of Sobieski, they took position
on the heights which connected Hotin with Jvanyets.
Twelve thousand warriors obeyed their commands; among
these were two thousand chosen infantry. From the
Dniester toward the south stood the allied regiments of
Wallachia, who left the Turkish camp on the eve of the
battle to join their strength with Christians. At the
flank of the Wallachians stood with his artillery Pan
Kantski, incomparable in the capture of fortified places,
in the making of intrenchments, and the handling of cannon. He had trained himself in foreign countries, but soon
excelled even foreigners. Behind Kantski stood Korytski's
Russian and Mazovian infantry; farther on, the field hetman of the kingdom, Dmitri Vishnyevetski, cousin of the
sickly king. 'He had under him the light cavalry. Next
to him, with his own squadron of infantry and cavalry,
stood Pan Yendrei Pototski, once an opponent of the hetman, now an admirer of his greatness. Behind him and
behind Korytski stood, under Pan Yablonovski, voevoda of

Rus, fifteen squadrons of hussars in glittering armor, with helmets casting a threatening shade on their faces, and with wings at their shoulders. A forest of lances reared their points above these squadrons; but the men were calm. They were confident in their invincible force, and sure that it would come to them to decide the victory.

There were warriors inferior to these, not in bravery, but in prominence. There was Pan Lujetski, whose brother the Turks had slain in Bodzanoff; for this deed he had sworn undying vengeance. There was Pan Stefan Charnyetski, nephew of the great Stefan, and field secretary of the kingdom. He, in time of the siege of Kamenyets, had been at the head of a whole band of nobles at Golemb, as a partisan of the king, and had almost roused civil war; now he desired to distinguish himself with bravery. There was Gabriel Silnitski, who had passed all his life in war, and age had already whitened his head; there were other voevodas and castellans, less acquainted with previous wars, less famous, but therefore more greedy of glory.

Among the knighthood not clothed with senatorial dignity, illustrious above others, was Pan Yan, the famous hero of Zbaraj, a soldier held up as a model to the knighthood. He had taken part in every war fought by the Commonwealth during thirty years. His hair was gray; but six sons surrounded him, in strength like six wild boars. Of these, four knew war already, but the two younger had to pass their novitiate; hence they were burning with such eagerness for battle that their father was forced to restrain them with words of advice.

The officers looked with great respect on this father and his sons; but still greater admiration was roused by Pan Yarotski, who, blind of both eyes, like the Bohemian king[1] Yan, joined the campaign. He had neither children nor relatives; attendants led him by the arms; he hoped for no more than to lay down his life in battle, benefit his country, and win glory. There too was Pan Rechytski, whose father and brother fell during that year.

There also was Pan Motovidlo, who had escaped not long before from Tartar bondage, and gone to the field with Pan Myslishevski. The first wished to avenge his captivity; the second, the injustice which he had suffered at Kamenyets, where, in spite of the treaty and his dignity

[1] More likely Yan Zisca, the great leader of the Hussites.

33

of noble, he had been beaten with sticks by the janissaries. There were knights of long experience from the stanitsas of the Dniester, — the wild Pan Rushchyts and the incomparable bowman, Mushalski, who had brought a sound head out of Kamenyets, because the little knight had sent him to Basia with a message; there was Pan Snitko and Pan Nyenashinyets and Pan Hromyka, and the most unhappy of all, young Pan Adam. Even his friends and relatives wished death to this man, for there remained no consolation for him. When he had regained his health, Pan Adam exterminated chambuls for a whole year, pursuing Lithuanian Tartars with special animosity. After the defeat of Pan Motovidlo by Krychinski, he hunted Krychinski through all Podolia, gave him no rest, and troubled him beyond measure. During those expeditions he caught Adurovich and flayed him alive; he spared no prisoners, but found no relief for his suffering. A month before the battle he joined Yablonovski's hussars.

This was the knighthood with which Pan Sobieski took his position at Hotin. Those soldiers were eager to wreak vengeance for the wrongs of the Commonwealth in the first instance, but also for their own. In continual battles with the Pagans in that land soaked in blood, almost every man had lost some dear one, and bore within him the memory of some terrible misfortune. The grand hetman hastened to battle then, for he saw that rage in the hearts of his soldiers might be compared to the rage of a lioness whose whelps reckless hunters have stolen from the thicket.

On Nov. 9, 1674, the affair was begun by skirmishes. Crowds of Turks issued from behind the walls in the morning; crowds of Polish knights hastened to meet them with eagerness. Men fell on both sides, but with greater loss to the Turks. Only a few Turks of note or Poles fell, however. Pan May, in the very beginning of the skirmish, was pierced by the curved sabre of a gigantic spahi; but the youngest son of Pan Yan with one blow almost severed the head from that spahi. By this deed he earned the praise of his prudent father, and notable glory.

They fought in groups or singly. Those who were looking at the struggle gained courage; greater eagerness rose in them each moment. Meanwhile, detachments of the army were disposed around the Turkish camp, each in the place pointed out by the hetman. Pan Sobieski, taking his position on the old Yassy road, behind the infantry of

Korytski, embraced with his eyes the whole camp of Hussein; and on his face he had the serene calmness which a master certain of his art has before he commences his labor. From time to time he sent adjutants with commands; then with thoughtful glance he looked at the struggle of the skirmishers. Toward evening Pan Yablonovski, voevoda of Rus, came to him.

"The intrenchments are so extensive," said he, "that it is impossible to attack from all sides simultaneously."

"To-morrow we shall be in the intrenchments; and after to-morrow we shall cut down those men in three quarters of an hour," said Sobieski, calmly.

Night came in the mean while. Skirmishers left the field. The hetman commanded all divisions to approach the intrenchments in the darkness; this Hussein hindered as much as he could with guns of large calibre, but without result. Toward morning the Polish divisions moved forward again somewhat. The infantry began to throw up breastworks. Some regiments had pushed on to within a good musket-shot. The janissaries opened a brisk fire from muskets. At command of the hetman almost no answer was given to these volleys, but the infantry prepared for an attack hand to hand. The soldiers were waiting only for the signal to rush forward passionately. Over their extended line flew grapeshot with whistling and noise like flocks of birds. Pan Kantski's artillery, beginning the conflict at daybreak, did not cease for one moment. Only when the battle was over did it appear what great destruction its missiles had wrought falling in places covered most thickly with the tents of janissaries and spahis.

Thus passed the time until mid-day; but since the day was short, as the month was November, there was need of haste. On a sudden all the trumpets were heard, and drums, great and small. Tens of thousands of throats shouted in one voice; the infantry, supported by light cavalry advancing near them, rushed in a dense throng to the onset.

They attacked the Turks at five points simultaneously. Yan Dennemark and Christopher de Bohan, warriors of experience, led the foreign regiments. The first, fiery by nature, hurried forward so eagerly that he reached the intrenchment before others, and came near destroying his regiment, for he had to meet a salvo from several thousand muskets. He fell himself. His soldiers began to waver; but at that moment De Bohan came to the rescue and prevented a panic. With a step as steady as if on parade, and keeping time to the music, he passed the whole distance to the Turkish intrenchment, answered salvo with salvo, and when the fosse was filled with fascines passed it first, under a storm of bullets, inclined his cap to the janissaries, and pierced the first banneret with a sabre. The soldiers, carried away by the example of such a colonel, sprang forward, and then began dreadful struggles in which discipline and training vied with the wild valor of the janissaries.

But dragoons were led quickly from the direction of Taraban by Tetwin and Doenhoff; another regiment was led by Aswer Greben and Haydepol, all distinguished soldiers who, except Haydepol, had covered themselves with great glory under Charnyetski in Denmark. The troops of their command were large and sturdy, selected from men on the royal domains, well trained to fighting on foot and on horseback. The gate was defended against them by irregular janissaries, who, though their number was great, were thrown into confusion quickly and began to retreat; when they came to hand-to-hand conflict they defended themselves only when they could not find a place of escape. That gate was captured first, and through it cavalry went first to the interior of the camp.

At the head of the Polish land infantry Kobyletski, Jebrovski, Pyotrkovchyk, and Galetski struck the intrenchments in three other places. The most tremendous struggle raged at the main gate, on the Yassy road, where the Mazovians closed with the guard of Hussein Pasha. The vizir was concerned mainly with that gate, for through it the Polish cavalry might rush to the camp; hence he resolved to defend it most stubbornly, and urged forward unceasingly detachments of janissaries. The land infantry took the gate at a blow, and then strained all their strength to retain it. Cannon-balls and a storm of bullets from small arms pushed them back; from clouds of smoke new bands of Turkish warriors sprang forth to the attack every moment. Pan Kobyletski, not waiting till they came, rushed at them like a raging bear; and two walls of men pressed each other, swaying backward and forward in close quarters, in confusion, in a whirl, in torrents of blood, and on piles of human bodies. They fought with every manner of weapon, — with sabres, with knives, with gunstocks, with shovels, with clubs, with stones; the crush became at moments so great, so terrible, that men grappled and fought

with fists and with teeth. Hussein tried twice to break the
infantry with the impact of cavalry; but the infantry fell
upon him each time with such "extraordinary resolution"
that the cavalry had to withdraw in disorder. Pan Sobieski
took pity at last on his men, and sent all the camp servants
to help them.

At the head of these was Pan Motovidlo. This rabble,
not employed usually in battle and armed with weapons of
any kind, rushed forward with such desire that they roused
admiration even in the hetman. It may be that greed of
plunder inspired them; perhaps the fire seized them which
enlivened the whole army that day. It is enough that they
struck the janissaries as if they had been smoke, and overpowered them so savagely that in the first onset they forced
them back a musket-shot's length from the gate. Hussein
threw new regiments into the whirl of battle; and the struggle, renewed in the twinkle of an eye, lasted whole hours.
At last Korytski, at the head of chosen regiments, beset
the gate in force; the hussars from a distance moved like a
great bird raising itself lazily to flight, and pushed toward
the gate also.

At this time an adjutant rushed to the hetman from the
Eastern side of the camp.

"The voevoda of Belsk is on the ramparts!" cried he,
with panting breast.

After him came a second, —

"The hetmans of Lithuania are on the ramparts!"

After him came others, always with similar news. It
had grown dark in the world, but light was beaming from
the face of the hetman. He turned to Pan Bidzinski, who
at that moment was near him, and said, —

"Next comes the turn of the cavalry; but that will be in
the morning."

No one in the Polish or the Turkish army knew or
imagined that the hetman intended to defer the general
attack till the following morning. Nay, adjutants sprang
to the captains with the command to be ready at any
instant. The infantry stood in closed ranks; sabres and
lances were burning the hands of the cavalry. All were
awaiting the order impatiently, for the men were chilled
and hungry.

But no order came; meanwhile hours passed. The night
became as black as mourning. Drizzling rain had set in at
one o'clock in the day; but about midnight a strong wind

with frozen rain and snow followed. Gusts of it froze the
marrow in men's bones; the horses were barely able to
stand in their places; men were benumbed. The sharpest
frost, if dry, could not be so bitter as that wind and snow,
which cut like a scourge. In constant expectation of the
signal, it was not possible to think of eating and drinking
or of kindling fires. The weather became more terrible
each hour. That was a memorable night, — "a night of
torture and gnashing of teeth." The voices of the
captains — "Stand! stand! — were heard every moment; and
the soldiers, trained to obedience, stood in the greatest
readiness without movement, and patiently.

But in front of them, in rain, storm, and darkness, stood
in equal readiness the stiffened regiments of the Turks.
Among them, too, no one kindled a fire, no one ate, no
one drank. The attack of all the Polish forces might
come at any moment, therefore the spahis could not drop
their sabres from their hands; the janissaries stood like a
wall, with their muskets ready to fire. The hardy Polish
soldiers, accustomed to the sternness of winter, could pass
such a night; but those men reared in the mild climate of
Rumelia, or amid the palms of Asia Minor, were suffering
more than their powers could endure. At last Hussein
discovered why Sobieski did not begin the attack. It was
because that frozen rain was the best ally of the Poles.
Clearly, if the spahis and janissaries were to stand through
twelve hours like those, the cold would lay them down
on the morrow as grain sheaves are laid. They would not
even try to defend themselves, — at least till the heat of
the battle should warm them.

Both Poles and Tartars understood this. About four
o'clock in the morning two pashas came to Hussein, — Yanish Pasha and Kiaya Pasha, the leader of the janissaries,
an old warrior of renown and experience. The faces of
both were full of anxiety and care.

"Lord!" said Kiaya, first, "if my 'lambs' stand in this
way till daylight, neither bullets nor swords will be needed
against them."

"Lord!" said Yanish Pasha, "my spahis will freeze, and
will not fight in the morning."

Hussein twisted his beard, foreseeing defeat for his army
and destruction to himself. But what was he to do? Were
he to let his men break ranks for even a minute, or let them
kindle fires to warm themselves with hot food, the attack

would begin immediately. As it was, the trumpets were sounded at intervals near the ramparts, as if the cavalry were just ready to move.

Kiaya and Yanish Pasha saw only one escape from disaster, — that was, not to wait for the attack, but to strike with all force on the enemy. It was nothing that he was in readiness; for though ready to attack, he did not expect attack himself. Perhaps they might drive him out of the intrenchments; in the worst event defeat was likely in a night battle, in the battle of the morrow it was certain.

But Hussein did not venture to follow the advice of the old warriors.

"How!" said he; "you have furrowed the camp-ground with ditches, seeing in them the one safeguard against that hellish cavalry, — that was your advice and your precaution; now you say something different."

He did not give that order. He merely gave an order to fire from cannon, to which Pan Kantski answered with great effect instantly. The rain became colder and colder, and cut more and more cruelly; the wind roared, howled, went through clothing and skin, and froze the blood in men's veins. So passed that long November night, in which the strength of the warriors of Islam was failing, and despair, with a foreboding of defeat, seized hold of their hearts.

At the very dawn Yanish Pasha went once more to Hussein with advice to withdraw in order of battle to the bridge on the Dniester and begin there the game of war cautiously. "For," said he, "if the troops do not withstand the onrush of the cavalry, they will withdraw to the opposite bank, and the river will give them protection." Kiaya, the leader of the janissaries, was of another opinion, however. He thought it too late for Yanish's advice, and moreover he feared lest a panic might seize the whole army immediately, if the order were given to withdraw. "The spahis with the aid of the irregular janissaries must sustain the first shock of the enemy's cavalry, even if all are to perish in doing so. By that time the janissaries will come to their aid, and when the first impetus of the unbelievers is stopped, perhaps God may send victory."

Thus advised, Kiaya and Hussein followed. Mounted multitudes of Turks pushed forward; the janissaries, regular and irregular, were disposed behind them, around the tents of Hussein. Their deep ranks presented a splendid and fear-inspiring spectacle. The white-bearded Kiaya,

"Lion of God," who till that time had led only to victory,
flew past their close ranks, strengthening them, raising their
courage, reminding them of past battles and their own
unbroken preponderance.   To them also, battle was sweeter
than that idle waiting in storm and in rain, in wind which
was piercing them to the bone; hence, though they could
barely grasp the muskets and spears in their stiffened hands,
they were still cheered by the thought that they would warm
them in battle.   With far less desire did the spahis await
the attack, because on them was to fall its first fury,
because among them were many inhabitants of Asia Minor
and of Egypt, who, exceedingly sensitive to cold, were only
half living after that night.   The horses also suffered not a
little, and though covered with splendid caparisons, they
stood with heads toward the earth, puffing rolls of steam
from their nostrils.   The men with blue faces and dull eyes
did not even think of victory.   They were thinking only
that death would be better than torment like that in which
the last night had been passed by them, but best of all
would be flight to their distant homes, beneath the hot rays
of the sun.

Among the Polish troops a number of men without sufficient clothing had died before day on the ramparts; in
general, however, they endured the cold far better than the
Turks, for the hope of victory strengthened them, and a
faith, almost blind, that since the hetman had decided that
they were to stiffen in the rain, the torment must come out
infallibly for their good, and for the evil and destruction of
the Turks.   Still, even they greeted the first gleams of that
morning with gladness.

At this same time Sobieski appeared at the battlements.

There was no brightness in the sky, but there was brightness on his face; for when he saw that the enemy intended
to give battle in the camp he was certain that that day
would bring dreadful defeat to Mohammed.   Hence he
went from regiment to regiment, repeating: "For the desecration of churches! for blasphemy against the Most Holy
Lady in Kamenyets! for injury to Christendom and the
Commonwealth! for Kamenyets!"   The soldiers had a
terrible look on their faces, as if wishing to say: "We can
barely restrain ourselves!   Let us go, grand hetman, and
you will see!"

The gray light of morning grew clearer and clearer; out
of the fog rows of horses' heads, forms of men, lances,

banners, finally regiments of infantry, emerged more distinctly each moment. First they began to move and
advance in the fog toward the enemy, like two rivers, at
the flanks of the cavalry; then the light horse moved, leaving only a broad road in the middle, over which the hussars
were to rush when the right moment came.

Every leader of a regiment in the infantry, every captain,
had instructions and knew what to do. Pan Kantski's
artillery began to speak more profoundly, calling out from
the Turkish side also strong answers. Then musketry fire
thundered, a mighty shout was heard throughout the whole
camp, — the attack had begun.

The misty air veiled the view, but sounds of the struggle
reached the place where the hussars were in waiting. The
rattle of arms could be heard, and the shouting of men.
The hetman, who till then had remained with the hussars,
and was conversing with Pan Yablonovski, stopped on a
sudden and listened.

" The infantry are fighting with the irregular janissaries;
those in the front trenches are scattered," said he to the
voevoda.

After a time, when the sound of musketry was failing,
one mighty salvo roared up on a sudden; after it another
very quickly. It was evident that the light squadrons had
pushed back the spahis and were in presence of the
janissaries.

The grand hetman, putting spurs to his horse, rushed
like lightning at the head of some tens of men to the battle;
the voevoda of Rus remained with the fifteen squadrons of
hussars, who, standing in order, were waiting only for the
signal to spring forward and decide the fate of the struggle.
They waited long enough after that; but meanwhile in the
depth of the camp it was seething and roaring more and
more terribly. The battle seemed at times to roll on to the
right, then to the left, now toward the Lithuanian armies,
now toward the voevoda of Belsk, precisely as when in time
of storm thunders roll over the sky. The artillery-fire of
the Turks was becoming irregular, while Pan Kantski's
batteries played with redoubled vigor. After the course of
an hour it seemed to the voevoda of Rus that the weight
of the battle was transferred to the centre, directly in front
of his cavalry.

At that moment the grand hetman rushed up at the
head of his escort. Flame was shooting from his eyes.

He reined in his horse near the voevoda of Rus, and exclaimed, —

"At them, now, with God's aid!"

"At them!" shouted the voevoda of Rus.

And after him the captains repeated the commands. With a terrible noise that forest of lances dropped with one movement toward the heads of the horses, and fifteen squadrons of that cavalry accustomed to crush everything before it moved forward like a giant cloud.

From the time when, in the three days' battle at Warsaw, the Lithuanian hussars, under Prince Polubinski, split the whole Swedish army like a wedge, and went through it, no one remembered an attack made with such power. Those squadrons started at a trot, but at a distance of two hundred paces the captains commanded: "At a gallop!" The men answering, with a shout, "Strike! Crush!" bent in the saddles, and the horses went at the highest speed. Then that column, moving like a whirlwind, and formed of horses, iron men, and straightened lances, had in it something like the might of an element let loose. And it went like a storm, or a raging river, with roar and outburst. The earth groaned under the weight of it; and if no man had levelled a lance or drawn a sabre, it was evident that the hussars with their very weight and impact would hurl down, trample, and break everything before them, just as a column of wind breaks and crushes a forest. They swept on in this way to the bloody field, covered with bodies, on which the battle was raging. The light squadrons were still struggling on the wings with the Turkish cavalry, which they had succeeded in pushing to the rear considerably, but in the centre the deep ranks of the janissaries stood like an indestructible wall. A number of times the light squadrons had broken themselves against that wall, as a wave rolling on breaks itself against a rocky shore. To crush and destroy it was now the task of the hussars.

A number of thousand of muskets thundered, "as if one man had fired." A moment more the janissaries fix themselves more firmly on their feet; some blink at sight of the terrible onrush; the hands of some are trembling while holding their spears; the hearts of all are beating like hammers, their teeth are set, their breasts are breathing convulsively. The hussars are just on them; the thundering breath of the horses is heard. Destruction, annihilation, death, are flying at them.

"Allah!" "Jesus, Mary!"—these two shouts meet and mingle as terribly as if they had never burst from men's breasts till that moment. The living wall trembles, bends, breaks. The dry crash of broken lances drowns for a time every other sound; after that, is heard the bite of iron, the sound, as it were, of thousands of hammers beating with full force on anvils, as of thousands of flails on a floor, and cries singly and collectively, groans, shouts, reports of pistols and guns, the howling of terror. Attackers and attacked mingle together, rolling in an unimaginable whirl. A slaughter follows; from under the chaos blood flows, warm, steaming, filling the air with raw odor.

The first, second, third, and tenth rank of the janissaries are lying like a pavement, trampled with hoofs, pierced with spears, cut with swords. But the white-bearded Kiaya, "Lion of God," hurls all his men into the boiling of the battle. It is nothing that they are put down like grain before a storm. They fight! Rage seizes them; they breathe death; they desire death. The column of horses' breasts pushes them, bends, overturns them. They open the bellies of horses with their knives; thousands of sabres cut them without rest; blades rise like lightning and fall on their heads, shoulders, and hands. They cut a horseman on the legs, on the knees; they wind around, and bite like venomous worms; they perish and avenge themselves.

Kiaya, "Lion of God," hurls new ranks again and again into the jaws of death. He encourages them to battle with a cry, and with curved sabre erect he rushes into the chaos himself. With that a gigantic hussar, destroying like a flame everything before him, falls on the white-bearded old man, and standing in his stirrups to hew the more terribly, brings down with an awful sweep a two-handed sword on the gray head. Neither the sabre nor the headpiece forged in Damascus are proof against the blow; and Kiaya, cleft almost to the shoulders, falls to the ground, as if struck by lightning.

Pan Adam, for it was he, had already spread dreadful destruction, for no one could withstand the strength and sullen rage of the man; but now he had given the greatest service by hewing down the old hero, who alone had supported the stubborn battle. The janissaries shouted in a terrible voice on seeing the death of their leader, and more than ten of them aimed muskets at the breast of the cavalier. He turned toward them like dark night; and before other hussars could strike them, the shots roared, Pan Adam reined in his horse and bent in the saddle. Two comrades seized him by the shoulders; but a smile, a guest long unknown, lighted his gloomy face, his eyeballs turned in his head, and his white lips whispered words which in the din of battle no man could distinguish. Meanwhile the last ranks of the janissaries wavered.

The valiant Yanish Pasha tried to renew the battle, but the terror of panic had seized on his men; efforts were useless. The ranks were broken and shivered, pushed back, beaten, trampled, slashed; they could not come to order. At last they burst, as an overstrained chain bursts, and like single links men flew from one another in every direction, howling, shouting, throwing down their weapons, and covering their heads with their hands. The cavalry pursue them; and they, not finding space sufficient for flight singly, gather at times into a dense mass, on whose shoulders ride the cavalry, swimming in blood. Pan Mushalski, the bowman, struck the valiant Yanish Pasha such a sabre-blow on the neck that his spinal marrow gushed forth and stained his silk shirt and the silver scales on his armor.

The irregular janissaries, beaten by the Polish infantry, and a part of the cavalry which was scattered in the very beginning of the battle, in fact, a whole Turkish throng, fled now to the opposite side of the camp, where there was a rugged ravine some tens of feet deep. Terror drove the mad men to that place. Many rushed over the precipice, "not to escape death, but death at the hands of the Poles." Pan Bidzinski blocked the road to this despairing throng; but the avalanche of fugitives tore him away with it, and threw him to the bottom of the precipice, which after a time was filled almost to the top with piles of slain, wounded, and suffocated men.

From this place rose terrible groans; bodies were quivering, kicking one another, or clawing with their fingers in the spasms of death. Those groans were heard until evening; until evening those bodies were moving, but more and more slowly, less and less noticeably, till at dark there was silence.

Awful were the results of the blow of the hussars. Eight thousand janissaries, slain with swords, lay near the ditch surrounding the tents of Hussein Pasha, not counting those who perished in the flight, or at the foot of the precipice. The Polish cavalry were in the tents; Pan Sobieski had triumphed. The trumpets were raising the hoarse sounds of victory, when the battle raged up again on a sudden.

After the breaking of the janissaries the vizir, Hussein Pasha, at the head of his mounted guards and of all that were left of the cavalry, fled through the gate leading to Yassy; but when the squadrons of Dmitri Vishnyevetski, the field hetman, caught him outside and began to hew without mercy, he turned back to the camp to seek escape elsewhere, just as a wild beast surrounded in a forest looks for some outlet. He turned with such speed that he scattered in a moment the light squadron of Cossacks, put to disorder the infantry, occupied partly in plundering the camp, and came within "half a pistol-shot" of the hetman himself.

"In the very camp," wrote Pan Sobieski, afterward, "we were near defeat, the avoidance of which should be ascribed to the extraordinary resolution of the hussars."

In fact, the pressure of the Turks was tremendous, produced as it was under the influence of utter despair, and the more terrible that it was entirely unexpected; but the hussars, not cooled yet after the heat of battle, rushed at them on the spot, with the greatest vigor. Prusinovski's squadron moved first, and that brought the attackers to a stand; after it rushed Pan Yan with his men, then the whole army, — cavalry, infantry, camp-followers, — every one as he was, every one where he was, — all rushed with the greatest rage on the enemy, and there was a battle, somewhat disordered, but not yielding in fury to the attack of the hussars on the janissaries.

When the struggle was over the knights remembered with wonder the bravery of the Turks, who, attacked by Vishnyevetski and the hetmans of Lithuania, surrounded on all sides, defended themselves so madly that though Sobieski permitted the Poles to take prisoners then, they were able to seize barely a handful of captives. When the heavy squadrons scattered them at last, after half an hour's battle, single groups and later single horsemen fought to the last breath, shouting, "Allah!" Many glorious deeds were done, the memory of which has not perished among men. The field hetman of Lithuania cut down a powerful pasha who had slain Pan Rudomina, Pan Kimbar, and Pan Rdultovski; but the hetman, coming to him unobserved, cut off his head at a blow. Pan Sobieski slew in presence of the army a spahi who had fired a pistol at him. Pan Bidzinski, escaping from the ravine by some miracle, though bruised and wounded, threw himself at once into the whirl of battle, and fought till he fainted from exhaustion. He was sick long, but after some months recovered his health, and went again to the field, with great glory to himself.

Of men less known Pan Rushchyts raged most, taking off horsemen as a wolf seizes sheep from a flock. Pan Yan on his part worked wonders; around him his sons fought like young lions. With sadness and gloom did these knights think afterward of what that swordsman above swordsmen, Pan Michael, would have done on such a day, were it not that for a year he had been in the earth resting in God and in glory. But others, taught in his school, gained sufficient renown for him and themselves on that bloody field.

Two of the old knights of Hreptyoff fell in that renewed battle, Pan Motovidlo and the terrible bowman, Mushalski. A number of balls pierced the breast of Motovidlo simultaneously, and he fell as an oak falls, which has come to its time. Eye-witnesses said that he fell by the hand of those Cossack brothers who under the lead of Hohol had struggled to the last against their mother (Poland) and Christendom. Pan Mushalski, wonderful to relate, perished by an arrow, which some fleeing Turk had sent after him. It passed through his throat just in the moment when, at the perfect defeat of the Pagans, he was reaching his hand to the quiver, to send fresh, unerring messengers of death in pursuit of the fugitives. But his soul had to join the soul of Didyuk, so that the friendship begun on the Turkish galley might endure with the bonds of eternity. The old comrades of Hreptyoff found the three bodies after the battle and took farewell tearfully, though they envied them the glorious death. Pan Adam had a smile on his lips, and calm serenity on his face; Pan Motovidlo seemed to be sleeping quietly; and Pan Mushalski had his eyes raised, as if in prayer. They were buried together on that glorious field of Hotin under the cliff on which, to the eternal memory of the day, their three names were cut out beneath a cross.

The leader of the whole Turkish army, Hussein Pasha, escaped on a swift Anatolian steed, but only to receive in Stambul a silk string from the hands of the Sultan. Of the splendid Turkish army merely small bands were able to bear away sound heads from defeat. The last legions of Hussein Pasha's cavalry gave themselves into the hands of the armies of the Commonwealth. In this way the field hetman drove them to the grand hetman, and he drove them to the Lithuanian hetmans, they again to the field hetman; so the turn went till nearly all of them had perished. Of the janissaries almost no man escaped. The whole immense camp was streaming with blood, mixed with snow and rain. So many bodies were lying there that only frost, ravens, and wolves prevented a pestilence, which comes usually from bodies decaying. The Polish troops fell into such ardor of battle that without drawing breath well after the victory, they captured Hotin. In the camp itself immense booty was taken. One hundred and twenty guns and with them three hundred flags and banners did Pan Sobieski take from that field, on which for the second time in the course of a century the Polish sabre celebrated a grand triumph.

Pan Sobieski himself stood in the tent of Hussein Pasha, which was sparkling with rubies and gold, and from it he sent news of the fortunate victory to every side by swift couriers. Then cavalry and infantry assembled; all the squadrons, — Polish, Lithuanian, and Cossack, — the whole army, stood in order of battle. A Thanksgiving Mass was celebrated, and on that same square where the day previous muezzins had cried: "La Allah illa Allah!" was sounded "Te Deum laudamus!"

The hetman, lying in the form of a cross, heard Mass and the hymn; and when he rose, tears of joy were flowing down his worthy face. At sight of that the legions of knights, the blood not yet wiped from them, and while still trembling from their efforts in battle, gave out three times the loud thundering shout: —

"Vivat Joannes victor!"

Ten years later, when the Majesty of King Yan III. (Sobieski) hurled to the dust the Turkish power at Vienna, that shout was repeated from sea to sea, from mountain to mountain, throughout the world, wherever bells called the faithful to prayer.

Here ends this series of books, written in the course of a number of years and with no little toil, for the strengthening of hearts.

THE END.

THE NOVELS OF HENRYK SIENKIEWICZ

AUTHORIZED AND UNABRIDGED TRANSLATIONS
By JEREMIAH CURTIN.
PUBLISHED BY LITTLE, BROWN, & COMPANY.

Just ready: a New Volume

Hania.

Translated from the Polish of HENRYK SIENKIEWICZ, author of "Quo Vadis," "With Fire and Sword," etc., by JEREMIAH CURTIN. Crown 8vo. Cloth, with portrait. $2.00.

"Hania," the new volume by Sienkiewicz, has been carefully translated from the Polish by Jeremiah Curtin, whose translations of "Quo Vadis," "With Fire and Sword," and the other writings of Sienkiewicz, have been so highly commended for their spirit and faithfulness by scholars and critics throughout the country. It is uniform in size and binding with Mr. Curtin's translations of "Quo Vadis," and the other works of Sienkiewicz, Library Edition, and contains a portrait of the author and his daughter, reproduced in photogravure from a photograph taken last summer in the Carpathian Mountains.

The volume comprises over five hundred pages, about one-third being occupied by the story which gives the book its title, "Hania." It is a story of strength and tenderness and powerful characterization, its scene being laid in Poland. In addition to "Hania," the volume includes the author's latest story, "On the Bright Shore," a romance of Monte Carlo; a philosophical religious story of the crucifixion entitled "Let Us Follow Him," which suggested to Sienkiewicz the idea of writing "Quo Vadis"; a sketch entitled "Tartar Captivity," the germ of "With Fire and Sword" and the other volumes of the great historical trilogy; a humorous novelette entitled "That Third Woman," etc.

The new book by the distinguished Polish writer is of great interest and power, and will doubtless have a wide sale. With the volumes previously issued it gives in a series of admirable translations a practically complete set of the novels and romances of Sienkiewicz.

Let Us Follow Him.

Translated from the Polish of HENRYK SIENKIEWICZ, by JEREMIAH CURTIN. 16mo. Cloth, extra, gilt top, with photogravure frontispiece by EDMUND H. GARRETT. 50 cents.

Although "Let Us Follow Him" is included in the new volume by Sienkiewicz entitled "Hania," its publication in a separate volume has been deemed advisable for the reason that this story gave to its author the idea of writing "Quo Vadis," the literary sensation of the time.

The period of "Let Us Follow Him" is that of the death of Christ. Antea, the wife of a Roman patrician, ill with terrible visions, is advised by a physician to seek the air of Jerusalem. There she and her husband meet Pilate, who tells them of the doctrine of the Nazarene, Jesus, and his condemnation to death. They are present at the crucifixion, and Antea gives honor to the condemned Nazarene, saying, "Thou art Truth."

"Quo Vadis."

"Quo Vadis." A Narrative of the Time of Nero. By HENRYK SIENKIEWICZ, author of "With Fire and Sword," "The Deluge," etc. Translated from the Polish by JEREMIAH CURTIN. Crown 8vo. Cloth, $2.00.

One of the greatest books of our day. — *The Bookman.*

In all respects a surpassing work of fiction. — *New York Herald.*

His understanding of the Roman heart is marvellous. — *Boston Transcript.*

One of the strongest historical romances that have been written in the last half century. — *Chicago Evening Post.*

Absorbingly interesting, brilliant in style, imposing in materials, and masterly in their handling. — *Providence News.*

The portrait of Petronius is alone a masterpiece of which the greatest word-painters of any age might be proud. — *Philadelphia Church Standard*

A book to which no review can do justice. A most noble historical romance, in which the reader never for a moment loses interest. — *Detroit Free Press.*

One of the most remarkable books of the decade. It burns upon the brain the struggles and triumphs of the early Church. — *Boston Daily Advertiser.*

With him we view, appalled, Rome, grand and awful, in her last throes. The picture of the giant Ursus struggling with the wild animals is one that will always hold place with such literary triumphs as that of the chariot race in "Ben Hur." — *Boston Courier.*

The world needs such a book at intervals, to remind it again of the surpassing power and beauty of Christ's central idea. . . . A climax [the scene in the arena] *beside which the famous chariot race in "Ben Hur" seems tame.* — *Chicago Tribune.*

Every chapter in it is eloquent with meaning. . . . The feasting at the imperial palace, the contests in the arena, the burning of Rome, the rescue of Lygia, the Christian maiden, — will hold their place in memory with unfading color, and are to be reckoned among the significant triumphs of narrative art. — *The Boston Beacon.*

Without exaggeration it may be said that this is a great novel. It will become recognized by virtue of its own merits as the one heroic monument built by the modern novelist above the ruins of decadent Rome, and in honor of the blessed martyrs of the early Church. There are chapters in "Quo Vadis" so convincing, so vital, so absolute, that by comparison Lew. Wallace's popular book seems tinsel, while Ware's honest old "Aurelian" sinks into insignificance. — *Brooklyn Eagle.*

With Fire and Sword.

The only modern romance with which it can be compared for fire, sprightliness, rapidity of action, swift changes, and absorbing interest is "The Three Musketeers" of Dumas. — New York Tribune.

WITH FIRE AND SWORD. An Historical Novel of Poland and Russia. By HENRYK SIENKIEWICZ. Translated from the Polish by JEREMIAH CURTIN. With photogravure portrait of the author. Crown 8vo. Cloth, $2.00.

"With Fire and Sword" is the first of a trilogy of historical romances of Poland, Russia, and Sweden. Their publication has been received throughout the United States by readers and critics as an event in literature. Action in the field has never before been described in any language so briefly, so vividly, and with such a marvellous expression of energy. The famous character of Zagloba has been described as "a curious and fascinating combination of Falstaff and Ulysses." Charles Dudley Warner, in "Harper's Magazine," affirms that the Polish author has in Zagloba *given a new creation to literature.*

Wonderful in its strength and picturesqueness. — *Boston Courier.*
A romance which, once read, is not easily forgotten. — *Literary World.*
One of the noblest works of historical romance ever written. — *The Pilot.*
One of the most brilliant historical novels ever written. — *Christian Union.*
A tremendous work in subject, size, and treatment. — *Providence Journal.*
Not a tedious page in the entire magnificent story. — *Boston Home Journal.*

The force of the work recalls certain elements of Wallenstein. — *Boston Journal.*

The first of Polish novelists, past or present, and second to none now living in England, France, or Germany. — *Blackwood's Magazine.*

He exhibits the sustained power and sweep of narrative of Walter Scott and the humor of Cervantes. — *Philadelphia Inquirer.*

The word painting is startlingly like some of the awesome paintings by Verestchagin. We do not feel over bold in saying that some of the character-drawing is Shakespearian. Where, outside of Shakespeare, can such a man as Zagloba be found? — *Christian Advocate.*

A novel that like Thackeray's "Henry Esmond" or Scott's "Ivanhoe" can be returned to again and again. — *Boston Gazette.*

Such a writer as Sienkiewicz, the Polish novelist, whose works belong with the very best of their class, and who has a kind of Shakesperian freshness, virility, and power of characterization, is sufficient to give dignity to the literature of a whole generation in his own country. His three novels on the Wars of the Polish Commonwealth, and his superb psychological story, "Without Dogma," form a permanent addition to modern literature. — *The Outlook.*

3

The Deluge.

THE DELUGE. An Historical Novel of Poland, Sweden, and Russia. By HENRYK SIENKIEWICZ. Translated from the Polish by JEREMIAH CURTIN. A sequel to "With Fire and Sword." With a map of the country at the period in which the events of "The Deluge" and "With Fire and Sword" take place. 2 vols. Crown 8vo. Cloth, $3.00.

"The wars described in 'The Deluge,'" says the translator, "are the most complicated and significant in the whole career of the Commonwealth." The hero of the book, Pan Andrei Kmita, is delineated with remarkable power; and the wonderful development of his character — from the beginning of the book, when his nature is wild and untamed, to the end, when he becomes the savior of the King and the Commonwealth after almost unequalled devotion and self-sacrifice — gives this great historical romance a place even above "With Fire and Sword."

Pan Michael.

PAN MICHAEL. An Historical Novel of Poland, Russia, and the Ukraine. By HENRYK SIENKIEWICZ. Translated from the Polish by JEREMIAH CURTIN. A sequel to "With Fire and Sword" and "The Deluge." Crown 8vo. Cloth, $2.00.

This work completes the great Polish trilogy. The period of the story is 1668–1674, and the principal historical event is the Turkish invasion of 1672. Pan Michael, a favorite character in the preceding stories, and the incomparable Zagloba figure throughout the novel. The most important historical character introduced is Sobieski, who was elected king in 1674.

Pan Michael (continued).

The interest of the trilogy, both historical and romantic, is splendidly sustained. — *The Dial.*

A great novel. It abounds in creations. It is a fitting ending to a great trilogy, — a trilogy which teaches great lessons. — *Boston Advertiser.*

May fairly be classed as Homeric. — *The Boston Beacon.*

There is no falling off in interest in this third and last book of the series; again Sienkiewicz looms as one of the great novel writers of the world. — *The Nation.*

From the artistic standpoint, to have created the character of Zagloba was a feat comparable with Shakespeare's creation of Falstaff and Goethe's creation of Mephistopheles. — *The Dial.*

Without Dogma.

Emphatically a human document read in the light of a great imagination. — Boston Beacon.

WITHOUT DOGMA. A Novel of Modern Poland. By HENRYK SIENKIEWICZ. Translated from the Polish by IZA YOUNG. Crown 8vo. Cloth, $1.50.

A psychological novel of modern thought, and of great power. Its utter contrast to the author's historical romances exhibits in a most striking manner the remarkable variety of his genius.

A triumph of psychology. — *Chicago Times.*

A masterly piece of writing. — *Pittsburg Bulletin.*

Belongs to a high order of fiction. — *New York Times.*

Intellectually the novel is a masterpiece. — *Christian Union.*

Self-analysis has never been carried further. — *Colorado Springs Gazette.*

Worthy of study by all who seek to understand the human soul. — *Boston Times.*

One of the most remarkable works of modern novelists. — *Kansas City Journal.*

Bold, original, and unconventional, and displays the most remarkable genius. — *Boston Home Journal.*

In her beautiful simplicity, her womanly strength and purity, the woman stands forth, Beatrice-like, in strong contrast to the man. — *Baltimore American.*

Both absorbing and instructive. Distinctly a notable contribution to the mental and ethical history of the age. — *Boston Courier,*

Children of the Soil.

A great novel, such as enriches the reader's experience and extends his mental horizons. One can compare it only with the great fictions of our great day, and in that comparison find it inferior to very few of the greatest. —W. D. Howells in Harper's Weekly.

CHILDREN OF THE SOIL. Translated from the Polish of HENRYK SIENKIEWICZ, by JEREMIAH CURTIN. Crown 8vo. Cloth, $2.00.

"Children of the Soil," a novel of contemporary life in Poland, is a work of profound interest, written with that vividness and truthful precision which have made the author famous. The great question of the book is, What can a good and honorable woman do to assist a man in the present age in civilized society? The question is answered thoroughly in "Children of the Soil."

A work of the very first order . . . which posterity will class among the *chefs-d'œuvre* of the century. In this romance are manifested the noblest and rarest qualities that an author can possess: a wonderful delicacy of psychological analysis, an incomparable mastery of the art of painting characters and morals, and the rare and most invaluable faculty of making the characters live in the printed page. — *Le Figaro,* Paris, May 4, 1895.

There is not a chapter without originality and a delightful, honest realism. — *New Haven Evening Leader.*

It must be reckoned among the finer fictions of our time, and shows its author to be almost as great a master in the field of the domestic novels as he had previously been shown to be in that of imaginative historical romance. — *Chicago Dial.*

Few books of the century carry with them the profound moral significance of the "Children of the Soil," but the book is a work of art and not a sermon. Every page shows the hand of a master. — *Chicago Chronicle.*

There are few pages that do not put in an interesting or amusing light some current doctrine or some fashion of the hour. — *New York Critic.*

Not only as a finely elaborated and manifestly truthful depiction of contemporary Polish life, but as a drama of the human heart, inspired by the supreme principles of creative art, "Children of the Soil" is decidedly a book to be read and lingered over. — *Boston Beacon.*

It is a book to sit with quietly and patiently, to read with conscience and comprehension awake and alert, to absorb with an open heart. — *Providence News.*

This is a narrative long but full, rich in vitality, abounding in keen and exact characterization. — *Milwaukee Sentinel.*

Yanko the Musician.

His energy and imagination are gigantesque. He writes prose epics. — Chicago Evening Post.

YANKO THE MUSICIAN, AND OTHER STORIES. By HENRYK SIENKIEWICZ. Translated from the Polish by JEREMIAH CURTIN. With Illustrations by EDMUND H. GARRETT. 16mo. Cloth, extra, gilt top, $1.25.

CONTENTS. — I. YANKO THE MUSICIAN; II. THE LIGHT-HOUSE KEEPER OF ASPINWALL; III. FROM THE DIARY OF A TUTOR IN POZNAN; IV. A COMEDY OF ERRORS, A SKETCH OF AMERICAN LIFE; V. BARTEK THE VICTOR.

A series of studies of the impressionist order, full of light and color, delicate in sentiment, and exquisite in technical expression. — *Boston Beacon.*

The stories are deeply intellectual. — *Philadelphia Public Ledger.*

The note of patriotism, of love of home, is strong in all these stories. *Chicago Figaro.*

Full of powerful interest. — *Boston Courier.*

Models of simplicity. — *Brooklyn Eagle.*

The simple story of the lighthouse man is a masterpiece. — *New York Times.*

They have all the charm of the author's manner. — *Public Opinion.*

The tale of Yanko has wonderful pathos. — *Chicago Herald.*

Lillian Morris, and Other Stories.

LILLIAN MORRIS, AND OTHER STORIES. Translated from the Polish of HENRYK SIENKIEWICZ by JEREMIAH CURTIN. Illustrated by EDMUND H. GARRETT. 16mo. Cloth, extra, gilt top, $1.25.

CONTENTS. — I. LILLIAN MORRIS; II. SACHEM; III. ANGEL; IV. THE BULL-FIGHT.

The reminiscence of Spain which describes a bull-fight in Madrid is a realistic and rather brilliant sketch, — one of the most effective accounts of the Spanish national sport one is likely to find. — *Review of Reviews.*

"Yamyol" in this new collection is written with awful intensity and marvellous power. This little tale is a masterpiece of literary work, and its effect on the reader extraordinary.

All the stories are remarkable. — *Literary World.*

Opinions regarding Mr. Curtin's Translations.

From the Author.

I have read with diligent attention all the volumes of my works sent me (American Edition). I understand how great the difficulties were which you had to overcome, especially in translating the historical novels, the language of which is somewhat archaic in character.

I admire not only the sincere conscientiousness and accuracy, but also the skill, with which you did the work.

Your countrymen will establish your merit better than I; as to me, I can only desire that you and no one else should translate all that I write.

With respect and friendship,

HENRYK SIENKIEWICZ.

With Fire and Sword.

The translation appears to be faithful, for none of the glow and vigor of the great Polish novelist are missing, and the work is indeed a triumph of genius. — *Chicago Mail.*

Mr. Curtin's admirable translation of this brilliant historical romance may be said to have taken the literary critics of the day by storm. — *Portland Advertiser.*

Mr. Curtin deserves the gratitude of the English-speaking public for his most excellent and spirited translation. We have to thank him for an important contribution to the number of really successful historical novels and for a notable enlargement of our understanding of a people whose unhappy fate has deserved the deepest sympathy of the world. — *Chicago Evening Post.*

Mr. Jeremiah Curtin shows uncommon ability in translation; he conveys in accurate and nervous English the charm of the Polish original, frequently exercising much ingenuity in the treatment of colloquial idioms. — *Literary World.*

The English-reading world cannot be too grateful to Mr. Curtin for rendering this masterpiece among historical novels into such luminous, stirring English. He has brought both skill and enthusiasm to his work, and has succeeded in giving us a thorough Polish work in English dress. — *Pittsburg Chronicle Telegraph.*

Mr. Curtin's style of translation is excellent and apparently faithful, and he is entitled to the thanks of the English-reading public for revealing this new and powerful genius. — *Providence Journal.*

It is admirably translated by that remarkable, almost phenomenal, philologist and Slavonic scholar, Jeremiah Curtin, so long a resident of Russia, and at one time secretary of legation there. — *Brooklyn Eagle.*

The Deluge.

Mr. Curtin has done the translation so well that the peculiarities of the author's style have been preserved with great distinctness. — *Detroit Tribune.*

This story, like its predecessor, has been translated from the Polish by Jeremiah Curtin in a way that makes its stirring or delightful scenes appear to have been written originally in English. — *Brooklyn Daily Eagle.*

Too much cannot be said in praise of the conscientious and beautiful work of the translator. — *Chattanooga Times.*

Of Mr. Curtin's share in "The Deluge," there are no words to express its excellence except "it is perfect." Fortunate Mr. Sienkiewicz to have such an interpreter! Fortunate Mr. Curtin to have such a field in which to exercise his skill! — *Boston Times.*

Mr. Jeremiah Curtin has accomplished his task with that sympathy and close scholarship which have always distinguished his labors. — *Boston Saturday Evening Gazette.*

The translation is full of sympathy, of vigor, and of elegance. The translator has accomplished the difficult task of preserving the spirit of the original without failing in the requirement of the tongue in which he was writing, and the result is a triumph of the translator's art. He has done a great service to the English reader, while he has at the same time made for himself a monument which would cause his name long to be remembered, even had he no other claims upon public gratitude. — *Boston Courier.*

Pan Michael.

The fidelity of Mr. Curtin's translation to the original can only be judged by internal evidence. That would seem to be conclusive. The style is vigorous and striking. — *Cleveland Plain Dealer.*

Children of the Soil.

The translation is quite up to Mr. Curtin's excellence. — *Brooklyn Eagle.*

Like all Mr. Jeremiah Curtin's work, the translation is excellent. — *New York Times.*

Mr. Curtin has made his translation with that exquisite command of English and breadth of knowledge characteristic of him. — *Boston Beacon.*

The translation is beyond criticism. — *Boston Home Journal.*

Short Stories.

The style of all the pieces, as Englished by Mr. Curtin, is singularly clear and delicate, after the manner of the finished French artists in language. — *Review of Reviews.*

Mr. Curtin has certainly caught the verve of the original, and in his rendering we can still feel the warmth of the author's own inspiration. — *New Haven Register.*

The translation from the Polish of all of Sienkiewicz's works has been made by Mr. Jeremiah Curtin, and it is sufficient to say that it has received the unqualified praise of scholars both in this country and in England. — *Boston Home Journal.*

Lightning Source UK Ltd.
Milton Keynes UK
UKHW052214220321
380773UK00024B/794